ALSO BY ANNE EASTER SMITH

Daughter of York
A Rose for the Crown

THE KING'S GRACE

Anne Easter Smith

A Touchstone Book

PUBLISHED BY SIMON & SCHUSTER

NEW YORK LONDON TORONTO SYDNEY

 Touchstone
A Division of Simon & Schuster, Inc.
1230 Avenue of the Americas
New York, NY 10020

First Touchstone trade paperback edition March 2009

TOUCHSTONE and colophon are registered trademarks of Simon & Schuster, Inc.

For information about special discounts for bulk purchases, please contact Simon & Schuster
Special Sales at 1-800-456-6798 or business@simonandschuster.com.

Designed by Mary Austin Speaker
Map by Paul J. Pugliese

Manufactured in the United States of America

10   9   8   7   6   5   4   3   2

Library of Congress Cataloging-in-Publication Data
Easter Smith, Anne.
    The king's grace / by Anne Easter Smith.
        p.   cm.
    "A Touchstone Book."
    Includes bibliographical references.
        1. Plantagenet, Grace, 1465?–ca. 1492—Fiction.   2. Warbeck, Perkin,
1474–1499—Fiction.   3. Pretenders to the throne—Great Britain—Fiction.
4. Great Britain—History—Henry VII, 1485–1509—Fiction.   I. Title.
    PS3605.A84K56   2009
    813'.6—dc22   2008033603

ISBN-13: 978-1-4165-5045-7
ISBN-10:   1-4165-5045-3

For Ann Wroe
with thanks for her inspiration, insight and support

Acknowledgments

*I*f I had a therapist, she would be the first I would thank, but instead I shall thank my husband, Scott, for putting up with hair-tearing and teeth-gnashing throughout the eighteen months it took me to tell Grace and Perkin's story. Dissecting this very complicated slice of fifteenth-century history proved far more daunting than I first imagined, but if I have succeeded I must acknowledge the help of many people, not the least of whom is my always-cheerful, ever-encouraging editor, Trish Todd, who set my feet back on the right path several times after panic calls for help. And without author Ann Wroe's help and enthusiasm for this project and her amazing book *The Perfect Prince* (Random House, 2003), I would have been lost.

I will acknowledge help during my research in geographical order. In Binche, Belgium: Etienne Piret, *echevin de culture,* who gave me copies of drawings and maps of the palace and town from the period; the ladies at the tiny Bibliothèque St. Ursmer, who went out of their way to hunt down old histories of the city; and our hosts at Les Volets Verts, who made the two aforementioned connections possible. In Lisbon, Portugal: the delightful and knowledgeable Adelino Soares de Mello, a friend of Ann Wroe's, who insisted on sharing many, many hours of his time and wealth of knowledge of his beautiful city with us, tracking down exactly where Edward Brampton and Pero Vaz would have lived on the Serros los Amirantes. Sadly, the way I chose to write the book meant I did not spend more time with Perkin in Adelino's charming city. In England: my love and thanks to my friend Roxy Gundry, who trundled around Exeter with me, imagining Perkin's attempts to attack the high city walls with his ragtag army, and who then drove me to Yorkshire (accompanied by her two impeccably behaved dogs) to research that part of the country where the York family had so many supporters. To Richard and Jenny Howarth, who own the awe-inspiring ruin of Sheriff Hutton castle, where Grace's story begins, my thanks for welcoming us and giving us cups of tea in their charming house on the property. I would like to acknowledge Nita Napp of Grantham, Lincolnshire, for her expertise on the Welles family history, and Bill White, a curator at the Museum of London and fellow member of the Richard III Society, who spent a morning giving me an in-depth tour. The museum is a fascinating place and a mine of information for history lovers.

To be honest, it would not have occurred to me to tell Perkin Warbeck's story had it not been for my sister, Jill Phillips. While I was on a research trip for *Daughter of York*, she arranged for me to meet some of the cast of the BBC docudrama *Princes in the Tower* at a dinner party, who were in the throes of filming the last few days of Perkin's life, including the hanging. Everyone at the table except me was a professional actor, and the cast members—Mark Umbers (Perkin), Roger Hammond (Bishop of Cambrai), and one of my movie-star crushes from the sixties, John Castle (Dr. Argentine)—plied me with questions about Margaret of York and what I knew of the Warbeck story. I confessed "very little" then, but the germ of a book was born! As always, my love and thanks to Jill, who never stints on her hospitality while I am in England for research.

I must again acknowledge the help of Maryann Long, midwife and teacher, and nurse practitioner Claire Denenberg in matters medical. Likewise the many members of the Richard III Society who are so generous with their knowledge of the period, especially Pamela Butler, Brian Wainwright, Lorraine Pickering and Joan Szechman. My thanks, too, to Cathy Thibedeau, a former English teacher with a passion for literature, who helped ferret out appropriate quotations for the section pages of the book.

And last but never least, all love and thanks to my agent, Kirsten Manges, who never fails to answer a call or e-mail or give me a confidence boost when I need it.

Contents

The House of York in 1485

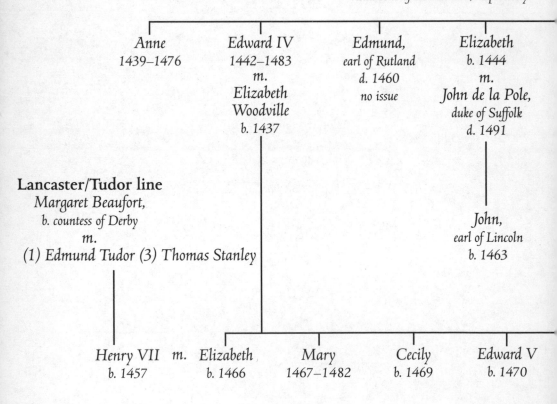

Richard, ═══

duke of York, d.1460
son of Richard, earl of Cambridge, and
Anne Mortimer, descended from the 4th &
2nd sons of Edward III, respectively

Anne
1439–1476

Edward IV
1442–1483
m.
Elizabeth
Woodville
b. 1437

Edmund,
earl of Rutland
d. 1460
no issue

Elizabeth
b. 1444
m.
John de la Pole,
duke of Suffolk
d. 1491

Lancaster/Tudor line
Margaret Beaufort,
b. countess of Derby
m.
(1) Edmund Tudor (3) Thomas Stanley

John,
earl of Lincoln
b. 1463

Henry VII   m.   Elizabeth
b. 1457   b. 1466

Mary
1467–1482

Cecily
b. 1469

Edward V
b. 1470

Cecily Neville,
daughter of Ralph, earl of Westmorland

Margaret	George,	Richard III	5 others
b. 1446	duke of Clarence	1452–1485	d. in infancy
m.	1449–1478	m.	
Charles,	m.	Anne Neville,	
duke of Burgundy	Isabel Neville,	daughter of Richard,	
d. 1477	daughter of Richard,	earl of Warwick	
	earl of Warwick	d. 1483	

Margaret,	Edward,	Edward,
countess of Salisbury	earl of Warwick	prince of Wales
b. 1473	b. 1475	1476–1484

Margaret	Richard,	Anne	George	Catherine	Bridget
b. 1472	duke of York	b. 1475	1477–1479	b. 1479	b. 1480
	b. 1473				

Dramatis Personae

York family
see genealogy chart
   and
      Grace Plantagenet, *illegitimate daughter of Edward IV*
      John of Gloucester, *illegitimate son of Richard III*

Lancaster family
see genealogy chart

Miscellaneous (asterisk indicates fictional character)
In Yorkshire
      Sir John Gower of Stittenham, *constable of Sheriff Hutton castle*
      Lady Agnes Gower, *his wife and attendant of Elizabeth of York*
      Sir Robert Willoughby, *steward in Henry VII's household*
      *Hugh Jones, *his squire*

*Alice Gower, *wife of George Gower of Westow*
*Edmund Gower, *her older son; Rowena, his wife*
*Tom Gower, *Alice and George Gower's younger son*
*Cat Gower, *their daughter*

In London
　　Elizabeth Woodville, *Edward IV's queen*
　　Lady Katherine Hastings, *widow of Lord William Hastings*
　　*Edgar, *a groom*
　　John Marlow, *prior of Bermondsey Abbey*
　　*Brother Damien, *monk at Bermondsey*
　　*Brother Oswald, *overseer of gardens at Bermondsey*
　　*Brother Gregory, *overseer of stables at Bermondsey*
　　*Wat, *head groom at Bermondsey*
　　Sir Edward Brampton, *Anglo-Portuguese courtier, entrepreneur, Perkin's employer*
　　William Caxton, *printer*
　　*Judith Croppe, *sister to his son-in-law*
　　*Matty, *Grace's first maid from Lincoln*
　　*Enid, *Grace's Welsh maid*
　　John, Viscount Welles, *Cecily Plantagenet's husband and step-uncle to King Henry*
　　Anne and Elizabeth Welles, *their daughters*
　　Thomas Grey, earl of Dorset, *oldest son of dowager Queen Elizabeth*
　　John Morton, archbishop of Canterbury and later cardinal, *King Henry's chief adviser*
　　Robert Cleymond, *the earl of Warwick's servant/guardian at the Tower*
　　Thomas Astwood, *Perkin Warbeck's servant/guardian at the Tower*
　　Doctor Rodrigo de Puebla, *Spanish ambassador to England*
　　John Skelton, *King Henry's poet laureate*
　　William Parron, *King Henry's astrologer*

In Burgundy
　　"Jehan LeSage," *Margaret's ward or "secret boy"*
　　*Pieter Gerards, *Sir Edward Brampton's agent*
　　Henriette de la Baume, *Duchess Margaret's chief attendant*

Guillaume de la Baume, *her husband and Duchess Margaret's chevalier*
Henri de Berghes, bishop of Cambrai, *Duchess Margaret's confessor*
Philip, duke of Burgundy, *Duchess Margaret's step-grandson*
William Warham, *King Henry's envoy to the court of Burgundy*

Perkin Warbeck's Journeys

*Atlantic
Ocean*

SCOTLAND

Stirling○ •Falkland

•Edinburgh

Ayr•

River Tweed

Sheriff Hutton•
York•

North Sea

1485–1487 --------→
1489–1491 ·······→
1495 ———→
1497 -·-·-·→

N E S W

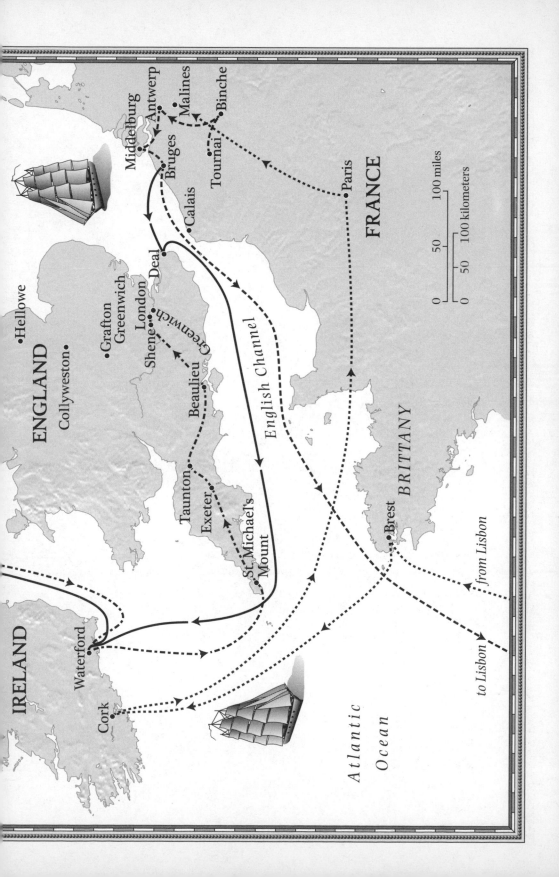

IRELAND

ENGLAND

•Hellowe

Collyweston•

•Grafton
Greenwich•
London•
Shene•
Beaulieu•

Grafton
Greenwich
London
Deal
Shene
Greenwich

Taunton•
Exeter•
St. Michael's
Mount

Waterford•

Cork•

Middelburg
Antwerp
Malines•
Binche
Bruges•
Tournai•
Calais•

FRANCE

Paris•

English Channel

BRITTANY

Brest•

Atlantic
Ocean

from Lisbon

to Lisbon

0   50   100 miles

0   50   100 kilometers

PROLOGUE

The lamb that belonged to the sheep whose skin the wolf was wearing began to follow the wolf in the sheep's clothing.

—AESOP'S FABLE

Burgundy

SEPTEMBER 1485

A crow's incessant caw outside the palace window magnified the boy's misery as each raucous note only served to punctuate the pronouncements made by the woman seated in front of him. Kneeling before her upon the sweet-smelling rushes, Jehan raised hurt blue eyes to the duchess's impassive face and, young as he was, failed to read the sadness in hers.

"You must leave me, Jehan," Margaret of York said in English, the language in which she always addressed him. Her tightly clasped hands were aching to caress his golden head and ease his fear, but she did not trust herself. "You are too young to know why, my child, but one day I promise on His Holy Cross, you will know."

"Am I never to see you again, aunt?" Jehan said, his lower lip trembling. For seven happy years he had been cocooned in the warmth of the dowager duchess of Burgundy's kindness, at her palace of Binche. His first five years in the Carfours section of Tournai had faded into vague memories as he played, studied, sang and prayed in the isolation of the duchess's most remote dower property. He had been lonely at first, but he came to look on his chaplain and tutor Sire de Montigny as a father, and, when the duchess was able to return for a visit, on Margaret as a mother. She had encouraged him to call her "Aunt Margaret" in private once he became accustomed to her, but he addressed her as "Madame La Grande," "your grace" or "madame" when they were not alone. He had never dared ask her why he had been chosen to come and live like a young prince, and she had never told him. It was a secret; he was her secret boy.

"One day, when the time is right, Jehan, you will understand everything. But now, fetch that stool, pour us some of that new cider and sit by me. I will tell you what I have arranged for you."

As he obeyed, Margaret of York's thoughts turned once again to the terrible events of the last two years that resulted in the continuation of the civil war in her homeland between the two rival branches of the royal Plantagenet family—the houses of Lancaster and York. Her brother, King Edward, who had won the throne in 1461 from Henry of Lancaster, had died suddenly aged only forty and left what he thought was a secure Yorkist throne to his young son, also named Edward. Not a month later, a bishop admitted witnessing a contract Edward had made with a woman prior to his marriage with Elizabeth Woodville, the queen. Suddenly, on the eve of his coronation, young Edward, together with his sisters and younger brother Richard, were declared illegitimate and thus unable to inherit the crown. During the turmoil the two boys were placed in the royal apartments at the Tower of London, for their safety, and they had not been seen since that summer of 1483.

Margaret's youngest brother, also named Richard, was proclaimed king as next in line to the throne, and she thought her family's York dynasty was guaranteed. Who could have guessed that Richard's son, Edward of Middleham, would die unexpectedly a year later and put Yorkist England in a precarious position? Margaret knew all too well about leaving an insecure dynasty: her husband, Duke Charles, was killed in battle eight years ago, leaving Margaret's unmarried stepdaughter as his heir. Without a strong male leader, Burgundy was left vulnerable in those first few months until Margaret succeeded in marrying Mary to Maximilian, the heir of the Holy Roman Empire.

Then last month, in England, the unthinkable happened—Henry Tudor, earl of Richmond and the exiled Lancastrian heir, returned to England, challenging Richard's right to wear the crown. He conquered Richard's army at Market Bosworth and was proclaimed king. Margaret had flinched as she read how Henry had treated her brother following his death on the battlefield: *"Naked, he was tied on a horse like a downed stag, his body riddled with wounds from the many sword thrusts that cut him down before he almost single-handedly reached Tudor . . ."* so the Burgundian ambassador had written. Poor Richard, she thought; he did not deserve that.

Jehan returned, offering a cup. She took it and shook off the vision of her brother's bloodied body to focus on the youth's handsome face. She was proud of her boy—he learned his lessons well. He spoke fluent French and English now; his Flemish was passable, but she had directed the tutor to teach him history and literature in French. He had even surprised her on one visit by reciting an ode by Horace in Latin.

Margaret knew who Jehan's real father was. She had let him believe the boatman who worked along the Schedlt in Tournai had sired him, although it had broken her heart to hear how many times this man, when in his cups, had beaten the boy. She chose not to tell him that his mother had died not long after little Jehan had come to Binche, but to simplify matters said that the boatman's new wife, Nicaise, was his mother. Once—not long ago—she had asked him what he remembered of his early childhood in Tournai. He had screwed up his eyes, thinking hard. "I remember going to bed hungry. I remember my father's face when he was angry, and the stick in the corner by the fire that he beat me with." He shuddered. Then his face brightened. "And I remember a little lady with a monkey," he said, and Margaret smiled. "Aye, Fortunata—my servant—and Cappi," she had explained. She could not erase everything bad from his mind, but she was satisfied. Some of the painful memories would never go away, she knew, but most of the happier ones were of Binche.

She had always planned to tell him one day who he really was, but now it was too dangerous. It was better to send him away while he still believed that his parents were the Werbecques of Tournai—until the day when she might need him to know more.

"Now that you are older, you must learn the ways of the world. You cannot remain here forever, Jehan," she told him gently. "As we have discussed many times, you are not my child—I chose to care for you and try to do my Christian duty by you, 'tis all." The boy nodded sullenly. "I cannot give you titles and a household, so now that you are almost a man, you must make your own way. Soon you will be taken to Antwerp by a respectable merchant, and then you will become page to Lady Brampton, who is English. Her husband, Sir Edward, was in the service of my brothers, but because of the new king he must stay away from England. Lady Brampton is kind enough to employ you for my sake, and I know you will be in safe hands. She knows you are well tutored but she thinks you are from the choir school at Tournai." Jehan frowned, trying to take in all this information. "I am afraid I told that little white lie, child, to protect you. For the next little while, you will learn how to be a page. One day, you may rise to become a knight," Margaret said, smiling at the incredulous boy. "Aye, I can see you would like that. Sir Edward is an important merchant who lives part of the year in Burgundy and part of the year in Lisbon. Would you not like to see the world, Jehan?"

"Where is Lisbon, Aunt Margaret? Is it far away from here?" Jehan was still afraid, but he was curious, too. He loved the stories he and de Montigny had read about Greek heroes and King Arthur's knights, and many a night he had gone to sleep dreaming about finding the Golden Fleece or the Holy Grail and sailing away on his own adventure. The thought of becoming a knight was titillating.

"Certes, I would have thought you had learned that Lisbon is in Portugal, Jehan. 'Tis where all the famous navigators sail from when they go to Africa or in search of the western way to the Indies. You do know that my mother-in-law, Duchess Isabella, was a princess of Portugal, do you not? Aye, I see that you do. Perhaps Sire de Montigny should have shown you where Portugal is on a map when he gave you that history lesson." She paused, frowning. "Now where was I?"

Jehan gazed at her, committing to memory every line on her thirty-nine-year-old face, her graying fair hair visible around her elaborate jeweled headdress, and those slate gray eyes that softened every time she looked at him. How he loved her! How beautiful she was, he thought. How kind. Certes, she was every boy's dream for a mother. And then an overwhelming sadness crumpled his face as he remembered that he must go away.

"Sweet Jesu, I beg of you do not weep, or I shall leave the room!" Margaret exclaimed, hoping she sounded suitably fierce, while inside she wept, too. He could not possibly know what happiness he had brought into her childless marriage. Not a day went by that she did not thank God for sending the boy to her. "You are almost a man, Jehan, and men do not cry."

Seeing Jehan swiftly wipe his nose on the back of his hand and sit up straight, Margaret nodded and continued. "That is better. You must be brave, Jehan. We do not know what life may bring you, but I always want you to remember that I taught you to be strong. Do you remember when you broke your leg? You were only six, but very brave. Now you must believe I am doing what is best for you, even though you may question why your life may not be as comfortable as this," she told him, indicating their rich surroundings.

"It would not be good to boast of being my ward," she continued, "and in truth it will be better if you do not speak of it at all. Remember instead your humble beginnings—or what you can of them. All men are jealous by nature, and you will not make friends if you put yourself above others. They may think you are lying, because to them you will be only a page, and thus it may put you in danger." She gave in to her longing and stroked the immaculately curled fair hair, regretting she might never again have the pleasure of combing it.

"And in all circumstances, do not dissemble, do not shy away from duty, do not believe everything anyone tells you and do not forget to pray every day. Listen to your heart, my child, for it is good and pure."

How much should she tell the boy, she wondered? Looking into that innocent face, she knew the answer in a trice: nothing. "I will follow you every step of the way because you will write to me of your adventures. We shall have a special code so no one else shall read what we say to each other." She saw the glint of excitement in his eyes at hearing of the secret pact. Margaret understood what interested boys, having spent most of her childhood in close contact with her two younger brothers, George and Richard, during her early years in England. "There may come a time when I have need of you. I would like to know that you would come to me at such a time, if I asked." She saw him nod vigorously and smiled. "Nay, do not be so hasty. In truth, you owe me nothing, Jehan." Jehan opened his mouth to disagree, but she stopped him. "Nay, 'tis I who owe you a debt so deep you could not begin to understand. The joy you have given me these seven years is immeasurable. But I do ask that you consider my request in the future, and I hope you would assent because of the love we have shared, 'tis all."

"I would lay down my life for you, Aunt Margaret," the boy whispered hoarsely, going down on his knees and crossing himself. "Cross my heart and hope to die."

Margaret took his hands in hers and chuckled. "Certes, that will not be necessary, my dear. But I am touched all the same. Now come, give me a kiss, for I must go and greet the visitors from England. They will have news of my family—what there is left of it," she murmured. She raised him up and accepted his kiss.

"One last thing, my child. 'Twill be easier for you if, when you leave here, we give you back the name you were known by when I found you. You were Pierre, do you remember?"

"Aye, aunt, I do remember," he said, his dull left eye under its oddly creased brow catching the light—the eye was the only flaw in an otherwise beautiful face. "They called me Pierrequin, didn't they?" he asked, now thoroughly mystified.

"Quite right, sweeting," Margaret concurred. "And so, from today, you shall be Pierrequin again." She glided towards the door, ending the conversation and leaving unspoken the one-word question he would have asked had he dared:

"Why?"

PART ONE

. . . the first night that ye shall lie by Igraine ye shall get a child on her, and when that is born, that it shall be delivered to me . . .

—SIR THOMAS MALORY, MORTE D'ARTHUR

1

Sheriff Hutton

SUMMER 1485

*G*race wondered if she would ever get used to the wind in Yorkshire as she leaned into it, feeling it loosen the hair pinned beneath two cauls on either side of her head. It had begun long before they approached the city of York on their journey from Westminster in June, and it seemed to her that it had blown steadily from then until now. Granted, she was standing unsheltered on the southern rampart of Sheriff Hutton castle, one of King Richard's strongholds, perched high on a hill. On a clear day, like today, she could just see the towers of the mighty York Minster a dozen miles over the treetops of the Forest of Galtres. She often came up here to contemplate her change of fortune, and to thank God for her blessings.

A little more than a year ago she had been an eleven-year-old orphan living on the good sisters' charity at the abbey of Delapre outside Northampton; she was astonished when she was told she was to have a new home. A young man, dressed more richly than she could ever have imagined, stood waiting as she bade farewell to the nuns—many of them weeping—and then took her up in front of him on his horse. Escorted by a body of four horsemen, Grace and her knight cantered out of the convent gate and onto the road for Grafton.

"It seems you are not any orphan bastard, Grace," the abbess had told her sternly that fateful day. "Your father was King Edward, may God rest his soul—adulterer though he was. God has smiled on you, my child, for his saintly widow has sent for you and will do her duty by you." Mother Hawise turned away. " 'Tis more than can be said for the father," she muttered. She chose not to enlighten Grace that her royal father had more than adequately compensated for the child's keep through the years; she was peeved the abbey would now lose the pension. Grace hardly had time to ponder the astounding news as she quickly packed her few belongings in a cloth bundle and hurried out to the waiting escort. She turned and waved once more at the blue-garbed group in the abbey courtyard, and then never looked back.

Grace had been tongue-tied for weeks after arriving at Grafton, the country estate of the once dowager Queen Elizabeth, wife to Grace's dead father. At first Grace had not dared ask why her mentor was now addressed as Dame Grey, but she bided her time, knowing full well her curiosity would get the better of her one day. Staring about her at the rich hangings, silver plates and enormous beds, Grace had been overwhelmed in those first anxious days. Delapre Abbey had not been a well-endowed community, and thus she had never known such opulence as this existed. She was given a new gown and shoes in place of her faded blue habit and clogs, and she now slept in a soft tester bed made up with sheets as white as snow, shared with one of her new half sisters instead of squeezing herself between two other novices on a pallet of straw in a dormitory that slept sixteen. She kept pinching herself to make sure it was not all a dream, and it was weeks before she would open her mouth except in prayer or to answer Elizabeth's questions. Her sisters ignored her at first, uncertain how to treat this newcomer suddenly brought into their midst. But the respect—and fear—that they had for their lady mother meant that they came to accept her, especially as she did not put on airs or, indeed, say much of anything.

When she was informed that she would now be known as Lady Grace Plantagenet, she had shaken in her shoes. But in due time Grace learned how to curtsy and address each member of the household correctly and recognize her new title. At first the only people she felt comfortable with, because they did not speak to her directly, were the servants, although Grace observed them whispering behind their hands and, as insecure children do, thought they were gossiping about her and making fun of her bastardy. Although by then she had learned the astonishing fact that all her half siblings were also bastards. One day while working in the herb garden, Grace had plucked up her courage and asked an attendant how that could be.

The woman had looked about her quickly before confiding in the girl the story of Edward's first betrothal contract with another. "I remember my mistress's terrible anger when a messenger came to tell her one cold January day in sanctuary that Parliament had declared her marriage with the king illegal, and that from now on she would no longer be addressed as queen dowager but plain Dame Grey—her name from her first marriage, you understand," she told Grace. "She broke down and wept when the man left, screaming at the children: 'Certes, now you are all bastards! And may Edward rot in hell!' The worst news of all for my poor mistress was that her two sons were still held in the Tower by that usurper, Richard. We watched her fall down on her knees, begging God to restore them to her. 'Twas pitiful to see; she suffered mightily, my lady." Grace had been taken aback by this tale. And though she was unsure what *usurper* meant, it comforted her that she was not the only one with the shame of bastardy weighing on her. And she had more and more sympathy for the woman who had shown her such charity by taking her in.

Still, Grace's shyness often left her tongue-tied and made her wish a large hole would open in the ground and swallow her. One day Elizabeth snapped at her: "Child, come out from behind that arras. No one will bite you. You must learn to be proud of your royal name, not pretend you are part of the wall." Grace was doubly mortified and shrank behind an expressionless mask and further into her shell. She cried herself to sleep that night, awed by her new surroundings and bewildered by her new position.

Then, when she had turned twelve at the feast of the Epiphany, Elizabeth had deemed it right and proper that Grace should join her older siblings at court. By then Grace had learned the ways of the house, to whom she must speak and to whom she should curtsy. She had become friends with her three half sisters, Catherine, Anne and Bridget, and the idea of starting all over again in even grander circles terrified her. Long since, she had decided she was too old to cry into her pillow, but she did send up several prayers to her favorite saints that Elizabeth might change her mind about her leaving Grafton. However, the next day she had quietly prepared for her departure, bundling up her few belongings and taking pleasure in the new gown Elizabeth had ordered for her. Her younger siblings were sad to see her go, because while Elizabeth's attention was diverted by Grace, they enjoyed a modicum of freedom from their mother's eagle eye. Mostly Grace kept her thoughts to herself and used her keen powers of observation to watch and learn everything she could so that she would eventually fit in. If the convent had taught her anything, it was that keeping herself to herself shielded her from hurt.

The lavish life at court had terrified her at first; it was far more imposing than Grafton, she realized, and she longed for a return to that accustomed routine. Her other half sisters Bess and Cecily, who were several years her senior, tolerated her, but her timidity was always an impediment, and she was relieved to find herself ignored by them most of the time. Queen Anne had been kind, but soon after Grace's arrival Richard's beloved wife had succumbed to the wasting sickness and the court was plunged into mourning. Then, with the imminent threat of an invasion by Henry of Richmond from his exile in Brittany, the Yorkist royal children were sent to the safety of the northern stronghold of Sheriff Hutton.

Now Grace stared over its ramparts to the vast expanse of forest, vaguely aware of the bustle in the inner bailey beneath her. She had only just begun to understand how many people kept the castle thrumming: masons, carpenters, alewives, armorers, chandlers, launderers, wheelwrights, joiners, potters, blacksmiths, cooks, grooms and the ale connor, who tested the ale for too much sugar, were all housed inside the castle walls, as were the armed guards, squires and knights and the royal party and their attendants. Only when darkness came did the daily work grind to a halt, and then a screeching owl, a wolf's mournful howl, the screams of a woman in labor or the lilting sounds of lutes and rebecs would break the silence.

"Daydreaming again, Grace?" The young man's voice startled her and caused her to blush. "What fanciful creatures are you looking for today?"

"You mock me, sir," Grace answered softly. "Why must you always treat me like a child? I am only three years younger than you."

John of Gloucester laughed at her chagrin and put his arm around her. "Have you not heard, little Grace, that only those who are most cherished are teased? 'Tis well known you are the quietest, most charming person at Sheriff Hutton, and so I tease you. It does not mean I take you for a child or that I dislike you, cousin. I wish I knew more of what went on in that mysterious mind of yours."

It was the longest conversation she had ever had with John, and Grace wished they could stand there all day. She was acutely aware of his arm about her shoulders and his fingers affectionately pulling at a wisp of dark hair that had finally escaped its cage.

"I was thinking about the wind, John," she said. "Do you think it ever stops blowing? I have lived all my life in the south, and there only on stormy days is it like this. Last night I was certain a dragon was outside my window, it did roar so. I have heard the wolves howl in the forest, and I pray they never venture near the castle, but this was an unearthly sound. Was it simply the wind?"

She raised her brown eyes to his and cocked her head in a way that called to mind an inquisitive bird. He squeezed her shoulders lightly and then let her go. "Aye, 'twas the wind. I have lived in the north since I was six, and I do not even notice it anymore. But see how it puts the roses in your cheeks, Grace." And he pinched one, making her smile. He picked up a stone, leaned over the parapet and dropped it into the moat far below.

"What news of your father, John?" Grace asked, joining him. "Has Henry of Richmond landed yet?"

The bastard son of King Richard straightened, an angry scowl crossing his face. "We do not have news of the weasel yet," he growled. "But Father is at Nottingham, ready for him—you may be certain of that. Henry will wish he had never decided to leave Brittany by the time Father has finished with him. The king is the best soldier in the world; even my uncle Edward—your father—said so. But to answer your question, little one, when I am called to join my master, Lord Lovell, we will know that Henry has landed." He brushed the dust from his leather jerkin. "Until then, sweet cousin, why not go and see what your half sisters are about. Those two are as thick as thieves, and I often see they leave you to your own devices. Besides, you are in danger of an accident up here by yourself."

Grace looked down at her feet, not wanting John to see the truth of his words in her expression. At nineteen and fifteen, Bess and Cecily were not inclined to give the new young member of the family much attention.

"You and I have something in common," John was saying. "We are both royal bastards. We have to stick together. I am used to it, and my father never made me feel different from my little half brother. You are not so fortunate, because you have no parent to support you. 'Tis odd that the queen dowager—I mean Dame Grey. I keep forgetting," he corrected himself. " 'Tis odd that she took you in. She has enough children of her own, and she is not easy with them, so my cousins tell me. I hope she is dealing kindly with you, even though you are her husband's bastard." Grace bit her lip. She was used to the fact now, but hearing the moniker out loud still troubled her. The nuns had impressed upon her that it was a bad word and that bastard children were born of sin. They had nightly prayed for her salvation and for her mother's sinful soul.

"At least you know your father," she whispered. "At least your father wanted you."

John was immediately contrite. It was true, his father adored him and had, earlier that year, appointed him Captain of Calais, a singular honor—especially for a bastard. He gave Grace an apologetic smile; her doll-like fragility always inspired a brotherly protectiveness in him. "Pray forgive me, cousin. I did not mean to upset you. If it helps, I must tell you that my father abhorred your father's behavior. He told me his brother did not deserve to have as sweet a child as you."

"King Richard said that? Why, I did not think he even knew my name." Grace's spirits lifted. "Did he really say that?"

"He did, you silly girl. Besides," he added, a hint of amusement in his voice, "don't forget, Bess and Cecily are now also bastards—though theirs is a different story, as all the world thought Edward and Elizabeth were married. We now know 'twas not the case. Young Ned was thus a bastard and could not wear the crown. That is why Father was asked to be king."

Grace recalled the conversation with the attendant in the herb garden at Grafton and was relieved she did not have to appear ignorant in front of John—she wanted so desperately to impress him. Before moving off

that day, the woman had also told her: "Young Edward was twelve and
his brother, Richard—Dickon, we all called him—nine when your Uncle
Richard"—she spat his name—"decided to keep them 'safe' in the Tower.
'Tis certain King Richard had them done away with!" Grace had been horrified by the accusation, but after she met the king at Westminster, she had
difficulty believing he was capable of such a heinous act.

"They say 'tis all lies, John," Grace said, nervously looking up and down
the rampart walkway. "They say Uncle Richard made up the pre-contract
story so he could take the crown."

John's face turned dark with anger, his slate gray eyes, so like his
father's, flashing dangerously. Grace was again struck by the resemblance
between John and King Richard, although John was more handsome and
of sturdier build.

"How dare they!" John cried, but seeing Grace's fear, he gentled his
tone. " 'Tis the truth, cousin. Your father was contracted to another in
secret before he wed Aunt Elizabeth. Bishop Stillington was witness, and
so that is that. 'Tis natural Beth and Cecily rail against their new position. In truth, I do not blame them. But they should be careful of what
they say while under my father's protection. We are all fortunate to be under his protection—especially Ned and Dickon. And," he said, brightening, "think how fortunate *you* are that Aunt Elizabeth sought you out and
took you away from those awful nuns. You would have hated being a nun,
Grace, I know you would. You are much too clever—and too pretty."

He tucked her arm in his and helped her down some of the steeper
steps inside the tower until they reached the courtyard. "I have archery
practice, but you must go and find your sisters and stand up for yourself,
my little . . . wren." At that moment, John finally realized that this brown-
haired, brown-eyed, unfussy girl reminded him of the smallest, most unprepossessing of English birds.

He grinned. "You and I will be friends, won't we? Know that you have
a brother here whenever you need one." And without thinking, he tipped
up her chin, gave her a quick kiss on the mouth and walked away, leaving
her dumbfounded.

He kissed me, she thought rapturously; John kissed me. She touched her
lips reverently, watching him walk confidently through the other henchmen waiting by the dog kennels for the captain of archery to supervise

their practice that afternoon. With a backslap here, a laugh and a greeting there, Grace could see John was very sure of his position among the other nobles' sons who were in training for knighthood.

"Tom! Tom Gower, I pray you keep me company," he called, and a lanky youth with a shock of corn-colored hair ran lightly to John's side, his bow slung over his shoulder and a lurcher dogging his heels.

Grace drew in a breath, brushed the sandstone dust from her plain kersey gown and, determined to take John's advice to heart, walked confidently back to the apartments she shared with her half sisters. Would she ever get used to this? A king's daughter—how could that be? She had trouble remembering her pretty mother, who never recovered from being abandoned by her family and had withered and died at the convent when Grace was five.

Grace grimaced to herself now as she climbed the spiral steps to her chamber on the third floor of the castle. Aye, I am a king's bastard, but I would rather have been born a commoner and known my father. John is blessed to be close to his father, she thought, which brought her to their present situation and her half sisters' constant question: How long would King Richard keep them all in the north?

A few minutes later, seated on a stool near the formidable Lady Gower and sorting through her embroidery thread, Grace surprised her siblings by asking the older woman about the danger to them should Henry Tudor invade. "Will we go to the Tower?"

Agnes Gower chuckled and patted Grace's hand. "King Richard is the gradeliest soldier king we have had since the fifth Henry," she declared in her broad Yorkshire burr, and the other ladies nodded in agreement. "This Tudor has been threatening to come for nigh on two years, child. No one believes he will really invade, and certes, no one will defeat our Richard in his own country. 'Tis almost laughable. Now stop fretting and ply your needle; 'tis unthinkable for one so young to concern herself with such matters."

Grace recognized yet again the affection with which these northerners spoke about her uncle, and found it difficult to believe he might have had something to do with the disappearance—or even death—of her half brothers. She was satisfied with Lady Gower's response and let the matter rest, although she did spend several minutes more on her knees that night begging St. George to be on Uncle Richard's side should Henry Tudor invade.

WHETHER GRACE'S NEWLY found confidence had impressed her sisters, she knew not, but the very next evening, when the light supper of rabbit pie and slices of pheasant had been cleared away and two of the attendant ladies took up a lute and a recorder and began to play, they chose the moment to teach her to dance. Their cousin, Margaret of Salisbury, orphaned daughter of George of Clarence, refused to join them and instead pulled a book from her sleeve and stuck her nose in it.

Tapping her foot lightly to the music, Bess waited for the beat, and then, taking Grace's hand, she bowed stiffly. "You must curtsy at the same time. Aye, that's right. I will play the gentleman," she said in a mock tenor. "You must never look at your partner, Grace, but at the floor. The gentleman will lead you and not allow you to bump into anyone."

Cecily stood on the other side of Grace and told her to watch the steps carefully. Grace felt herself move to the music of a *basse danza*, rising and falling on the balls of her feet, and her spirits lifted. Learning the steps seemed to come naturally to her.

" 'Tis no wonder you were named Grace," Cecily cried when the lesson was over. "I think you have found your true calling."

"She speaks the truth, Grace," John agreed, surprising the three dancers as he stepped into the room with several other henchmen. One of them was the ten-year-old Edward, earl of Warwick, who immediately ran to his sister Margaret's side. "Forgive us for intruding, but when we heard the music, we could not deny ourselves," John explained. He came forward and took Grace's hand. "And you should all have gentleman partners. Come, lads, let us show these fair ladies how it should be."

Bess beckoned to young Edward, who looked terrified and hid behind his sister. Shrugging her shoulders, Bess turned and fixed her eye upon Tom Gower, who bowed low over his extended leg and led her to their place behind John and Grace. Cecily pouted. Tom was her domain, her glare told Bess, but with her inbred courtesy she accepted the hand of another young squire and began the intricate steps of a country dance.

"What have you learned, young Grace?" John asked, noting with surprise that her fingers were clammy with perspiration. "Ah, I see your teachers have told you not to look at me. 'Tis the custom, I know, but I find it tedious. How can one have discourse with"—he eyed her tall head-dress with contempt—"a hennin?" Grace giggled and raised her eyes to his. "God have mercy, but you are bold, Lady Grace. But I am glad you have heeded our conversation of yesterday. Good girl."

Grace thought she would faint with pleasure. From the moment she had set eyes on the handsome John of Gloucester at Westminster earlier that year, she had given him her young, impressionable heart. Why could he not see how much she loved him? She noticed that many other young ladies at Sheriff Hutton also favored him, and she had seen him kiss one behind the buttery. Why wasn't she older, she railed in her daydreams. Why wasn't she prettier?

"If that is how you like me, cousin, then I shall be bold," she countered, blushing at her own audacity.

John was serious. "Nay, Grace. I like you just the way you are. You must not change for me, little coz, nor for any man. I only meant you must not allow others to walk on you as though you were a Turkey carpet—espe-cially not your sisters. Having spirit can get a person into trouble. I should know; I am the product of a most spirited lady."

"Your mother, John?" The music came to an end, as did the conversa-tion.

"Aye, my mother," he replied as a warm smile suffused his face. "Re-mind me to tell you about her one day."

The grinding sound of the portcullis being raised on the other side of the bailey startled the dancers in the large solar. John and Tom climbed the steep steps up into the window embrasure to peer out.

"A dozen horsemen," John reported, "wearing the crescent argent of Percy, I think. If they come so late, it could be news from Nottingham. Sweet Jesu, can the Tudor have landed?"

John sprang down from his perch and, without an apology to the girls, ran from the room followed by his friends. The door banged shut behind them, leaving the women stunned by the possibility John might be right.

"Quiet, Jason!" Bess snapped at Tom's dog that was left whining on the wrong side of the door. The lurcher turned sad brown eyes on her and slunk off to lie down.

"Your future husband is coming to claim you, Bess," Cecily teased, breaking the tension. "I wonder how he is? Short, fat and ugly, I dare say," and her tinkling laugh put Grace in mind of Dame Elizabeth.

Lady Gower was too preoccupied with discussing the possible invasion with the older ladies to upbraid Cecily, but Grace saw the look of fear that crossed Bess's beautiful face and sidled close to slip her hand in her sister's. Bess looked down at the girl and managed a grateful smile.

"Sweet Jesu," Cecily sighed. "Can you not see I was only jesting? John may have been mistaken about the visitors. 'Tis almost dark, and they may simply be travelers seeking shelter for the night." Grace felt Bess's hand relax in hers and heard her murmured acquiescence.

But Cecily persisted with her original thread. "You know well and good that we must all marry where we are told, so why not see the amusing side, sister dear."

"Bess, Cecily, I beg of you, don't fight . . ." Grace's attempts to interrupt fell on deaf ears and she knew she had been forgotten yet again.

"Do not mock me, sister *dear*," Bess snapped, loosing Grace's hand and taking a step towards Cecily. "Uncle Richard found you a husband whom you abhor." Cecily tossed her head but did not disagree. "And that's why you chose to come up here with me, instead of becoming a loving wife to Ralph Scrope," Bess declared. "It was only because you begged me to ask for your company that our uncle let you come. You were fortunate, too; the contract was arranged during Lent, so you could not be married. But you cannot put it off forever. *Your* husband may come and claim you any day," she finished triumphantly. "Therefore, pray cast your stones elsewhere, and not at me." Enjoying seeing her sister's mulish pout, she added: "You are too addlepated to see that the only way Henry of Richmond will be my husband is if—I repeat *if*—he wins the crown, for he is an upstart nobody. And if he does win, it could only mean"—she lowered her dark blue eyes down to the rushes at her feet—"that Uncle Richard was dead."

Cecily forbore her retort on Bess's undue fondness for Uncle Richard, a dangerous infatuation Bess had formed in the months before the death of his queen that spring. Her innocent flirting had led his enemies to believe Richard had contemplated marriage with his niece. The scandal had caught Richard off-guard in the midst of grief for his wife, and ultimately his councilors had advised him to make a public denial. A few weeks later, under the pretext of keeping Edward's children safe, Richard sent Bess and the others to Sheriff Hutton. "Out of sight, out of mind," those same councilors had advised him.

Lady Gower finally curtailed the tiff: "Enough, ladies!" she commanded. "You are behaving like children." At that moment there was a knock on the door, and a servant entered to summon Bess and the other royal children to the great hall. Lady Gower led the girls out of the room, and with little Edward traipsing behind, they wound down the spiral stairs, through an archway and into the hall that hugged the west wall of the inner ward. It appeared John had been correct in identifying the visitors, for their oldest cousin and guardian, John de la Pole, earl of Lincoln, was surrounded by Percy men as well as the knights and henchmen of Sheriff Hutton.

The earl bade them welcome. "Henry of Richmond has been sighted off the coast of Wales, cousins. My uncle, the king, has sent for us, and we are to join him in Leicester on the morrow. It cannot be long before Richmond finds safe haven, and I fear we must do battle." He looked around at his younger cousins, who were gazing at him expectantly. "Until the outcome is known, you are the guardians of the York line and must remain here in the safe north. I am leaving Sir John in command with sufficient fighting men to protect you."

For the first time, a frisson of fear crept up Grace's spine. Lincoln then addressed Bess and Cecily directly. "I charge you, cousins, to take especial care of young Edward. As son of our late Uncle George, he is one of the heirs to the crown." Lincoln paused, reflecting on his own role as Richard's heir, named such after the king's only legitimate son had died the year before.

With the summons to join Richard and as governor of the royal household in the north, Lincoln knew he must make safe the royal children—especially young Warwick. He guessed Henry might look upon the boy as a rallying point for Yorkist adherents should, Heaven forbid, disaster overtake both the king and himself.

He looked around at the anxious faces and a slow smile spread over his lean, tanned face: "Bastards and traitors, all of you!" he teased his cousins and was gratified when they all laughed in relief. Then he embraced the girls, paying particular attention to Bess, who clung to him, crying.

"Soft, Bess, we shall return, never fear. We shall kick Tudor's arse all the way back to Brittany, I swear to you. I have left enough of a garrison to defend you from the Scots should they decide to attack and defile you"—he broke off and laughed again, seeing her dismay. "Ever the jester—pay me no heed, cousin." He kissed her and repeated his directive more seriously: "You must be the stalwart now and take care of the youngsters. We shall not be long, I promise."

Unable to contain his excitement, John of Gloucester cheered: "For England!" and unsheathed his short sword, thrusting it into the air. "For Richard, rightful king of England!" The rest of the company took up the cry, setting the rafters ringing with their shouts. Grace's dark eyes glowed with pride for her family, and for the first time she truly felt a part of it.

WITH TOM GOWER's uncle, Sir John Gower of Stittenham, in charge, life at the castle returned to its daily routine. The girls spent their mornings in the shady garden plying their needles, reading aloud and practicing the lute under the watchful eye of Lady Gower. The nuns had taught Grace to read the scriptures, but now she thrilled to the stories of Master Chaucer and Thomas Malory. Cecily had a flair for drama, and she brought the tales of King Arthur and his knights to lurid life, causing their older attendants to chide the girls for their noisy laughter. After the midday dinner, they put on their wide-brimmed straw hats and wandered through the hamlet outside the castle gate, where villagers touched their foreheads or curtsied as they passed, and into the meadows in front of the woods. The ubiquitous Yorkshire sheep grazed unconcerned while the intruders gathered posies of cow parsley, ox-eyed daisies, heartsease and scentless mayweed.

Tom Gower was often their escort on these meanderings, a task he did not relish; he had felt demeaned enough at being left behind with the younger henchmen while his friend, John, and other squires and knights had ridden off to probable glory against the invading forces of Richmond. Aye, he thought each time, being given the duty of bodyguard to three girls was insulting beyond the pale. It did not help that his comrades teased him mercilessly, or that Cecily flirted incessantly with him. Certes, it was flattering that a Plantagenet princess had singled him out, but unlike John, Tom had not reached the age when a pretty face took precedence over improving his prowess with sword and dagger. He usually spent this tedious time throwing sticks for Jason or practicing his slingshot skills. When the girls begged, he taught them all how to fish, although there was not much to catch in the brook that ran in front of the castle.

One day at the end of August, however, Tom was rewarded for his mundane meadow duty. He was the first to see and hail the riders who emerged from the forest, riding hard for the shelter of the castle. The sisters, hearing his cries, picked up their skirts and ran back across the waving grass in the wake of the horsemen. Grace had immediately recognized John, and she ran as fast as her short legs could carry her to keep up with her sisters.

"A victory!" Bess shouted, her hair coming loose from her hat and streaming in a golden river behind her. "I smell a victory!"

Scattering hens and goats in their path through the village, the soldiers clattered into the castle yard and slithered from their sweat-flecked mounts. The guards housed in the tower next to the gate ran to help them, and grooms sprang to take hold of the horses' reins. The John who stood swaying with fatigue on the uneven cobblestones was very different from the one who had ridden out to glory ten days earlier. Tom was already there to steady him and, looking at John's ashen face, he knew the news was not good. A sudden pall settled over the castle as the onlookers waited for the young Captain of Calais to speak.

"What is it, John?" Bess cried, running through the archway under the gatehouse, past the well and to his side. "Is Richmond beaten? Say he is beaten. I command you to say it!" But she knew as soon as she had spoken that it was not so.

"King Richard . . ." John faltered as he spoke his father's name and then, seeing the expectant, loyal faces staring at him, rallied to continue with his awful report. "King Richard is slain, the army is routed and Henry Tudor already wears the crown. We are lost . . ." His voice trailed off as gasps and groans echoed across the bailey. Villagers had crept through the gate, unmanned as it was, and stood stock-still when they heard the pronouncement. Grace overheard one say, "He was a good lord to us, was Richard of Gloucester, God rest his soul." She crossed herself and muttered the rote response, "Amen to that." Poor John, Grace thought, how he worshipped his father!

Bess gave a loud cry and fainted on the spot. Several burly men surged forward, and one had the honor of carrying the young woman who might be the next queen of England out of the hot sun and into the great hall. Cecily was distraught and began to wail, jogging John out of his misery enough to slap her face. She froze in horror, and then she was in his arms and he was consoling her.

"Pray forgive me, Cis," Grace heard him say quietly, "but we must be strong for our people here. We are the leaders now, and Grandmother Cecily would not want any of us to weep at this moment. I know not what has become of your Ralph, but from the disdain you show every time his name is mentioned, I shall assume you could not care less." Cecily had the grace to fall silent as John put her gently from him. "Come, let us go inside and I will tell the sorry tale." He passed her to Tom, who escorted her to the hall to join Bess, and then turned to face the castle retainers who stood waiting for their orders.

"Our sovereign lord, King Richard, died valiantly on a field named Redemore Plain near the village of Market Bosworth in Leicestershire," he cried. "He was foully betrayed at the last by someone he called friend. With him in battle fell one of his most faithful lords, Jack Howard of Norfolk, may God rest his soul." He turned to Sir John Gower and went forward to take the older man's hand. "Sad news, sir—your cousin Thomas was also slain fighting for his king. I have no doubt his body will be returned anon to his home in Stittenham. Pray accept my condolences."

Gower signed himself and shook his head. " 'Tis a black day for England, my lord. I will send Tom to break the news to my cousin's wife. They are newly wed, you know. What of my lord of Lincoln?" he asked tentatively.

"I am not certain. There was a rumor he was slain, but others said he was taken prisoner. I pray Tudor has mercy on him—and Howard's son, Thomas of Surrey, who also survived. The rest of us will surely be attainted."

"Attainted? For fighting for one's king?" Gower spluttered. "Surely you jest, my lord. 'Twas Richmond who was the traitor!"

"I would not discredit that cream-faced craven with any act of cowardice," John cried, his grimace spoiling his good looks. "He never lifted his lily-livered sword arm to strike a blow at anyone on the field. Father should have killed him!" His voice had risen to a cry of anguish, which left the group silent for a moment before Sir John began to shout orders for the gates to be closed and more guards placed upon the ramparts in case Henry Tudor took it in to his head to find and kill more of the York line than just its leader.

Amid the flurry of men running to obey their orders and fetch weapons from the armory, Grace stood unnoticed, watching John with sad eyes. With all of her passionate young heart, she wanted to take away his pain. His eyes were full of it, and as though he knew he was being observed, he turned them to her concerned young face. At once his expression softened and he unclenched his fists.

"What, no tears, no swooning? You are braver than your sisters, little wren. Come, let us go inside." He put his hand on her shoulder and steered her towards the hall, and the men broke ranks to let them through. Grace could feel his fingers trembling, and she gently covered them with her own.

"I am so sorry, John. I cannot imagine your sorrow after seeing your father die." She felt his hand grip hers more tightly and heard the catch in his throat.

" 'Tis like being in hell, Grace. And 'twas not my only loss, God help me."

She made a logical guess. "Lord Lovell?"

"Nay, he escaped, God be praised," he said, quietly. Then he sighed. "My sweet sister, Katherine, has been taken by the sweating sickness. My father and I learned this the day before we marched out to face Richmond. My mother braved the road from Suffolk to tell us herself. Father was consumed with grief, and 'twas then I fear he lost all reason." He did not admit that he had cried in his mother's arms when she broke the news. He shook his head, scarcely believing he had lost his father and his sister within one short month.

Tears pricked Grace's eyes as she heard his words. She quickly brushed them aside as they mounted the few steps to the great hall's doorway. A trestle table had been hurriedly set up to receive Bess's inert form, and she was beginning to revive with the help of an attendant who held a singed feather under her nose.

"I did not know you had a sister, John. Was she younger than you?" Grace asked quickly, not wanting to let him go just yet.

John's voice was dull as he answered Grace. "Nay, I was the younger—by two years. She was the image of our mother." Leaving her to digest the information, he strode towards the group around the table just as Bess sat up and looked about her, puzzled.

"Praise be to the Virgin," exclaimed the gap-toothed attendant with the feather, fussing with her mistress's coif. "You swooned, my lady, 'tis all."

"Ho, there!" John called to a servant hovering at the kitchen end of the hall. "Fetch us some ale and food." The servant bowed and scurried off, and Tom and others set up benches around the table.

"Sit, sit," John said wearily. "We have ridden hard for two days. I have no doubt that after we have refreshed ourselves, my comrades and I shall take to our beds."

Grace sat next to Tom and watched John pick at a frayed piece of Lovell's snarling-dog badge on his tabard. Except for the scraping of the benches on the floor as the group settled, silence reigned, as all eyes were riveted on John's tired young face. Slumped in his seat, he waited patiently until the servers had finished bringing ale, cold savory pies and wedges of sharp-smelling cheese, and the other retainers had silently filed into the hall.

"What I know of the thick of the battle, I heard from those fleeing it," John began suddenly, making them all jump. "To my everlasting regret, I was not present, having been forbidden to fight by my father, God rest his soul." His eyes focused on a knot in the wood on the tabletop. Grace heard Tom draw in a sympathetic breath; she guessed he would probably not have been permitted to fight, either.

"We had the advantage, so I was told," John went on, still staring at the table. "We outnumbered Richmond's rabble nearly two to one, and our position was on a hill overlooking a marsh on our left and plain in front, whereon the enemy was marshaled. Beyond the swamp to the south lay my Lord Stanley's divisions, protecting my father's left flank, and to the west sat his brother, William, ready to support the right. With my father's troops directly behind, Howard's van fanned out upon the hill facing Oxford's ranks at the bottom of it. We, the squires and the armorers, were camped almost a league away near Sutton Cheney, behind Northumberland's rear guard." He sneered as he pronounced Henry Percy's title and looked up at his audience. "Aye, you notice my disdain? 'Tis not half the disgust and hatred I have for those whoreson Stanley brothers!" he cried, leaning forward and slamming his fist on the table. Bess recoiled at the unexpected show of temper but was reminded so much of John's father in that moment, she stretched out her hand and touched his arm gently. "Soft, John," she said, full of pity. "If 'tis too painful for you—" she broke off as John shook his head and continued grimly.

"Richmond himself was nowhere to be seen. My father sent out scouts to report on his position and as they were returning to say that he was cowering far behind his forces, it seemed Oxford broke Howard's line and Howard himself fell. 'Twas then the Stanleys showed their true colors by not moving a muscle to come to Howard's aid. And Northumberland sat on his rear at the rear"—he gave a grim smirk at his own choice of words— "and waited." He shrugged. "I suppose I should give him his due: it could be he was unable to see."

John paused, looking at the stony faces around him. He knew the hardest part of the story was yet to be told. Aye, 'twas hard, but when he had first heard it he had never been prouder of his father. "I know not what goes through a man's mind when he is on the verge of madness—or possible death—but what my father did then will only be described as folly by some or extreme bravery by others, who knew him better." Now the stony faces became animated. "Having been informed as to Henry's exact whereabouts, the king rose high in his stirrups and cried, 'We shall find Tudor for ourselves and slay the invader!' Then he led a mounted charge of his squires and knights down the right side of Ambien Hill, across the plain— and vile Will Stanley's front—and into the thick of Henry's guard."

The open mouths at the table told John he was doing the story justice. He took a deep breath. "It seemed Henry's men could hardly believe their eyes, for they almost allowed Father to cut his way through to their lord. The banner of the Red Dragon was his goal, where he knew Henry would be lurking. He seemed not to notice he was surrounded by Tudor's men on all sides. Wielding his battle-ax, 'tis said he hewed a path through them as though they were naught but waving wheat. At one point he was even confronted by a giant of a man—Henry's champion Sir John Cheyney—and Father felled him in a single stroke, though he was half the man's size."

John paused again, watching as some crossed themselves and others whispered to their neighbors. He found that as he described his father's valiant actions, the blood coursed through his veins and purged away some of the anger and bitterness he had experienced in the wake of the battle, when he had first heard of Richard's sacrifice. It helped that it was not the first time he had been forced to describe his father's death; he tried not to think of his beloved mother's anguish as he had broken the news to her in secret a few hours before he fled from Leicester.

"Go on, John," Bess whispered. "Although I almost cannot bear to hear it."

John shook his head in sorrow. "Ah, Bess. If you only knew how close he came to putting an end to the whoreson Tudor. But he was betrayed. Betrayed by those Stanleys, who, perceiving their new lord was in danger, came rushing to his rescue. Father was fighting Henry's standard-bearer when they bore down on him, knocked him from his horse and closed in with a hedge of spears and swords. His men heard his cry of 'Treason!' but there was nothing they could do." His voice lowered to a whisper, and Grace had to lean in to hear him say, "I did not see his body, but 'tis said it was hardly recognizable, there were so many wounds."

Grace put her hand over her mouth and stifled a cry.

"Poor Uncle Richard," Cecily whispered. "How craven of those men. They could have let him die with dignity. He was the king; they should have had respect for God's anointed."

"Dignity? Respect?" John shouted, rising and throwing his heavy chair aside. "The Tudor turd does not know the meaning of these words. He had my father stripped naked and slung, tied like a downed stag, over the back of Gloucester Herald's horse. The loyal herald was then forced to carry his master thus back into Leicester, ahead of the new king and his train. Henry was even wearing Father's crown, God damn his filthy soul to hell!" Tears were streaming down his face by now, and, ashamed of his emotions, he strode towards the stairs leading to his quarters. Those standing moved aside to let him pass. Bess half rose to follow him, but Tom was there before her, motioning to her to sit and hurrying to catch up with his friend. Stunned, the listeners tried to process the horrifying details of Richard's last ride—into battle and out of it.

Grace had not known her Uncle Richard very well; he was the king in magnificent robes who had moved about the palace at Westminster surrounded by a retinue of squires and knights and who had more on his mind than making a newly found bastard of his brother's feel at home. She was a little frightened of this man who had sent two children to the Tower. Why did no one here at court ever speak of them? If Bess and Cecily could be here now, why couldn't they? The mystery of the boys was a dark secret in this family, and therefore, she admitted with guilty pleasure, fascinating. But once, the central character in this mystery had come into the solar, where she and her sisters were wont to spend a rainy day, and he had spoken most kindly to her, chucking her under the chin and saying she had a look of her father. She remembered slate gray eyes under a worried brow on which sat the simple gold coronet, and thought her uncle looked careworn. She had been awed by his presence, though his great power was sheathed in his kindness to her, and her knees had almost given way.

"*Kyrie eleison.*" Her small but clear voice nudged the company out of their own memories of the thirty-two-year-old king, taken before his time. The shocking news had sparked in Grace a longing to draw on the only comfort she had known in her religious upbringing: prayer. There were some in the room who had never heard Grace say a word before this, and she felt everyone's eyes on her. Less steadily, she persisted: "We should pray for King Richard's departed soul."

Bess looked at her with new respect and took up Grace's prayer. "In the midst of life, we are in death. *Miserere nobis.* My sister is right," she said, holding out her hands to Grace and Cecily. "We must go up to the chapel and pray that Richard Plantagenet, last son of Grandfather York, may rest in peace. Let us hope he is now in Heaven, walking with his father and his brothers."

"Amen," the others murmured, forming a procession behind her.

The castle retainers were left whispering among themselves. How long before Henry Tudor sent soldiers north to find these royal cubs? Would they, as the guardians of the York children, be treated as traitors? Certes, praying for the dead king's soul was laudable, but the children should be also praying for their own well-being here on earth.

2

Sheriff Hutton

AUTUMN 1485

For three days following his retreat to his chambers, no one saw John except for a page who was assigned to take him food and drink. Sensing he had an ally in Grace, Tom Gower sought her advice about John on two or three occasions.

"He will not see me, in truth," Tom said on the third day, finding her playing with a spaniel pup near the kennels. "I fear for his reason. 'Tis the way his father behaved when his queen died, Lady Bess told me. Perhaps he will speak to you, Lady Grace."

Grace felt herself flush and was glad she did not have one of those complexions that turned bright red. "Me? Why do you think John would talk to me? 'Tis my belief he hardly knows I exist," she answered, allowing the furry brown ball in her arms to cover her face with wet kisses and hide her trepidation. "Certes, Lady Bess knows him better, and is more important than I." She looked at Tom's honest, strong face from under her lashes and was touched by the concern in his bright blue eyes. He truly cares about

John, she thought, surprised. What little she had seen of men since her departure from the convent had led her to believe they were all brain or brawn and very little heart. Her mentor, Dame Elizabeth, was always disparaging them in front of her daughters, warning the girls to "beware the fickle, false intentions behind those charming smiles."

"I speak the truth, Lady Grace," Tom was saying. "John has told me he trusts you more than any of his cousins. In Jesu's name, please help him. He is in danger, for if Henry comes here to claim his bride, it would not do for King Richard's beloved son to be among the faces he sees. Knowing John, he would as lief run Henry through than kneel in homage to him. He has his father's tendency to act rashly." Tom's serious expression softened into a sardonic smile at the thought. "What say you, my lady? Will you do it?"

Letting the puppy loose to find its siblings, Grace straightened up and brushed off a few silky hairs it had left on her blue kersey overdress. "If you think I must, Tom, then aye, I will go to him. But wait outside the door, in case he is angered by my intrusion."

Tom grinned. "Certes, I will be there. You can count on me. Shall we go now?"

Grace nodded and followed him across the courtyard to the northeast tower. As fortune would have it, they encountered the page with a pitcher of ale before he could knock at John's door. Tom took it from the boy and thrust it into Grace's trembling fingers. Giving her a smile of encouragement, he tapped quietly on the solid oak. Without waiting for a response, he opened the door wide enough for Grace to slip through, then closed it behind her.

The room was shuttered against the late-afternoon sun, but even so it was stifling, the rushes too old to mask the odors. Grace peered through the gloom to find her bearings. A movement in the chair beside the empty fire grate told her where John was seated and she took a few tentative steps towards him, clutching the pewter jug to her thumping heart.

"John?" she whispered. " 'Tis I, Grace. I have come to bring you ale."

"Put it on the table." John's voice was flat, but Grace was happy to notice it contained no anger. Encouraged, she went to the table, poured a cup and carried it to him. He was dressed in a rumpled shirt and green breeches more suited to a peasant than a nobleman. He did not bother to look at her but put out his hand to take the drink.

"Nay, you shall not have it until you have the courtesy to look at me and say my name," she said. Where did that come from? She panicked. Dear God, what madness made me say that?

John lifted his head and stared at her in disbelief. "What did you say?"

"I said I will give you the ale if you greet me properly," she repeated, less bravely. She decided she would make a run for the door if he exploded, knowing Tom would be there to rescue her.

Whether because of the gentleness of a female voice or her unthreatening presence, or because John's grief had simply worn itself out, he suddenly laughed. Not a cruel, harsh laugh of anguish, but a genuine laugh of pleasure. "Grace, my little wren, what brings you in here—and unchaperoned?" he teased. Grace was so relieved that she almost dropped the cup.

She smiled radiantly. "Ah, John, I am so glad to hear you laugh. And I am happy you are not angry with me. All of us have been worried about you—but none more than Tom and I." She gave him the cup and ran to open the door. "Tom! He is well again. Come and see for yourself."

Tom strode into the darkened room and almost tripped over John's faithful greyhound, which had not left its master's side for three days. " 'Tis right glad I see you hale again, John," he said, grasping his friend's arm in salute. Then he wrinkled his nose in disgust. " 'Twould seem your dog has not seen the outdoors for some time. The chamber stinks to high Heaven." He went to the window and propped open the heavy wooden shutter, letting in the light and air. "That's better." He snapped his fingers at the dog, which lifted its narrow head inquisitively. "I will take Bran and let him run with Jason. I shall return anon." At the mention of his name, Bran rose nimbly to his feet, but sought John's side. In the light, Grace could see that John's chin was in need of a scrape.

"Stay a moment, Tom," John said softly, fondling Bran's ears. "I have to thank you. Grace tells me you have thought me lost these past three days. I, too, thought I was, but I needed to grieve alone and speak to God in my own way. I regret I gave concern, but I assure you, I am mended. Again," he said more curtly, embarrassed at his outburst, "my thanks."

Tom inclined his head in acknowledgment, whistled to Bran and left the room. He did not close the door, for he did not want Grace compromised without him standing guard.

"Pull up that stool, Grace. If you have nothing better to do, I have a need to talk to someone about my family. I am not an orphan as you are, but certes, I feel like one." John slapped a couple of fleas on his calf that had been disturbed by the activity in the room. "Damn fleas!" he said. "I swear I have been eaten alive these past two days."

Grace smiled, sat down on the stool in front of him and gathered her skirts tightly around her ankles to avoid being similarly attacked. She turned her solemn brown eyes to his face and characteristically cocked her head. She waited, hardly daring to breathe, afraid to spoil the intimacy.

"You did not know my father, did you?" John began and saw her shake her head. "I have had a goodly time to think about him these past few days, in truth, and to try to understand him. He was a great man, but he was quiet and serious and did not allow many to come close to him. I believe it made some people distrust him, and I wonder if 'twas why he was betrayed in the end. He was very different from your father, who was loud, enjoyed the company of others and was not afraid to indulge in the pleasures of life. I suppose one knew where one stood with him, whereas my father . . ." He shook his head.

"There is nothing wrong with being quiet and serious, John. Look at me," Grace countered. "I think I have a good heart, but I do not say very much."

John laughed. *"Touché, ma belle,"* he replied. "Although you were unafraid to stand up for yourself a moment ago." He thought for a moment, studying his fingers, and then chose to confide in her. "When my father was with my mother, he was a different person. The last time I saw them together was when I took Mother to his audience chamber at Leicester Castle, two days before the battle. As soon as he saw her all the worry on his face seemed to dissolve, and his smile made him look young again. I knew then I had been born of real love—both me and"—he bowed his head—"my poor sister, Katherine, God rest her soul."

"Where does your mother live, John?" Grace said, crossing herself and hoping to divert his attention from the loss of his sibling.

"She lives in Suffolk, not far from the coast, in a house on Jack Howard's estate—he is . . . was . . . the duke of Norfolk," he explained, and Grace nodded. " 'Twas exactly like her to disavow Jack Howard's advice about traveling to Leicester at such a dangerous moment. But she was determined that Father should not hear of Katherine's sudden death from anyone but her. She told me first, and I know my sorrow was but a drop in the pail compared to his. He loved Katherine greatly—his first child, and his only daughter. I was standing outside the door and heard his suffering upon the news. 'Twas savage." He gazed at a point in the fireplace as he remembered the scene. Afraid for his mother, he had quietly opened the door a crack and seen her comfort Richard; they had even shared a kiss.

"My mother is not of gentle stock," he said, bringing his gaze back to Grace's face. "And yet somehow she befriended Howard's wife. One day Mother was an invited guest at Tendring Hall and met my father when he was hunting there with Sir John. Father loved hunting—especially with his falcon." His voice fell back into a monotone.

"What is she like? And what is her name?" Grace asked, again hoping to steer the conversation to the living and away from the dead.

"Mother is stout-hearted!" he said, his face lightening. "And her name is Kate . . . Katherine Haute, of Snoll's Hatch in Kent, she used to tell people. Her father, my grandfather Bywood, was a farmer, but I never knew him. 'Twas mother's forthrightness that often got her into trouble, so they tell me, but it also made people love her. They say I am more like my father, but I have inherited Mother's love of singing. She has the voice of an angel, and Father told me once that he fell in love with her the first time he heard her sing."

Grace's eyes shone. "Sing something to me, John. I would hear your gift."

Unabashed, John began to sing in a strong tenor:

"Our King went forth to Normandy,
With grace and might of chivalry;
The God for him wrought marv'lously . . ."

Suddenly his voice became choked with tears, and the next words were almost inaudible.

"Wherefore England may call and cry,
Deo gratias."

He buried his head in his hands, and tears fell from between his fingers. Grace sat stupefied, every nerve in her body itching to put her arms around him and comfort him, but her reserve got the better of her. A few seconds later she was glad she had refrained from her urge, for he sat up straight, wiped his face on the sleeve of his shirt and grinned sheepishly.

"Forgive me for being addlepated, Grace. I should not have attempted that particular song, in truth. It always reminds me of the time Mother put me in Father's care when I was six, and I had to say good-bye to everything I knew. She sang it to me the night before we parted. Foolish of me. Am I forgiven?"

"Dearest John," Grace whispered. "There is nothing to forgive. My mother died when I was so young, I do not remember her. But there is still a pain in my heart for my loss. And I never knew my father."

John looked at her curiously. "I have often wondered why Dame Grey sent for you, Grace. Do you know? After all, would she not want to forget her husband's infidelities? You would be a constant reminder."

"I heard from an attendant that 'twas a promise Dame Grey made to my father upon his deathbed. He knew where I was and had paid the abbey to keep me, so I was told. Dame Grey was keeping a promise, I believe, and I thank God daily for it—even if I do feel a misfit sometimes."

"Aye, little wren, 'tis ironic how very lonely one can be even in a big family. And now my sister is gone, I am even more alone—" he broke off, sighing.

"But you have me," Grace whispered.

"Aye, so I do. I am a lucky man," he said, holding her chin in his fingers. Grace willed him to kiss her, but footsteps along the corridor caught their attention and John rose when Bess and Cecily ran in to greet him. He has forgotten me already, Grace thought miserably, rising from her stool.

"We have been so worried, John," Bess admonished him, beaming at Grace. "Tom told us that Grace had the magic touch, and I am right glad to see you looking well again. We have news of Lord Lovell to tell. It seems he was able to hide among the returning Howard force into Suffolk and has sought sanctuary at Colchester, as have the Stafford brothers."

"Praise be to the Virgin," John said, crossing himself. "I am right glad to hear it. And what of our cousin Lincoln? Is he fled, taken"—he paused for a second before daring to ask—"dead, as was rumored?"

"Nay, he is alive. Henry keeps him close by, so the messenger says," Bess replied.

"What is that vile smell?" Cecily suddenly interrupted, her face screwing up in disgust.

"Cecily!" exclaimed Bess. "Where are your manners? 'Tis not your place to find fault. You know Mother taught us that."

Cecily pouted, used a corner of her veil to cover her nose and flounced off to the window. "Aye, but she isn't here, so where is the harm?" she retorted.

Bess looked shocked but decided to ignore her. Grace was used to Bess's dutiful demeanor and felt sorry for her. It must be hard to be the eldest of so many children, she decided, and have to be a model for the rest.

"I have not been as fastidious as I might these past three days, 'tis all, Cis," John answered, grinning. "Forgive me. Come, let us get some fresh air."

"Aye, before I swoon," said Cecily, and eyeing a pile of Bran's excrement in her path, she lifted her skirts well above the rushes and hurried from the room.

FOR THREE WEEKS those in the castle tried to settle into their usual routines. September's sun warmed the reapers as they gathered in the sheaves of wheat, and in other fields ploughmen forged their straight furrows, making them ready to receive the hardy rye seed. Ax and adze felled trees and made logs for the winter fires that would burn from November to spring. Grace wondered how cold it would get here, and she shivered when she thought of how the wind would change direction and come down from the north to chill their bones.

But thoughts of winter were far away as she strolled around the inner bailey one afternoon and watched the turner with his pole lathe making mugs and bowls, the blacksmith raining a blow on a red-hot horseshoe, a laundrywoman carrying a basket of linens on her head and a wheelwright mending a cartwheel. The craftsmen knew her by now and called "Good morrow, Lady Grace" in their strong Yorkshire dialect, and she smiled, acknowledging their salutations. Hearing her title always gave her a start, and she thought she would never get used to her new status. She found she actually missed the work in the garden that used to take up much of her day at the abbey, but here she was not required to lift a finger—except to hem a gown or embroider a kerchief.

She arrived at the kennels to check on her favorite pup and was about to gentle him away from his mother's tit when a villager ran headlong through the gate, shouting, "The king's messenger be coming!" He was accosted by a guard and prevented from advancing farther, but by then the watchtower sentinel was also alerting the castle to an unexpected visit. He blew on his shawm, its raucous reedy racket causing Grace to stop up her ears and a dog to howl.

"John!" she mouthed, frightened, "The king must not find him here." Taking to her heels, she raced into the northwest tower, up the narrow twisting stairs and out onto the rampart. John, Tom and two of Tom's Gower cousins had gone hunting after dinner at noon and had not yet returned. She scanned the forest but realized all she could see were the tops of the trees. The retinue of Henry's men must surely have passed through the forest from York through Strensall, so perhaps John had seen them and remained hidden. Odds bodkins, she thought, why have I not yet learned to ride? John had promised to teach her, but until he did, she could only ride pillion behind a groom or, on occasion, Cecily, who was an excellent horsewoman. The huge beasts terrified her. The nuns had owned a large ox that pulled the convent cart into Leicester on market days to give the leftover convent produce to the poor. The beast was placid, and Grace had been put on its back once by Sister Benedict, one of the younger nuns, who had taken the child under her wing. But when the ox swished its tail at some pesky flies and struck the little girl, she lost her balance and fell off. She had been afraid of large animals ever since.

Realizing her mission was futile, she ran helter-skelter down the spiral stairs to her chamber to alert her sisters. "The king is come!" she said breathlessly.

Bess dropped her needlework onto the floor and the lutenist missed half of the strings on a downward chord, creating a discordant twang that lent an ominous note to Grace's pronouncement.

"The . . . the k-king?" Bess whispered. "Henry is here?"

"The villager said 'the king's messenger,'" Grace explained. "I thought the king would follow behind."

"You witless girl," cried Bess's tiring woman, throwing her arms around Bess and glaring at Grace. "A messenger from the king means the king is *not* here. You have frightened my poor sweeting half to death."

Tears sprang to Grace's brown eyes and she begged Bess's pardon. Hiding her unhappiness, she walked quickly from the room, noticing Cecily's smirk at her older sister's dismay. I hope Cis's betrothed is a toad, Grace thought uncharitably, even though she had met Ralph Scrope of Upsall at court, and he had done nothing to deserve such an unkind moniker. She paused at the tower entrance to watch the horsemen dismount and the grooms lead the horses away. A stout man with a long drooping mustache was solemnly greeted by Tom's uncle as "Sir Robert," and Grace found out later the man's name was Willoughby and that he was steward of the king's household. Catching sight of Grace in the doorway, Sir John Gower hurried up to her and requested that she and her sisters ready themselves to meet the king's messenger.

"I will send for you all anon, my lady, as soon as Sir Robert has slaked his thirst," he directed her, and stomped off towards the great hall.

Bess's lovely face was pale with fear when Grace gave her the message, but her ladies gathered round, untying her sleeves at the shoulders, unlacing the tight bodice and slipping her skirts to the floor. They chose a deep crimson damask gown with blue facing and trimmed with miniver to show off her stature and porcelain skin. She had inherited the best of both her handsome parents, and with her wavy golden hair tumbling to her knees, Grace thought she had never seen anyone so beautiful. In no time at all, the ladies coiled the unruly tresses into a knot on the back of Bess's head and pinned a fashionable short hennin over it, which hid all that glory from the prying eyes of men. A simple wire frame attached to the hat supported the pure white gauze veil that stood out from her face. A collar of gold set with pearls and sapphires completed the portrait of a princess— oldest child of King Edward the Fourth.

As the attendants were busy dressing Bess, Cecily, Grace and Margaret helped one another into more fetching gowns, and a little later, when the sun was dipping below the west wall, all four stepped across the great hall's threshold.

"I am ready to face the enemy. Wish me well, sisters," Bess whispered as Sir John Gower came forward to take her hand and lead her to Sir Robert.

"For inspection," Cecily muttered angrily. "As if she were a horse or a cow."

Grace shuddered and her heart went out to Bess, standing there so regally, being ogled by the middle-aged Willoughby. Cecily and Margaret took a few steps forward and Grace followed, hoping she was well hidden behind Cecily's larger girth. Sir John sent Tom to escort them to cushioned stools against the wall and out of the bright light of the massive chandelier dripping wax from a hundred candles. They could not hear what was being said to Bess, so Cecily started to bat her eyelashes at one of Sir Robert's knights, but Grace folded her hands on her lap, stared at her fingers and retreated inside her comfortable shell.

She thought back to a conversation she had had with Bess one day in the meadow when Cecily had been confined to the castle during her courses. They were making a garland to help cheer their sister, and Grace suddenly noticed Bess was crying.

"What it is, Bess?" she asked, full of concern. "May I help you?"

Grace's gentle voice and sympathy only caused Bess to sob more, and to avoid Tom Gower noticing and causing Bess embarrassment, Grace left her spot on the grass and knelt in front of her sister, taking the older girl in her arms.

"Come now," Grace soothed, sounding more like a mother than a girl of twelve. "You can tell me. I swear on the Virgin I shall not breathe a word to anyone. What is it?"

She stroked Bess's forehead and pushed a wayward golden strand of hair off the girl's wet face. Then she proffered Bess her kerchief. "Sweet Bess, blow your nose and tell me of your troubles. Like as not I shall not understand, but Sister Benedict always said 'tis good to tell your heartaches to someone." She paused, knowing that the good nun may have had God in mind as a listener, but she pressed on. "When you share, it becomes someone else's care."

Bess did as she was told and blew her nose. Then, her tears spent, she contemplated the young girl in front of her. "You are a curious child, Grace. So green, and yet so wise. In truth, I know not how to treat with you sometimes. You are not so clever as Cecily and yet you are cleverer." She shook her head. "I am not making sense, I dare swear. But since you ask, I will tell you why I am distressed. I cannot speak of these things to Cis, for she either laughs at me or becomes as watery as the conduit in the Chepe."

Grace had no idea what Bess was talking about, but she nodded sagely. "I am listening, Bess," she said. "Is it about King Rich . . . I mean, Uncle Richard?"

"Nay, it is not!" Bess was emphatic, her brows snapping together. "What do you know of that, pray?"

"Nothing very much," Grace assured her, as she sadly realized her presence at Westminster must have gone unnoticed during the months before Queen Anne's death, when the subsequent rumor about Richard and Bess was circulated. She wished she had been more forthright during those times, but she was learning. She had accepted that she was an inconsequential member of this royal brood, and as such had done her best to stay out of everyone's way at court.

"I regret I made no impression upon you back then, Bess. But I was there; I saw what happened," she said quietly.

Bess was aghast at her faux pas. "Forgive me, Grace," she cried. "Certes, you were there. My mind is elsewhere, I have to confess." She sighed. "I have thought much about my feelings for our uncle since we were all sent here, and I see 'twas naught but a young and foolish fancy I had. Nay, my thoughts were far from the king, in truth." She hesitated, ashamed of herself for crying in front of the younger girl. "I was remembering a time long ago, when I taught our brother—sweet little Dickon—how to make a daisy chain, like this one. And it reminded me that I may never see him or Edward again."

Grace nodded. "One of your mother's ladies told me she thought Uncle Richard had . . ." she did not dare finish.

"I do not want to believe it, Grace," Bess answered sadly, "but where have they been all this time? It has been two years since we've had word of anyone seeing them at the Tower."

"Perhaps they were sent away for some reason," Grace ventured, her curious mind already conjuring up several. There was nothing Grace loved more than a mystery, and finally someone was addressing this one. "You cannot give up hope yet, Bess."

Grace's earnest little face made Bess smile. "I suppose you are right. 'Tis possible Uncle Richard sent them to our Aunt Margaret in Burgundy. I did hear such a rumor after we left sanctuary. But why would he not tell us?"

"I know not. But why were you in sanctuary, Bess? No one has ever explained that to me. Anne, Catherine and Bridget did not tell me much except that it was cramped and cold. Were you all there?"

"Aye. Certes, except for Ned; he was in the Tower." When Bess saw Grace's puzzled frown, she elaborated: "You see, when Father died so unexpectedly, Mother quickly sent word to her brother, Uncle Anthony—Lord Rivers—at Ludlow, where Ned was under his guardianship, preparing for the day when he would be king. Who would have guessed that day would come so soon?" she mused, shaking her head. "But no mind. 'Tis said Mother wanted to be regent, and so needed to have Ned with her in London to win over the people and Parliament. She asked Anthony to hurry to London with Ned. But, you see, when he was dying, Father named Uncle Richard as Lord Protector, meaning he would rule until Ned reached his majority and Mother would have no power. And so she 'neglected' to send a messenger north to Middleham and hoped Rivers and Ned would reach London first. 'Twas a rash decision that led Uncle Richard to believe Mother and Uncle Anthony were acting treasonously." She paused for Grace to take this all in. "That is the side of my mother I do not understand—or, God forgive me, admire," she remarked, tearing apart a daisy. "Why would she do such a thing? Uncle Richard was a good man; he would not have treated her unkindly." She caught Grace's surprised expression at this confidence and muttered: "Pray forgive me, I am thinking aloud."

She contemplated a chewed thumbnail and then continued: "Uncle Richard was warned of Mother's actions—'tis said by Will Hastings— and hurried south. He met up with the Ludlow party on the road at Stony Stratford, and when he saw the large army Uncle Rivers had with him, he understood Mother's intentions, arrested Rivers and sent him here." She glanced up at the castle, her blue eyes pensive.

"But sanctuary, Bess. You have not told me why her grace had to go into sanctuary?" Grace's knees were numb, but she was so eager not to miss a word, she could not move.

"Because she was afraid of what Uncle Richard might do to her," Bess said. "She was so fearful when she heard what had happened at Stony Stratford, and that Richard was on his way to London with Ned by his side, she knew she had lost. Certes, 'twas her ambition that put us all in danger." Bess's mouth was set in a firm line, and she held her head high. "If I do become queen of England, I shall not engage in scheming and politics. I have seen how much it hurts people. I do not believe for one moment Uncle Richard would have harmed any of us, but she must have believed she was trying to protect us all by seeking sanctuary. 'Tis the only reason I have been able to accept, in truth."

Grace nodded. "Aye, perhaps you are right." Her mind bounded from one thought to another and she returned to the possible whereabouts of her half brothers. "You say 'tis possible Uncle Richard sent Ned and Dickon to Burgundy—to the Duchess Margaret," she said, pouncing on the chance to find out more about this relative who was always spoken of with such awe. "What is she like—Aunt Margaret, I mean? Have you met her?"

Bess chuckled. "Aye, when I was fourteen she came back to England for a few months, and we were in awe of her lavish wardrobe. I remember Mother being jealous of all her jewels. But it was her wit and intelligence that were the talk of Father's court. I heard Jack Howard say that had she been a man, she would have made England a great king. To me she was kind enough"—she shrugged—"and I remember her being tall and handsome—not beautiful like mother, but impressive. She left England to marry Duke Charles, but he was killed in battle nine years later."

"I think I would have been afraid of her," Grace said.

Bess patted her knee and leaned forward conspiratorially. "And they say she and my Uncle Anthony were . . . well . . ." she stopped when she remembered Grace was only twelve and an innocent. ". . . um, close."

Grace's eyes widened with shock. "Were they not married to each other?" Her strict convent upbringing often made her the butt of sibling teasing, so she often kept her thoughts to herself, but it was hard to imagine these transgressors not being afraid of going to Hell.

Bess shook her head, laughing. "So prim, Grace! Our father was not the only one who . . . um . . . let us say, looked elsewhere for love. Certes, Uncle Richard had his leman, and Aunt Margaret had her paramour, too. Poor Uncle Anthony. Certes, but you know now what happened to him." She saw Grace shake her head. "After he was accused of treason, Uncle Richard imprisoned him"—she pointed dramatically to a window in the guard tower—"in *there* until he was beheaded at Pontefract."

Grace turned her curious brown eyes to the window in question and noted the bars on it. "How sad," she said. "But perhaps he deserved it." Then Anthony, Lord Rivers, was quickly forgotten as she begged for more information on her brothers.

"We hardly saw Edward at all once Father sent him to Ludlow Castle when he was only three to be groomed as prince of Wales and the next king," Bess told her, folding and refolding her kerchief on her lap.

"Three!" Grace exclaimed. " 'Tis no wonder your mother pined for him. You must have known little Dickon better, to be sure. What was he like?"

"He looks like Father—and I think he will be like Father. He is a prankster and loved to make our lives a misery. His favorite game was playing hide-and-go-seek, and he could crawl into the tiniest of spaces and never make a sound, so we gave up looking for him. Then he would whine to Mother that we were being mean to him. I confess I was so happy when he was taken away from us in sanctuary and sent to join Ned in the Tower. Mother was distraught, but, in truth, even she was relieved he was gone. It was hard enough, all of us living there crammed into those few small rooms, without Dickon creating havoc every day." Her tears began to fall again. "Now I wish we could have him back, and I pray for his return every night." She sniffed and wiped her nose unceremoniously on the hem of her dress, making Grace giggle. "He did love to sing, and had a beautiful voice. He also loved me to sing him to sleep. I would only have to hum a few notes of 'Douway Robin' or another lullaby and he would close his eyes and drift off in no time at all. He looked so angelic then, with his flaxen hair and great long lashes lying upon his cheek, that 'twas hard to remember he had annoyed me earlier in the day."

"I am sorry for you, Bess, truly I am," Grace said, shifting her aching legs gratefully.

"And now I may have to marry this hateful Henry, who I have never laid eyes on," Bess groaned.

"Perhaps you could ask Henry to find the boys," Grace said absently, and was startled by Bess's peal of laughter.

"Oh, Grace. You are such an innocent. Certes, Henry would like nothing more than if the boys are never seen again. 'Tis true, we have all been declared bastards, but still, two male York heirs at large would cause him many sleepless nights." She sniffled again, then blew her nose. "I do not even understand why he is allowed to be king. He has but a tiny trickle of royal blood in his veins, and that came by a bastard of John of Gaunt.

By rights the bastard Beauforts—and Henry is a Beaufort, in case you did not know—were expressly forbidden to ever claim the crown. But, by the sweet Virgin, look at them now!" Her voice rose in anger, her tears forgotten.

Grace listened attentively. So much about her family was incomprehensible to her—not the least of which was how many bastards loomed large in it—but she was learning fast and could not wait to lie in bed and remember it all.

"It seems my mother was conspiring with Henry's mother, the countess of Richmond and Derby, to arrange this match," Bess said and then smirked. "Mother has always loathed that woman. She calls her Scraggy Maggie—her name is Margaret Beaufort, and she is tall and thin, you will see." Seeing Grace nod, Bess was again ruefully reminded that the girl had met the Beaufort woman at court. "Why they brewed such a scheme, I cannot imagine," she went on. "But Henry is said to have promised to marry me—he promised in front of a bishop in Rennes that first Christmas of Uncle Richard's reign. Do you think they consulted me? Nay. I was but their pawn, and when Henry's first attempt to invade back in Eighty-four came to naught, I thought the whole plan would come to naught, too. Damn him for trying again," she cried, flinging the petals of a daisy into the wind and watching them swirl away.

Tom Gower heard Bess's raised voice and loped towards them with the awkwardness of a youth who has not yet grown into his long limbs. Grace helped Bess to her feet, and they gathered up the garland.

"We are ready to go back, Tom," Bess called, her pique subsiding. "You are bored, are you not?" Tom gave her a sheepish grin.

"Down, Jason!" Grace admonished Tom's lurcher, who bounded towards her. Despite its size, she was unafraid of the tall, lean hunting dog, who did not have far to jump to lick her face as she ruffled its coarse gray coat.

Tom called the dog off. "There is a storm brewing, Lady Bess. I must return you to the safety of the castle or my uncle will give me a thrashing," he said, pointing to the southwest. By the time they reached the inner bailey, the first raindrops were spitting against the castle walls.

THAT NIGHT GRACE had trouble falling asleep. She often did when she had something on her mind to put right. There was the time when Sister Benedict's rosary had gone missing. The nuns searched high and low, and

Benedict became more and more distraught. It had been a family heir-loom, and everyone knew one of the stones was a ruby. One of the novices was brought before Mother Hawise, accused by a mean-spirited sister of stealing the beads. The novice was one of Grace's bedfellows and she had worked alongside her in the garden all that day, so Grace knew the girl could not have been the thief. The accused was locked in one of the cells until the sheriff could spare the time to question her. Grace smuggled food through the tiny grille in the door and tried to console her friend. The next day in the garden, she racked her brain for an obvious solution—first believing it was the mean-spirited nun herself who had stolen it. And then she had seen the bird hopping on the ledge of one of the dormitory win-dows, where it had built its untidy nest.

" 'Tis a jackdaw!" she cried, dropping her basket of peas and running towards the building. Several nuns watched her go, smiling indulgently. Grace was a child, and animals and birds fascinated her. But Grace tugged at Sister Benedict's habit and bade the nun to follow her. The taller nun was able to reach up and pull the nest through the bars on the window, and sure enough, woven into the hair, twigs and other debris was her precious rosary. Grace had been the toast of the convent that day, and her fascina-tion with puzzles had begun.

And the mystery of the missing boys was exactly the kind of puzzle that she would enjoy gnawing on, like a dog with a bone. As she lay pondering, she thought that solving it would make her family so proud of her that she would never feel left out again. With all the certainty of a twelve-year-old, she knew that if she tried hard enough, any problem could be solved—as simply as finding a rosary in a bird's nest.

"WE ARE TO proceed to London at the end of the week," Bess told her sisters once they were back in their apartments. "Sir Robert will escort us, and we shall be lodged at Mother's old residence, at Ormond's Inn. I know not what is in store for us, in truth, and nothing was said of any marriage between Henry and me," she said, relieved, allowing Grace to unlace her tight bodice.

"Praise be to God," Cecily cried, pulling off her headdress and letting her silvery hair loose. "I, for one, will be happy to leave this backwater for London."

"Backwater?" Grace queried from behind Bess. "This is a magnificent castle, and we have everything we need."

Cecily tossed her head. " 'Tis a backwater, Grace, and full of Yorkshire turds!"

"Cecily!" exclaimed Bess and Grace together.

"Pray curb your tongue," Bess admonished Cecily and checked to see that the door was well and truly closed. Lady Gower might be in earshot, and she was a proud Yorkshirewoman.

"Pah!" Cecily retorted. "Certes, you feel the same way. You told me so."

"I told you in confidence, Cis. In our position you cannot go through life saying exactly what you think. That behavior is for peasants. When you take up your duties as Ralph's wife, you will be allowed to say only what your husband tells you you may," Bess lectured.

"You may behave that way, Bess, but I shall do and say as I please," Cecily retorted. "I do not care a fig what my husband will say." She cocked her snoot at an imaginary husband, causing Bess to roll her eyes and Grace to giggle. "I am weary of you telling me what to do. I am not a child," she pronounced as she flounced up the two steps to the garderobe carrying a candle to light her way into the small dark recess carved out of the thick wall, where the privy was hidden.

"She has been like this ever since Mary died," Bess confided in Grace. "You never knew our sister Mary—she was born between Cis and me, and she and Cecily did everything together." Bess looked grave. "She died from a fever in Eighty-two, and Cis was heartbroken." She paused. "We all were. Mary was Father's favorite: full of life and forever laughing. Cecily tried to be like her to gain Father's favor, but instead she became impertinent and willful."

Grace absorbed the information and resolved to be more patient with Cecily. For a year now, she had been learning what it was like to be a sister and part of a family, and she could not bear to think of losing any of them. The Benedictines had treated her variously with kindness or indifference, depending on their inclinations, but truth be told she had never felt a part of the order, nor had she heard a calling. Mother Hawise's constant reminders of Grace's base-born beginnings became a cross the girl learned to bear bravely, but instead of looking on her keeper gratefully, Grace had hardened her heart against her. She had dreaded the day when she might be forced into taking vows. Over the years, she grew a shell into which she would crawl at night and pray to St. Sibylline of Pavia—who had also been an orphan—for deliverance from the place. When Elizabeth's messenger had come, she was convinced the saint had heard her plea.

Loud voices interrupted their conversation, and both girls ran to the window, leaving Margaret of Salisbury to peer over her bedclothes in fear.

"What is it?" Cecily called from the garderobe. "Who is shouting so?"

From their chamber on the third floor they could not make out the scene in the dark courtyard below, other than a few torches held aloft by seemingly invisible hands.

"I will go and see what is happening," Grace said, surprising Bess with her fearlessness. She pulled her shawl from its peg by the doorway, covered her head and slipped out to the stone staircase. The stairs were lit with flambeaux, allowing her to wend her way round and round until she came to a small embrasure that, if she stood on tiptoe, gave her a clear view of the group of men in front of the great hall. She gasped when she recognized John, grim-faced in the center, his dagger drawn and Tom by his side.

"Aye, I am King Richard's son," he was saying. "His *bastard* son. Henry Tudor can have no quarrel with me!"

"Lord John, I beg of you, sheathe your dagger," Sir John Gower said calmly, coming between John and the guards menacing the young men. "Do not make this more difficult for yourself." More quietly, he told John, "Albeit you are the late king's bastard, you are a natural rallying point for all Yorkists, and thus you represent a danger, my lord. Have a care."

At that moment Robert Willoughby came striding across the courtyard from his quarters, demanding an explanation for the commotion. Gower stood in front of John, facing Willoughby, and attempted to make light of the situation. " 'Tis the hunting party come late, Sir Robert," he stammered, clearly nervous. "The lads meant no harm. The bum-baileys got lost in the forest, 'tis all. I will take them to task, have no fear." He walked forward, smiling more confidently, as if to accompany the older man back to his apartment, distracting him from John. "Pray get some rest, sir; you have had a tiring day."

Grace held her breath in her hiding place and sent up a prayer to keep John safe and turn Sir Robert's footsteps away. But all had reckoned without John's pride.

"I am able to speak for myself, Sir John, I thank you." John brushed Gower aside and gave Sir Robert a stiff little bow. "John of Gloucester, sir. I am son of our late and beloved King Richard. May he rest in peace."

Grace gasped at his audacity. "Oh, John," she whispered. "How foolish of you. You might have escaped."

Sir Robert stared at the young man before him and gave him a small bow in return. His orders made no mention of the young Captain of Calais, who was thought to have fled with Lovell into sanctuary, and he was at a loss to know what to do with the boy. Henry had been explicit that only Bess and "the sisters that lodge with her there," as well as Warwick and his sister, Margaret, be escorted to London, "in their own time. No hurry, Willoughby," Henry had said. "We do not wish to offend. Be gentle with them." Young Gloucester was not part of the plan, and Sir Robert needed time to weigh his options.

"Take him to the guard room for the night," he decided. "Gower, attend to his needs. We will talk more in the morning." He put up his hand as Sir John tried to say something. "And there is an end to it," he declared, turning on his heel and hurrying back to bed.

Gower instructed Tom to see to John's comfort. In the torchlight he saw John's angry face and put a restraining hand on the young man's shoulder. "Go quietly, I beg of you. Chances are you will simply accompany your cousins to London. As you say, the king can have no quarrel with you."

Four guards marched John to the guard tower and out of Grace's sight. Will they put him in the same cell Anthony Rivers occupied? she wondered, horrified. Would the same fate befall her beloved John? She shivered and realized she was chilled by both John's circumstances and the October night air. She hurried upstairs to relay her news.

THE NEXT DAY Sir Robert sent a messenger to London with the news of John of Gloucester's capture, and he calculated he would be long gone before a new order could arrive at Sheriff Hutton. "He will be in your charge, Sir John," Willoughby said, pleased with himself. " 'Twill be your first test of loyalty to our new sovereign. The lad will remain where he is until you know the king's pleasure, is that understood?" Gower nodded assent but swore nothing.

Taking Henry's edict to heart, Willoughby seemed in no hurry to depart for the south, tarrying instead to hunt in Galtres Forest or fish in the Derwent a few miles east of the village. He was intent on making a good impression on the young woman who would, if Henry kept his long-ago promise, become queen, and so refused to rush her.

"The king's grace has given me permission to ease your journey in any way I can," the jovial Willoughby told the lovely young woman who sat at his right hand at dinner on the second day. "I have made arrangements for the finest carriage in York to be fitted out for you and your sisters, my lady. We shall not go until all is packed, and you need not leave anything behind." His pale rheumy eyes twinkled at her. "I know how long a lady's wardrobe and accoutrements take to pack—my lady wife tries my patience at times, I must confess. In the meantime, I shall take advantage of the fresh Yorkshire air and expect to provide a buck or two for the table during my brief stay." He picked up the thighbone of a pheasant and carried it greedily to his mouth, leaving some of the gravy clinging to his mustache. Then he dipped a large hunk of bread into his trencher and sopped up the remaining savory juices noisily, smacking his lips and grunting in pleasure. "Good country fare," he announced finally, not noticing Bess's obvious disdain for his table manners, and waved at a ewerer to bring the finger bowl. "Would you care to join me in the hunt one day, my lady?"

Bess surprised him with a dazzling smile. " 'Twould please us all, in truth, Sir Robert. Although I think a few hours of fishing would please me the most."

"Fishing, eh?" Sir Robert slapped his thigh. "Do you use a worm or a fly, Lady Elizabeth?" He doubted that one as refined as Bess would deign to handle a worm.

"Both, Sir Robert," Bess replied without batting an eye. "One cannot learn how to fish properly without baiting one's own hook. Tom Gower has taught us all how to fish for trout this summer, and I confess it is a pleasant way to spend an afternoon."

"Sir John's young nephew, is it?" And seeing Bess incline her head in agreement, he continued: "Then we shall have Tom Gower show us the best spots in the river, say, two days hence? I have business in York on the morrow."

"Certes. We shall be happy to go with you, Sir Robert." She seized the lighthearted moment and, turning her dark blue eyes to his admiring gaze, continued airily: "But I have a boon to beg of you. My sister, Lady Grace, is most distressed by her cousin of Gloucester's confinement in the guard house."

At the mention of her name, Grace looked along the table, straining to hear. Her eyes were still red from her sleepless night of worry for John, when she had tried to stifle her frightened tears into her pillow.

"I wonder if you would grant her an interview with Lord John to satisfy her that he is not being mistreated," Bess said, a little more loudly.

Sir Robert was taken aback. Talking about fishing with Lady Elizabeth was one thing, but talking of state business was quite another. He coughed uncomfortably, trying to cover his inability to think of a reason why he should not grant this request. He was within his rights to refuse, but what harm could there be? Little Grace was but a child, and she did look as though she had been crying. He thought of his future; Elizabeth was certain to be queen and, judging from her beauty, she would have Henry wrapped around her little finger in no time, he deduced. Perhaps she would remember him kindly after she was crowned. Wiping his mouth carefully on his kerchief, he suddenly smiled, showing several gaps in his teeth. "Certes, Lady Grace may see her cousin, my lady," he said, magnanimously, and then leaned into Bess, chuckling, "as long as she doesn't help him escape. Ha!"

Bess gave a responding titter, trying not to reel away from his bad breath. "Aye, that would be a dilemma for you, would it not, Sir Robert? I assure you, Lady Grace has no more plan for John's escape than"—and she pointed to a spaniel worrying a bone—"than that dog there!" And they both laughed.

Sir Robert was entranced by Bess and could deny her nothing at that moment. "I see nothing wrong in allowing all of you to visit the lad whenever you want," he said, waving his hand to include Bess and Cecily. "There will, of necessity, be a guard outside the door, you do understand?"

Bess clapped her hands delightedly. "You are too kind, Sir Robert." She called to Grace at the end of the table, "We may see John whenever we like, my dear Lady Grace, thanks to Sir Robert's generosity."

Grace's usually serious face was transformed by a radiant smile, causing Sir Robert to notice her for the first time. By Christ's nails, she will turn heads in the not-too-distant future, he thought; her mother must have indeed been a beauty—must have been to turn lecher Edward's head. "Well, then," he said, satisfied, "and there is an end to it!"

As soon as the meal was over, the benches stacked and trestle tables collapsed, Grace ran to the kennels, picked up her special puppy and presented herself at the guard tower door, where a large yeoman stood sentinel and eyed her suspiciously.

"Eh, lass, why be you here? It be no place for a child," he growled, working a stringy morsel of meat out from between his teeth with a grubby fingernail and not recognizing her. "You canna come in here."

"But I can," Grace asserted, lifting her chin and holding the dog tightly. "Sir Robert Willoughby has given me permission to visit your prisoner."

The guard's mouth dropped open. "Did he now?" he said in disbelief. "We'll see about that. Ho! Dan'l Miller, rouse your arse and come out here. There be a little lady to see us."

"How dare you," Grace said, standing her ground. And with the greatest difficulty she pronounced her name, complete with its title, just as Daniel Miller appeared in the doorway. "I am the Lady Grace Plantagenet."

Daniel gulped, recognizing her at once, and cuffed his friend. "You dolt, Sam Withers. She be right. She be King Edward's bast— er, daughter." As Sam touched his forelock and muttered an apology, Daniel addressed Grace: "I be sorry, m'lady. Why're you here?"

At that moment, Sir Robert's squire arrived on the scene and corroborated Grace's statement, chuckling at the girl's enthusiasm. "Sir Robert gave his permission only a few minutes ago, lads," he told the guards. " 'Tis true, any of the royal ladies may visit John of Gloucester. But there must be a guard outside the door at all times."

"Aye, sir," Daniel and Sam said in unison, and straightening his helmet Daniel made way for Grace to precede him through the lower garrison chamber and up the spiral stairs to the second floor. Unhooking a ring of keys from a nail, he selected one and put it in the keyhole. "Visitor, my lord!" he said loudly, peering through the small grille at eye level. "A lady." And not waiting for a response, he pulled the heavy oak door open and ushered Grace in, slamming the door behind her. The puppy wriggled out of her arms and, happy to be free, ran around in circles, chasing its tail.

Grace was surprised by the size and comfort of the room. She had imagined John in a dank, sunless cell, chained to a wall down which the

damp would have created green slime. Instead she saw him standing by a
curtained bed, an abandoned book lying on top of the wool blanket. The
room also boasted a table on which sat writing materials and a silver flagon
and cup, and a high-back cushioned chair placed next to a small fireplace.
Sunlight streamed in through the open south window, and the larger east-
facing window afforded a view over the outer bailey and village beyond.
Certes, she thought, there are bars on the windows, but this is not the
prison of my nightmares.

"Grace!" John's hands were outstretched in greeting, and she ran to
take them, squeaking with excitement.

"Are you well, John? Have they tortured you?" she asked anxiously,
scanning his face and neck for cuts and bruises.

She was a little hurt when he laughed outright, lifted her up and swung
her around, assuring her he had not been harmed. The spaniel yipped at
his feet and promptly relieved itself on John's shoe. John promptly dropped
Grace and scolded the pup, pushing its nose in the puddle. "Bad dog," he
admonished it, and tapped it under the chin, making it yelp. " 'Tis how
you train them, Grace," he said, seeing her dismay. "He'll learn in time,"
he said kindly. "Now, how did you manage to bribe the guard? I have had
only one visitor since they dared to put me in here—Tom was allowed to
bring me my things," he said, indicating a few clothes hanging on a peg.
He used his foot to push some of the rushes on the floor over the dog's
puddle.

"Bess asked Sir Robert if we could come, and he said we could on condition we did not plot your escape," Grace told him. She lowered her voice. "I
would be happy to help you escape, if you want, John."

For a moment, John was tempted. But seeing the diminutive young girl
and her innocence laid bare for him, he dismissed the idea out of hand.
Instead he bantered with her for half an hour, hiding his anger at being so
treated by Henry but understanding the reason. He had spent the night
cursing his folly that he had not flown the coop long before Sir Robert had
arrived, but although he liked to think himself a man, there was still a
boy's fear not far beneath the surface, and staying with his family had been
his first instinct. He had no one but these cousins now that his beloved
father and sister were gone, and he could not place his mother in danger
by fleeing to her.

"No one is going to harm me, Grace. And no one will harm you, I promise. We are of no consequence in this fight for the crown, you and I. They believe I could rally my father's supporters if they let me go free, 'tis all. So here I sit." He rose and paced the room as he had seen his father do many times. "Now if only we knew the whereabouts of your two half brothers, Henry might truly have something to fear. If they are still in the Tower, he is in no hurry to parade them in front of his new subjects. They have no love for him yet, but Ned and Dickon are their beloved King Edward's sons, and I warrant the people would turn a blind eye to the illegal marriage to Dame Grey . . . . But what is the use? We know not where they are housed, and that is that. Certes, Henry's other worry is Edward of Warwick. I wonder what he has in store for Uncle George's boy, poor child. In truth, because of his father's attainder, he is not eligible . . ." He pondered this out loud, almost forgetting Grace was still there. When his glance fell back on her, he changed the subject. "When do you leave for London?"

"On Friday, so we are told. On Thursday Sir Robert is taking all of us fishing on the Derwent," she said. "I wish you could come."

John made a face. "Fishing? 'Tis for faint hearts, little wren, although Tom Gower has honed his skill well and makes it mildly amusing. The thrill of the hunt is infinitely more gratifying, Grace," he said, staring out of the window and onto the Galtres forest. "But 'twill be a change of pace for you girls. Send them a kiss from me."

Grace sensed her visit was at an end, left the chair and moved to the door, the pup under one arm. "Farewell, John. I shall come tomorrow—and bring the others. We can play cards if that would amuse you," she said.

"Aye, it would," John said. "Except Bess always wins. You have brightened my day, little wren." He tipped up her face and smiled at her. Grace's heart stood still; would he kiss her on the mouth as he had done a few weeks ago? But instead he dropped a brotherly kiss on her forehead and knocked on the door for the guard.

As she made her way back to the kennels, she suppressed her disappointment by imagining herself in his arms and his mouth on hers. Wait until I am thirteen, she wanted to tell him, then you will see that I am not a child and you will want to kiss me.

. . .

AFTER BREAKING THEIR fast with cold meat pie, bread and ale, Sir Robert and the small fishing party rode under the gateway, through the outer bailey and the village and onto the road east towards the forested hills that hid the Derwent from view. The bracken along the way was turning brown, and the hedges of hawthorn, holly and field maple were looking threadbare, just as the wildflowers had lost their blooms and the grass its spring. Flocks of sheep grazed on the wolds, and starlings crowded the sky. The day was overcast and cool, but as long as the rain held off, Bess declared, nothing would stop her from enjoying perhaps the last day of her carefree life.

"Certes, but you are gloomy today, Bess," John had told her the day before as they all sat in his cell and played cards. A cold wind howled outside, signaling the end of the fine autumn weather. "What ails you? You always love this game. Is it because you are losing?" He tried to coax her out of her melancholy, but her usually pleasant expression was marred by a scowl.

"If the wind changes, you will stay that way," Cecily taunted her, eliciting a snort from John. Cecily was indignant. "Do not mock me, John; Mother told us 'twould be so." She threw down a queen and crowed triumphantly. "Now best that!"

Bess suddenly squealed with glee and swooped up the card. "Even though she is an ugly queen, I will take her, and I shall win," she declared, her mood lightening.

John looked admiringly at his lovely cousin and remarked: "When you become Queen of England, Bess, I shall propose they use a likeness of you instead. Elizabeth, the queen of hearts! What think you, Grace?"

Grace jumped. She had been an observer in the cousins' game, as she had only recently learned to play, and so she shot John a grateful smile for including her. "Bess would indeed be more pleasing," she said, peering over Bess's shoulder. "I wonder who this old harridan was."

"Looks like Scraggy Maggie to me," Cecily exclaimed, and then regretted reminding Bess of her future mother-in-law, when her sister flung her cards down on the table and announced she was ready to leave.

She seems in much better spirits today, Grace thought as she held tightly to Bess's waist while riding pillion and tried not to look down at the ground far below. They were abreast of Sir Robert, who kept Bess engaged in a conversation that she had a hard time hearing. Instead, she amused herself by listening for birdsong. She was able to identify the flute of the thrush, the warble of a blackbird, the chirrup of a lark and the harsh caw of a crow along the way.

Cecily was riding her own horse next to Tom, while two grooms brought up the rear. Grace could hear her light laughter and could only imagine her flirtatious remarks. She could not understand why Tom did not take off at a gallop—or at least move up in the procession to talk to Sir Robert's squire, who rode behind his master. John would not stand for it, she was sure, but then, John is more of a man. Tom must have read her mind, she thought, as he kicked his horse's flank and trotted ahead of Cecily and up to the squire just as they passed by St. Michael's Church in the village of Cramburn. Soon they were atop the Howardian Hills, and then the road led down through the oaks, pines and ash that forested the slopes to the wide Derwent below.

Eventually reaching one of the only bridges for many miles, Sir Robert sharply reined in his horse, as did Bess, and Grace clung on for dear life. Tom rode up to Sir Robert and suggested they fish from the other bank.

" 'Tis grassier for the ladies if they want to sit, and there are shallower pools where they may fish safely," Tom advised Willoughby. He pointed over the next hill. "My home is in Westow, not a league from here. By your leave, sir, I would dearly love to ride and bid my family farewell at some point during the day. They do not know I am going to London. I would be happy to have the ladies' company on the way, if they find the fishing irksome."

"Why, Tom Gower," Bess retorted, "do you have such little faith in our ability to catch anything? We shall be perfectly content to stay here with rod and line all day, shan't we, Grace?"

"Not I," Cecily muttered behind her. "A visit to Tom's manor would make a pleasant diversion. What say you, Grace?"

Caught in the middle, Grace resorted to a quick silent Hail Mary to save her from disappointing either sister. But it was Tom, not the Virgin, who came to her rescue: "No matter; we should begin with the task at hand." And he spurred his horse and led the way over the bridge to a sheltered spot along the lower-lying eastern bank. The grooms untied the fishing gear from one packhorse and baskets of food and utensils from another.

Hooking their cumbersome skirts over their belts, the girls put on thick boots to wade in the water. Even so, the river soaked their petticoats, which clung around their calves and ankles.

"I swear I wish I were a man," Cecily complained, envying the men their longer boots and their breeches.

"Aye." Bess laughed, nodding in the direction of a groom relieving himself upon a tree. " 'Twould be easier."

The overcast day proved favorable for fishing, and there were squeals of delight whenever someone caught a fish. Grace watched Tom with admiration as he cast his line far out into the river in a fluid motion. He caught her eye and grinned happily. Aye, this is where he belongs, she thought, smiling back. She did not enjoy baiting her hook in the least, but watching Bess digging through the muddy mound of worms for a juicy one gave her courage to follow suit. An hour later, she was so surprised when she felt a nibble on her line that she jerked the rod out of the water too violently and fell over backwards, landing in a soggy heap in the shallow pool. She squealed when she felt the cold water on her thighs and backside. Tom was there in a flash to pick her up. He could not resist chuckling at her expense, and soon everyone was laughing—even Grace.

"I fear your fishing is over for today, Grace," he said. "We need to get you some dry clothes."

Seizing the moment, Cecily cried: "Then 'tis time we visited your mother, Tom. Perhaps she has something to lend Grace."

Sir Robert nodded his assent and turned to his squire. "Hugh, go along with Tom and the ladies. I shall be content to stay here, for I have found an excellent hole over there that is teeming with fish."

"I shall remain with you," Bess declared, "if you will allow me to share your spot." Sir Robert beamed and offered Bess his arm to help her over the rocks. She looked at Cecily's pout and said, "Nay, Cis, do not look so sour-faced! I am enjoying every minute here. You go with Grace."

Grace squeezed some river water from her skirt before one of the grooms lifted her up behind Tom, but she was still wet from her navel to her knees, although the boots had kept her legs and feet relatively dry. The three horses cantered off along the river path and up past Kirkham Abbey to the tiny village of Westow. The Gower manor was hard by Badgers Wood and Grace was not expecting such a large and rambling house. A low wall fronted the stableyard and a few ducks and geese flapped noisily out of the riders' path as they came to a halt by a well-worn mounting step. Tom slipped easily from his saddle and caught Grace as she slid from her perch, now shivering badly. Hugh had already helped Cecily down, and she was looking around her with interest.

" 'Tis much bigger than I imagined, Tom," she said. "You Gowers must own half of Yorkshire."

"Aye, we are a large family, in truth," Tom said. "I think I have upward of three dozen cousins in the region. And most of them are also named Thomas."

"Sweet Jesu!" Cecily exclaimed, laughing, just as a tall, big-boned woman exited the house and called a welcome.

"Tom, my son! How glad I am to see you," she said, stretching out her arms and pulling her to him. "Your father and I were much relieved to hear you did not go south to fight. Too young, praise be to God." She continued to embrace him, pinching his cheeks and giving him kisses.

Tom was clearly embarrassed, and Grace was amused to see him blush and gently disentangle himself. "Mother, I would present to you the ladies Cecily and Grace, King Edward's daughters," he said awkwardly, indicating each in turn.

Alice Gower was momentarily nonplussed. She thought she knew the names of all Edward's children, but could not remember a Grace. However, she affected an untrained curtsy to both young women and resolved to ask Tom about Grace later. "I give you God's greeting and welcome you to my humble house, my lady," she said, first addressing the older of the two girls. "I am Alice Gower, an it please you. May I offer condolences for the loss of your uncle, our good King Richard. He will be sorely missed in these parts." Then she turned to Grace and threw up her hands in horror. "By the Mass, you are soaked through. Oh, you poor child. Come along with me; we shall soon have those wet clothes off, and a hot bath ready for you. Tom, I will leave you to entertain the Lady Cecily and . . . forgive me, sir."

"I am Hugh Jones, at your service, madam. Sir Robert Willoughby's squire," Hugh answered her, bowing slightly.

Alice had no idea who Sir Robert Willoughby was, but she waved a hand in acknowledgment and hurried Grace inside, bustling about, giving orders to the scullery maid to heat water for a bath and calling to her own maid to fetch Mistress Cat's chemise and green gown.

"Cat is Tom's sister," she explained, shooing her charge up the stairs and holding up Grace's wet skirts. "She is with George—my husband—in York today. Cat has a head for accounts, and George takes her with him to learn more about the trade—wool, you know. We are hoping we will find a good match for her soon—there is a merchant in the guild who has his eye on her for his son." She paused only to take a breath. "Tom is the youngest of my brood, and a good boy. We were honored when our cousin of Stittenham agreed to let him train with the other boys at Sheriff Hutton, in truth. Very honored. But, listen to me prattle, my lady." She laughed, herding Grace into a cheery upstairs solar and pushing her towards the fire. "There, now warm yourself," she ordered. "Let me untie your wet skirts and rub your poor shivering legs. How you came to be so wet can only have something to do with Tom and fishing, if I know my Tom." She tut-tutted, but with a good deal of affection. "Certes, 'tis unconscionable for him to take ladies of your noble blood wading in the Derwent."

Grace had not opened her mouth since dismounting outside, for she did not know how to interrupt this garrulous woman whose mothering instinct oozed from every pore in her kind face, bustling body and hard-working hands. Grace basked in the larger woman's focus, and her heart was touched by Alice Gower's protective ministrations. She had been too young to remember a mother's love; the nuns had been fond of her, but it was a strict order and no favoritism towards the child was allowed. Dame Elizabeth was not unkind, but her maternal instincts were channeled into the betterment of her children's futures and not for their immediate comfort—and Grace's future was the lowest of Elizabeth's priorities.

" 'Twas my fault, not Tom's," Grace said, smiling shyly. "I had a fish and I did not heed Tom's advice to reel it in slowly. I pulled on the rod and line so hard I lost my balance, and"—she looked down at her wet petticoats—"I sat down."

"No harm done, then." Alice chuckled, dropping the skirt to the floor. "Now off with your bodice and chemise, there's a good girl." Before Grace knew it, she was standing naked in the middle of the room. Alice fetched a shawl from its peg and wrapped Grace in it. "Ah, here is the first of the bath water," she said as a knock came at the door. "Pull the tester curtains and wait on the bed until we are ready for you." Grace did as she was told, wrapping the sheet around her and climbing onto the high bed, which was covered in a colorful tapestry. From behind the curtains she could hear Alice ordering the servants to ready the bath and smiled to herself as she imagined John's amusement at her adventure.

In less than an hour she was dressed in Cat's apple-green gown—albeit two sizes too big—her hair neatly pinned under her velvet bonnet and a fresh-scrubbed flush to her cheeks.

"Here she is, right as rain," Alice announced, leading the way down the stairs to the hall where Cecily, Tom and Hugh were enjoying hot mulled wine. The two men scrambled to their feet as Alice advanced into the room, and Hugh walked to the fireplace to replenish his cup from the copper pot hanging over the flames. "Now, Tom, 'tis time to return these ladies to the castle. I am glad indeed that you came to bid me farewell, my dear boy, and your father will be disappointed to have missed you. Come, give me a kiss and receive your mother's blessing. I beg of you, do not forget your humble home and family on the road to London. You will come back to see us, will you not? And, although I know it pains you to pick up a pen, you owe your parents the honor of a letter or two when your duties allow." Used to his mother's never-ending conversations, Tom waited a second to see if there were more parental demands, and true to form there was one: "Give your loyalty only where it is deserved, Tom Gower. You come from a proud Yorkshire family, and I pray you never forget it."

Three pairs of Yorkist eyes glanced quickly at the Lancastrian squire, but he was draining his cup and smacking his lips, and Tom hoped he had not heard. He embraced his mother and thanked her for taking care of Grace. Cecily rose and put on her riding gloves, and Hugh hurried to open the front door for her. She turned and bade Alice thanks and farewell before preceding William out to the courtyard. Grace bobbed a curtsy and began to thank her hostess, but Alice was flustered for the first time.

"Nay, my lady, 'tis I who should be thanking you, for gracing my home . . ." She was cut off by a grin from Tom and a giggle from Grace. Looking from one to the other, the light dawned and she clapped her hands in delight. "Ah, I see, *gracing* was the right word, was it not? Nevertheless, my dear child, 'tis I who should do you reverence." And she sank into another awkward curtsy. "I wish you God speed on your road to London."

"Mistress Gower, I am a person of no account, I can assure you," Grace said, taking the older woman's hands and raising her up. "Tom and I are good friends, and I would wish you to look upon me as simply Grace. You have been very kind to me today, kinder than anyone has ever been in my life, in truth. I am only too sorry I cannot thank Cat personally for the loan of her dress. It shall be returned on the morrow, pray tell her. But I can thank *you* from the bottom of my heart for taking in a stranger thus. I must also thank my special saint, Sibylline, that I met you, and I promise to make sure Tom stays out of trouble when we are in London."

Tom stared at Grace in amazement. It was the longest speech he had ever heard from her, and judging from his mother's expression, it had left her astonished as well. Alice stammered a few words of acknowledgment, squeezed Grace's hands and then, regaining her composure, began to propel the pair out of the house, thrusting the bundle of wet clothes into Tom's hands. "You must be on your way before it gets dark, children," she said, wrapping her shawl around her in the sharp wind. "God bless you, Tom. I shall pray for you."

"I think your mother is the nicest person I have ever met," Grace announced once she had settled behind Tom on the horse, his warm cloak around her. "I am only sorry I shall probably never see her again."

"Never say never," Tom called over his shoulder, "as Mother would say!"

3

London

T he York family party spent nine days traveling to London. They left the north in pleasant autumn sunshine, but cold rain began to fall the farther south they traveled, and the dreary mist mirrored the feelings of dread they had for their uncertain future. Grace lost count of how many times they stopped to wrestle the carriage out of the ruts that seemed like innocuous puddles until a wheel discovered their deceptive depth. Sir Robert had kept his promise, however; the wainwright had fitted out the chariot with ample cushioning and heavy canvas sides that kept most of the weather out.

Young Edward of Warwick alleviated the boredom by changing his mode of transport every few hours. He alternately clambered into the girls' crowded carriage and used a peashooter to drill dried peas through the small air slots at the escorts' backs, sat atop a cart laden with household belongings and "helped" the driver with the reins or rode with Tom, safely tied to the front of Tom's saddle. Dame Elizabeth had explained to Grace that the boy was simple—touched in the head, she said. Certes, he did not have the understanding of a child of ten, Grace decided, looking at him now, but it seemed to her he preferred to see life in his own way and was the happier for it. Indeed, for the most part, she would describe Edward's personality as sunny. In contrast, his sister Margaret's expression appeared to announce that there was a bad smell permanently under her tiny, retroussé nose.

"In truth, ever since the queen—Aunt Anne—took them into her household when they were orphaned, Margaret has thought she was too good for us—especially now that we have been proclaimed, well, you know what," Cecily whispered to Grace one evening at Vespers in the castle chapel. This earned her a frown from Lady Gower, and Cecily assumed a look of such piety that Grace choked back a laugh. She smiled now, remembering the scene, and was glad Margaret had chosen this day to ride with Lady Gower in the carriage behind.

Grace had been intrigued by Lady Gower's litter: it was the size of a trestle table, with a canopied top and sides and long handles at each corner that were strapped to either side of a horse in front and a horse behind. Grace had ridden in it for an hour or so on the second day, but the swaying contraption caused her to relinquish her breakfast in a hedge. Cecily had laughed, but Bess had fussed over her and walked with her for a spell until Grace's stomach had calmed down.

Her thoughts turned often to John. Just as Willoughby had hoped, no word had reached Sheriff Hutton from the king in response to the news of John's taking, and he was relieved to leave all in Gower's hands. There had been a tearful farewell on the morning of their departure, and John had been allowed to join them in the chapel for Mass.

"I shall escape from here—never fear, little wren," he had whispered to Grace as he embraced her that final time. "Look for me in London ere long." Grace had not breathed a word to anyone of the exchange, and her faith in him never wavered.

As the small cavalcade rode through the towns en route to the capital—Doncaster, Bawtry, Newark and Leicester—townsfolk stopped what they were doing to run and see who was approaching. Bess had the escort roll up the sides of the chariot so the people could see them.

In Leicester, when they recognized the king's banners, people stood and cheered—some less enthusiastically than others. The citizens of that city had not long finished the macabre business of burying the dead from Bosworth Field, and their recent memories of royalty were of Henry's return to the city after the battle and his ignominious treatment of the slain King Richard that had not endeared him to his new subjects. But then the word was whispered that King Edward's daughters were in the large carriage and they roared their approval. The cry " 'Tis young Elizabeth!" was heard above the din, and people surged forward to get a better look at the gracious young woman whom they hoped would be their queen. Bess smiled and waved at their welcome, while Grace cringed behind the corner support, afraid the carriage would be toppled. Cecily was enjoying the limelight and laughed and threw farthings to some children staring open-mouthed at the richly clad occupants of the vehicle. The fresh young faces in the brightly colored carriage with their sunny smiles and kind gestures were a diversion on the dreary day.

"Smile! Wave!" Cecily advised Grace. "Have no fear, they don't know who you are—and they would not care. Father always told us not to be shy in front of our subjects. 'They want to love us, so give them your best smiles,' he would say."

Grace peeked out timidly and fluttered her hand. "Is this not the place where Uncle Richard was laid out after the battle?" she asked as they passed by the Grey Friars church. A few monks were standing by the gate, silently gazing at the Yorkist princesses from under their hoods.

Bess crossed herself and her smile faded. "Stop the carriage!" she commanded suddenly, and Grace was surprised by her tone of authority. "Stop, I say!" Tom heard her cry and turned his horse to see what the trouble was. "I wish to pay my respects to my uncle, if he . . . his body . . . is still here," she told him. "John told us he was taken by the Grey Friars for burial. I pray you ask the good brothers yonder if I may enter the church."

Tom nodded and rode over to the monks. One ran inside to fetch the abbot while the other two bowed a welcome to the royal visitor. Bess strapped on her pattens over her soft leather shoes and, with Sir Robert as her escort, walked on her high wooden soles through the muck in the street towards the church. "Are you coming with me, Cecily? Grace? And you, Margaret and Ned? Uncle Richard should know he is not forgotten," she said.

Tom took Cecily's arm and the others quickly followed. Sir Robert stood discreetly under the doorway and did not follow them in. Soon the little group was huddled, hoods up against the drizzle, in front of a newly dug grave in a small garden behind the church. A simple stone marked its head and a withered spray of white roses lay atop the mound.

The abbot hurried forward from the chapter house as fast as his stubby legs and rotund belly would allow and bowed low to Bess. "My lady, I am honored by your visit," he said humbly. "As you see, we have given his late grace, King Richard, a Christian place to lie in for his eternity. We do not have funds for a monument. But our brotherhood will care for his last resting place as long as we are in residence here. He was a noble prince, and it did pain us to see his corpse so ignobly treated upon his return from Redemore Plain." He crossed himself. "*Requiescat in pace. Domine, fiat volutas tua.* Thy will be done."

"Amen," the group answered, crossing themselves as they contemplated the mound of earth, each with his or her own memories of their uncle.

Bess fell to her knees in the muddy grass, tears pouring down her cheeks. Her repeated "*Requiescat in pace*" sounded more like "Richard, my true passion" to Grace, and judging by Cecily's sharp glance at her sister, she knew she had heard right. The kindly abbot put his hand on Bess's head and blessed her. Grace had hardly known the dead man, but her half sister's distress brought tears to her eyes, and she wiped her nose on her sleeve.

The quiet mood was broken by a sudden wail from Margaret. "Dear God, what will become of us? He and Queen Anne were so kind to Ned and me," she blubbered. "How I *hate* this Henry Tudor. I hope he dies like King Richard, with lots of stab wounds all over his miserable body."

Everyone was shocked by this outburst, and the abbot was at a loss for words. But Grace was intensely moved by the anguish in Margaret's voice and immediately put her arm around her. Instead of rejecting the sympathy, Margaret turned into Grace's arms and sobbed on her shoulder. "Come, Margaret," Grace whispered. "Let us find a seat in the church, where we can pray together for Uncle Richard. I am sure he would like that."

Margaret allowed herself to be led back inside the candlelit church, with little Edward traipsing along behind, and Grace chose an exquisite statue of the Virgin holding the baby Jesus in her arms to whom to make their supplication.

Margaret and Grace never became fast friends, but from that moment on, Margaret accepted Grace as a member of the family.

NOT FAR OUT of Northampton, Grace pointed out the road that led to the convent where she had grown up.

"Let us make a pilgrimage to Grace's old home," Cecily said with a perfectly straight face. Her high laugh startled Grace, who thought she was being serious. "Certes, Grace," she said, pulling a face. "Who wants to spend time with some boring old nuns?"

Grace smiled guiltily. "Aye, Cis, many are boring. But Sister Benedict . . ."

"Oh, sainted Sister Benedict! She who can do no wrong. I'll warrant she has committed several of the venial sins already, and she is only twenty," Cecily taunted.

Bess was truly shocked. "If I become queen, Cecily, I shall forbid you to appear in public with me, if you prattle on with your blasphemy. I am sure the good sisters lead a chaste and pure life. They certainly sent Grace to us thus. And now look what you have done," she said, glaring at Grace, who was trying to cover her laughter. "Grace, Cecily is not a good example for you. Certes, one impertinent clack-dish in the family is sufficient."

"Aye, your grace." Cecily mimicked the primness. "I pity poor Henry. He is getting a shrew, in truth." She knew raising Henry's name would send Bess down into the dumps, and she was right. Bess went silent. They know how to hurt each other, Grace thought, watching the two, and she wondered why they persisted, realizing she had much to learn about sibling rivalry. She listened to the familiar sound of the Northampton bells announcing the Terce—the same chimes that had accompanied her daily tasks for her first ten years of life. She wrapped her cloak more tightly around her and once again sent up a prayer of thanks to St. Sibylline for delivering her from a cloistered life.

"I hope Mother is expecting us," Bess said a few miles from Grafton. "She will not be pleased if we surprise her. The manor house will be full to bursting, although 'tis for only one night."

Cecily chuckled. "Aye, Mother hates surprises. But Sir Robert told me he sent a messenger ahead two days since. I wonder how she will take the summons to court from the king? Surely she must rejoice at this turn of fortune, and I imagine there is much tearing of hair and gnashing of teeth at the manor while Mother's ladies ready her for the journey."

" 'Tis true, Dame Elizabeth can sometimes be demanding of her ladies," Grace piped up. "The girls and I learned to keep out of the way on those days. But," she added, not wishing to criticize her mentor, "she was kind to them, too."

"I am happy for her that she is to be at court with us," Bess said. "And I shall have need of her," she murmured to herself. She had learned much about being a wife and queen from Elizabeth. Unlike Cecily, who chafed at Elizabeth's demands, Bess respected her mother, even if they sometimes disagreed. She had been old enough to understand what a profligate her father was, and she prayed nightly that whomever God—or Edward—chose as husband for her, she would not have to endure such infidelity. She found herself staring at Grace, a product of that sinning, and, again, she felt awe at her mother's ability to accept the living proof of it under her own roof. Aye, there was a kindness to the beautiful queen whom others had often derided as ambitious and greedy. Elizabeth Woodville had more than held her own with Edward Plantagenet, for all she was not royally born. There were some who said she was the most beautiful jewel in the land, and Bess did not doubt it. But there was nothing soft about that beauty, and when the news had come that Edward had been pre-contracted to another before their own marriage, Bess had shivered at the diamond-hard expression on that lovely face.

Grace caught Bess gazing at her and cocked her head, a question in her dark eyes.

"I was thinking about Mother," Bess admitted. "She has endured much these past two and a half years. More than most women have to bear. First her husband dies unexpectedly in the flower of life, leaving her in the care of councilors and bishops who have no wish to see a boy king upon the throne. And Father names Uncle Richard—far away in the north— Protector, and not Mother. Then Uncle Richard arrives, convinced Mother and her family are plotting to overthrow him, arrests Mother's dearest brother, Anthony Rivers, and executes him. And finally her two little sons are taken from her and then, by all accounts, disappear. Aye, 'tis enough turmoil for anyone to bear in a lifetime, let alone in a few short months." The young women went silent then, contemplating this truth.

"We are at Grafton, ladies," Tom's voice came through the canvas walls after another mile or two. The carriage rumbled slowly over the cobble-stoned courtyard and came to a stop. "The rain is tapering off, so you should not get too wet. But I advise pattens. Sir Robert is already inside, greeting your lady mother."

Gowns were smoothed, veils were hurriedly affixed to heads and pattens were strapped to feet. Two guards began rolling up the wall nearest the steps into the great hall, and when the two older girls were helped down from the cumbersome vehicle, they ran in out of the rain and straight into their mother's arms. Grace and Margaret followed at a discreet distance, and soon little Edward, Lady Gower and the other attendants were crowding into the brightly painted hall. The younger girls squealed when they saw Grace and ran to hug her, bringing tears of happiness to her eyes. She truly was part of the family, she realized, and she smiled and laughed as the children chattered gaily about their exploits and pulled her towards the welcoming warmth of the fire. Elizabeth turned towards the noise with a frown, but when she saw Grace her face softened and she called out: "God's greeting to you, Grace. Come, let me look at you." She stretched out her hand.

Grace dropped a curtsy before kissing Elizabeth's hand.

"Nay, we shall have none of that, sweeting," Elizabeth said, putting her arms around the girl. "You are as welcome as my own daughters. Is she not, Bess? Cecily?"

The older girls nodded and smiled, and Grace felt as though her heart would burst not only through her skin, but through her tightly laced bodice as well.

"I thank you," she said, beaming. "I thank you with all of my heart."

AT LAST THE spires of London were sighted through the October mist, after the cavalcade, increased in size by Dame Elizabeth's household, passed by St. Albans and Barnet, sites of some of the bloodiest battles ever fought on English soil. Tom had never seen London before, and he reined in his palfrey upon Highgate Hill to gaze on the scene in front of him, marveling at the city's size. As they rode closer he could see the walls clearly, rising out of the great ditches that surrounded the city, and the sheer numbers of carts, horses and pedestrians joining them on the road told him he was no longer in York. His horse shied away from a beggar, running with sores, who virtually threw himself in Tom's path whining for alms. One of Sir Robert's men used his horsewhip to make the man move, and Tom flinched. They crossed Smithfield marketplace, where three blackened corpses, much of their flesh eaten away by carrion crows, swung from a gibbet.

He turned to look at the young women in the carriage and saw that they were averting their eyes and covering their noses and mouths with kerchiefs. Street vendors shouted their wares from behind colorful barrows; a pie man made his way carefully through the throngs with a square board balanced on his head, upon which sat a stack of freshly baked pies; and several children amused themselves by launching rotten vegetables at a sad old man pinned in the stocks. A peddler juggling and jangling the knickknacks that were strung all over his body ran up to the carriage and tried to tempt Cecily with ribbons, gloves and furs. She was happy for the diversion from the gruesome gibbet and gladly parted with a halfpenny for a length of blue ribbon and a colorful wooden comb. Slowly the procession of escorts, carriages, carts and packhorses wended its way to Elizabeth's townhouse, Ormond's Inn, a stone's throw from the city wall and hard by the Holy Sepulchre. A granted property from her husband's parliament, she had spent many pleasant years under its roof when she was queen.

The three-storied house appeared small from the outside, but once through the gatehouse, Grace could see there were two extensive wings and a garden beyond the courtyard. The steward greeted Elizabeth reverently. "Welcome home, your grace," he said and, ignoring the frown from Sir Robert, bowed Elizabeth and her brood into the hall. The pantler was sent running to fetch refreshments from the kitchen, and jugs of cider were set out on the great hall tables; in this house, Elizabeth would be treated like the queen she had been, the steward had informed the staff, and he eyed King Henry's man with disdain.

Soon an array of pies and sweetmeats were laid out for the group, and the freshly brewed cider was quickly downed. Sir Robert conversed politely with Bess and her mother but soon made a move to leave. He bent to murmur something in Elizabeth's ear, and her head snapped up in surprise. "The king commanded this?" she asked, glancing in the direction of little Ned who was happily playing with a top. " 'Tis ridiculous, sir. He is only ten and . . ." She touched her finger to her head meaningfully. "He needs to be with his family. I hardly think 'tis necessary to put the boy in the Tower, do you, Sir Robert?" she finished indignantly.

" 'Tis for his own safety, madam," Sir Robert blustered, taken aback by Dame Grey's flouting of his orders. " 'Tis the king's wish. And there is an end to it!"

The room went silent. All were thinking about two other boys who were taken to the Tower for safekeeping. They waited breathlessly for Elizabeth's answer.

"Aye, for safety's sake!" she cried, and she threw back her head and laughed. Grace was frightened by it: it was not Dame Elizabeth's usual silvery laughter—the laugh Cecily had inherited—but a cruel, harsh laugh full of hatred and hurt. Sir Robert was unnerved and, much to Grace's astonishment, for she had not thought it could happen to a man, he flushed red in a mix of embarrassment and anger. Bess recognized that her mother was in a fighting mood and quickly rounded up her younger sisters and shooed them from the room. Ned would have gone with them, but he saw that Margaret was still standing with Grace and ran to her side.

"Why is Aunt Elizabeth laughing like that?" he asked his sister. "I don't like it."

"Soft, Ned," Margaret shushed him. " 'Tis important. Listen."

Sir Robert was flustered, but he knew this Woodville woman could not gainsay him. She was at the king's mercy, and she must know it. He must put her in her place, he decided. "The earl of Warwick is next in line to the throne, Dame Grey," he said with icy politeness. "The king's grace is anxious nothing shall befall him. I can assure you he will be well cared for, and he will have his own servants. And there is an end to it."

Margaret suddenly ran out in front of him. "And what about me?" she cried. "I am his sister. I refuse to be parted from him. He is the only family I have left." Sobbing bitterly, she fell to her knees. Ned darted to her side and glared at the outraged Sir Robert, whose patience was fast running out. "I will not go with you, sir!" Ned declared, his fists balled and his feet wide as his boyish voice rang around the hall. "I shall stay with my sister and"—he took a beat—"there is an end to it."

Grace hid a smile behind her hand. He is perhaps not as simpleminded as you thought, Dame Elizabeth, she exulted. Good for you, Ned, she wanted to call. Ned's outburst made Elizabeth laugh until she cried, but Bess could see they were tears of pain, not of humor.

"Enough!" Sir Robert bellowed, his arms akimbo and his large belly heaving beneath his short gown, Elizabeth's laughter still hanging in the air. "I have done my duty by all of you this past fortnight, caving to your every whim, protecting you the length of the realm, seeing to your comfort and taking more time than I needed to gentle your journey, and I am rewarded by"—and he bent down and poked his finger into Ned's chest—"impertinence from a child and"—he straightened up—"by mockery from a fallen woman of no further import."

A gasp went up from the stunned assembly, and Willoughby, aware he had overstepped his bounds, seized the moment. He picked Ned up as if the boy were a feather and strode across the hall, the long toes of his boots slapping against the tiles.

Elizabeth's laughter vanished into a snarl. "You shall rue this day, Sir Robert." She pointed an accusing finger at his retreating form. And to Ned she called, "Tell my boys, if you should see them, they are not forgotten. And neither shall you be, Ned, I swear on your sweet mother's grave."

"His grace shall hear of this," Willoughby spat over his shoulder as Ned wriggled and flailed his fists at his captor. "I am doing naught but my duty by him. And there is an end to it."

This time no one laughed, or even smiled. Elizabeth fell crying into Bess's warm arms, and Grace crept forward to comfort Margaret, whose pinched, white face stared fearfully in the direction of her brother's screams, now fading away. "Shall I see him again, Grace?" she whispered. "Certes, God could not be so unkind, could he?"

"Nay, Margaret. You shall see him again, I swear," Grace said vehemently. "Even if we have to climb the Tower walls ourselves!"

HENRY IGNORED THE occupants of Ormond's Inn while he planned his coronation. He had provided a small retinue of servants for the women, and the girls were sad to see Tom Gower leave to escort his aunt back to Sheriff Hutton. He left with a letter from Grace to John in his pouch.

"Pray tell him we have not forgotten him," she had begged. "And may God go with you on your journey, Tom. Only He knows when we shall meet again." Then she gave him two kerchiefs upon which she had embroidered her initials and a violet and yellow heartsease. "One for you and one for John," she said shyly. She pointed to the flower. "I have decided 'tis to be my special emblem. Did you know it is called a *pensée* in French, which means 'a thought.' I hope you might give me a thought when we leave. See how it looks like a tiny animal's face?" she rambled on, wishing she could stop. She took a deep breath. "You and John were kind to me this summer, and I shall never forget it."

It was a brave statement from a retiring person, and Tom had grinned and awkwardly taken the gifts, stuffing them with the letter into the leather bag at his waist.

ELIZABETH SEETHED AS day after day went by without a visit from the king. "Why did he send for you if it was to leave you dangling?" she asked Bess for the hundredth time. Bess shrugged and got on with her needlepoint. Grace glanced up at Elizabeth from her mending and again marveled at the woman's beauty. So pale was her hair, it was hard to distinguish whether it was still the silvery mane that had entranced a whole generation of young men or if it had simply turned white. She wore it pulled so tight under her turbaned headdress that it lifted the creases from her brow and around her eyes, but it made her look younger than her forty-three years. Grace wondered if it was as painful as it looked. She well remembered the first week she had spent with her older sisters at Westminster almost a year ago, when they had held her down to pluck the offending two inches of hair from her hairline and reduced her eyebrows to faint lines. Uncontrolled tears had coursed down her cheeks as they used ivory pincers to remove each hair. " 'Tis hard the first time, Grace," Bess had said kindly, "but 'tis better than shaving it. Then it grows back faster, and you have to shave again."

"But why do it at all?" Grace had dared to ask and had cringed at Cecily's contemptuous snort; vanity was not a vice Grace had been allowed to contemplate at the convent. After her ordeal, she was so certain the Devil would be hiding under the tester bed ready to reach out and pinch her during her nightly devotions that she disappeared into the alcove that held the prie-dieu and prayed for forgiveness as soon as her sisters turned their attention from her. There she noticed the exquisite painting of the Virgin that formed one of the panels on the triptych depicted Mary with exactly the same hair fashion, and she stared at it in disbelief. She had gingerly touched her bald forehead and shed a few more tears for her lost tresses.

Now, she ventured to admit, she was relieved to look like everyone else. Anything was better than being stared at, she told herself. As it was she was the only sister with dark hair, and on more than one occasion some well-meaning soul had remarked how she must take after her grandfather York, who had passed on his dark looks to his son, King Richard. She didn't like to tell them that in fact she looked just like her mother, or so the nuns had informed her. Only Elizabeth had refrained from mentioning her parentage, and Grace was astute enough not to mention it, either. She longed to ask her mentor or her sisters about her father but, other than the few times she heard Elizabeth curse her dead husband, she never dared bring the subject up herself. She cherished the description of her little brother, Dickon, that Bess had given her the afternoon in the Yorkshire meadow, and before she fell asleep she would busy her active young mind with the puzzle surrounding his and Edward's whereabouts. But then often those waking dreams were crowded out by thoughts of John in his prison. She prayed for him nightly.

"Mother, may we go and watch the coronation procession?" Cecily asked airily, breaking Grace's reverie.

Elizabeth frowned at this impertinence but decided to let it pass and allow Cecily the courtesy of a response. "You must understand, child, that I cannot give you leave to mingle with the citizens," she said firmly. "Anything could happen, and we must not anger Henry should he hear of it. His victory at Bosworth may mean he is king, but it does not mean everyone is pleased. It would appear from my intelligence that his subjects are restless and rebellious. If we go among the people without his permission, he may choose to believe we Yorkists are surreptitiously stirring up more unrest. We dare not give him just cause to change his mind about wedding Bess. Our family fortunes depend on it."

"Bess isn't his yet, Mother!" Cecily cried. "Why, he has not even sent a message of love or intent to her, and we have been here nigh on three weeks. I pray you, let us go and watch. We will take care, I promise."

Elizabeth's icy stare bore a hole in her daughter's imploring face, and her mouth was set in a thin, firm line. Cecily cast her eyes down to her lap and muttered an apology. Bess was aghast and attempted to change the subject. Elizabeth waved off her interruption impatiently and addressed Cecily. "How dare you gainsay me, daughter, when I gave you a reasonable answer to your first brazen question," she snapped. "I do not know what happened to your manners during your sojourn at Sheriff Hutton, but I do not like it. Nay, I do not like it all. Perhaps we should send for your husband to deal with you. But he has not shown his face since Bosworth, so we are stuck with you, more's the pity."

Grace saw two large tears drop onto Cecily's apple green gown, making dark stains in the tabbied taffeta. It was the first time Grace had seen the spirited Cecily cry, and it took all her resolve not to go and comfort her.

Then, as quickly as her anger had been aroused, Elizabeth sought to mollify. " 'Tis hard for all of us, Cis, and I like it not just as much as you. But unlike those who do not have our privilege, we are not born to do as we please. There is a price to pay for our nobility. However, I thank God every night that I can lay my head on a pillow that smells sweet, snuggle under coverlets of fur, eat the finest delicacies known to man and be clothed in the softest silks and satins. Ask Grace if she prefers living here to life in the convent. Look at her face, Cecily, and I think you have your answer." She paused, looking around at all the upturned faces of her brood. "We have all been under a dark cloud since your father was taken from us, and we all need to pray fervently that Henry Tudor fulfills his promise to marry Bess at the earliest opportunity and brings us back into the light. It is for your own good that I refuse you permission to roam the streets like peasants.

"But," she said, a gleam in her eye, "I do not foresee Henry caring whether or not Grace is among the throng. Once Bess is queen, Henry will be obliged to find husbands for *my* children, but he will be under no such obligation to Grace." She turned to Grace, who was biting off her thread with her teeth and looking wide-eyed at Elizabeth. "You could go and be our eyes and ears, Grace. What say you?"

AND SO GRACE found herself dressed in her old blue gown from the convent, now much too short for her, and a plain flannel cloak borrowed from a servant girl. Her hair hung loose down her back with a white linen coif covering it and tied under her chin. Escorted by a burly man named Daniel who carried a staff and whose booming voice and ferocious expression moved people out of the way in a trice, Grace ventured out that day in late October, a weak sun attempting to shine on the occasion.

Londoners were out in force. Despite having only recently participated in another coronation, any excuse for a day away from the drudgery of their lives was cause for celebration, and they were in full voice when the first trumpets and shawms announced the beginning of the procession. Grace watched as heralds, sergeants at arms, squires, aldermen and knights strode solemnly past her position on the steps of All Hallows on Watling Street and on to Westminster. She thought she had become accustomed to the lavish finery of courtiers during those few months at court, but she stared openmouthed with the rest of the citizenry at the opulence of Henry Tudor's entourage. Silks, satins and velvets of every color trimmed with fur, ribbons and laces adorned the men who rode by on their colorfully caparisoned horses. Jewels flashed from fingers, necks and hats, making Daniel mutter to his neighbor in his London accent: " 'E's spared no expense, 'as 'e? Don't give a toss for the rest of us, do 'e? Just as long as 'is arse is on the throne, 'e's larfing." A few grumbles followed this little speech, but soon the music and the excitement grew to such a fever pitch Grace knew the king must be near.

Preceding the king were the Lord Mayor of London and Garter king of Arms with the lords Derby and Nottingham, Oxford and . . . Grace gave a little squeal, " 'Tis Lincoln! John of Lincoln!" A couple of spectators turned to look at her and, realizing her mistake, she immediately began to cough shielding her face from the prying eyes. When she thought it was safe, she looked up and watched her cousin parade slowly past, his face impassive and his eyes staring straight ahead as he sat astride his big black courser. At least he is safe, she thought; Bess will be glad to hear that, although riding with his enemies must have been unsettling for him, she decided.

"The king! The king!" the murmuring became a roar as Henry Tudor, once earl of Richmond and now king of England, came into view. Drums and tabors thrummed a slow beat in time with the steps of the four knights who carried a high canopy emblazoned with the royal arms over the bare head of their sovereign. Trumpeters blew an earsplitting fanfare from platforms set up along the route. People craned to get a glimpse of him, and Daniel ended up lifting Grace up off her feet so she could see. The tall, bony man with a thin face and long, wispy, mouse-colored hair, clothed in a long purple gown trimmed with ermine, walked unsmiling through his subjects, gravely inclining his head to the left and the right. At twenty-eight, Henry looked old to Grace, although he was not the hideous monster Bess and Cecily had imagined. His hooded, pale blue eyes scanned the crowds—almost fearfully, Grace thought. Aye, he looks like someone expecting to be attacked. She remembered something John had said to her once: "To be born royal is to court an early death." In her naiveté, she had not understood, but, with the disappearance of the two young princes in the Tower and the untimely death of Uncle Richard, she was beginning to see the truth of John's pronouncement.

"God save the king! God save the king!" The cry was contagious and, much to her astonishment, she found herself joining in with the hundreds of fickle Londoners who had shouted the same words to another king just as jubilantly only twenty-eight months earlier.

HENRY WASTED NO time in calling his first Parliament in November, and by December, two of the many decisions made by the members directly affected the ladies at Ormond's Inn. Henry was finally taken to task by his Commons for waiting so long to fulfill the oath he took in Rennes Cathedral, so he agreed to wed Bess in the new year. It was then only seemly that Elizabeth be reinstated as queen dowager, and Henry set his lawyers about repealing Richard's Act of Titulus Regius in which Edward and Elizabeth's marriage had been deemed illegal and their children ineligible to inherit the crown. Indeed, he ordered every single copy of it destroyed.

The shocking news from those first days of Parliament for many of the Yorkist families was that Henry had dated his reign from the twenty-first day of August—the day before the battle of Bosworth. He refused to recognize Richard as king, and in all edicts and official documents referred to him as "Richard, late duke of Gloucester." Thus Henry was able to attaint as traitors to himself anyone who had not fought with him on Redemore Plain or had not reconciled with him following the battle.

"Lincoln and his father, Suffolk, have made their peace with Henry," Elizabeth explained to Grace when she questioned the presence of the earl and duke in the procession. "But the likes of Jack Howard—the duke of Norfolk who died fighting for Richard—and his son, Thomas of Surrey, are attainted, as are many of our old friends." She reeled off a list of names that meant nothing to Grace until Francis Lovell was mentioned.

"He is John's patron, is he not?" Grace asked timidly. "John of Gloucester, my lady," she clarified, seeing Elizabeth's frown. "He was with us at Sheriff Hutton." She was annoyed to feel herself flush.

"Aye, and still there under arrest by Sir Robert Willoughby's command," Bess told her mother. "John did not even fight at Bosworth—he was at the rear with the other pages and squires, guarding the supplies. I wonder if Henry has set John free?"

"I cannot possibly imagine why Henry has a quarrel with John, except that he has Richard's blood in his veins. Perhaps you might ask for John's liberty as a boon, Bess, now that you are formally betrothed. He is a good boy." Elizabeth sighed and looked at the clock on the table. " 'Tis early yet, but with your first meeting with Henry arranged for the morrow, Bess, I think 'tis time we took to our beds. Grace, send in my women, if you will. And I would like you to serve me the all-night." Grace rose, curtsied and left the room.

Just before she closed the door, she heard Elizabeth say, "For all she is a by-blow, I cannot help but like the girl. There is a sweetness about her that is pleasing to me. Cecily, you could learn much from Grace. And now, girls, get you to bed."

Before she could be discovered eavesdropping, Grace flew down the passage, her heart singing.

KING HENRY AND Bess stepped out to the music of lutes, recorders, *vielles* and the droning symphonie. Bess had chosen a shimmering green and gold gown to wear for her first meeting with her betrothed, and Henry was magnificent in a dark blue velvet pourpoint, its sleeves slashed to show white satin underneath. The room was brightly lit with hundreds of candles, as the winter solstice shortened the daylight. The meeting had gone well, and Henry's frequent smile showed his councilors and Elizabeth that he was well pleased with his bride. Only her sisters knew how terrified Bess had been when she was first ushered into Henry's presence.

"You were right, Grace," Cecily whispered. "He is not hideous at all. In fact, he is quite pleasant-looking—if you like tall, thin men."

"You like tall, thin men, Cis," Grace retorted. "You flirted all summer with one."

Cecily's irrepressible giggle made Elizabeth turn and frown at them both, but by then Henry was escorting Bess through the courtiers to the dais where they would preside over the evening's entertainment in the king's audience chamber, and the buzz of conversation saved the girls from further reprimand.

"Oh, Tom," Cecily scoffed. "I flirted with him only because there was no one else in that backwater. He was pleasant enough, but dull. I couldn't even persuade him to kiss me."

Grace gasped. "Kiss you? You asked him to kiss you? How brave you are, Cis."

Cecily tossed her head and laughed. "Do not think, my sweet innocent, that I did not see you casting moon eyes at John. How shocking! He is your cousin, and thus forbidden fruit," she teased.

Grace blushed, but Cecily's words alarmed her. "One cannot love a cousin?" she echoed. "I was told by one of the nuns that brothers and sisters may not wed, but they said nothing of cousins."

"Aye, 'tis against the laws of the church. Even Bess and Henry must seek a papal dispensation, for they are related in the fourth degree of kinship—in other words, cousins," Cecily explained upon seeing Grace's bewilderment. "You and John are first cousins, and if you have the addle-pated notion that you might wed him, I do not suppose you would be able to buy a dispensation with all the gold in the treasury!"

Grace's heart fell like a stone into her stomach. But as she stood quietly in a corner while Cecily was led onto the dance floor by Henry's chancellor, Thomas Lovell, she began to understand why John had treated her like a sister. It had nothing to do with her being so young and, as she judged herself, unappealing, and everything to do with their blood relationship. How foolish I must have seemed to him, she thought miserably, staring at the points of her soft satin slippers, peeking out from the hem of her fur-trimmed gown.

"You have grown, my dear Lady Grace," a familiar voice interrupted her thoughts, and she looked up into the handsome face of her cousin John of Lincoln. "May I lead you out to dance?"

"M-me, my . . . my lord Lincoln?" she stammered, looking about her as though there was another Grace nearby. "You wish to dance with *me?*"

"Certes, cousin. Cecily tells me you dance beautifully. Why don't you show the court how *all* the daughters of King Edward can shine?" he said kindly, holding out his hand as an *estampie's* lively tempo accompanied the dancers' steps and high hops. "Besides, I feel more comfortable with my family than with"—he glanced in Henry's direction, lowering his voice—"his."

His meaning was not lost on Grace, young as she was. I was right, she thought; 'twas indeed hard for him to process with his enemies that coronation day in London. She looked forward to revealing this tidbit to Bess and Cecily later.

Grace thought better of her decision when Bess twirled into the chamber the sisters were sharing at Westminster for the night. Cecily collapsed onto the huge bed, peeling off her hose with no semblance of dignity, her gown and petticoats in enough disarray to show off her lithe legs. Grace allowed a tiring woman to unpin her hennin and unlace her stiffened bodice. Bess was in no mood for sleep, they could see, and all Bess's attendants could do was follow her around the room, catching one of the sleeves she'd unlaced herself or the pearl earbobs she flung carelessly into the air.

"I think I am in love," she cried, finally standing still long enough for her women to untie her skirt and carry it carefully to the chest brought from Ormond's Inn. "Henry was very personable, I thought," she said. "And he is quite handsome, *n'est ce pas?* He paid me so many compliments, my head must have grown this evening. And he dances so well, does he not?"

Cecily and Grace shared a secret smile. "Aye, he dances well enough," Cecily said. "But I do not find him handsome. He looks a little like a weasel, in truth."

"A weasel!" Bess was indignant. "A weasel? Oh, you are just jealous because you do not like your husband, Cis."

"Pah!" Cecily said defiantly. "Certes, 'tis fortunate Henry was forced to wed you, for you were well on your way to being an old maid. I am only fifteen, and I still have my looks."

Her emotions strung taut that night, Bess gave an uncharacteristic shriek and flung herself at Cecily on the bed. Grace and the attendants stood staring in amazement at the sisters as they pulled each other's hair, pinched arms and legs and used pillows to pummel one another, squealing in pain or satisfaction when blows found their mark. Suddenly the door opened and Elizabeth walked in, her hair falling around her shoulders to her waist over her blue silk robe. The attendants fell to their knees, and Grace gave her a nervous curtsy.

"What is the meaning of this outrageous behavior? Get up, both of you. Immediately!" Elizabeth commanded, her eyes blazing with anger. " 'Tis my belief the whole palace can hear you, much to my shame. Shame on you, Bess. And you are to become England's queen? 'Tis not to be believed."

The two young women had leapt from the bed to the floor as soon as they heard their mother's voice and were now prostrate before her. The attendants crept from the room, giving one another meaningful looks. They had no wish to come under the queen dowager's menacing gaze. Grace shrank back, too, but Elizabeth put out her hand and stayed her, though not unkindly.

"Well, Grace, I think I may count on you for a fair explanation of this lapse of reason. You will tell me, please, what happened."

This was exactly the sort of situation Grace hated. The nuns had instilled the fear of the Devil and his hellfire for any lies she might tell, and yet she wanted to protect her sisters from their mother's wrath. She looked up at Elizabeth, who was waiting.

" 'Twas naught but a game, madam, and we meant no harm," was all Grace could think to say as she made the sign of the cross with her thumb between her fingers behind her back.

" 'Twas my fault, your grace," Cecily suddenly said from the floor. "I started it."

"Nay, I started it," Bess said, getting up on her knees. "I am giddy from the wine, Mother, and was feeling so happy that I spoke without thinking and may have hurt Cecily's feelings."

"Nay, 'twas my fault," Cecily insisted. "I am very sorry, Bess. Am I forgiven?"

Elizabeth stood by, quietly watching this little scene before turning on her heel and walking to the door. "I shall be glad when you are safely wed, Bess, and have a husband to control you. And we shall have to ask Henry to reunite Cecily with Ralph as soon as possible. Although 'twill take a man of steel to keep *her* in line," she said sternly.

As Grace held wide the door, Elizabeth glanced down at her and said, "Nicely done, Grace. May God give you a good night." And she swept out, leaving Bess and Cecily clutching each other in contrite camaraderie.

• • •

HENRY BECAME A frequent visitor to Ormond's Inn that Yuletide, getting to know his bride and, Grace noted, succeeding in evading Elizabeth's eagle eye on more than one occasion. He came with but a few esquires on these visits, and these young men kept Elizabeth, the girls and their attendants occupied while he walked and talked with Bess through the gallery and hall, bending his head to whisper things that made her laugh. Several times they went out of earshot, making Elizabeth look up from her embroidery frame and frown.

Then, one afternoon before Christmas he came unannounced, seeming to know Elizabeth had taken Cecily to visit the sick at St. Benedictus's hospital nearby. Grace and Margaret were playing a game of fox and geese, and Bess was practicing the lute, having begged her mother's indulgence to remain home that afternoon. Elizabeth had searched her face closely and stroked her cheek. "I pray you are not sickening for something, Bess. 'Twould not bode well for you to give Henry any qualms about wedding a healthy young woman who will bear him an heir."

"Nay, mother. I am perfectly well," Bess assured her. "But 'tis exactly because I do not want to fall ill at this moment that I choose not to visit the sick today. I crave your pardon. May I keep Grace here with me?"

Elizabeth had nodded, kissed her eldest and hurried out to do her duty, Cecily a step behind her. Grace had been puzzled by the little smile that played about Bess's mouth as she waved them off. As soon as Henry strode in, the steward barely able to announce him, all became clear to Grace.

"Your grace, what an unexpected pleasure," Bess murmured as she made a deep reverence. Henry smiled as he raised her up and, without a word to anyone, pulled her arm through his and left the room. The attendants, who had also fallen on their knees when they had seen their king, began whispering among themselves. Lady Alice, Bess's chief attendant, made up her mind and, with consternation, hurried to the door. Two of Henry's guards barred her way with crossed halberds.

Indignant, she demanded to be let out of the room. "My lady is unchaperoned, sirrahs," she pronounced, and was met by stony stares from the men. "How dare you keep me from my mistress!" she cried. "The king shall hear of this!"

" 'Tis the king's pleasure that you stay here, madam," one of the guards replied, unmoved. "We have our orders."

Near tears, for she feared Elizabeth's wrath should the dowager queen find out, Lady Alice threw up her hands and joined the other women by the fire.

Grace rose silently from her place, walked towards the guards and, for once glad of her smallness, smiled innocently at them and whispered: "I have need to go to my chamber, kind sirs. Will you let me pass? I am the Lady Bess's little sister," she added conspiratorially.

The guards looked at each other and back at her, and seeing naught but a wisp of a girl looking guilelessly up at them, they made a quick decision. Uncrossing their halberds, they allowed her to go, leaving Lady Alice complaining loudly in her wake. She scampered down the passageway in search of Bess and Henry. She had no idea what she would do when she found them, but she knew it was not seemly for the two to be alone. All was quiet at this end of the house, but just as she was about to turn back and go down to the great hall, she heard a low moan, and then another and then something akin to a cry of pain.

"Bess!" Grace muttered, an icy finger of fear clutching at her throat. "He must be hurting Bess."

But all had gone quiet except for some murmurs from within the solar usually reserved for guests. She turned the wrought-iron handle and, hearing the click of the latch, pushed the door open a crack. What she saw made her abandon her mission, turn and flee as fast as her legs could carry her down the stairs and into the great hall, empty at this time of day. But she could not get the scene upstairs out of her mind: Bess lying on her back on the bed, her petticoats up around . . . Grace did not know what people called their privy parts . . . and Henry, half undressed on top of her, heaving his buttocks in the same primeval manner she had seen dogs mount their bitches. She felt sick. But more than that, she felt certain that this was not supposed to happen until after one was wed. And why did Bess cry out in pain? Oh, I should have stopped him. I should have gone in and pulled him away, I should have . . . But as she calmed down, she suddenly laughed, imagining the scene. "Your grace, I pray you, get off my sister!" she would say, and he would reply: "And who are you to tell the king what he can and cannot do with his betrothed? Be off with you or it will be off with your head!" Nay, she would never breathe a word of what she had witnessed; 'twas not her affair, she concluded, and she thanked St.

Sibylline for not revealing her presence at the door. As she climbed back up the stone stairs to the second floor, she grimaced. Perhaps I shall not marry after all, she thought, if I have to endure such a monstrous act. She did not envy Bess the marriage bed.

IF BESS HAD qualms, they did not show upon her wedding day on the snowy eighteenth of January. She was radiant in white cloth of gold with a cloak of white fur lined with purple satin to keep her warm for the few paces from St. Margaret's Church across the courtyard to Westminster Palace.

The papal dispensation was barely dry when Henry plighted his troth to Elizabeth of York, oldest daughter of King Edward the Fourth, in the sanctuary. Henry had allowed the people to enter the inner walls of the palace on this occasion, as he wished as many of his subjects as possible to witness the unification of the houses of Lancaster and York. He knew this match would help quell the rumblings and stabilize his crown, and he was right: the Londoners cheered their young queen lustily as she smiled and acknowledged their good wishes.

Only Henry, Grace and Cecily—and perhaps the laundress who washed Bess's petticoats following Henry's secret visit in December—knew that Bess did not go to her husband a virgin. But only Bess knew that she also went to him already carrying his child.

4

Middelburg

YULETIDE 1485

Right noble lady and beloved aunt,

    I give you greeting this Christmas season from the cold and snowy north. You will be surprised to know I am not in Bruges but in Middelburg. There was plague in Bruges and Lady Brampton was afraid, so I was sent with her and some other servants to Middelburg. I became ill, so Master John Strewe, the merchant who is a friend to Lady Brampton, was kind enough to take me in. Do not worry, aunt; I do not have the plague, but after many weeks of sickness I am well enough to learn to be a page. We are very close to Lady Brampton's house, and she came to see me twice. I will return there at the end of the week.

    I do not like this island, aunt. Have you been here? The castle takes up too much space and so the houses are crowded and not beautiful, like in Binche. There is always fog here from the sea or it is raining or snowing, and the walls in my chamber have green patches that are slimy. I have seen rats as big as cats in the streets, and there are many mouses in this house. The Dutch people are not friendly like those in Brabant, but perhaps 'tis because I do not know their language well. Master Strewe speaks French and English, and I am happy to talk with him, now that I am not with fever. They say I almost died. I am certain my illness was because I was homesick for you, ma chère Tante Marguerite. I cried many nights after we parted at Binche. But Lady Brampton seems kind, I cannot deny it. But she does not love me like you love me, because I am only a page. The household addresses her in French, but she likes to practice English with me.

I was very happy for the new warm clothes you gave me, and more than anything for the thick wool stockings, which I wear to bed every night. I am used to the bedbugs now, but the stockings help keep them from biting my legs. I share a bed with one of Merchant Strewe's apprentices. He is the same age as me but he speaks only Dutch. He is teaching me a few words, and I am teaching him some French. Lady Brampton has promised me that I will be with her for the Twelfth Night celebration, and afterwards she is expecting that we return to Bruges. That will make me very happy.

How is my dog Pepin? I think about him all the time. I hope Chevalier de la Baume is kind to him. I miss Sire de Montigny also, but I do not miss his Latin lessons. I know it is important for me to know Latin, because you said it was, but it does not help me here in Middelburg. Perhaps in Lisbon it will be useful.

I will write again after I have learned my duties. Please write to me soon! Until then, I send you my dutiful love. Semper te adstringo, which I hope means I am bound to you always, my dearest aunt.

Your devoted nephew ~~Jehan~~ Pierrequin

5

London and Winchester

SUMMER AND AUTUMN 1486

After a particularly wet spring, the summer's sun was a welcome relief to Londoners tired of wading through mud in the street and lying in straw beds soggy from leaks in thatched roofs. The gong farmers had cause to complain, however, as they plied their carts full of human waste in and out of the city gates to the ditches that encircled the walls. Putrid steam from the rain-sodden refuse rose in the heat to intoxicate the swarming flies, and even the stalwart carters needed kerchiefs over their noses and mouths as they shoveled off their loads. On days when the wind blew from the south and east, Ormond Inn's casements were shut against the stench that marred the otherwise tranquil location of the house. A few cases of plague had been reported inside the city gates in July and August, causing the queen dowager to forbid her immediate attendants access to the town.

When Bess moved her household to Westminster Palace, she took Cecily with her as her companion. Cecily was euphoric when Henry informed her that Ralph Scrope of Upsall was not good enough for the queen's sister, and, besides, had the man not been forced upon her by King Richard against her will? When Cecily readily acquiesced—in front of witnesses— the legal process of dissolving the marriage began.

"Promise you will not tell Cis, Grace," Bess confided to her half sister one day, not long after this joyful news was given to Cecily. "Henry is not dissolving the marriage out of charity, but because he has a grander prize for his sister-in-law."

Grace waited, her head cocked, as was her wont.

"Cecily is to wed Henry's half uncle John, the Viscount Welles," Bess whispered.

Grace could not help but exclaim: "Poor Cis! 'Tis Scraggy Maggie's brother, is it not? But he is *old*, Bess, and he has the same long teeth as his half sister." She grimaced, trying to imagine the gaunt, balding lord kissing Cecily.

Bess sighed. "Aye, he is close to forty years, I think. But Cecily is sixteen and needs a noble husband. He is as close to the king as a man can be," she said, defending her husband's decision.

"In truth, Cis may think she was better off with Ralph Scrope," Grace said, half to herself.

"Don't be ridiculous, Grace," Bess retorted. " 'Tis the position, not the man, that matters in marriage. Remember that." And Grace had wisely held her peace. She was not sure Cecily would see things Bess's way.

And she was right.

"Holy Mary, Mother of God, what did I do to deserve that scrawny skeleton?" Cecily railed at Grace a few days after Henry had broken the news. "His breath smells of pig's urine and I could have sworn I saw a louse drop from his head once. What is worse, Grace, is that his lands are in the Lincolnshire fens. I shall probably end up sucked into a bog."

Grace bit her lip to keep from laughing. Cecily flounced about the room, kicking at the rushes and crying foul. Grace poured some wine and coaxed her into a chair, speaking sympathetic words as Cecily gradually fell silent. "Bess wants you with her," she soothed. "You may not have to go north, Cis. Look on the bright side: you will have your own household now, and maybe your own child."

The mention of children caused Cecily to wail once more. "But that means I have to . . . oh, you know. The idea horrifies me. Oh, Grace, what shall I do?"

Kicking herself for her thoughtless remark, Grace was unable to respond to Cecily's satisfaction, so the older girl got to her feet and without any more ado announced she was returning to the palace. She left Grace staring after her with astonishment tinged with compassion.

WHEN CECILY REMOVED to Westminster with Bess, Grace remained with the queen dowager and missed her sisters' company. It seemed Elizabeth was loath to let Grace go, and Cecily was full of sympathy. But Grace was more accepting of her fate after Elizabeth explained the situation in no uncertain terms.

"We know not if Henry—or more likely his dried-up mother—would view a bastard of Bess's father as suitable attendant on his queen," Elizabeth told her. Grace bit her lip. She could not remind the dowager that Bess herself was officially still a bastard, according to King Richard's law.

But by March, all was put right and Henry's parliament restored not only Elizabeth and her children's good names but all of Elizabeth's manors and properties that were forfeited during Richard's short reign.

When the news reached Elizabeth, she spent the day praying in her little chapel and her brighter mood gave Grace the courage to persevere in her research into her family. "May I beg an indulgence, your grace, and ask an ignorant question?" She was relieved when Elizabeth nodded graciously. "King Henry must be certain your two sons are"—Grace choked on *dead* and tried to find an alternative—"out of the way," she finally chose, "for, if I am right, one of them might . . . could return and demand his rightful crown now all your children are no longer bast—" Grace stopped, horrified, as Elizabeth's usually impassive face crumpled in anguish.

"My boys, my beautiful boys!" she sobbed. "Certes, they are dead, Grace. Or else where are they? Richard promised me they would be safe. How foolish I was to give my baby boy up to him in sanctuary—he said it was for Edward's sake, his brother who was lonely at the Tower. And I believed him, God help me. When the archbishop—old Russell—came that last time, I knew I could no longer fight Richard." She paused to blow her nose. "They pulled my boy from me, Grace. He was weeping, I was weeping and I gave him one last kiss, telling him I knew not when we would be together again. And so Richard had his way—and I have not seen either boy since." Her grimace marred her beautiful face. "I had not hated Richard until that day he snatched my baby from me, in truth," she said. Then she leaned in to Grace and her voice was softer. "There is no proof that Richard harmed them, but he took my boys, and, woe is me, he took my crown and my dignity. 'Tis hard to forgive." Her pale blue eyes lowered to Grace's upturned face again, and she took the girl's chin between her delicate fingers. "Aye, you are correct, child. The king would be in a boat without an oar if one of them had been found alive after Bosworth, and 'twould not surprise me if 'twas Henry and not Richard who ended their sweet lives," she murmured. " 'Tis true I hated Richard for taking them, but I cannot justify all that I knew of Richard and believe him a cold-blooded murderer. In truth, he worshipped his brother, and I cannot think he could have so dishonored Edward's memory. Nay, they are either still alive and abroad somewhere, or they sickened and died in the Tower—perhaps even after Henry took the crown. If they are abroad, I might add, Henry would do well to send his spies to look for them now that my children are once again legitimate, for my son Edward could rightly return and claim his throne. At least one of my children wears a crown—or should I say *will* wear one, if he ever deigns to give Bess a coronation. I suppose queen consort is better than nothing." Then, without warning, she rose to her feet and ended the discussion. "Lady Katherine! I am for bed. Come, attend me," Elizabeth called to her chief attendant, who was conversing quietly with the other ladies. She chuckled, her good mood restored as quickly as it had disappeared, and finished her celebratory cup of wine. "Young Lady Grace asks too many questions."

Retrieving the cup from Elizabeth, Grace looked sheepish. "I crave your pardon, madam. Mother Abbess always said I should think before I open my mouth. Pray forgive me." Her dainty head tilted to one side and her brown eyes penitent, Grace was the picture of contrition, and Elizabeth smiled in spite of herself.

"You are forgiven, child. Now off to bed with you. I have kept you too long."

"God keep you this night, your grace," Grace murmured and slipped quietly from the room.

Grace knelt by the bed she shared with her half sister, Anne. After so many years of practice at the abbey, she was able to reel off the rote prayers while she examined several more pieces of the puzzle of her new life.

"YOU HAVE A letter, Lady Grace," the steward announced one brilliant day late in August, disapproval written all over his face. "Her grace, the queen dowager, has allowed me to give it to you."

Grace was nonplussed. Who would write to her? she wondered. Thanking the steward, she took the missive and wandered down the wooden steps that led from the house into the private herber. In order to be closer to Bess, Elizabeth was now leasing Abbott's House at Westminster within the confines of the cathedral, and just over the wall from the palace. Grace found her favorite excedra and, sitting down, stared at the letter's seal and her name written in a neat hand. *Lady Grace Plantagenet, in the care of her grace, Queen Dowager Elizabeth.* It was the first time she had seen her name written, and it made her tingle with pleasure. Indeed, this was the first letter she had ever received, and she wanted to savor the excitement for as long as possible. A more impatient person would have torn it open and read it four times by now, she thought, amused at her own foolishness. She finally turned it over and broke the seal. Then she could not refrain from reading the signature and, with a gasp of pleasure, she hugged herself with joy. John! He had not forgotten her.

As Elizabeth had suggested, Bess had persuaded Henry that John of Gloucester posed no threat and so begged that he be let out of his prison at Sheriff Hutton. Henry had agreed to send him to Middleham Castle, where John would be more comfortable but still under surveillance. Henry had even agreed to give John a small pension, which Bess allowed was generous of her husband. Then came the news that Francis Lovell had escaped sanctuary and was fomenting rebellion in the Yorkshire dales, a region Francis knew well from his knightly training at Middleham and his wife's family estates nearby. Henry, on his progress, quickly moved troops to put down the rebels, hoping to trap Lovell and his cronies. Grace had held her breath when she had heard these tidings, wondering if John had been able to escape and join his master and other loyal Yorkists in the region. But Lovell, with the rebels scattering, had fled farther north, to the Furness Fells, and then disappeared. Grace had not dared ask Bess what had become of John. "Out of sight, out of mind" was a maxim Sister Benedict had taught her so that she could avoid being singled out during one of the mother abbess's many rampages. She thought the less John was mentioned at Henry's court, the better for him.

"John! John has written to me," she told a peacock that strutted with proud disdain a few feet from her, his long iridescent tail trailing behind him as he searched for food in the grass. "Oh, listen, I beg of you," she called, but the peacock sauntered off.

"*My sweet cousin, Grace, I greet you well from Middleham. It seems our new king granted me leave to return here, but I am still under suspicion and unable to leave. I was throwing crumbs for the birds today, and I was reminded of you.*" I doubt you would know me now, John, Grace thought, as you have not seen me for a year. I shall be fourteen in a few months and I have grown like a weed, the queen dowager tells me. Not upward, but outward. She chuckled, glancing down at her generous breasts. "*I received your letter and your gift of the kerchief from Tom, and I thank you for your kindness. Tom continues to train at Sheriff Hutton and will be squire to our cousin of Lincoln in due course. You will see him in London ere long, I dare swear.*" Tom is coming to London, Grace thought, pleased. Perhaps he will find time to take me fishing. She smiled, remembering the day she fell into the Derwent. "*I suppose you are informed about my master's treasonous activities this summer. He is gone from here now and can no longer harm our dear lord and sovereign Henry, praise be to God for his escape.*" Grace gulped. She could not believe John would use words like *treasonous* when referring to Francis Lovell, to whom John was so devoted. The lord had been his father's best friend, so Grace was told. She frowned, re-reading the text, as John knew she would. Then she saw a new meaning in the phrase *praise be to God for his escape.* "Certes," she said aloud, pleased with her discovery. John had been cleverly ambiguous as to whose escape he was thankful for; upon first reading, it would appear to be Henry's. He writes this in case the letter falls into the wrong hands, she thought, intrigued.

"*I cannot complain of my treatment, but I long to see my family once more. You are all in my prayers. Lastly, if it is possible that you speak to our cousin Jack of Lincoln, perhaps you could relay this piece of humor. His dog spends his time frolicking in a field of marguerites, and I believe he is seeking Jack there. The faithful hound is lost without him. 'Tis not all that important, Grace, but for the dog's sake I hope you will tell him.*"

Farewell, my little wren, I pray one day I shall be permitted to be among you all again. Your loving cousin, John."

Grace's puzzled frown accompanied her back to the house as she attempted to see what was funny about a poor dog's infatuation with daisies.

"WHY CAN I not have the babe here or at Westminster, Henry?" Bess had asked her husband when he'd informed her of his decision to send her to Winchester for the birth of their first child. Cecily had been in attendance on her sister that day and relayed the conversation to Grace the next time they were together.

"What did he say? Why do you think he wants to move Bess to Winchester, Cis?" Grace asked. They were lying beneath an oak tree near the herb garden, enjoying the warmth of a late-summer afternoon. She looked forward to Cecily's visits, when she would hear all the court gossip. "Is it not foolish to travel during the last few weeks of pregnancy? Could it not bring the child early?"

"What a green girl you are, Grace," Cecily scoffed. "Bess is not due for at least another month."

"Then 'tis a monstrous big babe she is carrying." Grace chuckled. "She resembles a ship in full sail."

"Aye, she does." Cecily laughed. "And she spends most of her day in the garderobe, pissing. But to answer your question, sister, Henry told Bess that Winchester was where King Arthur sat with his knights of the round table and that it would be good for England for their first child to be born there. And if 'tis a boy, he will be named Arthur. Henry actually believes he is descended from King Arthur. Pah! What a notion—his grandfather was a groom and his grandmother a princess of France on his father's side, and his mother is descended from bastards."

"Soft, Cecily," Grace warned, putting her finger to her lips. "You must have a care. Her grace, your mother, is convinced Scraggy Maggie has planted spies in our house."

"What do I care about that old termagant? She is a thorn in everyone's side, and"—she chose to lower her voice to give her opinion—"Henry cannot go to the jakes without her permission."

Both girls rolled over onto their stomachs, laughing again. They could hear the monks chanting in the cathedral behind them, and a blackbird entertained them with its fluty warble overhead. Elizabeth was in the house giving instructions to her steward for packing up the household for the journey to Winchester. Henry had flattered his mother-in-law by choosing her as one of the godparents to his firstborn, and she was eagerly anticipating the first grandchild of her marriage to Edward. Grace had been overjoyed to learn she, too, would travel with the royal party, especially as her three other half sisters had been sent off to Berkhampsted to be with Grandam Cecily. Grace had yet to meet the matriarch of the York family, and from all she had heard of Proud Cis, she was not looking forward to the time when she might.

"I suppose we shall have to tolerate Lady Margaret in Winchester," Grace said, grimacing. The first time she had met the domineering Margaret Beaufort, the woman had uttered but one single word: "Pretty." But her icy gaze from under hooded eyelids sneered, "another of Edward's by-blows." Tall and bony, she towered over Grace, and her once-attractive face was gaunt and starkly framed by a white widow's barbe. Her thin-lipped mouth rarely smiled, and each grudgingly affected smile revealed long, yellowed teeth. She looks like a horse, Grace thought, hoping that the simile would render the king's mother a little less terrifying to her. When Bess had told her mother that Lady Margaret would not be relinquishing her apartments to Henry's new queen, Elizabeth had gritted her teeth. "But those were *my* apartments—the *queen's* apartments," she responded angrily. "Not the queen mother's. You should have them, Bess. What arrogance!"

"I do not mind, Mother," Bess had soothed. "I prefer my rooms overlooking the river, truly I do."

"Then you are a fool to give her an inch, my girl," was Elizabeth's conclusion.

Cecily propped herself up on an elbow and grinned. "Ah, but Scraggy Maggie will not be at Winchester, Grace. 'Tis the best part about us going. I am sure when Henry told her that our mother was to be the godparent, she must have been so put out that she is not even attending the birth and has removed herself to the king's estates at Kenilworth. Good riddance, I say."

Grace laughed. " 'Tis hard to believe you will be her sister-in-law soon."

She was glad Cecily had finally accepted her fate and had resigned herself to being Countess Welles when the legal process of the Scrope dissolution and new marriage contract could be finalized. Henry did not seem to be in any hurry, and Cecily, who lived for the moment, often forgot she was betrothed.

"Aye, I shall be able to snap my fingers at her, like this," Cecily said imperiously.

"Neigh!" the two girls chorused, imitating Margaret Beaufort's high whine and collapsing in laughter.

"Grace," Cecily changed the subject. "Is that a new gown? Certes, green becomes you well."

Grace was flattered; it was the first time Cecily had commented on her looks. She smoothed the soft damask and nodded. "Aye. Your mother was good enough to let me choose the cloth. I am happy you like it. She has been so kind to me, Cis. She tells me my hand is neater than her clerk's, and she has entrusted me with the writing of several of her private letters. 'Tis a great honor."

Cecily arched her brows. "In truth, I am surprised. Mother trusts so few people now. She has never confided in me, but she has to Bess. Now Bess is married . . . she must need you. There is something in you that must please her," she said, for once choosing not to tactlessly remind Grace that Elizabeth had no reason to be kind to a bastard of her husband's. Attending Bess, under Lady Margaret's strict supervision, was teaching Cecily to hold her tongue and mind her manners. "And I am glad you are coming to Winchester."

"Me, too," Grace said. "I pray Bess has a boy to satisfy Henry. There are too many girls in our family, in truth. Little Warwick is the only boy, but we never see him."

"Aye," Cecily said, "and Margaret is stuck in Suffolk with Aunt Elizabeth. 'Tis sad what has become of them." She sighed, winding a stray tress of golden hair around her finger. "I try not to think about it, but I miss my brothers."

"Her grace tells me I was born on the Feast of the Epiphany in the same year as Dickon. How I wish I could know what he is like. Do you think they will ever find him and Edward?" Grace whispered.

Cecily shrugged. "I know Mother fears they are no more, Grace. Many people lay the guilt at Uncle Richard's feet, but I truly do not believe he harmed them. He was too kind to all of us—aye, even mother, after she came out of sanctuary. And he loved Father too well. I do not think Mother would have agreed to be at court with him if she imagined he had murdered her boys." She looked over her shoulder to make sure they were alone before murmuring, "I think they were taken away—maybe even abroad. Bess thinks I am foolish, but if I am not right, where are they? If they are dead, then why does Henry not bury them with honor and declare Uncle Richard a murderer? Because there are no bodies, 'tis why. And why did no one come forward after uncle's death and say he was made to murder them under pain of his own death? Henry would have been merciful. Indeed, he would have been relieved to know the boys were well and truly dead. If they are still alive, his throne is not really safe. Do you understand all of this, Grace?"

Grace nodded vigorously. "Aye, I think about it all the time," she said. " 'Tis a riddle, and I love solving riddles. If you are right that they are abroad, where would they go? And wouldn't somebody recognize them?"

"Nay," Cecily said, shaking her head. "They were very young, and so not often in public view. Dickon was always with Mother, so only those in her train might recognize him, and they are still with Mother. But Edward was at Ludlow for many years under Lord Rivers's supervision and only went through London once after Father died, when Uncle Richard rode with him into the city. Why, even I have trouble conjuring up their faces, I am ashamed to say, and so they certainly would not be known abroad. They could easily hide."

"But where?"

Cecily grinned. "You have not met our Aunt Margaret, have you?" Grace shook her head. "She's a clever one, I heard Father say. And she hates anyone from the house of Lancaster. If the boys are anywhere else but England, they are sure to be with her."

"But now that Henry has made all of you legitimate, why doesn't Aunt Margaret send Edward back to claim his throne?"

"That is the question of the age, Grace. I do not know."

A few days later, in a blaze of color, the mile-long cavalcade snaked its way through the rolling hills of Surrey, past the bustling market town of

Guildford and on its way to the ancient capital of England at Winchester in Hantshire. Henry led the way as the procession wound through the town and villages, with Bess comfortably ensconced in a large carriage, surrounded by her mother and sisters. Grace was honored to be among the royal women, comfortably reclining on cushions, although she did not care for the attention they got from the cheering townsfolk, who showered Bess with September flowers—the white and yellow yarrow, pale blue scabious and sweet-smelling honeysuckle. "God bless Queen Bess," they shouted, and occasionally Grace heard a lackluster "God save the king." The English loved their gracious sovereign lady, long known to them as King Edward's gentle daughter, but Henry had not yet earned their devotion. Grace could understand their reserve as she observed his rigid body and severe expression. His fierce and supercilious air was not aided by eyebrows that arched down to a point above his beaklike nose. When he did smile, it did not reach his eyes, which could pierce through even the most confident courtier and unnerve him.

"Grace, my dear sister," Henry had greeted her early in his courtship of Bess. "Certes, you are welcome at my court whenever you please. Bess speaks highly of you, although 'tis surprising"—he paused for effect— "seeing how low to the ground you stand." Then he had laughed, a high reedy laugh that did nothing to ease Grace's discomfort in his presence. She had curtsied and said nothing. Henry had moved on with nary a second glance. Over time, she had lost her trepidation and responded to his greetings with less reticence, but she knew he must find her company dull. She envied Cecily her gregarious nature and watched with astonishment as she pushed the boundaries of sister-in-law teasing to within an inch of being disrespectful. Henry never rebuked her, although her mother often did. "He is the king, Cecily, and deserves your respect and deference. I pray you do not live to rue it, for he has been known to hang a man for less," Elizabeth had admonished her. " 'Tis my devout wish that the marriage with Welles take place soon." And Cecily had rolled her eyes at Grace behind her mother's back.

Now and then Henry would dismount and walk beside the carriage, commanding that the gauzy curtains that kept out the dust and flies be rolled up so he could check on Bess's comfort. He does care for her, Grace thought, noticing that his blue eyes never wavered from his wife's face as she responded to his concerned questions. Every few hours he would call a halt, and the ladies were helped down from the chariot to stretch their legs and make use of a hole in the hedge to slip into a field and relieve themselves. It was on one of these breaks that Grace, wandering back along the column of courtiers, carts, servants and stragglers, saw the earl of Lincoln emerging from a field and lacing his codpiece. Recognizing her and seeing her embarrassment, he promptly turned his back to finish his task.

"How now, pretty coz," he said when he reached her side. Tilting her chin, he bent and kissed her. "I have not seen you much at court. Are you not in attendance on Bess?"

Grace smiled up at him. A handsome man, she thought, but not as handsome as her John. He had grown a beard, which made him look older than his twenty-four years. "I am in attendance upon the queen dowager, my lord," she replied, feeling small next to his above-average height and knightly bearing. "Having one sister in her train is enough for Bess, I warrant."

"And Cecily is enough sister for anyone, I dare swear," he said, grinning. "She always has been a handful."

"My lord—Cousin John," Grace was determined that she would not be intimidated by his age and stature. "I am most happy to see you, because I have a message to give you, and if I had waited much longer I might not have remembered it . . ." She trailed off, afraid she was gabbling, and calmed herself. " 'Tis important, and I am happy to see you."

"Aye, I gather you are happy to see me," Lincoln encouraged her with a smile. "As I am you, little coz. But now, I pray you the message, Grace— and, more to the point, its messenger."

Grace took a deep breath and started again. "I received a letter from my other cousin John—John of Gloucester," she clarified.

Upon hearing John's name, Lincoln's face tensed. "What does he say?" he asked, looking about him for eavesdroppers.

" 'Twas an odd message. Let me see if I can remember it correctly." She did not dare reach into her bodice, where she kept the letter next to her heart at all times, so she thought carefully. "He said it was naught but a little humor, but I was to tell you that your dog spends his time frolicking in a field of marguerites—daisies, you know—and John thinks the dog is seeking you there. 'The hound is lost without him,' were his exact last words. Does that make any sense, cousin?" Grace had been staring up at the wispy clouds overhead as she concentrated on delivering the message and so was surprised by Lincoln's expression when she looked back at him. His eyes had narrowed and his smile turned into a hard line. He grasped her arm—a little too roughly for her liking—and frightened her.

"Have you told anyone else about this message, Grace?" he said quietly, glancing over her head to the front of the procession and then behind him. "I hope you have not."

"Nay, my lord. You are hurting me, my lord," she whispered, and John immediately dropped her arm, patting it gently in apology. "What does it mean, cousin?"

"Can you keep a secret, Grace? Or perhaps I should not burden you— perhaps you are too young. But I dare swear that if John trusted you with this, so can I."

Grace nodded and crossed her heart. "I would never do anything to hurt John. And I am of no consequence to anyone at court, so who would think to question me?"

"I believe you are right," he agreed, brushing a few stalks of hay from his jacket. "You are nimble-witted, Grace. And you might be very useful to our family, if the need ever arises." He looked at her intently, calculating her worth. "The dog John refers to is Lord Francis Lovell." He paused when he heard her intake of breath. "You know him? Aye, certes you do, because he is John's lord. The dog is the badge of Lovell, Grace, and I believe the field John describes is Burgundy."

"How do you know that, cousin?" The riddle was beginning to unravel.

"Because the marguerite is the badge of our Aunt Margaret," Lincoln told her, and was amused to see her eyes widen in delight at his interpretation of the message. "You have remembered well, little Grace, and you have carried out a very important task, for which I thank you. Uncle Richard was right about John: he's a clever lad."

"I do not understand why John did not simply write to you, my lord." Grace was thinking out loud. "It did not make any sense to me, but you understood at once."

"No one cares about a love letter from a young man to his lady, coz. But don't you see, a letter from Cousin John to me would have been censored and deciphered before it reached me—if it ever did. Such an odd message to another might have been considered suspicious."

Grace nodded, her tremor of fear overcome by her pleasure that Lincoln thought it was a love letter. Then she remembered the part in the letter about Tom. "I hope you do not think me forward to ask about my friend Tom Gower of Westow. Is it true he will be in your service soon?"

"Aye, he will join my service in London after Henry's brat is born. His uncle asked me to employ him, and in thanks for the Gowers' loyalty, I am glad to do it. He is a good lad." He picked a harebell from beneath the hedge and gave it to her. "Now, you must return to the carriage before you are missed. I am still a person of suspicion for Henry, and I do not want him to think we are plotting his downfall, you and I," he teased her. As he bent to kiss her, he whispered, "Promise me you will not tell anyone of this. I must appear to be Henry's man now, but this news is of great importance to me and to our followers."

"I swear on Saint Sibylline's holy name," Grace whispered back, crossing herself. " 'Tis my special saint—of orphans," she explained, seeing Lincoln nonplussed. "And, my lord," she told him confidently, "do not forget that I, too, am a York." Then she turned, picked up her skirts and ran back to the carriage, hugging her secret and glowing with pride that she had been entrusted with it.

Lincoln's eyes followed her slender form as he settled his soft hat on his head and hoped he would not regret the conversation.

" 'Tis a boy!" The cry was taken up and passed from the birthing chamber to those anxiously awaiting the news in the chapter house of Winchester Priory, chosen for Bess's lying-in because crumbling Winchester castle had long since been abandoned as a royal residence. Henry was jubilant; he had sired an heir—and in the first year of his reign. What could be more perfect than that this boy was born in England's ancient capital? Winchester had not seen an heir to the throne born there since the third Henry in 1207, Prior Thomas Hinton had told his guests proudly. "All thanks be to the Almighty," he crowed.

"Praise be to God, a boy," was all Bess could muster after her ordeal. She had not seen her mother's sad eyes as she watched the wet nurse put Arthur to her breast. Fourteen years before, Elizabeth had lain in that same chamber and given birth to a little girl who did not live to see that Christmas. She was lying in her tiny sarcophagus next to Edward's at Windsor, and one day Elizabeth herself would join them.

"Arthur, his name shall be Arthur," Henry exulted, raising his jewel-encrusted cup and exhorting those present in the refectory to do the same. His relief was palpable after many hours of hearing Bess's pain echoing through the quiet cloisters of the priory in the cathedral grounds.

Henry was chagrined his mother was not there to share in the joy of his son's birth. He had explained her absence to Bess, who had been as curious as her sisters about it, as being a natural reluctance on her part to witness a first birth when she herself had come so close to death during her labor with Henry at the tender age of fourteen. "Perhaps the next one," Lady Margaret had said to him, "when a child slips more easily into the world. I shall go to Kenilworth and cede my place to Bess's mother. Besides, 'twill be a sound diplomatic gesture, Henry."

And so Henry had agreed, as he so often did when his mother gave advice. He would be eternally grateful to his parent for orchestrating his journey to the throne, and he knew she had a mind as agile as any man's and wanted only the best for him. There was nothing he could refuse her, it seemed. He even condoned her walking only half a step behind Bess instead of the customary full step, and clothing herself as richly as the new queen. Bess had admitted to Cecily—who had in turn told Grace—that she was afraid of Lady Margaret's influence with Henry.

"I believe he will never turn to me for counsel as Father did with Mother," Bess confided to her sister a few months after her marriage, when Henry was away on his progress through the country. "As long as his mother is there, he has no use for another woman's guidance. In truth, I am learning not to care, and now that I am with child, I see my role as a good wife and mother to Henry's children. 'Tis enough."

Lady Margaret had been right. Elizabeth, the queen dowager, was exultant that she would be at the birth without the domineering presence of the king's mother. Elizabeth would never forgive Margaret for duping her into plotting against King Richard in the autumn of 1483, after Richard had been crowned and Elizabeth's two sons were placed in the Tower for safekeeping. She had been led to believe that Richard's cousin and closest adviser, the duke of Buckingham, would rebel against the king to help her little son Edward regain his throne. Lady Margaret and Bishop John Morton had also duped the duke of Buckingham, who went to his death when Richard put down the rebellion. The two were working to put Henry on the throne, not the young prince, and rid England of the York dynasty in favor of Lancaster. Although Elizabeth's involvement was never proven, rumor had it that she had been in communication with the plotters from sanctuary. Despite this, Richard had treated her and her daughters with deference after they left the abbey's safety.

"It could have been a lot worse for me, Grace," Elizabeth had admitted one evening as they enjoyed the late summer light in the herber of the abbott's house. "I was grateful Richard and his wife were kind to the girls. I only wish I knew what has become of my boys," she said, and Grace had watched as Elizabeth sank into melancholic ruminating, as she did each time their names came up.

ELIZABETH'S SONS WERE momentarily forgotten when she stood triumphantly beside the enormous black marble font inside the cathedral, which was reputed to have the longest nave in all of Europe. Unprepossessing on the outside, Winchester's interior was a marvel of sky-high fan vaulting atop the delicately sculpted capitals of the stone columns. The royal party had waited a full fifteen minutes for the late arrival of one of the other godparents, John de Vere, earl of Oxford. Elizabeth glared at him, but the earl was in such high favor with Henry that she dared not voice her opinion of his rudeness. They all processed up the nave, stepping on myriad colorful tiles decorated with geometric patterns and mythical beasts, and through the exquisite rood screen into the quire. Behind the altar in the retroquire, just visible through another screen, was the newly positioned shrine of Winchester's patron saint, Swithun. Grace craned her neck to see it, knowing this was the saint on whose holy day, the fifteenth of July, the whole of England prayed it did not rain. She amused herself by reciting the well-known rhyme in her head:

> *Saint Swithun's day if thou dost rain*
> *For forty days it will remain.*
> *Saint Swithun's day if thou be fair*
> *For forty days 'twill rain no more.*

Aye, 'twould ruin the harvest, she mused.

The organ thundered a welcome to England's newest prince, who screamed his displeasure at being awakened thus from a nap in his Aunt Cecily's arms. Cecily carried the child to the high altar in the procession behind the bishop of Exeter—the old bishop of Winchester having died not a fortnight before—where she relinquished him to his godmother, Elizabeth. Flanked by Oxford and the third godparent, Lady Margaret's husband the earl of Derby, the queen dowager placed him on the velvet cloth that covered the holy table, where the baby squirmed in his swaddling clothes, crying with rage. Elizabeth smiled indulgently, picked him up and hugged him to her, the floor-length silk christening gown pooling around her feet. She looked radiant, Grace observed, almost like the vision she must have been when, as a new widow, she had stood with her two little fatherless boys under an oak tree and won the heart of King Edward riding by. Grace wished she could have seen her then. How could Edward have deserted such a beauty to sire a child with my mother? she suddenly thought, as she and the others intoned the *pater noster*. What makes men desire us so? On her knees, her rosary playing between her fingers, she hoped—and prayed—that if Henry chose a husband for her that he would remain faithful to her. Adultery was a mortal sin, she had been taught. So why did so many indulge in it?

"Grace, did you hear me?" Elizabeth's tone was sharp as she turned to speak to the girl. "Pick up my train. 'Tis caught somewhere."

Grace saw that her own kneeler was the culprit and stood to release the purple satin gown. Elizabeth then rose to receive the baby back from the bishop, who had just finished dunking Arthur's whole head in the holy water, further enraging the child.

"My lord bishop, pray bring the ceremony to a close as fast as you can," Elizabeth hissed at the gray-haired Peter Courtenay, who was taken aback at this irreverent request. But, having served as dean of Windsor under Edward, he well knew the queen dowager as intransigent. Not wishing to jeopardize the possibility of being appointed to the recently vacated bishopric of this most important of dioceses, he spoke the blessing at a spanking pace, making several of the nobles present smile into their prayer-folded hands.

As the party came out into the gray Sunday morning, a lone magpie flew down onto the grass beside the path, and Elizabeth gasped.

"One for sorrow," she murmured and crossed herself. "Pray God this is not an omen for Arthur."

"Amen," Grace and Cecily chorused hastily, signing themselves, and Grace surreptitiously spat out the bad luck into her hand.

Henry had stayed away from the christening ceremony to be with his wife, but now he and Elizabeth presided over the banquet that day in the chapter house. Grace was asked to wait on Bess in her chamber so that Cecily could also attend the feasting, and she gratefully hurried to Bess's bedside.

"How was it, Bess?" Grace asked about the birthing process. "It sounded very . . . uncomfortable." She decided *agonizing* might not be tactful.

Bess laughed and immediately reached her hand under the bedclothes to touch her tender pubis. "Uncomfortable? Nay, 'twas how I imagined the rack, Grace. Just you wait." She grimaced. Then she smiled. "Is the baby not beautiful? He is my heart's delight. In truth, he resembles my brother Richard when he was born." She looked over at the carved oak cradle being rocked by one of the ladies on the far side of the room.

"Aye, he is bonny," Grace lied, her thumb between her first two fingers. In fact, she had never seen such an ugly red face before, its nose flattened into obscurity. The boy did not look anything like the cherubic statues of the Christ child she was used to. And it seemed to her that he never stopped screaming, when his face became one wide, gaping hole. But she smiled and patted Bess's hand. "You must be happy you have a son."

"Aye. Now Henry believes the succession is safe." Bess lowered her voice so her attendants could not hear. "There is a rumor that our cousin of Warwick has escaped the Tower and has been seen on the isle of Jersey. 'Tis not good news for Henry. He thinks there is another rebellion fomenting."

Grace was horror-struck. "What does this mean? Little Ned is attainted because of his father, is he not?"

Bess nodded. She was pleased that Grace now understood the full ramifications of a conviction of treason. Ned's father, George of Clarence, had indeed been attainted and was eventually executed by his own brother King Edward; the father's attainder was passed on to the progeny, unless lifted by the king.

"So who would follow an attainted boy?" Grace persisted.

"Anyone who was an adherent of York, Grace. They would not let that stop them." Bess pushed a wayward strand of golden hair from her face up under her cap. Her face was glum. "Henry and I thought our marriage would heal those wounds and stop these rebellions, but they never seem to cease."

Grace was silent. She was thinking about her two cousins named John. Aye, they would take up the cause of Warwick, she thought, and she felt a tiny frisson of fear.

HER FEAR GREW a few days later when she and Cecily were given leave to walk to the market in the center of the city. Once one of the largest in England, the market's small size reflected the downturn in the city's fortunes. Nevertheless, the two girls, escorted by a burly guard, spent a pleasant morning away from their duties exclaiming over trinkets, ribbons and gewgaws and spending their groats on greasy hot roasted finch and a shared capon pie.

"Make way, make way," their escort growled as they eased their way through the customers jostling for the wares on the carts and stalls laden with everything from ginger, cinnamon, pepper and almonds to vegetables and salted cod, mullet and conger eel. Clothed in their plainest gowns, the girls did their best to melt into the crowd, but even so their elegant garb attracted some curious looks. They stopped to admire the three-level gothic market cross climbing to the sky past the rooftops of the surrounding houses. A jolly carter tried to sell them a slab of golden butter, but the girls demurred, thanking him and moving on.

"Fortunes! Have your fortunes told! A farthing for your fortune," a woman in tattered black rags called to them, reaching out a bony hand with a beckoning finger. Cecily squeezed Grace's hand in anxious excitement.

"Do we dare?" she whispered, eyeing the old crone with trepidation. The woman's coarse gray hair straggled out of a filthy hood, pushed back to show a wizened face and black, beady eyes. She smiled at Cecily, revealing one diseased incisor in an otherwise toothless mouth. Grace had taken one look at the hag and attempted to hide behind Cecily's larger frame.

"Nay, Cis," Grace muttered. " 'Tis against God's law. And besides, she looks none too clean."

As Cecily turned to cajole Grace into changing her mind, the fortune-teller spotted Grace, and her smile faded. Approaching the girls as near as the grumpy guard would allow, she pointed at the smaller girl and intoned something incomprehensible. Grace clutched Cecily's arm and tried to pull her away, but then the woman's face softened and Grace could see that she might have once been quite lovely. The woman's black eyes were mesmerizing, and Grace found she could not break her gaze. Something deep inside her stirred and she was afraid.

"Come here, child," the woman coaxed. "You have naught to fear from old Edith."

Cecily, curious, gave Grace a push forward and stayed the guard, who was ready to manhandle the old woman out of the way. Grace landed within arm's reach of Edith, who gently led her to a quieter spot.

Grace trembled, close to tears. "Good woman, I am a Christian, raised in an abbey. I fear for my soul should I listen to what you say," she stammered. She turned imploring eyes on Cecily, who was beginning to regret her action.

"You think I cannot see your goodness, my lady. I have a gift—some say 'tis of the Devil, some say 'tis from God. I also see you in great danger, and 'tis my duty to warn you of it."

Grace turned back and shook the old woman's hand from her arm, although, she noted, it had been a surprisingly gentle touch. The genuine concern she now saw in Edith's eyes reassured her somewhat. She reached for her rosary—always attached to her belt—and was comforted by the familiar cold beads. Holding on to them tightly, she whispered: "Danger, Goody Edith, what do you mean?"

Edith took Grace's small hand and peered closely at it. Cecily peeked over Grace's shoulder, fascinated.

"I see a room with colored walls, far away," Edith began. "There be a dog—a greyhound, I think. Nay, mayhap it be a hunting dog. His master be angry and sad." She traced a line on Grace's hand. She tensed. "Now I see blood—a lot of blood, and a boy leading soldiers. A battle, I think."

"She is addlepated, Grace," Cecily hissed. "What boy is she talking about? Ask her."

"Soft, my child," Edith admonished Cecily sternly. "Do not cloud my mind with your questions." She did not know she was talking to royalty; she knew only that they were girls of obvious wealth, judging by their attire. Cecily was not about to enlighten her, thinking the old crone would run away and spoil the fun. Edith concentrated on the palm. "I see another boy, older, in a place with strange trees, strange people in strange clothes. It is hot, very hot, and the boy often goes to the water to look at the ships."

"Aye, goody, but where is the danger for me that you spoke of? Boys and a dog," Grace was certain one was John. "Boys and a battle and boats. Where am I in all this?"

"Christ ha' mercy! You shall see two of them sent to their Maker." As Grace gasped, Edith squeaked with glee. "Executions! They be executions," Edith exalted, looking up at Grace and grinning hideously. "It be dangerous for you to know them, but you will help them. Better not make friends of young men, my lady," she admonished, and her loud cackle made several people turn and stare at the little group. She put out her hand for payment and looked expectantly at Grace.

Grace had gone white when she heard these portents and was rooted to the spot. Cecily reached over and put a penny in the old woman's hand. They both watched as she attempted to bite it with her one tooth and her gums; then she squirreled it away in the folds of her dirty gown and, with a final cackle, disappeared into the crowd.

"I should like to go now," Grace whispered, clutching at Cecily's sleeve. "I do not feel well."

"Oh, don't be such a goose, Grace," Cecily scoffed. " 'Twas a pack of lies. It made no sense at all. Put it from your mind." But she motioned to the guard to lead them back the way they had come. Truth be told, she was as unnerved by the fortune-teller as was her sister.

GRACE COULD NOT get the old woman's predictions out of her mind. She lay awake in the bed she was sharing with another of Elizabeth's attendants and stared at the eerie shadows cast on the ceiling by the dying embers of the brazier. A crucifix was nailed to the wall, and Grace prayed to the agonized figure of Christ to keep watch over John and to eradicate all memory of the afternoon. She was convinced the young man with the dog was John. But was he one of the young men who would die? And who was the other boy? Her restlessness was disturbing her bedmate, so she turned to her rote prayers, which had always stood her in good stead through her lonely years at the convent.

"*Ave Maria, gratia plena . . .*"

By the time she had recited the prayer twice, she was asleep.

The next day she woke to find her courses had begun, and for once she did not complain. Certes, 'tis no wonder the old woman saw blood, and some of her anxiety was stemmed.

IN MID-OCTOBER THE royal household began the tedious chore of packing up to return to London—to Greenwich this time, and the queen dowager's Palace of Pleasaunce, a gift from Edward to his bride some twenty years before. The queen dowager herself would return to the abbott's house at Westminster, her ceremonial duties as Arthur's godmother fulfilled. Grace had scarcely had a moment to think of that day in the market, and her mood had not remained gloomy for long. Elizabeth spent many hours with her daughter and grandson, and it was natural that Grace be part of the family group.

But unfortunately, Elizabeth's favoring of her young stepdaughter had embittered one of the queen dowager's closest friends.

Katherine Hastings, widow of Lord William Hastings, boasted the highest pedigree: she was a Neville, sister of Richard Neville, the great earl of Warwick, and niece of Cecily of York, and was, therefore, cousin to both kings Edward and Richard. She had long served Elizabeth, and the two women had commiserated with each other over their profligate husbands, who had eaten, drunk and whored together as only best friends can. The friendship between the two women was prickly at its beginning, Grace had learned, due to a long-held animosity between the Woodvilles and the Hastings over land. But whatever the ill will between the queen and the chamberlain, the friendship between the women had flourished over the years. It was Katherine who had consoled Elizabeth upon Edward's untimely death; yet within a month, Elizabeth found Katherine weeping on her shoulder for the extraordinary execution of William for treason, on the orders of Richard of Gloucester. In sanctuary, Elizabeth had invited Katherine to keep her company as the events of that tumultuous year unfolded.

Once, in a private moment with Elizabeth, they had talked of their husbands' infidelities. "Do you love him, Elizabeth?" Katherine had asked in that moment of truths, and was surprised at the hard glitter in the queen's eyes as she responded. "I loved John Grey with all my heart. I love Edward with the rest of me. In truth, my family benefits from this marriage, and I enjoy being queen," she said, fondling the ears of a terrier that lay on her lap. Her face grew wistful. "After my beloved first husband was killed at Saint Alban's, I vowed I would not love again. I swear Edward has never known, nor will ever know, and so you must promise to take this knowledge to your grave, Katherine. Swear on this cross." She reached out the cross at the end of her rosary to her companion, and Katherine reverently touched the gold and swore. " 'Tis the guilt I bear in this deception that allows me to be generous to Edward's bastards."

How Elizabeth had put up with those acknowledged bastards who strutted about the court under her nose while their father was alive, Katherine had never understood. Elizabeth's answer to the question had been: "Edward loves me and returns to me no matter where else he puts his pestle. I hate him for it, but I cannot stop him." Katherine, too, hated Will for his wenching, and her commiseration with the queen strengthened.

But to take the fruit of one of those lecherous liaisons under her wing *after* Edward had died was beyond Katherine's comprehension. She had enjoyed being the queen's confidante, especially after their husbands' deaths, and to watch this young woman worm her way into Elizabeth's confidence created a growing animosity in her towards Grace.

Now Katherine stared after the departing figure of Grace, determined that, as one of the highest-born ladies at the court, she was not to be shunted aside for this base-born slip of a girl. "May all whores rot in hell," she muttered as the door closed, leaving her with the lesser ladies of Elizabeth's entourage.

6

Bruges

NOVEMBER 1486

Right noble lady and beloved aunt,

I was so happy to receive your letter. I am sorry you were unwell for a time, but hope you are better. How glad I was to see you this summer in Malines! Sir Edward was good to let me come, if only for a few days. You taught me so much about your family in England, and by the time I left, I began to think of them as my own. It is strange to think I am the same age as your nephew who disappeared from the palace in the Tower of London. It must make you sad. I must thank you once again for your kindness towards me—and especially for the flagons of wine you provided for my needs. Do not worry, aunt, I did not drink all of them!

I promised I would tell you if I had any news of interest, but in truth, my life as a page is very routine. I fetch and carry whatever Lady Brampton needs, and I sometimes accompany her to the market. She says she does not trust her servants to pick the best cuts of meat or the freshest fish. Are all English ladies like this? I have heard some of the Flemish ladies laugh at her behind their big sleeves, but she tells me that she is an exiled merchant's wife who must watch her florins, and she says she cares not a fig for what they say. I love the market, except when the Belfort bells ring right overhead. I have to put my fingers in my ears or I would go deaf. Last week I saw some of the merchant adventurers from England in their purple livery on their way to the Prinsenhof, or perhaps they were visiting Mijnheer van Gruuthuse at his enormous house. Have you been inside it, aunt? It is not as big as Binche or Malines, but it is magnificent—and he is not even a duke!

Lady Brampton often calls on me to be a messenger for her, and yesterday she told me my English is almost perfect. She is surprised that I can read so well in French, but I heeded your advice and did not tell her I could also read Latin. Sir Edward makes me learn swordplay at a school in the Sint Jakobstraat beside the church and, I cannot tell a lie, I am a good student. Meester Grolinge says it must be in my blood, because I am so quick to learn. I laugh to myself, because I know my father was a boatman. Forgive me, aunt, for not showing modesty like you taught me.

As you asked during my visit to give you information that you think is interesting, I wanted to tell you that I was waiting on Sir Edward not a week since, and he was in conference with a brave knight from your home—from England. His name is Sir Francis Lovell, and it seemed to me he and Sir Edward were excited about a plan to rid England of the king. I think Sir Edward forgot that I speak English, and also because I am naught but a servant and I am not supposed to listen to anything while I am in attendance. How can you not listen, aunt, when they speak loud enough to hear? I did not understand it all because they used names I had not heard before, like Warwick and Lincoln. I am sorry if this is not helpful, but I did my best.

The cold and rainy season is well upon us again, so I hope we will soon go to Lisbon, because Lady Brampton says the sun always shines there and the sky is always blue. But I think we must go again to Middelburg, and I hate that place.

Know that I will love you always, and may God have you in his keeping, my beloved aunt.

Your Perkin (so Lady Brampton calls me now)

7

London and Bermondsey

1487

*A*small, disconsolate figure on a white palfrey hunched against the biting February wind and stared straight ahead at the guards in the green and white Tudor livery who marched slowly along Watling Street in front of him. It was not an unusual sight to see small groups like this making their way to and from Westminster and the Tower, but the youth's age and the beating tabors told Londoners this must be Edward, earl of Warwick, whom the town criers had announced would be paraded through the city streets to prove he was still very much alive and in King Henry's keeping. The citizens had all but forgotten this Yorkist prince, hidden in the Tower, until the rumor that he had escaped in the autumn and was hiding on the Isle of Wight had piqued their curiosity. More alarming still for Henry were the new rumors that someone claiming to be Warwick had been greeted in Dublin with open arms by the York-supporting Irish. After Lovell's rebellion of the previous spring, Henry could not afford to be anything but vigilant, and he took any rumor—no

matter how preposterous—seriously. To snuff out the rumor, the Great
Council at Shene decided that the solution was to prove to the people that
Warwick was still in the Tower.

"Poor little Ned," Elizabeth lamented as she stood at the window of
her house at Westminster, watching stray snowflakes waft down onto the
herber below. " 'Tis said he is thin and pale. He must not venture outdoors
to take the air much at the Tower. In truth, I doubt he knew why he was
showing himself to the citizens. The boy is slow-witted, 'tis true, but he
means no harm to anyone."

Grace was not of the opinion that there was anything wrong with Ned,
but she kept her eyes on her embroidery and her thoughts to herself.

Katherine Hastings agreed with her friend. "He is a simpleton, and I do
not understand why Henry does not let him join his household, where he
can keep an eye on him. Indeed, the boy's sister, Margaret, enjoys Henry's
favor. And she dotes on baby Arthur." Her pale eyes fell on Grace sitting
quietly by, and she suddenly snapped: "Her grace's cup is empty, Grace. Do
your duty by her, I pray you."

Grace got up quickly and took Elizabeth's cup. She was dismayed by
Lady Hastings's tone and wondered what she had done to deserve it. Elizabeth did not hear the rebuke; she was imagining the sad sight of her
nephew forced to ride for hours through the cold winter day. "I wonder if
my boys are still there in the Tower?" she said in a monotone. "Warwick
would know."

Grace cast anxious eyes at her mentor as she poured wine from the
pitcher. At any other time, she might have commented on how the cobalt
Venetian glass and the plum red wine put her in mind of the York colors,
but instead she silently carried the goblet to the melancholic Elizabeth and
sat back down.

A knock at the door startled the women, and Elizabeth's steward ushered in a young squire. When she heard his name, Grace could not forbear
a small squeak of recognition. "Tom!" sneaked out before she could stop it,
and Katherine silenced her, saying, "Quiet, girl."

Tom was on one knee in front of Elizabeth, but not before he had given
Grace a surreptitious grin. Hat in hand, he gave his name: "Your grace,
Thomas Gower of Westow at your service. I am here on behalf of my mas-
ter, my lord of Lincoln."

"Aye, Master Gower, I recognized Jack's badge," she said as she took the scroll of parchment from Tom's outstretched hand. "Where is my nephew? He was supposed to meet me earlier. 'Tis unusual for him to be late."

Grace heard the note of concern in Elizabeth's voice and recalled a short letter Elizabeth had privately dictated a few days earlier, summoning John to "talk with me on an urgent matter." Grace had been intrigued but had diligently penned the date and time of the meeting as requested and now remembered it was this day.

"My lord sends his deepest apologies, your grace. He said the letter would explain." As Elizabeth broke open the seal and read the contents, Tom backed away, bowing as he went.

"Ladies, you may leave me," Elizabeth commanded. "Stay, Grace, I may have need of pen and ink. Prepare a parchment, please."

Katherine sat where she was, not including herself in the dismissal. When Elizabeth smiled amiably at her and waited, she rose with great dignity and swept past Grace, almost knocking the young woman over.

"I shall call you e'er I need you, Katherine. I must compose my thoughts so I can chastise my errant nephew in just the right terms," she said with the same sweet smile. " 'Tis naught but a family matter and would be tedious for you. And Grace is a good scribe," she added.

There was no denying Grace's writing skills were far superior to the older woman's, and so dropping a well-practiced curtsy, Katherine left the room, glaring at Tom as he held the door for her.

"*Right trusty and well beloved nephew,*" Elizabeth dictated. "*I pray this reaches you before you take ship. My answer in this matter must always be nay, as my duty is to my daughter, our sovereign lady. Would the child was my own sweet Edward, for then you would have my complete support. I cannot help you further, but wish you God speed. Written from Westminster this tenth day of February.*"

Grace dipped the quill in the inkpot and wiped the excess off on the side before handing it to Elizabeth. The queen dowager signed her name with its underlined flourish and then frowned. "God's bones!" she muttered and scrawled beneath it:

"*Postscript: Have no fear, I shall burn your letter, as you should burn this.*"

She rose from her chair and flung Lincoln's letter into the fire. Grace sprinkled some sand onto the parchment and waited until the wet ink had been absorbed before carefully folding it. Affixing it with a drop of molten wax, she passed it to Elizabeth, who sealed it with her gold signet ring.

"Call Thomas Gower, Grace. This needs to leave the house quickly, before Henry's spies find it. I can of course trust you, can I not?" Elizabeth held Grace's unwavering gaze in hers and nodded, satisfied. "Good girl. Now go."

Grace saw Tom waiting down in the hall and waved to him, aware that several of Elizabeth's household were mingling there. He ran up the wide staircase and gave her a quick bow. He had grown another two inches since she had seen him last, and Grace could see that he now shaved his face and his once-lanky body had filled out and was shown off to advantage in his short green doublet and parti-colored hose. She had to acknowledge that he was quite handsome, but as always when she evaluated a young man, she compared him to John, and none could measure up. It did not occur to her that Tom, in his turn, might be noticing how womanly her figure had become or how a few tendrils of her dark curls had escaped her gabled headdress and were clinging artfully against her graceful neck.

She gave him a friendly smile. "How are you, Tom? I hoped I would see more of you when I knew you were to be with my lord Lincoln here in London." She was aware that they were being watched, and Elizabeth's fears of a spy in the household had taught her to be wary. She took his arm comfortably in hers and said in an audible tone, "How is your mother? I am so thankful for what she did for me that day. See, I have written her a letter to express my gratitude. I expect you will take the time to address it correctly for me." And giving him a meaningful look, she handed him the letter, the seal hidden from view.

Tom grinned and understood immediately, for he saw that the name written on the letter was not Alice Gower but John de la Pole, earl of Lincoln. "Certes, Lady Grace," he said in an equally loud voice. "I will make sure she gets it. I regret I cannot linger in your pleasant company, though, as my master needs me."

"*Adieu*, Tom, until we meet again," Grace said brightly. She was amused when he kissed her hand. "Do not overplay the scene, Tom," she whispered, smiling. "A simple farewell would have sufficed. No one is bothering to watch us anymore."

He released her hand and took his leave, but not before she saw him flush. Oh, dear, she thought, I have angered him, and she opened her mouth to apologize, but he was gone with the letter tucked safely into his doublet.

. . .

"I KNEW YOU had a spy in my household, Henry!" Elizabeth cried, rising
up from her knees with surprising agility, after being summoned to the
king's private apartment. "What have they been saying about me? That I
spend too much of your money? That I drink too much? That I do not pray
enough? That I pine for my sons and rail against my husband who left me
here on earth alone? Are any of these crimes, my liege?"

"I did not give you permission to rise, madam," Henry said, his hooded
eyes boring through her and his mouth set in a grim line. "But as you are
now standing, I will give you permission to sit. Dorset"—he snapped his
fingers at the man by the door—"bring a chair for your mother." Dorset obeyed, helping his mother settle into the wide cross-framed chair.
The dowager was surprised and perturbed that her son was present at the
meeting, and she arched her brow at him. He gave an imperceptible shake
of his head in return.

Grace was never sure of Thomas Grey, Marquis of Dorset, Elizabeth's
oldest son. He had always treated her like a nonentity or an unwanted
visitor. A handsome man about thirty, he had championed Henry's cause
when Richard had taken the throne, taking part in Buckingham's rebellion and fleeing to Brittany to join the exiled Henry. Elizabeth was bitterly disappointed that, despite Thomas's attempts at loyalty, Henry had
always looked upon her oldest child with suspicion and not elevated him
at court.

Elizabeth edged forward on the leather seat. Cecily was in attendance
on Bess, and Katherine and Grace had been allowed into the antechamber
for the private audience. Margaret Beaufort stood at her son's shoulder like
a vulture, her face an even colder mirror of his. Grace shivered; she did not
know if it was due to the frosty February temperature or the atmosphere
inside the room. It was indeed a private family gathering, and Grace's instincts told her this was not a good omen.

Bess was seated on her throne next to Henry and her eyes watched her
mother anxiously. "My dear lord," she coaxed, but her husband silenced
her with a raised hand.

"You know why I have called you here, your grace," Henry said with
icy calm, continuing his unblinking gaze at Elizabeth. "If you were not my
dear wife's mother, I would not hesitate to try you for treason."

A gasp went up from all but Henry, Bess and Margaret. Bess's eyes dropped to her lap, and her fingers plucked nervously at her dress. Henry placed his own long fingers over hers to calm them. Again, Grace saw evidence that Henry must truly love his wife and was glad for Bess. Dorset took a step back from his mother's chair and hoped the king was not including him in her folly.

Elizabeth's face paled, but she continued with her bravado. "Treason, your grace? What nonsense is this? I have committed no treason, I swear."

Henry reached into his wide sleeve and pulled out a letter that made Grace cover a squeak with her hand. Thankfully no one had eyes for her, sitting in a dark corner of the room with Lady Katherine.

"This letter came into my hands, madam. Do you deny that is your signature—your seal?" He opened it, turned it over for all to see and thrust it at her.

Elizabeth recoiled in horror. "I d-do not," she stammered, now visibly afraid. "How . . . ." She did not dare to finish, praying to the Virgin that Lincoln had not been caught.

"A servant of Lincoln's brought it to us before the earl set sail from Ipswich. I only regret 'twas too late to detain him on English soil. *Sal traitre!*" Henry spat. "It appears he has gone to Flanders and that meddling sister-in-law of yours, Margaret of Burgundy."

Inwardly, Elizabeth praised God. Outwardly, she blustered. "Then you see from my letter that I refused John support, Henry. I cannot deny he asked for it, but you can see for yourself I refused it. I have done nothing wrong."

Elizabeth had calmed herself and knew she had a point. She was almost certain nothing in the letter had incriminated her in anything specific. She racked her brain and prayed she had not mentioned the names Lambert Simnel or Francis Lovell or Margaret. Grace would know what she had written, but short of snatching it from Henry's bony fingers, she could not be sure.

Grace was stunned. Dear God, I cannot believe Tom Gower betrayed his master and Elizabeth. He wouldn't, he couldn't—but who else handled the letter besides Tom and me? Her mind was a jumble of imaginings, and her heart was heavy. She forced herself back to the awful reality that Henry might punish Elizabeth, and that she and Tom might be to blame. It was then that she became aware of Katherine's gaze upon her, and she turned to look at Lady Hastings and froze. Suspicion was clearly written all over her face. *Why, she thinks I betrayed Elizabeth!* Grace realized with shock. *She must have seen me with Tom and guessed the letter I was giving him was Elizabeth's. Our little game of pretense didn't work,* she concluded, and could not conceal a groan.

"Lady Grace, did you want to say something?" Henry's voice pierced her misery, made her jump to her feet and sink into a deep reverence. She could not say a word but stared at the king with frightened eyes.

"She is the one who penned the letter, your grace," Katherine said, also going down on her knees. "She is the only one who knew what was in it. And I saw her give it to Lincoln's man. 'Twas certain they were more than mere messengers, if I may be so bold. I saw them talking and laughing like old friends. If you ask me, 'twas Lady Grace who betrayed her mistress."

Grace found her tongue. "I swear on Saint Sibylline's grave I did not, madam," Grace said to Elizabeth, who managed a wan smile of acceptance. Then she addressed Henry. "Tom Gower and I *are* old friends, your grace. Tom was with all of us at Sheriff Hutton. With Bess—I mean, the queen— and Cecily—I mean, the viscountess—and . . . all of us." *Oh, no,* she thought, *my nervous tongue is running away again.* She tried to rein it in, but it betrayed her. "We went fishing together, we rode together. He helped me when I fell in the river, he . . ." She could see Henry's patience was running out, but she hadn't finished. "He is a good, loyal person, and he would never betray anyone. I swear we had not seen each other since we left York- shire, until I gave him the letter. Your grace, my lady," she addressed her sisters, "tell his grace, I beg of you," she pleaded, out of breath.

Bess chose to intervene. "She is right, my lord. Tom was with us that summer," she said, touching his arm and giving Grace a moment of relief. However, she then turned to her half sister and leveled a gaze at her with those sincere blue eyes. "But Grace, you should be grateful Tom gave up the letter. It proves he is a loyal subject to my husband, does it not?"

It was then Grace understood that Bess was lost to their family cause; Henry Tudor and her child were her family now. She would digest this before she slept that night, but all she could do now was murmur, "Aye, your grace."

Henry was all business from that moment. "Only the people in this

room shall know the true reason for your banishment, madam," he began, turning back to Elizabeth. Grace heard Katherine's sharp intake of
breath. Elizabeth slumped back in her chair, all pretense of queenly bearing sapped from her at the pronouncement. "I have decided you shall find
a holy house of your choosing and live there, where you will not have influence at my court ever again. Your daughters may visit you from time to
time, but you will cease your meddling in affairs of state. Your estates shall
be forfeit—although I shall bestow them on your daughter, my wife, so
they shall remain in your family, and I will give you as generous a pension
as my privy purse will allow."

That will not be much, Grace thought, knowing Henry's reputation for
tightly pulled purse strings.

"*Et quoique je n'ai pas de preuve,*" he now addressed the retreating Dorset in his preferred French. "I cannot allow you freedom of movement at
this time, my lord. We hear many rumors of discontent up and down our
kingdom, and because of your kinship to the dowager, I must keep a close
watch on you."

Dorset fell to his knees on the rushes. "My liege," he pleaded, blanch-
ing, "I know nothing of these dealings with Lincoln. My mother acted
alone. I swear my loyalty to you is unmatched, and I beg—"

"In faith, you have given the appearance of loyalty, my lord," Henry cut
in, "but I can take no chances. You shall be lodged in the Tower until this
pretender is unmasked and brought to our justice." Grace saw Thomas
finger his dagger, then think better of it and let his arm swing back to his
side.

A stifled groan turned Grace's attention to Elizabeth and she watched
helplessly as Elizabeth's beautiful face crumpled in defeat. She could not
bear to see her benefactress so humiliated and, without waiting for permission to rise, she got to her feet and ran to comfort the distraught dowager.
Bess constrained Henry from forbidding the kind gesture, and he leaned
back, relieved the unpleasant episode was over. His mother acknowledged his efforts with a squeeze of his shoulder. He sighed and patted her
hand. In truth, he had expected more of a fight from his fiery mother-
in-law, but her lack of defiance told him—told everyone—that she was
guilty.

"Why do you not just execute me, Henry?" Elizabeth asked dully. "Like any other traitor." She fixed her eyes on Grace's bent head at her knee, not wanting him to see the resignation in them.

"We do not execute women—as yet—Elizabeth," he said grimly. "But we can prevent further meddling by sending you away." He saw her flinch at the use of her given name; he was already treating her as an inferior. "Tomorrow, the council will be told that you are disgraced and will be retiring to an abbey. They will be told that you incurred my displeasure because of your past cooperation with the usurper Richard."

Elizabeth's head snapped up then, and, pushing Grace aside, she straightened her back and turned flashing eyes on Henry. Her daughters—and now Grace—recognized the danger signs. Bess frowned and shook her head at her mother, hoping to warn her, but Elizabeth was past caring. A peal of harsh laughter erupted from her and took Henry by surprise. For once, he found himself speechless, and looked to Bess for help.

The laugh was gone as quickly as it had come. "Cooperating with Richard, your grace? Me? What can you mean?" Elizabeth arched a finely plucked brow and sarcasm dripped from her mouth like honey from a spoon. "Ah, yes. Let me see. For taking my children into sanctuary to protect them from his greedy clutches. For allowing him to drag my little boy from my side while I screamed and fought. For supporting Henry of Buckingham's rebellion against him, along with your mother and Bishop Morton. For risking my very life by agreeing to betroth my daughter to you, an exile, while Richard was still on the throne. For listening while he made a declaration renouncing my marriage, bastardizing my children and reducing me to the status of dame. I can quite see how you might mistake these for 'cooperation,' your grace."

Bess stared in horror at her mother, but Henry was on his feet.

"*C'en est assez!* Enough!" Henry shouted, his pasty face now red with anger. "*Va-t-en!* Out! You ungrateful woman. I would have no more of you, and the court *will* have no more of you."

His raised voice alarmed the guards outside and they burst into the room, halberds at the ready. He waved them back but, offering Bess his arm, stalked past Elizabeth and Grace and out of the room, Cecily and Margaret hurrying to keep up with them. Cecily turned at the last and sent her mother a sympathetic look before disappearing into the corridor. Katherine and Grace supported Elizabeth as she rose on unsteady legs and gave her son a blessing before the guards escorted him out. Her face was ashen as the threesome made their way back to their barge.

"If I have been betrayed," Elizabeth whispered, " 'tis by my daughter's weakness. My daughter, who sits on the throne only because I risked my life in scheming for her marriage to that weasel. God damn him to hell-fire!" she spat.

Grace crossed herself and sent up a prayer, hoping to cancel the blasphemy and spare her mistress further heavenly punishment.

"Aye, Elizabeth. And that traitor Thomas Gower, whoever he may be," Lady Hastings muttered, glancing over at Grace, who pretended not to hear.

But she, too, was beginning to doubt Tom's innocence. She was learning not to trust anyone at court and to keep her own counsel. She grimaced. So, it was back into seclusion behind abbey walls for her, she reflected. And she thought she had come so far!

BERMONDSEY VILLAGE WAS adjacent to the lively borough of South-wark, which Grace observed at her leisure as the royal carriage lumbered through the crowded streets after crossing London Bridge. A crowd was gathered at a respectful distance from an enormous chained and muzzled black bear, tormented by two dogs lunging viciously at its exposed belly. Every now and then a swipe from its powerful paw sent a howling dog hurtling into the spectators, who turned it around and sent it back into the fray. Grace dragged her eyes from the grisly scene and fixed them upon a buxom wench with a breast hanging out of her bodice and her ragged gown split open to expose a fleshy leg to any passerby interested in ex-changing her talents for a few coins. Curious citizens gawped at the royal party as it wended its way up St. Margaret's Hill. They did not know that the carriage and few carts were transporting the once all-powerful wife of King Edward to her forced retirement. The group passed the newly roofed St. Mary Overie, the pillory, the well, the bull-baiting ring, the breweries and the many inns and taverns—the Swan with Two Heads, the White Hart and the Tabard—on their way into Long Lane. Grace had so many questions on her lips, like: "The Tabard Inn is where Master Chaucer's pilgrims began their journey, is it not?" "What do you suppose the man in the stocks has done?" and "How does that man walk on those tall sticks?"

But Elizabeth had sunk into despondency as soon as she returned to her house following her audience with Henry, and no one dared speak to her unless she invited it. When the small company left the busy thoroughfare and turned into Long Lane, the walls of the abbey could be seen looming over fields and woodlands in the near distance, and Grace's heart sank.

"Certes, Elizabeth," Henry had said upon the farewell meeting with his mother-in-law before the court removed to Shene. "We have no need of an unmarried bastard of Edward's here. 'Tis not my duty to care for her. By all means, take her."

Bess had turned sorrowful eyes on Grace, whose own eyes told the queen: *"Your mother has been good to me, and I will protect her if you will not."* Bess was dismayed by the look and had the grace to lower her head. Elizabeth had embraced her oldest child fondly despite her previous ire towards her, and Bess for once cared not that Henry saw her tears. He frowned and gently pried the two women apart, wholly possessing Bess's attention once again. He may love her, Grace thought, but only when he can control her. "You may visit your mother from time to time, my dear. Dry your tears; 'tis not as though she will vanish from your sight," Henry had chided her.

Selfishly, Elizabeth had not thought of Grace's comfort in her request, only of her own misery, but Grace had been proud that Elizabeth wanted her. It was only now, as the gates of the Abbey of St. Saviour closed behind her, that she felt trapped. She was all too familiar with life in a cloister, and she could not believe she was returning to it so soon after being liberated. Instead of the gray-habited nuns of Delapre, it was the black hoods of the Benedictine monks that greeted the dowager queen and her few attendants that blustery March day. Elizabeth had chosen Bermondsey Abbey because, in its twelfth-century charter, it was ordered to provide hospitality to any descendants of the great de Clare family, and Elizabeth's husband, Edward, had been a member.

Elizabeth was gracious to Prior John Marlow, who came from nobility, as did many of the monks at Bermondsey. He was so fat it was hard to know where his chin began and his belly left off, ample evidence that one ate well at the abbey.

The prior blessed the new arrivals as soon as they stepped from the carriage, and then led the way to the few rooms that would be Elizabeth's new home. The abbey, with its monastery and priory house, sat on several acres, and outside its walls were the fields and orchards that fed the cloistered community. A small army of laymen kept the abbey running smoothly, all living in cottages or huts within the shelter of the abbey walls. Grace was pleasantly surprised to see grooms, cooks and gardeners milling around the buildings, working alongside the monks; and in the fields, harrowers, clodhoppers and ploughmen were readying the fields for sowing.

"Bermondsey is one of the wealthiest prior houses in the kingdom," Cecily had confided to Grace when she had visited Ormond's Inn before her mother's departure. Elizabeth had been too distracted by choosing what to take to Bermondsey to spend time with her daughter, so Cecily had herded Grace into the garden to pick daffodils. Nodding and bobbing in the March wind, the flowers had sprung up all over the lawn in the first few warm days of the English spring. Accompanied by Cecily's young maid, the two young women walked and talked among the golden blooms, occasionally stooping to cut one with small iron shears.

"Mother will be well looked after; never fear. I only wish you could go with us to Shene, Grace. How will you find a husband hidden away in an abbey?"

Grace had stared at her sister in astonishment. "Find me a husband? But you heard the king: I am but a banished bastard with no dowry. Who would want me now?"

"Never forget you are a Plantagenet, Grace," Cecily retorted. "There are only a few of us, and someone will be proud to wed you, bastard or no."

Grace grinned. "I think perhaps I will be better off in an abbey than forced into the bed of someone like Viscount Welles," she replied, and ducked a clod that was aimed at her. "When will you two wed, pray?"

Cecily shrugged, taking off one of her crimson crackows and wiggling her cramped toes. "The later the better. He has been showering me with gifts, though," she said, chuckling. "Look at this brooch—the pearl is as big as a duck egg. He does not seem to be as penny-pinching as his uncle, in truth. Maybe it won't be so bad."

LYING IN THE pitch-black of a rural night several weeks later, Grace was courting sleep by conjuring up such vivid memories as the conversation with Cecily as she tried to get comfortable in her truckle bed. She was still not yet used to the rope-slung cot with its palliasse of straw under a mat-

tress of spiky chicken feathers, and she swore she could feel every knot
as she tossed and turned. She yearned for the large, carved wooden bed
topped with a goose-down mattress that she had slept on at Ormond's Inn
with another of Elizabeth's attendants. In their new quarters, even Elizabeth had to share her bed, which she did with Katherine Hastings, and
Grace's cot was stowed underneath during the day.

Grace was missing her weekly conversations with Cecily, who had
brought the court gossip to Ormond's Inn and whose descriptions painted
pictures for Grace that stayed with her for days afterwards. Hearing news
from someone close to the king was not the same as hearing it from a
traveler sharing the monks' hospitality for a night. She remembered the
gasp of disbelief that went up when one such passing merchant told the
company that the boy claiming to be the young earl of Warwick had been
crowned "King Edward the Sixth of England" by the Irish nobility in Dublin's Christ Church Cathedral.

"But we saw the young earl with our own eyes in London not two
months ago," one diner said. "And he is back in the Tower. It cannot be the
same lad."

"Pah! 'Tis certain the boy in Ireland is false. But 'tis said not one of
those Irish rebels raised a sword in allegiance to our sovereign lord Henry,"
the man cried. "Certes, we all know what a nest of York arse-kissers those
peat-burners are." Several pairs of anxious eyes swiveled in Elizabeth's direction, but she calmly continued eating her food, guest of honor at Father John's table. No one could see her clenched fist under the table due
to the elaborate linen laid upon the abbot's table including an exquisitely
decorated frontal cloth that hid the diners' legs and kept them free from
draughts.

"My good man," Prior John's voice erupted from his many chins and
thundered across the hall, silencing the speaker. "You are in the company
of the dowager queen of England, widow of our much-loved sovereign,
King Edward." He did not need to remind the embarrassed merchant that
Edward had been the head of the house of York. Elizabeth nodded her
thanks to the abbot, who called for more food. Plates of pheasant, duck
and suckling pig were set upon the head table, but Elizabeth waved it away.
Her confinement had done nothing to fatten her already dwindling flesh,
despite the abundance of food provided daily by the rich abbey. When

Grace combed her mentor's hair these days, she noticed how limp and white it had become, and although Elizabeth always attempted to look her best for these public dinners, her gowns hung off her bony shoulders and she had no breasts to fill the bodices. It was as though her appetite for life had died that day in February.

Laymen came to gawp at the diners and see how the nobility enjoyed the fruits of their poorly compensated labors. Then they queued at the kitchen door to receive the gravy-soaked trenchers that otherwise would have been added to the rubbish heap.

Elizabeth was not the only noble to have fallen on hard times or simply taken sanctuary to retire from the world, and thus she had stimulating company. "The pretender's name is Lambert Simnel," Elizabeth told one of those later that day. "But fear not, my lord, I dare swear my son-in-law will not allow him to set his foot this side of the Irish Sea." Then, seeing Lady Katherine's worried frown, she had hurried on, "Indeed, I know nothing more."

ONE EVENING, AS the daylight waned and the ladies could no longer see to work their needles or read, Elizabeth sent her two tiring women to their beds in the chamber next door, which they shared with another resident's servants. She yawned and stretched, kicking off her worn velvet shoes and holding her feet out to the dying embers of the fire. May was a fickle month for weather, and some nights still held the threat of frost. The small chamber warmed up once the fire was stoked and now the glowing coals gave off a rosy light.

"Play something for me, Katherine," Elizabeth asked. "I am not quite ready for bed, and some music would be pleasant."

Katherine picked up her lute and began to tune the strings, deciding what to sing.

"Shall I unbind your veil and brush your hair, madam?" Grace asked Elizabeth, who smiled and nodded. Katherine settled the instrument on her knee and played a jaunty introduction. Then her warbling alto filled the room:

"When nettles in winter bear roses red,
And thorns bear figs naturally,

And broom bears apples in every mead,
And laurels bear cherries in the tops so high,
And oaks bear dates so plentuously,
And leeks give honey in their superfluence . . ."

She paused for effect before emphasizing the final line of the stanza:

"Then put in a woman your trust and confidence."

Elizabeth feigned indignation: "Fie on you, Katherine! Why denounce womankind thus? Certes, 'tis men that this ditty describes, not us," she exclaimed, chuckling nonetheless.

"There are more verses, my dear Elizabeth, each more impossible than the last. Would you care to hear them?"

"Nay, I do not like your song, for in truth I believe you and I were more trustworthy than our men. Think back, Katherine, to those nights when our husbands deserted our beds for whores."

Grace was carefully folding Elizabeth's soft lawn veil on the bed and wondered if the conversation would continue because she was in the room. But either Elizabeth knew she could trust the quiet young woman or she forgot Grace was there, because she continued to berate Edward and Will's "adventures with other females," as she termed them. "I remember the time when I was carrying Dickon—when was that, late Seventy-two, early Seventy-three, it must have been, not long after Lord Gruuthuse's visit, and George's Isabel was also with child—and Will was home from Calais. He and Ned went drinking and they came back wine-soaked. Will all but carried Edward to his chamber, making such a din that I ventured out of my own bed and along the hall to see what was happening. I entered Edward's chamber to find my dearest husband prone on the bed and an equally wine-sodden Will dragging one of Ned's hose off him, both laughing like jackasses. Certes, 'twas humiliating for both of them. But I could not forbear smiling, for they were so tickled-brained, neither could focus their bleary eyes upon me."

Katherine's disparaging "Pah!" showed she could not imagine what Elizabeth would have found funny.

" 'Ned,' I said clearly but quietly in order to calm them, 'what is the meaning of this? Where have you been? You have woken half of the palace with your drunkenness.' " Elizabeth chuckled, remembering. "They both sat up on the bed like naughty boys and told me—between guffaws—how they had played a trick on Ned's brother, George, that night. But try as I may, I could not extract the story from them, except that it had to do with a Flemish girl and a tun of wine."

"Frieda," Katherine said suddenly, bitterly. "Her name was Frieda."

Elizabeth sat up abruptly, almost pulling the comb out of Grace's hold. "Ouch, girl, do be more gentle," she snapped, but then she turned her attention back to Katherine. "How do you know her name? Do you know what happened?"

Katherine turned away to lay the lute beside her so that Elizabeth could not see her eyes. "Nay, that is all I know," she lied. "I had long stopped my ears to Will's conquests in the city, but I interrupted a conversation between him and his squire as he was asking the man to find a Flemish girl named Frieda not long after that incident. 'Twas probably a mere coincidence," she said vaguely.

Elizabeth accepted the explanation, but Grace did not. She had come to know Katherine's tones of voice well over three years in close quarters and knew the woman was lying. She was intrigued, loving the mystery of it all, but Elizabeth was bored by the affair, and, yawning, she waved the comb aside and stood to be disrobed. Her drab gray gown was unhooked and puddled about her feet. She shivered in her fine lawn smock, and, keeping her stockings on for warmth, climbed into bed.

" 'Twas a long time ago now, Katherine. And what does it matter? Both men are dead, God rest their souls. Besides, I suppose I should not tell these kinds of stories in front of Grace. After all, we must not forget Ned was her father, and her mother another of his little *adventures*." The last word was delivered with such truculence, Grace wanted to run from the room in shame, but instead, as was her wont, she buried the hurt deep inside and busied herself with her truckle bed. The queen dowager still knew how to wound.

8

Bermondsey

SUMMER 1487

One day in late May Grace was learning the art of beekeeping from a gentle friar named Oswald and so did not see a young horseman enter the gates of the abbey in the wake of a cart piled with tuns of wine. His garb was Lincoln green, proclaiming him an archer, and his hood concealed most of his long black hair while a beard hid his face. Hailing a groom, he slid off his palfrey's back and handed over the reins, giving a few instructions as to the care of the animal. He was greeted by Brother Geoffrey, the guestmaster of the abbey, who assumed he was to house a weary traveler for the night. Nodding amiably, the man followed the friar's pointing finger and ran up the steps and into the hostelry, seeking his room. "Dinner is at noon, Master Broome," Geoffrey called after him.

Grace was nonplussed when she stepped back into Elizabeth's apartments and found a grubby piece of parchment addressed to her on the table by the door. Elizabeth was resting on her bed, with Katherine seated beside her, reading from their favorite book, Malory's *Le Morte d'Arthur*:

"So they rode till they came to a lake, the which was a fair water and broad, and in the midst of the lake Arthur was ware of an arm clothed in white samite, that held a fair sword in that hand. Lo! said Merlin, yonder is that sword that I spake of. With that they saw a damosel going upon the lake. What damosel is that? said Arthur. That is the Lady of the Lake, said Merlin; and within that lake is a rock, and therein is as fair a place as any on earth, and richly beseen; and this damosel will come to you anon, and then speak ye fair to her that she will give you that sword . . ."

Katherine paused when Elizabeth held up her hand.

"A moment, I pray you, dear Katherine. We can learn more of Excalibur later. Grace," she called, as Grace took the missive to the window to better decipher the handwriting. "That was delivered but a few minutes ago. Who is it from? The brother said 'twas for you, not me. Whose heart have you set aglow, my little one? Ha! I see you are blushing. Come, tell us all about him. Certes, it will cheer this dull day, I have no doubt."

Katherine pouted. "I thought you liked my readings, Elizabeth," she groused, annoyed that Grace's entrance had interrupted the romantic tale.

Without a moment's thought, Grace lied for the first time in her young life. " 'Tis one of Lord John's squires. He has been casting sheeps' eyes at me for a week now. 'Tis of no import, your grace, and he writes ill."

Disappointed there was to be no gossip, Elizabeth sank back into her melancholy and waved to Katherine to continue with the narrative as Grace thankfully escaped out onto the covered walkway. "I can always count on Grace to avoid gossip," the dowager muttered after her. "But then, in truth, 'tis why I like her." Katherine scowled.

Outside, Grace opened the note: *"Grace, I must see you. Come to me tonight in the undercroft when the bell strikes the Compline and the monks are safe in prayer. Say nothing of this to anyone. Your long lost cousin, John."*

"*Sancta Maria, gratia plena,*" Grace murmured, kissing the paper. John is here! He wants to see me, she exulted. Then she frowned; why is he so secretive? Her grace, the queen, would have no quarrel with John. Indeed, she would venture to say no one at the abbey would have a quarrel with the bastard son of dead King Richard. Then a shiver of delicious excitement ran through her and, tucking the letter into her bodice, she ran down the stone staircase to the back courtyard and straight to the privy. She was one of three women sitting on the plank in the smelly outhouse, hanging their backsides over the cesspit. And no one noticed that she used a cloth parchment instead of hay to wipe herself and thus cleverly disposed of John's secret missive.

She was glad Elizabeth chose to take her cold supper in her chambers that night, because no one but his family would have recognized John in the refectory after two years from court. But the minutes dragged into hours, and Grace could not wait to see him.

UNSEEN AS SHE descended the undercroft steps, she slipped from pillar to pillar like a shadow. The soft light from her swinging lantern caught a rodent's red eyes as the animal cowered in a corner, and Grace shivered. Rats—she hated them. They reminded her of her childhood at Delapre, where she was often sent to fetch parsnips or turnips for the daily soup from its equally unpleasant root cellar. She passed the vermin quickly, pulling her cloak more tightly around her with her free hand. The cellar of Bermondsey was no place for a young girl to be at midnight, and despite her excitement at seeing John again, she was beginning to regret her impetuous decision to a meet him in secret.

A noise stayed her steps and she hid behind a column, forgetting her light would give her away to a guard—or anyone else creeping about the musty cavern at such an hour. She held her breath.

"Grace?" Her whispered name echoed eerily among the sacks and casks stacked in lumpy piles upon the dirt floor. "Is that you?"

Grace let go of her breath and stepped out from her hiding place. "Certes, 'tis me," she replied. "Who else did you think would be addlepated enough to come down here at this hour and risk excommunication for violating the Compline law?"

John could not help but laugh, a sound that was muffled by the thick stone walls and the monks chanting in the church above them. "Little wren, you appear to have grown up since I saw you last. Are you not at least glad to see me?"

Grace stared at the figure in front of her. His black beard and long hair hid the face she had imagined so many times in her dreams, but she would have known those gray eyes anywhere. Without a thought for convention, she put down her lantern and ran into his arms.

"Why, I do believe you have missed me, coz," John said, laughing. He kissed her forehead, as he always did, and then her generous mouth. It was the kiss of a cousin, she knew, but it lit a fire in her that made her gasp. She stepped back to study him in the dim light.

"Aye, I have missed you with all my heart," Grace whispered, her lashes casting dark shadows across her cheeks. "I thought never to see you again, John. How did you find me? Why are you come? Why are you dressed like this?"

John swung her around, laughing at her questions. She had grown up, his little wren, and she was very pretty, he noted. "Come, let us sit, and I will satisfy your curiosity, never fear. I have made a comfortable nook of sorts over here," he said, taking her hand and leading her to several sacks of straw that he had fashioned in the shape of an oversized chair. Carefully putting the lantern on a small cask, they sank back into the sweet-smelling hay. Grace was intoxicated by the nearness of him and shivered, which John attributed to the cold. When he put his arm around her shoulders, it was all she could do not to snuggle even closer. He smelled of horses and leather, and she hoped he would notice the lavender water she had sprinkled on her hair and gown before she had crept from her chamber. She still could not believe he had come to her at Bermondsey.

"Why have you sought me in particular?" she asked, hoping she didn't sound too eager. "Are you in some sort of trouble?"

"There you go again, Grace. Questions, questions! Aye, I wanted to see you in particular because our cousin Jack suggested you might be able to help me. I dare not show my face in London—although I fear I am much changed since last I was at Father's court." He laughed when he saw her nod vigorously. "I received word from Jack that he and Lord Lovell are planning to go to Ireland with the help of Aunt Margaret. They have a boy with them—"

Grace stopped him. "Oh, John, they are already there. Did you not hear? The boy you are talking about has been crowned King Edward the Sixth in Dublin."

John removed his arm and swiveled around to face her. " 'Tis Warwick, not just any boy. 'Tis little Ned, and he is the rightful king of England. So, 'tis done, is it? Then I must guess where they will invade, for I will be part of Ned's bid for the throne. Damn Tudor! He kept a close watch on me these last eighteen months, but thanks to my father's friends in the dales I was able to escape from Middleham a month ago. Henry is looking for me, but I am small fry compared with Lincoln, Lovell and an army ready to kick his bony rump off the throne. I doubt not he knows about my escape, but he will not waste valuable men looking for me."

Grace waited until he finished before she gently let him down. "But Ned is still in the Tower, John. Lincoln himself spoke to him in February, at Henry's command. Henry made poor Ned ride through the streets so the people could see with their own eyes that the earl of Warwick was firmly in the king's hands. I wish it were different, John, but I am telling you the truth. The boy in Dublin is an imposter—and his name is Lambert Simnel."

John listened intently but did not appear disillusioned. " 'Tis no matter, Grace. If the Irish believe it, or if they believe *in* it—the cause, I mean—then they can invade, win against Henry, take the real Warwick from the Tower and crown him in London. Don't you see? He is only a figurehead. Why, he cannot even wield a sword yet—what is he, twelve now? 'Tis the York cause that is important, not the boy. I must try to join them, either in Ireland or where it is they land." He was on his feet now, stirring up the dust on the floor with his rough peasant boots. He began to pace, hands behind his back, a mannerism he had inherited from his father.

"How can I help?" Grace ventured. "I am cloistered here now and have little contact with anyone outside the abbey. The only person I see from time to time is Cecily."

John stopped pacing and snapped his fingers. "Cecily! Certes. Is she married to Welles yet? Nay? Good; we should enlist her help, because she is close to the king. Can you get her to visit in the next two or three days? Time is of the essence, now that I know the army is in Ireland. Oh, say you will send for her, I beg of you. I think she will be my friend, don't you?"

He was bending down to her, his hands gripping her upper arms and his face a few inches from her own, and she was intoxicated by their closeness. Kiss me, John, she wanted to whisper. Let me show you how I love you! But he merely repeated the question, his intense gaze searching her face for an answer to his plea.

"Aye," she murmured, tears pricking her eyes. "She is your friend and will come, never fear."

"What is wrong, my wren?" John let her go but tipped up her chin, seeing the tears. "Did I hurt you?"

Grace winced at the irony. Aye, you have hurt my foolish heart, but 'tis my own fault, she wanted to say. Unable to trust her voice, she shook her head.

He moved away from her, all business again. "May I count on you to bring Cecily here? I can stay at an inn for a few days without attracting attention."

Grace sat down on the straw chair and tried to remain calm. She had been unprepared for the intensity of her feelings for John when he had kissed her in greeting. Was she such a harlot that she wanted him to touch her . . . everywhere? Wanted to feel his mouth on her breast, wanted to run her hands over his young, hard body? Dear God, such lustful thoughts— and on holy ground.

"Well, Grace?" John's tone was more urgent. "I cannot tarry much longer."

She stared at her neatly folded hands. Think, you goose, he is waiting for you to answer.

" 'Tis Elizabeth's birthday next week," she suddenly remembered. "It would be a natural time for Bess and Cecily to visit. Is that too late, John?"

"Perfect!" John cried, and then looked about anxiously when Grace put her fingers to her lips. He lowered his voice. "I knew coming to you was the right thing. What day next week is the birthday?"

They made a plan and then John saw Grace safely back to her staircase by the light of a waning moon.

"My thanks, little coz. Until next week," he whispered. He looked at her with deep affection. "By Christ's nails, you are all grown up, and, I might add, quite lovely," he said and gave her a tender squeeze. "God give you a good night."

She stared after his dim shape. "And you, my dearest John," she whispered into thin air.

GRACE PLEADED A headache the next morning and Elizabeth excused her from attending Prime. Left alone, she wrote a letter to Cecily, ran down to the abbey gate and waited for John to pass by on his horse as planned. Only a few field hands were to be seen when she passed him the letter and he cantered off. Then she held her breath as she waited for a response. John had his own methods of expediting the letters to and from

Shene, and he had not bothered Grace with them. Whatever they were, it appeared he was successful, because within two days she received Cecily's reply. John again boldly entered the gates dressed as a groom and gave the letter to one of the monks.

"How kind you are to remember our mother's special day, Grace. The king is at Kenilworth and he has just called for Bess and his mother"—Grace giggled when she saw the (SM) for Scraggy Maggie that followed—*"to join him there. He has had disturbing news from Ireland, but I can tell you of this when I see you, because I am to stay behind this time, and so I am able to come with an attendant and a small escort. I suppose I can lodge at the abbey with mother for a night or two? I am looking forward to seeing you again, dear sister, and I hope you are not dying of boredom in your cloister. Look for me on Tuesday. Your devoted sister, Cecily."*

Grace hugged herself. Her part of the plan had worked. On the eve of the birthday, John was to again meet her in the undercroft and know Cecily's response.

Once again, she waited until all was silence in the community before she crept out of bed and tiptoed from the room carrying the pisspot. If she was caught coming back in, she could say she was emptying it. She was astonished at her own bravery as she felt her way along the side of the residence in the pitch-black night and then made a dash for the back of the abbey. She could not believe she was the same girl who had thought there were dragons outside her window at Sheriff Hutton.

She was there early, she knew, and finding the tinderbox John had left for her, she lit the lantern that was still on the cask in front of the straw chair. A couple of rats scuttled away and she heard noises among the wine casks and hoped that whatever they were would avoid the light. John's quiet greeting got her to her feet, and she started towards him. This time he merely took both her hands and, kissing her fingers, led her back to the straw bale.

"May I be bold, my sweet cousin?" His tone was kind, but serious. "I saw something in your eyes when we last met that warned me you perhaps think of me as someone other than a brother; am I right?" Grace's openmouthed silence made him nod. "I see that I am. I cannot properly express how flattered I am, little wren, but I must assure you that you deserve better than I. And when you find such a man, you will know that I speak the truth. If circumstances were different, 'tis possible I could love you in the same way, but I do not. I say this not to hurt you, but to warn you." He grinned. "You do not truly know me, and perhaps if you did, you would not love me so blindly. My life of late has been too solitary and I am ashamed to say I take my pleasures where I may." He turned her to him, wiping the tears that were coursing down her cheeks with his thumb. "But never believe I do not love you, because I do. 'Tis simply not the love you should know from a man. I would take you because you are a desirable woman, but I love you because you are my little wren and my cousin. Can you understand?"

Grace was so taken aback by this speech that she was at a loss to say anything for a moment and nodded miserably. He took her in his arms then, and held her close, listening to her heart break.

" 'Tis so unfair," she sniffed into his coarse tunic. "I am born a bastard, lose my mother and my childhood in a nunnery, and then find a family, friendship and riches beyond my wildest dreams, only to have them taken away and end up where I started—in an abbey." She heaved a sob. "But cruelest of all is loving someone who cannot love me."

"What we have is just as valuable, Grace—believe me. We have both suffered many heartaches due to our base birth, but in you I found a true friend and ally. I beg you to believe that your friendship means the world to me." He gently put her from him and whispered, "Why do you think you were the first person I came to for help?"

Pulling herself together, she replied: "I think I understand. But I tell you this, John of Gloucester, my love for you will never change, and if you ever need me I shall always come. Do *you* understand?"

John was visibly moved, his own unwanted tears not far. She is a treasure, he thought, and I wish she were mine. "Aye, Grace, I understand," he told her. "And you have my devoted friendship for as long as I shall live." He lifted her hands to his lips and kissed them reverently.

She used her sleeve to wipe her nose. "Cecily will be here tomorrow," she announced as if nothing had happened. "Bess is for Kenilworth, where the king is, with Scraggy Maggie, so she will not come. In truth, 'tis better for our plan if she is not here." John nodded, his eyes showing pleasure at this news. "Cecily did not say more in her letter but it seemed significant that Henry, having news from Ireland, called for his wife and mother."

John leapt to his feet. "By the Rood, that *is* good news. Let us pray Cecily knows more and can give me hope that I may join Lovell and Lincoln. Now you must go. I shall sleep on the straw tonight and mingle with the other field hands as soon as the cock crows. If I tend the field outside the gate, I shall see Cecily arrive and we can put our plan into action. I have borrowed a gown, as you suggested." He did not enlighten her as to how he had come by a woman's gown; it would only have twisted the knife in further.

Grace smiled at his enthusiasm, but her heart was heavy. "Let us hope the weather is fair, or I know not what we shall do."

"God is not that unkind, Grace, for all you believe He is. Now go quickly—I am so full of thanks, I know not how . . ."

She disappeared up the dark stairway before he could find the words.

"THE DRONE MEANS they are busy making honey inside the skep," Grace explained to her two companions, gathered round several beehives in the herb garden. "The skep needs air around it, but it should not be too close to the ground. And if it sits on a plank, like this, 'tis not easy for mice and other animals to steal from it." From behind the long, opaque muslin veil that hung down over the wide-brimmed straw hat and covered the upper part of her body, Grace took note of where others worked in the garden and, seeing one of the brothers moving out of earshot, she whispered. " 'Tis safe to talk now."

Cecily giggled behind her own protective covering. "John, is that really you in that gown? Grace says you now sport a beard. 'Tis hard to imagine, cousin."

"Aye, 'tis I, and do not tease, Cis. I feel foolish enough already. And certes, I shaved my beard before donning this disguise. Grace, are you sure you cannot see I am a man beneath this gauze?"

"Nay, John. Other than being a little taller, you look the same as we do. We do not have much time, and my knowledge of beekeeping is little at best, so let us pretend we are moving from skep to skep and I will lift a lid for you to see the wax comb and honey. Keep your hands well hidden under the gauze. My gloves will protect me."

They moved to the next hive and pretended to peer closely at it, Cecily unconvinced that she was not going to get stung.

"Do not anger them, Cis," Grace cried, as her sister squealed and flapped her long veil at a few insects buzzing around her head. "They are hard at work and do not wish to harm you, unless they are angered."

"I think this was a silly idea, Grace," Cecily said, and Grace knew she was pouting. "Why do you need to hide, John? Certes, Bess would see you were well treated."

"I do not want to be anywhere near that usurper brother-in-law of yours. I want to help upend his arse and put Warwick on the throne. If I am where he can see me, then I cannot join with our supporters, can I? I beg of you, Cis, do not ask any more questions of me—I must move fast, if I am to be of any use to Lincoln. Now pray, what is the news from Ireland?"

"Oh, very well," Cecily acquiesced. She told them that the boy, Lambert Simnel, after being crowned in Dublin, was now at the head of an army made up of Irish lords and their men, an army of German mercenaries sent by Aunt Margaret and Yorkist lords Lovell and Lincoln with their forces. She chuckled. "I wish I had seen Henry's face when he learned that the army had set sail from Dublin and has landed somewhere near Furness."

John let out a not very feminine whistle. "So the invasion is real. Praise be to God."

"Henry is so frightened that he had writs posted up and down England forbidding any rumors or stories to be circulated that speak of an invasion," Cecily went on. "He has ordered mayors and bailiffs to track down the tale-tellers and use the pillory to extract the source of the rumors from them so that he can find and hang them."

"Christ's nails!" John exclaimed, causing both Grace and Cecily to shush him. "This means he fears this army greatly. I must away north again and join it."

"There, see the honeycomb?" Grace said suddenly, taking the top off the tightly woven straw skep and pointing. Her loud voice made the other two look around to see a monk walking towards them. "Brother Oswald, this is my half sister, the Lady Cecily, and her attendant. I have just finished telling them the little I know about your bees. However, we have disturbed them enough, don't you think?"

Brother Oswald bowed low, showing his shiny tonsure, and without waiting for a response Grace bade him good day and walked off in the direction of the residence, with Cecily and John in her wake. She heard John's admiring "Well done, little wren" and glowed. She led them close to the abbey and stopped near the undercroft door, pretending to point out an architectural detail.

"Cousins, I will leave you in a few minutes," John said, checking that the coast was clear. "But you should know I will carry your courage with me on my way north. Wish me well; I know not when we shall meet again. But let us hope it is soon—and at the head of a triumphant York-family procession into London! Farewell and God be with you."

"Be careful, cousin," Cecily said, removing her protective veil. " 'Tis treason you are contemplating . . ."

John gripped her arm. "You swore to keep silent on this, Cecily. I must know I can count on you. My life may depend on it."

"Certes, I shall not betray you, John. I swore on our fathers' graves," Cecily retorted, pulling away. "Now go, I beg of you, before someone sees through your disguise. 'Twas an addle-brained—"

"May Saint George protect you, John," Grace interrupted her, reaching out and taking his hand. "Give us word when you are able that you are safe. You will be in my prayers."

"Fiddle faddle, Grace! I thought you had given up on God," John joked, hiding his trepidation for the road ahead. "Now, walk me to the undercroft, I beg of you."

They turned the corner by the undercroft stairs and, in a flash, John was gone.

"Fiddle faddle?" Grace said, taking off her hat and gauze and trying to sound nonchalant. In truth, she wanted to run down the stairs and embrace John one more time.

"His mother's favorite expression," Cecily said. "He used to say it a lot when he was younger."

NEWS OF AN invasion reached the abbey two days after Cecily's visit, and Grace pretended to be as surprised and worried as everyone else. What would it mean for them all? The English had settled down with their new king and were loath to restart the civil war between the red rose and the white.

As the tallest tower at the abbey could be seen for miles, it was part of the country's alarm system, and that night it was one of hundreds of beacons lit up and down England to announce the invasion and serve as a call to arms for those close enough to join Henry on his march north to stop the rebels.

The next day the abbey received a visit from the sheriff of Southwark, and Grace was grateful that Cecily had given John the invasion news early. It meant a two-day start for him. The sheriff entered the refectory at dinner and, with permission from the abbot, asked if anyone had seen a young man calling himself John Broome. Grace held her breath. John had explained that broom was the English translation of *planta genistra*—the flowering bush for which the royal Plantagenet house was named. He had been pleased with his own ingenuity.

There was great consternation among the brotherhood before stout Brother Geoffrey stepped forward and said, "Certes, I remember the man lodged with us for but one night. He was a quiet guest and gave no offense."

"Pah! No offense, Brother? He is a spy!" the sheriff cried, horrifying his listeners. "He was staying at the Bull's Head and stole a gown from the innkeeper's wife. One of the tavern wenches allowed he had tumbled her and asked her to steal it for him, saying he was on secret business. He threatened her with his knife, she did say."

Grace gasped, hardly believing her ears for a moment. But then she looked at the piggy-eyed sheriff with his fat belly and unshaven face, enjoying the attention of the lords and ladies at the abbey, and guessed he was exaggerating the story for effect. She was certain John would never threaten a defenseless girl with a knife. It was true John did not tell her where he found the gown, but she was convinced John had meant only to borrow it. She dismissed the accusation, although to her great regret, she was sure the part about tumbling the tavern wench was true.

"I crave your pardon, Father John," Elizabeth said suddenly, causing the company to swivel all eyes her way. "I do not know who this John Broome is, but to falsely accuse someone of being a spy because he stole a gown is contemptible. He may be a thief, but you need proof to bring such a damning accusation, sheriff. What is your proof?"

The sheriff was about to dismiss the woman in the widow's barbe who had dared to interfere with his investigation when someone close to him whispered her name. Apologizing, he withdrew backwards from the hall, bowing awkwardly, followed by an amused prior.

"Sweet Jesu," Elizabeth said when he had gone. "What drivel!"

By the time the feast of Corpus Christi was celebrated and the two armies were closing in on each other, the occupants of the abbey were making wagers as to who would win should a battle ensue. Prior John did not forbid gambling in the refectory and threw in a couple of coins. "The last time this happened, an invader won. And let us not forget William of Normandy, called Conqueror. I shall wager the invader will win again." A great deal of money was thrown on the tables, with a brother running around, eagerly recording the bets.

Elizabeth threw down a noble and loudly sided with the king. "He has the advantage, Father John. From all I hear, the rebels are a rabble—the Irish barely have clothes to cover them, let alone good weapons; the Germans may be well trained but, in truth, they do not have the numbers. As for the traitors Lincoln and Lovell"—Grace and Katherine both drew in their breath, knowing full well Elizabeth had prayed beside her bed for their victory the night before—"they fight for an imposter, and thus no one will support them. Besides, Henry is my liege lord and husband to my daughter. Certes, I pray for his victory," she cried. "We all should. Nay, Father John, I believe I shall be richer in a few days—and half of my winnings I shall, of course, donate to the abbey treasury," she added to scattered applause. "And now I beg your indulgence, Father. I am overcome with the heat and need to step outside. Come, Lady Katherine, Lady Grace, let us find a shady place in the garden and read awhile."

The company rose with her and respectfully moved aside as the dowager queen and her attendants processed from the refectory. Grace hoped Elizabeth had not heard the unkind comment that was whispered by a man to his companion as she passed by. " 'Tis said the Grey Mare is here precisely because of her dealings with Lovell and Lincoln. I cannot believe she prays for a royal victory. 'Tis naught but show." He is right, Grace thought, but she admired Elizabeth for trying to stem that story.

9

Lisbon

1487

*I*have been in Lisbon for a year now, and I should be writing to Aunt Margaret, but instead I write secretly in the pages of the book Lady Brampton gave me when I left her service. It was she who taught me that writing one's innermost thoughts releases the spirit, and I know now that she was right. And so Madame la Grande will have to wait!

On Sundays, after my new master, Admiral Pero Vaz da Cunha, has released me from my duties, I come to write in my favorite place upon the rampart of the Castelo de São Jorge built by the Moors above the River Tagus on the highest of the several hills in this colorful city. To my right I can look over the poorer parts of the city, the large market square and hospital in the valley to where the land climbs high again to the Carmelites Convent of Sta. Maria do Carmo, the church of Sta. Catarina and the big new houses on the Serro do Almirantes, which means Admiral's Ridge. Appropriately, as they are both admirals, Sir Edward and my master live there! On days like today, the red-tiled roofs and white walls of the houses on the green hills stand out against the blue sky. In the winter, as I have seen many times, the fog rolls in from the ocean and the city disappears and then the rains come—hard, driving rain, and one is glad of one's cloak.

The guards at the Castelo gate down the hill know me now and call me the Lowlander. In the summer, King Jão moves the court to his beautiful palace at Sintra, perched on a hill to the west of the city, and so I can come and sit in relative solitude. It is the best view in the whole city! Up here I can watch the local fishing barcas with their angled masts skimming along the Alfama shore to my left and larger caravels and carracks arriving at and departing from the quays at Belém, west towards the sea. The people of this kingdom are proud of their seafaring heritage—from the lowest fishermen to the famed explorers—and live or die by it. How I long to go exploring with the great Diogo Cão! 'Tis said he is the first to sail into the mighty Rio Zaire along the west coast of Africa, claiming the land for Portugal. I have seen Bartolomeu Dias, with his big broken nose, and Vasco da Gama walking and talking together on the quays of Belém. They are like gods to me.

I still remember the creaking timbers, the sea spray in my face, the rhythmic shanties of the sailors as they toiled and the noise of the wind filling the sails of the ship that brought me here from the Low Countries when I was not yet thirteen and still such a boy. The voyage took two weeks, and I wish I could have stayed on board forever. I am proud to say I was one of the few who did not have the *mal de mer*, and Sir Edward took me into his confidence and told me many stories of the English court to pass the hours. I kept my promise to Aunt Margaret and pretended I did not know anything about England. But, of course, I know much, including the most fascinating tale about the two sons of King Edward who seemed to have vanished after they were put in the Tower of London. What puzzles me is that when King Richard was defeated and killed three years ago, why were the boys not released? I wonder if they are still alive. And then Sir Edward told me that the boys' oldest sister is now Queen Elizabeth of England. How strange fate is!

Admiral da Cuhna was eager to have me because I can read and write—all thanks to Aunt Margaret—and speak French and English. With his one eye, fierce features and a temper to match, he is often called *Bisagudo*, which means Hatchet-face. I have to confess, he treats me well, although it is said he has beaten many of his mariners and is feared greatly on his ship. I think he was surprised that I had learned so many manners at Sir

Edward's house, and how to be a page: keep your nails clean, do not turn your back on anyone, never speak first to your superiors and certainly do not spit at table. *Bien sûr*, I did not tell the admiral that it was second nature to me, as I had learned everything at the dowager duchess of Burgundy's palace of Binche. I am proud that I can keep such a secret. God and all his saints bear witness that I would never betray my dearest aunt. It has often made me curious as to why she kept me so secret. The rumor in the village was that I was her bastard child! Although I do not remember my parents, I know my father was a boatman and that Werbecque is my name. Sire de Montigny told me I was a charity child and not to question the duchess's actions, but to thank God for my blessings, which I did nightly. But only I know how deep my love was for Aunt Margaret, and hers for me. It grieves me to think perhaps she no longer thinks of me; perhaps she has another charity child now. Perhaps. But I like to think I am wrong, because even though her letters come less frequently, they are still affectionate.

Today, if Aunt Margaret is correct, I am fourteen and am starting to enjoy the attention of girls and know that, in this land of black-haired and black-eyed people, they consider me handsome because I have fair hair and blue eyes—even if one of them is not always true. I am not as tall as I would like, but I have a few hairs on my chin and my voice has pleasantly deepened. I hope it will not be long before I know love.

I suppose I must close my book now, find my cipher and write to Aunt Margaret. I will tell her about my duties with the admiral, how I am trying to learn Portuguese and about the burning of a heretic in the Ribeiro square. I witnessed hangings in Middelburg and Bruges, but this was my first execution by fire. I am ashamed to say the terrible screams of the prisoner and the sickly smell of burning human flesh made me vomit. I hurried away when several spectators began to laugh at me. The victim was a Jew who would not convert and had written heretical pamphlets against the teachings of the Church. It made me glad that Sir Edward had converted in England and could boast King Edward himself as his godfather. There are many mutterings about the Jews, who mostly live in the Alfama district. It is expected they will be forced to leave soon, but where will they go?

And now to my duty letter, but I don't think I will tell Aunt Margaret about the girls!

10

London

SUMMER 1487

No one could remember a hotter June. It was only a few days until midsummer's eve, with the hottest months of July and August yet to come and an interminable stretch of sweltering, dusty days to look forward to. The discussion behind Elizabeth's closed door was all of the up-coming battle—that there would be a battle, no one had any doubt. Elizabeth's mood swung between elation at a possible Yorkist victory, which would surely free her from her present incarceration, as she termed it, and despair that she would die of boredom inside the sandstone walls of the abbey residence. Even tales of Arthur and his knights could not take her mind off events that might be occurring north of London, and Katherine had been indignant when Grace had timidly suggested that reading about Master Chaucer's more peaceful—and amusing—pilgrims might take the dowager's mind off the present.

"Why must you always undermine me, Grace?" Lady Hastings hissed while Elizabeth was distracted by an annoying fly in the room. "I know better than you what the queen likes to read. If you know what is good for you, pipe down." And Grace had reddened and bitten her tongue.

That afternoon Grace begged to be allowed to walk the half mile to the river, where she could dabble her feet in the Thames's cool, clear water and wrap a wet cloth around her head. Elizabeth was not wearing the heat well and had spent many hours in her darkened room, swatting flies and having Katherine or one of the other ladies fan her.

"Aye, you may go," Elizabeth said, brightening. "There must be news from the north soon, and maybe you will hear something in the village before it reaches us here in the wilderness."

Katherine frowned. "She has not finished her needlework, your grace. And was she not supposed to pick fresh herbs for our pillows, and—"

She got no further because Elizabeth raised herself onto her elbow and snapped: "Let the child go, Katherine. She is young and does not mind the heat. If you are insinuating that you, too, would like to walk to the river, then by all means accompany her, but enough of your whining. 'Tis tiresome and boils my blood, which is hot enough already," she complained, sinking back onto her pillow. "I swear, 'tis hotter than Hades in here."

Katherine shrank at the reprimand and assured Elizabeth she had no wish to leave her side.

The queen grunted. "Go, Grace, with my blessing—and keep your ears open."

From behind her fan, Katherine glowered at Grace, who curtsied to Elizabeth, picked up her straw hat and veil and gratefully quit the chamber. Why does lady Katherine hate me so? she thought as she pushed her unruly curls up under the wide hat, glad of its shelter from the noonday sun. She could have told the older ladies that despite the heat, there was always a breeze along the river, but she had no wish to be accompanied by the Hastings harridan, as she had begun to call Lady Katherine. Is it because I am young or that Elizabeth seems to like me? she wondered. Nay, there is something else. It was a puzzle, and usually her mind was always ready to tackle one, but she had tackled this one so many times she decided she might never know and so skipped along between the fields of young corn and barley, occasionally bending to add another of her favorite heartsease to her nosegay until she saw the Thames below London Bridge sparkling in the sunlight. Just seeing the water cooled her, and she was about to cross the square and into Tooley Street when she heard a horse's hoofs thudding along the path behind her.

Jumping off to the side of the narrow road to let the rider pass, Grace shaded her eyes to look up at him and, gasping with surprise, stared right up at John's familiar face. When he saw her he reined in his horse so sharply that it reared up on its hind legs, terrifying her. He swung his leg over the saddle and jumped down onto the path. His hair was much shorter, and the shadow on his chin told her it had not seen a blade for at least two days. His clothes were torn and dark with dirt and what looked like sweat, and his horse was flecked with foam.

"Praise God I have found you, Grace, thanks to a field hand who saw you pass," he said, pulling her to him urgently enough to make her drop her flowers and lose her straw hat. Her dark curls tumbled down her back and he inhaled their scent of rosemary. All he wanted to do was lose himself in their silky softness and forget the past week's dreadful events. "All is lost," he murmured. "Our cause is finished."

Grace tensed. Her intuition told her to stand perfectly still and not say a word for a full minute. If John needed her embrace, who was she to deny it? Then, gently, she pulled away.

"Come, John, let us go to the river and talk," she cajoled. "Your horse must need water, by the looks of him, and"—she tried to lighten his mood—"you could do with a wash."

Grasping the rein, John stroked the horse's mane and encouraged him away from his grassy snack. "Aye," he said with a small smile, "I expect I could." He pointed to the horse's left front leg. "And he is in need of a new shoe." He rescued a couple of the abandoned heartsease and fixed them into Grace's hair.

As they walked, John looked about him warily, staying in his horse's shadow, but other than a few field hands weeding in the barley, they were alone. "Lead on, little wren," he said.

She took him downstream from her usual spot, afraid he might be recognized by those from Southwark who still sought him. They walked away from London Bridge and came to a cut in the riverbank that was sheltered from prying eyes by high reeds. As the tide was ebbing, John let the horse slide down the bank to the water's edge, where it could slake its thirst.

Neither had spoken since leaving the field: John was weighing how much he should tell Grace, and Grace knew he needed to think.

"You do not have to say anything, John. I understand 'tis hard. But I came here to cool my feet, so rest awhile if you want while I dip them in the river." Tucking her overdress into her belt and removing her shoes and stockings, Grace padded onto the mud, grimacing with disgust as it oozed between her toes. But she let out a sigh of pleasure when the cold water ran over her feet. She stood ankle-deep, watching the boatmen on the river pulling on their oars. Smiling, she turned back to John to share her experience and her smile widened into an "oh!" of guilty pleasure. He was coming towards her, his bare torso glistening with sweat and his coarse breeches barely sitting upon his narrow hips.

"Sweet Jesu," she muttered. Look away, my girl, or you will be confessing lust on the morrow. She hastily turned back to the boatmen and noisily splashed water on her face and neck. When he got to the water, John launched himself into the clear, inviting ripples, disappearing for a few seconds before surfacing and flipping his wet hair out of his eyes with a practiced toss of the head. Grace could not take her eyes off him, and when he stood up with his back to her to plunge in again, she gulped. A dark red welt as big as a man's fist was visible on his left shoulder.

"John!" Grace cried, splashing her way towards him, her waterlogged skirts impeding her progress. "You are hurt. Let me see."

He stood up and shook his head. " 'Tis naught, Grace, in truth. Not when you have seen what I have seen." He dismissed her concern and pulled up the breechclout that had all but disclosed the rest of his body to her. "God's bones, but this feels good," he said, and dived back into the river before she could come closer.

Grace made her way back to the bank and bravely picked up the horse's rein and tugged until the animal followed her to where she could tie him to a beached log. "Good horsey," she said, with confidence, but still she could not bring herself to pat the huge animal. She picked up John's jacket and surcote to shake out the dust, and it was then she realized the dark patches were blood, not sweat. A hole in the padded jacket corresponded to his wound, and there was a black substance embedded around it. Tar, she supposed, to cauterize the wound.

John took his shirt from her outstretched hand and grinned sheepishly when she showed him the bloodstain. "Aye, I was wounded—an arrow found me, I have to confess. It saved my life, but I run ahead of myself." He put on the linen shirt, which clung to his wet body, and Grace had to look away again. "Sit, and I will try and remember all that I have seen and done."

When he had ridden away the day of Cecily's visit, he had taken the road north to Leicester, knowing—as his father had done two years previously—that the town in the middle of England was a good place from where to move an army easily in any direction.

"I was right. Henry was there, and so I joined his army as an archer," John said, chuckling. "I gave my name as Broome and attached myself to a group of archers from London. I had only a little money, so this was a good way to have food and information and not be noticed. Clever, no?"

Grace nodded enthusiastically as she wound her wet scarf around her head and pushed her curls under it.

"I got there none too soon, for Henry marched us out the next day, to Nottingham. I heard the rebels were picking up men still loyal to my father through Lancashire and the dales of Yorkshire. I know well how secluded the route through Wensleydale is, from my time at Middleham. We heard the rebels were thousands strong and it gave me heart to hear how afraid Henry's men were of them." John paused to take a drink from his pigskin flask.

"How were you going to leave that army and join the other?" Grace asked. "Would your comrades not accuse you of deserting, or worse?"

"You are not simply a pretty face, are you, wren?" John said. "I, too, was wondering the same thing when we got word in Nottingham that the rebels were approaching the Fosse Way a few miles north of the city. Henry announced his intention of marching out of the city the following day, the fifteenth, to confront them. That night I feigned drunkenness at one of the many taverns near the castle—my father called it his castle of care, for it was there that he and Aunt Anne heard of their little Ned's death," he explained, and Grace saw pain in his face when he spoke of his father. "But I digress. With the few coins I had left, I filled my new comrades' cups several times, watching as they became intoxicated and feigning the same. Three of them fell asleep at the table and the fourth was busy in the bodice of a whore . . . I crave your pardon," John quickly apologized. "A tavern maid."

Grace nodded. "Continue, John. I am not an innocent; I know what a whore is."

"It being high summer, it was still light, and so I stumbled back to our camp, pretending to lurch from house to tree to hedge or whatever I could fall upon. When I got there, as I had hoped, there were a few sober guards who laughed and teased me about my condition and then ignored me when I slumped to the ground near one of the weapons carts."

Grace was enthralled, imagining the scene and John's mummery. "How clever, John," she said. "They thought you were dead to the world."

"You have the measure of it, sweet Grace. As soon as it was dark, others returned in a true drunken state and were soon snoring to wake the dead, so I took a sword and a few arrows for my bow and stole away. Praise be to Saint Christopher for the fine weather and a moon to see my way. Our intelligence was that Lincoln had moved rapidly south from Doncaster and was camped in Sherwood Forest. The scouts were certain Lincoln and Lovell would avoid engaging Henry at Nottingham—the city sits high on a rock, with the castle guarding its southwest corner, and so it seemed to me they were aiming for Fosse Way and a direct route to London. Having hunted in the area with Father, I knew where the road was, but I knew the army must cross the Trent to reach it. If I followed the Trent northwards, I was bound to come across the force as it looked for a good fording. 'Twas easy to follow the river, and with the dense forest to shield me above its banks, I moved through the night quite swiftly. If Jack was to cross the Trent, I knew he had to do it between Nottingham and Newark."

"Why did you know that?" Grace asked.

John was impressed. Most females he knew would have wanted him to skip the strategic details. "Because the king was at Nottingham, and not only is there a large fortified castle at Newark that commands the river, Grace, but the bridges near it were washed away in the floods of Eighty-six. Therefore, if Jack wanted to reach Fosse Way, which the Romans conveniently built as a straight road south to Leicester and on to London, he had to cross between those two points. And I was right!" John got up and stretched, picking up a pebble and launching it into the river. He swung round to face Grace. "You should have seen my lord Lovell's face after I walked into the camp and was taken to him. I looked worse than I do now, in truth. I only hoped he would recognize me. My clothes were in tatters after scrambling along the river rocks and catching them on thorn bushes and tree branches all night." His eyes shone as he recalled the reunion with his erstwhile master. " 'John of Gloucester, by the Rood,' he cried and called to Cousin Jack. 'My lord Lincoln, come and see who has sauntered into camp to join our cause.' It was so good to see them both again, and they soon found these clothes, armor and a horse for me. Lovell is much changed, Grace—ah, you did not know him previously, but he is a gray-beard now." He paused and his face fell.

"What is it, John?" Grace said, at once concerned.

"In truth, I know not if he lives or is dead. But that comes later—much later. Let me tell the tale as it happened." He picked up a stick and began to draw lines in the mud. "We crossed the Trent at the Fiskerton ford here, which I guessed would be low in summertime. Martin Schwartz, the commander of the German force that Aunt Margaret sent, was an impressive man, Grace. And his soldiers would put the fear of God into any brave soul. I met with the Irish commanders, who paid me great reverence because of my father. In truth, we Yorks are dear to the Irish because of our grandfather's fair dealings with them when he was governor all those years ago."

Grace had no idea what he was talking about but she urged, "Go on."

"But you must know that, far from attracting the hoped-for supporters from the north to our cause, precious few joined them on the march from Furness Fells. Thus, we only had nigh on eight thousand men on our side. And an odd assortment they were, too. The Germans, Flemish and Swiss were disciplined enough and skilled with crossbows, halberds and pikes, but we lacked enough English longbowmen, cavalry and artillery. Worse, many of the Irish had no armored protection, and primitive weapons, and, certes, many of the poor devils were half-naked. They were a sorry sight, indeed." He shook his head. "But more serious than this—only now is it apparent to me—was our lack of military commanders to lead this hodge-podge army."

"Didn't Cousin Jack fight at Bosworth—and Lord Lovell?" Grace asked, in her heart knowing these tidings did not bode well for a happy end to the story.

"Aye, they did. And two more valiant soldiers you could not see. But it is very different to lead an army than to fight in it, Grace. When we are learning military skills as a donzel—as I did under my lord of Lovell's patronage—we read accounts of long-ago battles and their tactics, but to lead one must have more than courage and written descriptions. You must understand your enemy, your position, your weaknesses and strengths and when is the right time to do what. No one except Martin Schwartz had ever led an army—and, I think, Richard Harleston. So our English lords had to defer to a German mercenary, which may not have sat well with our English soldiers. Now you know our weaknesses, and if you were Henry, you would exploit them. And exploit them he did."

Grace was a little bewildered by all of this, but kept her gaze on John and hoped she appeared perceptive.

"Let me explain," John continued. He drew Fosse Way as a straight line that, had the Trent not bent into a loop around Stoke, would parallel the river about a mile away. Tracing a large circle between the river and the road just to the south of Stoke, he jabbed at it and said, "Here we formed our lines. The whole army upon a hill in one big wedge, which meant we had no one flanking us to call on for aid. From the hill, we could see Henry approaching—thousands upon thousands winding along the riverbank."

John then slowly drew squares on his makeshift map, two to the east of the road and one each to the south and west. "The largest force facing us was commanded by Oxford," he began, and Grace drew in a sharp breath. He nodded. "Aye, the same who crushed my father's van at Bosworth and killed our loyal Jack Howard. He is the most skillful commander in the realm, and he was in charge of Henry's vanguard of six thousand—almost as many as our total army, we estimated. On his right and left flanks"—he got up to make crosses to illustrate their positions—"was the cavalry. The king's own force was arrayed behind the van, and we saw him ride up and down the ranks, rallying them with a speech." He gave a short laugh. "Our 'king' Simnel gave no such encouragement—in fact, Lincoln chose not to show him in front of the troops, in case they lost heart. The boy had no learning and was obviously not who he claimed to be. The southernmost force here"—he pointed to it—"was commanded by Lord Strange. Oh, Grace, because of our vantage point on the ridge, we could see all our foes ranged before us in twice as many numbers."

"Were you afraid, John?" Grace whispered, thinking she could hear horses snorting in their caparisoned trappings and the jingle-jangle of metal armor, and see the sun glinting off weapons and shields, and banners and pennants curling in the wind. "You must have been afraid."

John threw himself back down on the ground. "Aye," he muttered with shame in his voice. "Aye, I was never more afraid in my life. I saw grown men vomit in fear, and more than one soil his breeches. 'Twould have been clear to a dimwit that we were doomed." He stared over the water at the wharves on the other side. "And then they began to move towards us, step by step and yard by yard. I think I will hear that relentless clanking as long as I live. As the ranks became clearer to us, we could see, between the lines of billmen, rows of archers—English archers, the best archers in the world, Grace. The silence in our ranks was terrible, more terrible even than the sudden eruption of bloodcurdling battle cries from our allies the Scots and Irish. As you can see, because of the bends in the river, we had nowhere to retreat to, which was surely a strategic blunder on Jack's part." He shook his head in despair. "Schwartz ordered his crossbowmen to fire, which stayed the front rows of the enemy for a brief moment, but those weapons take time to reload and gave Henry's archers time to let go their own deadly arrows. In that first volley, I was hit and fell forward. Mercifully, I swooned and did not feel the feet that ran over my back to attack the enemy. Someone heard me cry out when I awoke and thought my shoulder was on fire, and I heard a broad Scots brogue shout, 'Hold on, laddie. I'll pull you out of this.' And he did. But not before I saw . . ." He dropped his head in his hands and groaned, unable to finish.

"Saw what, my dear John? I would know your sorrow." Grace put her arm around his shoulder and he relaxed into its comforting hold.

"Ah, Grace, what sorrow indeed. I saw Lincoln, our loyal cousin Jack, run through by an English pike." He raised gray eyes to hers and she was not surprised to see his tears. They sat for a few minutes while she rocked him back and forth, both with their own memories of their cousin. Then John pulled himself together and described his last sighting of Francis Lovell.

"The battle raged for three hours or more, they say. A surgeon—a butcher from Dublin, I was told—removed my arrow and filled the hole with tar. I swooned again, I hate to admit. When I awoke, the carnage about us was terrible to see." He weighed his next words and chose to leave out the nightmarish scenes of bloodied heads with staring eyes, arms and legs without owners, horses screaming in agony, men slipping and sliding on the spilled guts of others and everywhere the ghastly smell of death. Instead he told her: "Thousands upon thousands of dead and wounded—and because of our position, with Henry in front and the river behind, the retreat meant many drowned. And then I saw Lovell. I could not raise myself to cry his name but he was on his horse and plunging into the Trent—at its deepest part. I cannot believe that, with the armor both on him and his horse, he did not drown." He clutched Grace and sobbed. "Oh, God, 'twas the worst day of my life—even worse than when I heard my father had perished at Bosworth."

"Soft, dear cousin, you are safe with me here," Grace soothed him, stroking his hair. Shocked as she was, she tried to commit all to memory so she could report back to Elizabeth. Elizabeth! How long have I been gone? I pray they will not send out a search party, she thought, panicking. Perhaps they think I have drowned! But when she looked at the sun's position, she saw it had actually been only an hour since John had found her.

She gently removed herself away from his tense body and got to her feet, untucking her overdress and retrieving her hat. These actions gave her time to think. John must not be found here, because he was in danger from both the sheriff of Southwark and, more important, the king. He had fought against his king, and she knew that was treason. But where should he go? He had a horse, which was an advantage, but it needed shoeing. He could take it to the abbey blacksmith, but she was fearful he would be recognized from his first visit. Might she be able to pretend she had found the horse, abandoned? But that would mean she would have to walk the terrifying animal all the way back to the abbey alone. She wasn't certain she was brave enough. But you have to be, for John, she chided herself. Certes, the animal had not bitten her just now when she had tied it up. Maybe she could accomplish this and Prior John would have no reason to think she was lying about finding the horse. She sent a prayer up to St. Sibylline to protect her from God's wrath for the intended lie, but she was convinced helping this good man was the Christian thing to do, and so God would surely forgive her. She sat back down a little behind John so she could raise her skirts and put on her stockings without revealing her bare legs to him, but he was still staring across the water, his mind's eye stumbling over dead bodies on the battlefield. Aye, the horse might be shod, but where would he go with it? she wondered, losing faith in her plan. He cannot hide his identity forever, she reasoned. Someone will recognize him and give him away.

"I must go to Aunt Margaret," John said suddenly, startling Grace out of her planning. "Certes, that is what I must do. I will be safe there."

"Why, that is perfect, John!" Grace cried, anchoring her second shoe and standing up. "You can take a ship from here. There are always ships going to the Low Countries."

John stood up and faced her. "I cannot go without money, Grace. I have to pay my way, and I shall need some when I arrive. I cannot present myself to the duchess looking like this. I have not a penny to my name."

"I would give you all that I have, John, you know that, but I am living on Elizabeth's—and thus the king's—charity. I have nothing of value to give you or to sell. Perhaps you could sell your horse."

"Dearest Grace, you are the sweetest girl in the whole world, without a doubt," John cried, her kindness cheering him and a smile brightening his face. "But I shall need my horse in Flanders, and I would pay a captain to take me and the palfrey aboard." An idea crossed his mind. "Do you think Aunt Elizabeth would lend me some money? She seemed to like me when I was at court with Father. She was not so fond of Katherine—my sister—but my father said 'twas because Kat was young and beautiful and Elizabeth was past her prime. I care not, but I do believe she might help me, if she knew my plight. What say you, Grace? Would she help me? You know her best."

Grace's first instinct was to reject the idea, mostly out of concern for Elizabeth's health and well-being at present. But when she pondered further, she recalled that Elizabeth had always enjoyed scheming in secret, and perhaps helping John escape might alleviate her melancholy. She smiled happily up at him.

"Aye, John, if I can speak to her alone and describe your plight, I am certain she would not refuse. She seems to hold me in some esteem, although the same cannot be said for Lady Hastings," she said, grimacing. "That is why I must have Elizabeth's ear alone."

John reached for her hand and pressed it to his lips. "It seems I am always in your debt, little wren."

"Fiddle faddle!" Grace said, grinning, and was delighted to hear John laugh outright for the first time that afternoon. "Aye, Cecily told me about it being your mother's favorite saying. And now I shall tell you the rest of my plan for shoeing your horse."

Not long after, they parted. John agreed to lie low until dark and once again meet her in the undercroft after Compline. By then, she promised, somewhat recklessly, that she would have some money, food and the newly shod horse ready for him.

"Cross your fingers for me, John," she called back along the towpath, holding the horse's rein as far from the animal as possible, "and send a prayer to Saint Martin of Tours that the horse gets safely to the abbey."

John waved. "Nay, I shall pray to Saint Sibylline to protect my orphan wren!" he muttered to himself, not wanting to put Grace in danger by shouting. And then, ducking back out of sight, he curled up in the grass and fell fast asleep.

MATTHIAS, THE BURLY blacksmith, was happy to shoe the stray horse for Grace. He had been amused when the young woman had come through the gates and into the bustling courtyard towing a good-looking palfrey. He nudged his neighbor: "Bain't that be the Grey Mare's attendant? A daintier maid I have yet to see."

"I hear she be one of King Edward's bastards. And judging from her looks, his prow must have found port in quite a beauty," Toby said, slapping his thigh and chortling at his own wit.

"The poor girl is no horsewoman, by Christ. She looks to be leading a dragon from the way she be holding the rein. The beast must be tired or lily-livered not to have made his escape. Ah, but it seems he has need of my services, my friend. Look, she comes our way." Matthias bowed politely as Grace approached, and it was all he could do not to laugh when she flipped the rein to him.

"Master smith, I will leave this poor animal in your care. He was alone and lame in a field along the river with no one near to claim him. I called, but it appears that either the horse is a runaway or his owner is. Can we stable him here?" Grace gave him her sweetest smile, and both the blacksmith and his assistant were charmed.

"Someone will come for him, never fear, little lady," Matthias assured her, lisping through toothless gums. "He be fine-looking and so will be missed. You can leave him to me." He slapped the horse on the neck and then ran his practiced hand down the left foreleg to gentle the hoof off the ground. "Aye, the shoe is worn through. I will have another one on in no time."

"You are very kind, sir. I thank you." Grace smiled and hurried back to the abbey residence and Elizabeth's chambers. One task accomplished, she thought, relieved. Now to face the next. As she mounted the staircase to the second floor she heard a door bang and, looking up, saw Katherine Hastings on her way to the same staircase she was climbing. Grace assumed she was going to the privy, which might not give her enough time to explain John's story to Elizabeth. However, when Katherine saw Grace she threw up her hands.

"Mother of God, but you are worse than a plague of fleas, Grace. Where have you been? Elizabeth has been asking for you this past half hour. I am so weary from fanning her that she has sent me to doze in the garden. 'Tis your turn to please her. She is crosser than an unmilked cow today. I shall be gone an hour, so pray stay out of trouble. And before you see her grace, I would comb your hair and brush the grass off your wet skirts. 'Tis likely you have been rolling in the hay with some lout, by the looks of you."

Grace opened her mouth to protest, but Katherine had already passed her and was stalking off to the garden. Thank you, sweet Mother of God, or whoever is looking after me today, she thought. My lie about the horse must not have been so prodigious. She ran along the walkway to Elizabeth's room and knocked.

"Come!" the queen dowager called. "Ah, there you are, Grace," she said from her high-backed chair as Grace slipped into the room and made her obeisance. "I was beginning to worry about you. Mistress Beauchamp, you may go, and thank you for keeping me company. These young girls never seem to run out of energy, do they?" Mary Beauchamp demurred as Elizabeth put out her hand to be kissed and, not giving Grace a second glance, the elderly woman left the room. "She is kind, but a bore, Grace. As you can see, I am feeling better than I was and made Katherine get me off the bed and into the chair. She, on the other hand, was swooning from the heat and could no longer keep her eyes open, so I sent her off to sleep in the garden, for I could not tolerate her snores. Sweet Jesu, but we all rack each other's nerves in this dreary, small place, do we not?" She sighed, not expecting an answer.

Grace refilled Elizabeth's empty cup and picked up the fan Mistress

Beauchamp had abandoned. She knew she must act now or she might not have another chance to be alone with the dowager, so she took a deep breath and plunged in. "I beg your grace's pardon for delaying my return, but I had no choice." She saw Elizabeth frown and, without waiting for a question, whispered, "You see, I was overtaken by someone on horseback who is near and dear to all of us and in danger, and I could not refuse him my help."

Now she had Elizabeth's attention. The queen sat up in her chair, her eyes alive and her senses alert. "Him? Who, Grace? I pray you, do not dissemble."

" 'Tis John of Gloucester, your grace. He is fleeing the battle that ensued not three days ago near Nottingham." She stopped. She needed to know absolutely on which side Elizabeth's loyalties lay. Perhaps her first instinct had been right: Elizabeth had no desire to anger her son-in-law or her daughter further and thus would not help John. Grace held her breath.

"Johnny," Elizabeth murmured, conjuring up the youth of whom Richard had been so proud. Then there was anxiety in her voice. "Dear God, is he well—is he wounded? But more to the point, did Lincoln win?" But the disappointment on her face as she answered her own question gave away her leanings. "Nay, he could not have won, or that news would have reached us by now and all London would be in an uproar. With Henry the victor, life goes on as usual." Grace nodded sadly and Elizabeth groaned. "All the plans were for naught, and here I shall stay until I die, I have no doubt."

"Aye, you have the measure of it, madam. And I shall relate the whole sad tale later, if you wish, including"—she reached out and covered Elizabeth's hand with her own—"the death of your nephew—and my cousin—Jack of Lincoln." Elizabeth groaned again and shook her head in disbelief. Grace knew she should allow the queen to grieve or ask more questions, but she was on a mission and so soldiered on. "But now, I have— nay, John has—a boon to ask, and I must ask while we are alone. No one must know John is here—as, certes, he is in danger."

Elizabeth pulled herself together. "I understand, Grace." She was full of questions, but she began with the most puzzling: "Why you, Grace? How did John know where to find you?"

Grace told her of their friendship in Sheriff Hutton, of his letters to her and how she had relayed his important message to Lincoln on the road to Winchester. She made Elizabeth's eyes widen with the tale of the meetings in the dead of night in the undercroft and of her fear when the sheriff had come from Southwark seeking John Broome. At that Elizabeth clapped her hands. "Ha! There is no doubt Johnny has Plantagenet blood in his veins. Clever indeed!"

Then she was all seriousness. "Where is he now, and what does he intend to do?"

Someone was approaching on the walkway, and both women stopped to listen. The footsteps passed by and faded into the distance. Their eyes met in an acknowledgment that no one was at the door, and the discussion continued. Grace told Elizabeth of John's plan, and of his need for money. Without a second thought Elizabeth left her chair, went to the bed and, in front of an astonished Grace, pressed a knob on the elaborate headboard causing a secret drawer to slide out from under the wooden side support of the bed. Grace turned away, not wanting to invade Elizabeth's privacy. If the queen dowager was keeping money secretly, it was none of Grace's business. She was only too glad Elizabeth did have more money than the meager pension Henry had bestowed on her to live at the abbey, because it meant John could be helped. Grace briefly wondered if the money had been part of the royal treasury that Elizabeth and her brother were known to have taken in Eighty-three, when she had gone into sanctuary and he had fled to sea. At this moment, though, she did not care and was happy to hear the clink of coins as Elizabeth counted some out. She looked back only when she heard the click of the drawer closing.

"This should buy him his passage and keep him from starving until he reaches Margaret. Henry would hang him if he found him, and Johnny never harmed anyone. Nor is he a threat, but Henry would perceive him to be, and Henry is afraid of any man whose name is either York or Plantagenet. Tell John to ask Margaret to write to me. I need to know if she has knowledge of my boys. If Richard did send them abroad, he would have sent them to her. I was certain this boy Simnel was one of them, and 'twas why I agreed to help Lincoln at first, but when I learned he was naught but the son of an Oxford tailor I withdrew my support. An unconvincing pretender, indeed."

Grace took the handful of gold nobles, tied them tightly into a kerchief so they would not jingle and put them in the pouch at her waist. "I know John will thank you with every step he takes until he is safely in Flanders, your grace." She was aware Elizabeth was looking at her intently, and she flushed. She was even more disconcerted when Elizabeth suddenly exclaimed: "Grace Plantagenet, you are in love with your cousin Johnny, are you not?"

Grace was speechless. She cast her eyes down to the wooden floor and moved some rushes around with her toe. She lifted her head, and her expression was one of such confusion that Elizabeth laughed. "Aye, I am right. But, my child," she said more gently, "if I know Johnny, yours is not the only heart he has stolen." Grace's wet eyes answered for her. "Ah, little Grace, life is cruel, is it not?"

Grace gave a rueful nod.

A GRATEFUL JOHN folded Grace into his arms a few hours later. But only after he had devoured the meat pie, cheese and ale that she had brought, put the money in a pouch that hung around his neck and tucked it inside his jacket and listened to the message he was to convey to Aunt Margaret.

"I shall ride to Gravesend and find a Flemish vessel to take me to Burgundy. No one will know me in Kent, and it will be safer than crossing London Bridge and finding a vessel on a wharf in the Pool. You will know I am safe when Elizabeth hears from Aunt Margaret. That shall be the sign. I know not whether Henry knows I was at Stoke or not, but I shall not take the chance of staying here to be attainted. Attainted! How foolish to attaint a bastard—what do I have that the king could possibly want?"

"Your name," Grace whispered. "Never forget you are a Plantagenet."

John grinned. "Never fear, little wren, 'tis engraved on my heart. As are you, from this moment on. I must tell you again how lucky your future husband will be, for you are a jewel." He chuckled when she blushed. He had no wish to hurt her, and he needed to leave now. "Remember to be angry that someone stole the horse you brought back. We do not want you to come under any suspicion. And now, I must away. Only God knows when we shall meet again, but we shall, I promise, we shall."

"You will be in my heart always, John, and in my prayers." She tried to think of anything to keep him with her and suddenly remembered to ask: "What about Tom—Tom Gower? Was he there? Did he . . ." She faltered, dreading to know if yet another friend had perished.

John smiled. "Nay, Grace, he was not even there. It seems that on his way through Wensleydale he got word that his father had died, and Cousin Jack gave him leave to make sure his mother was well cared for. So he was excused and did not catch up with us. I hope he is safe in Westow—and stays there."

Grace nodded, satisfied. "Then I must let you go. Farewell, and God speed."

She waited until he had hurried through the cellar and up the steps to the deserted courtyard before collapsing onto their makeshift chair and sobbing silently into the straw.

A MONTH LATER a letter was delivered to Grace by an abbey guest from Flanders. Grace ran to the stone seat under the shelter of the yew in the privy courtyard and opened it with trembling fingers. Pressed in the folds of the parchment was a single heartsease. *"My thanks, little wren"* were the only words written on the page, but they were enough to assure Grace that John was safe.

PART TWO

For as well as I have loved thee, mine heart will not serve me to see thee.

—SIR THOMAS MALORY, MORTE D'ARTHUR

11

Lisbon

1490

Right noble and beloved aunt,

Your letter finds me exceedingly well as I sit in my customary spot upon the ramparts of the Castelo de São Jorge watching the ships come and go from the wharves down the river to the sea. It also finds me about to embark on another adventure.

I am to be apprenticed to a merchant and sea captain from the duchy of Brittany named Pregent Meno. Going to sea will be a dream come true for me and I hope this will meet with your approval. I understand from Sir Edward that I have to thank you in part for my good fortune. Once again, dear aunt, I am in your debt. When will I ever be able to repay you? It happened like this: Sir Edward took it upon himself to recommend me to Captain Meno, telling him that I had connections to the dowager duchess of Burgundy. Impressed with that information and after an interview, I am happy to tell you that the merchant decided I should become his apprentice. You see how Sire de Montigny's years of teaching me mathematics has helped me learn accounting!

I must learn many things about commerce here in Lisbon before I can travel abroad. My new master trades in cloth, and I have marveled at the hundreds of bolts of silk, satin, damask and velvet that line the shelves of his warehouse in Belém. One day, I swear, I shall wear beautiful clothes again. Many of the bolts reminded me of the gowns you used to wear at Binche, and they brought back happy memories of my time there. But I have a sad confession to make, dearest aunt. I can no longer conjure up your face as I used to when I first left you. It has been four years after all, and I suppose you, too, have forgotten how I look. I do not think you would know me now if you saw me again, in truth. I am no longer the innocent boy Jehan, of that you can be certain!

As for Sir Edward, do you know that King Henry has forgiven him and he is free to go to England once more, although he is in such high favor with King Jão, I know not why he would want to leave Lisbon. It seems that a few months ago, when the king's ambassadors were visiting from England, Sir Edward entertained them at great expense. I was a little disappointed in his behavior towards these men of Tudor's—I know you would not have approved of such a show from this staunch supporter of the house of York. But his efforts were rewarded by a pardon from King Henry, and the last thing he did before he left Lisbon to visit Bruges on his business was to arrange for my employment with Pregent Meno. This led me to believe that his actions were not entirely selfish. Could he be going back to Flanders to spy for you? Certes, you cannot answer that, for even though we have used our cipher and our secret addresses success-fully all these years, there is always the chance that someone might take an interest in letters from an aunt to her "darling boy" as you used to call me.

It heartened me to learn from your letter that Lord Francis Lovell was with you last year and that you gave him a safe conduct to go to Scotland. The rumor that reached us in those months after the battle of Stoke was that he had drowned. And you tell me that the bastard son of King Richard is with you now. John of Gloucester has long intrigued me—but you speak so highly of him in your letter that I worry he is taking my place in your affections! I often think of those two poor princes imprisoned in the Tower. Do you have news of them? My former master, Admiral da Cuhna, was convinced they are dead, but Doña Catarina confided to me that she and her "Bisagudo" believe one or both of them still live. I have always felt a bond with the younger one—the duke of York, is he not—because he was born in the same year as I. Did I tell you that when I first went to live with the Bramptons, Sir Edward remarked on a likeness between him and me? 'Twas puzzling, aunt, because he knows I am just a boy from Tournai.

In other news from abroad, we heard of the death—nay, murder—of James of Scotland in battle, and that his fifteen-year-old son, the new King James, was the leader of the rebels. Astonishing that a son would so conspire against his own father. I also learned of the birth of a princess to King Henry's queen in November.

In April, when the fog rolls away from the Tagus and the winds are fair, I shall sail with Captain Meno, so I shall be here to receive a letter should you need to send me one until then. After April, I know not where I may be, and my whole being thrills with the anticipation of adventure.

I pray you are well and that your charge, the young duke of Burgundy, grows into a fine young man. If he receives as much affection from you as I did, he must be a happy boy indeed. Written in Lisbon, this twelfth day of December in the year of Our Lord, 1489, from the ramparts of the Moorish Castelo de São Jorge, my special place high above the river where I come every Sunday after Mass to watch the ships come and go from the sea.

Respectfully and with love, your Perkin

Binche, 1490
Right well beloved nephew,

I greet you from Hainault in this chilly month of March. Every time I come here I am reminded of you. Your room is as you left it, and I refuse to let anyone change it. I particularly remember the conversation we had in it when I explained that you had to go away. I shall never forget the sadness in your eyes, and it was then I knew you truly loved this old woman. Aye, I am in my forty-third year and feel age in my very bones, especially when the cold winds blow like today.

I was pleased to receive your letter and to know you will be fulfilling your desire to go to sea. Be careful, my boy! Do not climb too high or engage in any brawls. Mariners can be brutes. 'Tis fortunate you told me when you would leave, because this letter is of the utmost importance. The time has come when I have need of you, my dear child. I pray to God that you have not forgotten your promise to me all those years ago in Binche. The Sunday after you are in *receipt of this, you should return to your favorite writing spot that you have de-scribed so many times and wait. I do not want you to change your routine that day, but you may be joined by a stranger. Listen to him well, for he knows my mind.*

Pierrequin, you believe your life will be changing because you are going to sea, but it will change more than you will ever guess. This is all I dare write now, but remember, be at the meeting place on Sunday next.

Your faithful and loving aunt

I notice that in this letter Aunt Margaret gives nothing of our identities away—I know she must have been at Binche, because it is her favorite palace in the province of Hainault. How clever she is! But I am now consumed with curiosity as I sit here on the wall of the Castelo and wait. Certes, I have not been able to sleep or eat since I received the letter. What can the duchess possibly want from me? What do I have to offer her? All I know is if she asked me for the moon, I would give it and the sun to her. She has my complete duty and devotion.

There are more people here today, as the king and his court are in residence. But no one pays me any mind—I always wear my old badge so the guards think I am from the house of da Cuhna, a name well respected at King Jāo's court.

But wait! Sweet Jesu, I see a stranger approaching . . .

12

London

SPRING 1490

Sir Edward Brampton seeks an audience, your grace," the prior's favorite, Brother Damien, purred after bowing low to Elizabeth. Like a satisfied cat, Grace thought, watching him lick his sensuous lips at this juicy piece of information and straighten back up. An Adonis, Katherine had deemed him, and she could never reconcile his looks to his chosen vocation. " 'Tis no wonder the abbot desires him," she had declared.

Grace had been shocked the first time she discovered that men of the cloth defied God's holy law of chastity: it was common knowledge the priest who was assigned to serve communion at Delapre Abbey had sired a child, but when Grace had overheard Elizabeth tell Katherine that Father John took this handsome young monk to his bed, she was at once fascinated and repelled by the thought.

"Sir Edward Brampton?" Elizabeth repeated, surprise in her voice. "Here? To see me?"

"Aye, your grace. Shall I fetch him? He is with Father John," Damien mewed.

Elizabeth nodded and characteristically put her hand up to her head covering to fluff out its silky folds. She had taken to wearing a widow's barbe with a simple silver circlet anchoring it to designate her rank and hide her scrawny neck. But her hollow cheeks and rheumy eyes and the creases around her mouth gave away her age and failing health. She had lost three teeth that year, and so she rarely smiled.

"I pray you, fetch my mirror, Katherine," she said, easing her aching body out of the chair and disturbing her lap dog. The animal found itself sliding off its mistress's bony knees onto the wooden floor and yipped in annoyance. Lady Hastings held up the polished silver hand mirror and Elizabeth fussed with her wimple, asking for her favorite pearl and ruby brooch. "Grace, work your magic on my face, child. I would not have Sir Edward be shocked by my appearance after all this time. I believe the last time I saw him was at Richard's court, before he ran off to Flanders to avoid Henry's punishment."

"Aye, he was a useful man to both your husband and his brother. A loyal servant of the house of York, for all he was a Jew," Katherine remarked. Then, seeing Elizabeth's look of reproof, she demurred, "a converted Christian, certes, thanks to Edward."

"He must have made his peace with Henry, I am guessing, although visiting a traitor such as I must not endear him to my son-in-law," Elizabeth mused. "Perhaps he is now spying for Henry. I would not put it past that adventurer."

Grace listened absently as she smoothed white ointment on Elizabeth's face, which, she admitted, besides being the fashion, did hide some of the lines. But she secretly thought the effect was more like a death mask, and she experienced a quiver of fear. What would become of her if Elizabeth died? She was completely dependent on her mentor and received only a few nobles a quarter out of Henry's meager two-hundred-and-sixty-pound annuity to his mother-in-law. Elizabeth was obliged to pay the abbot for her small entourage's board and lodging from it. The ladies' everyday gowns were mended and patched, and only when Elizabeth received a visitor would she allow Grace and Katherine to robe her in a carefully folded gown left in the large carved wardrobe chest from her former glory days.

"I have no time to change my gown," she said, sighing. "Sir Edward always told me I looked most beautiful in blue. This dull gray will look dowdy, in truth." She frowned. "I wonder why the hurried visit?"

She had no time to ponder, as men's voices were heard upon the stairs outside and a knock came soon after.

Elizabeth checked her reflection once more, straightened the brooch and, sitting down, arranged her skirts gracefully around her. "Come!" she called, sounding calmer than she felt. Grace, Katherine and the other two attendants flanked her as Sir Edward was ushered in. Grace immediately recognized a man who had spent many years at sea. He was handsome in a swarthy way, small but sinewy, with the merriest eyes she had seen at the abbey in all the time they had been in residence. She liked him instantly.

"Your grace," he greeted her, going down on bended knee, hat in hand, and kissing her outstretched fingers. "I see your beauty has not diminished since last I saw you."

Grace and Katherine were so heartened at the sound of Elizabeth's tinkling laughter that their eyes met in a mutual smile of relief. When Elizabeth laughed, it was a good day at the abbey.

"You scoundrel, Sir Edward. I see you have not lost your ability to flatter a lady. Even one as old and hagged as I!" she replied, motioning him to stand. "To what do I owe the pleasure of a visit? Come, sit by me, I pray you. Pull up that chair," she said, pointing to the larger of the two remaining chairs. "You may see to what penury I am reduced, Sir Edward. My son-in-law will have me dress in rags and sit on the floor ere long. Whereas you seem to have flourished in your enforced absence from our shores." And she laughed again.

Sir Edward smiled, but his sharp eyes had already noticed the shabbiness of her clothes, the furniture and hangings on the bed, and he was shocked. "How often do you see your daughter, the queen, madam?" He could not believe Elizabeth Woodville's daughter would allow her mother to live thus.

"Bess has been a few times—less of late, 'tis true, but she has recently given birth and Henry keeps her close," Elizabeth said, determined to defend her daughter, who had not set foot in the abbey for almost a year. "And I was allowed out for a meeting with the French ambassadors at Westminster last November, not long before little Margaret was born. Let me see, that was six months ago," she said brightly. "And I saw my grandson, who is a delightful child. I hear the new baby, too, is healthy enough."

"Aye, she is healthy, your grace," Sir Edward reassured her, trying to keep the sadness from his voice. "And the queen is churched and back to her duties at court."

Grace noticed a hint of an accent in Sir Edward's speech and wondered why he did not sound as English as his name. Perhaps all Jews speak with an accent, she mused, fascinated by this man in his exquisite murrey velvet doublet, edged with vair, and a ring on every finger. He must be exceedingly rich, she decided, admiring the wide gold collar around his neck and the jeweled garter circling his thigh.

"Grace, dear, do I need to present you twice?" Elizabeth admonished her and Grace started, turning embarrassed eyes on the visitor. She saw Katherine smirking at her over Elizabeth's head, their fleeting friendly moment forgotten. "Sir Edward, forgive my young friend; she has a vivid imagination and lives in another world sometimes. Certes, I do not blame the child, because abbey life is dull for one used to the delights of court life." She sighed. "I present Lady Grace Plantagenet to you again, Sir Edward, and perhaps she will respond this time."

"I crave your pardon, Sir Edward," Grace apologized, stepping forward and curtsying. "I am honored to meet you." And she hurriedly retreated behind Elizabeth, hoping Sir Edward's black eyes would stop assessing her. Aye, I am a bastard, she wanted to blurt out, now pray stop staring! But he was smiling kindly enough, and she relaxed the grip on her belt.

"Lady Grace," he murmured and then turned his attention to Elizabeth.

"I would speak with Sir Edward in private, ladies," she said, nodding to the two nearest the door. "Katherine and Grace will stay. Although, I dare say," she added, chuckling at Sir Edward, "that people our age have no more need of chaperones, *n'est ce pas*, my dear sir."

When the door closed on the two servants, Elizabeth got to the meat of Brampton's visit. "I hope we may dispense with formalities now, sir. Why are you here?" she urged. Katherine and Grace stood discreetly at the back of the room, but they could still hear every word. "Knowing your loyalty to my husband and his brother, I cannot think Henry has sent you to give me his good wishes." She lowered her voice. "Or are you now as good a spy for him as you were for Edward?" She held his eyes with her astonishing blue ones.

Sir Edward was on his knee in a trice, hat once again in hand. "Your grace, you cannot believe that I would betray you after all King Edward did for me. You must believe I am here with news that I thought might cheer you, 'tis all. In truth, I did not seek permission from King Henry to visit you, but it is well known at court that he does not deny you visitors. I regret I have not come sooner, but I have been . . . well, let us say . . . forced to stay abroad until this year." He grinned and Elizabeth bade him sit again. "I thought it prudent to first present my apologies and duty to King Henry in person following my pardon. He was kind enough to find lodging for me within the palace for a week or so. But as soon as my audience was ended, I was determined to speak with you at the earliest opportunity. Perhaps I should have sent my servant to you before my visit. Certes, I had no wish to alarm you."

"Forgive me, Sir Edward, but you cannot blame my anxiety. I was betrayed before, and look what happened to me. I needed to hear the loyalty in your voice, and indeed I am right glad to see you. I pray you, continue with your news."

"Very well, madam. I am recently come from Guisnes . . ." he paused when he saw Elizabeth frown. " 'Tis one of the two castles that guard Calais, your grace."

"I know that, Sir Edward," Elizabeth said, a more little impatiently than necessary, Grace thought. "But why should that be of interest to me?"

" 'Twas a conversation I had with the governor of the castle, Sir James Tyrell," Sir Edward replied, ignoring her tone and pleased to see the queen dowager sit up at the mention of one of King Richard's favored councilors. "Without revealing anything that could return to haunt him, Sir James led me to believe that one of your sons is still alive."

All three women gasped, and Sir Edward swiveled round to look at Grace and Katherine, seeming to have forgotten they were there. Katherine hurried to Elizabeth, her eyes shining, and grasped her hand. "Ah, Elizabeth, your prayers have been heard!" she cried.

Grace sank down on a stool and observed the group: Elizabeth had blanched whiter than her makeup, her eyes wild with hope, and Katherine was chafing her friend's hand and repeating "Dear God, dear God!" while

Sir Edward stirred the rushes with his toe, waiting for the queen to speak. Can this be true? Grace's heart pounded; one of her half brothers was found!

Elizabeth was momentarily speechless, so Sir Edward continued: "I have also had word from merchant colleagues in Bruges that your sister-in-law is putting it about that her nephew, the young duke of York, lives. Although his whereabouts seem to be a mystery," Sir Edward told her. "When I heard the second rumor, I knew 'twas time I came to see you. I wish I had more to tell you, but I do not."

Elizabeth still could not speak. She allowed Katherine to keep patting her hand but she stared straight ahead at the door. Finally she turned to Sir Edward and whispered: "I thank you, sir. You have brought a ray of hope so bright into this small chamber that I can barely see for its brilliance." Then she said, and Grace strained to hear her sotto voce, "I never believed Richard could have killed his brother's children in cold blood. About a year after their disappearance, I dreamed Ned was dead, and then Doctor Argentine said he had treated the boy for a wasting disease in the Tower. My brother, Lord Rivers, told me that at Ludlow Ned complained often of pain in his face, but with some oil of clove rubbed on his gums, it was eased. 'Twas naught but toothache, I imagined. Lately, in my heart, I knew Ned was dead. But my little Dickon . . ." she trailed off, too moved to say anything more.

" 'Tis a miracle indeed, your grace," Sir Edward said. "But the tale could have stern consequences should Henry learn of it. I beg of you to keep this to yourself until I can discover the truth. I am a friend at Duchess Margaret's court, so perhaps I can glean more. And you have my word that, should you desire to send a letter to her, I can guarantee its safe and secret arrival."

Elizabeth turned grateful eyes to him. "I have no doubt you can, Sir Edward. My husband counted on your discretion many a time. I will compose something to the duchess—she and I had a friendship many years ago—and I will send Grace with it. Shall she find you at Westminster?" Sir Edward nodded. "Good," she went on, her voice returning to its usual calm. "Then expect her within the week. We do not want Father John or Brother Damien to suspect anything untoward took place today—I fear they spy on me for the king, and by leaving it several days, they will not connect your visit to Grace's brief absence. Tell her where she should find you."

"Let us say that after three days I will wait for her every day at noon at the Sign of the Red Pale next to the abbey at Westminster. William Caxton, who owns the printing shop, is an old friend, and I have business with him."

"Aye, I know the man. Grace will be there in three days, if all goes well. And now, dear friend, I think you must go." She beckoned to Grace and Katherine. "Let us all pretend to make merry for a few minutes for the benefit of anyone passing or listening at the door."

Sir Edward rose to the occasion with a few suitable anecdotes for the women, and they supposed their false laughter fooled any eavesdroppers. Then the courtier dropped another kiss on Elizabeth's outstretched hand before leaving her presence and cantering through the abbey gatehouse into Long Lane.

Elizabeth sat staring at the closed door for several minutes before she could speak. Grace poured a cup of sweet hippocras for her and Elizabeth took the proffered cup, raising it high in celebration. Then, as Katherine's jaw dropped, she downed the contents in one swallow, wiping her mouth with the back of her sleeve. She grinned up at Grace with the lopsided smile of someone pleasantly in her cups, rose and began to pace about the room. Grace now saw a glimpse of the woman who had delighted in playing political games during her nineteen years as Edward's queen and in King Richard's reign. Her eyes glittered—from more than just the wine—and her fists were clenched by her sides. When an uneven floorboard tripped her for a second and she became unbalanced, she reached out for the wall to steady herself but then turned and paced purposefully back to her chair.

"Something tells me Margaret is at the bottom of this, ladies," she said. "She is a wily one, our Meg. Edward always said she was the cleverest of all his family. Still, I cannot quite believe that my little Dickon is alive. After all this time!" She frowned. "Why has whoever has him waited so long to produce him? Certes, he would have been a natural choice to lead Lincoln and Lovell at Stoke."

"Perhaps because he was still such a boy, madam," Grace offered timidly. "I remember you telling me when I first came to Grafton that all was lost to you because Ned was a boy king."

Elizabeth looked at the diminutive young woman with respect. "Do you forget anything you are told, Grace? Aye, you are probably right, but Simnel was a boy, standing in for Warwick, who was also a boy. Nay, it does not make sense. Where could Dickon have been hidden for so long? I want so much to believe he is alive, in truth, but it seems too fantastical."

"Dickon would be sixteen now, Elizabeth, and could rule without a regent. He would be ready to return, if indeed he exists," Katherine said, blowing her nose noisily into a kerchief. She had shed the tears of joy Elizabeth had not.

Her tipsiness forgotten, Elizabeth rose. "I am in need of prayer, ladies. Terce is past, and the church should be empty. Perhaps Father John would not mind if we availed ourselves of its holy comfort. Come, let us go and pray for guidance from the Virgin."

GRACE COULD HARDLY wait for the planned visit to Westminster. She had not been out of the abbey for more than half a year, when she had attended Elizabeth at court on the visit of her kinsman and French emissary, François of Luxembourg. "Certes, Henry invites me only to allay any suspicions my cousin might have if I do not pay my respects," Elizabeth had complained when the messenger brought the invitation. "Pray God he sends me a new gown for the occasion, or François will be asking questions when he sees me thus." Indeed, two bolts of cloth were furnished for the occasion by a clothier from Southwark, and a tailor was tasked with making Elizabeth and Katherine new gowns. The clothier was so pleased with the commission that he willingly provided Grace with a cinnamon-colored gown of satin de Bruges and a gabled headdress to match at no extra cost.

"You look like a little brown bird," Elizabeth had exclaimed when Grace was dressed. Unexpected tears stung Grace's eyes, as she was reminded of John. "I suppose I must conform and wear naught but widow's weeds," Elizabeth groused, although the requisite purple the merchant had chosen was anything but drab. A violet damask overdress was raised at the front to show an even deeper purple satin skirt underneath, and a delicate gold crown sat atop her wimple. Despite her wraithlike body, she was still beautiful, Grace thought.

" 'Tis better than gray," Elizabeth admitted, when Grace held the polished mirror for her. She then chose to adorn herself with the entire contents of her secret drawer, saying: "I may never have the chance to wear these jewels again, and I may need to sell them if Henry is any meaner with his money." She had found a small brooch set with amber and pinned it to Grace's bodice. "I had forgotten I had this trinket. It suits you more than I, so you shall have it. You have been a good, uncomplaining girl these three years." Grace fingered the petals of the brooch with awe. She had never owned anything so beautiful and gratefully kissed Elizabeth's hand. Katherine had sniffed with displeasure and Elizabeth, in a generous mood, had given her a pair of pearl earbobs that were worth considerably more than Grace's brooch. "Now come, ladies, our carriage awaits," Elizabeth had commanded, and the three women went out into the cold November afternoon.

Now it was June, and the larks were singing high above the meadows, twittering barn swallows swooped in and out of the abbey stables and lambs frisked beside their shorn dams. The bare-chested weeders in the wheat field methodically stomped on the tops of the weeds, pulling the roots up behind them in the crooks of their long wooden hooks as they moved on to crush the next offending plant.

Grace secured her linen coif under her chin, pushed her straw hat down on top of it and hurried out of the gate to the farmlands beyond. There was plenty of work to be done, which would take her mind off the coming meeting in Westminster. Brother Oswald had seen a love of the land in Grace when he had first taken her into the garden to teach her the art of beekeeping, and Elizabeth was happy enough to let Grace toil there during the hours she had no need of the girl. She and Katherine would make fun of Grace when she came back from washing the lambs, tending the vegetable patch or feeding the chickens with mud on her face, strands of wool carpeting her kirtle or green stains on her hands.

"You will make some farmer a fine wife one day," Katherine had remarked once, smirking as she tuned the strings of her lute. "As King Henry seems to have forgotten about you, no doubt a farmer—or a merchant—is all you will end up with. Or perhaps the nuns will find you useful when you have to take the veil." Elizabeth was gone to the privy and did not hear these unkind remarks, but Grace had chosen to ignore the insinuation that she would end up a spinster and responded: "I am happiest when I am busy, Lady Hastings, and husbandry seems to be what is most needed here at the abbey. I am not ashamed to learn how one must work with animals and plants in order to live." She looked at the lute and added: " 'Tis more valuable than . . ." she hesitated for a moment, as she did wish she were more musical, and then finished, ". . . embroidery." She had expected the usual rebuke, but Katherine had merely grunted and continued plucking and humming.

Today Grace swung open the little gate that enclosed the runcival-pea patch and began tying up the long stalks to small branches that had been cut for the purpose and staking them in the rich soil. Two other women, wives of the laborers who lived in huts outside the abbey walls, acknowledged her with little bobs. Grace waved and called "Good morrow to you, Joan, Maud. And a fine morning it is."

"Aye, my lady," Joan responded, giving Grace a toothless grin. They were used to her now, but when she had first begun to work among them, the field hands had been uncomfortable. She had soon put them at their ease with her friendly yet respectful questions about their tasks and then by working as hard as they, even though she was only there for a fraction of their long, backbreaking day. Well used to this labor from her years at Delapre, she was an invaluable member of the group. Although she did not mind tying peas, gathering beans, planting leeks and lettuce or digging up turnips and carrots, she loved working with the animals the most— except for horses, which still terrified her. Her small, quiet presence did not frighten the new lambs or calves, and she had been thrilled to be present at the birth of a calf the year before.

She found the hours flew by when she was outside, and her face and forearms naturally turned the color of beechnuts, eliciting despair in Elizabeth's voice. "And now you will be going to Westminster looking like a peasant," she admonished her young attendant. "Pray God no one from the palace recognizes you. Which reminds me, Father John has been kind enough to lend one of the grooms to me as your escort. If anyone questions you, you are going to William Caxton's shop on an errand from your mistress. No names, no places. Do you understand?"

Grace had nodded and then gone to the wash basin and poured some water into it to scrub her hands and clean her nails. "I do not mind that you spend your time rubbing elbows with peasants, but do not allow your hands to become like theirs. You must take care of your hands, Grace. If we go back to court, worn hands will never get you a husband."

"Aye, your grace," came the dutiful response, although they all knew they were never going back to court. In the past year, Elizabeth had had to let the other two attendants go—one to be married and the other because she could not afford to keep her. "Damn Henry's eyes," Elizabeth had hissed one particularly trying day, "and may his prick shrivel up and die!" Grace had paled at the curse. There were times when she did not like Elizabeth at all, despite feeling sympathy for the woman. She presumed coming down so far in the world must be humiliating indeed for the once all-powerful queen.

The night before Grace was due to go to Westminster, the three women spent extra time in prayer. "Dear Mary, Mother of God," Elizabeth murmured, staring at the small painting of the Virgin on the wall, in whose arms sat a rather overweight Christ child with golden curls and bright blue eyes, "watch over Grace as she undertakes this mission for me to find my long-lost child. Bless my son and intercede for me with our Lord and Saviour that He might bring young Dickon and me together again. Let him know his mother's love once more.

"*Ave Maria, gratia plena . . .*" she intoned and was joined by Grace and Katherine as they prayed the rosary together. Then each conversed silently with God before Elizabeth crossed herself and blew out the prie-dieu candle.

"Tomorrow I shall write to Meg," Elizabeth said from the bed as Grace drew the curtains around the two women and prepared her own crude truckle bed. "God will guide my thoughts, and you will guide the pen, Grace. Now let us try to sleep. God keep you."

"God give your grace a good night, and you, Lady Katherine," Grace replied, releasing the last curtain, and then, wrapping herself in her cloak, she lay quietly on her mattress contemplating the next day until sleep claimed her.

She dreamed of John in the meadow at Sheriff Hutton running towards her, calling her name, and Bran running circles around him as she bent to gather daisies. When she looked up only the greyhound was loping through the long grass and wildflowers. "John!" she called, thinking he had dropped to the ground to hide from her. "Where are you?" Silence. "John!" she screamed in a panic, and, tossing the daisies into the wind, she ran to where she had seen him last. As she reached the spot, a strange young man appeared from nowhere with golden hair and an angelic smile.

There was something odd about his eyes, but she was too intent on finding John to look more closely. "Where is John?" she demanded. "And who are you?" The young man said. "You know who I am, Grace. I am your half brother, Dickon. John sent me to you." He reached out his hand to her and she tried to take it, but Dickon disappeared as well, leaving her rooted in the meadow with Bran still prancing around her. Then a cock crowed in the castle behind, startling her out of her trance.

Grace's eyes flew open, and she realized the cockcrow was not in her dream but in the abbey's barnyard. Daylight was creeping over the sill, and she closed her eyes and tried to go back into her dream. What had happened to John? How could she dream so clearly about a brother she had never met? No one had painted his portrait, so she did not know what he looked like, and yet she believed the man was Dickon. He reminded her of someone, but she could not put her finger on whom, and, as with all dreams, the harder she fought to remember the details, the faster it faded away, leaving her nonplussed and very curious.

"My dearest sister, we greet you well. I thank you for reporting the safe arrival in your country of my young kinsman, John, two years ago. I pray he is well and enjoying the benefits of your hospitality." Elizabeth paused, watching as Grace's neat script flowed off the nib of her quill and caught up with her dictation. It was an hour past Prime and the bread and cheese that were to break their fast were still sitting in the wooden bowl on the table where Grace was seated, making the girl all the hungrier. Elizabeth had sent Katherine to the refectory to eat with the other residents in order to write this all-important letter to Margaret. "Dear Katherine, do not look as though I am punishing you," Elizabeth had told Lady Hastings. " 'Tis better for you not to know the contents. For if the missive falls into the wrong hands and I am found out, you will have a clear conscience and cannot be punished." A fleeting look of relief belied the words of indignation Katherine spoke to the queen, assuring her of her complete devotion and silence, but a second later she had curtsied and was gone. Elizabeth had smiled and murmured "Ever the expedient, Lady Hastings" to the closed door.

Grace raised her warm brown eyes to the older woman and gave a quick nod to say she was ready. "Stay your pen, Grace. I must make sure I reveal nothing of importance. It must not put anyone in jeopardy—not Meg, Sir

Edward, my little Dickon or me—for I believe Henry still hates the house of York and would not hesitate to execute any of us if he felt threatened."

"Even me?" Grace squeaked. Elizabeth looked down at the sweet face with its trusting but frightened eyes and softened.

"Nay, Grace. You are the innocent in all of this. You are doing my bidding, and as a bastard *daughter* of my late, lamented husband, you pose no threat to Henry. But I must know that I can trust you." She paused and saw Grace nod her head vigorously. "Good. I do not believe you or your friend—Tom, was it?—betrayed me back in Eighty-seven, but Christ's nails, somebody did!" She thumped her fist on the table, making the wooden bowl jump and disturbing the flies that were enjoying the cheese. Elizabeth waved them away with her hand as they attempted to land again. "Damn flies," she groused. " 'Tis the curse of living on a farm."

Grace respectfully smothered her laugh. She thought Prior John would be horrified to hear his abbey spoken of in such demeaning terms. She dipped her quill in the sepia ink and wiped the excess off on the rim of the bottle.

"You must know that I am aware of a rumor that my errant son is enjoying foreign hospitality. I am told you may be able to help me bring him home. In truth, I have not seen him for many a moon, and it pains me that he has been lost to me all this time. If you know of his whereabouts and can tell him of his mother's love and willingness . . ." Elizabeth stopped. "Nay, strike that last word and substitute *eagerness*," she directed Grace. *". . . to restore him to his rightful place in the family, I shall be eternally grateful to you, my dear sister. Much depends upon his safe return, as you are only too aware.*

"I think fondly upon our times together those many years past, and wish that we lived closer. My circumstances have changed and I am no longer able to travel to see you, as well my health is not as it should be. We are both getting old, in truth. I look forward to hearing from you with the news I so long to hear. Your loving sister, Bess," she concluded. " 'Tis what Edward called me. Meg will know," she explained, as Grace looked up, puzzled. "I think that is as guarded as I can be and yet perfectly clear, do you not think?" She did not require a response, but sank down heavily on the bed, her energy spent. "No one but you and Katherine will recognize your hand." *And John, if he sees it,* Grace exulted.

Grace lifted the quill and stared at the page. She did not dare to look up at Elizabeth for fear of giving away her concern for her mentor's health.

Elizabeth's clothes hung about her shoulders like a scarecrow's, and she had had several fainting spells that spring. Instead she asked, "To whom should I address it? And with what shall I seal it, your grace?"

"Use the base of the crucifix on your rosary. It needs to be metal, but the square base of the cross will do nicely as a tool," Elizabeth said, making Grace raise one eyebrow at the use of a holy object to, in fact, deceive others. But she did as she was told, and the letter was sealed tight. She waited for the final instruction and turned to the dowager.

"I had not thought about the address, Grace," Elizabeth moaned. " We need to put something on the front."

Grace suddenly brightened. "Why do we not use Broome again? Would Aunt Margaret understand that it was for her?"

Elizabeth was moved to sit up and swing her legs over the side of the bed. Her eyes were shining. "You are a clever girl. Certes, she would know. Sir Edward will make sure it is put into her hands. Write upon it Dame Meg Broome and then hide it on your person until you meet Sir Edward. Ah, how I wish 'twas I who was going to Westminster. You are fortunate, my child, because no one will know you." She looked at the hour clock and gasped. "Your escort will be waiting for you, Grace. Are you ready to go?"

Grace nodded. She had put her tooth stick, a comb and some clean hose in a small bag, and she tucked the letter between her chemise and her tightly fitted bodice and slipped on her pattens over her plain round shoes. Her russet wool gown and simple linen cap and veil gave her a rustic appearance, and she could have passed for a farmer's wife or daughter. Elizabeth nodded her approval and bent and kissed her forehead, a gesture Grace had not enjoyed since they'd come to the abbey three years before. She stood on tiptoe and kissed Elizabeth on the cheek. "I will do my best for you, your grace," she whispered. "I pray it helps return Dickon to us."

"Amen," Elizabeth agreed, and they both crossed themselves.

GRACE AND HER burly escort walked the mile to Southwark in the drizzle. As was usual in London, the weather changed from day to day, and the blue skies of yesterday had given way to a gray overcast and the lightest of rains. As they walked down St. Margaret's Hill and onto High Street, Grace was able to take in her surroundings in more detail than she had from the covered carriage that had taken Elizabeth and her attendants to the palace at Westminster the previous foggy November.

Elizabeth had insisted Grace should wear nothing that set her apart on this dangerous errand, and Grace observed that in their brown wool garb she and Edgar, her taciturn servant, blended right in with other towns-folk. Only the higher-born could afford the expensive dyes like saffron and kermes red, although a cleric in his crimson would also stand out.

As they neared the bridge and passed the pillory, Grace watched as a jeering group of citizens lobbed rotten eggs at the mournful face of the man standing with his face and wrists stuck through the holes of the cross board. The wrong-doer's plight so dismayed Grace that she begged Edgar to escort her into St. Mary Overie to pray for him. Edgar mumbled in assent, but as soon as he saw her safely inside the south transept door he announced that he needed to slake his thirst at the Swan tavern across the road. Before Grace could protest he had taken off, assuming his charge would be safe in the house of God. She stood still to take in her surround-ings and become accustomed to the gloom; there was no sun streaming in the glorious windows this day. However, she was not expecting the ca-cophony of banging, hammering, talking and laughing that greeted her as she stepped out of the transept and into the nave. Dozens of carpenters were scrambling along scaffolding beams high above her as they worked on the new wooden roof. Grace turned and hurried down the south aisle to a quieter spot to pray.

Half an hour later, her supplications for the man in the stocks made, she returned to the transept door to wait for Edgar. When he eventually came, he reeked of ale and stumbled on the steps. Grace made him sit down and, to his surprise, proceeded to berate him, even slapping his slacked jaw several times as she did so. Then she hauled him to his feet and commanded him to lead her to the wharves. "If you put another foot wrong, my man, Father John will know of this lapse. I trust you told no one of our journey while you were tossing back the ale?" Edgar's baleful look and shake of the head told her she could expect no more trouble from him, and he even bowed and mumbled an apology. A curious onlooker passing by wondered why the big man allowed his daughter to pummel him so, and Grace thought she heard Edgar tell him, "She's as prim as a nun's hen," but she was too intent on continuing their journey to question him again. The man chuckled and passed by into the church. Handing the groom his sturdy stave, she waved him ahead of her, hoping he was sober enough to find the way to the water. "Not another word," she said.

On the north side of the church, the alleys were narrow and the walls dank with slime from their proximity to the river. Grace was not sure what she was stepping on as they went, but the stench led her to believe it was not merely mud, and she was glad of her high wooden pattens. She pulled out a kerchief she had soaked in rosemary water for just such an occasion and held it to her nose. She heard a thwack behind her and turned to see Edgar grinning smugly. "A rat, my lady. I killed a rat." Grace shuddered and was glad she had not seen it. She inclined her head in acknowledgment but then reminded him, "Edgar, do not call me 'my lady.' I am simply Mistress Grace, remember?"

The groom nodded. "Aye, mistress. I forgot." Grace sighed, wishing Father John could have chosen a more quick-witted man than Edgar.

As they approached the wharf below the Clink prison, she was glad to see more people, as the alleys were ideal for concealing cutpurses, though big Edgar with his quarterstaff had given her some reassurance. They stood in the queue for a boatman to ferry them to Westminster, and only when the groat fare was paid and the six-person boat was being expertly pulled through the water away from shore did Grace feel her tension ease. The drizzle had stopped, and she shook out the moisture on her shawl and settled into the seat in the stern. It was not long before the houses of Southwark dwindled into woods and fields on the southern bank and the massive spire of St. Paul's dominated the London side of the river. They passed Baynard's Castle, the city residence of the York family, and she gazed at its impressive white walls and crenellated towers that rose in splendor from the water. She had been inside the castle once, when she was taken with her half sisters to pay respects to their grandmother, Cecily, who had made a rare visit to London from the duchess's reclusive life at Berkhamsted. Grace had been awed by the imperious woman whose legendary beauty was still evident despite her seventy years, and the girl had spoken not a word during the hour-long visit. "Yet another of Edward's by-blows, I suppose," the duchess had muttered to herself, but all Grace had heard was the final "Poor child."

Thoughts of her family led her to her present adventure. She turned to look over her shoulder at the whitewashed walls of William called Conqueror's Tower receding in their wake. Could her half brother Dickon still be alive? And Ned? So many rumors had flown about since their disappearance in Eighty-three: Uncle Richard had ordered their murder, Harry of Buckingham had done the deed—or was it Margaret Beaufort? Or indeed, following Bosworth, could it have been Henry Tudor himself? Then there were those who believed the oldest had died of natural causes and that the younger had been sent away to safety by Uncle Richard. Grace liked that story the best, and her thoughtful reasoning told her that if they had really been murdered by Richard, then Henry surely would have accused him of it publicly and put the rumors to rest. Henry must not have been sure they were dead, she concluded, and a shiver of excitement went through her. Perhaps this story from Sir Edward Brampton was true, and young Richard of York was somewhere safe in Calais or Flanders. Her brother had every right to the throne now that Henry had overturned the illegitimacy claim against Edward and Elizabeth's children so he could marry Bess. Small wonder Elizabeth did not want this errand discovered, Grace mused; it would put Henry in a very awkward position if Richard of York were brought home successfully. Grace shivered with trepidation as she realized that anyone remotely connected with the prince's return could be accused of treason. She hoped her steady head would not let her down. In her deep gratitude, there was nothing she would not do for Elizabeth.

"William Caxton is an old friend of Aunt Margaret's," Elizabeth had explained to Grace before sending her on this errand. "He is well respected in London for his printing press, and his workshop at the Sign of the Red Pale is visited by nobles and merchants alike. My oldest brother, Anthony"— and Grace nodded, knowing he was the one who had been locked up at Sheriff Hutton—"was a patron of his. You have seen me reading his translation of *Cordiale*. 'Twas Caxton who printed it. You may go there without suspicion, and Sir Edward will keep his end of the bargain, I trust."

Now the boat was pulling for the north bank as the slate roofs of the palace of Westminster and the massive abbey beyond grew closer over the prow. Grace was tempted to see if Cecily was at court, but she put it from her mind. Cecily and Grace had laughed together when the marriage with Viscount Welles had finally taken place late in 1487, because they realized that as John was half uncle to Henry, Cecily was now half aunt to her own sister, Bess. Grace did not envy her sister the aging viscount as a husband—twenty years difference was a lifetime to the girls—but she did envy Cecily's recent motherhood.

" 'Tis not a true marriage without children," Elizabeth had remarked after a year without a sign of a Welles child. "At least, so the Bible tells us. I cannot believe one of my girls is barren, so I blame it on Welles." She had put up her index finger and let it curl slowly limp, making Katherine laugh. So when a letter had come early in 1489 announcing that Cecily had borne a daughter at John Welles's mother's family residence of Bletso, Elizabeth was much relieved.

"My own Cecilia has done her duty by your son, Dorset. Three healthy children," Katherine had said upon the news, although she did not mention the babes who had not survived. Elizabeth's eyes had shone with pride, as they always did whenever Thomas was mentioned: she adored her oldest son, child of her first love, Sir John Grey. Dorset was back in the king's graces, she was happy to know, but Henry still did not bestow the favors on him that his proud mother felt were his due, and it rankled.

The busy wharf was alive with courtiers and their ladies stepping into and out of their richly decorated barges, and with merchants followed by apprentices carrying bolts of cloth and other merchandise to tempt the noble residents of the palace. Coopers rolled barrels off shouts whose sails were now dropped, and wharf workers hauled stone from the barges that had brought it from the midlands. Grace and Edgar threaded their way through this melee towards the abbey. It was close to noon and Grace's stomach was growling. Barrows and stalls loaded with vegetables, fish, poultry and cheese lined the streets where housewives bartered with the stall-keepers in raucous voices. A cook-shop boy was crying out "Hot pies! Boiled sheep's feet! Roast thrush," a stack of steaming hot pasties balanced on the board on top of his head. Grace bought two, and a sweet tart from another vendor, and she and Edgar found a bench where they could sit and eat. Grace saw Edgar eye the swinging bush sign hanging from the eaves of a building across the street that announced a handy alehouse, but she frowned heavily at him and was amused to see that he was cowed by it. She was always in the deferent position, and to have someone—especially someone of Edgar's imposing height and girth—look up to her was rather gratifying. She was thirsty, however, and so told the man, "Go and ask in the alehouse where we might find the Sign of the Red Pale, and fetch us both a pot of ale while you are there. But you will return to me immediately, do you understand?" Her own authority impressed her. Edgar grinned, took the silver penny she gave him and disappeared inside the dark tavern.

The sun was attempting to pierce the lifting clouds, and she removed her shawl and tied it around her waist, as she did when she was in the fields. Edgar returned a few minutes later with the beer and they both quaffed the amber liquid quickly. The imposing mechanical clock in the square outside the palace gate told Grace it was nearly noon and thus time to seek out the print shop.

"It be not far from here, mistress," Edgar said, pointing to the abbey. "No more'n five minutes." And he was right. The wide vertical red line down the center of the white sign swinging above a door in the building adjacent to the abbey advertised William Caxton's shop, and telling Edgar to wait outside and not to wander off, Grace pushed open the door and went inside. Her heart was beating loudly, but she must have looked perfectly serene, as an apprentice sidled up to her.

"Can I 'elp you, mistress?" he asked, taking in her plain, worn gown and damp coif. She did not look like a customer who could read, and other than being a rather tasty morsel, he was not prepared to waste much time on her. "Be you in the right place? This be a print shop. You know, where we print books."

His tone was patronizing, and Grace drew herself up to her full five feet in her pattens and gave him a supercilious stare. "Certes, I am fully cognizant of that fact. I wish to see your master, sirrah. I have come to do business with Master Caxton, and no one else. Might I assume from your manners that you are not he?" Her more refined speech had established her superiority. Twice in one day, she thought proudly. The young man bowed and hurried to the stairs that led to Caxton's office.

Grace looked about her with interest. The great press dominated the workshop and was being overseen by a tall thin man with piercing eyes. She edged closer to the apparatus, whose wooden frame stood almost six feet high. On a table nearby, another apprentice was fitting soft metal letters into a chase. As Grace watched him smear ink over the framed letters, a grizzle-haired man with a full white beard came slowly down the wooden staircase, supported by the apprentice.

"May I help you, mistress? I am William Caxton, the owner of the establishment," he said, unhooking a stick from a peg and leaning on it as he walked.

"Good day, Master Caxton. I am here on an errand from my mistress, her grace the dowager queen Elizabeth," Grace replied softly when the apprentice had moved away to help at the press. She had been expecting to find Sir Edward there, give him the letter and then start back for the abbey. She prayed Caxton knew of her mission and would allow her to wait upstairs for Brampton. She would not put the letter into anyone's hands but his.

"At your service, my lady." Caxton bowed gravely. "You are the Lady Grace, I trust?"

"Aye, sir."

"Fear not. You are safe here, child," the kindly printer told her, responding to her anxious glances at the others. "This is Master de Worde, my foreman. He looks fierce, but take no notice; 'tis from staring so long at sheets of printed paper to make sure each is perfect. Wynken, show our visitor how the machine works."

Grace smiled her thanks and went closer to the press. The apprentice laid the now well-inked chase of words into its place and a page of paper upon it, and the foreman pulled down on the heavy bar attached to the screw, pressing the platen quickly onto the page and releasing it. As Grace watched, Caxton gently peeled the paper off the type and held it up for her to inspect. She gasped. It was as though someone had spent hours writing this neat script, but because of the skill and speed of the apprentices in setting the type and the astonishing invention of the press, the page was complete in minutes.

The paper fluttered in her hand and Grace knew the door onto the street had been opened, letting in the wind. She turned and, to her relief, saw Sir Edward Brampton walking towards her, a ready smile on his face.

"Lady Grace, 'tis a pleasure to see you and know that you came here safely," he began quietly out of earshot of all but Grace and Caxton. "Ah, Caxton, I see you have been showing our young friend this marvelous machine. Did you know this man is renowned throughout Europe for his books, my lady?"

"Pshaw!" Caxton laughed off the compliment. " 'Tis her grace, Madame la Grande, who deserves all the praise. Without her patronage, I would still be peddling goods as a Merchant Adventurer in Bruges! I would still be unmarried and not have my lovely daughter."

"Madame la Grande?" Grace asked. "Who is she?"

"Why, she is your aunt, my lady," Caxton exclaimed. "Her grace, the duchess Margaret of Burgundy. A most intelligent and beautiful woman.

'Twas she who took me from the Waterhall in Bruges—where the Merchant Adventurers lived, you see—and gave me a position at her court so that I could work on translating the *Recueil*—or *History of Troy*, as it is known in English. Wait, allow me to show you." Caxton fetched a book from the shelf and put it into Grace's hands as if it were made of gold.

With reverence, Grace opened the embossed leather volume and read the introduction to the first book ever printed in English: "*At the commandment of the right high, mighty and virtuous princess, his redoubted Lady Margaret, by the grace of God, duchess of Bourgoyne . . . meekly beseeching the bounteous Highness of my said Lady that of her benevolence listened to accept with favor this simple and rude work here following . . .*" Grace looked up at Caxton and was touched by his expression. " 'Tis humbly said, Master Caxton. I trust my aunt was pleased with your dedication?"

"I am proud to say she shed a tear upon first reading it, just as I will if you continue to remind me of that memorable moment of my life, my lady," Caxton said, laughing. "Now I must return to my accounts, or this poor fellow here"—he indicated de Worde—"will not be paid this quarter. Lady Grace, Sir Edward," he murmured, bowing. "I am always at your service."

Another customer came into the shop, and again the apprentice hurried to greet the newcomer. Sir Edward led Grace to a quiet corner, consternation on his face.

"I fear you are come on a fool's errand, my lady," he said, "for which I am deeply sorry. I have received word from my wife in Lisbon that I am required there, and I shall now not be returning to Bruges as I thought. I assume you have come with a letter. Aye, I thought as much. It pains me greatly to break my word to her grace, but I must—and ask her forgiveness."

Grace's expression of dismay stirred something in the old sea dog's heart and he picked up her hand and patted it. "Let us walk in the abbey gardens and think how we might resolve this. I know it would distress your mistress if you returned with this news. I saw how much she was counting on getting word about her son from Burgundy. Her health is not good, I could see that."

Grace shook her head. "She does not eat, Sir Edward, and she complains of dizziness and shortness of breath."

Sir Edward nodded. "Her heart has been broken too many times, I fear.

It has weakened over the years." He took her hand and tucked it under his arm and called farewell to de Worde, who hurried to see them out, where Edgar was waiting.

"I have been fortunate enough to speak to your sister, Viscountess Welles, while I have been at court. She is also a very lively young lady," Brampton said.

Grace smiled and sighed. "Aye, she is, and I miss her very much. She and I became fast friends until our lives forced us apart. She has come twice to see her mother and me, but she spends much of her time in Lincolnshire at her husband's estates, I understand, which," she confided in her companion, "would not please her one little bit. She hates being away from court."

"I told Lady Cecily of my visit to your mother and how dismayed I was to see the penury in which I found her. I hope she has influence with the king, and that he will relent and allow her grace, the dowager, a place at court again."

"Hmmm" was all Grace said in response.

The herber behind the abbey was a pleasant place, and Grace remembered her time at the abbot's old house with Elizabeth well. So much had happened since those early days when she had first been taken in. It was hard to believe six years had passed. Sir Edward's squire fell into step behind his master and Grace, and Edgar lumbered along a few paces behind the squire. It was nigh on two o'clock and Edgar was thinking about the return journey and the pot of ale waiting for him at his tiny cottage under Bermondsey's walls. He didn't much like the look of this foreign gentleman, with his ridiculously high plumed hat, and he was not going to let Grace out of his sight. He wiped his nose with the back of his hand and then cleaned it down his belted tunic. He lounged against a wall, just far away enough to be visible and yet close enough to come to Grace's rescue if necessary.

Grace led the way to her favorite excedra and sat down while Brampton paced back and forth, deep in thought. "I have an idea," he said suddenly. " 'Tis a bold one, and you may dismiss it out of hand, but I have the means to make it work."

Grace's young eagerness delighted him, and he took her hand and kissed it. "Queen Elizabeth must be thankful to have such a pretty and lively attendant, my lady. I was fortunate enough to have a page once who was curious and eager to learn, and he reminds me . . ." He stopped. "*Jesu Christus*," he exclaimed in Portuguese. "I wonder what happened to young Pierrequin."

Grace frowned. "Your plan, Sir Edward. What is your plan?" she said, dismissing the remark about the page. "I dare not return to her grace without hope of delivering this letter. 'Twould break her heart—and her spirit," she added, touching her chest.

"It would take an act of courage to embark on this adventure, and I do not know how brave you are, my lady," he said, raising a quizzical eyebrow. He was amused when Grace leaped to her feet and faced him. "Soft, Lady Grace, I see you are no milk-sop. Sit down again and listen."

"GRACE! MY DEAREST sister," Cecily cried when Grace was ushered into the room. "I am so glad to see you, although"—she stood back to look askance at Grace's plain brown gown—"I trust all is well with mother? You look as though you have fallen on hard times."

If you came to see her occasionally, my dear Cecily, perhaps you might find out for yourself, Grace thought indignantly. But she was too happy to see the gregarious Cecily, well into another pregnancy, to chide her out loud. In truth, Elizabeth had received word from Henry's treasury in February to say her pension was to be raised to four hundred pounds, but, as was typical of all things in government, she had yet to see a penny of the increase.

"How I have missed you, Cis!" Grace said, kissing Cecily warmly on both cheeks. An unexpected lump came into her throat; she had not realized until now how much she longed for company of her own age. She touched the long draped sleeve of Cecily's fashionable square-necked gown, admiring the rich red kermes silk, delicately woven with white flowers, and envying the ermine-trimmed, stiffly gabled headdress. The jeweled collar that lay prominently upon Cecily's full breasts was worth a king's ransom, Grace was sure. I could be wearing a similar garb if I weren't in attendance on the cloistered queen dowager, she thought fleetingly and was instantly guilt-ridden.

Eyeing the curious attendants, she whispered, "You *do* know why I am come? Or I will have spent a night in a dingy room at the White Horse for nothing. Edgar—my escort from the abbey—and I had to share straw pallets in the room with four other travelers. I could not sleep for the snoring of one fat woman and the bedbugs eating me alive. Even the dormitory at the convent was better than that." She crinkled her nose in disgust.

Cecily let loose her high laugh and took Grace in her arms again. "You should see your face, my sweet girl. It would sour milk! Aye, I was expecting you. Come and sit with me, and tell me about *Mother*," she said, staring meaningfully at Grace. She turned to address her astonished attendants. "For those of you who do not recognize this lady, Grace is my half sister, and I am right glad to see her. Now, we should like some privacy. You may leave us." The women curtsied to their mistress and to Grace and left, disappointed.

Grace could hear them chattering after the door had closed, and grinned at Cecily. "This will be all around the palace in a matter of hours, I have no doubt," she said. "I pray Henry will just think I am here with a message from the queen dowager."

"Oh, a pox on Henry! He will not even care; his mind is on France and Brittany these days, and trying to arrange for Arthur to marry the Spanish infanta," Cecily said, easing her ungainly body down on the bed with a satisfied grunt and patting the brightly colored counterpane for Grace to join her. "Now tell me everything. Sir Edward was infuriatingly vague, but I did glean that Mother's well-being was at stake and that I should see you as soon as I could. I told him that I will go to Bermondsey and tell her where you are. 'Twill be safer if I go. Two visits from Sir Edward in as many weeks will give Henry's spies plenty to twitter about," she said. "Pray God Mother is not angry; I do not think I could support her ire at the moment." She winced, her hands caressing her belly. "This one is a kicker. Can you feel him? My sweet Anne never gave me such trouble."

Grace blushed at the idea of touching Cecily's distended stomach, but she was glad she did, for the thrill she got from feeling the babe's foot protruding determinedly through the taut skin was a joyful one. "So you think this is a boy?" she asked, and Cecily nodded confidently.

"I pray you are right, dearest Cecily," she said and changed the subject. "Before we proceed with the reason for my mission, what news can you give me of Bess? Is she happy? Does she enjoy motherhood? Why does she not come and see her mother more? Does Henry forbid her?"

Cecily frowned. "As John Welles's wife, I am not at court so much, as you know. Hellowe—his seat in the flat fens of Lincolnshire—is a world away, God help me. It is so dull there, I would even prefer Sheriff Hutton," she groused, making Grace chuckle. "Bess is always glad to see me, but 'tis not so much Henry who guards her against her own family but that bat-fouling baggage of a mother-in-law. And"—she snorted, and Grace smiled, having forgotten Cecily's way with words till now—"do not forget, she's Jack's stepsister as well. 'Tis all so incestuous, Grace, and I dare not speak a bad word about any of them *to* any of them for fear it will be repeated. But most of all I fear the Beaufort bitch."

"Aye, Scraggy Maggie," Grace murmured. "Certes, she is the queen through Bess, I can see that. Poor Bess; she was always the dutiful one among us. I pray you, give her a kiss from me and tell her I pray nightly for her and her babes. I do not, however, pray for her husband. He has treated the queen dowager very ill indeed."

Cecily nodded. "Bess will be glad to know that you pray for her, Grace—as do I."

Grace untied and took off her cap. Unpinning her dark curls, she shook them out and breathed a sigh of pleasure as they tumbled free. Cecily pounced on a louse that fell off the linen cap and crushed it between her finger and thumb. "Ugh!" Grace groaned. "It must have come from the tavern straw. Dear Cis, pray comb my hair and make certain there are no more. They are the very devil to be rid of." While Cecily ran the rosewood comb through Grace's unruly tresses, Grace asked: "Now, tell me, how much do you know of my upcoming adventure? And will you help me?"

"I would do anything to spite Henry for forcing Jack on me," Cecily snarled. "I hate my life as it is, and if there is a chance our brother, Dickon, might take back the throne for York, then, aye, I will help you! The first thing I'd ask him is to grant me a divorce."

"But you would be excommunicated, Cecily," Grace said, aghast. She could not conceive of such a fate, but Cecily merely shrugged.

"Do not take everything I say so seriously, Grace," she answered. Then a secret smile replaced her grimace. "Besides, life is not quite as bad as I paint it. Now, let us concentrate on the matter at hand. You need a different gown, new stockings and chemise, a pair of nice crackows and a more elegant head covering. You really do look like a peasant in that." She chuckled. "One of my tiring women is about your size and, as I recently gave all my attendants new clothes, she will be able to spare you some old ones. How soon do you go to Burgundy?"

Grace put her finger to her lips. "Hush, Cecily, not so loud," she begged. "Sir Edward told me when he fetched me this morning that a Merchant Adventurer's ship will be leaving for the Low Countries on the tide this evening. He has arranged for me to be a passenger, as his first wife's niece." She wore a worried frown. "Sweet Jesu, I hope I remember that my name is Grace Peche. The abbey groom who came with me here will accompany me. And William Caxton—ah, I see you know the printer—is arranging for his son-in-law's sister to be my tiring woman for the journey. We shall all meet at the Sign of the Red Pale at four of the clock."

Cecily clapped her hands and jumped off the bed. "I wish I was going on this adventure with you, Grace Peche!" she cried.

Going to a silver coffer on the table by the window, Cecily opened it with a key hanging from her belt and took out a velvet pouch. She counted out several rose nobles and slipped them into it. Then she held up a silver necklace decorated with blue enameled flowers, and earbobs to match, and nodded. "I can spare these without my lord noticing. You must look like Father's daughter when you are presented to Aunt Margaret, or you will not get past the first usher." She put the jewelry into the pouch with the money and drew the cord tight.

Grace drew in a breath. "Aye, Aunt Margaret. I hope she is not as awe-inspiring as she sounds." She took the proffered pouch and flung her arms around Cecily's neck. "I am a little fearful, in truth," she whispered on a sob. "Pray for me. Oh, Cis, I am afraid I may never see you again. I have never been on a ship before."

"Such folly!" Cecily retorted. "People sail back and forth to Burgundy all the time. I only wish I could go. Besides, maybe Aunt Margaret will find you a young count who will take you away from your dreary life at the abbey."

That made Grace laugh. "Aye, and I am the fairy queen," she said, but she felt better.

"And did you not tell me that Cousin John is with Aunt Margaret's court? You had a soft spot for him, I seem to remember." Cecily let out a peal of merry laughter when she saw Grace's telltale blush. "Surely you do not still carry a torch, Grace? Ah, I see that you do. Such a pity, for I know a man who carries one for you."

Grace's eyes widened and her blush deepened. "You do? How is that possible, sister, when you and I have been apart for so long and, certes, do not move in the same circle anymore?"

"Tom Gower, Grace. Remember? He is now one of my husband's squires!" Cecily was triumphant when she saw Grace's look of amazement. "Once, in idle conversation, I reminded him of our visit to his farm that day, and he blushed in the very same way you do now. And I know 'twas not for me."

"I have not thought of him for many months. I cannot believe you speak the truth, Cis. Surely he is wed by now?"

Cecily shook her head. "My Lord Welles keeps him too busy. Besides, he is the second son of a lesser branch of a Yorkshire family. He is not sought after by many, and may remain a bachelor. Or"—she giggled—"go into the church. So, to save him from that fate, I requested that Jack take him into our household after our cousin of Lincoln's untimely death at Stoke." She smirked. "Jack was feeling generous in those first few months of our wedded bliss"—she spoke the last two words with such sarcasm, Grace could not forbear to smile—"and agreed. Tom's father died, you know, and his eldest brother now owns the manor."

Grace nodded. "John told me. I am pleased he is in your household now, but I cannot think you are right about his liking for me." She chose not to admit that Cecily was right about the torch she carried for John. 'Tis best kept to myself, she decided.

The two young women spent their precious time together reliving old memories of the days at Sheriff Hutton and the changes in their fortunes since then. Cecily told Grace that Edward of Warwick was still housed in the Tower and well guarded, but that his sister, Margaret, was under Bess's wing and a marriage was being contemplated with another relative of the Beauforts. "I tell you, 'tis incestuous," Cecily repeated with vehemence. "Poor little Margaret; she has become obsessed with her Bible and prayer."

Grace crossed herself and asked the Blessed Virgin to watch over the young woman and her imprisoned brother.

A knock at the door stopped the conversation, and Cecily called out, "Come." A young woman as diminutive as Grace stepped into the room, followed by two servants carrying a plain wooden chest. The men bowed and retired, leaving the attendant to close the door behind them. She curtsied and stood quietly by while Cecily hurried to the coffer and flung open the lid. " 'Tis perfect, Kate, thank you!" she cried, pulling out a pale blue taffeta gown edged with dark blue velvet. "This was the gown I thought of immediately when I knew my sister Grace was in need. And this other one," she said, throwing the blue to Grace and holding up another dress of dark red worsted wool, "will be for traveling. And this hood is pretty enough. You may go now, Kate. Lady Grace is only borrowing these, and will return them anon."

"Aye, my lady," Kate said, nervously curtsying again. Although barely thirteen, she knew she had no right to question why the clothes were needed. She slipped out and closed the door.

"And now I must commit to memory the reason for my journey," Grace said, smoothing out the somewhat crumpled letter on her lap. Such a hurry-scurry about one small piece of paper, she thought, but then, a crown could topple because of its contents.

13

Burgundy

SPRING 1490

Sir Edward led Grace, Edgar, and Caxton's relative, Judith Croppe, to the waiting boat at the Westminster wharf and settled them on the cushions for the short voyage to the Pool of London. It was William Caxton who had devised a plausible reason for Grace's visit to the Duchess Margaret, and that reason was in a bag tied securely to her belt. Grace could feel the comforting weight of the leather-bound book against her leg as she thought back to the scene at the workshop.

" 'Tis well known her grace loves books, my lady," the old man had told her. "When you seek an audience, you should mention my name and that you have a gift from me. She will welcome this particular book, of that I have no doubt." Grace had turned to the title page and read *The Moral Proverbs of Christine de Pisan* and nodded earnestly, although she would have preferred a copy of *Morte d'Arthur* to while away the hours on the upcoming voyage.

"You knew my lady aunt well, did you not, Master Caxton?" she asked.

"Was she a . . . will she . . . ?" Her stammering expressed her anxiety at meeting the imposing duchess.

"Aye, I know her," Caxton said, fingering a small ruby ring that hung on a chain around his neck and smiling. "She was most generous to me in so many ways. I would not be here were it not for her. Not only did she display a fine mind, but she had an admirable sense of humor as well. Never fear, Lady Grace. When she sees this book, I promise you will see her softer side."

"I hope you are right, sir," Grace said, and carefully replaced the book in its bag.

Caxton leaned forward and whispered: "I happen to know Duchess Margaret has a partiality for rose-petal jam, should you wish to—forgive the pun—sweeten the audience with her."

Grace had given him one of her most brilliant smiles, and it was in that smile that Caxton knew she was truly her father's daughter.

The velvet pouch with Cecily's money was safely tied around Grace's neck and tucked under her bodice. She only wished her heart would stop racing and her stomach heaving. Sir Edward patted her knee as the boat-men pushed off with their oars.

"Courage, my little one," he said. "Master Ward, the captain of the *Mary Ellen*, will see to your comfort, and you have my letter of introduction to my agent in Bruges. You should be there in two days, if all goes well and the winds are favorable."

He reached into a purse at his waist and brought out a small packet. " 'Tis the powder of galingale for the *mal de mer*. Take it when you sail past the Isle of Thanet and leave England behind; it will settle your bile."

Perhaps I should take it now, Grace thought, as her fear mounted and her belly turned somersaults. "I thank you, Sir Edward," she murmured. "You are very kind."

They were approaching London Bridge, with three-storied houses perched precariously atop it and its many narrow arches spanning the river from Bishopsgate to Southwark. "Up oars!" cried the boatmen in unison as the boat shot through the fast-moving water beneath the bridge, and then they dipped them again while chanting "Rumbelow, furbelow" to regain their rhythm. Grace could see the tall tower of Bermondsey Abbey on the south bank in the distance now, and she wondered what the queen dowager would say when Cecily went to tell her that Grace was on her way to Burgundy. She trembled to think of Elizabeth's possible anger and sent a prayer Cecily's way. Brampton, believing she was cold, wrapped his short mantle about her.

"There she is," he said, pointing to a small caravel anchored close to the Wapping wharves, the flags and pennants on its two masts fluttering in the wind. He hailed the ship and a heavy rope ladder was heaved overboard.

"I will go first, Mistress Grace," Judith Croppe offered, seeing Grace was unsure of how to proceed. "I climb a ladder to my bed every night. Certes, this must be much the same. Follow me." And to the surprise of the men in the boat below, she fearlessly negotiated the knots on the swinging ladder and was hauled up on the deck by two swarthy mariners. It was only ten feet to the lowest part of the gunwale, but to Grace, swaying in the small boat beneath, the ship's side looked like a mountain.

Suddenly Edgar picked her up, threw her easily over his shoulder and clambered up one-handed. She closed her eyes and prayed, listening to Sir Edward laughing below. A sailor soon had her in his arms and set her lightly on the wooden deck. Edgar's trusty staff and the bundle of clothes were passed up as Sir Edward called a greeting to the master of the ship. Grace peered over the gunwale and stammered her thanks and farewell. She had felt safe and comforted by Brampton's easy confidence these past two days; now she felt small and vulnerable, watching the rowing boat pull away. Brampton and his servants would leave on the tide bound for Lisbon the next day, Grace remembered, as she gave him a final wave.

When the ship stood out to sea past Margate, Grace felt the waves beneath her roughen and the ship creak and groan like an old man rising from his chair. Far from being frightened, as she had imagined, she was exhilarated by the spray in her face, the billowing sails and the wind across the bow. She thought about taking Brampton's powders, as she was convinced she would need them as a first-time sailor, but when she saw Judith's green face and white knuckles gripping the gunwale, her concern was all for her companion. She took the packet from her pouch and went to fetch a cup of rainwater from the barrel lashed to the mast. Stirring some of the gray grains into it, she handed it to Judith and advised her to drink it all. As the young woman examined the contents suspiciously, Grace turned to see poor Edgar retching over the side and immediately ministered the rest of the packet to him. Heeding Sir Edward's words that fresh air was best when the *mal de mer* struck, she settled both the servants in a sheltered nook on the foredeck out of the wind and found some old sacks to cushion their heads. They both stared up at her miserably, and they looked so wretched she had a hard time not smiling.

"I am sure the galingale will help you. Sir Edward promised it would," she said cheerfully. "Is there anything more I can do for you?"

"A bucket, mistress, if you please," Edgar moaned, heaving again. Grace looked about and saw a sailor tying off a line nearby and asked him to fetch a pail. The young man grinned, seeing the two seasick passengers huddled together. "Aye, mistress, leave it to me."

Grace wandered back down to her quarters, a small cabin she and Judith had been given next to the captain's. She removed her mantle and felt a momentary pang of guilt when she realized she was still in possession of Sir Edward's handsome cloak. She folded it up carefully and covered it with the rough blanket on the hammock. It would add to her appearance when she sought an audience with Aunt Margaret, she decided. Her stomach was grumbling and she realized she was hungry. Had it really been so many hours ago in Cecily's apartments when she had last eaten anything? The sun had gone down on the late June evening and the stars were starting to appear. Master Ward stomped down the companionway and called to her from behind the curtain that served as a door for the ladies' privacy.

"Would you and your attendant like to join me and the other gentleman passenger for supper, Mistress Peche?" he asked. "The food is always good on the first night out from London."

He was unprepared for the speed with which Grace appeared on his side of the curtain. "I would indeed, Master Ward," she enthused. "But my tiring woman, Judith, is under the weather. She and our escort are as comfortable as possible on deck. I pray they will be able to sleep."

"Ah, the *mal de mer*." Ward laughed. "Aye, sleep will come—'tis often the first sign of seasickness, mistress. I see you are not suffering. Have you made other sea voyages, then?" He took her arm and conveyed her into his cabin, where two young cabin boys were setting out a haunch of meat, a pie, loaves of fresh bread and cheese for their captain and the London goldsmith, her fellow passenger, who was also going to Bruges. Grace saw the boys were no more than ten or twelve years old and was astonished to discover that most began their sailing apprenticeships so young.

After satisfying her hunger and sharing a glass of mediocre wine with the two men, she begged to be excused and fell exhausted into her hammock, pulling the soft wool mantle around her. "Dear Saint Sibylline, intercede for me with our Lord and Saviour and His gracious mother, Mary, for I do not believe I can stay awake long enough to pray . . ." She was asleep before she could whisper *"Amen"* into the pitch-black cabin.

THE WIND WAS fair and Master Ward was confident they would sight land by the end of the second day, and he was right. The flat lands of Flanders were a long, low line upon the horizon as the ship beat its way up the coast to the harbor of Sluis. "We are not small enough to be able to sail down the canal into Bruges, Mistress Peche, but we will unload at Damme," the captain told her as she stood watching the first foreign land she had ever seen grow into recognizable beaches, with marshland and fields beyond, and the occasional church spire. It did not look much different from England, she mused.

"Do you speak French?" Ward asked. "The language of Bruges, or *Brugge* as it is called by the Flemish people, is Dutch, but most will speak some French. Indeed, 'tis the rule of the French-born dukes of Burgundy who turned this into a frog-speaking land," he explained. "Our own Princess Margaret—King Richard's sister—made this very same journey more than twenty years ago to marry Duke Charles, the present duke's grandfather. I remember seeing the procession in London all those years ago when Lady Margaret sat behind the great earl of Warwick, as he led her through the streets to receive our farewell. 'Twas before you were born, I have no doubt, mistress. We thought 'twere a grand affair, but 'tis said it was a poor show compared with the welcome parade the people of Bruges gave their new duchess. Ten days of feasting and jousting followed! Imagine that."

"Imagine," Grace echoed with awe, pretending this was the first time she had heard of Aunt Margaret's magnificent *joyeuse entrée* into her new country's wealthiest city.

HER OWN ENTRY into Bruges was far more mundane. The *Mary Ellen* sailed into the Zwin estuary and up as far as Damme, where the passengers disembarked and goods were to be unloaded on the flat barges that plied the lowland waterways. Edgar and Judith gratefully stumbled down the gangplank and onto solid ground. Grace bade Master Ward farewell and paid one of her rose nobles for the voyage for all three.

"There is Sir Edward's man, mistress," the captain called after her, pointing to a rotund, rosy-cheeked man in a short black gown and high hat who was checking barrels as they were rolled down a parallel ramp. "Heer Gerards!" He called loudly in Flemish, "This is Brampton's niece. You are to take her to Brugge."

Gerards looked at Grace with interest. He had not known Sir Edward had a niece—and certainly not such a pretty niece. He waddled over and gave a small bow. "*Mevrouw*, I call myself Pieter Gerards. I in your service am." His English was passable, and Grace breathed more freely. She had hoped he would not speak French to her, as she could read it tolerably well, but she could not speak it as fluently as her sisters did, as the nuns had been keener on knowing Latin than French.

"I thank you, Master Gerards," she said as confidently as she could. "I am Grace Peche. Here is a letter from Sir Edward explaining my visit. I trust you can help me complete my mission. These are my servants, and they will be accompanying me."

Gerards took the offered letter and broke open his master's seal. He let out a whistle when he read the instructions. "*You are to escort my niece, Grace Peche, to Madame la Grande's court and arrange for an audience. I would deliver my message to her grace, the dowager duchess, myself, but our business interests in Lisbon have necessitated my returning there immediately.*" The rest of the letter explained the nature of the trading problems in Lisbon, with further instructions on how to proceed with them in Bruges. Finally he wrote: "*I am counting on you to give Mistress Peche every courtesy and to see her back safely on a ship to London as soon as possible.*" The merchant puffed out his cheeks and let the air out slowly as he translated and took all of this in. Grace looked around the bustling port and admired the new town hall with its gothic ornamentation.

"I take you now to be refreshed to a *herberg*. Come, please," he said, ushering Grace along a side street by the hall. She assumed *herberg* was a house, and when Gerards pointed to an imposing stone house with large, high windows she was pleasantly surprised. However, he passed it by, saying, "Princess Margaret of York by your country is together with Duke

Charles married therein," he told Grace proudly. Grace was intrigued and stared back up at the building, imagining the scene. Already she was experiencing so many connections to the only member of her father's siblings she had not yet met.

"Your uncle say you to see the old duchess. She in Malines is resting. It is long way from Brugge, but we there will go in *morgen*—in morning." Grace's heart sank; she had hoped she would be able to deliver the letter there in Bruges. Sir Edward had not said anything about Malines.

When Gerards reached the entrance of a spotlessly clean lime-washed building a few doors away, its telltale sign swinging above them, he repeated *"Herberg!"* and opened the thick wooden door. Ah, an inn, Grace thought. 'Tis like *auberge* in French. They entered the low-beamed public room, where several people were sharing bowls of food on long tables. Judith and Edgar eyed the food eagerly after two days of purging. Edgar had grumbled to Judith on the way that "my belly is flattened against my backbone. Look't, my tunic hangs off me now." Judith admitted that she, too, was ravenous, although she could not see where Edgar had pared down one inch of his substantial girth.

Gerards ordered food and ale for them all and counted a few ridders out for the landlord. "I to the work must return, *mevrouw*. You keep yourself here. I return, *ja?*"

"*Ja* . . . I mean, aye," Grace replied. "We are in your hands, sir."

Puzzled, Gerards turned his palms up and inspected them, shrugged and left.

Several hunks of bread and cheese, a rabbit pie and a bowl of mussels later, the trio of travelers felt better. Edgar had downed most of the blackjack of ale by himself, and Grace did not admonish him this time after his suffering on the ship.

"Edgar, who is your overseer at the abbey?" she asked him. "I pray her grace the queen dowager will explain your absence to him. If you lose any wages because of this, know that you will be well rewarded for your service to me. In truth, I could not make this journey without you guarding me. But I warrant taking commands from a lady is not what you are accustomed to, am I right?" She smiled at him, hunched over his horn cup of ale, and his shoulders straightened and he lifted his head proudly.

"Nay, Mistress *Peche*." He grinned, hoping she would notice he had remembered her new name, and she nodded an acknowledgment. "Brother Gregory holds the purse strings in the stables. He be not kind, and no one dares cross him. He has threatened us with Hell, and I be not inclined to go there," he said, shuddering at the thought. "I be an undergroom, but I hope to be head groom one day, and . . ." he stopped. He had never voiced this ambition to anyone before. He waited for her to berate him for speaking so freely, but she sat patiently waiting for him to continue and so plunged ahead. "In for a penny, in for a pound!" he said under his breath. "If I do your bidding well, mistress, will you speak for me?" he said, gabbling on before he lost his nerve, and her nod of assent encouraged him to continue. "The others mock me and call me a simpkin, but I can talk to the horses, you know," he told her, leaning forward and almost knocking over his cup in his childlike eagerness. "They listen to me."

"I have seen you, Edgar," Grace replied, her head cocked and her eyes guileless. "Perhaps when we return you could tell the horses not to frighten me so. I love animals, but horses . . . Well, they are so large, you see, and I am so . . . small," she explained.

Edgar stared at the lovely young woman in front of him. He was only a lowly groom, and he knew she was really the Lady Grace Plantagenet, daughter of a king, and yet she was speaking to him. His simple mind tried to digest this extraordinary fact, and the only way he could think of expressing his undying devotion was to clamber off his bench, lumber around to her side, kneel and kiss the hem of her worsted gown. Several customers watched this little scene with amusement; Grace looked on with embarrassment.

"I pray you return to your seat, Edgar. We do not need to attract attention," she said, more sternly than she intended, and his face clouded a little. "Master Gerards should be here anon, and so you should drain your cup." She gave him a quick smile and he got up off his knees and sat back down next to Judith, who had not said a word since attacking her piece of pie.

Gerards was as good as his word, and an hour later he returned and escorted Grace to a barge that would convey them all to the Waterhall in Bruges, where the English Merchant Adventurers lived and worked. Their boat was pulled by a Flemish great horse, which was led along the three-mile towpath by its owner. As they drew closer to the towers of Bruges, the bells began to ring out the Terce. Soon they were gliding under the Dampoort gate and along a canal that boasted high, step-gabled brick houses on either side, graceful trees and pairs of swans that reached their long necks around to clean their feathers. Grace thought she had never seen such a beautiful place.

"You will in my house sleep, *Mevrouw* Peche. Tomorrow we to Malines journey, *ja?*" Gerards told the young woman, whose beauty and connection to Brampton were making him believe she would be an excellent choice of bride for his son, although he worried, with her dark skin, whether she might be a Jew.

Grace thanked him, looking forward to a comfortable bed after her time in the ship's hammock.

Whether it was the unaccustomed beer made with hops or the eel pie that Mevrouw Gerards served for supper, Grace did not know, but that night she tossed and turned and dreamed of the old hag who had told her fortune in Winchester. "You will see both of them go to meet their Maker. It be dangerous for you to know them, but you will help them. Better not make friends of young men, my lady." Ugly Edith's face melted into Elizabeth's fair one. "You will help me, Grace? You will bring me news of my son," she pleaded, reaching her arms out to Grace, "before I go into my grave?" As she stepped back, Grace could see a freshly dug hole behind the queen and before she could stop her Elizabeth began to float, featherlight, downwards into the earth. Screaming, Grace desperately tried to catch the dying woman's hand, but there was nothing to hold on to. Elizabeth's ghostly body drifted down and down . . .

"Mistress Grace, wake up!" Judith whispered in the dark, shaking Grace's shoulder. "You were dreaming, 'tis all."

"I am very afraid, Judith," Grace said, sitting up and clutching her servant's arm. "I dreamed of death."

"Sweet Jesu, 'tis a bad omen," Judith muttered, crossing herself. She slipped out of bed and felt for the tinderbox. Within a few seconds she had lit a taper and padded across to fetch Grace a cup of ale. "Drink this, mistress. 'Tis said if you tell your dream it will not come true. Come, tell me quickly before you forget."

"Maybe tomorrow, Judith," Grace answered pretending to yawn. She could not risk revealing her identity by retelling her dream. "But say an *ave* for me."

. . .

GRACE WAS CONVINCED Master Gerards had led them around in a circle when the towers and spires of Malines came into view late in the afternoon. They had passed neat farms and fields that ringed the city before slowing their horses to a walk to cross the moat bridge and ride through the fortified gate in the city wall. Except for the canals, the city was similar to Bruges, and Grace was impressed by its gothic grandeur. The market square matched Bruges for space and splendid buildings. St. Rumbold's cathedral rose majestically behind it, and as the little group rode past, its double carillon of bells rang out over the city from its monumental tower, stopping conversation for those directly beneath. Grace was astonished at the multitude of people crowding the streets and asked Gerards if there was a special occasion that had brought so many to the town. He turned back to her riding pillion on his sturdy jennet and explained that while Bruges was the heart of commerce in Burgundy, Malines—or *Mechelen*, as the Flemish called the city—was the seat of legislative government.

"Forgive me, sir, but I thought you said Ghent had that honor," Grace said, wondering why this country did not have one central city like London.

"Ghent seats the judges, *mevrouw*. Here the councilors of the duke sits," he said in his broken English. "There is the council chamber," he said, pointing to the newly refurbished cloth hall.

A steady drizzle began as they turned their backs on St. Rumbold's and made their way towards the Veemarkt, which at this late hour was empty of its livestock, and finally to the ducal residence. Grace was disappointed when they were turned away at the palace gate. Come again on the morrow, they were told. Madame La Grande will see petitioners after Matins. A friendly guard told them where there was suitable lodging for the night, and Edgar, with Judith seated behind his sturdy back, and Gerards urged their horses in the direction of the inn.

That night the travelers slept on mattresses of clean straw in a room that overlooked the Dyle River. Grace hardly slept a wink, unused to the loud snoring that came from Edgar and the noises from the taproom beneath. She made sure William Caxton's book and Elizabeth's letter were well hidden underneath her and lay contemplating her meeting with Aunt Margaret. She tried to imagine the scene, but a handsome, familiar face kept intruding on her thoughts.

John, she told him, go away! 'Twould be too good to be true were you
indeed here.

FIRST THING THE next morning, Grace acted on one of the more practical
thoughts that had come to her during the long night. "Judith, you must go
with Edgar and find me some rose-petal jam," she announced. Glad of the
chance to explore the city, Judith took the coin Grace gave her and set off,
with Edgar following a customary step behind.

Gerards had found a well-lit corner of the taproom, now void of noisy
drinkers, where he could sit and enter items into a small accounting book
and wait with Grace for Judith to return. His admiring look had told Grace
that the blue silk dress she had donned for the audience with Margaret met
with his approval. She wished she could have practiced the little speech she
had prepared for this meeting, but she was fairly confident Aunt Margaret
would do all the talking and that she would assume her usual role of listener. Instead she recited the letter from Elizabeth in her mind again.

An hour later, Grace and Gerards were in a second antechamber in the
palace, after Gerards had given their credentials to an usher and they had
left Judith to wait in the first hall, full of anxious petitioners. The usher
took in Grace's fashionable gabled headdress, on loan from Cecily, the elegant gown and her aristocratic bearing, and nodded. The retainer knew
Madame la Grande's door was always open to anyone from England, and
he had recognized Sir Edward Brampton's name.

"*Passez, Monsieur, Madame*," he said in the language of the court. Grace
smiled her thanks to him as she and Gerards proceeded through the archway and into the duchess's presence chamber. She gasped in delight at the
magnificent room, its painted columns decorated with golden fleurs-de-
lys, the two-headed eagle of the Hapsburgs and the white rose of York.
Colorful banners hung from the ceiling and, at the end of the room, a
canopied dais was set with a carved wooden throne. Standing in front of it
and conversing with a kneeling courtier was a tall woman, a little stooped
by her advancing years, but still an imposing figure, clothed in black and
gold damask with sable at her neck and hem.

Gerards, too, was obviously impressed and whispered to Grace that
it was his first time in the dowager duchess's presence. A space cleared
in front of the dais as the courtier kissed Margaret's hand and bowed

his way backwards out of her purview. Another man came forward, took Gerards's and Grace's names and announced them to the duchess and her small retinue. Gerards escorted Grace forward, bowed and immediately fell to his knees, allowing Grace to take center stage. Her knees wobbling, she moved forward and executed a low curtsy, staying on the floor until a surprisingly youthful voice gave her leave to rise.

Grace raised her eyes to Margaret's gray ones and immediately recognized the likeness to Uncle Richard's. Otherwise, Grace thought, she resembled Grandmother Cecily, with her fair English skin, blond hair—now turning white—and unusual height.

"Mistress Peche," Margaret said in English. "We greet you well. How is your uncle? Sir Edward has done this court and England many good services through the years. I trust he is well?" Margaret paused and frowned. "I trust you do not have bad news for me, my child?"

Grace looked around her and, observing she was not attracting much attention, lowered her voice, murmuring, "With the deepest respect, I would talk to you in private, your grace. 'Tis a matter of importance to our family."

Sweet Jesu, that was not what I should have said, Grace thought miserably. That came out all wrong. She stammered an apology, her eyes pleading. "I beg your pardon, madam. I mean . . ." she faltered, and Margaret reached out, took her hand and encouraged her to join her on the dais.

"By all that is holy, child, you do not have to be so frightened of me. I am no ogre. You have a family problem that you would like my help with? Is that it, my dear? Are Sir Edward or his wife in trouble?"

Grace looked down at Gerards, still on his knees in front of the steps, and was at a loss as to how to tell Aunt Margaret who she really was and yet keep up the masquerade with the merchant. As if Margaret could read her mind, the duchess suddenly turned to a blond giant of a man close to the dais and said: *"Guillaume, venez nous accompanier jusqu'aux mes apartements."* Turning to Grace, she said, "Come, mistress. We shall take some refreshment in my chambers. Your escort can wait, can he not?" She then astonished Grace by addressing Gerards in his native Dutch, who nodded his willingness to wait, got up off his knees and gave Grace the tooled leather bag he had carried for her into the palace. He stared after Grace and bowed with the rest of the court as Margaret exited.

Each room Grace passed through seemed more opulent and magnificent than the one before. And she had thought Westminster, Windsor and Shene grand! The poster bed in Margaret's private chamber was an enormous piece of furniture hung with green velvet curtains, into which were woven her marguerite device. Grace entered behind the duchess and her lady-in-waiting, a pretty woman who was several months with child. "Henriette is my chevalier's wife," Margaret explained as Guillaume swept Margaret a bow and left the room after blowing Henriette a kiss. "They are quite sweet on each other. 'Tis a change to see such devotion between a husband and wife." She sighed, caressing the ears of a wolfhound that whined in pleasure when he saw his owner. "Are you married, mistress? I am, as you must know, widowed these many years. Aye, Lance, I am happy to see you again, too. Now lie down, there's a good dog. Lancelot is from England, and so he listens only to English commands," she confided.

Grace could not believe this woman who was talking to her so amicably was the dragon lady of Bess's and Cecily's childhood memories. She stood while Margaret settled herself in a high-backed chair and Henriette placed a footstool under her mistress's feet.

"I have to stand on that dais all morning, listening to petitions and complaints. You have provided me with a respite, my dear Mistress Peche. My feet seem to grow more delicate every passing day. *Merci*, Henriette," she thanked her attendant. "We shall enjoy a cup of wine together, and then I must return. Now, what is it that you must tell me?"

Grace opened the bag and first drew out the jam. "I did not know, madam, if I would be able to give this to you myself, but please accept it with my deepest respect. A mutual friend told me 'twas a particular favorite of yours."

Margaret's eyes lit up at the sight of the jar. "Rose-petal jam, is it?" she cried, seizing it and untying the cloth lid. Then she looked curiously at Grace. "Who, pray, of your acquaintances knew about my penchant?"

A mischievous smile curled Grace's mouth as her earlier fear dissipated at the expression of the duchess's childlike glee over a simple jar of jam. "The same acquaintance who wished to give you this," she said and removed the book in its velvet pouch from the larger bag. She held it out, saying, "And to be remembered to you with all duty and devotion," surprising herself with her eloquence.

"A book," Margaret cried, drawing it out and holding it close to her chest. "It cannot be from your uncle; he does not know of my passion for rose-petal jam." She opened the embossed leather cover and saw the title page. Grace saw a deep blush rise from the bosom of Margaret's square-necked gown and suffuse her entire neck and face in a rosy glow. "*The Dictes and Sayings of the Moral Philosophers,* translated by Anthony, Earl Rivers," Margaret read aloud. "William Caxton," she murmured, and Grace saw tears in the duchess's eyes. "Tell me 'twas Caxton himself who gave you this, Mistress Peche?"

Grace assented but was puzzled. Surely Aunt Margaret and William Caxton . . . nay, it is not poss—. Certes, she suddenly realized, 'tis Anthony, Lord Rivers, for whom my aunt blushes and weeps. She curled her mouth into a knowing smile, remembering the conversation with Bess those many years ago at Sheriff Hutton.

Margaret drew in a sharp breath. "Do that again, mistress," she commanded, surprising Grace. "You put me in mind of someone." She thought for a moment and then chuckled. "Why, certes, it must be Sir Edward."

Grace seized her moment. "Nay, madam, 'tis another Edward whom I resemble. I am afraid I have had to come to you in a disguise. I am not Mistress Grace Peche, but Lady Grace Plantagenet, your brother Edward's—"

Margaret's mouth had dropped open, but she finished Grace's sentence without thinking. "Bastard!" she exclaimed, staring at Grace with new eyes. "Certes, you are Ned's, although how you lack for inches, I cannot conceive. But your smile is his." She clapped her hands together, laughing. "My niece, Grace! How delightful this is!" Then she frowned and lowered her voice. "But why the masquerade? Why are you come?"

"I am come to give you a message, your grace. I was sworn to secrecy by my mistress," she said, glancing at Henriette, who was seemingly focused on the sewing of a tiny gown. She had no intention of mentioning Elizabeth's name to anyone but Margaret.

Margaret turned to Henriette. "*Cher Madame de la Baume, veuillez chercher mon neveu, s'il vous plaît,*" she said pleasantly, and Henriette rose at once, curtsied and left the room. "Never fear, Grace. Henriette does not speak a word of English, but you are right not to trust those you do not know. And, in some cases, those you do," she muttered to herself.

Grace told Margaret the whole story and how she became Elizabeth's messenger. "So I thought it safest to commit the letter to memory, your grace."

Margaret was amused but impressed. " 'Twas as well you did not fall into Henry's hands, my dear, or you might have been shown the rack," she teased her. "Sadly such a possibility is not out of the question. Since the alliance with England last year, my son-law-law Maximilian has been loath to complain to Henry about spying on our court. He has also suggested that I curb my enthusiasm for giving Henry headaches. The archduke and I agree on many things, but my loyalty to the house of York is not one of them, more's the pity." Margaret was pacing in front of the fireplace, its sculptured hood bearing her motto, *Bien en aviengne*, in painted relief. "But I ramble—the price of getting old, I fear. You have done well, Grace. Certes, it took courage to come all this way by yourself. Now, quickly, before you forget, what were the letter's contents?"

When Grace had recited the letter word for word, Margaret arched a finely plucked brow and gave a short laugh. "Elizabeth always enjoyed a conspiracy. A coded letter would have been amusing for her to word. And no one will know your hand. How clever of her!"

With her burden relieved, Grace was eager to tell of her part in the addressing of the missive. "We chose Dame Meg Broome, hoping you would understand the wordplay," she said.

Margaret mouthed the words, puzzled, and then her face lit up: "Broome, *planta genistra*, Plantagenet. Certes! Ingenious."

Grace blushed at the compliment.

"You have had quite an adventure, Grace," Margaret said, looking at her niece with admiration. "You have your father's blood in your veins, in truth." She began to pace again, and Grace decided it must be how her aunt liked to think and was reminded of John. Finally she stopped and weighed her words. "As we have some unaccustomed privacy, I think it best to give you a verbal message to return to Elizabeth, and I believe I can trust you to remember it." She winked. "It is this: Tell her she has every reason to hope; I believe her younger son is alive and well." Grace's expression of joy caused Margaret to hold up her hand. "I regret I can tell you no more about him, but suffice it to say that when the time is right we shall see about overturning the Tudor's throne. Tell her to hold steadfast, and I will do all in my power to return England to Yorkist rule. The less she knows, the safer it is for her. We do not want Henry torturing her—or you—for information, now, do we?" She chuckled when she saw Grace's horror. "I am but jesting, my dear."

There was a knock at the door and both women jumped. "What gooses we are, to be sure." The dowager laughed and called, "*Entrez.* Ah, there you are, nephew. I think you must know this young lady."

Throwing etiquette to the wind and squeaking with excitement, Grace flew into the arms of an astonished John.

"Aye, I see that you do," Margaret said softly, smiling at the scene. Henriette stood in the doorway, staring at the young people, puzzled by the whole episode, but then bustled to Margaret's side to tell her she was expected again in the presence chamber. Sighing, Margaret allowed her attendant to straighten her turbaned headdress before leaving the room and admonishing the young people to "behave yourselves."

"I cannot believe my eyes," John said, holding Grace at arm's length. "What is my little wren doing in Malines? And in a gown that is quite unworthy of you, in truth. Has Aunt Elizabeth fallen even lower that she could not dress you better for a visit to the most fashionable court in Europe?"

"Clothes do not make the man, John—or the woman," Grace retorted. "I am still the same person, even if you do not approve of my gown. And her grace is not responsible for it, if you must know."

"Temper, temper!" John teased, grinning down at her. "I've told you before, I like you when you are indignant. Nay, spare me your blushes, Grace, and tell me what you are doing here."

Indeed Grace did feel underdressed beside her cousin's brilliant blue satin pleated jacket, trimmed in gold and pearls, its slashed sleeves revealing shimmering white silk beneath. His well-shaped legs were encased in parti-colored hose and his codpiece was tied with a jaunty bow. A soft black beaver hat topped his long and fashionably curly hair, and although she acknowledged he was still the handsome John of her dreams, Grace thought she preferred him in his plainer English garb. He took her hand and drew her onto a cushioned settle, where she had to repeat her adventure for the second time in half an hour. John's eyes were wide with astonishment when she finished. He let out a whistle, and Lancelot obediently eased himself off the tiled floor and loped towards him. "Nay, my dear old hound, I did not mean to disturb your sleep." He laughed, scratching the dog's coarse hair just above his tail. The dog lifted his huge head heavenward in ecstasy. "Ah, you cannot reach this spot, can you, boy?" He continued massaging the dog's bony haunches and told Grace, "I am speechless. You have shown more fortitude than many of the knightly fellows I rub elbows with. And now I assume you must make your way home the same way."

Chagrined, Grace made a face and nodded. She had not wanted to think about the return journey. "I suppose I must, for it would not do to be found out as Grace Plantagenet on this side of the channel, when no one in England knows I left there—except for Cecily, Sir Edward, Master Caxton and by now, I hope, the queen dowager. Aunt Margaret tells me Henry has spies everywhere," she said, looking about her nervously.

John laughed. "Do not imagine that Aunt Margaret and Maximilian do not have their own in England, my innocent wren. But aye, it would not do for anyone to know you have been here."

"Certes, my absence will have been noticed at the abbey, but I suspect her grace will cover it cleverly."

"I have no doubt." John snorted. "Her life has been filled with deceit."

"You may think so, but you cannot deny Elizabeth has been good to me," Grace retorted.

"You are too good-hearted to know what the rest of us think, Grace. She has denied you a life with your sisters, or others of your age. You could have been here with me, or with Cecily and her ancient viscount. Aunt Elizabeth likes you because you do not gainsay her and do as you are told, and so she selfishly keeps you by her side." He smiled at her. "I warrant those monks aren't much fun, are they?"

Grace chuckled. " 'Tis true, but I have learned much about vegetables and lambing in the meantime."

They were still laughing when Henriette returned followed by servants carrying steaming dishes of food.

"Your aunt wishes you to eat without her, *messire*. She is hearing the grievance of a merchant from Antwerp who claims he was cheated by a member of her household. The man has obviously not heard that it is unwise to challenge her grace on the loyalty of her servants," she said, laughing. "I pity the poor fellow."

John pulled the settle up to the table to see what Margaret's chef had prepared for them. "We can think about your return to England after we have sampled Bernard's fare," he said, lifting the lid off some venison in frumenty and inhaling the delicate aromas. He lowered his voice and turned back to her. "But for now, know that I am right glad to see you again, Grace. I would not be here if it had not been for you, and I owe you my life."

"Oh, pish," she replied modestly. "I must thank you for the note; 'twas gladly received."

He lifted her hand and kissed her fingers, charmed by the blush that crept up her neck but, guessing the cause, he moved a few inches away. "So, cousin, has Elizabeth found a bridegroom for you yet?"

"Nay, you know you are in my heart always, however hopeless," Grace whispered, and it was his turn to redden. "I, too, imagined you would be husband to some lovely Flemish noblewoman by now. Surely Aunt Margaret knows many who would be glad to marry a Plantagenet prince."

"Aye," he admitted ruefully. "She has put several forward, and even my bastardy does not seem to turn them away. I have learned that the good Duke Philip had twenty-three bastards—aye, three and twenty—here at court, but only one legitimate child, Duke Charles, who was Aunt Margaret's husband. So we are in good company, it seems." And they both laughed.

"So you are not promised?" Grace asked.

John grinned. "Nay, I am not. I told my aunt that I would only wed an Englishwoman, and she has not attempted to fob me off on anyone since. I am twenty years old and know I should think about a wife, but in the meantime . . ." he paused, spearing a piece of meat on his knife and waving it about. "In the meantime . . ."

His smirk irritated Grace, who pushed away her trencher, got to her feet and exclaimed: "In the meantime, because women throw themselves upon you, you do not see the need. Is that what you would say?"

John's fork stopped midway to his open mouth as he stared at her and did not heed the milky gravy that ran down onto his sleeve.

"You still take me for a green girl, John, when I am a grown woman and should have a husband of my own," she declared, two pink spots appearing on her cheeks. "Why do you boast of your conquests in front of me?"

John was at once contrite. "Forgive me, Grace." He got to his feet and took her clenched fists in his own to stop them from trembling. "I would not hurt you for the world. You are the best friend a fellow ever had. Forgive me?"

Henriette cleared her throat, and the pair sprang apart, remembering they were not alone. *"Pardonnez-moi, Messire Jean, mais le repas refroidit,"* she apologized, pointing at the food.

MARGARET INSISTED GRACE stay at the palace that night and sent word to Pieter Gerards that he was to wait at the inn with Judith and Edgar until Grace was returned to his care. "I would read you a letter from a young protégé of mine after I have shown you the gardens and we have taken some fresh air. There has been plague in the city, I have heard, and my doctor allows me to walk only when 'tis not hot or cloudy, and then not at noontime. Now is perfect," Margaret said after putting her head out of the window. "John, will you accompany us?"

The carillon of St. Rumbold's rang the None as the small group stepped into the formal gardens behind the residence. "I do like it here," Margaret said, sniffing the air, which was perfumed with roses. "Ten years ago this month, I had just landed in England for the first time since my marriage." She sighed, absently pulling petals from a half-spent rose. "I have not been since, but I fear 'tis not as I remember, and so I stay here."

John chuckled. "Aye, aunt. From all I hear, you would be most uncomfortable there, as it appears Henry looks upon you as the sharpest thorn in his side. I doubt he has forgiven you for the Lambert Simnel affair."

"But that was not all my doing, nephew!" Margaret retorted. "I lent my support, aye, but I knew the boy was a pretender from the start. Did you not see him? He had all the bearing of a kitchen lad—which is where he ended up, *n'est ce pas?* I hoped Lincoln and Lovell would be victorious and release the real Edward of Warwick from the Tower." She looked around and, seeing only the requisite retinue of her own attendants trailing behind her, said low: "I have a far bigger burr to place under Henry's saddle, when the time is right."

"Will you tease us, aunt, or spill the beans?" John asked boldly. Grace was in awe of his easy way of talking to their imposing aunt, but the duchess appeared to enjoy John's familiarity.

"Not so fast, nephew. My plan is not fully hatched, although, certes, you will play a part in it. Aye, I see that pleases you." Margaret chuckled, and Grace saw that her aunt had lost several teeth. "As you may guess, the news that Dickon of York has been found must be significant to it. But I want Henry to chew on his nails for a good, long time once this rumor reaches him and before we act."

"You know where he is, don't you, Aunt Margaret?" John gasped, and Grace trembled with excitement when she saw the answering smile.

"I will say no more, impertinent boy," the duchess retorted, "beyond that soon it will be put about that my nephew—he who all thought had perished with his brother in the Tower of London—is alive. That should put the fox among the hens," she told them, rubbing her hands together. "Also, you should expect to go on a journey in the not-too-distant future, John, when the plans are ripe." She turned to Grace. "And by giving Elizabeth my message about her son, you, too, will be playing your part. Let the rumors begin! We shall send you back to Master Gerards on the morrow, but I will insist he put you on a ship out of Antwerp. 'Tis faster from here. Now smile for me, child, it reminds me of my brother."

"Tell me more of him, I beg of you, your grace," Grace said, hoping she was not breaking with court convention. "I never knew him, you see."

"I would have thought Elizabeth could have given you a more intimate portrait," Margaret said, her eyes twinkling in her long oval face. She may not have been beautiful, Grace decided, but with her height, golden hair, creamy English skin and large gray eyes, she must have attracted attention when she was younger. "As his sister, I saw a different side to him, I am sure. He was brilliant in the early days, Grace, especially on the field of battle—a born commander, and his people loved him. We had some arguments in our day, and often he behaved like a child, but for all his magnanimity—especially in the case of our brother, George—you learned not to push him too far. I felt the lash of his tongue on more than one occasion," she admitted with a rueful smile. Then she shook her head, her sapphire earbobs catching the light.

"But he let himself and his people down with his choices sometimes, not the least of which was his choice of friends. Will Hastings encouraged the philanderer in Edward, in truth, and the drinking and eating to excess. The last time I saw him he was grossly fat, and he knew his humors were not in balance. It was three years before his death, but the signs of a decline were there for all to see. I know not if he thought he was immortal or he did not care, but the day he died, it was a blow to our family," she said on a short, sardonic laugh, "and that is an understatement." Her walk had slowed during this long speech and, shading her eyes with her hand, she pointed to a stone bench in a shady spot under a linden tree and made her way towards it. "Are you satisfied, Grace?" she asked kindly. "Is there aught more I can tell you?"

"Lady Hastings is the queen dowager's only other attendant, your grace, and she does not like me. The two only speak ill of their husbands, I am sorry to say, so I am glad to have another view of my father," Grace told Margaret.

"My dear child, 'tis not your character Katherine Hastings dislikes, 'tis the daily reminder of her husband's—and Edward's—inconstancy that irks her. She is a Neville, Grace, and in her eyes her family name was soiled by Will's behavior. She is visiting her anger at her husband on you, 'tis all. I am sorry for you, my dear, and I hope Elizabeth treats you better."

John guffawed. "Aye, if you think keeping poor Grace locked away like a nun is kind."

"It is not our place to question the queen dowager's actions, John," Margaret said sternly and changed the subject. "Now, let us sit. I tire easily these days. My grandson Philip ran me ragged for many years after his dear mother died, but soon he will be ready to take on the mantle of majority and rule Burgundy instead of his father—if Maximilian will ever let him." She sighed and sat down, arranging her patterned satin gown in graceful green and gold folds about her and inviting Grace and John to sit on the grass at her feet. The attendants gathered in a group at a respectful distance from their mistress, and Grace noticed that Henriette and her handsome husband stood a little apart in close conversation.

Margaret drew a scroll from a velvet pouch on her belt and smoothed it flat. Then she took out a pair of silver-rimmed spectacles and held them up to her eyes while her two young companions waited, Grace picking a sprig of lavender and holding it to her nose.

"The greeting is the usual respectful salutation," Margaret said, scanning the first few lines, "and I shall be translating this into English from French as I go, so forgive the clumsy reading." She did not give her niece and nephew the writer's name, nor did she say the letter was in code—not French at all—but as John and Grace sat at her feet, they could not see the words. "My protégé is learning to sail the ocean with his master, a Breton merchant," she said, "and I thought his descriptions might impress you,"

"When I am the lookout and at the highest point of the main mast, my feet lodged firmly in the rigging, the wind tearing at my hair, billowing my smock about me and trying to tug me loose from my perch, I feel at one with the ship, the waves and the very universe. Dare I say it, I am as close to God as any man on earth. You told me once I was the son of a boatman, and I truly believe I was born to be at sea. The first time I had to leave the safety of the deck, find footholds on the hundreds of knots in the rigging and see my fellow mariners become as ants below me, I did not think I had the fortitude to reach the tiny crow's nest above the yardarm. Did you know there are crows up there, your grace? Every ship carries one or two in a cage, and one of the tasks of the lookout is to feed the birds. They are there so that when our ship stands out to sea, the sky is overcast and we cannot see the shore, the bird is let loose and flies straight in the direction of the land. The first time I saw this, it amazed me. The bird was not mistaken, nor are they ever, so says the mariner with whom I share my hammock."

"Can you not hear the wind in his words, feel the waves under his feet?" Margaret said proudly, lowering her spectacles. "He is indeed a poet." She looked back down at the letter.

"But the most awful and awesome experience by far is a tempest at sea. In the midst of the torrents of water poured upon us from the heavens, the rivers of seawater that swept all in their path over the decks, the flashes of lightning as bright as day and the cracks of thunder enough to deafen Neptune himself, I felt God all around us, and I was not afraid. It seemed to me I was being saved for a higher purpose than mere death by drowning in something as natural as a storm."

Grace crossed herself, but John's focus was riveted on Margaret's face and the writer's imagery. "What higher purpose can there be than to die trying to survive God's wrath, for surely that is what storms are—God's wrath shown upon us poor sinners?" John whispered. "Methinks your protégé is a little too full of pride. But I agree, he is a poet."

Margaret looked peeved and her response was terse. "You do not know him to berate him thus, John. I know him like my—" She stopped herself. "Would you hear more, or no?"

Grace was puzzled. Whoever this person is, Grace thought, watching her aunt intently, he means as much to her as any of us—her own family. She knew the dowager had borne no children of her own but that she had been like a mother to her stepdaughter, Mary. And then, upon Mary's untimely death from a riding accident, Margaret had been given the charge of Mary's two babes—Philip and another Margaret—by their father, Maximilian, who now ruled Burgundy as regent. It was said his stepgrandmother had more influence on Philip than his father had. These were Margaret's surrogate children, as everyone knew, and when her namesake was taken from her at age three and sent to live with her future husband, Charles of France, she was brokenhearted. So, who was this man—a boatman's son and a common mariner by all accounts, but one who could read and write? How Grace wished she were brave enough to ask, but etiquette forbade such questions of one of the most powerful women in the world at one of the most formal courts in Europe.

"Certes, Aunt, we would hear more, and I beg your pardon," John said dutifully.

Margaret reached out and patted his hand. "I am not angry, John, just a little tired," she lied. "There is only a line or two more that is of interest to you, my dears."

"*We came to Cork in the green country of Ireland. Everywhere I go I am reminded of you. Your family is much beloved here, so my master, the merchant Meno, tells me. But they have an odd way of speaking and many only speak the Celt, so I am mostly content to stay quiet, watching and learning as Master Meno trades his cloth, and I scribble the accounts. 'Tis a strange thing, your grace, but when you tread on dry land again after many weeks at sea, your body wants to sway with the waves, and I find myself listing from side to side along the wharf as though it is heaving. They tell me it will pass in a few days, and I am hoping 'tis so, for it is disturbing and not at all amusing—except to those watching me.*" Margaret folded the paper and laughed. "The first time I went on board ship was to come here for my marriage with Charles. I remember thinking I was born to be a sailor—for about an hour! And then I was not seen again, except with my face in a bucket, for a full day. And my dear Fortunata—my servant—could not go on the river in a barge without turning green.

"Now, *mes enfants*, I think we should return to my apartments and I will challenge John to a game of chess. We need to find a place for Grace to lay her head tonight as well." She rose and stretched her long torso from side to side, grimacing as she did so. "The bones are old and no longer move the

way they should. But what would you two young people know about that?"
she said, reaching her hands out to both of them. "Come, let us walk, and
Grace shall give us news of my other nieces."

GRACE HAD TROUBLE sleeping that night, mostly due to the labored
snores of the elderly attendant with whom she shared her bed. John's face
danced before her in the dark, and she indulged in fantasies as she tried
to go to sleep. In her imagination, instead of pulling away from her on the
settle that afternoon, he pulled her to him, whispering: "I wish with all
my heart you were not my cousin so I could wed you tomorrow. Let us run
away together to a distant shore and live in a cottage by a river. My love,
my Grace, my little wren." The thought of a river made her think of that
scorching day by the Thames after Stoke, and she saw John again, water
running off his strong young torso and his wet breeches clinging to his
thighs. But this time he was coming towards her, his eyes full of love, his
arms outstretched, and she went into them, lifting her face for his kiss. As
John bent to her breast, which had somehow been freed from her bodice
in her dream, a tingling sensation hardened her nipples and sent clear
messages of desire through her entire body as she lay still in the bed. Take
me, take me, she whispered to the dream John, but a snort from her bedmate jolted her from the fantasy and she gritted her teeth in frustration.
It can never be, she told herself miserably. He does not love me, and we
are first cousins. By the sweet Virgin, how many times have I hated being
the bastard daughter of King Edward? But never so much as now, when I
am denied the right to love his brother's son. How cruel were the fates at
my birth! How cruel God is! she railed silently, then crossed herself for her
impiety.

She must have kicked her bedmate in her anger because the woman
stopped midsnore, muttered in her sleep and turned over, only to start the
racket again. Grace giggled, turned away on her side and closed her eyes.
She heard the watch call out an hour that sounded like "three" to her English ear, and willed herself to sleep for the two hours before cockcrow.

GRACE GAVE MARGARET deep reverence after breaking her fast alongside her bedmate in a small hall reserved for Margaret's ladies in waiting.
Her stomach was still full from the rich food the night before and now,

after the smoked herring, cheese and bread for breakfast, she thought she would not be able to eat for a week. It seemed to her that life was lived more extravagantly in Burgundy than in England—at least at the dowager duchess's palace of Malines—and she marveled at the amount of gold leaf on the walls and ceilings, the diversity of dishes, the excessive fashion and even the water piped in to her washbasin in the attendants' quarters.

Margaret had given her several gold florins for her return journey, insisting that Gerards be compensated for his extra night at the inn. Judith and Edgar, too, would be paid from the duchess's generous gift, "and the rest, my dear Grace, you should take as thanks from an old aunt who enjoyed your company, if only for one day. From all you have told me, you will receive nothing for your years of service to Elizabeth, thanks to her miserly son-in-law. If Elizabeth's health is as bad as you report, you must think of your own future when she—" She stopped when she saw Grace's look of dismay and reached out to stroke the girl's cheek. "It surprises me you have not had suitors for your hand, being that you are of royal stock and pretty as a gillyflower, in truth. If you were to stay here with me, I warrant I would find you a willing husband inside a sennight."

"I thank you, *madame*, but I am content to do my duty by her grace; she has been good to me," Grace replied, carefully adding the coins to the remainder of her English nobles in the pouch under her bodice. A dumpy little man was approaching, whose face might have served as a model for one of the gargoyles that leered down from the roof of Bermondsey. Grace waited to be dismissed, but Margaret turned and greeted him like an old friend.

"*Ah, Messire de la Marche, veuillez attender un moment, s'il vous plaît,*" she said. Her chamberlain bowed and withdrew to the window. "And now, my duty calls, Grace. You have my message for Elizabeth committed to memory, I hope, and rest assured I shall write to my niece, young Bess, and make sure she takes better care of her mother—without revealing my source, *bien sûr,*" she added, seeing Grace's consternation. "I wish you God speed, and for the journey to Antwerp, you shall have a small escort." She put out her hand for Grace to kiss and said in a louder voice, "Farewell, Mistress Peche. I pray you give my greeting to Sir Edward, your uncle. My nephew, Lord John, will see you reach Heer Gerards safely."

Grace murmured her farewells and, feeling John take her elbow, backed away to the door. The last glimpse she got of her aunt was of the tall dowager bending down to plant an affectionate kiss on her wolfhound Lancelot's massive head.

"I may see you sooner than you think, little wren," John murmured as they walked through the antechamber to the large hall beyond, where Gerards was waiting. "Our lady aunt has work for me in England—or perhaps Scotland, where my old master, Lovell, now is. There have been many Flemish vessels sailing back and forth between here and Scotland ever since James came to the throne. I am anxious to be gone from this court and back home to England. But as I left in disgrace, I shall have to be careful." He smiled down at her. "If I need help, I know where to go," he said, pressing her hand. "Now, which one is your Pieter Gerards?"

There was no chance of even a fond embrace in the crowded hall, where several people turned to look curiously at the bastard of Gloucester and his pretty companion. Grace felt a rising panic that she would not ever see him again. "You will have a care, my dear John," was all she could whisper. "If anything should happen to you, I should not want to live."

"Fiddle faddle! Don't you know I was born lucky—so my mother tells me. No need to fret, my wren. I shall reappear at some inauspicious moment in your life and you will wish me far away."

Grace's face was a picture of dismay. "Oh, no, John! I shall always be happiest when you are near me," she insisted. "You are never far from my thoughts."

John laughed. "I hope you never have cause to rue that remark, coz," he teased her and, looking around, he asked, "Now where is your friend?" He did not wish her to sense the fear in his heart, too, that he might never see her again.

GRACE WAS REUNITED with Judith and Edgar at the inn, and they were most relieved to see her. The night before Heer Gerards had been grumpy upon his return, thinking that Sir Edward Brampton had stretched his patience with this pointless jaunt. He had shouted at Edgar, been rude to a tavern wench and complained to Judith after Edgar had stomped off to sleep in the stable. However, he and Judith had been consumed with curiosity as to why Margaret had taken such an interest in this young Englishwoman, and he tossed and turned on the unforgiving straw mattress upstairs that night, plotting to persuade his stubborn wife that Mistress Peche might be a suitable bride for his son once Judith had assured him that Grace was a good Christian. Judith's curiosity did not last long, however, and she was asleep in a trice, wrapped up in her cloak on the other side of the straw, after praying for a quick and safe return to London and resolving to tell Grace of the man's interest.

Gerards was impressed that the duchess had provided them with an escort as far as Antwerp and, with Grace riding pillion, sat on his horse as if he were a lord. The black and scarlet colors of Burgundy on the guards' tunics caused heads to turn with interest, and the merchant thought he should acknowledge their gawping by removing his tall beaver hat and waving it grandly. Grace hid her giggles in his mantle and was glad when they left Malines behind. She turned to look over the horse's rump at the great tower of St. Rumbold's rising from the walled city, and a lump in her throat changed her laughter to sadness as she thought of John waving farewell from the steps of Margaret's palace. She committed to memory his strong chin, square face, sensual mouth and dark gray eyes—those eyes that alone marked him as the son of King Richard—and whispered "I love you" into the wind.

Then she turned away and looked towards Antwerp—and home.

14

Bermondsey

SUMMER 1490

As the roofs and spires of London hove into view around the last bend before the Pool, Grace drank in the vista as one parched for the sight.

"See how the Tower gleams in the sunlight, as though it had received a lime wash but yesterday. And there's Saint Mary le Bow, and yonder the steeple of Saint Paul's," she cried, pointing the landmarks out to Judith, who was gladder to see terra firma approaching than the stunning sights of her city.

But when the carrack docked at a wharf close to the Billingsgate Market and the putrid smell of dead fish assailed their nostrils, Grace admitted she would be happy to put her feet on dry land again—English land. So much had happened to her and so different did she feel that it seemed to her she must have been gone for a year instead of a mere ten days. She blinked. Have I really walked the streets of Bruges, heard the bells of St. Rumbold's, made two sea voyages and been in the presence of her grace, the dowager duchess of Burgundy? It hardly seems possible, she thought. Perhaps it has all been a dream. But then the shriek of a fishwife brought her rudely awake.

"Get yer filthy 'ands off me barrow, yer maggot-ridden pisshole!" the voice floated up to the trio on the deck, waiting for the gangway to be secured, and Judith laughed.

"Aye, we are indeed back in London, are we not, Edgar?" she asked.

"And I wouldn't be nowhere else," he replied, grinning. "Never thought I'd be glad to see the rat-infested streets o' London again, Mistress Croppe, but I am right glad, that I am."

The captain appeared at Grace's side and invited her to disembark with his help. She thanked him and paid him three of the florins from Aunt Margaret's purse for their voyage.

"I am grateful to you, Judith, for your company on this enterprise," Grace said to the young woman when they stood on shore. "I am sorry the sea voyage did not agree with you, but the homecoming was less of a trial, I trust. I pray you convey my respectful greetings to Master Caxton and tell him his book was received with pleasure by the duchess. Now, I beg of you, let us accompany you back to your home. I am loath to leave you alone in the middle of Billingsgate."

Judith chuckled. "Mistress Peche, I am well known here by the mongers and their wives alike, for I come to buy every Friday. My brother's house is hard by in Pudding Lane and is but a stone's throw from this place. I shall bid you farewell and God speed here and now. I shall be pleased to see my own home again, in truth, for all 'twas a lark we were on." She gave Grace a bobbing curtsy, said good-bye to Edgar and hurried off between the stalls and baskets piled high with cod, mackerel, skate and hake, and was soon swallowed up in the lanes and alleys behind Thames Street.

Edgar was sent to find a boatman who would ferry them across the Thames to the wharf at Tooley Street, and Grace waited with the bundle of clothes until she heard Edgar's "halloo" from the river. Fifteen minutes later they were standing on the dock on the south bank, where Grace paid the boatman and told Edgar to lead the way back to the abbey.

Once on the path, Edgar dropped a discreet step behind Grace, his hulking presence a comfort to her. She had grown fond of the simple stable hand and sincerely hoped Elizabeth would reward him well for his duty to her. As they came to the abbey garden, Brother Oswald spotted her and came hurrying flatfooted along the path to greet her.

"We have missed you, Lady Grace," he cried, his long pointed nose almost meeting his chin in a wide smile of welcome. "Father John said you were visiting your sister at Westminster. I trust you had a pleasant stay?"

Ah, so Elizabeth did concoct a plausible story, Grace thought, relieved. "Aye, brother, the Lady Cecily was well, and 'twas good for me to have a change of scenery." And more than one scene, she thought, hoping she had not deceived the good monk with her enigmatic answer. "But I am sure there are things that need my attention in the field and garden. I shall look forward to joining you on the morrow, Brother Oswald. But now I must hurry back to the dowager's side. I have been gone longer than expected."

Brother Oswald inclined his tonsured head and nodded amiably. "Until tomorrow, my lady."

Reassured that Elizabeth had explained away both her and Edgar's absence to Father John, she was not prepared for the reception her body-guard was subjected to upon passing the stable doors.

"Get in here, you lazy lout!" Wat, the head groom, strode out and headed towards Edgar, fists clenched at his sides and ignoring Grace. "Brother Gregory be in a foul mood this past week after you didn't come back as expected. Where've you bin?"

"How dare you speak to my servant thus!" Grace stepped between him and Edgar, a full foot shorter than both men, and in unison they fell back a step. " 'Twas all arranged with Father John and her grace, the queen dowager. Edgar, follow me. And you, sirrah, will move away at once. You smell of horse piss."

Both Edgar and Wat stood rooted, their jaws dropped open in astonishment.

"Aye, my lady," Wat stammered, finally retreating several paces. He said not a word as Edgar, cocking a snoot at him, followed Grace to the abbey residence.

"Thankee, mistress," he said when they were out of earshot. "I was afeared Brother Gregory might send me packing. And then what would I do?"

"You will not be sent packing, I promise you," Grace said, more confidently than she felt. "And if you are, I have no doubt you could find work onboard ship." She smiled as she said this, knowing he could not see her.

"Go to sea!" Edgar yelped. "Nay, mistress, I would rather be chained up in the Clink than go back on a ship."

"I am teasing you, Edgar," she said, mounting the stairs to the dowager's rooms. "You had best stay down there and wait for a sign from me. And do try not to get into trouble."

"Trouble?" Edgar said, looking around at the empty yard, puzzled. "What trouble, mistress?"

Grace laughed. "Oh, Edgar, you are such a delight to tease," she said. And seeing his fallen face, she immediately felt contrite. "Forgive me, but please believe me, I tease you only because I like you."

She was rewarded with a simple grin of happiness and a touching of his temple. "And I like you, too, mistress," he called as she disappeared into Elizabeth's room.

"Grace, my dear child!" Elizabeth cried from her bed, where she was lying fully dressed while Katherine read to her. Her little white terrier sprang off the bed and ran circles around Grace's feet, yapping happily. "Praise be to God you are safely back. Katherine, help me to my chair and lock the door. Let us hear what Grace has to tell us."

Grace rose from her curtsy, picked up the dog and cuddled it before helping Katherine ease Elizabeth to her feet. She looks so much older and thinner, Grace thought, and yet I have not been gone a fortnight.

"In truth, I am glad to see you again, your grace. And you, Lady Katherine," she said, giving the pinch-faced woman a smile. "Indeed it warms my heart to be back in familiar surroundings." Katherine grunted a response.

Elizabeth was settled into the cushions of her chair, where Poppy scrabbled at her mistress's gown to be lifted into her lap. "Katherine is aware of your mission, Grace," Elizabeth said, but did not feel the need to explain her motive. In truth, she had been shocked and upset upon hearing Cecily's news of Grace's unexpected journey, and Katherine had again been there to console her.

Undismayed, Grace pulled up a stool and told her tale. "And so, the message from my aunt, Duchess Margaret, is that your son is indeed living, although she claims not to know his present whereabouts."

Elizabeth's eyes filled with tears, but she smiled through them and whispered: "Thanks be to the sweet Virgin, Mother of God. She has heard my prayer. Did Margaret think Sir Edward spoke the truth that Dickon had been kept at Guisnes?"

Grace nodded. "The word in Malines—so my cousin John said—is that Dickon was kept at the castle in Calais on secret orders from King Richard. Aunt Margaret did not deny this when we questioned her, but she did not confirm it, either. 'Tell Elizabeth to hold steadfast, and I will do all in my power to return England to Yorkist rule' were her very words. She said no more, because she had no wish to put you in danger."

Elizabeth stroked Poppy's long white hair and, at the last statement, inclined her head, the folds of her white wimple almost enveloping her gaunt face. "Aye, she would think of that. Meg and I always looked out for each other, and I missed her when she left for Flanders. 'Tis comforting she still cares," she said softly. " 'Twas her love for Anthony that allowed her to see me in a kinder light than other members of her family did."

Katherine drew in a sharp breath of disapproval, which made Elizabeth laugh. "Katherine the saint! Katherine the sanctimonious! Does this knowledge shock you, my dear Lady Hastings? Aye, my brother and Edward's sister were lovers—but unlike our inconstant husbands, they waited until both were widowed, or so Anthony led me to believe."

Grace looked at her lap and smiled, remembering the expression on Margaret's face when she had opened William Caxton's gift. He must have known, too, she thought. Elizabeth winced as she shifted in her chair. "Certes, Grace, you have done well. I must confess Cecily knew my wrath when she came knocking at my door with the preposterous story of your departure for Flanders." She grinned ruefully. "I never quite understood the meaning of *flounce* until she demonstrated it for me upon her leaving. I am sorry, for 'twas at Sir Edward I was truly irked."

Katherine interrupted with a snort: "*Irked* does not adequately tell the tale, my dear Elizabeth. I seem to remember you calling him a craven, onion-eyed clotpole for sending a girl to do a man's work."

Grace chuckled and Elizabeth looked shamefaced. "Is that what I said?" she said. "I suppose I owe Cecily an apology, but, by the Rood, I do not think Brampton could have executed the mission any better than our Grace here. My compliments!" She put her hands in prayer position and bowed over them, looking straight at Grace, who blushed and thanked her.

"Let us say the Angelus together and then Grace must find Father John and allay his fears that Grace has absconded with Edgar for good."

Grace's hand flew to her mouth and she jumped to her feet. "Edgar! I completely forgot about Edgar," she cried. "He has been waiting downstairs all this time. In truth, I could not have done this journey without his protection, your grace, and he is so afraid he will be sent from the abbey for it. The head groom threatened him with dismissal as we arrived earlier. Can you not intervene with Father John, I beg of you? He is a good man—a simple one, but a good man."

"My dear Grace, you will be a great deal more successful with Father John than I by pleading just as you have with me now. Go, child, and say I sent you. I am too weary to do battle for a simple groom. I know not why you care about him; he is merely a common man, and of no account. I would hear no more of him," she complained, waving Grace away. "Katherine, I need my powders or my head will surely crack."

Katherine glowered at Grace and pushed her roughly towards the door. "Get thee gone, Grace," she hissed, unbolting the top of the door, which Grace could not reach. "Certes, I wish you had stayed in Flanders. We were going along quite well without you."

I'll warrant you wish I had drowned, Lady Hastings, not merely remained abroad, Grace thought. She tried to take into account Margaret's words of explanation for the woman's ill will towards her, but her heart was hardened and she left without a word.

GRACE LOVED THE summer season most of all. Seeing all the seedlings she had so diligently nurtured into full-grown plants—stalks heavy with peas and beans, or heads of lettuce and cabbage full and lush—gave her the sense of accomplishment that watching a tapestry grow never could. Then, seeing the fruits of her labors either in pottages or stews on the refectory tables for the abbey community to enjoy or given as fodder to the animals was an added satisfaction. She had stored a wealth of knowledge from her work in the fields and knew that leeks and cabbages must be removed from the ground in June, that onions were good from December to March, that cutting—not tearing—the lowest beans from their stalks would double the crop and that she should save some of this summer's seeds for next spring's sowing. She loved the smell of the newly mown hay, the earth and even the horse manure that was spread on the tilled ground in the autumn. The song of a thrush, a blackbird and the warbler all delighted her and kept her company as she toiled.

Being alone also gave her the chance to think independently and day-dream to her heart's content. If she was not reliving the precious moments with John in Malines, she was mulling over all she had learned of Dickon, her half brother. It seemed certain now that he was still alive and somewhere on the other side of the Channel. Or was he? If the last place a report of him had been noted was Calais, might he have already taken ship and landed in England to seek his rightful crown? Grace dismissed that notion; 'twould not be wise to come without an army behind him. And there had been no talk of an army being mustered to help him while she was with Margaret. Nay, whatever is afoot as far as Dickon is concerned is still an illusion, she concluded, as it would seem no one had actually set eyes on the young man. She shook her head. 'Twould be nigh impossible to keep such a secret, she thought, but Aunt Margaret certainly believes it—as did Sir Edward. And he has no reason to care if 'tis true or not, she reasoned. Thinking of Margaret, a conversation at the private supper she had shared with the duchess came to mind and made her determined to ask Elizabeth about Uncle George of Clarence. She straightened her aching back and wiped the perspiration from her forehead.

"Royal visitors!" came a cry from the field closest to Long Lane. "The queen! The queen is come."

"Bess, here?" Grace muttered, shading her eyes and recognizing the royal banners. "Lord have mercy, Elizabeth will not be ready to receive her." Handing her basket of peas to a fellow picker, she picked up her kersey skirts and ran as fast as she could back to the residence, stopping for a moment at the well to splash water on her face and neck and get the dirt off her hands. Bess would have to be greeted by Father John first and then be properly announced, she knew, so if she and Katherine were quick, they could ready Elizabeth for her daughter's visit.

"My finest gown!" Elizabeth commanded upon hearing the news. "Why, oh, why did she not give me notice? 'Tis most unseemly and unkind. She gives me no respect," Elizabeth whined as Grace released the ties on her drab gray skirt and Katherine opened the wardrobe chest and lifted out the purple gown from the tailor in Southwark.

"Perhaps she has good news, your grace, and wanted to come as soon as she could to tell you," Grace suggested hopefully. However, Bess had not been to the abbey for two years, although her letters were frequent and affectionate enough. It seemed Henry—or his mother—had her firmly under his control, and she had dutifully provided him with a son and a daughter, both of whom were healthy.

"By the blessed Virgin, Grace," Elizabeth exclaimed, "why do you always hear a lark when 'tis a jackdaw cawing? And hurry with my bodice— Bess will be here in a trice."

Katherine curled her thin lips into a smug smile that only Grace could see, adding to Grace's annoyance. A year or so ago, she would have been devastated by Elizabeth's jibe, but now she gritted her teeth and tightened the laces of the queen dowager's bodice into a vise, causing Elizabeth to suck in a sharp breath of pain.

"Looser!" she cried. "Do you want me expiring before my daughter gets here? I know not what has come over you, Grace. It would seem wandering far away has addled your brain or given you high-flown ideas of your own importance."

Now Katherine was positively grinning with unabashed glee as she shook out the purple gown. "Aye, for a slip of a bastard, she does put on airs," she said, and then shrieked in fear when Grace flung herself at her, intent on wiping the smile from her bewhiskered face. Katherine dropped the dress and grabbed Grace's small arms, pinning them to her sides and knocking off Grace's coif, but then she was at a loss as to how to proceed. Grace kicked her hard on the ankle and the older woman yelped in pain but held on grimly.

"Grace, stop this instant!" Elizabeth cried, aghast, going to help Katherine, her too-tight bodice impeding her movements. "How dare you behave thus? Stop, I say!" She succeeded in dragging Grace from Katherine's grip and slapped her face soundly.

"Your grace? Mother? May I come in?" Bess's voice penetrated the scuffle and all three women turned in horror as the queen entered the room, with the curious Prior John peering over her shoulder. "We did knock twice, but . . ." Seeing the state of her mother, standing in her chemise, the widow's wimple askew and her breasts almost forced over the top of the constrictive bodice, she quickly took a step backwards and curtly dismissed the astonished abbot. Crossing himself, he fled back along the walkway to the stairs as Elizabeth, Grace and Katherine sank into deep reverences. Grace stared at the rushes on the floor, regretting she had not cut fresh ones now that she could see them up close.

Bess reentered the room, calling back over her shoulder in amusement. "Cis, you must see this!"

Cecily walked in behind her sister and stared at her mother's disheveled appearance, Grace's tumbled curls and Katherine's bleeding cheek. "Odd's pittikins, what happened?" she asked, trying hard not to laugh. "It has all the appearance of a catfight."

Mortified, Elizabeth got to her feet and with some dignity went to embrace Bess. "Cecily, have you forgotten all your manners?" she chided her younger daughter. "The queen must always speak first. I hope you are teaching your daughters properly."

The Viscountess Welles, stepaunt to the king, hung her head, mumbled an apology and wandered to the window to pout.

"Mother, we do not need to stand on ceremony here," Bess said after receiving her mother's kiss and noting Cecily's sulks. "I, too, should like to know what happened." She eyed Elizabeth's bodice. "Come, let me help you with your gown. I came at an inopportune moment and without warning, is that it?"

"Aye, Bess," Elizabeth lied. "We were hurrying to make ready for you, 'tis all."

A loud harrumph from Katherine told another story, but Elizabeth ignored her, calling to Cecily to stop sulking and come and greet her. Cecily did as she was told and Elizabeth tried to coax her out of her ill humor, a little chagrined that she and Cecily always ended up thus.

"My felicitations on the birth of my granddaughter, by the by. And my thanks for naming her after me." She kissed Cecily's stony face. "Next time you will give John a son, never fear. Remember, I had three lovely daughters before I produced a son."

Cecily managed a smile and helped Bess dress their mother, first loosening the binding bodice laces.

"Dearest mother, you are dreadfully thin," Bess said, concern in her voice. "Are you not well?" She turned to Katherine. "Do you not have sufficient to eat here, my lady?" she asked, and Grace almost laughed. Despite the older woman's trim figure, she never pushed food away, and Grace had seen her finish Elizabeth's half-eaten plateful on many occasions.

"There is plenty to eat," Elizabeth answered testily. "God does not give me an appetite most days, 'tis all." She shrugged and declared in her old authoritarian way, "I eat enough. Have you no word of greeting for your half sister?" She nodded at Grace, still on her knees. "Or perhaps it has been so long you have forgotten what she looks like."

Bess ignored her mother's insinuation as she looked in surprise at Grace. Then she put out both her hands to raise her sister and embraced her warmly. "I did not know you with your hair so long and—dare I say it—so unruly. And you as brown as a nut! I took you for an Italian, in truth. Although where Mother would have found an Italian attendant I know not!" Grace had to look up at her regal sister, and she dimpled at this last. Italian? Jew? I wonder what is next, she thought.

Bess had aged, Grace noted anxiously, and there were dark circles beneath her beautiful dark blue eyes. But her smile still lit up the room as she studied Grace's unkempt appearance. "Has no one told you that young women of noble blood are supposed to be fashionably pale and delicate? It should have been easy for you to stay that way inside the walls of an abbey, but you have the robust constitution, face and hands of a peasant girl. If I did not know you better—or know my mother's strict upbringing—I would think you had been working in the fields. For certain you have been outside a great deal this summer, and one can only wonder why." Bess was nonplussed when her mother and Lady Katherine laughed aloud.

"You are right, Bess. I have been working in the fields—every day, when it does not rain. Do not look so shocked, dear sister, 'tis not a sin to toil with one's hands. And the queen, your mother, is good enough to let me go."

Bess was astonished, and Elizabeth cast sheep's eyes at her. "Mea culpa, Bess. I did not have the will to deny her. Life here is dull as ditchwater and, as you have witnessed, Grace and Katherine are often at odds. 'Tis tiresome for me."

Katherine opened her mouth to defend herself but wisely shut it again. She knew she would feel the lash of Elizabeth's sharp tongue if she dared contradict her patron.

"So, it was a fight we interrupted," Cecily exulted, coming out of her sulk. "What is there here to fight about?"

"Mind your own business, Cecily," Elizabeth snapped. "Now, Bess, will you not sit and take some wine? The quality is poor, but you are welcome to try it." She motioned to Grace to pour them some of the abbey wine—a thin, pink liquid that smelled musty. Bess wrinkled her nose but gamely sipped some. "How is my grandson? And the babe Margaret? I wish with all my heart I could see them both," Elizabeth grumbled. Then she grimaced. "I am filled with jealousy that their other grandmother may dandle them on her knee any hour she pleases while I languish in this place," she said, dismissing the room with a wave.

"Mother, I pray you do not talk thus. You know I have no sway with the Lady Margaret," Bess said sadly.

"Nor with your husband, it would seem," Elizabeth muttered. More hopefully, she said, "I would know why you are here on such a whim, daughter. *Bien sûr*, we are delighted to see you." She smiled. "Has the king mellowed where I am concerned? Is that what you are come to say? That I can return to court? Can you not see to what penury I am reduced? Certes, I am too old to cause trouble for Henry now." She leaned in eagerly. "I beg of you, tell me I can return."

Bess had to look away in a moment of guilt. She could not bring herself to admit that her mother was right: she had no sway with her husband. The two times she had attempted to bring up a reconciliation, Henry had given her one of his cold stares and a one-word answer: "Nay." Indeed, she had come today of her own accord while Henry was away from the capital, but her mission was an awkward one and so she had begged Cecily to accompany her, saying it was high time the two of them visited their mother. Cecily had been all too glad to leave her dull husband's side for the jaunt and had been merry company on the way. Now Bess worried a fingernail as she composed her thoughts. It was then that Grace, sitting on a stool opposite her, noticed that all Bess's fingernails were chewed to the bone. The younger Bess had occasionally bitten the nail of her thumb in times of anxiety, but this excess told a sorry tale. For all her crown, children, palaces and wealth, Bess was an unhappy woman.

"I am here because I overheard a conversation between Henry and one of his spies a few days ago," Bess began, lowering her voice. "There is a rumor afoot in Burgundy that Dickon—our little Dickon—is alive somewhere on the Continent and that Aunt Margaret is circulating that rumor."

The four other people in the room, as if rehearsed, feigned surprise or shock.

"Dickon alive!" Elizabeth cried, grasping her wine goblet and swallowing a mouthful. "How is it possible, after all this time?"

Cecily and Grace exchanged glances and Grace nodded her head once in thanks for her discretion. She was impressed that the garrulous Cecily had been able to hold her tongue. Cecily, too, expressed unmitigated surprise and joy at hearing the news of Dickon, but Grace noticed that Bess was silent during the exclamations of excitement. Elizabeth shushed them all, afraid of eager ears at the door.

"Bess, dear, you do not speak. Are you not glad your brother is alive?" Then she put her hand to her mouth. "How foolish of me. Certes, you cannot be happy, for Henry's crown may be at stake—and thus your own. Forgive me for my lack of tact—I was merely expressing a mother's joy."

Bess smiled wanly. "You know I rejoice to know my little brother is alive, but in truth I do not know what will become of it. Henry will watch all of us like a hawk—afraid we will be plotting behind his back. I dread his return from the progress—especially if he knows I have been here. Since those dark days of the pretender Simnel and your enforced exile from our court, I have been mortified by my lack of courage where you are concerned, dearest mother. You must know that I pray nightly for you and for the strength to win Henry over. But it seems he listens only to his mother—"

"That dried-up crone!" Elizabeth spat. " 'Tis unnatural when a man cannot cut those leading strings. Your father turned to me for counsel as soon as we were wed. I would not have stood by and allowed his mother to come between us, you may be certain of that." Bess nodded glumly.

Grace wondered if Elizabeth knew what Edward's subjects had thought of his queen while he was their king. She had been privy to several rude remarks about the queen dowager made by the laborers at the abbey as she worked among them, and even Edgar had blurted out one day on their journey from Burgundy that he had not expected the Woodville woman to keep such pleasant company as the Lady Grace. When Grace had questioned him, he had reddened and touched his forelock. "Beg pardon, mistress. Bain't my place to say aught about the lady, but us Londoners never took to the Grey mare. Notions above her station, is what we thought. And she weren't even his proper wife!" She knew she should have reprimanded the groom for his insolence, but she also knew he was an honest man and, after all, she had invited him to speak his mind. In as stern a tone as was necessary, she said, "I beg you to keep such foolish thoughts to yourself, Edgar. You are speaking of the queen's mother." "Aye, mistress," he had replied, and then he'd confided, "you need have no fear, us Londoners love our own Queen Bess."

Now Grace looked from mother to daughter with a more informed eye and saw how their contrasts outweighed their similarities. Both were beauties, but Bess radiated warmth and shone from the inside; Elizabeth was cold and calculating underneath her dazzling smile. Aye, Elizabeth had schemed and fought hard for her siblings' and children's best interests—and none could fault her for that—but the animosity shown her as Edward's upstart wife had hardened her, whereas Bess's compassion exuded from every pore; only a few, including Grace, were ever the recipient of Elizabeth's.

"Are you telling me that you must give up the fight to release me from this place, daughter?" Elizabeth said after the conversation had subsided. She put her hands in prayer position and tapped the tips of her fingers together. "Henry cannot think I can do anything from here? I am cut off from the outside world, and no one even remembers where I am. Certes, he has left me poor enough that I cannot help support an invasion. So, 'twould be more prudent of him to have me live close by you, Bess, and thus be able to keep an eye on me," she concluded triumphantly. "What say you?"

Always thinking, Grace marveled. I wish I had her agility of mind.

"I had not thought of that possibility," Bess said, looking with admiration at her mother. "You mean I could counsel Henry to 'keep our friends closer but our enemies closer still'? I believe that is the adage."

"Aye, and Henry will be impressed with your clever thinking, my dear. Mark my words, this could be the beginning of your having more influence." She got to her feet, her cheeks pink with excitement. "Dear Mother of God, I have not felt this good since the visit by Sir Ed—" She remembered just in time and swallowed the rest.

"Sir Edward Brampton, Mother?" Bess said, finishing the name. "Aye, we knew he was here, but not why."

Elizabeth's eyes widened but she recovered her composure quickly enough to laugh it off. "Aye, he came to flirt with me, Bess. He always did have an eye for me back when I was queen and still beautiful. He came to cheer me, 'twas all. It made me feel like a girl again." She bent down to her daughter and took Bess's chin in her hands. "You would not begrudge your old mother a few compliments, now, would you?" She was at her most cajoling.

Bess gave her mother a kind smile and took Elizabeth's hand and held it to her cheek. "I would not be so churlish, mother. In truth, you do not have much to look forward to, and Sir Edward is quite the gallant! I suppose he told you Henry had pardoned him for supporting the usurper Richard?"

"Why, Bess!" Cecily cried from her seat on the bed, artfully diverting the topic. "What happened to 'my dearest love'—which is what you used to call Uncle Richard? How fickle you are, dear sister."

"How dare you speak to your queen thus, Cecily!" Bess said, surprising everyone with her tone. "That was many years ago. I am a wife and a mother now. You have no right to—"

"Pish!" Cecily said. "Come, Grace, show me your vegetable patch. 'Tis unbearably hot in here." She took Grace's hand and pulled her towards the door, disappearing through it. Grace first curtsied and then retrieved her coif from the floor. Elizabeth was shaking her head, while Bess sat defeated in her chair, nibbling on what was left of a fingernail. "Let them go, mother," she said. "Cecily is incorrigible, but she is right. I did think I loved Uncle Richard." She smiled. "I was young, and when Father died, he was kind. But now I have Henry and am content," she said firmly. "Let us talk of other things. Lady Katherine, how is your health?"

Grace caught up with Cecily at the bottom of the staircase, where Bess's other attendants sat on the bench in the shade of the old yew tree. The ladies rose and came hurrying to Cecily's side, but she waved them away. "Lady Grace and I are going for a short walk alone. You may wait here." They curtsied and Cecily tucked Grace's hand in her arm. "Lead on, Farmer Grace," she joked.

Grace giggled. "Do I really look like an Italian?" she asked. "They say the women are very beautiful." "Pah!" came the response. Several people bowed and wished Grace a good day as she and Cecily passed through the main courtyard and out to the fields beyond the gatehouse.

Once they were out of earshot, Grace asked, "Did you receive the borrowed clothes? I sent them with a carter who said he was for Westminster. I did not know if you had disappeared back to Lincolnshire or not."

"Aye, Kate received them safe. But enough of these details—you must tell me all about your journey," Cecily demanded. "And leave nothing out!"

As they walked arm in arm past the pea patch, a pen where three bristly pigs rooted noisily in the dirt and towards a field ripening with corn, Grace recounted her adventure.

A figure in the Welles's livery, the blue bucket and golden chain badge on his sleeve, was skirting the barley field and coming towards them, a frolicking lurcher alongside him.

"Tom!" Grace called out in surprise. "Tom Gower, with Jason. Cecily, you did not tell me Tom was with you."

Cecily's sly smile told Grace she had planned this encounter carefully. "I told you he was in Jack's service, Grace. Why should he not be along?"

Remembering Cecily's recent confidence that Tom carried a torch for her, Grace groaned. "Look at me," she cried, as Tom approached them. "Oh, Cis, why could you not have told me? I would have at least put on a more suitable headdress. Sweet Jesu, I must look a fright. How is my coif? Look at my hands! Oh, Cis, how could you?"

"I thought you didn't care about Tom," Cecily said, laughing at her. "Don't fret, you may look pleasing to a man who comes from a farm in Yorkshire."

The hair was still an unkempt yellow thatch and the eyes were the same remarkable cornflower blue, but the lanky boy Grace remembered had turned into a man of considerable stature with a light brown beard framing a strong, pleasant face. He is not handsome like John, she thought, but certes, he is good-looking. He had grown more since Stoke and now he towered over her as he bowed and wished her a good day.

"God's greeting to you, Tom," Grace said, giving him a quiet smile. "How long has it been since we saw each other—two years, maybe?" She knew full well it had been the day she had entrusted Elizabeth's incriminating letter to him.

"More than three, my lady," Tom replied. "I am happy to see you again." His frank, admiring stare unsettled Grace. Come, Lady Grace Plantagenet, she told herself, why should you be unnerved by this man of little consequence? 'Tis only Tom Gower, your fishing friend from long ago. It must be his height, she decided; he made her feel like a child. She drew up every inch of her five feet and even managed to step out of the furrow she was standing in, adding three more inches. She covered her unease by bending down and paying attention to Jason, who had immediately recognized a friend and had tried to jump up and greet her. "Down, boy," Tom said, and the dog immediately obeyed.

"Cecily told me you are in her husband's train," Grace said, catching sight of her dirty fingernails and trying to hide her hands. "I also heard that your father died, and I am sorry for that, truly I am." Her voice sounded unnaturally squeaky to her, but the more she tried to lower it, the more she gabbled on. "How is your mother? And your sister—Cat, is it not? Your brother owns the farm now, doesn't he? And here is Jason. 'Tis Jason, isn't it? Sit, Jason! Good boy, Jason." Oh, no, she thought, somebody stop me talking! For the love of Saint Catherine, button your lip, Grace, I pray you. She looked up helplessly at Cecily, who let forth a peal of her famous laughter, which made Tom start chuckling, too. Soon all three were laughing, and Grace's unease melted away.

"Holy Mother of God, Grace, when you decide to talk, you would talk the tail off a cat. Forgive her, Tom, she has been locked up for too long in here with my mother, her old bat of a companion and a cloisterful of monks," Cecily explained, wiping her eyes. She flicked her perfectly manicured hand in her sister's direction: "So Grace hides in the fields with the sheep and cows, and this is the result. What think you, Tom? Does she not look like a milkmaid? I say she will not find herself a husband looking thus. Do you agree?"

"Cecily!" Grace spluttered.

Tom's fair skin flushed scarlet and he replied, "I think you do Lady Grace an injustice, my lady," which made Cecily laugh all the more. "Aha, I was right," she crowed at Grace, as Tom's color faded and he looked in bewilderment from one to the other.

Grace glared at her sister. "Pay no attention, Tom, I beg of you. The sun has no doubt addled her wits." She felt sorry for him, as his blush and stammered response had so clearly given his feelings away. She reached up and slipped her hand through his arm companionably. "You don't mind if I take your arm, do you, Tom? These ruts can trip one up so quickly. Did you come to keep us company, or do you have a message for us?" she asked, hoping to alleviate his awkwardness. "And please, call me Grace, as you used to do."

A shiver went through his arm as she touched him, and it buoyed her confidence that this giant of a man, four years older than she, trembled at her touch. How different from John, she mused, who was never far from her thoughts.

"Aye, my . . . I mean, Grace," Tom said, grinning foolishly down at her. Sweet Jesu, Cis was right, he does carry a torch, Grace thought. She raised a questioning eyebrow, and he remembered why he had come. "I was sent to fetch Lady Cecily; the queen is ready to return to Greenwich."

"Cis, did you hear?" Grace called, as a little ahead of them Cecily threw another stick for Jason to prance after. "Bess is waiting for you."

"If the queen commands, then we must obey," Cecily cried, executing an exquisite curtsy to a bean pole on the edge of the vegetable patch. "Nay, Tom, you stay with Grace, and Jason shall keep me company. Come, boy," she addressed the hound, whose tongue lolled out of his mouth as he stood over the retrieved stick, willing her to throw it again. She flung it once more and followed Jason through the field, her headdress streaming behind her like a pennant in the wind.

" 'Tis hard to believe she is a viscountess, is it not?" Grace chuckled, keeping the conversation light, but Tom only nodded. She wondered if he found her closeness unsettling and, not wanting to give him any false hopes, loosed her hold on him and bent to pick a tall corn cockle from among the barley stalks. They walked on in silence for a few minutes, Tom tongue-tied and Grace debating whether she should mention she had seen John in Bruges. She would have to lie about her journey's purpose if she did, she decided, because she was not sure she could trust Tom. She had never been able to discover whether he had indeed betrayed Elizabeth in the matter of the letter. So, in the spirit of fairness to him, she took the bull by the horns and, with a sharper tone of voice than she knew was necessary, stated: "Tom, if you and I are to be friends, I must settle something that has eaten at me since the queen dowager was sent to the abbey." She took a deep breath and, seeing Tom stopped in his tracks, turned to him and whispered. "Was it you who turned over the letter I gave you from Elizabeth to Henry's spies?" As soon as the question fell from her lips, she knew it had not been Tom. The anger in his eyes and the grim set of his jaw told her she had insulted him, and she was immediately contrite.

"I . . . am . . . sorry, Tom, but you were the last person who had the letter, and 'twas I who put it into your hands. What would anyone think? Lady Hastings accused you in front of the king. I tried to defend you—truly I did—but the prickly seed of suspicion has never left me."

His hand on his heart, Tom gave his reply through clenched teeth: "I swear to you, Grace Plantagenet, that I did not betray your mistress nor my master. Henry's spies were so close to capturing Lord John in Suffolk that he fled on foot and they discovered the letter among other papers in his saddlebags. No one betrayed him—or the queen dowager. I am mortified you would question my honor."

Grace was ashamed. "Pray forgive me, Tom. I should not have doubted you. You are an honorable man, in truth, and I am happy to put the matter to rest once and for all." She turned back to the path. "Come, let us catch Cecily, and I will tell you of my adventure."

Then, making him promise not to breathe a word of what she was about to relate, Grace told of her meeting with John at Duchess Margaret's court, where, she lied, she had been invited to meet her aunt and convey Elizabeth's greetings in person.

"He was in such good spirits, although chafing to return to England," Grace told Tom, detailing John's fashionable dress and life of luxury at the Burgundian court.

Already much chastened by her accusation, Tom's dejection was not helped by Grace's enthusiastic description of his rival, John.

"The last thing he said was that our aunt was sending him to join Lord Lovell at King James's court in Scotland," she continued brightly. "Did you know Lovell was not drowned at Stoke, as 'twas rumored?"

Tom shook his head in surprise. " 'Tis good news indeed," he said, although his flat tone belied his words.

She sighed, not noticing his monotone, and murmured, "How I wish with all my heart John would come here instead."

Now Tom bristled. "Your aunt is right," he said curtly. "John should not come to England, or Henry might arrest him for spying."

"Certes, he knows that," Grace said, a little impatiently. Then she held up the flower, twirling it in front of her nose. "I made him promise he would not put himself in danger," she said to the delicate pink petals, although it was clearly meant for Tom's ears. "I could not bear it if any harm befell him."

Tom kicked a pebble out of the way with his hard-soled riding boot. Looking askance at his grim face, Grace frowned. "Why the stone face, Tom? Are you not pleased to know John is safe and well?"

"Certes, Grace! What do you take me for?" he replied, hurt. "But it seems I am not half so pleased as you seem to be. 'Tis plain you wear your heart upon your sleeve."

"I am not ashamed of it," Grace told him. "But why should you care?" She gave him a sidelong glance and laughed, a little more heartlessly than she meant to. "Ah, Tom, I believe you are jealous," she teased.

"You do me wrong, Lady Grace," he answered roughly. "Perhaps I have been foolish to wear *my* heart upon my sleeve, but I do not deserve your cruelty for it. You may rest assured I shall never mention it again." His sincerity humbled Grace, and she wished she had bitten her tongue. Where had this exchange gone so wrong, she wondered? They had reached the courtyard, where he bowed stiffly and stalked off to join Cecily on her way back to Elizabeth's apartments.

Feeling even smaller than she had a few minutes ago, Grace stared after him miserably. What have I done? I did not mean to hurt him; I only wanted him to know he should douse that torch he carries in the nearest river. But who can understand the ways of men? she asked herself, as if she were the expert in affairs of the heart. "Not I!" she said out loud and flounced off to find Brother Oswald in the herb garden. "A pox on too-tall Tom!"

TRYING TO SLEEP in the sultry night air, Grace mulled over the day's events, her chemise damp from perspiration. Elizabeth had been morose when Grace finally returned after waving Bess and Cecily off. Riding beside the horse litter, Tom had stared straight ahead, and Grace did not dare to call out a farewell. Her heart had been heavy; she had not wanted to spoil the friendship, but she was at a loss as to how to repair the damage, as she did not know when she would see him again.

"He will recover, Grace," Cecily had assured her after Grace quickly whispered the tale. "I will see if I can arrange a suitable marriage for him," she said with a mischievous grin.

"I wish you would," Grace answered as they embraced, and their the little cavalcade moved off. Bess gave Grace a sweet smile from the litter before leaning back on the cushions and closing her eyes. She had forgotten how much her mother could tire her out.

Grace sought solace in the fields after the carriage disappeared down Long Lane, watching the reapers rhythmically cut the corn with their smooth-edged sickles. Pots of grease, bags of sand and whetstones for sharpening the small curved blades were placed strategically around the field, and many of the reapers were bare-chested in the heat of the noon-day sun, their chausses unbound from their belts and tied off below the knee. There were many more workers than usual, men recruited from the neighboring farms and villages to help with the harvest, which was early this year after the hot, dry summer. She hitched her overskirt into her belt and began filling a basket with fat pea pods, unable to resist snapping a few open and savoring the tender contents. The task calmed her and, after depositing the full basket with the head laborer, she walked back to her room.

Now Grace lay on her bed thinking about Bess and her devotion to Henry. She could not reconcile the love Bess declared for her husband with the sadness she saw in her sister's eyes. Something is wrong, she thought, but I pray I am mistaken. Bess does not deserve to be unhappy—unlike me. She grimaced in the dark, and her guilt over her unkind treatment of Tom returned to worry her before she fell asleep.

She dreamed of the grassy field again, and there was John smiling at her from afar. This time he did not disappear from view but turned and shouted at someone else. A second man appeared, holding a sword that glinted in the sun. Grace could not see his face, as it was hidden behind a salet, the visor closed. John shouted again, this time in anger, and went for his sword to face the stranger, but Grace found that she was holding it. She tried to run towards him with it but her feet were rooted to the spot. She cried out for help: "Help him! Somebody please help him!" A shadowy figure carrying a noose appeared near John, and looping it about John's neck, he began to tug him out of the way of the knight's sword. It was Tom Gower. "I will help him, Grace," Tom yelled at her, laughing hideously. "I will help him to the gallows!" Then the knight lifted off his helmet and laughed along with Tom. Horrified, Grace saw that it was King Henry. She willed her legs to move and excruciatingly slowly began to run towards John, but she was too late. Henry pointed his sword at John's belly and ripped it open, spilling his guts upon the green grass. Grace screamed and woke up, tears streaming down her face, her heart racing and her shift drenched in sweat.

"Soft, Grace, what is it?" Elizabeth called from the bed. "You screamed to wake the dead—and you certainly woke me. Katherine, fetch the child some wine. Mother of God, but it is hot in here. Small wonder Grace has bad dreams." She sighed, knowing that whatever sleep she might have had that night was at an end with this disturbance.

Katherine grudgingly climbed out of bed to carry out Elizabeth's wish. "Here's wine for you, Grace," she said, yawning. Grace sat up and took the cup, the sweet liquid soothing her, although she knew a potion of hot thyme would ward off more nightmares. Then, hearing Elizabeth turn over, Katherine bent closer and whispered, "Her grace has had an exhausting day and needs her sleep. How inconsiderate of you to wake her!"

"Certes, I wish I had not either, but 'tis God who controls our dreams, Lady Katherine. And this was a bad one," Grace shot back.

"The Devil's handiwork, more like! I saw you dallying with that squire alone in the field. I watched you from the window. You should be more discreet where you do your whoring!"

Grace gasped at the woman's gall, but she was in no mood to continue the fight that had begun that morning. She turned towards the wall and gave the woman a terse good night. How I hate you, she thought, and how I wish I could leave this dismal place. It was the last supplication she made to the Virgin before she drifted off.

If the Virgin heard her plea that night, she waited until autumn to respond. A messenger arrived from Greenwich with a letter from Cecily that caused Elizabeth to first frown, then nod thoughtfully and take a long, hard look at Grace, who was busy mending a stocking. "Katherine, I pray you go and tell the abbot I shall be dining with him today," she said to her attendant. "It has been a long time, and I fear I may have offended him by my persistent absence."

Katherine's face fell at the dismissal; she was put out she would now not know the contents of the missive, but she curtsied and left the room. Grace looked up from her work, made curious by Elizabeth's unusual request. It had indeed been months since she had dined in public, preferring to be served alone by Grace or Katherine, while they took it in turns to take their meals with the rest of the community.

"Come here, child," Elizabeth said. "I have some news for you."

Grace's wide eyes betrayed her apprehension until the dowager gave her an encouraging smile. "Many would think it good news, Grace, so do not look so fearful."

Elizabeth watched her young attendant carry a stool forward and sit carefully upon it, arranging her faded green dress around her. Pretty thing, she thought, not for the first time; and there is a look of Ned about her when she smiles. She sighed, as she always did when she thought about her dead husband.

"It seems your sister and her husband are offering you a way to leave me that you would be very foolish to refuse," Elizabeth began.

Grace gazed at the skeletal woman in front of her, dismayed always by the hollow cheeks and lifeless eyes. "Leave you, your grace?" she exclaimed, finding the end of her belt and twisting it between nervous fingers. "I could not do that. 'Tis my duty to serve you, after all your goodness to me." She tried to hide the panic in her voice. Leave? Oh, dear God, 'tis all I know. She glanced around the room, its drab surroundings now seeming cozy and familiar. Thoughts flitted in and out of her brain like barn swallows around their muddy nests. Where shall I go? Why must I go? Then she knew. Henry must have found out about my journey into Burgundy, she thought. He must have spied on me. Someone has betrayed us! Sir Edward? Cecily? Oh, no, she realized suddenly, it must have been Tom. Dear God in Heaven, he must really hate me!

But Elizabeth did not seem ruffled, and Grace reasoned she would be if they had been found out. Instead she was calmly saying, "I know you know your duty, my dear, and for four years I could not have wished for pleasanter company. But Grace, I am not long for this world, and you have your life ahead of you. We must do what is best for you." She handed Grace the letter. "Why don't you read it for yourself."

With trembling fingers, Grace reached out for the parchment. She glanced at the signature and saw Cecily's untidy scrawl at the bottom of the page. She frowned and began to read aloud:

"Right honorable and esteemed mother, the most high and mighty queen dowager, I give you greeting. This letter concerns our dearly beloved sister, Grace, and insomuch as you, too, love her, you will be pleased to know that Viscount Welles, my husband, has granted his henchman, one Thomas Gower of Westow in Yorks, permission to wed her." Grace put her hand to her mouth and gave a little cry. "Oh, no! Not Tom," she muttered, the room beginning to swim around her. She looked down at the letter, but all the words were a blur as she fought back tears. "Your grace, my dear lady, do not make me do this, I beg of you. I am certain Cecily is doing this to be kind, but . . ." She was at a loss for words and looked up hopefully at Elizabeth. "But I am not ready to be married. Or to leave you," she added hurriedly.

Elizabeth rose in one swift motion and swiped the letter from Grace's hand. "What is this nonsense, Grace?" she cried. "You have no right to contest Viscount Welles's proposal for you. He is the king's uncle, and Cecily is the queen's sister. Do be reasonable and see the sense in this. After all, you are sixteen and no longer a child. Why, I was married with a son at your age. Do you have any notion what is to become of you once I am gone? A nunnery, perhaps? Is that what you want? Nay, I didn't think so." She went to the window and read some more. "Cecily is prepared to give you a small dowry, and she wants you to live with her in Hellowe as part of the household. True, I could wish the fellow were higher born or could offer you more than the income of a manor or two, but Cecily says he is a good man with the right leanings." She arched her brow, intimating that those were Yorkist leanings. "Why, she said he was squire to John of Lincoln. Is that true?" Grace nodded miserably, and Elizabeth retorted, "Then that is enough of a pedigree for me."

She went to Grace's side and with great difficulty crouched down on her heels to Grace's level and took the young woman's hand. "Grace, my sweet child, why the sad face? Has this Tom Gower insulted you? Is he a monster? Tell me that he is, and I shall refuse to let you go. Otherwise, your future is not in your own hands—or in mine. You know that. You would be at the king's mercy once I die, and believe me, he would not think twice about wedding you to the highest bidder or consigning you to the nearest abbey. You would have no choice but to obey." She sighed as she looked at the sulky expression on Grace's face. "Speak to me, Grace. I will listen this once, for I owe you much, and I do not wish you unhappy. And, in truth," she could not forbear to add, "your leaving would inconvenience me considerably."

Grace's pulse quickened, for once ignoring Elizabeth's selfishness and clutched at a straw of hope. But then Elizabeth stood up and returned to her train of thought. "Our lives as women give us little in the way of control—surely you have seen that. Look at your own sisters: Bess was forced to marry Henry, as you know, Cecily the dull Jack Welles. And poor little Catherine was contracted to Juan of Castile when she was a baby! Aye, it was broken off when your father died, but then Henry promised her to dead King James's brother in Scotland, and"—she gave a sardonic laugh—"me to James himself, which thankfully came to naught when the man was killed at Sauchieburn. Catherine is only eleven, and who knows who will barter for her yet. We are but royal chattel, Grace, and you are more fortunate because you were born a bastard. Had your father still been king, you would have been a good catch for an ambitious man at court, as even a bastard royal has influence if the father is a king. Do you see?" She searched Grace's sad face, her generous mouth drooping and her large brown eyes close to tears, for some sign of acceptance of these hard facts. "But now . . ."

"Now I am nothing," Grace whispered for her. "I know that. But I am still not free to love where I will."

"Love comes eventually, from respect and familiarity—most of the time. You learn to love and count on each other. Why do you not think you could love this Tom Gower? You know him, I can see that, or you would not act the way you are. Is he an old man?" Grace shook her head. "Is he cruel?" Grace shook her head again. "Does he have one eye, warts and no teeth?"

Grace's mouth trembled in a semblance of a smile, and she shook her head a third time. "Nay, my lady, some would say he is handsome," she conceded. "But . . ."

"But what, Grace?" Elizabeth snapped her brows together. "You are beginning to try my patience. For the last time, what is *wrong* with this man?"

"I love John of Gloucester," Grace blurted out. "I cannot conceive of wedding anyone but him."

Elizabeth's bell-like laugh rang around the room, but it sounded like a death knell to Grace. Now the tears fell in great drops on her dress. " 'Tis no laughing matter, your grace," she said miserably. "You are going to say he is my cousin, and thus I cannot marry him. I know that already." She rose suddenly and stamped her foot. "Oh, life is not fair! I just want to die!"

"*Tiens!* All these years, and I never knew you had a temper," Elizabeth said, amused. "So now your secret is out—although I seem to remember guessing at it two years ago, did I not?"

Grace stared at the floor and gave an imperceptible nod and a loud sniff. For once, Elizabeth's maternal spirit was moved to open her arms and invite the weeping Grace into them. " 'Tis true, you cannot marry John," she said, rocking the young woman gently, "even though money can perform miracles with the pope. Sadly, we have none, and besides, John cannot offer you a home, children or stability. And women of our station need that, Grace. Who knows if you will ever see John again? Remember him as your first love, and keep that memory sweet and fresh." She paused as Grace let out an anguished sob. "Hush, now. Marry Tom Gower and have a family of your own. You are a born mother—look how well you take care of me. Would you not like to hold your own wee babe? Aye, what woman doesn't? I should know; I have held ten, although some be with the angels now." She put Grace from her and pulled a cambric kerchief from her sleeve. "Dry your eyes, child. You do not want Katherine to mock you more, do you?"

Grace looked up in astonishment, dabbing at her face and blowing her nose. "You notice?" she asked. "I thought you did not notice."

"What do you think I am?" Elizabeth retorted. "A ninny? Certes, I notice. She treats you abominably, but she is old and sour, and I do not have the strength or desire to change her. In truth," she told Grace brightly, "there is another good reason for you to become Tom Gower's wife. You can leave the old bat behind!" She was rewarded with a chuckle.

Grace took a deep breath. "As always, I am grateful for your wisdom, your grace." She stood on tiptoe and, without warning, kissed Elizabeth on the cheek. "You have been like a mother to me, and I thank you from the bottom of my heart." She noticed from the softening of her features that Elizabeth was moved by the gesture, and she was glad. The dowager had not known affection since before Edward died, and Grace knew well that Elizabeth's daughters were respectful but afraid of their mother.

There was a knock at the door, and Katherine's voice called, " 'Tis I, Lady Hastings. May I come in?"

Elizabeth recovered her composure and sat back down on the shabby cushions of her chair. Grace asked quickly, "I beg of you, indulge me one more favor: let me go into the garden and gather my thoughts before we go and dine with the abbot. I promise I shall think long and hard about all you said."

Elizabeth nodded and then called out, "Come."

GRACE FOUND A patch of grass in the shade of a hedge out of sight of the ploughmen and sat on the ground, hugging her knees to her chest. Questions tripped off her tongue in quick succession like raindrops off a roof. What did Cecily say to Tom? Why would Tom want to wed me after our miserable meeting? Why does Cecily think I would even consider marriage with him? What has her husband to do with this? How do I feel about leaving here? Do I want to wed now? Do I want to wed Tom? Do I want to wed at all? Sweet Jesu, what choice do I have? And finally, what it all came down to: "Why can't I be with John?" she cried in frustration to the clouds scurrying by in the autumn wind.

Calm down, girl, she told herself sternly. Think this through. Consider your present circumstances. You are no more than a servant, in truth, for all you have royal blood in your veins. And you have no means of your own. What if Elizabeth *should* die in this place? What then? Do you want to be a nun? "Nay," she snorted as she snatched up a daisy and began pulling off its petals. "If my lot was to be one, God would have left me at Delapre," she said aloud. Come, Grace, you have been praying to be released from here every night for two years, she told herself. Now here is your deliverance, and you are hesitating. What did you have in mind, pray? John! Always John. How many times had she daydreamed of John riding through the gate, clattering into the courtyard and, seeing her picking flowers, come running to sweep her off her feet? "You addlepate!" she cried, throwing the decimated daisy into the wind. "Daydreams are for children. John looks on you like a sister. You should be ashamed of yourself."

She forced herself to think about Tom. She went back in her mind to Sheriff Hutton and saw him again riding companionably with John, playing with Jason, the dog and boy so close they were always together, and teaching Bess, Cecily and her patiently to fish. She remembered laughing with him when she fell into the river and was reminded of the ease with which she could talk to him then. Alice Gower's face swam clearly into that day's memory, and she thought of the woman's kindness to her, a mere stranger, and of the warmth she had experienced in Tom's home.

"I liked the north country," she muttered, surprising herself. There was a freedom to the wildness and the wideness of the landscape that had captured her imagination—despite the constant wind. Ah, but was it because John loved it, too? But then, so does Tom. John had asked her about Tom in Malines, she recalled. "He and I spent many a happy hour at the butts or riding out on the moors. I am glad Cecily persuaded Welles to take him into his household. He is a good fellow." Isn't that what John had said? Aye, she had to acknowledge, Tom is a good fellow. She conjured up their last meeting and tried to think how she had thought about him before they had fallen out. Be honest, Grace—you were glad to see him when you first recognized him in the field, were you not? You were glad, too, when he came to Westminster with the message from John of Lincoln. Aye, she said to herself, I like him. I have always liked him. She frowned and plucked at the grass. Then why did he have to spoil their friendship by thinking he loved her? " 'Twas *your* fault, Tom, not mine!" she muttered. She acknowledged she had been unkind, but how else was he to know that she loved John and he should forget her? You just do not know how to treat with men, my lady, she acknowledged sadly.

She lay back on the grass and cupped her hands behind her head. A magpie flew by and she sat up in a panic. "One for sorrow . . ." she murmured, quoting the old saying, and was about to spit out the bad luck when, in a black-and-white flash, a second swooped out of nowhere and joined its mate on the field to enjoy the fallen grain among the shorn cornstalks. Grace breathed a sigh of relief: "Ah! 'Two for joy,' " she finished. "Perhaps 'tis a sign."

The bell clanged for dinner, cutting off further rumination, and she got up and brushed off her skirts. Perhaps I can be happy with Tom, she mused. Certes, 'twould mean being close to Cecily again. The thought buoyed her as she hurried back to join the diners in the refectory and mingled with some of the extra field hands eager to a catch glimpse of the rich folk at their food. The one question she had not yet answered was why and how Cecily had come up with this plan for her, and what had she said on Grace's behalf to mollify the wounded Tom. She would have to discover for herself later, she concluded.

"You may tell Cecily that I will wed Tom Gower, your grace," she whispered to Elizabeth as they waited for the ewerer to make the rounds for the ritual handwashing before the meal. "But if 'tis possible, I would like to wait until the summer."

"Good girl," Elizabeth said with a wicked smile. "Let the man wait. Let him truly desire you. It worked for me, and look what happened—I became queen of England!"

15

Bermondsey and Greenwich

CHRISTMAS 1490

*H*enry had given his gracious permission for Bess's mother and two attendants to spend the holy time with her at Greenwich as she was again with child and thus would not travel with Henry to his mother's favorite residence of Collyweston. The three women awaited the break from abbey routine with much anticipation.

"Praise the heavens," Elizabeth had said at that point in the letter. "We can make merry while the bitch Beaufort's bones turn brittle in her freezing northern abode." She sounded more cheerful than she had for many weeks after a severe bout of the bloody flux had laid her low. "That phrase tripped nicely off the tongue, do you not think, ladies?" she asked and repeated "the bitch Beaufort's bones" to herself, chuckling.

"How clever you are," Katherine gushed, making Grace wince at her toadying.

Elizabeth inclined her head in acknowledgment. "I always loved Greenwich as the best of my palaces," she had said, wistfully. "I called it my 'palace of pleasaunce,' for I was never happier than when in it." She eyed Grace's old green gown and grimaced. "We shall have to find you something else to wear, Grace. That is far too shabby for the court. In fact, I think you should burn the gown, for I am heartily sick of it." She chuckled. "Besides, you need to look your best when you see your Tom again." She winked at Grace, who blushed and groaned inwardly.

THE ROYAL BARGE was sent to fetch Elizabeth and her two ladies two days before the feast of the Christ child. Jack Frost had left his telltale mark upon the landscape that morning, transforming the tilled fields, grass and trees into a sparkling white fairy kingdom. A layer of ice covered the water in the well and in the animal troughs, and the smoke from the abbey chimneys created gray trails in the blue sky. An abbey servant had made his daily visit to Elizabeth's chamber to light a fire—an expense the queen dowager saw not as an indulgence but a necessity. Even the water in the basin had a thin film of ice upon it, and Grace shivered as she plunged her hands in to splash water on her face. Once the wood began to crackle in the small fireplace, all three women gathered round to warm their numb fingers. Being so thin, Elizabeth felt the cold the most, and Grace and Katherine spent many hours during the harshest months chafing the queen's feet, being careful not to irritate the painful red chilblains on several of her toes. The first winter there, Bess had visited and had been dismayed that her mother had to make do with a small brazier that spewed out noxious fumes unless the window was left open. She had paid the abbey mason to build a fireplace and chimney outlet so that Elizabeth might have some semblance of the luxury that she had been forced to leave behind.

After breaking her fast, Elizabeth was helped into her warmest garments. Grace and Katherine, too, wrapped themselves in their fur-lined cloaks and donned gloves and wool hoods. With Poppy tucked into her cloak, Elizabeth and her two attendants processed down the stairs, through the privy yard and around the building to the main courtyard. Teeth chattering, they climbed into the waiting horse litter, the two large beasts at the front and back of the covered contraption snorting white clouds as they stamped their feet and waited to move. Grace saw that Edgar was to lead them to the river and waved. He grinned and bowed his head, watching to see Grace helped safely into the litter and seated opposite the other ladies before he told the lead horse "giddyup."

As the horses were led across the courtyard and out of the gate, Grace could hear the deep, resonant chants of the brothers as they celebrated the Terce. *"Magnificat anima mea Dominum,"* they sang, and although she was used to the sound now, it still had the power to move her. And looking at the magical scene they were passing, she felt the hand of God touching them. *"Gloria Patri,"* she whispered to herself in awe.

Elizabeth's eyes lit up when she saw the gorgeously canopied royal barge, the king's arms emblazoned on the hangings, awaiting them at the Tooley Street wharf. "At last I am to be treated like a queen," she muttered, as one of their escorts stepped forward to open the litter door and Grace hopped out first, taking Poppy from Elizabeth. Knowing the two older women would be slow to exit the carriage, she took the opportunity to hurry to Edgar, patiently holding the lead horse's bridle and murmuring into its velvety ear. She had heard the groom had shown great courage during a fire in the stables the week before, when he had rescued two horses and several other animals, burning his hand in the process.

"Edgar, I regret I have not seen you since the fire. I wanted to commend you on your bravery that night." Seeing the bandage covering his hand, she frowned. "I hope Brother Benedictus is caring for that properly?" she asked. "Honey is recommended for burns." Edgar nodded, shrugging off the injury. "I hope it goes well for you with Brother Gregory and your wish to become head groom. I have put in a good word for you with Father John, so perhaps one day you will be rewarded."

Edgar's face fell. "Brother Gregory says I be stupid—a simpleton," he said. "He said I be too stupid to be in charge of the stable lads. And the boys mock me, too. You be the only one who says kind things, my lady." Then he brightened and stroked the shiny brown flank of the patient horse, which turned and nuzzled his shoulder. "But Admiral here don't think I be stupid, do you boy? And I see that animals be liking you, too," he said, as Poppy scooted up to a warmer place around Grace's neck and closed her eyes.

"Nay, Edgar, you are not stupid," Grace replied kindly, fondling Poppy's fluffy ears. She did not know what else she could do for the man, so she reached out and gingerly patted Admiral's neck, in the hope of assuring him of her sincerity. With Edgar there she was less afraid of the animal. The gesture had the desired effect, and Edgar grinned and touched his forelock as she moved away. "God bless you, Lady Grace, and may your Yuletide season be a happy one," he called after her.

"Why do you waste time with that groom?" Elizabeth snapped after Grace had hurried to the dock past the line of oarsmen and was helped into the roomy barge. "You have kept us all waiting."

" 'Twas Edgar, my lady," Grace answered, a hint of indignation in her voice. "I was commending him for his bravery in the fire. He saved several animals, in truth." She knew Elizabeth had taken her time getting into the barge, enjoying the deference paid her by the escort Bess had sent and by the master of oarsmen. She joined the two women ensconced cozily among the fur blankets and cushions and, depositing Poppy onto Elizabeth's lap, pulled up her hood against the cold morning breeze on the river.

"Now that Lady Grace has blessed us with her presence, Master Rowley, we may cast off," Elizabeth called, ignoring Grace's explanation. Instead, she said, "I know not why you must consort with peasants, Grace. Servants are servants; one should treat them well, but not as equals. Have I not taught you well enough to understand your place?" She sighed. "The sooner you are married and no longer my responsibility, the better."

Grace saw Katherine smile, and she hid behind her hood and grimaced at the intentional reminder of her betrothal to Tom. "I beg your pardon, your grace," she said. "I did not know you had gone aboard so quickly." *Grace, watch your tongue,* she thought, waiting for the expected admonition. Elizabeth chose not to dignify the cheek with a reprimand, she just sighed and sank lower into the warm blankets. Nothing would spoil this day for her; she was returning to court—even if it was only for a few days.

As the barge approached the Greenwich pier below the elegant white-washed palace, shawms heralded the arrival of the queen dowager. Their raucous fanfare brought people running to the wharf to cheer the visitors.

"Is my wimple straight? My hood folded back the way I like it?" Elizabeth fussed, turning first to Katherine and then to Grace. "Is Bess there to greet me?"

Grace scanned the courtiers arrayed at the bottom of the tower on the steps that led away from the water into the king's apartments but did not see the queen. Then another fanfare rang out across the water. The boat-men had shipped their oars while the tiller man guided them expertly the last few yards to the water steps, and now Grace could see a company of guards in the royal blue, gold and red livery, the axlike blades of their long halberds glinting in the sun, clearing a passage from the tower entrance to the wharf. A small group appeared from the building and Grace recog-nized Bess's tall figure in a gown of pale blue velvet trimmed with ermine bowing this way and that as courtiers gave her reverence. She was escorted by an older man with a lugubrious expression on his thin face. An outsized velvet hat sporting several feathers capped off his murrey velvet, ermine-trimmed robe.

"Aye, Bess is there, but I do not recognize her escort," Grace told Eliza-beth, who was preening in a silver mirror that Katherine held for her. Elizabeth pushed Katherine aside and tried to focus her eyes on the figures now waiting at the top of the steps. She had spent so much time in the con-fines of her chamber that she had trouble seeing long distances.

" 'Tis John Welles. Cecily's husband," Katherine said, knowing Eliza-beth was too vain to admit she could not see anyone clearly. "And Cecily walks behind them on the arm of . . . God be praised, your own Thomas," she cried, excited for the first time since the visit to Greenwich was an-nounced. "That means my Cecilia is also here—and my granddaughters."

"Thomas, here?" Elizabeth's face lit up. "It would seem the king has him high in his favor again, God be thanked."

The lines from the barge were thrown and secured, and gradually the boat was drawn to the landing dock. Elizabeth edged her way to the gang-plank and, with the help of the master, went ashore, followed by Grace and Katherine. Judging from the shocked faces of many of the retainers who craned their necks to get their first glimpse of the queen dowager in al-most four years, Grace was not the only one who recognized the change in her. But Elizabeth was smiling happily and climbing the few steps to Bess, unaware that she had caused anything but joy in the spectators. She gave Bess reverence, but the queen raised her up quickly, knowing how painful such a deep curtsy must be, and embraced her mother warmly.

"You are right welcome at our court, noble mother," Bess said. "You remember Lord John?" Elizabeth nodded, holding out her hand for him to kiss, Poppy held firmly in the other. Jack Welles bowed stiffly over it and gave her a good day. Poppy growled and bared her teeth; she did not like strange men touching her mistress. Grace heard someone titter. She and Katherine were still on their knees on the cold stone of the wharf, until Bess gave them permission to rise and kissed Grace on the cheek. When Cecily bent and kissed Grace, she whispered, "So what think you of my handsome husband?" and Grace almost laughed. It wasn't that Viscount Welles was hideous, she thought, but he was most certainly old for his forty years and had the look of his humorless stepsister, Lady Margaret, about him. She vaguely wondered if anything would make him smile.

"I confess I've seen handsomer," she whispered back.

Elizabeth was kissing her oldest son's cheeks, glowing with happiness. Katherine had told Grace in an unusual moment of camaraderie one morning, when Elizabeth was in conference with Father John, that Thomas Grey, Marquis of Dorset, was the queen dowager's favorite child. "Her firstborn, you understand. And son of the man she loved with all her heart. Aye, she grew to love your father, who was besotted with her"— she had rolled her eyes at the memories—"but John Grey always had her heart—and he was constant, unlike Edward. His death on Saint Alban's field was what changed her," she declared. "She vowed she would stop at nothing to give her two sons the most advancement she possibly could to compensate for their father's loss." Katherine had bent close to Grace then, who was busy sponging a stain off her gown, and whispered, " 'Tis said she and her mother used witchcraft to beguile the young king, Edward." Grace had gasped and crossed herself. "Aye," Katherine ended, gleefully. "Jacquetta Woodville was a descendant of the water witch Melusine." Grace had no idea who Melusine was, but with her silvery hair and tinkling laugh, Elizabeth might be thought of as having sprung from a sprite.

Katherine had then whispered: " 'Tis said Elizabeth refused him her bed unless he promised her marriage, and although he must have realized a marriage with her would have displeased the commons and the lords— not to mention his mother—he did indeed wed her in secret." Grace nodded. She had heard this tale from Bess, who had thought it the most romantic love story in all the world. But Lady Hastings was not finished: "The betrothal was held with her mother's blessing, at her mother's house and . . . perhaps with the help of a magic love potion." Grace crossed herself again. Dear God, she hoped Bess did not know about the witchcraft rumor—the virtuous young queen would be mortified.

Grace had been astonished at Katherine's revelations that day—not only that the older woman would betray her friend's confidences, but that she, whom Katherine had always disdained, should be the recipient of them. Grace had put it down to the fact there was no one else to gossip with, and Elizabeth had been excessively trying that day. She had said nothing but kept the knowledge in that treasure trove in her mind reserved for family.

Now she looked curiously at Thomas. He had visited the abbey once or twice a year, but Elizabeth had always sent her attendants away for those hours so she could enjoy her son by herself, and thus Grace had never formed any opinion of the man. He was tall and broad with strong features and a loud laugh, but his eyes were restless and untrusting. And Grace had seen the self-serving side of him when he had denied his mother at the time of Henry's angry decision to send her away.

"Let us go inside," Bess said, turning from the water and taking Jack's proffered arm. "Lord Thomas, I pray you escort our lady mother." At once the entourage shuffled into place behind the queen, and the colorful procession wended its way up the spiral staircase in the tower, through the king's presence chamber that faced the river and then around the corner into the queen's watching chamber, the largest of her private rooms. The court waiting there gave their queen reverence as John Welles escorted Bess to her canopied throne on the dais. She motioned to Elizabeth to take the other chair while Cecily, Katherine and Grace took their places behind the two queens. As they walked past the kneeling retainers, Grace heard one whisper to her neighbor: "Such shabby clothes. What has the Woodville woman come to?" Grace glanced down at her own new gown. Elizabeth had charmed the Southwark dressmaker into making the new gown quickly, and although the plain blue wool overdress had fashionably long trailing sleeves and a square bodice, it did not belong among the damasks, velvets and silks of every hue that surrounded her. And on the dais, Bess, in the radiant bloom of pregnancy, glowed golden as the sun next to her silvery, moon-pale mother.

As soon as the two queens were settled, a young woman came hurrying up to the dais escorting a little boy who was an exact miniature of a courtier in a short, belted blue tunic trimmed in sable, pale blue hose and a soft black hat. Around his neck was an exquisitely crafted gold collar of tiny roses. He bowed solemnly to his mother and grandmother and then went on one knee to await permission to mount the dais and kiss his grandmother's hand. Bess's face lit up when she saw him and she readily called him to her: "Lord Arthur, you remember your grandam, Queen Elizabeth? Come, give her a kiss, my precious boy." His severe courtly expression melting into a childish grin, young Arthur Tudor scrambled up the steps and clasped his mother about the knees. Grace could see he was a sweet boy, with fair curls and a sunny smile; only the pale blue eyes and slender build were reminiscent of Henry. For a second she wondered if he might remind Elizabeth of her own lost young sons—one of whom was lost no more, it would seem—but the dowager merely accepted the boy's kiss and returned him to his mother's knee.

While they awaited the call to dine, Bess called for music. She conversed quietly with her mother, allowing her courtiers the liberty to stroll around the room and talk among themselves or watch the antics of a jester who cavorted from group to group in his striped costume and shook the bells on his many-pointed hat and beribboned wand. Arthur laughed gleefully at the clown and was soon entertaining the court with his childish imitations of the performer's acrobatics. After an unfortunate tumble, when Arthur let out a wail of frustration and pain, Bess signaled to the nursemaid to remove him from the hall. He left screaming with indignation at being thus dismissed, and the court breathed a collective sigh of relief when the closing doors dampened the intrusive cries.

Katherine had negotiated a position directly behind Elizabeth, to be next to Cecily and accepted as Elizabeth's senior attendant, leaving Grace to stand a step away from Katherine's elbow. She could have strained her ears to eavesdrop, as she knew Katherine was doing, but instead her eyes roamed around the room, enjoying the luxurious surroundings she remembered from her life before Bermondsey. She saw now they were no match for the sumptuous furnishings of Duchess Margaret's palace, but they were a welcome change after months in the austere abbey.

She was scanning the faces and finery in front of her when she suddenly looked straight into Tom Gower's honest blue eyes. Her stomach turned over and the blood rushed into her face. *Certes, he is here, you* addlepate, she thought miserably; Cecily and the viscount are here. Where else would he be? And yet when she had seen the Welleses she had given no thought to Tom. Sweet Jesu, I am blushing, she realized, furious with herself. Ashamed, she lowered her eyes from his gaze, hoping he had not noticed. She could not say what she read in that look; he had not smiled, she was certain of that, but was there anger or dislike in his eyes? She could not be sure. When she looked up at him again he was being addressed by John Welles and his attention was riveted on his master. Cecily had advised Elizabeth in the betrothal letter that her husband had elevated Tom to squire of the body, and from the friendly way Jack was gripping Tom's arm as he spoke, Grace could see that the viscount thought highly of the young man.

With Tom focused on his master, Grace had a chance to look at him with new eyes. He stood a head taller than those around him, for once a black bonnet taming his corn-colored hair. She admitted his neat beard suited him, as did the padded blue pourpoint, its pleats forming a V shape from his shoulders to his trim waist and then flaring over his lower body. With his checkered hose and long trailing sleeves, he was a far cry from the plainly dressed youth at Sheriff Hutton. Her appraisal complete, she could say that although he was not John, she could do much worse. However, seeing him from afar was one thing, but sooner or later she knew they must come face to face, and it now appeared it would be sooner, and she dreaded it. What would she say? She had not had the chance to speak to Cecily alone since their arrival. She desperately wanted to know why Tom had been talked or coerced into wedding her. It would help her to know so she might prepare what to say to him. His steady gaze of a few minutes ago haunted her already and told her nothing that might alleviate her misgivings that he hated her and was wedding her against his will. She had been bitterly disappointed that he had not written to her himself to reassure her that he did indeed wish her to be his wife, but Elizabeth had scoffed when Grace complained.

"My dear Grace, 'tis not required once the betrothal is sanctioned by those responsible for the bride and groom's future. In the end, 'twas between Jack Welles, or"—she chuckled—"should I say Cecily, and me. By rights, you have no say one way or the other. But we have been through all this, and you have assured me there is no compelling reason for your refusal to wed Master Gower and therefore you shall wed him. Let me hear no more about it." And so, from his silence, Grace was certain that Tom must be a reluctant bridegroom. Now, without even a glimmer of a smile from him, she was even more convinced.

ON CHRISTMAS DAY, after the court had celebrated the eve of the Christ child's birth in prayer and thanks, the chamberlain approached the throne in the queen's audience chamber and announced that dinner was served. The players of rebecs, recorders and the new German crumhorns ceased their background accompaniment and hurried out of the room to set up anew in the minstrels' gallery above the great hall.

The women sat apart from the men for the feast, a tradition Bess kept this season in deference to her mother's more formal court of a decade ago. She and Elizabeth sat on the dais and chose Cecily and Grace to serve them. Katherine was grateful to stay off her feet and found her place at a table of other noble ladies. High above the diners, the king's choristers took their place with the minstrels and broke out into song, reminding the company why they were celebrating.

"Nowell, nowell, nowell, nowell,
This is the salutation of the angel Gabriel.
Tidings true, there be come new, sent from the Trinity
By Gabriel to Nazareth, city of Galilee.
A clean maiden and pure virgin, through her humility
Hath conceived the person second in Deity."

The voices rang out in the painted hall and floated up to the magnificent hammer-beam roof as if they were addressing God himself, and Grace felt her skin prickle.

Before the blessing was said, Elizabeth looked around the hall and a chuckle escaped her. "I remember well my coronation feast, Bess," she murmured, fingering the leaf motif of her gold and black enameled necklace, a square ruby glowing in the center. "I made Edward's sisters, Elizabeth of Suffolk and Margaret, serve me on their knees. They were there for hours, and Meg fell ill soon afterwards. Wicked girl! She made me think my command had something to do with her fever. But 'twas not my fault her humors were misaligned." Bess cringed at the thought of her mother's arrogant behavior as Archbishop Morton offered a long-winded grace.

Following the traditional soup of ground chicken and frumenty, and after the fish dishes of lamprey and eel had been greedily consumed, the company applauded loudly as cooks and their helpers brought in roast swans, peacocks and a heron, each redressed in their own plumage and looking so real Grace was afraid they might fly off the platters. But the highlight of the feast was the suckling pigs, and the enormous platters were borne in by several kitchen lads, followed by the two head cooks carrying the steaming roasted head of a boar, a garland of holly crowning it and its razor sharp tusks now used as decorative spikes for rosy apples.

> "The boar's head in hand bear I
> Bedecked with bays and rosemary;
> And I pray you, masters, be merry
> Quot estis in convivio."

The singers paused so the people below could take a collective breath and join in the joyful refrain:

> "Caput apri defero
> Reddens laudes Domino."

The fleshy cheeks of the animal were considered the delicacy from the beast, and a slice each was given to Elizabeth and Bess for their tasting. Using golden forks, the two queens each lifted a morsel to their lips and nodded their approval. The rest of the company waited until their messes had been filled before dipping in with their neighbors and transferring succulent pieces of meat to their own trenchers. The wine flowed freely, and Grace soon lost count of how many glasses she had consumed. When the tables were cleared and stacked with the benches against the walls, the dancing began. A lively *branle* sent many dancers to the floor. Behind Elizabeth's chair, Grace tapped her foot in time to the beat of the timbre and tabor, watching those who knew the intricate kicks, twists of the feet and swinging of the legs demonstrate why the French dance was known as the "brawl" in England.

Cecily bent to ask permission from Bess to take Grace onto the floor for the next country dance. "She has not had the chance to show her skill for three years. Your grace, sweet sister, do relieve us of our posts so we can join the others."

"You do not need to give me false flattery, *sweet* sister," Bess replied, smiling. "Certes, go and dance. I wish I could be among you, but . . ." She paused, touching her belly. "Henry would not be happy if I lost this babe. He is sure we will have a second son this time. What say you, Mother? Shall we let these two loose down there amongst all those young men?"

Elizabeth laughed and several heads turned upon hearing the once familiar sound at court again. "Aye, Bess. Grace needs to sow her wild oats before she is wed, and as for Cecily . . . ah, well," she said, winking at Bess. "Cecily is always Cecily, and will never be tied down." Cecily gasped then giggled, looking around quickly for her husband, who was deep in conversation with Archbishop Morton. "You may go, girls, but send Lady Katherine and her daughter to attend us. It will be amusing to hear the two mothers of our grandchildren vie over whose child is more perfect." And she chuckled again. Grace knew Elizabeth had had at least as much wine as she, but perhaps it was pure happiness at being let out of her cage that had caused the queen dowager's merry mood. Cecily took Grace's hand and ran down the steps of the dais towards a young man with coal black hair and eyes as green as the summer sea.

"Master Kyme, do lead us out to the dance," Cecily said, accepting his kiss on her hand. "This is my half sister, Grace, who is to wed Tom Gower. Is she not the daintiest thing you have ever set eyes on?"

Thomas Kyme turned to Grace and smiled, and Grace knew she had never seen a comelier man—not even John could compare to this paragon of masculine beauty. "Thomas Kyme, at your service, my lady," he murmured, taking her hand and bowing over it.

"Master Kyme is a neighbor in Lincolnshire," Cecily explained airily, but Grace doubted her sister could also explain her high color and nervous hands, which Grace observed with interest and not a little apprehension. Surely Cecily was not . . . nay, she could not be. You are dreaming, Grace, she thought. Cecily make a cuckold of the king's stepuncle? 'Tis cock-brained.

"I will lead the Lady Grace out, my lady," a voice said behind Grace, who jumped and turned to face Tom a few feet from her. "If she will accept," he added, bowing so low she could not see his face.

Cecily gave Grace a little push. "As the two of you will be dancing together for the rest of your lives, this would seem a good time to start. What say you, Grace?" Without waiting for an answer, she took Master Kyme's arm and hurried him away to join the set.

Tom lifted his head and looked straight into Grace's anxious eyes. It was as though the two of them were alone in the room. The gorgeously arrayed revelers moved liked shadows around them and the noise melted into a background drone. Neither spoke a word, and yet each understood the other in that silence. "I am sorry," her eyes told him. "I know," his replied. After a long moment, Tom slowly reached out his hand, his eyes willing her to take it. Her gaze never leaving his face, she put her hand in his and they walked towards the circle of dancers. His hand was warm and firm, and although her tiny one was lost in it, it was comforting, she decided, and relief flooded her.

As they prepared to join the circle the music came to an end and the men bowed their reverence and led their partners to find refreshment. Tom and Grace were left in the middle of the red and white tiled floor as the musicians struck up Grace's favorite *basse danza*.

"Do me the honor, Grace," Tom said simply, turning her to face the dais and holding up her arm in the first movement of the dance. She acquiesced by giving his hand a tiny squeeze as she rose up on her toes to perform the gliding steps of the slowest of the courtly dances, casting her eyes to the floor, as was customary. Drawing strength from each other, the two usually reserved young people found the confidence to begin the dance alone. Many present recognized Grace, but the last time they had seen her she had been a girl. Now they admired the comely young woman's fluid movements and perfectly proportioned—almost doll-like—figure, and one whispered that King Edward's bastard was surely born to dance. In her russet silk dress with the amber brooch pinned to her breast, she shone that night. Later, as Grace prepared Elizabeth for bed, the dowager told her of the pride she had seen in Tom's face as he partnered her.

"He is in love with you, Grace, make no mistake," Elizabeth remarked, tying her nightcap under her chin. "I hope you were kinder to him tonight than you were last time, in truth." Grace had nodded, although by then she was so befuddled, she could not have told Elizabeth exactly why.

If she had tried to correctly remember the steps of the dance, she possibly might have failed after so long without practice. But she was so acutely aware of Tom's hand touching hers and his eyes fixed upon her that it seemed her feet recalled the rise and fall of each movement on their own. In the first few moments she was relieved that he had overcome his anger towards her enough to approach and ask her to dance, but then her mind was filled with questions, half questions and an awful confusion of feelings. Why could she not conjure up John's face at that precise moment? And why had Tom's touch sent unexpected sweet sensations through her body, if Tom was only a friend? How, until now, could she not have noticed his long, strong legs or the chiseled features of his face, the delicious smell of orris root and leather and his gentleness? When had his friendship for her turned to love? She knew she must forget John, but how? He was her one and only love—or was he? Certes, he was! However, she admitted, Tom did not displease her. Sweet Virgin, let the dance go on forever, she begged, but then could not say why. She saw Elizabeth arch an eyebrow and give her a secret smile as they moved with the music towards the dais. She should not be looking up, she knew, and so she fixed her eyes firmly upon the rushes again.

When the dance finished, Tom turned her to him and they reverenced each other, Grace hardly daring to look up in case he could read her busy mind.

"You have not forgotten how to dance, Lady Grace," Tom murmured, kissing her hand. "You were always the most graceful of the sisters."

Grace looked at him warily. "I love to dance," she said simply, and as her courage began to resurface, she joked, "Although the monks make poor dancing partners, in truth."

Tom grinned and then was serious. "I would speak with you privately about our betrothal. When might that be?"

Grace was taken aback by his directness. "Ah, aye. Th-the betrothal," she stammered, and attempted to brush it off. "I know not when. I have my duty to the queen dowager. 'Tis her permission you must seek to speak with me, I believe. I do not think we should be alone. I kn-know not the way of things, you see."

"But you have agreed to be my wife, have you not?" he asked anxiously. "Lady Cecily gave me your answer." He had led her to a quiet window seat, unobserved by all but a curious few. He drew her down upon it.

"I . . . I am not ready to talk about this, Tom," Grace protested. "I pray you, speak to the dowager first. Why must you spoil the moment?"

She made to rise but he pulled her down. "Why should talking of our betrothal 'spoil the moment'?" he asked. She saw to her dismay that he was clearly annoyed. "My offer is honorable. Why can you not tell me you will wed me to my face?"

"Perhaps because you did not ask me to my face—or even with a letter," Grace shot back. "Certes, I do not know if 'twas you who made the offer or my sister, Cecily. I have not had time to question her yet, but I will. Do you deny she had a hand in this?"

Tom studied the signet ring on his little finger for a moment before he answered. "I cannot deny it, I am ashamed to admit. Your sister told me you wanted to leave the abbey and"—he paused, seeking the right words so as not to offend the young woman who owned his heart—"that in the circumstances, marriage would be your only escape. Knowing my . . . respect for you, she suggested . . ." He stopped, then forged on, "As a second son I might do worse than marry someone . . . someone with no . . ." He could not bring himself to say "prospect of wedding higher because she is base-born and of no value to a king who looks upon her as an encumbrance from the defeated house of York."

Grace felt tears behind her eyes but forced them back. "She offered a dowry for me, did she not?" she asked in a whisper.

Tom's eyebrows snapped together. "Hell's bells, Grace! You do not think 'twas the dowry that made me do it?"

Now Grace's dander was up. "How should I know why you did it?" she retorted. "I never heard a word from you, either before or after the betrothal proposal. The last time we saw each other you departed in anger, and I believed our friendship was over."

"But I did write to you!" he cried, his cheeks flushing red. "I wrote after the . . . the argument we had. I told you I regretted my outburst. Did you not receive it?"

Grace shook her head. "Letters are often lost at the abbey, it seems—so many comings and goings, I suppose. Even so, I still do not understand why you would wish to wed a woman whose heart is given elsewhere. Did you think an offer from you would change what is in my heart?"

It was Tom's turn to be indignant. "John! Always John! If I am so unexceptional in your eyes beside John, why did you accept my offer, pray? Was it merely the only alternative to taking the veil?"

Grace hung her head. "Something like that, Tom," she admitted miserably. "Elizabeth painted a dismal picture of my future, and I was afraid, in truth. I am sorry."

Tom's mouth curved into a smile, then he chuckled, and finally he threw back his head and let all his frustrations out in a belly laugh. Several heads turned in their direction, and people nudged and smiled at the merry laughter. Grace looked up, nonplussed. What had she said that was so funny? She cocked her head in her old way, asking, "Why do you laugh? 'Tis no laughing matter."

"If I don't, I shall cry," Tom told her, taking her hand. "Can you not see the irony? We have been forced into a situation that is painful for both of us simply because we thought it was the best we could do for ourselves given our sorry circumstances. What a way to start a marriage! You must see the funny side, Grace, or we are doomed to unhappiness before we begin our life together."

"But you did not need to wed, Tom," Grace said, acknowledging the wisdom of his words and liking him more for it. "You could remain a bachelor in Welles's service and forge a way for yourself at court. A wife is not a requirement for a man to get ahead in this world."

Tom cupped her chin in his hand. "Grace, Grace, my dearest girl. You must know the answer. I have loved you since that day you fell in the river and I took you to my home. I know you do not love me in return, and that I will always pale beside John, but if you will allow me to care for you and protect you and give me your friendship, then I shall be content." He was astonished by his own eloquent declaration and was suddenly shy. "By the Rood, I *do* wear my heart on my sleeve, don't I?" he said ruefully. "You were right that day in the cornfield, and I swore I would never do it again. Forgive me?"

Grace could not speak. She took the hand from her chin and, looking him straight in the eye, kissed his upturned palm. He bent forward and with utmost tenderness kissed her soft lips as if to seal the pact.

"Grace Plantagenet, will you do me the honor of becoming my wife?" he murmured, his mouth still on hers.

"I will, Tom Gower," she whispered back, and not heeding the titters of two young women standing near, she pressed her mouth to his to signal her acceptance.

Lying next to a snoring Katherine in the darkness of the small chamber assigned to the queen dowager's ladies in waiting, she thought back more clearly on the evening and marveled how, in the space of such a short time, she had come to accept and be grateful for her fate.

"Dear Saint Sibylline," she whispered, turning Tom's ring on her thumb. "It would seem this orphan has come in from the storm."

"Come keep me company, Lady Grace," the queen welcomed her half sister, who had been announced and entered the private chamber a few days later. "I trust your visit to Greenwich is a pleasant diversion for you."

Grace rose from her curtsy and went to embrace Bess, seated among large crimson satin cushions on the floor before the cheerful fire. In one corner of the chamber, hung with colorful tapestries of flowers and birds, an attendant softly plucked a lute and sang:

> "There is no rose of such virtue
> As is the rose that bore Jesu,"

and she was joined in the "Alleluya" by her two companions, busy with their needlework.

"God's greeting to you, your grace. 'Tis good of you to ask, and aye, the change of scenery is much appreciated," Grace said, smiling. She plumped up a cushion and sat down, spreading her skirts about her. Cecily had given her young Mistress Kate's blue dress again, and this time Cecily had told her sister to keep it. "Kate is to be married, and her bridal chest will not include anything that is not new. Her father has seen to that." Grace had accepted the gift gratefully; the garment increased her wardrobe to three gowns: the new gray worsted for everyday wear at the abbey; Kate's blue for high days and holidays; and the russet silk for royal occasions.

"How well you are looking! The gown becomes you, Bess," she said. "May I still call you Bess?"

"Aye, Grace, you may," Bess replied, chuckling. "Though it seems I will have to address you as Mistress Gower in a little while. Who would have thought all those years ago in Sheriff Hutton that you and Tom . . ." She smiled wistfully at the memories of those idle summer days in the meadows and hills of the north. She dared not admit that she longed for their solace more often than she ought.

"I would ask if you think 'tis what I should do," Grace began a little timidly, recognizing the inexperienced young woman of five years ago was gone; Bess was now a wife and mother of two, with a third on the way. She was a queen and had forsaken—or appeared to have forsaken—her Yorkist sentiments; her husband was her lord, and with a mother-in-law whose character was stronger even than Elizabeth Woodville's, she had buried her own needs and wants inside a beautiful and brave facade.

"Certes, 'tis what you should do, Grace," Bess assured her. "I fear for Mother's health. She is more than fifty now, is naught but skin and bone and cannot last much longer. You should know that I gave Cecily my blessing in this matter. Both of us are grateful for the service you have done our mother, but without our help you would have no future. We both agreed marriage with Tom was the best way." She paused and fiddled with the venice gold braid that made up her belt. Once again she had received a cold stare from Henry when she had broached the subject of Grace and a small dowry, but she could not bring herself to hurt Grace with that information. She lifted her eyes to her half sister's expectant face and put out her hand to touch her. "Dear Grace, you are always so uncomplaining, but you must tell me if Cis and I did you a wrong. We had to find you a husband, and we thought Tom Gower would suit more than a stranger."

Bess's kindness was too much for Grace. She flung herself into the queen's arms and said on a sob: "How can I refuse when you and Cis care so very much? I like Tom Gower"—she took a deep breath and pulled away—"and have no fear, we are disposed to wed. I will learn to love him, and he will be kind, I have no doubt." She wiped away a tear and smiled. "So be it. There, now, do you feel better?"

Bess nodded, relief written all over her face. "Then we should have a celebration—a betrothal celebration, before you return to the abbey," she exclaimed and rubbed her belly, chuckling. "I do not want to wait until summer—I shall be engaged elsewhere."

A celebration? Grace paled at the thought of hundreds of people staring at her and Tom. A formal betrothal was as good as a marriage contract and meant . . . Dear God, it meant Tom had the right to bed her. She gazed at Bess unblinking as thoughts ran rampant around in her mind. First and foremost, she had not wanted to contemplate lying with him. Why, oh why had she agreed to wed? Her imagination took hold for a second—perhaps she could disguise herself again and return to Malines, tell John again of her love and beg him to run away with her . . .

"Grace? Are you listening?" Bess's kind voice intruded upon her thoughts, and she blinked in surprise.

"I crave your pardon, Bess. What did you say?"

"I was saying that we should seek out Cecily and Mother and plan a small feast. No need to invite the entire court—only the family. What say you?"

"Must I . . . will Tom and I . . . do we have to . . . bed . . ." she stumbled over the words like a blind man in unfamiliar surroundings and looked so miserable that Bess laughed.

" 'Tis not so bad, Grace." She blushed, again stroking her belly. "And the rewards are great. Henry and I"—now it was her turn to stumble—"in truth, Henry *knew* me before our marriage," she said delicately. "We were so much in love, it seemed natural."

"Aye, I know," Grace said absently, still fixed on her own dilemma and failing to notice Bess's questioning frown. "But there is a difference. I like Tom, but I do not love him."

"What did you say? You knew Henry and I . . . ?" She leaned forward, whispering, "How did you know?"

Grace blinked and then smiled. "Have no fear—I kept it to myself. But I was concerned for you that day Henry arrived unannounced at Ormond's Inn and took you off somewhere. His captain took pity on me and let me leave the room. I saw you . . ." Now it was her turn to blush. "I did not know what was happening, but as you were not fighting or screaming, I decided you did not mind Henry being on top of you."

Both women laughed then, and Grace felt better. "I know more now, Bess," she said. "All I can hope for is that Tom is kind with me."

THE HEAVY OAK door closed quietly behind Grace and a tiring woman sent by Bess came forward in the firelit chamber to unlace her bodice and untie her skirts. She allowed the woman to lift off her linen chemise and replace it with one of finest lawn, and she shivered in pleasure as the flimsy fabric floated over her nakedness. It had been a gift from Bess, and, not to be outdone, Cecily had loaned her a bed robe of yellow silk that was much too long and so gave her an almost childlike air. The attendant unpinned her glossy curls and invited Grace to sit while she ran a comb of horn through her waist-long hair. Grace had bathed earlier in the day, before the festivities that had taken place in the gaily festooned solar in Bess's lodgings overlooking the orchard at the back of the palace. The oil of lavender that had been rubbed into her wet skin was still evident, its sweet smell filling the room.

For the ceremonial blessing of the marriage bed and with several witnesses around her, Grace lay in the bed of the small chamber she and Tom had been given for the night. The priest sprinkled drops of holy water from a copper bowl upon the green and red counterpane, after which Elizabeth, Bess and Cecily kissed her in turn and wished her luck, leaving her with the attendant for company. And she waited for Tom.

"Comb my hair again, Joan, if you please," she said, nervously climbing out of bed after only five minutes. "It soothes me." She thought back on the day, grateful for the attendant's silence and the rhythmic strokes of the comb.

Clothed in her copper silk, a gabled headdress edged with seed pearls framing her face and a pearl and enamel pendant—a gift from the Viscount and Viscountess Welles—hanging on a delicate gold chain around her neck, Grace had found herself much admired that afternoon. Bess was true to her word, and the group that gathered to give their blessing to the young couple was comprised of family members and a few attendants. Baby Arthur, in a long purple robe edged with ermine, entertained everyone with his joie de vivre, curious questions and attempts at dancing. Then mummers arrived during the feasting to reenact the legend of St. George and the Dragon. They coaxed Grace from her place of honor at the table to serve as the Fair Maiden of the tale, giving Grace several minutes of embarrassment in the center of the room as the dragon's unwilling victim. At last, after much posturing by the knight and bellowing from the dragon, bold St. George felled the animal with a sword thrust into its scaly heart. The beast, who was portrayed by two men at the front and back of the bright green costume, took several agonizing turns around the room before collapsing with a terrible scream, causing the onlookers to cheer and clap as St. George put his mailed foot upon its body and raised his sword high. "For England!" he cried. "For England!" the royal family repeated, raising their goblets. Bowing dramatically to Grace, St. George returned her to her place next to Tom, who had beamed with pride.

Tom! He would be here any moment, she realized, and she felt perspiration slipping down her sides. She must have started because the comb slipped out of the attendant's hand and clattered to the floor.

"I beg your pardon, my lady," the older woman apologized, bending to retrieve the object. "So careless of me."

"Nay, mistress, 'twas my fault," Grace assured her. "I confess I am a little anxious."

"If I may be so bold," Mistress Bayley offered, "I believe any bridegroom would be overjoyed to have a lady of your beauty and temperament as his wife." Bess had purposely chosen Joan Bayley for this task, and her instincts had not led her astray. "And if you would take advice from a wife of many years, a little dreaming of your own while your husband"—she searched for a phrase that was polite—"claims what is his right will make the act more bearable. Did your mother not advise you in these matters, my lady?"

Grace looked at the woman in surprise. It was unusual for someone of lower rank to thus address her superior, but she liked Joan's honest face and sensible words and swallowed her pride.

"Nay, Mistress Joan, I lost my mother when I was five. I was raised in a convent, and"—she chuckled—"the nuns were loath to talk about matters of the flesh."

"You poor little mite," Joan said kindly. "Then why don't you ask for guidance from our Lord's dear mother?" Grace did not like to remind her that the Virgin Mary had not had to endure the carnal act, so merely smiled her thanks. "But," Joan continued, leaning in and whispering, "if your husband does not please you, lady, then imagine someone else who might."

Grace gasped, wondering if the woman could read her heart, but she had no more time to wonder because there was a knock at the door and she knew Tom had come. She thanked Joan for her kindness and called, "Come." Was that thin, squeaky voice really mine? she asked herself. She cleared her throat and, with more conviction, called again, "Come." Joan curtsied as the door opened to admit Tom, and then she slipped out into the passage.

Tom had removed his parti-colored padded doublet and was now in his gipon—the high collar of his cambric undershirt showing under it—and his hose, their silver lacing points glinting in the flickering light.

"Grace?" he said softly, peering into the shadows. "Where are you?" Grace stepped into the light and Tom's eyes drank in the sight. "God's bones, but you are beautiful," he whispered and took a step towards her.

When Grace saw the love on his face and heard the tenderness in his voice, she lost her fear. I cannot be cruel to him, she decided; he is too good a man. And so she glided towards him, careful not to trip on Cecily's long robe.

"Let me help you, husband," she said, reaching up to untie the neck of his gipon.

Her closeness was too much for Tom, and he pulled her into his arms and whispered, "Sweet Jesu, how I love you" into her curls and inhaled her lavender scent. With her cheek pressed against the soft jacket and her arms barely meeting around his waist, she felt dwarfed; but once again, it comforted her. He tipped her face up to his and bent low to kiss her on the lips. She recognized it as a respectful first kiss, and taking Mistress Bayley's advice to heart, she pretended he was John. Her mouth opened under his and, without knowing how she knew to do this, invited in his tongue. As he slowly accepted her overture, she felt him harden against her and was surprised to feel her own mounting desire.

"I need to rid myself of my hose," he whispered. "They are the very devil to remove alone. I have heard them called 'passion killers,' and for good reason."

Grace giggled. "I have no experience, you understand, but let me try." Between the two of them they unlaced the two leggings and lifted the tight jacket over his head. He stood there in his soft shirt, which fell to just above his knees. Gently, he slipped the yellow robe from Grace's shoulders and ran his hands down her arms, feeling the warm skin under her flimsy chemise. Her full breasts with their brown-tinged nipples were just visible through it, and Tom could not keep his eyes from them. Grace timidly lifted one of his hands and placed it on her left breast.

"I can feel your heart, my love," he said hoarsely and, sweeping her into his arms, he carried her to the bed. There he knelt beside her and slowly removed his shirt.

"Ah, Grace, if you only knew how long I have wanted you," he said. "And now that you are mine, I am afraid of having you. You are a creature so fragile and precious that the thought of . . . of mounting you—"

"I will not break," Grace interrupted, amused. "But I hope you will be mindful."

He was darkly silhouetted against the firelight, but she could see how powerful his shoulders were after years of knightly training. She did not dare to look down past his flat belly, for she sensed he was fully aroused, and now she knew a moment of fear. Dear God, this will hurt, she told herself, but she put out her hand and stroked his chest. She knew that she, not he, would have to make the first move and, taking pity on him, she whispered, "Come to me, Tom. But be gentle with me."

And he was. The initial sharp pain was bearable, and now that the long wait for her was over, he took only a moment to climax, surprising Grace with his cry of pleasure. She had not even had time to think of John, and now there was no need. Tom's fingers found their target and soon she was moaning in her own astonished ecstasy.

"I fear I was a Johnny-come-early," he murmured, lying on his side with her nestling into him. "Tomorrow I will do better."

" 'Tis no matter, Tom, as long as I pleased you," Grace said sleepily. "May God watch over us tonight."

"*Amen*, my sweet wife," Tom said. "I swear I am the happiest person on earth."

Grace wanted to say she was, too, but she could not bring herself to lie.

BUT THERE WAS no tomorrow for Tom. The very next day, when Grace quietly joined Elizabeth, Cecily and their ladies in Elizabeth's apartments, Grace learned that Viscount Welles and his entourage would be leaving that morning for Lincolnshire in the company of Archbishop Morton. The cleric was Henry's chancellor and considered by many to be the most learned man in the kingdom. Under Edward, despite his solid Lancastrian leanings, he had risen to bishop of Ely and master of the rolls.

Cecily was standing by the window, staring out at the gray day, sulking.

"Ah, there you are, Lady Grace," Elizabeth called and, raising one elegant eyebrow, she added: "I trust you had a good if not entirely restful night?"

Grace blushed, curtsied low and stammered a noncommittal reply.

"Be a good girl," the dowager said, turning her gaze on Cecily. "Go and cheer up your sister. Sweet Jesu, I had forgotten how she can pout. Her husband and the archbishop will confer with the king at Lady Margaret Beaufort's house in Collyweston. Henry has need of his chancellor, it seems." She laughed. "That wily priest has managed to jump into every king's pocket since Edward forgave him for being a Lancastrian, God help him. I would not trust the man as far as I could throw him."

Grace was amused. She recalled Duchess Margaret speaking of Morton in exactly the same terms. " 'Twas he and Henry's sour-faced mother who fuelled the rebellion against Richard by fooling Harry of Buckingham," Margaret had told Grace and John. "Why Richard did not execute the turncoat Lancastrian on the same block as Buckingham, I shall never understand. When Morton fled to Tudor's side in Brittany, he showed his true red-rose colors and plotted to put Henry on the throne—with his witch of a mother. And now he lauds it at Henry's court as chancellor and archbishop of Canterbury. What a reward for treachery!" she had cried, and Grace had never seen such fury in a face. "If it were not for my two foolish brothers' favor and leniency, he would be dead, and Richard might be on the throne still."

Grace hurried to Cecily's side and drew her down into the window seat. "Is it true, Cis? Are you to leave today?"

"Aye," Cecily grumbled. "Jack cannot bear to be left out of any of Henry's plans. The truce with France over the Brittany succession ends this month, and 'tis feared that without England's mediation, the French king will conquer not only the duchy but its duchess as well. It appears this will infuriate Maximilian of Burgundy and, under the terms of our agreement with him, England will have to go to war. War! Why must men settle everything by fighting?"

Grace's eyes glazed over; she was not interested in France and Brittany, Charles and Maximilian. She had her own conflicted emotions to contend with. Besides, she despaired of Cecily when she was in one of her moods. She sighed at the same time she realized, with a jolt, that Tom must also be leaving. Was it a sigh of relief or of disappointment?

A sour expression marred Cecily's lovely face as she exclaimed: "Cock's bones! We shall not even be here for Twelfth Night!"

Lost in her own thoughts, Grace sighed again.

"Aye, 'tis a matter for sighing, Grace, or even weeping over," Cecily said, cheered that her sister was sympathetic. "Hell's bells!" Cecily exclaimed and then clapped her hand over her mouth in case her mother had heard. But Elizabeth was too busy with a mirror and instructing Katherine where to pin a brooch to her gown to pay attention to the young women on the window seat. "I forgot all about you and Tom in my misery. Forgive me. How did you fare last night, little sister? Do tell all, I beg of you. Dear God, you do not have to blush."

"I don't blush," Grace said indignantly. "My skin is too sallow."

Cecily laughed, and Elizabeth looked over at her and smiled. "You see how Grace can always coax one out of an ill humor," she said to Katherine, who pursed her lips into what some might have mistaken for a smile.

"Certes, you do not want me to rattle on about war when 'tis plain you are not listening, Grace," Cecily said, chuckling. "How was it last night? Aha, I see the way of it," she whispered, and when Grace said nothing but lowered her eyes and smiled, she could not resist crowing. "You did not find Tom as unacceptable as you thought. Is it not wonderful? Is it not close to Heaven when you feel his skin on yours? His hand caressing your thigh? His lips seeking your breast?"

Grace could only open her mouth in amazement. Surely Cecily could not enjoy the act that much with her bag of bones of a husband? Curiosity got the better of her, and she had to ask: "Jack pleasures you thus, Cis?"

It was Cecily's turn to lower her eyes and smile secretly. "Nay, Grace, I never said anything about Jack."

"Why, Cecily Welles, you have a lover!"

"Soft, you ninny," Cecily hissed. "Certes I do. But promise me to never breathe a word. I have not told a soul of your love for John, nor of your adventure to Aunt Margaret. I pray you will do the same for me."

Grace nodded and crossed her heart. " 'Tis Thomas Kyme, is it not?" she asked. "Certes, I will not tell. I knew it that night when you danced."

Cecily went pale. "Was it so plain to see?" she breathed. "We have loved each other since the moment we met. I do my duty to Jack, but once in a blue moon Thomas and I meet alone. Are you shocked, Grace?"

Grace's face acknowledged that she was, but she drew Cecily to her and murmured: "You secret is safe with me. Pray have a care you do not get with child by him instead."

"Pish, I am not such a ninny as that. I would never *lie* with Thomas. And now, back to you. Was Tom kind?"

Grace nodded. "Aye, 'twas easier than I had thought," she confessed and leaned forward to whisper, "but I had to help him, in truth, for he was more frightened than I."

Cecily chuckled. "Well, dear Grace, you will not have to suffer through any more nights for a while. Oh, I am so glad you will be coming to Hellowe, and I pray Mother lets you go soon." More seriously, she added, "I am hoping that being a wife will put John from your mind. Nay, do not deny it, you still hold out hope for our cousin of Gloucester, do you not?"

Grace did not have a chance to answer because there was a knock at the door and Tom was ushered into the queen dowager's presence. Bowing low, his beaver hat to his heart, he caught Grace's eye across the room and a tiny smile flitted across his face. Then he was all business.

"Your pardon, your grace, but I am sent to fetch her ladyship the viscountess. The archbishop's party is boarding the barges, and Lord Welles is ready to leave." Indeed, they could hear the sounds of pibcorns and shawms announcing Morton's departure.

"Cecily, dear, come and receive my blessing," Elizabeth called to her daughter. "And you, sir," she leaned forward and said softly, "go and bid farewell to your bride. I will send her to you anon, have no fear. But she is dear to me, and I am not prepared to let her go to you yet awhile. You must be patient."

Tom grinned. "She is dear to me, too, your grace. And I can be patient. Know that I will be as good a husband as I can to her, for your sake as well as hers." He bowed again and walked towards Grace, passing Cecily, who winked at him broadly.

"I am sorry we must part so soon, Grace," he whispered as he kissed her hand. "But I will carry the memory of last night until we can be together in Lincolnshire. Lady Cecily is making arrangements for us at Hellowe, and it may be we will have our own rooms in the manor."

"I know not when I shall come, Tom. Her grace must decide my fate, not us. But I am content that we are friends again and you go away with pleasant memories of our"—she paused and, stroking his soft beard, gave him a mischievous smile—"our virgin night together. 'Twas the first time for you, was it not?"

Tom's face gave him away, and she laughed. "Farewell and God speed. You will write to me, won't you?"

"Every day, sweetheart," Tom promised and then chuckled. "And this time I pray my letters find you." He turned his back on the room, hiding her from view, and kissed her waiting lips. "Farewell, my love."

"Farewell, dear Grace," Cecily cried, running to embrace her. "I shall count the days until you come to Hellowe in the spring. Your grace, you must not keep Tom and his wife apart for too long, promise?"

"Away with you, my lady," Elizabeth admonished her. "I'll have no more of your impudence." But Grace saw the smile in her eyes as Cecily swept out of the room, followed by Tom, who had to duck to avoid hitting his head.

Grace sat down hard on the window seat and wondered when she would see them both again.

16

Ireland

MARCH 1491

Most high and noble lady,

I greet thee well. I find myself in Ireland for this start of a new year, and while my master sups with those in Carrick castle below me, I came up on this grassy hillside to find the high crosses of Kil Chiaráin that are made of sandstone and marvelously carved with bosses and stories by long-ago Celtic people. The largest one stands ten feet high. From here I can see mountains to the south and east, the river Suir winding through the Golden Vale, the grass-roofed mud huts of the village of Carrick that surround the castle set upon a rock and in the far distance the sea. The March winds are cold and the almost constant rain keeps the land of Fitzgeralds and Butlers emerald green.

The Irish who live in this part of the country, I have learned, are influenced by the comings and goings of the earls of Desmond, Ormond and Kildare. These three hold almost as much land as the chieftains in the rest of the country. They call Gerald, earl of Kildare, the "uncrowned king of Ireland," and although he is no longer Henry Tudor's governor here, he has the support of those who

are of English descent and many of the clan chieftains. I tell you all this, aunt,
because I want you to know how I am following your desire to observe the lay
of the land for you as Master Waters instructed me in Lisbon when he found
me at the Castelo de São Jorge. Butler of Ormond, as you must know, followed
the Lancastrian banner into battle and lost against your father's supporter,
Fitzgerald of Desmond. I heard a Desmond also supported our house of York
again in Seventy and impaled twenty of Warwick's supporters afterwards.
Desmond country may be more sympathetic to our cause. His stronghold is in
the port city of Cork, and I will wait until we have to unload our cargo there
to observe how the York name is viewed. Never fear—I still guard the fine suit
you sent to me with Waters closely. The bag in which I keep it safe is pillowed
under my head each night.

Perkin paused, his pen hovering over the paper. His mind was crowded
with the instructions Margaret's messenger, John Waters, had instilled in
him that day at the Castelo de São Jorge. Much against his will, he had
become a spy, but he knew he must for his love and duty to Margaret of
Burgundy. She was the only mother he remembered—although he had a
foggy memory of someone who had spanked him once, but that was all.

Perkin watched a shepherd lead his flock farther up the grassy hillside
and then listened as the man took a pipe from the scrip that was slung over
his shoulder and began to play a mournful air. The music reminded him
of Brittany, and he vaguely wondered if the people were somehow linked.
Carrick was known for its wool, and the Franciscan friary produced a
fine ale, both of which Perkin availed himself as he sat with his back to
one of the crosses, woven blanket keeping him warm outside and a jug
of ale inside. What else should he tell Aunt Margaret, he wondered? Not
of the rosy-cheeked Irish girl he had romped with the night before in the
castle stable, he thought, grinning to himself as he dipped his quill in the
little pot of oak-gall ink he carried in the pouch at his waist. The uneven
surface of the cloth paper he had bought from a peddler was difficult to
write on, and the wind did not help his ability to write neatly and without
blots.

You will be pleased to know that, in Waterford not two days since, I heard
a whisper that the boy, Richard of York, was alive and well somewhere on the
Continent. Waterford is Butler territory and not friendly to your cause, and it

is why I will go to Cork when the time is right. For now, I wish you health, and
I hope for more news soon.

Your devoted and dutiful nephew, Perkin.

The abbey bells ringing out for Vespers from the valley startled him.
He had not realized it was so late. He carefully folded the letter and, hiding
it and his writing tools in the stiff leather bag with the false bottom, he
locked the compartment and covered it with the small bundle of food he
had not eaten. It would not do for the other mariners to see him writing,
for they would know him for an imposter at once. He hurried back down
the hill.

17

London and Lincolnshire

1491

Grace had attended another calving that winter, and she had grown fond of little Clover, as Grace named the bony white creature. She hoped Brother Oswald would keep her for the abbey's milking shed and not for market. Grace's vain hope was that by naming the animal she would prevent the monk from sending it off for slaughter when it grew. The milkmaid, Joan, had shown her how to feed the calf when it was first born, taking it to its dam and making it reach up to take the teat. "She be only able to suck if her head is raised, see," Joan told Grace. "Put her nose in the pail and she'd likely drown." The calf fed from its mother until the rich birthing fluid was gone and the abbey needed the ensuing milk. Grace learned from Joan how to teach the calf to lick the liquid from her raised fingers for several days, gradually lowering them until the calf could be changed to a tipped pail and eventually learn to drink from it without drowning.

Elizabeth complained every evening that Grace stank like a cow byre, despite the young woman's attempts at cleaning herself with handsful of snow before appearing in the royal apartment. The hem of her gown took on a brownish tinge over the winter weeks, but she went to bed happy to have been useful in the shed.

Now it was May, and Grace wondered how soon Elizabeth would let her go to Hellowe. After Elizabeth led them in prayer each night, she would try to keep warm in her truckle bed, with the blanket and Elizabeth's and her own cloak tucked around her. It had been a hard winter, and she had envied the two older women their shared bed and warmth. Often she could not sleep for the cold, and in those dark, silent moments when the abbey lay silent under a mantle of snow, she would try to imagine Lincolnshire, and her life with Tom. When her course had appeared in January with its usual dull pains, she knew she had not conceived and had sent a prayer of thanks heavenward. Cecily had been right—she did hold out hope that John would suddenly be there to whisk her away, and it would be awkward if she were with child. Addlepate! she chided herself. That would not happen any more than if the man in the moon could climb down to earth and bid her "good day."

It was warmer now, and the fur-lined cloaks had been safely stored in the wardrobe chest, but still she could not sleep. She rose and tiptoed to the jakes to relieve herself and then sat on the stool beside the last embers of the fire, hugging her shawl around her. It would not be long now before Elizabeth dismissed her, she believed. Why else would her grace have had the conversation they had that very morning after Matins?

"I do not wish to send you to your wedded bliss without a gift, my dear," Elizabeth had said, patting the cushion next to hers on the settle—a new piece of furniture Cecily had ordered made for her mother after last summer's visit. The queen saw Katherine stiffen. Feeling charitable, she invited the bitter woman to join the conversation, and it was a mollified Lady Hastings who pulled up her chair and sat down.

"You have been a good, kind girl to me all these years, never asking for anything—except on behalf of others," Elizabeth said, knowing Grace would understand she was referring to the money for John. "So today, I have made arrangements with Father John that you shall have a servant to take into your new life. A groom. Who do you suppose that is?" She sat back and watched the realization dawn on Grace's astonished face.

"Edgar!" Grace cried, breaking into a grin. "Do you mean Edgar?"

Elizabeth's smug smile and nod acknowledged the correct guess. "It is," she said. "You seem content, and thus my good deed is done. Katherine, what a fish face you pull! You have never liked Edgar since he dropped your mantle in the mud. Admit it."

Katherine gave a rueful grin. " 'Tis true, your grace. Certes, she is welcome to him, although I must allow he is good with horses." She turned to Grace and for once spoke kindly. "You are a fortunate young lady to have so gracious a mistress. My husband, Will, hired a groom for me when we were first married, but when I fell on hard times . . ."

"You mean when I forced you into exile with me," Elizabeth teased her. "We have no need for grooms as we did when we were at court. We both gave up much when the Tudor banished me."

Grace was stunned by her good news. Edgar would be free of Brother Gregory's stinging tongue and the stable lads' cruel mockery. She had no notion what to do with a groom, but she knew she would welcome Edgar's stalwart presence on her journey north. He would be her bodyguard, and she would feel safe.

She went down on her knees in front of Elizabeth and kissed the dowager's clawlike hand, noticing the swelling around the knuckles and the quick intake of painful breath as Grace picked it up. "How can I ever thank you, your grace?" she whispered, her eyes shining. "I shall be able to pay for Edgar from my dowry from Cecily, I suppose."

"Aye, Cecily and I planned this purposefully. Tom has a goodly income from Welles, and I have no doubt will afford a tiring woman for you. 'Tis the least he must do for one of royal blood. You should be comfortable. But you must learn to keep your accounts and not be a spendthrift so your household will grow. Watch Cecily, my dear; she has a good deal of common sense when it comes to spending, although"—she clucked her tongue—"none when it comes to her foolish heart." Grace hid a smile but was surprised Elizabeth knew her child so well.

Now Grace stirred the dying embers with the poker and pushed a wayward curl back under her nightcap. Aye, the time was drawing near, she thought, and although she wanted nothing more than to escape the dreary abbey walls, there was much she would miss. Having Edgar with her would keep the memories fresh, she hoped. She returned to the scene that afternoon, when she had gone to find Edgar and confirm what Brother Gregory should have told him by then, and chuckled. As soon as Edgar had seen her walking towards the stable, where he was checking for stones in the hoof of a broad-chested rouncy, he had gently replaced the hoof on the ground and run towards her. He pulled off his hood and fell to his knees on the manure-strewn ground. Grace could not be cross with him but gently told him to get up and move away from the dung, eyeing the soiled hem of his tunic. She would have to teach him how to serve a lady, she thought, but for now she came straight to the point.

"So, Edgar, you have heard your fate, I warrant," she said, looking up at him and glad his bulk blocked out the sun. "It seems our paths are destined to run together from now on. I trust you are not too dismayed to be leaving Bermondsey. We are to live a long way from London and all that you know. You must bid farewell to your family, you understand."

"I haven't got no family, my lady," Edgar assured her, grinning from ear to ear. Grace decided then and there that she would try to remember not to make Edgar too happy, as she could not bear the sight of those hideous teeth. "You be an angel, my lady, and I swear I will be a good servant." He winked at her. "Bin and got wedded, I hear," he said, bending to speak low and bowling her over with his bad breath.

"You must learn your manners, Edgar," she admonished him, taking a step back. " 'Tis not customary to wink, or address a lady in such bold language. We have been through much, you and I, but do not think it may give you airs. You will speak when spoken to and do my bidding without a grumble. Do you understand?" Edgar looked so crestfallen she felt sorry for him, but she stood erect and stared him down until he mumbled an apology and touched his forelock.

"Edgar, you clay-brained mammet, get back to work!" Brother Gregory's angry command froze poor Edgar's feet to the ground, and his eyes were full of fear. Grace took two steps to the side of her groom to become visible to the muscular, square-headed monk, whose turn it was to freeze in his tracks.

"Lady Grace," he said, acknowledging her with a quick bow of his head, "I did not see you. I crave your pardon. I thought Edgar—"

"Aye, I know what you thought, Brother Gregory, and I have no doubt Edgar would have been punished had I not been here to stand up for him.

Your reputation precedes you," Grace said, wondering where she was finding the courage to speak thus to one of the most senior of the order. She
caught a glimpse of Edgar's awed face and was emboldened further. "I shall
have great pleasure in removing this poor man from your cruel treatment
when I leave Bermondsey, which will be very soon. I trust he will not be
punished for speaking to his new mistress, or I shall take the matter to
Father John. This is supposed to be a house of Christian virtues and charity, but I have seen precious little of either from you. Good day to you,
brother." And she turned on her heel and walked off with as much dignity
as her short legs could afford her. When she turned the corner into the
privy courtyard and out of sight, she collapsed against the wall, her heart
pounding, and then she began to laugh and hug herself for her brave stand
against the bully of the abbey.

GRACE WAS OVERCOME with emotion as she received Elizabeth's blessing on her knees in the apartment that had been her home for four years.
She noticed a hole in the hem of Elizabeth's gown and with a sad rush
knew she would not be the one to mend it now. That would be Anne's
task. Fifteen-year-old Anne stood by her mother's chair, quietly watching
Grace say her farewells. She was a dutiful girl who had spent time in the
household of her aunt, the duchess of Suffolk, and was still waiting for a
husband to be found for her. During her father's reign, Anne had been betrothed for a short while to little Philip of Burgundy, but ensuing politics
had voided that contract. Now, as the fourth daughter of the dead Yorkist
king and with a new Tudor princess in the royal cradle with whom to forge
alliances, her future was of less importance to Henry. She had been surprised and dismayed to be summoned to live with her mother in Grace's
place. The de la Poles kept an unpretentious house, and the many children under their roof were less rigidly disciplined than Elizabeth would
have sanctioned. Anne was loath to leave there, and Grace had felt sorry
for her when she arrived with two packhorses piled high with belongings
that had no place at the abbey. Anne had expressed shock to Grace at the
change in her mother's appearance, and Grace told her that the death not
two months ago of her last remaining brother, Richard Woodville, had
grieved Elizabeth greatly. "Earl Rivers was the last of the Woodville line,
so her grace told us," Grace explained. Five sons were born to Jacquetta

and her handsome knight, and not one had male issue, Elizabeth had fretted.

This was a rare day when Elizabeth insisted on leaving her bed to bestow a proper blessing on the departing Grace. When the young woman looked up after receiving the queen's kiss on her forehead, she saw tears trickling down the former queen's gaunt cheeks.

"Ah, Grace, I have loved you well," Elizabeth said. "Truly you are like a daughter to me for all you were born of my husband's lust. You have more dignity than most noblewomen I know, and I let you go with a heavy heart. Be healthy and beget many children, my child. When you bring them to me, I shall be proud to be called Grandam."

Grace found she could not hold back her own tears, for she was certain Elizabeth, dowager queen of England, would not live long enough to dandle a Gower grandchild on her meager lap.

They exchanged one last embrace and then Grace was gone.

IN A FINAL generous gesture, the abbey afforded Edgar new livery for his new life, and it was a proud man who helped Grace up onto the sidesaddle of the pretty jennet Cecily had sent to transport Grace to Hellowe. He carefully placed Grace's feet on the planchette and then adjusted the strap of the cushioned saddle under the horse's belly. He would ride the rouncy that Cecily had also provided, with Grace's few belongings strapped behind him. The small armed escort flying Welles's lion rampant pennant started slowly through the abbey gate and past the fields into Long Lane. Grace was astonished to see so many field hands and monks lining the route, waving and wishing her luck. She had no idea these people had even noticed her during her four-year stay. The usual group of women she had worked alongside was waiting up ahead, and when she drew close one ran forward with a posy of cow parsley, ragged robin and poppies. "God bless you, Lady Grace. You be always one of us," she cried. Grace reached into a purse at her waist and gave the woman an angel. "Divide it among you, and may God bless you, too, Agnes. I will pray for a good harvest."

The crowds of citizens at the weekly market on Southwark high street parted respectfully as Grace's party trotted along the cobbled part of the busy thoroughfare that led onto London Bridge. They joined a column of other travelers, some on foot, some on horseback or in carts, rumbling slowly over the wooden drawbridge on to the massive, built-up bridge that was the only pedestrian crossing into London. Grace glanced up to see a blackened head of some criminal, the face now unrecognizable, impaled on a stake high above the gateway, and swinging in the wind the skeleton of a man left to starve to death in an iron cage. The man's arms were pathetically hanging out of the bars, as if begging for food. Grace averted her eyes, for although these were common sights in the cities and towns, she could never forget the lessons about Christ's love for his fellow man she had learned from the nuns. She could not imagine being the cause of a fellow human's death, and she was even upset by the agonized squeals from the pigs that were slaughtered every November to be smoked and preserved for the abbey larder through the winter.

Looking up at the three-story buildings of wattle and daub that lined both sides of the street over the bridge, Grace never failed to marvel how they didn't simply topple over into the Thames. Merchants had their ground-floor shutters open, displaying their wares on counters, while wandering vendors hawked hot pies and roasted birds on sticks to hungry passersby. They were soon inside the city wall, and traffic thinned out as they proceeded north past St. Margaret's on New Fish Street and the conduit at Cornhill and into Bishopsgate Street. Grace was relieved when the hurly-burly of London was left far behind and she could delight in watching lambs frolic in fields and deer leap away along the forest paths. They followed Ermine Street, the ancient Roman road that stretched from London through Lincoln to York. After two nights along the way, they passed the road to Fotheringhay, the seat of her father's York family. And then they turned off the road, busier now as they neared Stamford, to find Collyweston, where Cecily would be waiting for her. And Tom.

Of course he had not written every day, but he had communicated often in the months they were apart, and she had been touched by his attempts at love letters.

"*My sweetest wife*," was often his greeting, and he would invariably end with "*You have my heart*," "*I think of you daily*," or "*My love and devotion are yours always*." She wrote of her daily tasks, Elizabeth's health and her attempts at raising a calf. How could she falsely write of her love to this good man? So she focused on their friendship and her duty to him as a wife. She knew he was intelligent enough to read between the lines, but he could never accuse her of dissembling.

The road wended through woods and fields, tall elms standing out among the hazel and birches in the fertile Welland valley. Collyweston Palace was situated at the end of a long driveway, which ended in meticulously clipped knot gardens flanking the last hundred paces to the steps. The sun was setting and cast pink and orange tints on the walls and glinted off the many windows as they approached. Fluttering high over the central tower a silk flag bearing the royal lions of England proclaimed the presence of the king. Grace's heart skipped a beat. She had not been told of Cecily's command that the escort take her to Margaret Beaufort's residence until the journey was under way. "Lady Welles will meet you there," the captain had said. "She is a frequent guest of the Lady Margaret and wishes to accompany you back to Hellowe." Grace had been nonplussed. The last time she had talked to Cecily about Scraggy Maggie, Grace remembered, Cecily had made a face. She assumed Cecily was forced to attend the countess when her husband had business at Collyweston as well. It had not occurred to her that the king would be there, too, especially as Bess was in seclusion awaiting the birth of her child at her favorite residence of Greenwich. But birthing was a woman's cross to bear, Grace knew; after the pleasure of conception, most men deemed their work done. She had to admit the king and his mother frightened her, and she hoped Cecily would suggest they leave for Hellowe on the morrow so she would not have to face the pair.

Her fears were well founded, it seemed, because not an hour after she was greeted with great joy by Cecily and shown to the chamber, no bigger than a closet, where she would spend the night, Grace was ushered into the Great Hall, and Margaret's chamberlain announced her in overly loud tones.

"Lady Grace Plantagenet, your grace," he bellowed. Grace had given her name as Mistress Gower, but the chamberlain knew her well and made the correction. *Certes, the irony is that I shall always retain the name of my highest status,* she thought, *even if 'tis as a king's bastard.*

Henry and his mother stood under a canopy in the elegant, paneled hall, with her husband Lord Derby nowhere to be seen. Grace understood now why the countess of Richmond and Derby preferred to spend time here. The palace was more like a large mansion, beautifully imagined and lavishly decorated but warm and manageable.

"Ah, Lady Grace," Henry said, looking down at her from his above-average height. Grace was glad to note a warm tinge to his greeting, although she recognized the pinched look of worry about his mouth and eyes. Edgar had told her during their journey north that the commonfolk had not yet warmed to Henry, even though they liked the peace his reign had brought. " 'Tis said he fears the ghosts of those two boys what disappeared from the Tower," Edgar had confided. And well he might, Grace had thought.

Henry continued with his greeting: "*Soyez la bienvenue*—welcome," he translated quickly, "after all this time. Approach, and tell us how the queen dowager fares."

Grace kissed both his and Margaret's outstretched hands, and even Margaret gave her a smile of welcome. "Her grace the queen dowager is not strong, my liege. She spends much of her day in bed and is therefore wasting away. Lady Hastings and I do—did," she corrected herself, "what we could to keep her entertained and eating, but she grieves for Earl Rivers, who you must know passed away in March, and the shock has brought her low." She hoped her gown was not trembling visibly from her shaking legs and that she had given a coherent answer. Why was she so afraid of this man? Was it the crown he wore? The purple mantle trimmed with royal ermine? His stiff bearing and piercing eyes—even the unsightly red wart just above his chin? Aye, he is the king and anointed by God, Grace thought. Certes, I am right to be afraid.

Henry made a sympathetic sound but then changed the subject; Elizabeth was not his favorite topic. "Cecily tells us you are betrothed to one of Welles's squires. We are pleased for you, are we not, Mother?" He intertwined his long fingers together and, bending them backwards, cracked all his knuckles loudly, making Grace wince.

Margaret concurred. "Aye, we are. You have our blessing, Grace," she said as though she were the sovereign dispensing permission. "I trust you will find him a good husband, my dear. Is he here?"

Grace had not dared take her eyes from the king and his mother since entering the room, but now she glanced around and saw Tom watching her anxiously. "He is here, my lady, and if it would please you, your grace, I would have you meet him." Her own bravado surprised her.

The king nodded and Grace walked quickly to fetch a bewildered Tom, who fell on his knees before his liege lord. "Thomas Gower, is it?" the king asked. "Stand, Master Gower, I would give you and Lady Grace my blessing."

The king was tall, but Tom towered over him, which obviously amused Henry, who looked at them for a full minute before remarking: "You look more like father and daughter than husband and wife, in truth. But with a stalwart like this by your side, Grace, I should not fear for your safety, if I were you." He gave Tom a baleful stare and took the squire aback by remarking, "You rode with Lincoln at Stoke, did you not?"

Grace drew in a sharp breath, and she saw Lady Margaret's eyes narrow.

"I had the honor of being in Lord Lincoln's household, your grace," Tom said, and Grace was surprised at his steady voice. "However, I was not at Stoke, but at my home in Yorkshire, helping my mother on our estates after the sudden death of my father. Lord Lincoln gave me leave to go."

Henry weighed Tom's words and finally nodded. "So may I count on your loyalty now, Master Gower?"

Tom was on his knees again in a flash, swearing fealty to the king. Grace felt a twinge of irritation, and her mind flitted back to the incident of Elizabeth's letter and Katherine's suspicion that Tom had somehow betrayed the dowager. Tom had been John's best childhood friend; he had chafed over not being allowed to fight for King Richard at Bosworth; and he had been glad to follow Cousin Jack of Lincoln. He and his whole family were Yorkists, so why was he groveling to the Tudor so willingly? She determined she would question his arse-kissing. He must know where her loyalties lay, in truth.

"Where is your lord, Master Gower? I would speak with him," Henry said. He turned away from the women and addressed a man with a flowing white beard dressed in an extraordinary mantle emblazoned with moons and stars. Grace knew an alchemist when she saw one and remembered Cecily telling her that Henry never made a personal decision without consulting his. She watched Tom hurry off to extricate the viscount from a group by the door, glad not to have to answer any more awkward questions.

"An agreeable young man," the countess told Grace, who would have liked nothing more than to leave her side and join Cecily. Her sister was laughing and talking with a group across the room. "And I can see why Lady Welles has been anticipating your arrival. For all she has a large household, I believe she misses her family, and at times does not behave exactly as she should. You seem to have a level head on your shoulders, my lady, and I am counting on you to steer her out of trouble." Sweet Jesu, Grace thought, does she suspect Cecily and Thomas Kyme? But Margaret was smiling. "She makes my stepbrother obey her every whim, he tells me." She leaned forward and smirked. "But he adores her, have no fear. She is so full of life that she leads poor old Jack in a merry dance, 'tis all."

Grace could not believe her ears. Why, Scraggy Maggie has a sense of humor, she thought, and was bold enough to answer, "I will attempt to curb her excesses, my lady, although"—she smiled—"my opinion has not counted for much up to now." Seeing Cecily approaching, she said more loudly, "I must tell you, countess, Lady Cecily has been so kind to my husband and me, and I look forward to seeing Lord Welles's estate at Hellowe on the morrow."

"We shall leave in a day or two, Grace," Cecily corrected her. "Lady Margaret and I are working on an embroidered gown for the new baby, and I promised we would finish it in case Bess has the child early." And, to Grace's astonishment, Cecily gave Margaret a winning smile. "Is that not so, my lady?"

Margaret patted her arm and agreed that it was so.

"I thought you hated her, Cis," Grace whispered as they left Margaret's presence after a rotund courtier went down on one knee and begged for a private audience.

Cecily shrugged. "She is cold and aloof much of the time, 'tis true, but she can be warm and courteous when she is in private. In truth, she has treated me with courtesy, and we rub along well enough. It seems Jack is close to his stepsister and, as a member of Henry's Star Chamber, he must advise Henry, so 'tis necessary for us to be in his train often. 'Tis not my choice, you understand; merely my duty." She tucked Grace's hand under her arm and took her out to the gardens behind the palace that were bright with the colors of gillyflowers, irises, lilies and roses all glistening from a recent shower. "Let me tell you about your new home, Grace," she said, a wicked twinkle in her eye. "There is a farm, so I know you will be happy, little peasant."

Grace stopped and stood with her arms akimbo and a retort ready on her lips, but when Cecily threw back her head and let forth her familiar laugh, Grace forgot her indignation and laughed with her, realizing how much she had missed company of her own age at the abbey.

As a squire of the body, Tom was on duty in the viscount's bedchamber that night, so he was able to speak to Grace for only a few minutes before he went to the other wing of the palace, where the Welleses were housed. He found her in the long gallery, admiring the wall hangings, and, whisking her aside, kissed her hungrily. When she was unresponsive, he pulled apart and whispered: "Dearest Grace, what is wrong? I have longed for this moment for all these months. Have I offended you—again?"

Grace felt a pang of remorse, but she was ready to speak her mind and wasted no time. "I was not aware that your devotion to Henry Tudor ran so deep," she said scornfully. "It pained me to see you fall at his feet with such fervor, which told me how quickly you have forgotten your former friends and loyalties. You are wed to the daughter of a Yorkist king, who knows where *her* duty lies. I am disappointed; I thought I knew you better."

Tom blanched and checked over his shoulder to make sure no one was listening. "Henry is the king, Grace. Would you rather I had refused to bow down to him publicly and risk my neck? Or does my neck mean nothing to you?" When he saw her stubborn expression, he grimaced. "I see that it does not. And I thought we had come to an understanding, you and I." He took hold of her arm none too gently and bent close. "You are no longer at the abbey, Grace. You are in the real world, where one does what one can to survive. I will do what I must to protect what little advancement I have made and provide for you. I shall not go back on my promise to be a good husband to you, and if that means I kneel to my king and vow to serve him, I will do it. He, however, will never know what is in my heart." He looked at her sadly. "And I thought I knew *you* better."

Then he turned on his heel and walked away. Grace stared after him, her heart heavy. *Ah, you are cruel, Grace. Why must you be so cruel?* She well knew the answer; it lay over the sea in Flanders. A sob caught in her throat as she sank down onto a bench and whispered a prayer to St. Jude of lost causes.

THE NEXT DAY, as the household sat down to dinner and the ewerer was offering Grace the finger bowl, the sound of horses' hooves in the court-yard caught the diners' attention and everyone turned curious eyes to the door. They were not disappointed, as several knights entered, spurs clank-ing on the tiled floor, followed by a flustered steward.

" 'Tis Sir Edward Pickering," Grace heard a man say to his neighbor. "He who captured the whoreson traitors Chamberlain and White in Janu-ary. And you know what happened to them." He made a ghoulish face and dragged his finger across his throat.

"By Christ's nails, look who he has taken now," the other man mur-mured, nodding his head towards the back of the new arrivals.

Worming her way between the two, Grace was finally able to glimpse the object of their curiosity. His arms tied behind his back, a hood falling off his long dark hair, being rudely forced to his knees by two men-at-arms in Henry's livery, was John of Gloucester. The spectators gasped and whis-pered his name to those who could not see.

As soon as she saw him and before she could stop herself, Grace let an involuntary scream escape. "John!" she cried and fell to her knees.

Henry's chamberlain, Sir William Stanley, who had been standing nearby, gently raised Grace from the floor and attempted to remove her from Henry's line of sight.

"If I were you, my lady, I would distance myself from Lord John. He may be accused of treason," Stanley cautioned under his breath. "The king's spies sent word he had set sail from Flanders to an unknown destination along the northern coast."

"Treason?" Grace asked, her eyes wide with fear. "Why? Because he wanted to come home?"

Stanley put his finger to his lips. " 'Tis not wise to ask too many ques-tions. We shall know soon enough." He bowed curtly and walked away. This was the man who had come to Henry's rescue at Bosworth when Uncle Richard had come so close to personally killing Tudor, she recalled. He had turned his coat, and Grace had no doubt he must hate Richard's bastard niece for all he had shielded her. She shrank back through the courtiers straining to get a look at the kneeling prisoner, and no one noticed her until she felt her arm being gripped tightly and Tom's urgent whisper commanding her, "Come with me."

Grace was too stunned to resist and allowed Tom to maneuver her outside, into the courtyard. "Grace, are you all right?" he asked, concern in his voice. "I heard your cry. 'Tis rumored John is wanted for treason, although I cannot believe his flight from Stoke would count as treason. Attaint him, certes, but unless he is involved in a plot to overthrow Henry, let us hope he should be freed anon."

Grace was silent, her heart racing, as she knew that John must have come from the Duchess Margaret. Something was afoot, but what? She hoped her face would give nothing away to Tom. If she was to help John, she must pretend to be John's innocent cousin who was merely frightened at seeing him manacled. No one, not even Tom, must know she had been to Malines.

Tom lifted her chin with his forefinger and thumb and looked into her eyes. "If Henry allows it, and because of your kinship with John, I shall not forbid you from seeing him," he told her. "But as your husband—and, I admit, a jealous one—I cannot condone it. Can you understand the difference, sweetheart? The choice is yours to make."

"Thank you, Tom," Grace murmured and, reaching up on tiptoe, she kissed him on the cheek. She turned and went back into the hall without giving him an answer. Tom closed his eyes, leaned back against the wall and prayed his wayward wife would use the brain he knew she had.

Grace had gone only a few paces when Cecily pounced on her. "Where did you disappear to?" she whispered. "It seems John may have some intelligence about You Know Who and was sent here to spy for Aunt Margaret. Or so my lord husband thinks."

"Has John been formally charged with anything?" Grace whispered back.

Cecily shook her head. "He has denied any wrongdoing to his captors, but 'tis sure Henry will torture him. Ah, poor Grace, I beg your pardon, 'twas unfeeling of me," Cecily soothed when she saw Grace's stricken face. Then she shrugged. " 'Tis the way of things in a man's world, sister. Men are always fighting, politicking or whoring. And when they don't get what they want, a little torture thrown in might not hurt." She chuckled at her own wit, but Grace was not amused.

"You have an odd sense of humor, Cis," she retorted. Pulling Cecily behind a pillar, she whispered, "And rather than preaching, I would remember your part in what has brought John back to England." Then her courage failed her, and her face crumpled. "What has happened, Cis? Where have they taken John?"

Cecily drew Grace's arm through hers and, seeing curious eyes on them, said matter-of-factly, "Henry briefly accused John of plotting to overthrow him and ordered his confinement in the guardroom." She clucked her tongue. "Certes, it all must be a misunderstanding, and John's innocence will soon be proven. Come, sister, I believe the king and his mother are taking a turn about the garden. Shall we join them?"

Grace understood immediately and, nodding and smiling at a couple of courtiers she recognized, said brightly, "Aye, the fresh air will do us good."

IT WAS MARGARET Beaufort who persuaded her son to allow Grace to visit John later that day. "It could do no harm, Henry," she had said, when Cecily had charmed Margaret into asking the king. "Grace is but a weak-willed girl and besides, she has been closeted with the Woodville woman behind abbey walls all these years. Certes, she is no threat to you or anyone."

Henry had narrowed his eyes, Cecily related to Grace later, and hesitated for a moment before giving Cecily a curt nod. "Aye, she may go, but she may have only five minutes with him. Sir William," he called, beckoning to his chamberlain, "pray arrange for the Lady Grace to speak to the prisoner at her convenience today." Stanley had bowed and left the royal presence to find Grace.

Brimming with anticipation, Grace followed the fifty-year-old Stanley, younger brother of Lady Margaret's husband, out of the residential area of the house, through a dark, dank passageway and into the small armory, where several soldiers jumped to attention recognizing the king's chamberlain. Stanley scowled when he saw the dice and coins on the table, giving away the gambling the guards were engaged in. He swept them from the table and shouted: "You know his grace, the king, does not sanction games of chance, except at Yuletide. I have a good mind to have you all horsewhipped." Grace almost choked. What a hypocrite, she thought; it was well known in the family that Henry relished the chance to gamble. But, anxious to get back to Henry's side and be done with his paltry errand, Stanley fixed his eye on one young man and ordered him to take them to John's temporary prison. Scurrying to pick up his pike and the large ring of keys, the guard bowed and opened a thick wooden door to a staircase, eyeing Grace curiously. Two floors up, they arrived at another door with a grille the size of a man's face in it.

Stanley turned to Grace and was impressed to see the diminutive young woman standing proudly and without fear. "Remember, my lady, you have five minutes. Guard, make sure she has not one minute more, you understand? And wait here outside the door. Then escort the lady back to her quarters. I must return to the king." He gave Grace a polite bow and started back down the staircase.

"Visitor," the guard barked through the grille, inserting a key in the lock. "Five minutes be what's allowed." He pushed the door open far enough to allow Grace through and then slammed it shut behind her. He peered curiously into the room as he locked it again but ducked out of sight when John commanded him to go.

Grace stood rooted to the spot, horrified by John's unkempt appearance. Were those streaks down his bloody face from tears? He hid his hands behind his back, his legs wobbling as he took a step towards her before falling to the uneven stone floor and groaning in pain. Grace was down beside him to catch him in her arms as he fell forward, cradling his head against her breast. Neither said a word, and Grace's tears fell freely.

Finally she whispered, "They have tortured you, dear John, haven't they?" John nodded and sat back on his heels, bringing his broken hands out from behind his back and shuddering in despair. Grace stared in horror at the crooked fingers, the thumbs that had been pulverized by the screw, and reached out to touch them. John winced and shook his head.

" 'Tis more than I can bear, Grace." He tried to smile, but the gash on his mouth had reopened, and it was painful. "Who did you have to charm to see me, little wren? Have you beguiled the king?"

But Grace was on her feet and calling to the guard: "Bring me a bowl of water and some linen this instant, sirrah. The prisoner is in need of bandages."

The guard guffawed and retorted: "We don't bandage prisoners, my lady. They deserve what they get."

Grace stamped her foot and shouted, "You puny, clapper-clawed measle, you will do as I command."

"Soft, Grace, he will not heed you. And where did you learn language like that? At the abbey? Come here and comfort me," John cajoled. "Ah, but you are a sight for sore eyes, my sweet cousin." He frowned. "How is it you are here at Collyweston? Has the queen dowager died?"

"Come, sit, and I will tell you." Grace helped him onto the pallet, its straw at least fresh, and sat close to him, engaging his gray eyes and trying not to look at his hideous hands.

John's eyes widened when Grace spoke of her marriage to Tom and he tried to smile. "That wily Tom!" he exclaimed. "I knew he was sweet on you, and when I challenged him one night over many cups of wine, he admitted it. He is a good man, Grace—take my word for it."

Grace said nothing but nodded briefly; she did not want to spend their precious five minutes talking about Tom. "Why are you tortured, John? What do they accuse you of? I would help you if I could."

In a whisper, John told her that Aunt Margaret had sent him to find Francis Lovell and help smooth the way with James of Scotland for a possible landing by her nephew, Richard of York. "I have no papers on me, and so when they captured me I had nothing to show or tell. But Henry is no fool, and he believes I have come to overthrow him."

Grace gasped. "So, 'tis true, Dickon lives?"

John nodded. "He is now at Aunt Margaret's residence at Binche, but when word gets back to her that I am taken, I am sure she will not attempt to send Richard to Scotland. She will have to assume Henry would get the information from me"—he looked down at his hands—"one way or another."

Grace hardly dared ask, "And, did he?"

John's eyes filled with tears. "My father would be so ashamed of me, Grace. When they took a hammer to my fingers—" He stopped on a sob.

"Hush, my dear. Do not blame yourself, you are only human, which is more than can be said for *them*," she said, jerking her head towards the door. "Let me ask one more thing," Grace insisted, hoping to divert his attention from his shame and onto more practical matters. "Have you told them all that you know?"

John nodded miserably. "My mission from our aunt was to find Lovell and enlist his help in smoothing a landing in Scotland. I swear 'twas all. We don't even know if Lovell is still there, or even alive. I was supposed to find out and give him—" He broke off in a fit of coughing. He could not endanger Grace any further than he already had.

"Then maybe there is hope for you," Grace said, not noticing his evasion, "if I can beg Henry to pardon you. 'Tis common knowledge these days that Dickon is alive, so the only new information is that he might have looked to Scotland for help. Aye, your action was treasonous, but not so heinous that it couldn't be pardoned. I shall have to enlist Bess's help, for I have seen that Henry loves her—if he loves anyone," she said.

John had trouble stemming the flow of tears as he listened to Grace's suggestion; only his mother had loved him this openly, he was sure. His nose began to run, and he begged Grace to find the kerchief that he could not pull from its place inside his shirt and help him wipe his face. Gently removing the threadbare piece of cloth, she gave a little gasp when she recognized the kerchief she had embroidered for him all those years ago at Ormond's Inn. She gave him a peck on the cheek.

"What was that for?" he asked, puzzled, as he lifted his face to be cleansed.

"I cannot believe you still have this old kerchief, 'tis all," Grace replied, motioning to him to moisten a corner of the cloth with his tongue and rubbing some blood off his cheek. "I am flattered."

John looked sheepish. "In truth, I had forgotten you gave it to me, cousin. I am such an ingrate."

"Your time be up, my lady!" the coarse voice of the guard came through the door. "Bid your handsome sweetheart farewell. I have my orders."

The grinding of the key in the lock made Grace's heart sink. When would she ever see John again? Rumor had it that Sir Edward Pickering would be taking him to London, where the king would decide his fate, but she would not worry John with a mere rumor. She stood up and dropped a kiss on his dark head, the once glossy hair matted with dirt and blood.

"I will do what I can, John," she said, and she heard him whisper his thanks as she left the room. It was all she could do not to run back and take him in her arms. Mustering all her dignity in front of the guard, she descended the stairs in an unhurried fashion, but as soon as she was out in the fresh air she ran as fast as she could to seek out Cecily and beg for her help. In her frantic conversation with John, she had forgotten that Bess was far away in London in the throes of producing another royal child, but if Cecily could sway her husband, and Welles could persuade his half sister, then maybe, just maybe, Lady Margaret would persuade Henry to grant John a pardon. Certes, that is a lot of persuasion, Grace thought as she lifted her hand to knock on Cecily's door.

"Grace?" Tom's voice came from nowhere and made her jump. "I would not disturb Lady Welles now." He winked. "She is not alone."

Grace almost said "Thomas Kyme" but thought better of it. "The viscount is with her?" she said instead, and Tom nodded. She sighed; help for John would have to wait.

"It means I am free to be with you," Tom said shyly. "I have permission to fish; would you like to go with me?"

Grace was grateful he did not immediately bombard her with questions about her visit to the guardhouse and agreed to walk with him down to one of the palace's fish ponds. It seemed many others in the palace had chosen to rest that hot afternoon, and after finding Grace a straw hat and collecting his rod and basket, Tom led the way through magnificent terraced gardens, past a large dovecote and onto the path for the ponds. Jason bounded ahead of them, delighted by the unexpected outing.

"Do you remember our fishing expedition on the Derwent?" Tom asked, hoping to distract Grace from thoughts of John. He had spent many agonized minutes conjuring up images of the two together in the prison cell.

"How did you know I was thinking of the same thing?" she exclaimed in surprise, smiling up at him. "I well remember how cold the water was, and then how warm your mother was to me—a complete stranger."

Tom grinned happily. This was the Grace he had loved since that day. Perhaps they could avoid talking about John at all, he hoped. He told Grace of his sister Cat's marriage to the York wool merchant, which Tom's father had aspired to, and how glad his mother had been when she had heard of her son's betrothal to Grace.

" 'A gradely, bonny lass with no falsity' is what she wrote of you, sweetheart. She, too, remembers that day fondly, although not as fondly as I," he said, feeling brave. " 'Twas the day I realized I was a man, for I knew that I loved you, Grace."

Grace slipped her hand in Tom's and again enjoyed the comfort of it.

"Aye, so you told me. But I was so young—a child, even. You fell in love with a child."

Tom was so pleased with the turn in the conversation that he forgot to be careful. "But you were not such a child to think yourself in love with—" and he brought himself up short, cursing his slip of the tongue.

"With John," Grace finished for him. "Aye, I loved John, but he had no time for me. I was but a child in his eyes." She let go of his hand as they approached the pond and bent to pick a yellow flag iris. Several wild ducks flapped their wings, preparing to fly off the water as they heard the sound of voices, and a large frog leaped out of the stand of irises and fell with a plop into the water. Judging from the ripples all over the surface on the breathless summer day, the pond was teeming with fish, but Tom hardly noticed. He knew they could no longer avoid talking about John's presence, only a stone's throw from where they stood.

"They tortured him, Tom," Grace whispered, pulling off one of the flower's velvet petals and casting it into the water. "They broke his fingers with hammers. 'Twas pitiful to see."

Tom could not forbear comforting her then. Laying down his rod, he put his arm about her shoulder and she turned into him, whimpering.

"I am sorry, Grace, truly I am," he soothed. "I heard from my lord Welles that John was suspected of carrying information to Yorkist supporters, and that they must extract that information at all cost. Tudor is a hard man, I have observed. He cares not how his subjects like him, and indeed it seems he does all to make them hate him. It rankled many of us when he commanded all mastiffs in the kingdom to be killed. Those magnificent dogs were doomed to die simply because Henry had heard they were capable of killing lions. 'The lion is the king of beasts,' he declared, 'and nothing should kill a king.' "

Tom paused, shaking his head. He took off Grace's crumpled straw hat and coif and stroked her wild curls. "He is afraid for his throne and prays many times daily to Our Lady to keep it safe. And at any time of the day or night he asks advice of his astrologer. In contrast, he was kind to the Simnel boy after Stoke, and now the boy is one of his falconers. Odd, perhaps, but I believe he knew the boy was an imposter from the start—especially as he had young Warwick closely guarded in the Tower at the time—but now, this rumor is different. If the son of King Edward is indeed alive, then he has a greater claim to the English crown than Henry does. So, you see, he had to make sure whatever John knows, he knows, too."

Grace sniffed and used her sleeve to wipe her nose. She had listened intently to Tom's little speech and was tempted to tell him what she knew of Dickon, but she had been sworn to secrecy and, besides, she could not entirely trust him yet.

"What do you think Henry will do with John?" she asked, sitting down on the mossy grass and stuffing the hat back on her head to shade her eyes from the sun. "He knows nothing, in truth."

"You are not a green girl, Grace. Certes, he must know something, or else why did he risk returning?" He whistled at Jason, who had found a rotted bird carcass on the grass and had put his shoulder down to roll in the muck.

Grace lowered her eyes to her lap in case her face betrayed her. "He told what he knew, so he says, but 'twas nothing Henry did not know already." Then she looked up at him with hope in her eyes. "Oh, Tom, do you think I could persuade Cecily to ask Lord Welles to beg Henry for a pardon? I have promised John I will do what I can," she blurted out. "Or perhaps you could ask your lord? He seems to like you."

Tom turned away in case, in turn, his face would betray him. "You ask much of me, Grace. I cannot stop you cajoling your sister, but I cannot compromise my position with Lord Welles. I know John is your kin, but he is not mine. We owe each other nothing."

Grace leaped to her feet. "Not even friendship, loyalty or as comrades in arms? Where is your sense of chivalry and honor? Didn't they teach you that at Sheriff Hutton?" she cried, running to him and raining blows on his back. He turned swiftly and took her by the wrists, his anguished face a mirror of hers.

"At this moment, my loyalty and honor are to you, as my wife—the person I cherish most in the world. As much as I regret John's predicament, I cannot condone putting your own life at risk. Can you not understand? All I ask is that you give me your loyalty, if not your love, in return. You put both of us in jeopardy with your foolishness. 'Tis my duty to protect you, and I am telling you that by allying yourself with John, you risk the king's anger. John is not a boy. He has made his own choices, and I am sorry it has gone badly for him. Comfort him if you must—I will not deny you or him that—but do not meddle in the affairs of state, Grace, or you may end up like John. And it would kill me if I could not prevent it," he finished hoarsely.

Grace stared at him openmouthed. She had not thought of Tom as eloquent until now. His words rang true and made sense, despite her first instinct to attribute them to jealousy. *He truly loves me,* she realized in a flash of understanding. *John had appealed to her love for him, perhaps selfishly, but the poor, tortured man was on the brink of disaster, and who could blame him for grasping at a straw? Oh, God, please show me the right path,* she begged.

Whether it was God or her own heart that answered she would never know, but she pulled Tom's head to her and kissed him with an ardor she had not before experienced, even in her imagined encounters with John. And as if she were nothing but a dandelion clock, she felt herself lifted off her feet and carried into a hazelwood copse that hid their lovemaking from any prying eyes except for two nervous squirrels and a doe that sprang easily away.

Jason loped along behind but was sternly told to lie down at the edge of the woods, which he did, watching his master and mistress curiously from afar.

HENRY WASTED NO time returning to London, and John was among the dozens of people on horseback, in carts and on foot who accompanied the king. Satisfied that Gloucester had been questioned enough to glean the most important piece of information—that a pretender to the throne did exist—Henry had granted Cecily's plea to cease torturing the young man further. She had done this without encouragement from Grace, who thanked her from the bottom of her heart as they watched the cavalcade move down the long drive and onto the road to London from Cecily's room above the courtyard.

"Certes, Grace, did you not think I was capable of asking for clemency for John on my own?" Cecily said, peeved. "He is my cousin, too, don't forget. And I have known him a lot longer than you have. I am only too sorry Henry did not pardon him altogether. It seems he wants to discuss what to do with John with his advisers in London. He dare not bring John to trial here—the commoners would not stand for it." Seeing Grace raise an inquiring eyebrow, she explained: "With so little evidence, Henry would look foolish, and to bring charges against John anywhere within a hundred miles of Fotheringhay would court rebellion. Our family is revered hereabouts, and Fotheringhay was Uncle Richard's birthplace. The people consider John of Gloucester one of their own."

"Where will Henry keep John in London?" Grace asked.

Cecily shrugged. "I know not. But it will probably not be at the Tower, where Henry would think he and Warwick might concoct a plot to overthrow him. Poor Henry; he is afraid of his own shadow. He spent an hour on his knees in the chapel yesterday praying to the Virgin for another son to secure his throne. Jack complained of pain in his back after being so long on his knees." She patted Grace's hand. "Hard as it may be, sister, you must put John out of your mind. At this time, he is dangerous to know, and more dangerous to support. If I did not have the good will of Lady Margaret now, I would not have been able to approach the king on John's behalf as I did. You, on the other hand, have no influence with anyone at court—well, except me"—she smiled—"and a plea from you would have put both you and Tom at risk."

"You sound like Tom," Grace said, chagrined. "I wish we were not going to Hellowe and could follow Henry to London. Then I might be able to see John again, if I knew where they were taking him." She suddenly saw John hunched in the back of one of the carts, his ankles manacled and a rope around his arms and chest. "Dear God," she murmured, her heart going out to him. "There he is, Cis!" she cried and waved. "John!" she called, but he did not hear her and stared steadfastly at the back of a guard on the end of the cart, who was swinging his legs in rhythm with the vehicle's motion.

"Ah, Grace, why not turn your favor on Tom," Cecily said kindly, pulling her away from the window. "John is lost to you—to all of us now. I beg of you, sweeting, don't cry. You will be happy, you will see."

But Grace could not see; her tears were blinding her.

18

Binche

JULY 1491

*P*erkin walked slowly down the path in the sunken palace garden, its rose and knot beds sheltered from the wind and weather by the massive stone city wall. He inhaled the heavy scent of the hundreds of blooms that were carefully tended by the dowager duchess's gardeners. Seated by a fountain, the ever-present book upturned on her lap, was the duchess herself, her head tilted back and her mouth slightly open as she dozed. She did not hear him approach and the quiet moment gave him time to study her for the first time in six years.

At forty-five and after many troubled years of unrest in Burgundy, the premature loss of her husband and his heir—her stepdaughter, Mary—Margaret of York was showing her age. She had put on weight in a matronly way, and Perkin could see that the once-golden hair pushed back under her fashionable gabled headdress was now completely gray. But sensing his presence, her head jerked forward, her eyes flew open and a joyful smile curved her mouth.

"Let me look at you, Pierrequin," she enthused, speaking English as she always had with him, and invited him to sit by her. After a graceful bow over her outstretched hand, he kissed her on both cheeks and sat down. "You are a handsome boy, in truth. But then, you always were," she said, and put her hand up to stroke his hair. The familiar movement caused Perkin to start, color rushing to his cheeks.

"Aunt Margaret," he whispered hoarsely. "Never I think to see you again."

"Foolish boy," she replied, shutting her book and laying it aside. "I told you that one day I might ask something of you. At the time, I was only half serious—I had no reason to say it, except that selfishly it bound me to you. But now . . ."

"Aye! Now?" he inquired eagerly. "I have done what you asked me of with Master Taylor. I sailed the seas and went in Brittany, France and Ireland. I told you that Ireland—and especially Cork—is safe *de commencer* the plan. But what *is* the plan, *madame? Qu'est ce que vous voulez plus de moi?*" he asked, reverting to his more comfortable French, the language of his native Tournai.

Margaret frowned. "English, Perkin, please. I can see you have forgotten much, and you must practice again," she chided him. Then she patted his hand. "You want to know what more I want of you, and of course you have a perfect right. The information you have given me since John Taylor spoke to you is of import, but not as important as what I shall ask of you now." She looked about them and noted the distance of the nearest gardener before beginning.

"I have kept a secret from you all these years, my dear. When you were a boy, it would have served you nothing to have known, but now it is of the utmost significance."

Perkin trembled with excitement. "I remember a long time ago you called me your secret boy, but I think you were ashamed to show me because I am a poor boy—Pierrequin Werbecque—from Tournai. Sire de Montigny, my tutor, knew this, but he was kind always and let me play with the gardener's boy. Then I was Jehan. Jehan LeSage—John the Good."

Margaret sighed. "Aye, it was, but that was the name I gave you. I wanted you to forget your mother and father and think of only me as your family. Piers, or Pierre, was your name, and Pierrequin means 'little Pierre.' "

"I do not remember anyone but you, *ma tante*," he cried. "Who was my family?"

"Your mother married a boatman by the name of Jehan Werbecque, who is now a comptroller in the city of Tournai, so I am told. Not long after you came to me, she died. Your stepmother's name is Nicaise or sometimes she is called Katherine de Farou, but you do not know her, nor will you." Margaret played with the huge ruby ring on her finger—her betrothal ring, Perkin remembered. "But—and here is the secret"—she paused, weighing her words and wondering if she could really involve her darling boy in her outrageous plan—"you were born in London, where your mother, whose name was Frieda, lived with your grandparents— Flemish weavers. Your father was not Jehan Werbecque at all, but my brother George, duke of Clarence and brother of King Edward of England." The look of disbelief on Perkin's face told her that what she was saying had been understood, and she plunged on. "Aye, you are a bastard of the house of York," she told him, "and when George, who was my favorite brother, was executed for treason, King Edward begged me to care for you. In truth, Edward was the one who condemned his own brother to death, and his guilt and remorse were great." She looked at Perkin with tenderness. "The other reason was that I was never able to have children of my own, God help me, and Edward knew I would care for you as only an aunt—and one who longed for children—could. Certes, I am your real aunt, but I thought it would be less complicated—and, I admit, selfish— if I kept you to myself. Perhaps 'twas wrong, but at the time it seemed right."

She took a deep breath and watched his expression. Dear God, he looks like one of us, she thought. Even more so now that he is older. He did not have the stature of his father, but his looks were clearly of the York line— the long, soft blond hair was like George's, the petulant, full lower lip like Edward's and the strong jaw reminding Margaret of Richard. He even had the odd crease above the brow line that Edward always proudly announced he had inherited, although from whom, Margaret could not remember. There was an odd dullness to Perkin's left eye, but perhaps he had looked too long at the sun on board ship or been in a fight and damaged it, and his skin was almost too soft for a man's beard. Otherwise, he was a beautiful young man in her eyes, and she glowed with pride.

"Who else knows this secret?" Perkin asked, interrupting her long avising of him.

Margaret shook her head. "No one has ever known about you, except for Edward, George, your mother and me—and, certes, your grandparents at the time of your birth. I am the only one left alive, you see."

Perkin was dumbfounded. A royal bastard? It could not be true, he thought. For all these years I have thought I was a poor boatman's son and that the duchess took me in as a charity case. He had not questioned her act of kindness, but praised God for his good fortune.

"Your stepfather, Werbecque," Margaret went on, "agreed to take in your mother and you because your grandparents gave him money, but he was not a good father to you. You told me once that he beat you."

"I do not remember him," Perkin said, rising and beginning to pace. "I do not remember anything before here."

"My darling boy," Margaret said, watching him anxiously and thinking even his movements had a natural grace to them, as if he had known all along he was no ordinary man. "I see you are in shock. Perhaps we should wait a while before I tell you why I brought you back."

Perkin swung back to her, his brows snapping together. "Nay, aunt, I want to hear your plan now. I have waited too long." Realizing to whom he spoke, he changed his tone: "Whatever it is, I cannot say no. I promised you, remember?" And he crossed his heart, just as he had done almost exactly six years ago.

Margaret rose stiffly from the bench and replaced her book in its velvet pouch, attached to her belt. Then she took Perkin's arm and led him through the gardens to a spot where they could look out over the city wall to the green fields undulating in front of them.

"Do you remember the two sons of my brother Edward who disappeared from the Tower of London?" she began.

Perkin nodded. "I heard in Lisbon that King Richard suffocated them in order to be king."

Margaret frowned. "You have the story wrong, nephew. My brother Richard was offered the crown by parliament months before the two boys disappeared. He had no reason to kill them. In truth, we do not know what happened to them. There were no bodies, no evidence, nothing. My sister-in-law, the boys' mother, believed they were dead, but many believed Richard sent them away for safekeeping somewhere. But he died at Bosworth Field, so no one knows where they are."

Perkin was intrigued. "And now that Henry Tudor wears the crown, what do it matter?"

Margaret smiled. "*Does* it matter, Perkin, not *do*. Certes, it does matter—to me and to all who support my family. If we could bring forth one of those boys, then Henry's claim to the crown would be very much in danger, don't you see?"

"Aye, I see how Henry must worry. But what can you do from here? What can I do?"

Margaret clucked her tongue impatiently. "Can you not guess, boil-brain? You will be one of those boys and frighten Henry off the throne."

Perkin stared at her, stunned. "M-me?" he stammered. "You . . . you want *me* to pretend I am who I am not?" Then he suddenly remembered the rumors. "But just as Master Waters told me, the talk in the taverns and markets is that Richard, duke of York, is alive—and you know where he is. Why do you not use the real man? I do not understand."

Margaret chuckled. "They are only whispers, Perkin, started by me and fueled by people fascinated by the mystery of the missing boys. Now that I have people believing it, we are ready to show him to them. There is no Richard, duke of York—only you." She waited for this news to sink in and watched the myriad expressions flit over his face.

Finally, he spoke. "You would have me lie?" Perkin asked miserably. "You would have me pretend to be someone else?"

"Dearest boy, you have been someone you are not for all of your life. It will not be difficult, I promise you." She eyed him surreptitiously as he stared at the cows in the meadow and let the idea percolate. "You are every inch a Plantagenet, and even though you are George's son, no one will ever doubt you are not Edward's—if you have the tools to carry off the masquerade. Tools that I shall give you"—she paused for effect—"as well as Archduke Maximilian, who finally supports me in this."

She shook his arm gently as he stared off into the middle distance, his mind in a whirl and every fiber of his being screaming "No!" Her tone turned seductive: "I swear to you, my dearest, that in five years time you will be king of England."

Perkin slowly turned his horrified eyes to her expectant face. "And if I fail?" he asked in a whisper.

Margaret scoffed. "How can you fail? I warrant even your sisters would believe you to be their brother the minute they saw you. Henry cannot deny the possibility of Richard's existence because he has never proved or declared publicly that the two princes are dead. This means he believes deep down that they could be alive, and that is why he is afraid."

Grasping at a straw, Perkin asked, "Why do you choose the younger son and not Edward? What will they believe has happened to him?"

Margaret gave him an appraising look. "Well done, nephew. An astute question. 'Tis well known Ned was sickly that summer of Eighty-three. There was a doctor who tended both boys who believed Ned had a wasting disease of the face. 'Tis possible he died from that—and that is the story you will tell, as well as how you were taken from the Tower and into hiding, which we shall practice. Besides, you and Richard are the same age—Ned was two years older." She picked up his limp hand and carried it to her cheek. "With Burgundy on your side, the friends you say we have in Ireland and Lord Lovell paving the way for support in Scotland, you will have the backing of many leaders. There are friends at the French court—rebel Englishmen who hate Henry—who are ready to help a Yorkist cause, and the French king would like nothing more than to anger Henry. And I shall be your chief supporter and champion—with Maximilian's help. The time is right, Pierrequin, and all these things will help us to succeed. I will guide you and teach you everything you need to know. As soon as you are ready, you will go to England with an army and claim the throne back for the house of York." She leaned into him and whispered. "I say to you again, you *will* be king of England!"

She waited patiently while he gathered his thoughts, but when he turned his anguished face to her, her heart sank.

"I cannot do this, your grace," he said. "I am a simple man, and my mask will be cast aside as quickly as . . . as an ax will cut off my head!" He clutched his throat and choked down a sob. "All I want is to go back to my ship and sail away forever."

Margaret felt tears roll down her cheeks, and she could not say if she shed them in sympathy for his terror or in frustration that he might thwart her and Maximilian's plan.

"Ah, Jehan," she used his old name tenderly. "I fear you have broken my heart." And she turned away and descended the few steps to the garden path, dabbing her eyes with her kerchief. She could not blame the young man for refusing the task; it was a mammoth—and dangerous—one. But seeing him had made it seem all the more possible: he looked the part, and with some coaching, no one would deny he was the son of Edward of England.

As she walked slowly back to her palace, leaving Perkin to ponder her words, she remembered the scene in Seventy-eight when William Hastings had unexpectedly come to her in this garden and told her of Edward's request to take George's bastard son under her wing. She smiled. She knew she could persuade the young man; it was just a matter of time.

And of keeping a promise.

PART THREE

Wherefore, cousin, think on this matter, for sorrow oft-times causes women to behave otherwise . . .

—THE PASTON LETTERS,
FIFTEENTH CENTURY

19

London

NOVEMBER 1491

*G*race had forgotten how noisy and dirty London was. All summer long, in the peaceful pastoral setting of Hellowe, she had thought she missed the sights and sounds of London. When Viscount Welles had recited a poem that Henry had been particularly taken with,

> *London, thou art of towns a per se,*
> *Sovereign of cities, seemliest in sight,*
> *Of high renown, riches and royalty;*
> *Of lords, barons, and many goodly knight;*
> *Of most delectable lusty ladies bright;*
> *Of famous prelates in habits clerical;*
> *Of merchants full of substance and might:*
> *London, thou art the flower of Cities all.*

she remembered thinking, *Aye, a fair city, but perhaps the poet has not seen Bruges.* Even at the abbey there had been a hustle and bustle about the place, and not a mile away one of the busiest thoroughfares in the kingdom led to London Bridge through the hubbub of Southwark, with its stews and taverns, marketplace, bull-baiting ring and breweries. The laymen workers brought the latest news from the city, and visitors from all over Europe would seek hospitality within its walls. In Lincolnshire, news was slow to catch up to them, and so when Grace was told that a man calling himself Richard, duke of York, had landed in Cork in October and been acclaimed as the son of King Edward by the Irish lords and people alike, she trembled for John.

To give him his due, Lord Welles had kept Cecily abreast of John's situation through the autumn, knowing hers and Grace's concern for their cousin. When Grace learned he had been first lodged at Westminster, where the king was in residence—in a guarded room, she had no doubt—she was hopeful that Henry would soon release him as being no particular threat. But with the appearance of a pretender now very real, Henry had good cause to distrust anyone who bore the name of York, despite Bess having given him a second son to solidify his position.

Grace eased her right leg on the stiff sidesaddle, envying the men's ability to straddle the backs of their horses. Her rump was numb and her back aching by the time the Welles party trotted through the Newgate and into Chepeside. It was a mild day for mid-November, and Grace was glad of the sunshine that greeted them after leaving Hellowe in a drizzle that had accompanied them as far as Barnet the evening before. Despite her tightly woven woolen cloak, all of her clothes were damp and uncomfortable. She hoped Pasmer's Place, where the Welleses lodged in the city, would be warm and inviting. Jack Welles had galloped off to Westminster with his squires and secretary to join the king, leaving Cecily and her attendants with the small armed guard who turned under the portcullis of Newgate.

Along the Chepe and down Soper Lane to St. Pancras Lane, the weary riders coaxed their mounts through mounds of refuse in the muddy street, avoiding sudden showers from the contents of pisspots heaved out of second-story windows and shooing away urchins in bare feet and rags begging for coins. A mangy dog lifted its head from a discarded carcass outside a butcher's shop, and Cecily remarked that the merchant was sure to be fined for breaking the law.

Pasmer's Place was a new house in St. Sithe's Lane, a stone's throw from the Barge Inn on Bucklesbury Street, and Grace could hear raucous laughter coming from its taproom.

"Our apartments are facing the other way," Cecily assured Grace. "You will not hear the noise, I promise. How do you like my house?" she asked, gesticulating grandly with her arm. "Jack brought the slate for the roof from Collyweston. 'Tis the best in England," she said proudly.

The new stone gleamed in the sunlight and stood out among the wattle and daub buildings adjacent. Inside, Grace was impressed with the brightly colored ceilings and polished furniture of the paneled rooms, where the sun streamed in through the west-wing windows that looked out onto a secluded garden.

"You and I will share my bed while Jack and Tom are at Westminster," Cecily enthused, showing Grace around the townhouse. "I am so happy you could come with me this time, Grace. We have to thank my husband for this—he is in a bind with us praying every night for John's release and he praying for Henry's safety—but I think I was persuasive enough," she said, winking at her sister.

"I am grateful to you, Cis. Tom was not pleased that I came this time, because he knows it is only for John's sake that I come. But let us not talk of Tom, dear as he is. Let us see how the children weathered the journey. They are probably already asleep."

Cecily shrugged. She did not understand Grace's fascination with her daughters, whom the younger woman loved as if she were their mother, while she was quite complacent about leaving them in the care of nursemaids all day. Once a day she would go and see them in the nursery, and it never failed to amuse her to find Grace down on her knees, playing a game with the oldest Welles daughter, Anne. But she knew Grace longed for her own child and was curious as to why her sister had failed to conceive.

Grace knew the answer. After the passionate lovemaking they had enjoyed in the wood at Collyweston, Grace had felt guilty and returned to her preoccupation with John. Tom had not touched her since.

VISCOUNT WELLES STRETCHED his long legs out in front of him towards the fire and gave a satisfied groan. "Cecily, bring me some of that wine," he addressed his wife, who was tending to a pipkin hanging on a swing hook over the flames. "It smells so good. I swear the London air is damper than in Lincoln," he grumbled. "Every bone in my body aches after sitting on that hard bench in the Star Chamber all day. It may be colorful, but the damn room is draughty."

"And what was your business today, my lord?" Cecily asked, ladling some of the spicy wine into a cup. "It sounds tedious. But then, doing needlework, teaching our daughter to walk and overseeing the household is also tedious. There, there, my lord—taste this and forget your dull day," she clucked.

"I said the bench was hard, my dear, not that my day was dull," Welles responded with an edge to his voice. Grace could see he did not appreciate being treated like a child. "Certes, you and Grace would have found it most interesting." He took the cup and sipped it carefully. "Several decisions were made, including one that will end the life of your cousin John."

Cecily dropped the ladle on the hearth, splashing wine on her yellow damask gown, and Grace slipped off her stool onto her knees, moaning as if in pain. Welles gave a short laugh. "You see, I told you it wasn't dull. There were others who were also condemned for their part in this damnable pretender debacle. So he will not die alone."

"My lord, my dear husband, how can this be? I pray you were not one who called for John's death. Say you were not, I beg of you!" Cecily knelt before him, clasping his free hand to her cheek. "Is there nothing we . . . you can do?"

Grace rocked back and forth, weeping, her hair escaping from her cap and clinging to her wet cheeks. "John! Ah, John, my dearest," she whispered. Cecily persisted with her supplications to her husband, if only to prevent the viscount from hearing Grace's words. She knew Welles would not understand why Tom Gower's wife whispered another man's name with such passion.

"He may be your cousin, Cecily, but he is also a traitor. Certes, there is nothing I can do. Now do pull yourself together and see to your gown. And take Grace with you—I cannot tolerate women weeping," he dismissed them both and pulled his hands away from Cecily. "John will be hanged, drawn and quartered, like any traitor at Smithfield, two days from now." He took another drink. "I wish to hear no more about it."

"H-hanged, drawn and quar-quartered," Grace repeated, horrified. "But he is of royal blood. He should be . . ." but she could not even bring herself to utter the word *beheaded*.

"Blood of a usurper, you mean!" Jack Welles roared. "And attainted. He deserves nothing more than any other common traitor. We were all agreed." He pointed to the door and said, more temperately, "Now go, before I lose my patience."

Cecily rose and gently helped the trembling Grace to her feet. "Come, dearest, let us go and pray for John's salvation," she said and, propelling Grace through the door first, turned back and snapped, "and leave my husband to his warm wine."

Before he had time for a reprimand, she had slammed the door behind her.

Taking Grace's hand, Cecily pulled her towards a room farther down the corridor, begging her to stop crying and start thinking. "We have two days," she whispered. "If we put our heads together, I have no doubt we can plot a way out of this. How I wish Mother were here—she'd have thought of one already."

Jack Welles had mellowed after a cup or two of the hot, rich wine and told Cecily he would arrange for the two women to visit John in Newgate prison. "I pray you, my dear, do not allow your sister to dishonor our name. Her behavior earlier was disgraceful," he said, chuckling at his pun.

Cecily kept her head for once and let him have his little joke, although how he could mock Grace at such a time, she could not understand. "I promise, my lord," she answered respectfully, wincing as her attendant tugged at a knot in her long fair hair. Then she steeled herself as she did every time she knew he was hungry for her and, looking over at him where he sat on the bed awaiting her in his murrey silk bed robe, gave him a seductive smile. "Your generosity will be repaid, of that you may be certain."

It was another miserable day in the city, and the facades of the white-washed houses along the wide Chepeside thoroughfare were made gray from the rain. It was the only paved road in the city, and thus the servants carrying Cecily's litter moved faster than they had been able through the muddy lanes from Pasmer's Place. Citizens hurried from place to place enveloped in felted cloaks, the women trailing the hems of their homespun woolen gowns in the puddles. Grace warmed her toes on the hot stone tucked under the fur blanket and closed her eyes in the gloom of the heavily curtained litter. She had visited and revisited what she would say to John as soon as Cecily had given her the news that they were permitted to visit him. Even Cecily's optimism had diminished after a night of lovemaking had failed to sway her husband's resolve not to plead for John's life.

"But I thought you had a plan," Grace said as they broke their fast on bread, cheese and ale. Welles had long since ridden back to Westminster, after giving instructions to his steward to ready a litter for Lady Welles. "You told me you had a plan."

She had not slept a wink in the bed she shared with Cecily's chief attendant on those nights when Jack wanted Cecily, her own maid on a pallet under the window. She was afraid that if she fell asleep she would have the fearful dream of old about John with a noose about his neck and the sword ripping open his belly. It frightened her that she might have foretold his fate in those nightmares.

Cecily had shaken her head, her full mouth drooping at the corners. "My plan did not work," she admitted. "I am sorry, Grace."

Her crying done the night before, Grace smiled wanly at her sister and accepted the apology in silence. A servant knocked and entered to take away the remains of a jug of ale and a lump of cheese. If he noticed that the ladies had eaten more heartily that morning, he showed no surprise that half a loaf of crusty bread and a second hunk of cheese were gone. Grace had carefully hidden them in a bag at her waist. "In case John is not given enough food," she told Cecily as she wrapped them. Then she had returned to her room to get ready for their visit to Newgate and sat sad and silent as Matty dressed her hair and arranged the black velvet headdress over it. Edgar did not even receive the customary smile and greeting from his mistress that morning, and her swollen red eyes told him she had heard the news of the execution. A handheld litter was the quietest mode of transport, but this morning Grace would have preferred the clopping of horses' hoofs or the rumbling of carriage wheels to jar the morbid thoughts that were swimming around her head.

"Sweet Jesu!" Cecily's awed voice came from the other side of the vehicle now, startling Grace out of her reverie. "Do you remember the old hag in the market at Winchester, Grace? When Bess gave birth to Arthur?"

Grace's hand flew to her mouth. "Certes, I do. What made you think of her?"

"I cannot say. Perhaps the thought of an execution," Cecily replied.

"What did she say? Something about two men you would help. Ah, yes." Changing her voice to mimic the old woman, she quoted: " 'Executions! They be executions. It be dangerous for you to know them, but you will help them. Better not make friends of young men, my lady.' By all that is holy, it seems she was right."

Both women crossed themselves, and Grace reached for her rosary. She had helped John with his flights north to Stoke and east to Burgundy. "God have mercy," she whispered, "for if she is, it would seem no plan we can devise can save John at this late hour." Her throat constricting, she said, "Oh, Cis, it all seems like a bad dream. I wish we could wake and find we were once again in the safety of Sheriff Hutton, awaiting Uncle Richard's summons back to London. Why, oh, why did John have to go and get himself captured? There is no one to help him here."

Cecily shook her head. "Aye, no one. Jack was my only hope." The escort coming to a stop told them they were at Newgate, and they pushed aside the coverlet, arranged their skirts and blinked at the light when the curtains were pulled back. Edgar helped Grace out after Cecily's captain lifted her onto the steps of the prison so she would not soil her shoes.

Newgate's solid stone rose above them, its tiny barred openings in the wall proclaiming it escape-proof. It was said hundreds were kept in its dank, grimy cells, and many had known the pain of gruesome tortures like the rack within its bowels. Grace shivered and shrank close to Edgar's protective hulk. The captain announced the Welles party and the spike-studded wooden door creaked open to admit them. The stench inside made Grace retch.

They were ushered through the prisoner's holding room, where one or two unfortunate men were chained in a corner, awaiting their more permanent accommodations. One was groaning and attempting to stem the blood from a cut in his ankle caused by a too-tight manacle. A covered walkway led past a couple of large cells, one open—except for bars—to the wind and weather, in which huddled a dozen men around a small brazier. The guard laughed. "Those buggers be lucky to have the fire. Sir Hugh don't want his guests to freeze to death, do he?" he jeered at the poor inmates. "Thieves and murderers, all," he confided to the ladies, exposing toothless gums with his grin. On the open side of the walkway was a small courtyard, slimy with moss watered for decades by the piss of prisoners and their guards. Both young women held their tussie-mussies to their noses and followed the prison guard though the door at the end of the passage and into a cheery room with a roaring fire and a tapestry-covered table piled high with papers and massive tomes.

"God's greeting to you, Lady Welles," a rotund man with rosy cheeks and bulging blue eyes said, waddling forward and effecting a passable bow. He was unaccustomed to receiving royalty, and the king's sister-in-law was a rare treat indeed. He gave Grace a cursory glance but focused all his unctuous attention on Cecily. "We are honored by the visit of such a high and mighty princess as yourself, graced by God and all his angels—" he began loftily, but was cut off by Cecily, who inclined her head graciously but held up her hand.

"I am sure you are, Sir Hugh, but Lady Grace and I would like to see our cousin as soon as possible. I trust Lord Welles, my husband, sent word that we would come?"

Grace was shocked at the contrast of this comfortable room with the miserable conditions in the rest of the prison. How can the man sit here all day in all good conscience knowing what is on the other side of the door? she thought and loathed him on the spot.

A fleeting expression of annoyance crossed his perfectly round face before he was all smiles again. "Certes, my lady, I will have you escorted to Lord John's . . . ahem . . . place of detention," he said. "I trust you will find he is well looked after. He is our most prestigious prisoner at this time," he said, gloating. In a nastier tone, he barked: "Guard!" and instantly the door opened, admitting their previous escort, who bowed. "Take these noble ladies to see John of Gloucester. Have them wait in the anteroom while he is readied. 'Tis a more pleasant place for talking," he explained to Cecily. He muttered something to the guard, who nodded and then held the door for Grace and Cecily to leave. Sir Hugh bowed low, but then Grace saw him retreat backwards to warm his fat arse at the fire.

"Horrible man," she remarked to Cecily. "I suspect him of cruelty, for all his bowing and smiles."

They waited half an hour for John in the cold but relatively clean room assigned to them. Cecily whispered that she was surprised Sir Hugh had not searched them, or at least asked them to show him the contents of their belt bags. "If he had," she chuckled, "I would have hit him with mine."

It was obvious why Sir Hugh had made them wait when John was ushered in, having observed the other disheveled inmates on their way up to this part of the building. He had been washed, his hair was combed and he was wearing a clean shirt under his soiled, bloodstained gipon. But nothing could hide the despair in his eyes or the gauntness of his face, even though it was hidden by a heavy black beard. Cecily turned to the guard and in her most cajoling voice asked him to leave them alone. The guard looked mulish, but when Cecily drew herself up to her full height, slowly raised her arm and pointed to the door, commanding "Go!" he scurried out like a frightened mouse.

"Cecily, Grace," John said, going to them, tears close to the surface. "I never thought to see you again."

Grace gently led him to a stool, on which he sank down gratefully. His legs were weak from lack of exercise and food, and she noticed that his poor broken hands trembled as they touched hers. "Little wren," he whispered. "I have seen you so many times in my dreams."

Tears coursed down Grace's face and she pulled his head to her bosom and stroked his hair.

"Dear God!" Cecily groaned upon seeing John's condition. "I am so sorry for you, cousin. What have they done to you?" Cecily came to John's other side and the three clutched one another as if they would never let go. Then Grace extricated herself slowly and took the bulging pouch from her belt. She spread her kerchief on his lap and fed him hunks of bread and cheese, which he gobbled hungrily.

"You two are a sight for sore eyes," he said, finally managing a smile. "But this is manna from Heaven. What else do you have in there, Grace? A pardon, perhaps?"

The women looked aghast at each other, and then back down at him. Cecily shook her head. "Nay, John. We have tried, but it seems Henry cannot tolerate one of York blood alive to threaten his throne. It surprises me he has not yet found an excuse to get rid of poor Warwick, who is still in the Tower. I don't think you need to know what method of persuasion I used on my husband, but 'twas of no avail. We come to give you comfort, but not to give you hope."

John grinned bravely. " 'Twas only in jest I asked, Cis. You should not have remorse. My own folly brought me to this point. I only wish I knew what fate had in store for me."

The gasp from Grace told John his cousins knew more than he did.

He inclined his head. "Will you tell me, or will you kill me with your kindness?" he demanded, slapping at a flea hopping brazenly on his white sleeve. He grimaced as pain coursed through his fingers. "I have been here for weeks with no word of my destiny. I expected to languish here, forgotten, until I died of old age. It seems there is another plan, if your faces tell me true."

Grace turned away; she could not be the one to tell him. Cecily was shocked. "Was it not clear at your trial?"

John gave a harsh laugh. "Trial? What trial?"

Cecily's face went white with anger. "Hell's bells, and damn Henry," she cried. "He thinks he is above the law." She took a deep breath. "You have been condemned, dearest John. Condemned to die at Smithfield."

John swayed, dropping the bread and cheese, and Cecily reached out to catch him, holding him upright on the stool. When he had recovered, she continued: "The whoreson Tudor will not even give you a royal execution . . ." she stopped, knowing that he understood what a common traitor's death would mean.

He held Cecily's gaze with his, and the unspoken question in it was "When?"

She could not bear to look into those gray eyes then, so she rose before she said, in a barely audible whisper, "To-morrow."

When he groaned, Grace swung round and went to him, taking him in her arms and rocking him like a baby. All three fell silent as they pondered the awfulness of John's fate. Grace finally said: "I will be there, John. You will not be alone."

Cecily drew in a sharp breath. "How, Grace? Certes, Tom will not allow it. I know Jack would not permit me to go and mingle with the commoners. Pray be sensible."

Grace got up, her fists clenched and her mouth set in a stubborn line. "I will go, Cis. Edgar will take me, and I will disappear just as I did in Burgundy—and just as I did when Henry processed to his crowning, remember? No one knows me. I have always been invisible—why, even Bess forgot I was with you all during the scandal with Uncle Richard. But I am not invisible to John. He will find me wherever I am in the crowd. I know he will."

A chuckle made the two women turn to John, who had stood during

Grace's tirade. "*Tenez, mes cousines,*" he mocked them in French. "Do I not
have a say in who sees me die and who does not? I have no doubt that
if Grace wants to be there, she will be. Part of me wants you there, my
dear, but the other parts scream never in a thousand years would I put
you through such a hideous experience. 'Tis bad enough that I must endure . . ." As though he had only just considered the horror, the bile rose in
his throat and, turning from them, he vomited on the floor.

While Grace gentled him back onto the stool and knelt beside him,
Cecily went to the door and demanded water and a cloth from the guard.
Peering in, the man observed what had occurred and, touching his fore-
lock, regretted he was not allowed to leave his post.

"Unlock the door, you measle," Cecily barked. Then she turned her
sweet smile on him. "You and I will go and fetch it. These two are sweet-
hearts," she lied, winking at Grace. "You wouldn't be so surly as to deny
them a few minutes together, would you?"

The man was charmed and unlocked the door, and Cecily slipped out.

"Always thinking, cousin," John said, his voice rasping after the puk-
ing. "Thank you. Don't fret, Grace, I feel better," he told her. "I would pour
myself ale, but I can no longer lift a jug that big," he said, indicating the
drink Sir Hugh had ordered taken up for the royal visitor earlier. "I must
have eaten the food too quickly, 'tis all," he explained, knowing full well
he had not fooled the sisters. Grace fetched him a cupful, and he took a
mouthful of the pale liquid, swilling it around his mouth and spitting it out
on the floor. He was ashamed his fear was so transparent and tried not to
think on the grisly method of execution he would suffer—dear God, was
it really tomorrow? He forcibly expunged it from his mind, as he needed to
turn to more practical matters.

"Can I trust you?" he said urgently, handing Grace the empty cup.
"Before the guard returns, I must ask you to do something for me." From
a hidden pocket sewn into his gipon and cleverly concealed by an embroidered rose, he drew out a folded square of paper cloth. "This is why I
came back. I have kept it here, untouched, since I left Malines in June. I
thought about giving it to you that day in Collyweston, but then I was certain Henry would pardon me and I would find a way to deliver it. It must
go to Lord Lovell in Scotland; I know not how, but he is waiting for word
from me. They did not discover it, and I thank God, or Lovell would be

found out—he is thought to have died ere now." John saw the frightened look on her face and sought to reassure her: " 'Tis in code, Grace, so if it is lost, I doubt it can be read. If the task proves too daunting, then you must get word to Aunt Margaret why it failed to be delivered. Can you do this, Grace?" He stood up and held out the surprisingly pristine missive.

His trust seduced her so completely that Grace could not gainsay him, not recognizing the danger he was putting her in. She took the letter and nodded. "I will try my best," she said, tucking it down between her breasts. She had no idea how she would find Lord Lovell, but how could she tell John that? " 'Tis about my brother, Dickon, is it not?" she asked. "Is he coming soon?"

John shrugged, a sense of relief coming over him now that he had relinquished his failed task and knowing he could trust Grace. "I left before anything was determined. Before I even saw Dickon. That is why I had nothing to tell Henry's torturers, God damn them to Hell," he growled.

"Amen to that," Grace murmured.

John looked at her upturned face and sighed. "How you have brightened my life all these years. You and I are kindred spirits, orphaned bastards, never knowing our place and forced to follow whatever star our royal fathers chased after. You may be amused to know how many times I have thought of you and your goodness, surviving the frightening position you were thrust into with so much dignity. It inspired me to be a better man. How I wish I could congratulate Tom, for he is indeed fortunate."

"Nay, he is not," Grace assured him guiltily, and she took out her kerchief and cleaned his beard. "He loves me, I know that. But I do not love him as a wife should. How can I, when . . ." she hesitated, unsure if she should burden him with her feelings for him.

"Soft, Grace," John chided her. "You must forget what you once felt for me. I had hoped you had heeded me that night at the abbey. Know that I cherish you as a brother might his dearest little sister, but now you must look to Tom for the love of a man. Promise me you will, Grace?" He held her eyes with his until he saw her nod, a tear escaping down her cheek. "But promise that you will not forget me, for there are precious few who will mourn the loss of King Richard's bastard, in truth." Grace went into his arms then, and she dared not look up and see the anguish in his face. "There, there, little wren," he consoled her, holding her awkwardly.

They heard Cecily's voice outside the door and John released her. Cecily hurried in with a cloth and a bowl of water. "Is there anything we can do for you, cousin?" she asked, watching Grace wring out the wet cloth and gently wipe his face.

"I wish I could see my mother one last time, 'tis all," he mumbled from beneath the cloth. "But I doubt she knows I am here, or what is to happen to me. I wish I could see her beautiful golden eyes and hear her sing once more . . ."

The guard had entered and cleared his throat noisily. "It be time to leave, my lady. Sir Hugh—"

Cecily turned and gave him a withering look that sent him slinking back into the passage. But not knowing what more they could achieve, and with no hope of a reprieve, she thought it best to leave. "If I knew where to find your mother for you, I would. But I don't think there is time." She lowered her voice to a whisper, saying, "I am sorry, John, truly I am."

"Tell her I loved her all my life. Tell her that. You will find her at Tendring Hall, caring for Lady Howard, I think." He made the most of rinsing the cloth so they could not see his tears. "Tell her I was strong, I beg of you. And pray for me to be strong tomorrow and to remember I am a king's son. Ah, Jesu . . ."

Grace moved as if to go to him, but Cecily took her arm and propelled her towards the door. "May God bless you, John," she said with finality.

"And may he have mercy on your soul," Grace choked out. "Look for me tomorrow, dear John, I shall—" but Cecily did not allow her to finish.

"Do not promise something you cannot fulfill," she hissed in Grace's ear. "Come, let us go from this place, or I fear I, too, will lose control."

She led the distraught Grace back down the stairs, past the other pitiful prisoners and out onto the street, where they gratefully clambered back into the waiting litter. Just as the curtains were being drawn, Grace noticed a middle-aged woman with anxious amber-colored eyes wearing a widow's barbe and carrying a basket hurry up the steps to knock upon the prison door. Poor lady, she thought briefly; she is probably the mother of one of the inmates and is taking him food. Dear God, what a hideous place. She shuddered.

Cecily's hand found hers under the warm blanket and, without a word, the two women let their grief flow freely, comforting each other on the road home.

. . .

CECILY LIED FOR Grace the next day and told her husband the two of them would visit Bess and baby Henry at Westminster that morning.

"Do not go anywhere near Smithfield, madam," Welles said. "You know what happens there today."

"Aye, my lord," Cecily replied dully. "You do not need to remind us. We thought we might be of comfort to the queen. She loved John, too. We shall go and light candles for him at Saint Margaret's."

"Very well, my dear," the viscount assented. "Henry wants to hunt today, so we go to the forest at Shene. If it helps, he is grieving over this particular execution, and I hope our expedition in the country will take his mind off it. He looks on John as kin, as well, in truth."

Cecily shut her mouth for once; her customary "Pah!" died on the tip of her tongue.

Later, Welles, Tom and a small meinie trotted out of the gate of Pasmer's Place while Cecily and Grace watched from the upstairs window.

Tom had taken her aside before he left. "I wish I could stay with you today of all days, Grace, but I cannot gainsay my lord. I shall think of you every minute, and pray for John's soul. I am sure you will spend most of your day on your knees, and I pray it will comfort you. Courage, sweetheart," he had said, and he held her close before hurrying off to join the group.

When they were gone, Cecily took Grace to her garderobe and shut the door. Grace donned her plain gray gown and Cecily covered her with a drab cloak borrowed from a servant, finishing off the inconspicuous garb with a simple kerchief over her curls. Cecily nodded. "You will pass as a citizen, and with Edgar to protect you, you should be safe. I do not like you going, Grace, for I fear you will be marked for life by it. I have witnessed an execution such as this, and I had nightmares for weeks—and I did not even know the victims. Are you certain you must go?"

"Aye, Cis," Grace said, nodding vigorously. "I cannot let John die alone. I would never forgive myself. I may turn my back at the moment his life is taken, but I will be there."

Cecily embraced her and wished her God speed. Grace hurried down the back stairs to the kitchen courtyard and sidled out, looking for Edgar as arranged. He was there, as solid and reliable as always.

"This way, my lady," he said, ushering her through a door in the garden wall and out onto a lane behind the house. "There be nary a one who will see us this way."

It took them half an hour to walk to the marketplace, as they joined more and more Londoners anxious not to miss the spectacle at the scaffold.

"Edgar, you are to tell no one that we came," she commanded as they drew near. "Swear you will not."

"I swear, my lady mistress. But why are we here? An execution like this be no place for a lady," Edgar remarked, using his elbow to make a path for Grace through a group of noisy boys, playing a game of hot cockles. The blindfolded youth in the middle was attempting to guess who had slapped his outstretched hand, and Edgar could not resist joining in and slapping it for good measure. He grinned when the boys roared their approval.

Grace frowned at her servant. "We are not here to play games, Edgar," she snapped. "Have you no respect for those about to go to their Maker in such a hideous fashion? Although 'tis not your place to ask, I will tell you I am here to give comfort to my cousin John, one of the condemned. Now make us a path, sirrah."

Edgar hung his head, stung by her harsh tone. "I be sorry for you, my lady. I did not know," he mumbled, looking at her with a mixture of sympathy and admiration. But for once Grace did not feel pity for this simple man; she was too intent on preserving her own hard outer shell, even though inside every nerve in her body was frayed like an old rope. Furthermore, after a night spent on her knees begging God and John's own saint to end her love's misery quickly, she had lost her breakfast soon after eating it and was now feeling weak.

Upon entering the square they passed a building with a low abutment upon which several people were standing to get a better view. Among them, Grace recognized the woman she had seen at the prison the day before. This time, however, a young man with chestnut hair accompanied her, his eyes the same color as hers. Her son, Grace guessed, as she began to squeeze her way behind Edgar through the hundreds of people crowded in front of the high scaffold. Grace's stomach turned over when she saw the gibbet, its three nooses swinging loosely as they awaited their victims. She eventually came as close to the front of the crowd as she dared, and told Edgar to stop. Their neighbors reluctantly stepped aside to accommodate his bulk, and Grace stood in front of him, with a clear view of the stage, at the base of which stood a large brazier that sent clouds of smoke up into the cold blue sky. Several guards were warming their hands over it, but the tools of their grisly trade, leaning harmlessly against the scaffold's supports, revealed the real reason for the fire. An ax, several butchers' knives and large hooks would soon take their toll on a half-hanged prisoner, whose belly would be slit open, his entrails pulled out with the hooks and burned in front of the man as he still lived. With luck, he would expire before he was beheaded and his body was hacked into four quarters. His head would then be set upon London Bridge's gate, the other parts displayed in strategic places in the city.

Grace had decided that she would stay until John was cut down from the gibbet. She knew she would not be able to withstand the rest of his agony. She hoped that by arriving late she would not be there long, and it seemed she was right. Off in the distance, the slow beat of a tabor alerted the throng to the imminent appearance of the main attraction. Vendors bawled out their wares one last time, hoping for a customer for their pies, ale and roasted thrushes, and the crowd instinctively moved forward as one to get a better view of the somber procession. Grace clutched her drab cloak around her neck and braced herself for her first sight of John. He was the third of the three prisoners tied to wooden hurdles, surrounded by half a dozen guards and dragged along the street.

"Death to the traitors!" shouted one man near Grace. "Death to the traitorous bastards!" Jeers and catcalls followed, and John averted his gaze from the people as the guards untied him from the frame. Grace could see that he was now clean-shaven and wearing a shirt that hung just above his knees, but no breeches or hose. She had been warned by Cecily that he would be bare-legged. " 'Tis easier for the butchers to cut off—" She had stopped there, as Grace had gone as white as chalk.

"Th-they c-c-cut off his . . . member?" she'd whispered, bile rising in her throat. "Christ have mercy. Mankind is surely the cruelest of God's creatures." Cecily had comforted her then. Grace now saw her sister had been right, and her terror of what she would see almost sent her running from the place.

Then, suddenly, a man shouted: "Why, 'tis Richard's bastard! 'Tis John of Gloucester! Why were we not told?" And he poked the guard who was forcing the crowd back from the prisoners. "A king's son should have a private execution. 'Tis customary," Grace heard him say.

Edgar could contain himself no longer. He called angrily to the captain, who was pushing John. "What treason has John committed?"

"Who saw the trial?" Edgar's neighbor agreed. But the captain ignored them and the crowd went quiet. Grace's heart leapt with hope. Perhaps the mob would rescue John, she thought desperately; they would demand a trial, and he would live to see another day. Thank you, dear God, you heard my prayer, she rejoiced. But just as quickly as the information had created indignation in them, the Londoners again turned complacent.

"Too close to Richard for comfort," a woman at the back of the crowd yelled, and Grace was dismayed to hear the callous laughter that erupted.

Edgar attempted to keep up his heckling, but he soon gave up. The people wanted a spectacle and, thirsting for blood, their fickle thoughts turned to morbid fascination and John's unfair treatment was forgotten. Mocking cries and shouted insults rent the air as the first of the three condemned men stood in front of his noose and received the last rites from a priest, who was more intent on yawning than on what he was saying. Grace realized, with another rush of bile, that they were saving John for last.

The hanging of the first man was over in a trice, the mob sending up a rousing cheer. Grace stared, horrified yet riveted. The hangman swiftly used his knife to cut down the still-wriggling body, and two guards caught it as it dropped like a stone to the ground. Then the disembowler began his grisly work, and Grace almost fainted from the disgusting sight and the primeval screams the half-dead victim was able to let forth. The shriveled genitals were tossed into the fire, and then the man's stomach was slit from chest to pelvis and yards of bloody white entrails were hauled from the gaping wound and added to the flames. It was too much for Grace, and she sank to the ground in a dead faint. Edgar, mesmerized by the sight, did not notice until his neighbor nudged him, and with a cry of concern the groom picked up his mistress and cradled her in his massive arms. The crowd was pressing so close, he could not have made his way out of it, so he stood there and drew his cloak around her to protect her. She was revived by the sickly smell of burning flesh, but she hid her face in Edgar's chest as the rest of the sentence was carried out. She blocked her ears and hid her face through the second man's agony, and then Edgar whispered: "Your cousin, my lady. He be last."

"Hold me up higher, Edgar," Grace said as bravely as she could. "John must see I am here."

John stood tall on the platform and stared at the unfriendly crowd as the priest intoned the prayers of the dead. Grace willed him to look at her, but his eyes stared over the mob's head and he suddenly reached out his hand and called, "Mother!"

"He cries for this mother, the baby!" someone shouted, and many turned their heads to see who he was looking at.

"There she be," the neighbor said, nodding at a woman on the abutment. "See, the one with the white hair, next to the youth." Grace knew without looking that it was the same woman she had seen the day before at Newgate, and here earlier. It was Katherine Haute, Richard of Gloucester's leman and John's beloved mother. Tears poured down her cheeks. Poor lady, Grace thought; how can she bear to witness her son's awful death?

"Must be the whore who birthed him," the neighbor's wife agreed, cackling. "Seems she do not have the stomach for it. Look it, she be leaving." The unpleasant woman called loudly: "The craven whore be leaving. Good riddance! Death to traitors, death to traitorous bastards!" And the crowd took up her cry.

Grace stiffened in Edgar's tight hold and forced herself to look back up at the scaffold. The captain was conferring with the hangman, who nodded, and Grace saw silver flash between them. She assumed the man was being paid for his services, but she put it from her mind as she focused on John, again willing him to look her way. Then, as he was rudely pulled backwards to have the noose fitted around his neck, he saw her. A grim smile curved his mouth, and he locked his gaze on her, his eyes full of compassion. She gasped at that moment, remembering her dream of him, a noose around his neck, being led towards her by Tom. She trembled and, wriggling from Edgar's hold, railed silently at the heavens. Dear God, I foresaw this and I did nothing to stop it. Never losing his gaze, she forced him to look at nothing else but her.

"John!" she screamed, holding out her arms to him. "My dearest John!" He was still looking at her when the floor fell away and his body disappeared. The people around Grace moved away respectfully, murmuring and crossing themselves, and many did not notice until it was too late that the hangman had done his work too well this time, for the victim the guards cut down was already dead. There was a moment of quiet before fury erupted from the throats of the people who felt cheated out of the prize execution of the day.

The usual haze that fogged Edgar's mind dissipated for one crystal-clear instant, and he knew what he must do without being told. He swept Grace up in his arms and hefted his way to the front of the angry, booing crowd. Using the open space between the restraining guards and the scaffold, he ran under the platform, past John's inert body, and out onto the other side of the Smithfield marketplace, Grace's sobs breaking his big, simple heart.

GRACE WAS INCONSOLABLE for two days, and even Cecily became impatient with her.

"You dishonor Tom with your tears, sister," she reprimanded Grace late on the second day, entering the small solar Grace had been assigned once Welles returned from Westminster. "My lord Welles is ready to send you back to Hellowe. Indeed, I am ready to agree with him, for a change. You have not left your room for two days, nor have you allowed Tom to see you. 'Tis unkind, and disrespectful to your husband."

Grace turned her blotched face from the pillow to fix Cecily with an obstinate glare. "By all that is holy, Cis, you are not one to preach about disrespect. You treat the viscount abominably."

Cecily grinned sheepishly. "Touché," she acknowledged, but she was pleased she had succeeded in rousing Grace from her weeping. "I pray you, let Tom come to you. He is distraught, the poor man. You do not deserve to have such love. What say you, Grace?"

Tom's pleasant face floated into Grace's mind, and she was immediately contrite. His only fault was that he loved the wrong woman. She pulled herself together and slipped her legs out of bed to feel for her soft velvet slippers. Her shift was crumpled beyond help and her hair was a tangle of knots and curls that stuck out at all angles from her head.

"Certes, I think I shall tell Tom to wait until Matty has tidied you up. Perhaps a warm bath might help." She turned to Grace's maid, who had not left her mistress's side but to fetch food and drink, and gave some instructions before turning back to Grace. "There is one thing you need to know about this dreadful business that might bring you comfort," she said, coming to sit next to her sister on the brightly colored coverlet. She followed the pineapple outline with her finger as she spoke, afraid that she, too, might be overcome with emotion. Bess had been surprised that her two sisters had visited Newgate prison, but she and Cecily had wept together on the day of John's execution, and then they had lit candles for his immortal soul.

Cecily spoke steadily, as if she were addressing a child. "It seems the captain of the guard gave orders to leave John's body intact—except for his head. You knew the noose had killed him instantly, did you not?" Grace shook her head, but her spirits lifted. "Aye, it did," Cecily continued. "Edgar tells me he saw money given to the hangman just before John's turn—"

"I saw it, too," Grace cried. "But I thought it was the hangman's fee."

"Someone bribed the captain to pay off the hangman. It wasn't you, Grace, was it?"

Cecily was taken aback by Grace's harsh bark of laughter. "What money do I have to bribe anyone, pray? I must rely on others' generosity—your mother's, yours—to exist. Certes, if I had it, and if I had known it was possible to help John in this way, by God I would have spent it gladly." Then she modulated her tone. "Nay, Cecily, 'twas not I."

"I am happy to hear it. Jack was curious, and your name was mentioned." She put her finger to her lips and whispered, "It would not do to turn him or the king against you, Grace. These are treacherous times, with a pretender knocking on Henry's door, and no one is safe from his spies and suspicions. Bess and I have done our best to explain that you had more than just a cousinly love for John. Praise be to God, they laughed about it, but if they knew you had been to Duchess Margaret's court in secret—" She broke off as a quiet knock on the door told her Mathilda was announcing the arrival of the bath. "Come!" she called, and then murmured to Grace, "Have a care, Grace, and reconcile with Tom, I beg you."

AN HOUR LATER, her skin glowing with oil of lavender and her curls combed to a glossy sheen, Grace felt better. The lump in her throat and the ache in her heart could not be expunged so easily by a simple, scented bath, but she felt calmer and ready to face Tom. Fifteen-year-old Mathilda

pulled her mistress's blue gown over a clean and pressed chemise and stood
back to admire her.

"You may send word to Master Gower that I would see him, if 'tis convenient, Matty. Ask a page to send some wine and wafers."

Tom arrived at the same time as the refreshment and, sending the page
and Matty away, entered the room carrying the tray himself. Jason was at
his heels. Grace stood when she saw him; her eyes smiled a welcome even
though her mouth could not. The dog wagged its tail and went to her,
expecting the usual caress, but lay down by the fire when it saw Grace's
affection was not forthcoming.

"Thank you for coming, Tom," she said, smoothing the wrinkles from
the tapestried table cloth for Tom to land the tray. "I was not well, in
truth." What a foolish thing to say, she thought; he knows why I shut myself in here. But it was the best she could do at that moment, and she was
unsure whether he knew she had been at Smithfield.

"Aye, so they told me," Tom said, his clear blue eyes taking in her ravaged face. "And I can see that you have not been 'well.' I apologize again
for not being here with you during the ordeal, but I had no choice. I hope
I showed my concern and understanding on that day. However, I trust you
will recover from whatever ailed you?"

Grace felt the blood rushing to her face and she lowered her eyes, understanding full well his meaning. "It seems I have no choice," she murmured. "I trust . . . I trust you will be patient a little while longer. The pain
I have will take time to heal." She poured wine into two silver goblets, the
Welles crest engraved on the side, and held one out for him. "Let us drink
to an old friend, may he rest in peace."

Tom drew in a whistling breath. "Christ's nails, but you are stubborn,
Grace," he said grimly. "How long before John comes no more between us?
Aye, may he rest in peace, but I will drink to him leaving *us* in peace." He
swallowed the contents of the glass in a single mouthful and banged the
glass down on the tray, making Jason raise his big head off the floor.

Grace flinched and was immediately contrite. "Forgive me, Tom. I do
not mean to be cruel, but I cannot be less than honest with you. You do not
deserve lies and dissembling. I promise I will become the wife you wish, if
you allow me this time to grieve. What say you?" She put her hand on his
arm and searched his face for a softening.

"How much time, Grace?" he asked without moving a muscle. Grace was dismayed; he usually unbent at her touch. "I am the butt of much jesting by my fellow squires," he told her. "They question why I spend so many nights with them and not in your bed. 'Tis galling that I have no answer."

Grace bit her lip and turned away. "I have not prevented you coming to my bed, sir. It has been your choice to stay away. You know full well 'tis a husband's right to take his wife wherever and whenever he chooses. I pray you, do not blame me."

"Ah, Grace. I see that you do not understand me still. I am a man of simple values, and I have no wish to take what is mine unless it is freely given. When you offer it to me, you may be certain I shall return to your bed. Until then, pray excuse me. 'Tis my turn for the viscount's all-night, and I am late already," he said. "I wish you a good night and even pleasanter dreams. Come, Jason."

Grace swung round to see him at the door, giving her a small formal bow before exiting. Her tears spent on John, she ran to the bed and pummeled the pillow with her fists in frustration.

20

London

WINTER 1491–92

A few days later, escorted by Edgar and Matty, Grace went for a walk in the dreary December air to St. Mary le Bow, close by the Chepe. They passed several beggars lining Hosier Lane near the ruined tower of the Norman church, and Grace could not forbear throwing a groat to a man covered in sores with only stumps for legs. "Gawd bless you, mistress," he croaked, swiping the coin and tucking it into his filthy tunic.

She was greeted at the entrance by a monk, who opened a small door within the massive oak door for her to step inside the ancient church, named for the arches in its crypt. "Rector Fisher welcomes you to his church," the monk said earnestly. "He is hearing confession at this hour, if you care to wait."

Grace thanked him and moved inside, adjusting her eyes to the gloom. She dipped her fingers in the holy water and, crossing herself with it, genuflected in front of the gold crucifix facing her upon the altar at the far end of the church. Leaving Edgar and Matty to make their own peace with God, she glided down the side aisle to a statue of the Virgin in front of which were hundreds of lighted candles. She bought several from the monk seated at a table nearby and, after mounting and lighting them, stepped back to a kneeling bench and settled herself for her vigil.

Dear Lord God, keep Your servant John safe and raise him up upon the Day of Judgment to be with You, Your Son and all the angels, she prayed. And I ask You to take pity on this poor woman who wants to be a dutiful wife and yet cannot forget her first love. Is it possible and right to love more than one man? I am so ignorant in the ways of the world, and I need guidance, O Lord. As I look at the sweet Virgin's face, I shall take comfort from her and believe she will intercede for me with You.

Then she began to tell her beads and, during the rote *ave*, think back to all the encounters she had had with John: at Sheriff Hutton, where she comforted him in his grief over his father's death; their secret meetings in the undercroft of Bermondsey Abbey; his strong, young body wet from the Thames when he first began to trust her; her joy at their reunion at the palace of Malines; and his desperate straits at Newgate and their last moments together . . .

"Sweet Jesu!" she muttered, jerking her head up from her rosary and startling an old woman kneeling next to her. She had forgotten all about the piece of paper John had entrusted to her. Where was it now? She remembered taking it from its original hiding place before Matty undressed her that night and placing it inside her pillow. Hell's bells! she thought, using Cecily's favorite oath. Matty had changed her pillow during her two days in bed mourning, Grace remembered. It may have fallen behind the bed curtain or—fear gripped her heart—Matty or someone else may have found it. Confession was forgotten and she sped through the rest of the rosary so fast the old woman clucked her tongue in disapproval. I must get back to Pasmer's Place as fast as I can, Grace determined, crossing herself in front of the Virgin and hurrying back to Edgar and Matty, who were astonished to be leaving so soon.

As they stepped out onto the street and walked the few paces to turn the corner into Chepeside, Grace almost bumped into a woman, her head tucked into the hood of her cloak, making her way to the church entrance. The woman dropped her fur muff into the mud as she stumbled, and muttered: "Fiddle faddle!"

Grace gasped. "Pray forgive me, mistress," Grace said. "Are you not Katherine Haute, John of Gloucester's mother?"

The woman's eyes were wary as she nodded slowly. "I am, God rest his soul," she replied. "Who asks this? I do not know you, madam."

"I am the Lady Grace, John's cousin. My father was our sovereign, King Edward," Grace replied, wrinkling her nose at an unpleasant smell. She caught sight of a piss bucket a few paces from them hanging on the corner of the King's Head, next to the church. It was brimming over, awaiting collection by a fuller who would use it to set the dye in his cloth. "Shall we cross to the other side?" she said, pointing at it, and Kate gladly acquiesced. "John has told me so much about you, Dame Haute," she went on, "and I saw you at the marketplace—" Her hand went to her mouth and she looked about her. Nay, she thought, this is London, and all are strangers; you are too suspicious, Grace. No one here cares if you went to Smithfield.

"Aye, I was there, God help me," Kate replied pleasantly. "I am pleased to make your acquaintance, my lady. John mentioned you the last day I saw him at Newgate." She paused, her quick mind working, "Certes, now I remember, you were there that day, getting into a litter."

Grace smiled. " 'Tis indeed so, mistress." She was enthralled with the chance to meet John's mother at last, and uncharacteristically blurted out, "Forgive me for being forthright, but may I say you are as beautiful as John described you."

"I do not mind at all, Lady Grace." Kate was wistful. "Although 'tis usually me who is forthright. I believe I have that reputation." They both chuckled, but their laughter died guiltily when they remembered how they were connected.

"I could not bear to watch my son die, I have to confess," Kate said softly, taking her left hand out of the muff and looking at it. "Dickon, my youngest, took me away, but perhaps you can tell me if my bribe helped—"

Grace interrupted her eagerly: "So 'twas you paid the captain to end John's life by the noose and not the knife? Indeed, my dear madam, the captain and the hangman carried out your wishes. John was dead before they cut him down," Grace cried, marveling at the cleverness of the woman before her. "If ever a man needed an angel, 'twas on that dreadful day. May God bless you!"

"Praise be to God," Kate moaned, a tear escaping and rolling down her cheek. "I had no way of knowing." She stared at the circle of white flesh on her finger where a ring had resided for many years and held up the hand. " 'Twas a gift to me from Richard—John's father—that paid the bribe. I like to think the two of them are walking together again in Heaven as we speak. They were very close, in truth. I am grateful for this news. It will comfort me and my son as we mourn to know John did not suffer unduly."

It was the second time Kate had mentioned another son. Grace was puzzled. "I thought John had only a sister—may God have mercy on her soul, as well," she said, and both women crossed themselves. "He did not tell me he had a brother, except for his half brother, Ned, who died at Middleham."

Kate smiled. "John never knew about Dickon before that day in the Newgate—nor indeed did Dickon know about John. I kept the youngest a secret even from his father—until the eve of Bosworth Field. He is all I have left, and more precious to me than gold." Tears shone in her eyes. "And now, my lady, if you will forgive me, I must light a candle for John."

Grace put out her hand and touched Kate's arm. "I loved John with all my heart, Dame Haute, and he loved me"—she sighed—"like a sister. Meeting you has brought me some solace, and," she said, indicating the missing ring, "I thank you for your sacrifice."

Kate wiped her tears away with her hand and sniffed. "Ah, yes, unrequited love! 'Tis a cross many women have borne, my lady. But, in my own bold way," she said with a smile, "may I say that John must have been blind."

"Fiddle faddle!" Grace said, and was rewarded by wide eyes and a merry laugh. "Farewell, Dame Haute, and I hope we shall meet again."

"If you find yourself in Kent, Lady Grace, at a place they call Eastwell, you may look for us there in the spring. Meanwhile, God speed."

The two women reverenced each other—Kate because she knew her place and Grace because she honored John's mother—and went their separate ways.

BACK AT THE Welles residence, Grace searched her room, the bed sheets, her pillow and all her clothes for the parchment. Then she questioned Matty, who swore she had found nothing upon emptying the soggy filling from the pillowcase except feathers and grasses. Other servants had been in to clean after Grace had left her bed and gone out, so anyone might have picked up the secret letter.

"Perhaps one of them threw it in the fire, my lady," Matty offered, and Grace nodded grimly. She was certain that was the case, as she knew none of the servants was literate and might have taken the wadded up paper cloth as discarded rubbish. Her only consolation was that it was safer for the coded paper to burn than to fall into the wrong hands. But she worried in the dark as she lay next to one of Cecily's attendants. Why had she not secured it in the small coffer she kept for her few precious things, like Elizabeth's amber brooch? She slept fitfully, dreaming of Tom, scaffolds, candles and Kate Haute, and when Cecily came knocking at her door for Terce, she knew that she had finally fallen into a deep sleep and not heard the household stirring.

"Bess has summoned us to Westminster," Cecily cried, plumping down unceremoniously on Grace's bed. "The message was very brief, and I do not know why we must go, but we must. So arise, you lazy bag of bones," she said, jerking back the cover from Grace's small frame. "I confess, Pasmer's Place is beginning to bore me. Let us to the palace, Grace, and do hurry up."

Cecily swept out and Grace swung herself out of bed, her head pounding.

"Fetch me some yarrow tea," she told Matty. "And if the dispensary has a pinch of skullcap, my headache will likely disappear sooner." She padded over to the heavy marble washbasin set into the wall. She unstopped the copper faucet and ice-cold water gushed out from a reservoir on the roof. Aye, 'tis a marvel to have piped water, Grace thought, bracing her face for the freezing wash, but will it ever run hot? She thought not. She heard the door open as she groped for a drying cloth, and a wet nose nuzzled her hand instead. She started, turning round to see Tom standing in front of the closed door. She patted Jason's waiting head and scratched his ears with one hand as she dried her face with the other.

"I am glad to see you awake, Grace. I came before, but the attendant said you slept still." Tom's voice was measured, and his expression serious. "I pray you, let us sit while we are alone, for I have something of consequence to discuss with you."

Grace's heart sank. She was in no mood to quarrel, and with her head hurting as much as it did, she knew she would not put up a very good fight. But she went to the small settle he motioned to in front of the newly stoked fire and sat down, leaving room for him. Their legs touched and their eyes met for a brief moment. His were sad and hers anxious. He cleared his throat.

"I promised myself we would talk of John no more after yesterday," he began. "But something happened to change my mind."

Grace cocked her head and looked so vulnerable it was all he could do not to take her in his arms. Instead, he reached into the mailed belt bag at his waist and brought out the lost wad of paper. Grace gasped and snatched it from him.

Tom sighed. "I see you do know what this is. I prayed you had nothing to do with it."

"Where did you find it?" Grace whispered, turning it over nervously.

" 'Twas Jason," he said. "When I left yesterday, I noticed he was carrying something—he has a soft mouth, you see."

"Have . . . have you told anyone else?" Grace asked fearfully. "Viscount Welles?"

"Certes, I have not. I do not know what it is, except that it appears to be in code and has likely traveled far. If it had not been found in your room, Grace, I would certainly have taken it to his lordship. What is it?"

"I . . . I cannot tell you, Tom. I beseech you, do not ask that of me. I swore I—"

Before she knew what had happened, Tom wrested the letter from her inattentive fingers and threw it on the fire. "I should have done that yesterday," he cried hoarsely.

Grace cried out, jumped up to fetch the poker and tried to prevent the precious document from going up in flames. She was too late; the paper flared briefly and was blackened to soot in a matter of seconds.

"How could you, Tom? You have made me break my promise," she wailed, throwing the poker on the hearth and turning on him. Then she fell to her knees and wept unashamedly. She did not stop him helping her back to the settle, and even Tom was not expecting her response to his gentleness. She curled into his chest and allowed him to hold her while she cried. She was still clothed only in her chemise, and feeling her soft body through the flimsy material was torture for him.

"Hush, sweetheart. 'Tis astonishing to me that you have any more tears to shed. They are like to fill a river these past three days. Am I correct in thinking the missive came from John?" He felt her nod. "And am I correct to think you did not know the contents?" Again, she nodded. "At least John spared you that danger," he muttered angrily.

"He did not know what it contained either." Grace's voice sounded muffled in his padded pourpoint. "He was only the messenger."

"A valuable message," Tom remarked grimly. "It cost him his life, I warrant."

Grace sniffed and Tom felt her heave on another sob. Rocking her gently, he let the crackling fire and the rain pattering on the windowpanes be the only sounds to accompany their thoughts for several minutes, before her crying subsided and she lay still against him.

"Grace, my dearest wife, you must trust me," he begged, stroking her curls. Then he took a chance. "I am not unaware of your involvement in matters beyond the sea."

Grace slowly pulled her face from the tear-stained worsted jacket and raised her wide eyes to him. "Wha-whatever d-do you mean?" she whispered.

"The king has his spies, Grace. One of his most successful is Stephen Frion, who traveled between this court and Burgundy's many times over the years. It came to Henry's attention that Duchess Margaret had a pretty young English guest staying with her, calling herself Sir Edward Brampton's niece by marriage. Henry was suspicious—Brampton has long been associated with the house of York—and when he found out Brampton did indeed have a niece, but she has been virtually bedridden in her Northamptonshire estate for the last several years, he attempted to discover more. My lord, the viscount, as one of the king's chief advisers, was made aware of this—and that is how I was privy to it. He asked me to try to discover who the mysterious young lady was, but I was unsuccessful—until I saw Edgar."

Grace sat up, resuming her original position on the seat. "Edgar? What has Edgar to do with this, pray?" she asked warily.

"The young lady who traveled from England to Malines boasted a tiring woman and hulk of a servant. Frion's information also included an interesting account of how much time this young guest of the duchess spent in close company with her nephew, John of Gloucester."

Grace gasped. "Where do these spies hide, pray?" she asked, afraid, looking around the room to check for a possible peephole in the wall.

For the first time that morning, Tom laughed. "You are sometimes so wise, sweetheart, and yet oftimes so innocent. 'Tis possible some secret doors and spy holes exist in palaces, but more often 'tis a servant who is paid to listen while they go about their menial tasks—like serving supper and bringing firewood."

"So this Stephen Frion may have paid someone to watch me?" Grace asked when the information sank in. Although it perturbed her, she was secretly elated to have been the cause of annoyance to Henry. "I pray I never meet the man, or my secret identity will be revealed," she said, a mischievous smile finally appearing. "But they cannot have known my mission."

Tom could not resist. "And what was your mission, little adventurer?" he asked, wondering if she had let down her guard enough to tell him. He knew when she stiffened beside him that she had not.

"That, too, I cannot tell you," she responded, and was saved from further questioning by a knock on the door. "Come!" she called gratefully, and Matty entered with the infusion.

"One day you will learn to trust me," Tom murmured, covering her hand with his. "But for now, 'tis enough that you appear in better spirits. I shall be accompanying you and Lady Welles to Westminster, so I will see you anon." He picked up her hand and kissed it tenderly. "Until then."

"Until then," Grace replied, and after a beat added, "Thank you, Tom."

An hour later the small party was settled into Viscount Welles's boat and being rowed upstream to Westminster. The rain of the day before had subsided into a cold drizzle out of still-leaden skies, and Grace hoped that by the next day the winter sun would reappear. London in the winter was a dreary, damp affair, but she was thankful to be welcome at the Welles's modern residence, where a fireplace graced every room and the wood paneling and leaded glass windows kept out the chill wind. The Yuletide season was almost upon them, and Grace thought back to last Christmas when she, Elizabeth and Katherine had made merry at Greenwich. Had it really been a year since she and Tom were wed? Despite the promising first night, their partnership had plummeted, it seemed to her. There had been a little fillip that day at Collyweston when she had unbent in her stubborn determination to keep John always first in her heart and given herself willing to her husband, but John's dreadful dilemma had again pushed poor Tom into the background since then.

She stared at Tom's back farther up in the barge and noted the proud carriage and long, strong torso. She did not doubt there were ladies who would be happy to call him husband, but until she no longer pined for John, she could only feel dispassionate. As if he knew she was watching him, he turned around and gave her a small, anxious smile. Ah, Grace, you do not deserve even that, she thought guiltily, and so she smiled back and was ashamed to see how swiftly his expression changed from worry to hope.

The deafening sound of bells ringing out over the city for Matins jolted her from her daydreaming and she could see that they were passing Baynard's Castle, with the great spire of St. Paul's rising on the hill beyond. The palace dominated that part of the river, and Cecily remarked, "Grandmother Cecily's castle, a cold, draughty place, in truth. I always dreaded going there. 'Twas upon the steps of the inner courtyard that Uncle Richard was offered the crown by the parliament. 'Tis said our cousin of Buckingham waxed eloquent as their speaker that day."

The mention of King Richard brought back John's face, and Grace gritted her teeth. She forced herself to think of something else, and indeed the controversy over the crown that summer of Forty-three did turn her thoughts to her half brother, Dickon; it was rumored that he was still in Ireland, and being claimed as Richard, duke of York, by those lords.

"I wonder if Bess has new information about our brother," Grace murmured, using the roomy hood on her cloak as a shield for her voice. The fox-fur lining was damp and gave off a rancid odor, but she was glad of its warmth.

"Nay, I would have heard from Jack, although I believe Henry's wrath at their acceptance of the young man is beginning to cow the rebel Irish. 'Twill not be long before whoever he is will be unwelcome in Munster," Cecily whispered back.

Grace was astonished. "You do not believe 'tis Dickon, Cis? Why?"

Cecily shrugged. " 'Twould be too good to be true, 'tis all. Certes, we would have to see him for ourselves before we could be sure. It astounds me that Henry has not taken him, or forced Kildare and Ormond to detain him—they are two Irish earls, Grace," Cecily explained when she saw Grace's blank look. " 'Tis said he wears a fine suit of clothes and looks every inch a prince—a Yorkist prince, in fact. At first the Irish took him for Warwick again because he has a family resemblance, but that notion was quickly doused by Kildare, whose servants had been here to treat with Henry and knew Ned was still kept in the Tower, poor boy."

"I believe he is our brother," Grace said firmly. "Aunt Margaret is convinced, and so is your mother. I cannot believe Aunt Margaret would back another pretender, if she were unsure. She is far too sensible."

Cecily laughed. "Jack says Henry calls her Juno. You know, the goddess in Virgil who did all she could to thwart Aeneus's plans to found a new Troy. It made me giggle when I heard, and Jack was not pleased. Aunt Margaret does seem intent on overthrowing Henry, and I believe it was anger against her that made him act so harshly with John, for 'tis certain he knew she had sent him. As for the man in Ireland, I will tell you when I see him. He had an odd eye, I remember. But 'twas nine years ago, and he must look very different now." A shout from the oarmaster at the front of the boat to the shore interrupted them. "But soft, Grace, here we are at Westminster. No more talk of Dickon, promise me, unless Bess begins it."

Grace nodded and stood up to be helped from the barge by Tom. He lifted her onto the wharf with ease, and she walked alongside Cecily, their wooden pattens keeping their soft leather slippers out of puddles. As they were mounting the steps to the water entrance of the royal apartments, the dark skies opened. "Dear God," Cecily complained. "Will this rain never cease?"

ARTHUR WHOOPED AROUND Bess's elegant solar on his hobby horse, brandishing a wooden sword under the watchful eye of his nurse, while baby Henry, at six months a chubby, cheerful child, had been unswaddled and was enjoying kicking his legs in the air on his mother's lap and sucking on her rosary. Two-year-old Margaret, named for her grandmother who was not present, much to Grace's relief, stood quietly at Bess's knee and observed her aunts curiously.

"Such a domestic picture you make, dear Bess," Cecily said, reverencing her sister and then bending to kiss her and little Harry. "I know not how you have the patience for all these little ones."

Grace curtsied low and then she, too, embraced her oldest sister kissing her, on both cheeks. "Your children are bonny, your grace," she told her, and then crouched down to greet little Margaret, whom Grace privately thought was uncommonly plain. "How now, my lady. Do you know who I am?"

The child shook her head and looked up at her mother for help. "This is Lady Grace, sweeting, your aunt, and she thinks you are beautiful," Bess told her, caressing Margaret's cheek. "Thank you for the compliment, Grace, but all children are beautiful when they are this age, are they not? Pray sit, both of you," she said, waving to two wide leather-slung stools. Then she called for refreshment and took the moment while her attendants obeyed her command to say quietly, "I want you to know I share your sorrow over John, sister. Know that he is with the angels and that I pray for his eternal rest."

Grace thanked her but took Cecily's advice and did not mention her attendance at the execution. She had not often seen Bess in the years after Elizabeth's exile, and she was always awed by her regal composure and natural beauty. Her skin was flawless, and her deep blue eyes always held warmth and sincerity. Grace thought it was a pity the queen was so much under the thumb of her mother-in-law, because her kindness, piety and quiet intelligence, often eclipsed by Lady Margaret's domineering personality, were underappreciated. Grace remembered Elizabeth's anger when she heard that Bess had been cheated out of the more luxurious queen's chambers here at Westminster by the countess, but as she looked around at the French tapestries, green and gold curtains around the enormous tester bed, the table, chests and chairs of finest carved oak and walnut and blue and gold painted celestial ceiling, she could not imagine how much more elegant Lady Margaret's apartment could be. Again, it did not compare with the palace of Malines, but Grace was the only one of Edward's daughters to have seen it, so she wisely kept her peace.

"We are agog to know the reason for your summons, are we not, Grace?" Cecily said eagerly. "I pray do not keep us waiting or we shall die of curiosity."

Bess frowned for an instant. "Always so impetuous, Cis. Has my lord Welles not tamed you yet?"

Oh, no, Grace thought; the sibling rivalry again. And again, she attempted to mediate. "Certes, we are not dying, Bess. But 'tis a long row from the city to Westminster, and we had ample time to speculate, you see."

Bess relaxed and smiled. "Always the diplomat, dear Grace. Aye, I can see how the two of you might pass the time on the river in idle curiosity." Cecily and Grace exchanged a quick glance and then focused on the queen, who was saying, "I have to ask something of Grace, Cis, and therefore, like a fish, I shall let you off the hook."

Grace's stomach turned over when she heard Bess's words. Sweet Jesu, she must know I was in Burgundy; she must know I was at Smithfield; she must know I had a secret letter from John; she knows . . . But Bess did not dismiss Cecily, and Grace breathed more easily.

"Our sister Anne has not been well and she can no longer serve my mother at Bermondsey." Bess stated. "The queen herself has been in poor health lately, and has begged me to ask you to return." Bess was sad. "I do not think she has long to live, sisters, and if your husband can spare you, Grace, I should like to honor her wish. What say you?"

Grace knew Bess was being gracious by asking her: one did not refuse a royal request, so she smiled gratefully at her and inclined her head. "There is nothing I would not do for your mother, your grace. I owe her all honor and love. My husband cannot hinder my going—neither would he try. He knows the debt I am in." And he will probably be happier with me out of his life at the moment, she thought sadly. "When shall I go?"

Cecily clucked her tongue and cried, "How I shall miss you, Grace! I am quite used to you being with me, but I'll wager Tom will miss you more." She winked at Grace, who managed a smile.

"I am pleased by your unselfish nature, Grace. I know how hard it is to be separated from one's beloved husband. Henry and I dread being apart." Bess was busy extricating the rosary from Harry's iron grip and did not notice the gasp of incredulity from her sisters—nor Cecily's expression of disgust.

"Tom and I have our whole lives to look forward to," Grace said quickly. "How can I deny the dying wish of the only mother I have known?" And again she asked, "When?"

"Anne will come to Greenwich when my household moves there next week. I regret my lady mother is too ill to travel, so I am afraid you will spend Christmas at Bermondsey again, Grace. Rest assured I shall send some special gifts from the royal larder to you there. And to make your duties less taxing—as well as for Lady Hastings—I am arranging for another gentlewoman to be lodged with you from my own household. Does this sound fair, Grace?"

Grace rose and went to kneel and kiss Bess's hand. "Aye, more than fair, your grace," she said, smiling, and peeking up at Bess from under her lashes, she added: "I hope you remember how much I love marchpane."

"Then you shall have marchpane, Grace," Bess assured her, and then she made a face. "Nurse!" she cried. "I pray you, take this little monster away; he has soiled my new gown. And be good enough to send the Ladies Catherine and Bridget to us." She held Henry aloft, his lawn gown soaked through, and gave him a loud kiss on his fat cheek. "Away with you, Harry," she said as the nurse took him, and he bellowed his displeasure at the top of his very fine lungs. They all laughed and watched while he was whisked out of the room to the nursery.

A few minutes later the youngest of Edward and Elizabeth's daughters sidled into the solar and curtsied to their sister. Then they ran to hug Grace, whom they had not seen for a very long time.

"And what about me, sisters?" Cecily said, pouting. "Do I not get a greeting?"

Twelve-year-old Catherine grinned, showing perfect teeth and merry eyes in an exquisite face, and fell onto Cecily's neck, who squealed and begged her sister to have a care with her jeweled hood.

"How are you, dear Bridget?" Grace asked the quietest of all the siblings. Bridget was tall for her age and had the awkwardness of someone who knew not how to manage her new inches.

"I am well, Grace," the girl replied politely. "We heard you are wed. Is your husband handsome?"

Grace laughed. "Aye, Bridget, I suppose he is. But more important, little one, is that Tom is kind." Where do you find the gall to utter such platitudes, as though you deserved Tom? Grace chastised herself. "And how go your studies?" she asked, changing the subject.

Bridget became serious, a trait that had marked her from birth and caused Elizabeth and Edward to decide that she, of all their daughters, should take orders when she was old enough. Grace had felt sorry for the child, knowing well the life of a cloistered nun. But Bridget had accepted her fate with equanimity and was proud to tell people she was destined for the convent.

"*Tu es . . . très beau . . .* I mean . . . *belle,*" Bridget said. "*Oui, tu es très belle,*" she repeated with more confidence. "Master Frion taught me that."

Grace's eyes flared wide for a second, but then she hid her apprehension. "Master Frion?" she asked levelly. "Is he your tutor?"

"Nay, he used to be the king's French secretary, Grace," Bess called from across the room. "He is a clever man. But he fell out with his grace a year or so ago, and 'tis said he returned to France to work under King Charles. I believe he was a spy all the time."

"What's a spy, your grace?" Bridget asked the queen.

"Nothing to worry your pretty head with, sweeting," Grace said airily, but she sent up a prayer to St. Jude that the man was no longer at court.

"Speaking of France," Bess continued, "the king and his council are debating what to do now that Charles of France has married Anne of Brittany, for it will change the nature of our dealings with both countries. His grace wants to go to war to defend his old friends in Brittany from being overrun by France, but I ask you, what is the point if the two rulers are now wed?" She shook her head and sighed. "Certes, no one listens to me." Rising from her cushions, she turned her sweet smile on her four sisters. "Now, shall we dine, ladies?"

Cecily waited until she and Grace were back in the barge before asking: "What think you about returning to the abbey? 'Twas a shock, was it not?"

Grace nodded. "I had not thought to ever go back, in truth. But if 'tis only for a short . . ." she hesitated, not wanting to imply to Cecily that Elizabeth's demise was imminent.

"Do not fret on my account, Grace. Mother has long thought me the worst of her brood, and I have not felt affection for her in many years. Aye, I give her respect, but she could be cruel, and she compared me unfavorably to Bess at every turn. In truth, she showed you more love than she has ever shown me. Nay," she said, putting her hand over Grace's to stop her protest, "you do not need to deny it, or apologize. 'Tis well known, Mother loves her own self the best, and next she dotes on Dorset—though why, I cannot say. The man turned his coat and went to Henry in Brittany, and 'tis ironic the king has been suspicious of him since. That must tell you something of his nature. Untrustworthy, I heard Father tell Hastings one day when, as a child, I wandered into the wrong room to play."

Grace absorbed all this information on the way back to Pasmer's Place as, after divesting herself of her true feelings for the first time, Cecily sank into melancholy. She demanded a litter be sent to her for the short walk up the hill from the wharf, but Grace let her ride alone and chose to walk with Tom instead.

"I know I should have asked your permission, Tom, but I could not gainsay the queen or her mother, you must agree," she told him after explaining why she was leaving the Welleses.

Tom nodded. "Indeed, Grace, you were right to make your own decision. I would not have stopped you, and I thank you for knowing that. It gives me hope that you trust me a little."

Grace stopped still, frustrated. "I trust you, Tom, more than you think. I pray you, cease feeling sorry for yourself. It does you no credit." She continued walking and took his arm, annoyed at her own sharp tone. "We have a week to mend this breach we have somehow made . . . nay," she corrected herself, "*I* have made between us. If we could only have some time alone, we could talk more and try to understand each other better."

Tom covered the small hand on his arm with his free hand and squeezed it once. "I should like nothing more than time alone with you. But I fear that because of my duties, the only way is if we share nights together. If it would make my presence in your bed more agreeable, I might promise that we simply talk until we fall asleep."

Grace gave him a sidelong glance. "You would do that for me, Tom?"

"Certes, anything to stop the taunts from my fellow henchmen," Tom teased her, and jumped away as a precaution. Grace raised an eyebrow, but her eyes gave away her amusement. "Do we have a pact, then?"

They had turned into St. Sithe's Lane from Watling Street and could see the gates of Pasmer's Place before Tom heard the murmured reply: "Aye, we have a pact."

IT WAS LATE when Tom came to her bed that night. They spent it whispering of the day's events and of the dowager queen's condition and of Grace's dislike of Katherine Hastings. "I know not why she hates me, Tom. Her grace told me 'twas because I was young and she was no longer. And that she was jealous of my place in Elizabeth's heart." Grace hugged her knees, her curls falling around them under a simple linen nightcap. "In truth, I often wondered if Elizabeth even had a heart. But then she would talk about her little sons and the tears would flow, so it seemed she did."

"Tell me of your time at the other abbey, Grace. How was it you came to be raised by the good sisters of Delapre?" Tom watched her in the soft light of a single candle, anchored in its pewter holder and clamped onto the bedstead. Matty was on the truckle bed in the corner of the room, already fast asleep.

Grace shivered slightly, and so Tom pulled a corner of the silky coverlet over her shoulders and leaned back to sit cross-legged on his side of the bed. Thanking him, she told him what she knew of her mother and of her early life and finished by describing the day when the handsome young squire came to carry her away. "I thought 'twas all a dream, in truth."

Tom began to tell about his carefree childhood in a warm, loving household with his gentleman farmer father and his hardworking, generous mother, but soon Grace was stifling a yawn. "Pray forgive me, Tom. 'Tis not that your tale is tedious, but I am so very tired. May we continue tomorrow?"

Tom's heart soared. She wants me back tomorrow, he thought happily, and he agreed readily. True to his word, he let her snuggle beneath the covers on her side of the bed before getting in himself and leaving a chasm as wide as a third person between them. Blowing out the candle, he wished her a good night.

"May God and all his saints watch over you, too, Tom. Sleep well," Grace murmured. She lay on her back, acutely aware of his presence, and when she heard him turn away from her to sleep, her hand slipped along the sheets towards him. But she could not touch him, knowing that her reason for wanting to was only to reassure him of her gratitude. She was sure he would think she desired him, and she was still not quite certain.

And thus they spent the next three nights, each one breaking Grace's reserve a little more and allowing Tom closer. Grace found herself looking forward to their trysts during the day and storing up anecdotes and questions to put to him at night.

On the fifth night Tom was late and Grace began to worry something she had said the night before had kept him from her. But then she remembered he had gently kissed her cheek before wishing her good night and turning his back. His soft beard had tickled her, and she liked the smell of rosemary from his nightshirt. He said it warded off fleas, but Grace guessed he did not want to admit he found the scent pleasant. Although she had observed how big his hands were, the long conversations behind closed curtains gave her the leisure to study them, and she soon saw how carefully he kept them. It was another trait she found to her liking.

She heard the latch on the door click shut and saw the wavering light of his candle through the curtains coming closer until he quietly pulled one back on his side and got into bed. "I am glad to see you, Tom," Grace said, and she meant it. "I was afraid you would not come."

Tom clamped the candle onto the post and gave her a quick smile. She saw that he had something on his mind and asked if he would share it.

"Lord John is still at Westminster and sent me home to let Lady Welles know that he will lodge with the king tonight. As 'twas past curfew, he bade me stay here until first light." Tom grinned. "I made a feeble protest about my duty to him, but he did not have to command me twice. I could hardly tell him I did not want to miss one precious night with my sweet wife."

"How you exaggerate, Tom," Grace demurred as she propped herself up on one elbow. "But what keeps him there, pray?"

"Henry heard today that Charles of France has offered this so-called duke of York shelter there," Tom said. "His grace's stern measures with the Irish have made the man unwelcome."

Grace lowered her eyes to her finger tracing on the bed sheet and asked as innocently as she could, "Why do you say 'so-called'? Could he not be the real Prince Richard?"

Tom gave a derisive grunt. "Come, Grace, you surely cannot believe the boy has risen from the dead. 'Tis well known the two princes died in the Tower—by fair means or foul. Though I never said so to John, I am one who thinks King Richard had them dispatched."

Grace's brow snapped together and she sat up across from him. "Why, that is slanderous, Tom," she declared. "Where is your proof that Uncle Richard 'had them dispatched'? Could he not have sent them away instead—say to Calais or Burgundy—in case someone"—she lowered her voice to a whisper—"like Lady Margaret and her son saw them standing in the way of the throne?"

Now it was Tom's turn to be angry. "Never let me hear you utter such nonsense in this house," he hissed as loudly as he dared. "You are a guest in Viscount Welles's house, and I am his retainer. King Richard is dead and King Henry rules. Never forget that, Grace. Oh, I knew I should not have told you this. Why are you so bent on destroying us, our future? There is no future but Henry, and although I may not like it, I am at his mercy. Besides, I have sworn my fealty to him—and you were a witness." They glared at each other in the candlelight until Tom's expression softened and he put out his hand to touch hers. "Please, Grace, have a care."

Tears welled in Grace's eyes. " 'Tis easy for you to say, Tom. But this 'so-called duke of York' may well be *my brother*. If there is a chance for him to be reconciled with his family, with his mother; if there is a chance that he may be reconciled to his rightful crown, then who are we to be cowardly and deny him?"

"Cowardly!" Tom's voice rose and he snatched his hand away. "You call me coward, Grace? Now you have truly wounded me. Forgive me if I change my mind about staying with you tonight. I see that my company offends you. I wish you good night."

Before a chastised Grace could reach out her hand to stay him, he had taken the candle and was gone. She buried her face in her pillow and sobbed quietly. Let him come back, she prayed. I do not mean to hurt him, truly I don't. 'Tis not his fault he is not John. John! Oh, John, have pity on me, she begged, and let go of my heart.

She tossed and turned for another hour, fretting over the conversation with Tom. When she did finally sleep, she dreamed she was in a long hall, the walls of which were covered in dark tapestries. Peering out from behind each one as she passed was the king's mother, Margaret Beaufort. "I am spying on you, Grace Plantagenet," she crowed, and then swiftly hid herself again. Grace began to run, but the door at the end of the room never got closer, and then she noticed there were strange faces staring at her from mirrors, from between the branches of the chandeliers, on top of a cupboard that held the king's plate. All were whispering the word *spy* over and over, making the room sound full of snakes. Terrified, Grace called out to the one person she knew would save her. "Tom!" she cried. "Help me, I beg of you! Help me!" The door suddenly flew open and Tom stood there, not moving. She reached out her arms to him as the floor began to float under her feet, and she looked down to see blood covering the tiles.

"May you drown in your lover's blood, Grace. I have washed my hands of you," Tom's voice echoed as if in a vacuum.

"No!" she screamed at him. "John is dead. Help me!"

Matty finally resorted to slapping her mistress's face when her gentle shaking and calling failed to work. The sting of Matty's hand forced Grace awake and her eyes were momentarily blinded by the candle thrust in her face.

"Mother of God, my lady. But you did cry out like one faced with the flames of hell," Matty whispered. " 'Twas but a dream—a terrible dream. Are you feverish, mistress? Shall I fetch wine?"

Grace blinked and touched her burning cheek. "Did you hit me, Matty? It feels as though someone slapped me," she said, puzzled. Noting Matty's sheepish expression, she didn't know whether to laugh or reprimand her servant. Glad to know she had only been dreaming, she chose a middle path. "No harm done, I dare say," she admitted, smiling. Then she wagged her finger. "But pray do not ever think of doing it again."

Matty shook her blond head vigorously. "Nay, my lady. I am sorry, my lady. But I was afeared you would wake the whole house, you did cry so loud." She was agog to know the nature of the dream, but Grace did not share it. Instead she told her servant to go back to sleep and slipped out of bed to use the jakes. Matty inhaled a quick breath as the candlelight revealed that Grace's monthly course had taken her unawares. She drew back the curtains and took off the bed sheet, laying a large square drying cloth on the mattress in its place. Anticipating her mistress's need—Grace was as punctual as the full moon every month—she had already prepared a pile of clean torn cloths and now set them next to Grace along with the candle.

"Thank you, Matty," Grace said from her low perch. "You are a good girl, in truth."

"Aye, my lady. Thank you, my lady," Matty curtsied and then curled up on her little truckle bed and was asleep in a second.

Grace was intrigued by her nightmare, although she hoped she would never have it again, as it had seemed so real. She wondered if Tom had really washed his hands of her. And now, because it was the time when a woman must be left alone, her chance to mend the fence with him would not come soon.

CECILY WAS TO accompany Grace to Bermondsey despite her lack of enthusiasm for seeing her mother. A message had been dispatched to Elizabeth that Grace would not be arriving for a few days, but as Anne had left on the appointed day, their paths did not cross. Grace was disappointed to learn this; she had hoped to be brought up to date on Elizabeth's condition from a less antagonistic source than Katherine Hastings. But now that Elizabeth had been granted a third attendant through Bess's urging and Henry's wish to please his wife, perhaps Grace would hear the truth.

Edgar would remain behind. "The viscountess was kind enough to allow you to stay with her household while I am gone, and Master Gower will be responsible for you. Matty will remain here, too. It will not be for very long, for the queen dowager is ailing," Grace explained.

Before she could say any more, Edgar fell to his knees, and Grace was disconcerted to find they were still only eye to eye. How she wished she were taller! Still, she knew that, despite her lack of inches, she was ten feet tall to Edgar. Grace was astonished to see a tear fall down his jowly cheek, and she cocked her head at him. "How now, Edgar, what is the matter?"

"I be your servant, my lady. I don't want to stay here. I must serve you; I must protect you. Please take me with you," he begged, pulling off his hood and holding it to his heart. His sparse brown hair stuck up at all angles and reminded Grace of a patch of winter-dead reeds on a riverbank.

"Come, Edgar, you know the abbey. Why would I need protection there when I have Brother Gregory and his minions to fend off vagabonds? And I cannot believe you want to return and live among those unkind grooms again. Nay, 'tis my wish that you remain here," Grace said in what she thought was a firm tone.

At that moment Tom came around the corner by the stable and stopped when he saw her, with Edgar there on his knees. Her unpleasant dream still floating around in her head, Grace's first instinct was to turn her back on him, but then she admitted Tom could not be held responsible for his actions in *her* dream. So instead she beckoned to him, and he walked slowly towards her.

"Well met, husband," she said for Edgar's benefit. "Perhaps you would be so good as to explain to my groom why he must stay here while I am at the abbey. It appears he wishes to provide me with protection there. I told him he is being absurd, but he is insisting."

"Edgar is right, Grace," Tom said, much to her chagrin. "As your husband, I insist that Edgar go with you, if for nothing else so I may have news of you. He can be a messenger between us."

Edgar gave a loud grunt of approval that made Grace jump. "Aye, sir," he said with alacrity, bowing as best he could on his knees. "I will be a good messenger, I thank you, sir." He stood up, unheeding of his now muddied tunic, and grinned down at his mistress. "I be right, all right, my lady. And the Bible says a wife should obey her husband. Ain't that the truth, sir?" he asked so earnestly that Grace had to hide a smile behind her hand.

"You are right, Edgar, so ready yourself," Tom said sternly, ignoring Grace. "I think my wife should read her Bible more carefully," he added bitterly. And with that, he turned to leave.

"What, no farewell for me, Tom?" Grace murmured as Edgar hurried off. "Are you still so angry?"

Tom stopped and thought for a moment before facing her. "Aye, I am still angry with you. If you care to know—though I doubt it—being angry with you is not the same as not loving you. You go with my love, but also my anger. I regret the unpleasantness between us, but I do not know how to reach you, Grace. You seem bent on disliking me."

"Disliking you?" Grace said, taking a step towards him. "How wrong you are. I like you better than anyone else in the whole world. And when you left me the other night, I thought my heart would break. I am sorry for what I said, and if my monthly visitor had not intervened, I would have given you my apology sooner. I beg of you, Tom, do not send me away without saying you accept it. Please," she implored, her eyes watching his for any relenting. "Please."

Without a word he drew her to him then, a look of relief flooding his face. As they stood silently in the middle of the stableyard, her head on his chest and his arms holding her close, they did not see the amused glances of the stable hands or hear the whispered comments of a couple of laundrywomen passing by to hang up their washing in the kitchen garden beyond.

In that quiet moment, Grace knew she could finally move John into a locked compartment of her heart and open the rest to Tom. John would always remain there, but she understood now that he was dead and gone, and he had never really been hers.

BROTHER DAMIEN WAS the first to greet the two women who arrived on horseback on that cold afternoon in January. He oozed unctuous charm as he escorted them up to the queen dowager's apartment, professing to have missed Grace these months past.

"How kind of you," Grace murmured, although to herself she said, Pish! What a hypocrite. You were hardly aware of my existence all those years.

Edgar, in his new role as Grace's servant, was able to recruit one of his former fellow grooms to help him carry Grace's wooden chest up the stairs, and Grace was amused to see Edgar's smirk of satisfaction when the groom grumbled but obeyed.

Poppy's yapping alerted Elizabeth and Katherine to approaching strangers, but the terrier's furiously wagging tail and snuffling under the door told them the strangers were well loved, and thus they were not surprised when Grace and Cecily entered. Poppy launched herself at Grace's knees, then sprang vertically up and down with excitement until Grace bent down to gather the bundle of white fur in her arms. Thus encumbered, she sank into a low curtsy next to Cecily, as civility required, before she had had a chance to look at Elizabeth properly. When she did, she had to force the smile of greeting to stay curved upon her lips. Profoundly shocked at the dowager queen's deterioration, she waited until Cecily had greeted her mother before rising and kissing Elizabeth affectionately on both cheeks.

"Well met, Grace," Elizabeth said, her sunken eyes warm and her tone welcoming. "I wager you did not expect to have to sleep here another night when you left last summer. You see, your bed is still here"—she indicated the narrow wooden truckle bed at the foot of the poster bed—"although Anne complained of its size and hardness. 'Twas not the only thing Anne complained about. Sweet Virgin, but I birthed a spoiled child in that one."

"Bess told us Anne was sickly and should not stay," Cecily replied. "What ails her, Mother?"

"Christ's nails!" Elizabeth rasped impatiently. "There is naught that ails her except a sharp tongue. She is as healthy as a horse, and I predict she will outlive all of you."

Privately, Grace thought Catherine and not Anne was the healthiest of the siblings, with her rosy cheeks, clear eyes and merry mien. As for the sharp tongue Anne was accused of, Grace knew exactly from whom the girl had inherited it. Cecily had caught her eye and winked at the remark.

"Aye, she proved difficult company, my lady," Katherine said to Cecily. "Your lady mother was kindness itself, but the Lady Anne was frequently disrespectful. And with my poor dear Elizabeth not herself." She stroked Elizabeth's arm, watching her anxiously. *For all she is an old harridan,* Grace thought wearily, *she is entirely devoted to the queen.* She wondered if their relationship would mellow as their mutual affection for Elizabeth must surely supersede their previous animosity.

When Cecily left not an hour later, the attendants helped Elizabeth back to bed and Grace was horrified to know that she could lift the queen so effortlessly. She caught Katherine watching her from the other side of the bed and their eyes met in full understanding over the frail form under the covers. Leaving the third attendant, Alison Mortimer, to watch over Elizabeth, Katherine invited Grace to walk with her, greatly surprising the younger woman.

"I would show Grace how the stable has been rebuilt," Katherine lied, and Elizabeth waved a clawlike hand to dismiss them. "She will be asleep before we close the door, mark my words," Katherine said to Grace.

At least a wintery sun accompanied them on their brief walk, as they made their way to the herb garden through the main courtyard. Brother Oswald called cheerful welcome when he spotted Grace, and she again admired his fortitude for tending to the herbs and vegetables that still grew in this cold season, for he was now more than sixty years of age. She drew her fur-lined cloak around her and found Katherine eyeing it with envy.

" 'Tis handsome, is it not?" Grace said. " 'Twas a gift from Lady Welles. She has been more than generous since I went to be her companion. I pray you, take my cloak for today, Lady Katherine, and I will gladly wear yours. The wind is cold, in truth." Grace pushed the hood back, unhooked the silver clasp and swung the garment off her shoulders. Katherine did not protest but unhooked her own worn velvet mantle and encased her old shivering body in Grace's with girlish glee.

" 'Tis indeed a thing of beauty, Grace. I thank you." She reached out and touched Grace's arm, as the younger woman wrapped herself in the thin black velvet. "I now have a confession to make." She took a deep breath, and Grace wondered what was coming. "All these months after you were gone, I wrestled with my conscience for the manner in which I behaved towards you. I spent many hours with my confessor and on my knees, asking God for forgiveness and for the chance to make amends. It seems my prayers were answered, for here you are in person. In truth, I never thought to see you again." She paused to take a breath, but hurried on. " 'Twas only after you left us and the queen's spirits sank so low that I saw how much goodness there is in you. Lady Anne showed me how fortunate we were to have had you in our lonely exile. She is my dear friend's daughter, and yet she could show only a modicum of the love you showed a woman who is not your own mother." Her fingers tightened on Grace's forearm. "Will you forgive an old lady her unkind jealousy?" she asked. "For I believe now that is what it was."

Grace stared at the woman who had brought her so much misery for so many years and saw true contrition in her eyes. How much courage must she have mustered to tell me this, Grace thought, awed. As faded memories of Lady Katherine's cruel taunts and insults came crowding back, they seemed petty now, after all Grace had experienced since leaving the abbey. Katherine was watching her anxiously, the seconds eroding her confidence, and so she begged once again. "Please forgive me, Grace."

Grace's face softened into a sweet smile. "Certes, I forgive you. I am honored by your honesty and grateful for your apology. 'Twill make her grace's last weeks on this earth more peaceful, I'll wager—not to have us squabbling. Now, let us speak no more of it."

If someone had overheard the exchange without seeing the women, he might have thought Grace the older of the two. In a year away from the bitter older women she had acquired confidence and an understanding that not all in life was black or white. "You must tell me all that has befallen the queen to reduce her to this sad bag of bones," she said. She patted Katherine's arm, acknowledging the tears of relief in the older woman's eyes, and they resumed their walk.

IN APRIL, THEY thought Elizabeth's last hour had come. In the middle of the night, she called for Grace to light the candles and fetch parchment and a pen. Elizabeth had woken in a sweat, certain the Devil was hiding behind every piece of furniture and wall hanging to snatch her off to Hell. Katherine and Alison bustled about with the tinderbox and taper until every rushlight and candle had brightened the room.

"As God is my witness," the queen dowager cried in fear from her pillow, "I have done nothing to deserve the flames of Hades. I was faithful all those years to Edward, despite his infidelities, and I gave him many children." Grace went to her side and held her hand. "If I have sinned because I did my best to better my family, then I know not what it means to be a dutiful daughter and sister. Aye, I schemed to keep Richard from the crown, but only to protect my own children's right. And I entered into an alliance with that Beaufort woman to give Bess to her measle of a son, but only to raise up my own child, who in the end might wear the crown." Katherine took the bony hand out of Grace's so Grace could make ready her quill. But Elizabeth wasn't finished. "My only sin was the failure to be a good mother to my boys. How could I let them go—especially Dickon? If I could take back one decision I made in my life 'twould be the one on that June day. I should never have agreed to let Richard take Dickon, God forgive me. And now, I suppose, both boys are dead," she cried, a great sob racking her. "And I shall die without ever knowing."

Grace hurried back to the bed and set down her implements. "Nay, your grace, do not say that," she whispered, bending close to Elizabeth. The rancid odors of foul breath and incontinence almost caused her to retch, but she controlled herself and stroked the queen's perspiring forehead. "Remember your sister-in-law sent assurances that Dickon lives yet," she told the distraught woman. "And there is more news of him." She turned to Katherine, who raised her brows in surprise. "Aye, he has been recognized in Ireland—in Cork—and now it seems he is the guest of the king of France. People have seen him; people have declared he looks the image of his father—*my* father," she said, excitement in her voice, and she was cheered that Elizabeth's eyes had brightened with her words. "I promise your grace, Richard of York will come to claim his throne. 'Tis why you must stay well, so you can greet him—so that we all can greet him." She looked from one eager face to the next. Alison Mortimer had covered her mouth with her hand, her already bulging eyes now almost popping out of her head; Katherine, a lopsided grin on her face, was crying tears of joy; and Elizabeth, using all her strength to raise herself into a sitting position, stared openmouthed at Grace. "Is this true? Is he coming home?" she whispered.

Grace nodded, her eyes shining. "I do not know when, but he will come. So you must be well when he does. And I," she cried happily, "shall finally meet my brother."

The news made Elizabeth forget her will and, after an infusion of valerian root, she finally went back to sleep. "I will send a message to the royal doctors to attend Elizabeth soonest; she trusts these two men, and I have no doubt will make them executors of her will," Katherine whispered to Grace as they settled back on their truckle beds. Katherine had given up sharing the softer bed with Elizabeth once it had become so unpleasant to do so, and Grace could not blame her.

The next afternoon Elizabeth again called for Grace to sit down beside her to take down the details of her new will.

"How I regret I have nothing to leave you good ladies," Elizabeth said before she started. "But you know you have my gratitude—especially you, Katherine. I shall request that my body be buried beside my dear Edward at Windsor. 'Twas his wish, and mine, too. I would hope the king will allow this, but I doubt he will afford anything elaborate for me." She gave a snort of laughter. "Certes, I cannot afford but a winding sheet and crude wooden box to house me. But I should not like to make the journey to Windsor alone. I pray you, will one of you accompany my poor body?"

All three of her attendants agreed in unison, although Katherine reassured Elizabeth that she should not speak of dying yet. "There is color in your face this morning, my dear friend. Would you like to see in the mirror?" she asked.

Elizabeth had not called for a mirror for several weeks, and she shook her head again now. "You are a liar, Katherine," she said haughtily. "I do not need a mirror to know that I look like a hag. I can see it in your eyes every time you look at me. Now, Grace, have you finished trimming that quill? Why are you so slow today?"

Grace smoothed the vellum, anchored a curling top corner with the inkpot and nodded.

"*In Dei nomine, Amen*. The tenth day of April, the year of our Lord God Fourteen Hundred and Ninety-two. I, Elizabeth, by the grace of God Queen of England, late wife to the most victorious prince of blessed memory, Edward the Fourth, being of whole mind, saying the world is so transitory and no creature certain when they shall depart from hence . . ." Elizabeth paused, and then chuckled. " 'Tis true, I thought I would die last night."

She stroked Poppy's silky hair absentmindedly as she allowed Grace to catch up to her dictation and thought about her next sentence. " 'Item: I bequeath my body to be buried with the body of my lord at Windsor . . .' " She stopped, searching for the right words. Then she snapped her fingers, startling Poppy, who leapt off her knees and went to lie by the door. "I have it!" she cried. "Write this, Grace, and then Henry will have no choice but to carry out my wish. After 'Windsor,' write 'according to the will of my said lord and mine,' " she instructed, " 'without pomp entering into it, or costly expense.' Ha! Forever after, people will think kindly on me for eschewing a lavish funeral, and ill of Henry because he didn't spend the money on one. Then I shall immediately plead penury thus: 'Item: Where I have no worldly goods to do the queen's grace, my dearest daughter, a plea-sure with, neither to reward any of my children, according to my heart and mind, I beseech almighty God to bless her grace, with all her noble issue, and as with good heart and mind as is to me possible, I give her grace my blessing and all the aforesaid my children.' Do you have that, Grace?"

She waited as Grace, who was mouthing to herself the exact verbiage, painstakingly scratched out the phrases. Katherine chuckled and remarked that Elizabeth was a sly fox indeed. "Ah, but you do not know how sly I am, Katherine," Elizabeth murmured. "I shall name Bess one of my executors so that she will know to what depths her mother has fallen at the behest of her purse-pinching husband."

Grace did not like to say that Bess did not deserve the scorn her mother might subject her to; it was one of the paradoxes of Elizabeth that she could give with one hand and take with the other without regard to moral or personal considerations.

Elizabeth also named her son, Dorset, and three other men Grace did not know as executors. Then she commanded Alison to fetch Father John and Brother Benedictus, the infirmarer, to witness the document.

"I do not trust Brother Damien as far as I can see him—which with my bad eyes is not very far," Elizabeth said, amused by her own joke. "Prior John's long nose may be put out of joint, but 'tis his own fault for violating God's holy laws with the man."

Once the will was witnessed and placed in the secret drawer in the bed, Elizabeth seemed to rally. She even expressed an interest in taking a walk in the garden. Alison and Grace helped her into her second-best gown—she was saving the purple velvet for her next visit to court, she had informed her attendants, although they guessed Elizabeth would never again be well enough to go. The women did their best to make their mistress as presentable as they could—the abbey inhabitants had not set eyes on the queen dowager for many months—but despite a few cosmetic tricks that Alison had learned, they could not conceal the ravages of time and ill health that had eroded her former beauty. Her dove-gray dress and white wimple only served to swallow up her chalky face, although her large almond-shaped eyes were still her best feature. Grace placed the wide straw hat over the linen coif and threw a veil over the top of it, protecting Elizabeth from the bright April sun and curious stares.

"I would walk apace alone with Grace, ladies," Elizabeth said once they had half carried her down the stone stairs to the little yard. "Nay, Katherine, do not be offended. I need to speak of family matters, and Grace is family," she said, smiling sweetly at the prickly Katherine. Grace gave the queen a gnarled walking stick to support her left side, and took her right arm. Slowly they processed through the main courtyard, and many of the laymen workers doffed their hoods and touched their forelocks as the queen passed by. Elizabeth nodded this way and that, and Grace could see she was smiling beneath the gauze.

"How is your husband?" Elizabeth asked suddenly, taking Grace aback with her directness. "Why are you not yet with child, my dear? I pray you are not barren, like my poor sister-in-law, Margaret."

Grace stiffened. There was too much to explain, she knew. Elizabeth would not have the patience to listen to the complicated reasons for her failure to produce a child. After all, she had been married now—what was it? dear Lord, nigh on eighteen months? Nay, she does not want to know that Tom and I have spent only a few nights of intimacy together in that time, Grace thought. So, making a cross with her thumb between her fingers, she lied. "Tom insists on consulting the viscount's astrologer, and it seems the man has been unable to predict my fertile time," she said, not knowing where this preposterous explanation sprang from and begging God and Tom's forgiveness for her indiscretion. Tom consult an astrologer? She would have laughed if she hadn't been so afraid of going to Hell.

"All is well between you, then?" Elizabeth persisted. "If I were to guess, I would say you were not pining for your husband as one would imagine a young bride would. Is he deficient in bed, my dear? Do not be afraid to tell me, for my mother taught me many ways to solve that little problem."

Grace gasped. "N-nay, your grace," she said, horrified. "Certes, it must be my fault, for Tom . . . well, he . . . um . . . performs . . . I mean . . . there is no problem on that score," she finished in a rush, making Elizabeth laugh.

"I am glad to hear it for your sake, child. A good roll in the sheets can cure most ills in a marriage, I have found." She then lowered her voice. "What I really want to talk about is my son, Dickon. Is there more you are not telling me?"

Grace steered Elizabeth to the herb garden and a stone bench she'd often rested on when she used to help Brother Oswald tend the plants. The fragrant bay bush beside it and the aromatic angelica close by scented the air, and Elizabeth breathed deeply and let out a satisfied "Ah."

" 'Tis a pleasant spot, is it not, your grace? Are you comfortable?" Grace arranged the gray silk around the dowager's feet and picked an early lily of the valley to present to Elizabeth. "John went to his grave believing Dickon was alive," she began, and although she felt a pang of sorrow at the thought of him, she no longer grieved for him. "He was captured and tortured for the information he might have about this man who, 'twas rumored, was Richard, duke of York. John knew very little, so he told me, but he was charged by Aunt Margaret with joining Lord Lovell in Scotland to prepare the way for an invasion by the young duke."

"Dear God, so he gave his life for his cousin, brave boy. I know how your heart was broken, Grace. But John was not meant for you. Your Tom will suit you better, please believe me." She sighed, pushed the veil back from her hat brim and let the sun warm her face. "I fear there is naught I can do from here to aid my son's invasion. If I were well enough to travel I would go to France and see for myself. And if you had but met your half brother once, I would send you to tell me if he be Dickon or no. No matter; there are many who will know him when he comes, even if he is ten years older. Bess and Cecily will know him, and the doctor, Argentine. He had

Edward's odd brow and a lift to his right lip, but otherwise his body was unmarked, unlike Ned, who had a birthing mark on his upper arm."

Grace had many questions about Dickon, and as the two women sat quietly for half an hour, she learned other facts about the child—or those Elizabeth's fading memory could conjure up. He hated the smell of cloves and loved the taste of mint, and his favorite fruit was oranges. He had been a small-boned boy, although at age eleven, it was hard to know if he would grow up more like his father. "And one more thing," Elizabeth recalled, smiling. "How he loved to sing!"

She suddenly turned to Grace and gripped her wrist. "I would know if my son is this man, Grace. Promise me you will find out—one way or the other, even if I am dead." Her tone was urgent and her eyes pleaded.

"I will do my utmost, your grace," came Grace's quiet response. She was promising much to those waiting to go to God lately, she thought and grimaced, but she put her hand over her heart anyway. "I cannot refuse you anything after all you have done for me. If I have not thanked you enough during these years, I am most heartily sorry. You are thanked in my prayers each and every day."

Elizabeth patted her hand. "I know, Grace, I know. And if I understand that clever mind of yours as I think I do, you will unravel the mystery of the man across the sea." She turned away. "Pray God I live to see it."

A flock of starlings flew overhead, shrilly announcing their passage, and blackened the sun for a second. Elizabeth shaded her eyes to follow them, and then both women saw the single magpie as it chose to alight on the wall that sheltered the garden. They gasped in unison, and Grace quickly recited, "Good morrow, Master Magpie, how is your wife?"—the question that was supposed to ward off the bad luck.

" 'Tis time for me to return to my chamber," Elizabeth said, putting out her hand to Grace. "I have one more thing to ask of you, Grace. I would like to see my daughters. Can you send word to Cecily for me? I would like to see them all before I die."

21

Bermondsey and Windsor

SPRING 1492

Tom formed part of the escort that brought all of Elizabeth's daughters to the abbey on a glorious day in late May. Skylarks rose up from the fields, thrilling listeners with their soaring song, and lambs bleated as they frolicked beside their dams, each lamb's voice different and known by its mother. Grace had learned that lambs always waved their tails in ecstasy while they suckled, and she had laughed delightedly when Brother Oswald had shown her how to manually wag a lamb's tail so that it would accept milk from another source when the mother died in the lambing.

Word had spread of the visit by the royal princesses, and people from miles around abandoned their hoes, spades and weed-hooks or their barrows, laundries and spinning wheels to line the road from Southwark to Bermondsey. Bess, heavy with child, sat on a low, cushioned chair in the middle of the open carriage, its canopy richly decorated with the new Tudor rose and the lions of England, and she was surrounded by all her sisters—Cecily, Anne, Catherine and twelve-year-old Bridget. "God bless our queen. God bless good Queen Bess," they cried, waving their bonnets and throwing flowers onto the litter. Grace waited in the courtyard for the procession to enter, a posy of her favorite heartsease in her hand, and her heart swelled with pride for her family—and especially for Bess. How England loves its good, sweet queen, she thought. And she was ashamed of herself for thinking how little they had loved Bess's mother, Elizabeth Woodville, her mentor and protector. Ah, she told herself, but one of them was born royal and had nothing to prove; the other had royalty forced upon her and had spent her life trying to prove she was worthy.

All thoughts of Elizabeth and her daughter vanished as soon as she recognized Tom's tall figure astride a chestnut palfrey. Had she stopped to notice, she would have been astonished at the sudden rush of feelings she had for him, but in her hurry to reach him, with her arms outstretched and a delighted "Tom!" on her lips, she did not have time. In a graceful movement from his saddle, Tom bent down and lifted his wife like airy thistledown into his arms. The dainty heartsease fluttered to the ground, forgotten.

"My dearest Grace!" he greeted her before kissing her waiting lips. Grace twined her fingers in his untidy hair and kissed him back, thinking he would squeeze the breath from her. The sound of high-pitched laughter floated up to the oblivious pair, and then Cecily's commanding voice calling her made Grace pull away with an embarrassed "Oh!" The laborers, grooms and laundrywomen, not to mention several of the monks in the crowd, who had all come to respect Grace over the years, burst into spontaneous applause. Grace wilted into Tom's protective chest, hiding her eyes and her blush. Tom waved at them gaily and expertly guided his horse towards the stable, one hand on the reins and the other cradling his wife. Edgar was there to take Grace from him and was grinning from ear to ear.

"God's greeting, my lord," he said, bowing to Tom. "It be clear to all that my mistress be glad to see you again."

" 'Master Gower' or 'sir' will be enough, Edgar. I am no lord," Tom said, laughing. "I may be married to Lady Grace, but I have no right to a title as her husband."

Edgar frowned as he took this in. "That don't seem lawful, sir. A husband be more important."

"Edgar!" Grace exclaimed. "I pray you, know your place."

But Tom hushed her with a wink and, chuckling, leaned over to Edgar and said: "The sooner you learn that 'tis a woman who really rules the roost, all the better for you when you find yourself a wife. I do nothing without Lady Grace's permission, believe me."

"Tom!" Grace laughed. "Do not tease Edgar so. Edgar is my good and faithful servant, and I will not have you putting foolish notions in his head. Now go and see to her grace and Lady Cecily, before your behavior is reported to Lord Welles."

"See?" Tom muttered to the flabbergasted Edgar and, hanging his head, he pretended to slink off with his tail between his legs. Grace was left staring after him openmouthed, surprised and warmed by Tom's show of humor.

AN HOUR LATER, after Elizabeth was surrounded by her lovely daughters and wine and wafers were served in the privacy of the queen dowager's chamber, Grace slipped out with Katherine's nod of approval to go and find Tom. "I will tell her grace where you are. She will not notice you are gone, I warrant. She is contented as only a mother can be, God bless her."

Grace flew down the stairs and around the side of the residence to the courtyard. Now that the excitement of the visit had died down, the smith was back at work, and she could hear the swishing of a carpenter's adze as it smoothed the rough wood plank, the laughter of the laundrywomen and the clucking of the hens as they strutted around the courtyard pecking in the dirt. At the stable, the grooms were currying the queen's carriage horses, and Grace called out to Edgar, asking if he knew where Tom had gone.

"The last I saw him, mistress, was a-walking in the field yonder," he said, pointing towards the river. "It be not so long ago. Shall I fetch him for you?" Edgar rubbed his dirty hands on his tunic and then used a grubby sleeve to wipe his perspiring face. He reeked of sweat and horses and Grace waved him away. "Nay, Edgar, I will find him. Finish your work." She hurried off through the herb garden, snapping off a stalk of mint to crush between her fingers and refresh the air. She was very fond of Edgar, but his lack of bodily hygiene distressed her.

It was not long before she saw Tom, his long legs striding through the long grass towards a small cow whose leg was stuck in the mud.

"Clover!" Grace cried, hitching up her skirts and taking off running. "Certes, it looks like Clover. Tom! Tom! Wait for me."

Tom turned when he heard her and waved his hat. She caught up to him, breathless, and explained that this was the cow she had weaned the year before. Not heeding the wide swath of mud and cow manure that Clover was mired in, she waded through to the cow's side, speaking gently to it. Clover was unafraid and seemed to know Grace was there to help, and soon Tom was easing the animal's hoof out of the sucking muck as Grace slapped its scrawny haunches to get it to move. Eventually they succeeded, and when Clover slowly turned her head to gaze at them before lumbering off to greener pastures, they both collapsed laughing into the long grass.

"I could swear that cow knew you, Grace. 'Twas a look of love she gave you," Tom said, taking off his muddy short boots and wiping them on the grass. "Were you not afraid she would kick you?"

"I did not think on it," Grace said, shaking her head. "She needed our help and I was glad to give it. She might have broken her leg and ended up on the refectory table. I could not let that happen."

"What a good farmer's wife you would be—if only I had a farm," Tom teased her, and them tickled her nose with a grass frond. "Did you come to find me to say the queen is ready to return to London?"

Grace looked up coyly from under her lashes. "Nay, husband, I came to snatch some moments with you alone. I know we have much to talk about, and I have much to be forgiven—" She did not have a chance to finish, as Tom pulled her to him and began to kiss her. He kissed her forehead, each eye, her nose and her lips and then worked his way down to her breasts. Grace allowed him to touch her under her chemise and her body tingled all over when he caressed her brown nipples with his fingers. Gently he unlaced the back of her gown and drew off the bodice. Then he untied her chemise and eased it down over her arms, leaving her naked to her belly. Grace thought she would swoon with pleasure when he teased her breasts with his kisses, and she felt a rush between her legs as her desire mounted.

"Come to me, Tom," she whispered, helping him lift her heavy skirts. "I would have you make love to me like that afternoon at Collyweston. Do you remember?"

"Do I remember?" Tom laughed almost harshly as he untied his codpiece. "It has lived in my dreams every night since that day. Now, I pray you, my sweet Grace, stop talking!"

Grace thought she must have been in Heaven for the next half hour as she was pleasured over and over again in the sweet-smelling grass, a ceiling of blue above her and the song of a lark drowning her rapturous little cries.

"I love you, Tom Gower," she murmured into his corn-colored hair when he finally lay quietly on her naked breast. "Thank you for waiting for me to know it."

"I would have waited until the cows came home," Tom replied sleepily. And then he lifted his head and turned to stare off in Clover's direction. "I suppose you could say that I did."

Grace tweaked his ear, laughing, then pulled his head to hers and kissed him once more for good measure.

ELIZABETH HAD TURNED her face to the wall, Katherine said to Grace one day in early June. "Did you not notice how, after she had bidden her children farewell, she turned inwards?" she asked. Grace nodded, remembering guiltily how she had arrived back at the apartment flushed from her passionate rendezvous with Tom just in time to wish her sisters God speed. Cecily had wagged a finger at her.

"Why, Mistress Peasant, do look at your shoes, the grass stains on your gown and your badly laced bodice," she murmured as they stood near the door while Elizabeth, her face impassive, gave her blessing to her younger daughters. Little Bridget was sobbing, but Grace noticed Elizabeth did not touch or comfort her. *Truly she loves them,* she thought, recognizing the suppressed sadness in Elizabeth's eyes, which she dared not show them. *And yet she has shown me love; 'tis a puzzle, in truth.*

"I had to rescue a cow," Grace said, her face not moving a muscle and her tone as matter of fact as if she were describing the weather. Cecily guffawed, making her mother look up and frown, while Alison helped Bess out of the chair, the young queen's advanced condition causing her to reach round and support her aching back.

"There you are, Grace," Elizabeth said. "I trust your time with Tom Gower was productive?"

Grace demurred with a small curtsy as Cecily whispered to her, "Enough to produce a child, I'll warrant." Grace surreptitiously leaned back and poked her sister's thigh, trying to hide her laughter.

As Elizabeth turned her attention back to her blessings, Grace stepped up to Bess's side and slipped her hand in her sister's. Bess looked down at her and smiled. "I remember you doing that all those years ago at Sheriff Hutton when I was so frightened of my future," she said softly. "Now you do it to comfort me, as 'tis plain as a pikestaff we shall be grieving for my lady mother before long. Am I right?"

"You have the measure of it, your grace. I would have you know that your mother was always good to me, and believe me when I say I shall grieve as though she were mine, too." Tears pricked behind Grace's eyes as they watched Elizabeth from across the room. Catherine and Anne had risen and curtsied, but Bridget was still on her knees, crying. Bess let go of Grace's hand and went to help her little sister up. "We must leave, Biddy," she coaxed. "You can come again next week, if you would like." Bridget turned into her oldest sister's arms, and Elizabeth motioned Bess to take the child away. The meeting had exhausted her, and she wanted nothing more than to lie down and never wake up. The sisters and Katherine filed out, leaving Grace standing quietly by to watch over Elizabeth.

In a gesture of complete respect, Bess, who by rights should have been thus honored by Elizabeth, sank into an awkward reverence in front of her mother and asked for her blessing again. Instead of giving it, the queen dowager suddenly leaned forward and hissed: "You have been here nigh on two hours, daughter, and you have said nary a word about my son."

Bess was nonplussed. "Your son, Mother? Do you mean Dorset?" Bess responded evenly.

"Nay, I do not mean Thomas," Elizabeth snapped. "I am talking about Dickon, your youngest brother. Certes, I have heard that he has been seen in the Low Countries and Ireland. If 'tis so, then the crown belongs to him, not Henry. Surely Henry—and you as his queen—must be having a few sleepless nights?"

Seeing her sister struggling to stand, Grace ran forward to help.

"Aye, there is a man who pretends he is Richard of York," Bess retorted, using Grace's shoulder as a crutch, "but none of us who knew Dickon nine years ago has set eyes on him since, and thus Henry is dismissing him as a mammet of Aunt Margaret and her arrogant son-in-law, Maximilian." She turned and began to pace, and when Grace saw the telltale hand flutter to her mouth for the ritual nail-biting, she knew Bess was trying to hide her nervousness. "Henry is gathering evidence as we speak to denounce the man as a fraud—just like Lambert Simnel," Bess continued bravely. "Whoever this man is, he cannot be your son, madam. Your sons were murdered by Uncle Richard and Buckingham."

Grace gasped at Bess's tactless statement. Finding her feet and a last burst of energy, Elizabeth grasped Bess's wrist. "My son is still alive, I tell you!" she spat. "He will come, mark my words, daughter. And your measle of a husband can slink back into the Welsh wilderness whence he came." Exhausted, she sank down into the chair, and Grace hurried to fetch a cup of wine.

Bess gritted her teeth. "I honor you too much to quarrel with you, madam," she said, rubbing her wrist. "It would seem to me 'tis the bile in you speaking and not your true self, and so I forgive your lapse of courtesy. But do not forget I am now the queen, and when you insult the king, you insult me." She swiveled on her heel and made for the door.

Grace stepped in front of her, tears in her eyes. "I beg of you, your grace, put yourself in your mother's place," she whispered. "After many years of anxious wondering, she has heard that one of her sons may yet live. Can you not understand the hope she has in her heart?" she pleaded. Then, more boldly, she said, "Besides, we have no proof that he is or is not Dickon yet, so allow her to hope until then—please." Seeing her sister relent, she put her hand on Bess's arm. "Can you not see 'tis this hope that keeps her alive?" she murmured. "I beg of you, do not leave here angry, or you will regret it, for you may never see her again."

Bess looked down at Grace's hand on her arm for a moment, and Grace forced herself not to loosen her hold even though it felt like kindling on a fire. Then the queen looked into Grace's honest eyes and a small smile appeared on her lips. She shook her head and patted Grace's hand. "Certes, ever the peacemaker, sister. I should have Henry send you to France to negotiate with King Charles." She glided past Grace to her mother, but this time she did not go down on her knees. Instead she bent and kissed Elizabeth gently on both cheeks, then picked up one of the frail hands and carried it to her lips.

"Forgive me, Mother," she said quietly. "I lost my temper for a moment." She patted her distended belly. "This babe is to blame, I fear. As God is my witness, I would not leave you angry with me, and rest assured I shall pay dearly on my knees when I confess of my disrespect." She stood up and glanced at Grace. "Here is what I will allow. As Grace seems well informed with regard to this man"—she paused and spoke the words she knew Elizabeth was waiting to hear—"our brother, Dickon, should you choose to send Grace to talk to Aunt Margaret herself, you will have my blessing. I shall inform Henry that a visit by a niece to her aunt sometime in the coming months will do no one any harm. But we will expect to be fully informed upon her return. Is that clear?"

Elizabeth eyed her daughter with new respect. She dabbed at her eyes and nodded. " 'Tis good of you, Bess, but I am loath to part with Grace at present. Come, let me walk with you to the carriage so all can see your mother is not dying yet." She gave Bess a wry smile. "You are a good girl, Elizabeth, and your father would have been very proud of you. Indeed, I am proud of you. You are the consummate consort for a king—unlike me, who brought naught but trouble to my husband. And it seems both of us are fruitful."

Grace and Bess helped her out of the chair and, leaning heavily on both, Elizabeth made the slow and arduous journey down the stairs and into the main courtyard to see the royal entourage off. Tom was on hand to help the princesses back into the carriage and then, with a quick kiss and farewell to Grace, he sprang on his horse and led the way back to Southwark. Grace and Katherine stood on either side of the queen dowager, helping her to stand erect for a last glimpse of her daughters. The only woman in either group who did not shed a tear at that moment was Cecily.

ELIZABETH'S LAST FEW days took her in and out of lucidity—sometimes crying, sometimes praying, but mostly sleeping. Once, in the middle of the night, she whimpered for water to slake her thirst. "Bring me the pure spring water from Grafton," she begged, forgetting where she was, and when Grace hurried to her side, she clutched at Grace's cambric shift fearfully. "Are the windows and door closed? The Devil wants my soul, you know. Christ in his mercy, do not let the Devil in," she cried.

Katherine awoke then, but Grace motioned to her that she would keep vigil until the queen slept again, so the older woman turned over gratefully in her cot and resumed her snoring.

"My dear lady," Grace soothed, holding the horn cup to the queen's parched lips. Whatever was gnawing at her belly had woken her and was causing frequent spasms of pain to cross her pinched face. "Here is something to calm you, from Brother Benedictus. And I can assure you there is not a chink in the room wide enough for the Devil to slip through from outside." Indeed the room was stifling on that warm June night because Elizabeth insisted all windows be shut tight against the satanic forces she believed were threatening her. The pungent smell from the bed told Grace the queen had once again wet herself, and she fetched the newly washed shift from its peg on the post and gingerly helped Elizabeth out of the soiled one and removed the sodden bundle of rags from between Elizabeth's wasted thighs, depositing them into the jakes. Once Elizabeth was in clean linen, Grace fanned her perspiring face, hoping the potion would soon begin to work its calming magic. She gazed fondly at her mentor, who was resting back on the pillows, her pale face and even paler hair hardly distinguishable against the white linen.

"You are a good girl," Elizabeth muttered. "Come, stay with me through this night." She patted the bed beside her and insisted the curtains be drawn around them, although her other attendants were fast asleep. The candle guttered for a second in the breeze from the curtain and a little cry of fear from Elizabeth told Grace the queen did not want to be in the dark, so she steeled herself for an even more suffocating hour before the cock crowed.

"I want to tell you how much I loved your father, my dear," Elizabeth murmured, playing with one of Grace's long brown curls. "He adored me, you know, although 'twas often a puzzle to those who witnessed him seducing any pretty face that passed him by. Ah, yes," she apologized, "that was probably what happened to your poor mother, Grace." Grace cast her eyes down to her hands in her lap and listened quietly. "But he always came back to me." She sighed. "I suspect there are those who believe my mother cast a spell on him—you have heard, perhaps, that she was descended from the witch Melusine, have you not?" Grace nodded; she had been told a hundred times or more. But this was the first time Elizabeth had ever mentioned her mother's part in her marriage. " 'Tis said she wove magic to lure the king to wed me. But, in truth, 'twas Edward's own lust that drew him to me that spring in Grafton. Certes, all my mother did was extract a promise from me that there would be no bedding without a wedding." She gave a short laugh. "You did not know my mother, Grace. If you think I am a forceful woman, I am but a squall compared to the tempest that she was." She reached for her rosary and kissed the ebony crucifix before continuing. "Now, child, I shall tell you a secret that you will swear never to repeat." When Grace's face betrayed her trepidation, Elizabeth's tone was scornful. "Do not be lily-livered about this, my dear. You have the backbone to hear the truth, and I know you can keep a secret. So swear to me you will take this to your grave."

Grace nodded and, once again for Elizabeth, put her hand over her heart. "I swear, your grace," she whispered, although she prayed to St. Sibylline to make Elizabeth fall asleep immediately and forget all about divulging this secret.

When her next spasm passed, Elizabeth took a deep breath. "A few years after my marriage, my mother discovered that Edward had been contracted to another before he ever laid eyes on me. Her name was Eleanor Talbot, and she was also a widow. God be praised, she died a few years after Edward and I married. I learned the truth from my mother on her deathbed." Seeing the irony, she chuckled. "Much as I am now relaying it to you. Do not say a word, child," she insisted, seeing Grace about to deny that she was dying. "I know I am not long for the world. Indeed, I wish the good Lord would take me soon, for I am weary of this dull life and would now rather lie with Edward at Windsor for eternity." A wave of pain made her grimace, and Grace lifted up the bony shoulders and head to administer another sip of laudanum. Then she gently let the queen down, wiping her brow.

"Where was I?" Elizabeth frowned. "Ah, yes, Eleanor Talbot—or Butler, as she was when Edward was tempted to bed her. I swear to you, Grace, I knew nothing of this when I agreed to wed Edward. Aye, I was ambitious for my two sons by John, but not so ambitious as to break one of God's commandments."

Grace's eyes were wide. "Then what Bishop Stillington unveiled in Forty-three, when my father died, was true? And Uncle Richard did wear the crown by right?" Grace whispered, her mind racing. All those insinuations that he had usurped the throne and bribed poor Stillington to come forward at exactly the right moment and tell his story were untrue. Poor Uncle Richard. He went to his death at Bosworth still fighting to prove he was England's true king.

"Aye, Richard had the right," Elizabeth said dully. "But he did not have the right to put away my boys, even if they were bastards."

Grace brightened. "But it seems he did not 'put them away,' your grace. It seems Dickon survived whatever fate was in his path. I have heard it said that Ned was sickly and inflicted with a bone-wasting disease. Certes, 'tis likely he perished either in the Tower or elsewhere, wherever Dickon was also hidden." Grace was so absorbed in the certainty that one of her half brothers was alive that she failed to notice the mulish look in Elizabeth's eye.

"Are you not shocked by my secret, Grace?" the queen snapped. "Do you know what honor I do you by revealing it? I am admitting I was a bigamist and that my children were no better than you are—all bastards! I pray you, appear outraged or sympathetic or . . . anything," she groused.

Grace was at once contrite. "Your grace, I am indeed surprised. But as you tell me the lady in question no longer lives, and that you were ignorant of the event when you gave your hand to my father, I cannot condemn you. My father is another matter," Grace said, frowning. Then she took Elizabeth's hand and looked into those once-glorious eyes. "Remember, your daughter sits on the throne. The king legitimized all your children so that he could marry her and make his rump safer upon the throne. But if Dickon returns, what can Henry do? If he reverses the bastardy act, Bess can no longer be his consort and the mother of future kings. But if he does not, it means Dickon will have every right to state his lawful claim."

Elizabeth's eyelids were beginning to droop and her words slurred with the effects of the drug. "Do not think I have not pondered this question ever since I heard of this man's existence. Do I want to disinherit my daughter with this information and welcome my son back as king—although he does not have the right, in God's eyes—or do I go to my grave knowing I have passed on that responsibility to you? Now you know why 'tis important for you to go to Margaret. Promise me you will?" The exertion of this exchange had drained the queen dowager, and her eyes finally closed. "Let us recite the Angelus together and try to sleep," she said. Grace had to lean into her face to hear her mutter, "I am tired of this weight I have carried for so many years. I trust you may bear it less heavily." Then, fingering her rosary, she began, *"Angelus Domini nuntiavit Mariae."*

"Et concepit de Spiritu Sancto," Grace intoned the response of the dying queen's favorite prayer, crossing herself as she did so. She blew out the

candle, but she could not sleep for the rest of the night, while her mind processed all that she had been told. As the cock crowed and the abbey awoke, she sat up with a start. "Dear God," she whispered, "Bishop Stillington died last year." She turned her head to look down at Elizabeth, whose breathing was now so shallow, and realized: "When she dies, I alone will know the truth."

Deciphering the true identity of the young man across the sea now seemed even more vital. And, she thought grimly, I have given my promise that I will. She shivered—from excitement or fear, she wasn't sure.

"*MISEREATUR VESTRI TUI omnipotens Deus,*" chanted Father John, holding the Holy Chrism high above his head, while Brothers Damien and Benedictus stood behind him holding long candles. They answered with a sonorous "*Amen*" at appropriate intervals during the last rites of the most high and noble lady Elizabeth, dowager queen of England and beloved mother of the queen.

On the other side of the bed, kneeling by their dying mistress, Lady Katherine Hastings, Lady Grace Plantagenet and Mistress Alison Mortimer told their beads, their heads bowed. The dowager's doctor, Thomas Brente, was also in attendance. An occasional sniffle from Alison broke the monotony of the chanting monks and the tolling abbey bell, but Grace and Katherine had shed their tears earlier that morning, when it became clear their charge was slipping quietly away.

"Bless you, my dear friend," Elizabeth had murmured as Katherine had pressed the queen dowager's hand to her lips, wetting it with her tears. "I wish I had more to leave you than my gratitude . . ." She drew another labored breath and Katherine hushed her, stroking her forehead with her other hand.

Then it was Grace's turn, and she thought her heart must be made of marble, it weighed down her chest so heavily. She tried not to cry, tried not to conjure up again all the memories of those first days at Grafton when Elizabeth had rescued her from the convent, taught her to be a lady and given her a new life. They were all engraved on her heart, and she had vowed in her prayers the night before that she would never tolerate a bad word about Elizabeth from anyone from that day forth. She bent and kissed Elizabeth's cold forehead, one tear escaping and wetting the parchmentlike skin.

"Now, now, Grace, no tears." Elizabeth managed a smile with her admonishment. "I am counting on you to help carry out the wishes for my funeral. Do you remember them?"

"Aye, your grace, certes I do," Grace answered, attempting to smile back. "No pomp, no finery. A plain wooden box, and only two attendants on the boat to Windsor." Elizabeth nodded, satisfied, and closed her eyes. Grace continued: "However, you cannot prevent us from mourning you in whatever way we wish. I for one will light a candle for you daily, and you will be in my prayers until I die."

"What day is it, my child?" Elizabeth asked, each word a struggle.

" 'Tis the Friday of Pentecost."

"Then let me be buried on that holiest of Sundays. And may the white tongue of the Holy Spirit touch me and wing me to Heaven," Elizabeth whispered reverently. Then her eyes flew open and she attempted a laugh. "Sweet Mary, 'tis the very same day I was crowned, twenty-seven years ago. How droll." Her laughter gave way to a cry of pain, and she clutched Grace's hand.

Grace waited until Elizabeth was calm again. "Your grace?" Her voice was low and urgent. "I would ask a boon before you die."

"Ask," Elizabeth said, a little of her impatience returning. "For I have not much time left, and I must reconcile my soul to God."

"I am not your daughter, but, in truth, you have been like a mother to me. May I be given leave to call you 'Mother' just this once?" Grace held her breath. She was breaking all the courtesy codes with her request.

Now Elizabeth's tears began to flow and her serene face crumpled. "Nothing would please me more, child. Certes, you have shown me more devotion than any of my own daughters." A spasm of pain wracked her body and a thin trickle of blood oozed from her mouth. With her last ounce of energy she pleaded: "Send for Father John, I beg of you."

"Aye, Mother," Grace answered on her knees, sobbing. "And may the Virgin protect you on your journey to the Light." She rose and hurried out to find the abbot.

"*Indulgentiam, absolutionem et remissionem peccatorum nostrum, tribuat nobis omnipotens et misericors Dominus,*" Father John intoned now, touching Elizabeth's head, lips and heart with the holy oil.

Elizabeth's mouth curved into a soft smile, and it seemed the queen's beauty was miraculously restored in that final moment. "John, my love, I am coming," she murmured with her last breath. True to her heart, the once proud queen of England had called out the name of her first husband, and not the man who had raised her to the highest rank in the kingdom.

THE REGULAR SPLASH of the oars as they dipped into the limpid waters of the Thames lulled Grace into a somnambulant state as she sat to the right of the flower-covered coffin that was being carried upstream to Windsor, some forty miles from London Bridge. The abbot had sent word immediately to Greenwich, where the queen was in confinement, and to Thomas, marquis of Dorset, to inform both of their mother's passing. Dorset had spent a day with Elizabeth a few days before she died, and Grace had been gratified to see his grim face when he turned away from the bed to take his leave. She had never forgiven him for forsaking his mother when Henry had banished her to Bermondsey. So he should be sorry, she thought; but she had helped him with his short mantle and murmured, "Pray accept my sincere sympathies, my lord." He had given her a smile and a curt nod before hurrying from the room.

It had been decided that Katherine would stay behind due to her age, and to make sure none of Elizabeth's few possessions were looted once the news of her death was known. "I will throw myself on my brother-in-law Richard's charity," she told Grace when they were discussing their futures. "And you, Grace?"

Grace would not return to Bermondsey after Windsor, she told Katherine, because she belonged by Tom's side now that her duty to Elizabeth was over. "I pray he may reach Windsor to escort me home—wherever that may be," Grace had said. "Cecily is at Greenwich for the queen's confinement, but I know not if Tom is with his lord or no."

"Certes, 'tis possible you and I will be neighbors!" Katherine cried. "The Hastings have a manor in Lincolnshire, too, if you go to the Welles estates there."

So it was Alison who sat to the left of the coffin on the barge to Windsor—an unknown attendant, it was noted by those watching—who journeyed with Grace, bastard daughter of King Edward. Also on the boat were Doctor Brente, one of the executors of Elizabeth's will, and her second cousin, Edward Haute.

The scent of the dozens of white roses that the kind people of Bermondsey and Southwark had gathered from their gardens to place upon the bier of the Yorkist queen masked the smell of death from the crude coffin as the barge floated past Baynard's Castle, Westminster, and around the bend to Shene, the fairy-tale palace Elizabeth had so enjoyed, which stood proudly against the backdrop of lush Richmond Hill. The boatmen rowed to the dock, where everyone disembarked. It was their chance to relieve themselves and be offered food from the charterhouse priory nearby, whose prior—another of Elizabeth's executors, John Ingilby—joined them on the journey to Windsor.

Grace nibbled on a piece of rabbit pie but had little appetite as she watched a moorhen and her brood weave in and out of the reeds. Wooded islands floated in this wide part of the river, and Grace could see lambs gamboling in the fields on the other side.

"*Let lambs go unclipped, till June be half worn/The better the fleeces will grow to be shorn . . .*" went the old adage. Aye, your first shearing must be near, Grace thought, smiling to herself as she remembered the frantic flailing legs of the lamb she had attempted to truss and shear her first summer at Bermondsey. She turned away, leaving Alison to make a chain from among the thousands of daisies that bloomed in the overgrown lawn, and wandered down to the river's edge to dabble her feet in the cool water. It irked her that the boatmen made merry while they ate and drank, seemingly having forgotten the solemn occasion that had brought them there. She saw Edgar among them—he and others were in another boat that was following the funeral barge—and she frowned when she saw him raise a full flagon of frothing ale to his lips. Catching her eye, his hand froze halfway to his mouth and then he quickly set the drink down, slopping some onto the table. Grace turned away; it was a hot day and she should not begrudge the man ale.

Her thoughts flew back to the day before, after the three attendants had knelt in turn to pray for hours at Elizabeth's prie-dieu. Sadly, they noted, as women, they were not permitted inside the church while the monks kept vigil over Elizabeth's body. "Idle hands make the Devil's work," Katherine had said. "Open all the windows and take the linens to the laundry, Alison. Grace and I will gather fresh herbs."

The two women picked up baskets and small shears from the shed and meandered through the pretty walled garden deadheading, cutting fragrant herbs to freshen their chamber and pulling up weeds. As they worked, they reminisced about Elizabeth.

"How unkind of God to take her before she had the joy of seeing her young son again," Grace said, returning with all speed to her favorite subject. She glanced around and lowered her voice. "I wonder what chance there is that he can unthrone Henry?"

"That is treasonous talk, Grace, and you should beware," Katherine warned under her breath, putting her finger to her lips. "Our brown-robed friends are not averse to eavesdropping. Will always said he would never trust a cleric as far as he could see their shiny tonsures, and after what happened with Bishop Morton the day of Will's death, he was right not to trust them."

Grace clucked her tongue and shook her head. "The news of your husband's sudden execution must have come as quite a shock, Lady Katherine. He had been such a friend to my father, I wonder at Uncle Richard's strange behavior."

"Aye, 'twas shocking indeed, and I can never forgive Gloucester for that. Poor Will never even had a trial." She sighed. "But you are right, Edward and Will were the best of friends," she said, and grunted. "Forever whoring and drinking. You would have thought neither had a care in the world, instead of being the king and counselor of one of the most important realms in Christendom."

"I remember the story you and her grace told about fooling my Uncle Clarence one night in London. How they tricked him with drink . . . I forget the rest," Grace said, chuckling.

Katherine sat her large frame down on the same seat Elizabeth and Grace had occupied a few weeks before, in April, and Grace settled herself on the grass and played with a stalk of mint, inhaling its fresh scent.

"You mean the Frieda affair?" Katherine replied, rolling her eyes. "There is not much to tell. Edward and Will found George with this buxom Flemish girl, both very much the worse for drink, and offered to help them upstairs to bed. So Will tells me, Edward helped George with his codpiece, but as soon as the lad fell on the bed he was dead to the world, and the girl not much better. Knowing Edward wanted the woman, Will left the room while Edward pleasured her. Whoring was such an uncharacteristic thing for Clarence to do—he and Isabel adored each other, you know—but Edward could not resist allowing his brother to think he had done the dirty deed when he awoke the next day, and so he thought he would have the last laugh."

Grace was wishing she had not asked to have the story repeated. Her thoughts about her father's behavior were filled with disgust. Instead of stopping his younger brother from shaming himself with a whore and betraying his wife, Edward had encouraged it. And as if that act had not been heinous enough, he had taken advantage of a young girl in a stupor and allowed the guilt-ridden Clarence to believe he had sired a bastard. She hung her head and tore the mint leaves to shreds.

"Instead, my uncle Clarence had the last laugh—although he did not know it," she muttered. "You are sure the girl had a child, Lady Katherine?" The older woman nodded. "And your husband paid her off on behalf of my father."

Katherine harrumphed. " 'Twas the way of it. 'Tis always the way of it, more's the pity," she complained. "A woman is naught but a chattel—a pleasure tool for a man, whether he be husband or no."

At that moment, Grace agreed with her, although, in her heart, she knew all men were not the same. A warm glow spread through her as she thought of Tom, but for good measure she prayed he might never run afoul of a brother as immoral as Edward, king of England—her own father.

GRACE WAS SHOCKED by the secrecy and lack of reverence accorded the arrival of Elizabeth's body at Windsor. By this time it was late at night and only moonlight and a few half-used torches carried by a handful of old men illuminated the small funeral procession up the steep slope and into the massive castle on the hill. The coffin was pulled on a common hearse, a single wooden candlestick at each corner as its only ornaments. With undue haste, Elizabeth was interred next to Edward in the gloom of St. George's chapel, with only a priest and a clerk to oversee the proceedings. Why were there no bells tolling, no appearance even by the dean and canons of the chapel? Grace was not the only one who was shocked. She overheard one of the heralds, sent by Henry to report on the event, remark to another about the surprising "modesty of the burial of an English queen." Grace wanted to tell them, "Her grace was particular about keeping her obsequies simple. She was full of piety and humility, in truth, and she wanted no pomp or expenditure." But when she heard the herald blame it on Henry's close-fisted nature and ill will towards his mother-in-law, she grinned to herself, knowing this was exactly what Elizabeth had secretly wanted people to think.

Two days later a more formal Mass was said, and by then members of Elizabeth's family had arrived at the castle. From her vantage point atop the tower in the middle ward, Grace saw them step ashore at the same spot the funeral barge had docked, and she could now see the crude cottages clustered on the shore under the castle. Across the water, the graceful flying buttresses of the sixth Henry's Eton College vied for her attention with those of St. George's chapel to her left, built by his rival Edward inside the walls of Windsor. Acknowledging it was a beautiful spot and a favorite among her father's castles, she sighed and turned away to descend the tower staircase to greet her half sisters.

"Where is the king?" Grace said, frowning. And the other nobles who were in his Star Chamber circle, she thought. " 'Tis right that the queen should not come, but surely Henry must."

"His grace and his councilors are busy contemplating the invasion of France, Lady Grace." Thomas of Dorset's voice behind her made her jump. "Forgive me if I startled you. The king regrets he is unable to attend. No doubt, my lady mother would have understood. Excuse me, but now I must consult with Bishop Audley, who will conduct the memorial Mass." He bowed to the group and strode towards the south front entrance of the chapel.

"I know he's the only brother we have now," Anne murmured when he was out of earshot, "but I don't like him."

Grace decided this was not the time to remind them of Dickon, and instead took Bridget's hand and showed them the way to the royal apartments in the lower ward. At least Elizabeth would have several of her children praying for her soul that day, she thought sadly. How soon will she be forgotten? If Dickon is ever crowned king—it was possible, she told herself—he will build a fine monument to his mother, she had no doubt. "Then England will never forget," she whispered.

TWO DAYS LATER she traveled with her sisters back down the Thames to Greenwich. She had been unnerved by Thomas of Dorset's few words with her as he bade farewell to them on the wharf. "I know my lady mother talked with you about the man across the sea who is claiming to be Richard of York," he murmured. "What more do you know, my lady?"

"Only that, my lord," Grace said, her hackles rising in anger—and fear. She knew Dickon had last been located in France, where Charles was treating him as a royal guest. "Why, is there more?" she asked, her wide eyes as innocent as she could make them.

" 'Tis common knowledge the king's grace plans to invade France on behalf of his friends in Brittany, but the information on the imposter that he has received from his envoys at the French court . . ." Grace bit her tongue; she had almost blurted out, "You mean, spies, my lord!" Thomas lowered his voice even further: ". . . is that there is a conspiracy afoot, and several Englishmen with Yorkist sympathies have somehow turned up there and joined him. I would ask that you not upset the queen at Greenwich with this news. Indeed, I forbid you to talk of this man in front of her or my other half sisters. Do you understand?" He gripped her wrist in the folds of her black mourning gown so no one could see, and Grace winced in pain. Her heart was pounding in her throat, and she was afraid. She nodded slowly, and without missing a beat, Thomas suddenly smiled broadly, bent over and smacked a kiss on her unsuspecting cheek. "Farewell to you, Lady Grace, and God speed to Greenwich," he called loudly. "I cannot thank you enough for your care of my lady mother." Dropping her arm, he strode over to the other young women and bussed them all amiably before walking back up the hill.

From her perch on the queen's barge, Grace stared back at the hulking limestone castle, its central round tower gleaming against the sky, and told herself that Henry must indeed be concerned for his throne if he had to send such a warning through Dorset, who had finally fulfilled his mother's wish and found favor with the king. It seemed she alone was left with the desire to discover the truth about Dickon. Certes, none of her half sisters would benefit from his reappearance, she mused, but she could not forget that John died for his loyalty to York, and who was she to let him down? Or, certes, Elizabeth, who had earned her love and loyalty above all others? Nay, she was determined to understand the truth of what became of the Yorkist prince.

· · ·

ONCE AT GREENWICH, Grace faithfully recounted to Bess and Cecily the events surrounding their mother's death. Less than a month later, the cycle of life came full circle when, with Cecily and Grace in attendance, Elizabeth's granddaughter was born and named for her. Summer melted into autumn, and she and Cecily were still at Greenwich with Bess and her sickly child, and Grace wondered when she would next see Tom. Then Henry sailed for France and Grace learned that Tom had gone with Viscount Welles and the rest of the army, and she feared for his safety.

"Pah!" Cecily made sure only her two sisters were within earshot in the nursery where they watched Arthur, Henry and Margaret play. "Henry fight? Surely you jest. I heard he cowered behind Brandon, his standard-bearer, at Bosworth Field, and that Uncle Richard almost reached him by killing the giant bodyguard Cheney as well as Brandon. And at Stoke, after addressing his men bravely enough, he withdrew to some safe vantage point to watch."

"Enough, Cecily!" Bess commanded. "At least my husband did not flee as yours did—with ten thousand men."

"Sisters, please don't fight again," Grace begged, rocking the carved oak cradle that held the whimpering princess Elizabeth. "See, you have frightened the baby. With all due respect, I do not care a fig for either of your husbands' battle prowess; all I care about is that mine may be in danger."

As quickly as their rivalry had divided them, they were reunited by Cecily's wink. "I can remember a time not so long ago when our good little Grace could have given a rat's arse about Tom Gower," Cecily teased.

"Cecily!" Bess cried, concealing a smirk. "Watch your tongue in front of Arthur, I beg of you. But you are right, Grace has changed her tune. How now, Grace?"

Grace hid her blush by leaning into the cradle and easing the baby's swaddling bands. She was loath to talk about her marriage with Bess, although Cecily had wrested most of the juicy details from her over that dull summer in Greenwich's sleepy setting. Cecily knew how disappointed Grace had been when she had not conceived that day in the meadow at Bermondsey. And Grace had not seen Tom since, although loving letters had arrived at regular intervals, telling of his monthlong visit to Westow to help on the farm during harvest.

"How I wish you could be here with me at my home, my sweet wife," he had writ-

ten, and Grace had wondered why he had not sent for her. "*My lord Welles tells me Cecily would be bereft without you, and as she must attend on the queen, I had no hope of freeing you from your duty to the queen to come with me. One day, my love, I will bring you here, I promise.*"

"I love my husband, just as you do, Bess," was all Grace would say. "More I will not say."

A MONTH AFTER Henry's return from France following the Treaty of Etaples, the sisters were once again in the nursery when the door burst open and a lady in waiting curtsied low and told them breathlessly, "The king is come. He wishes to see you, your grace, and is on his way up."

Bess rose and smoothed her gown and felt for her headdress. "The king? Here? But he was not due to come for a week. We were to journey to Windsor together for the Yuletide season. I pray nothing is amiss."

Cecily and Grace hurriedly arranged the folds of Elizabeth's sarcenet hood and straightened its gold-brocade frame around her oval face. Wisps of fair hair curled in tendrils upon her forehead, and her golden eyes flitted anxiously to the door. "Make haste, sisters. His grace dislikes vain women," she urged.

Henry's face softened into a smile when he entered the room and took in the scene. With Bess's attendants clustered around her and Arthur and Margaret each holding one of their mother's hands, the group presented a charming tableau for an instant, before they all sank into their reverences to the king. Then Margaret ran headlong into her father's arms and Arthur danced around him brandishing a wooden sword. Grace was astonished at Henry's informality when he carried Margaret to greet Bess with an affectionate kiss and then dismissed his servants. *Certes, there is still love there,* she marveled. Then she found herself greeted by name before Henry relinquished his older daughter to her nursemaid and went to inspect baby Elizabeth. He tickled the child with one of his long bony fingers and was dismayed when a whimper and not a gurgle of glee was the response.

"She is a puny child, my lady. I trust the wet nurse is providing for her well?" After some private conversation over the cradle, his face turned serious.

"I promised you Christmas at Windsor, madam, and go there we shall.

But there is news from France that I must attend to first. However, I thought I could deal with it just as well here as at Westminster."

"But I thought you had signed a treaty with Charles," Bess said, pouring wine for him and inviting him to sit. "I trust he has not broken it already?"

Henry scowled, reminding Grace of her favorite gargoyle at Bermondsey. "Cracked it, perhaps, but not broken it," he said. "By agreeing not to aid any of my enemies, I believed he would hand the mawmet imposter over to me—the man has had the run of the French court for months, even availing himself of the courtesans, so I am told—but instead he allowed the measle to flee with his friends into Burgundy. They are no doubt dining with the diabolical Duchess Margaret as we speak," he said with clenched jaws. "*Nom de Dieu, qu'il est une peste.*"

"Hush, my dear lord. Why do you fret about him so? He will be revealed as a dissembler by Maximilian and his son, and it will all be over, mark my words," Bess soothed.

Henry swung round to address Cecily and Grace, who were keeping Arthur amused with colored building blocks. "What do you know of this . . . this deceiver? Do you believe your brother is still alive and kicks his heels and thumbs his nose at me over the Channel?"

Grace fumbled a block on top of her tower and it collapsed, making Arthur squeal with glee. Cecily sat back on her heels and, looking Henry straight in the eye, answered: "Nay, your grace. He is, as the queen says, a dissembler. I believe both my brothers are dead."

Grace gulped and mentally crossed herself. How could Cis have lied so convincingly, and without batting an eyelid? She busied herself gathering up the scattered bricks and murmured something unintelligible. She prayed Bess would not enlighten him, and her prayer was answered. Thankfully, Henry was, as always, uninterested in what she had to say, but accepted Cecily's word with a nod and a "*C'est bon.*" Then he suddenly slapped his forehead and exclaimed: "*Sacré coeur de Jesu!* Forgive me, sister; I forgot to mention that your husband asked me to send you to him in his apartments. And Lady Grace, Master Gower is attending him. If her grace can spare you, you should make haste." He grinned. "They are anxious to see you again."

Cecily sighed and got to her feet, but Grace was already in a curtsy before the king and queen, asking to be excused.

Bess nodded and, laughing, called to Cecily: "We have our answer after all, Cis. 'Tis plain as a pikestaff our little sister is besotted."

THAT NIGHT LORD Welles's wife joined her husband in his bed and his squire found his way into Grace's bed, where both couples enjoyed each other on differing levels of passion.

Tom could not hide his joy when he closed the heavy drapes of their tester bed from the prying eyes of the tiring woman curled up in a truckle bed by the fire and found Grace naked under the sheet. His hands explored every part of her, making her hold her breath in case a moan escaped. A single candle burned in the sconce, allowing them to feast their eyes on each other before they rolled over and over, savoring the feel of skin upon skin, his mouth upon her breast and her hand upon the most velvet part of him. How many times he moved her to climax, Grace could not say, but she counted four times for him before he fell asleep, exhausted, and the cock crowed. This is what the poets talk of, Grace mused, lying in the crook of Tom's arm, the candle long since guttered out. 'Tis what lovers know only in secret trysts and lustful liaisons, not, she had been led to believe, husbands and wives. How she hoped she would conceive this night! How loved a child of this union would be, she thought, dreamily.

22

Malines

NOVEMBER 1492

Margaret chewed the end of her quill, gazing out of the newly glazed windows onto the garden, drab now after nights of frost had killed the remaining autumn roses. She had been delighted to learn that her darling boy was enjoying the hospitality of the king of France, who was the first ruler in Europe to recognize the young man as Edward of England's son. She would have to remember to call him Richard now—poor boy, she thought; first Pierrequin, then Jehan, then back to Pierrequin and now he must get used to Richard.

Unfortunately, the tide had turned in France, and she needed to warn her nephew. Thus she must send this letter without delay, being careful not to reveal too much to her protégé in case it fell into the wrong hands and their years-long code was broken. She would send it via her former secretary and spy, Stephen Frion, who was now among Richard's adherents at the French court. He had been charged by Margaret to instruct Richard on all manner of things English, which he had learned during his time at

Edward and Henry's court. Frion was a gem, she acknowledged, and had fooled Henry completely.

She grimaced. What right have you to play with this boy's life, Margaret? she asked herself. Is your hatred of Henry so great that you would risk your own little Jehan to reclaim the throne for York? Then her beloved father's words echoed in her mind: "Never forget your blood kin. The most important people in your world are right here in this house—the house of York," he had told her. Her father had died fighting to claim the crown for York, and her brothers Edward and Richard had worn it instead— rightfully so. Now the Tudor turd dared to wear it—his claim as flimsy as gossamer thread! Nay, 'twas not to be borne, she told herself, and even though she knew this prince was not the duke of York, no one else did. Aye, she decided and dipped her pen in the inkpot with new purpose, Richard is the son of a royal duke—bastard or no—and can restore our family's birthright.

"Right noble and well beloved nephew, Richard, duke of York, I greet thee well," she wrote in her firm script. She must be formal in case this was intercepted. *"And I am satisfied that you are indeed my long-lost nephew, after hearing the testimony of my son-in-law Maximilian's secretary, who recently visited the French court and saw you there. However, I must see you for myself and shall know then if you be my brother's son or no. I pray that it is so and will rejoice greatly upon that day, which I hope will come soon.*

"But I digress. It has come to my attention that your brother-in-law, King Henry of England, has signed a treaty with your host, his majesty Charles, king of France, following Henry's recent siege at Boulogne, which he undertook last month to make good on a promise to Brittany by claiming his right to the French crown." So far, so good, she thought. Nothing confidential there—Richard must know this much. She gave a short laugh, threw some sand over the parchment to help dry the ink and spat out a piece of feather she had worried off her quill during her ruminations. The invasion all came to naught, certes, because it seemed King Charles was loath to fight the English in the north while his ambitions lie south, in Italy. In fact, he preferred to buy off the English, and Henry received a handsome pension to withdraw.

"However, another condition of this treaty of Etaples will force Charles to cease and desist aiding any of England's enemies, and my fear is that Henry looks upon you as a foe because of your rank and obvious claim to the English crown. It is my duty,

as a loyal sister of your deceased father, to warn you that if you remain in France any longer, Charles may have no alternative but to surrender you to King Henry as part of this agreement. It goes without saying that those faithful followers who have joined you there are also in grave danger. I therefore beg you, nephew, to make haste and come to my court at Malines, where you will be among friends. I shall look forward with all my heart to giving you a warm welcome.

"If all goes well here, and my son-in-law accepts you as Edward's son, then Henry must look to his crown."

She dared not add that Maximilian is not pleased that Henry treated with France and thus is ill disposed towards the king at this point. But could she win Maximilian over? He might balk at providing resources for an invasion of England, she knew, and he needed to protect his trade with her homeland. Despite her loyalty to her English family, Margaret had never shirked her duty to Burgundy, and if her son-in-law forbade her to help Richard she would not gainsay him. She dared not say in the letter what else she had arranged in case Maximilian refused his support: she had been treating with James of Scotland on her nephew's behalf through the faithful Lord Lovell, and as James would like nothing more than to irritate Henry, he was not averse to receiving the so-called duke of York at his court. From there, it would be easy to invade . . . but she was running ahead of herself, she knew, and she sighed.

"Prepare your bags and make haste, dearest Richard, before Charles decides you are a problem.

"Your devoted aunt," she hesitated, pen poised over the paper, and then signed herself, "Margaret of England."

23

England

March and April were blustery and rainy and then, early in June, the king at Kenilworth learned of a treaty signed by Charles of France and Maximilian, effectively ending the war between the two that had ravaged the countryside upon their borders for more than fifteen years.

June was also filled with rumors of an invasion by the man who was causing Henry concern and embarrassment from the Burgundian court, where he was being treated as a royal guest. Henry's spies had scoured the Low Countries in search of clues to this obvious puppet of Margaret of Burgundy; Henry was desperate to find anything that would be plausible enough to stop the murmurings up and down England of a York revival. Indeed, there had been a few hangings when men had even dared gather together to whisper Richard, Duke of York's name. Then when Sir Robert Clifford, one of Henry's own household, flew the coop to the young duke's side, Henry knew he must act. He secured the eastern ports against other defections or invasion and sent his ships to intercept those from Burgundy who were said to be carrying messages back and forth to James of Scotland.

"If only we had corpses," Grace heard him grouse to Bess one day in the spring, when the court had moved to Warwick Castle. "Your Aunt Margaret keeps taunting me to show her the princes' bodies."

"Aye, and because you reversed Uncle Richard's bastardy act against us all, you have created a legitimate prince, if he be alive," Bess had said, riling Henry more.

"I need not be reminded of it, my lady," he snapped at her, and Bess had fallen silent.

Now it was the end of June and Cecily had begged the queen's leave to return to Hellowe with her attendants for the rest of the summer, which Bess was gracious to give, albeit reluctantly. "I love your company, sisters," she had said on the day they left. "You will be sorely missed."

Grace would be glad to see the warm stone Lincolnshire manor house set among trees again. It had been almost two years since she had been there, and she hoped this time Cecily would make good on her original promise to find Grace and Tom a house of their own. She hugged herself. She was convinced she was with child, although she could not be certain, for after the *fausse couche* in March her courses had been none too regular. She thought back on that sad day when, after missing two courses, her bile had risen violently and, as she ran to the garderobe to vomit the warm blood had coursed down her legs and she knew she was losing the baby. Not heeding the mess she had made of her favorite blue gown, she collapsed onto the hard wooden seat and felt the tiny life she and Tom had created slip down the shoot, to be carted away by the gong farmer on his next round. She could not control her weeping, and Cecily found her there half an hour later mourning her loss.

"Certes, Grace, do not grieve so hard. I have had several false starts, but then I conceived two healthy daughters, in truth. This is your first time to conceive, is it not? Aye, then 'tis often the case that a womb is not ripe enough to form a child. I promise you, you will be more fortunate next time, and at least you know you are fertile." She talked and stroked Grace's hair, which had come unbound from under her coif and tumbled around her tear-stained face. "Would you like me to fetch Tom, dearest?"

Nay, Grace had shaken her head. She had not even dared to tell Tom she was pregnant yet, for fear of tempting fate. She had seen a lone magpie the week before, hopping down the path in front of her, and her heart had jumped into her throat. "Good morning Master Magpie, how's your wife?" she had murmured, but certes, it had not broken the bad luck.

"Be of good cheer, I beg of you," Cecily told her. "Imagine the grief a mother knows when she has held the child and then loses it. Her grief is truer, do you not agree?"

It was what Grace needed to hear. She wiped her eyes and took the bundle of clean squares of linen Cecily offered.

"I shall arrange for a bathtub to be brought for you. You will feel better," Cecily said as she slipped out of the cold stone alcove.

Cis had been right, Grace now thought. Her sadness had not lingered, and here she was, not three months later, already believing she was with child again. She still would not tell Tom yet, she decided. He would treat her with the utmost care, she thought with a smile, and she had enjoyed their nights of lovemaking until Lord Welles had moved on to Kenilworth with the king and Cecily had asked to go home.

Grace took great joy in making herself useful on the farm that belonged to Hellowe manor, and the head gardener gave her a small plot of land to work as she pleased. She and Edgar planted peas, leeks and beans, and she was often to be found there, bent double, with her skirts caught up in her belt, weeding and watering the tiny plants as they sprouted through the rich Lincolnshire soil. With one or two heartsease blooms stuck in the ribbon of her wide straw hat, and with her little greyhound puppy capering around her, she was a familiar figure in the fields, the cow byre and the sheep dip. They were close enough to the coast that Grace could swear she smelled the sea on windy days, and she began to feel a part of the gentle hills populated by hundreds of sheep—the wool from which had made the Welles family fortune.

One sultry morning in late June, after breaking their fast and saying morning prayers, Cecily watched her go from her solar window with a twinge of envy. She wished she had something she was passionate about to pass the monotonous days of summer. Not even Thomas Kyme was in the vicinity to dally with—he was tending to his business affairs in London for a month, and she missed him. She spent an hour or so playing with her two little girls, but that got tedious so she donned her pattens over her shoes and decided to see what Grace was doing.

As she passed the large dovecote and went under the archway into the kitchen gardens, she heard horsemen cantering up the stony drive. Calling to Grace to hurry back, she crossed the courtyard to the mounting block to await the visitors' arrival with impatience. Finally, something to break the routine, she thought.

Grace heard her call and let down her skirts, wiped her sweating forehead and told Edgar to keep weeding. Edgar rolled his eyes, but she ignored him. She knew he considered gardening beneath him, but with only a few horses in the stable and Welles's grooms to tend them, there was not much else for him to do. Grace gave him a stern finger-wagging, and he went back to work. She called to Freya, who had her nose in a rabbit hole, and went to join Cecily as fast as her clogs would allow.

The two men had just dismounted when Grace gave a cry of delight, as she saw Tom's mop of yellow hair over the saddle of one horse. Hearing her voice, he gave his groom the reins and strode across the yard to take her in his arms, knocking off her hat. After kissing her several times with no thought of propriety, he set her down, laughing.

"If you could only see your face, my dearest," he said, taking out a rather shabby kerchief and wiping a mud clot from her cheek. " 'Tis clear you wasted no time in returning to the peasant life. And I love you for it," he exclaimed, kissing her again, this time on the forehead.

"By Saint Sibylline!" Grace said, ignoring him as she stared at the piece of cloth in her hand. " 'Tis the kerchief I made for you at Sheriff Hutton. You have kept it all this time?" She remembered with a tiny pang that she had last seen its duplicate in John's hand in prison, but she had learned finally that John was in her past and that her present and future stood, nodding foolishly, by her side. "I am humbled," she said softly, as she moistened a corner with her own spittle and let him dab at her face with it. "But what brings you at a gallop—besides me, certes!"

"Aye, Tom, what news have you? Not bad, I hope," Cecily said, joining them. "Does my husband miss me?" she asked, mimicking a child and grinning. "Come, let us find you some refreshment; 'tis murderously hot out here. Grace, how can you abide toiling all day in the sun?"

"I don't think about it, Cis. There is so much to do, and every day God's gift of the sun brings forth my plants. How can I complain?" Grace said, picking up her hat. She tucked her arm in Tom's and followed Cecily up the steps and into the cool hall of the manor house.

Tom had two letters: one was to Cecily from Jack, and the second was from none other than the queen—to both of them. "Her grace knew my lord Welles was sending me to check that all was well at Hellowe, and she gave me this to give to you because, she said, 'I miss my sisters.' " Tom looked up eagerly when Cecily's steward ushered in two servants with pitchers of ale and some meat pies. Then he stood by discreetly.

Cecily ignored her husband's missive and cracked open Bess's seal. "Come sit by me, Grace. Let us see what Bess says." As the two women pored over the fine script on the parchment, their eyes widened, and Grace let out a long breath.

Tom watched them, puzzled. " 'Tis not bad news, I hope, my lady," he said.

Cecily let out a peal of her inimitable laughter, aware that the steward and two servants were very much within earshot. "Bad news? Nay. She writes that his grace the king lost a fortune, including one of his favorite rings, in two card games called Plunder and Pillage. What perfect names, don't you think? She says she wishes we could be with her because his grace is in such ill humor." And she laughed again.

Grace stared at her, aghast, before her open mouth managed to discharge some facsimile of merry laughter to fob off the servants. How could Cecily lie so blatantly? she wondered. Did she not fear the flames of Hell? Grace still remembered every lie she had told and prayed daily for forgiveness.

Tom frowned. "I am surprised," he said. "Her grace the queen seemed anxious when she approached me and asked me to make sure I did not lose the letter along my path."

Grace caught his eye and frowned, while Cecily jumped to her feet and dismissed the steward with a wave. "Let us inspect Grace's garden, if you are refreshed, Tom. I was on my way there when you arrived." She led the way outside and read her own letter as they walked.

Once in the seclusion of the garden, after making sure that Edgar was busy with a cartful of manure at the other end, Cecily read Tom the relevant passage from Bess's letter.

"I promised our mother before she died that I would allow Grace to go to our lady aunt's court in Burgundy and find what she could about this imposter. It has been weighing on me that we are dishonoring our mother and father, as well as our brother, if it indeed be he, and I cannot sit by and not know. The king knows my mind on this but he is loath to allow any of us but Grace to travel at this dangerous time. But as a boon"—Cecily paused to harrumph—"he agreed that if Grace reports faithfully to us what she sees and hears, Henry will sanction a visit to Aunt Margaret under the guise of an aunt's wish to meet her niece."

Tom whistled. "Praise be they do not know you have been before," he said, pulling Grace close. He did not say it aloud, but he was impressed that Cecily had kept her peace on this; she was not known for her ability to hold her tongue. "I pray they never find out," he finished.

"Or 'tis the rack for you, my girl!" Cecily joked, seeing Grace's worried look. "Let me continue. 'I think Aunt Margaret will allow this particular visit, because if she is dissembling about the man, she would refuse to receive any of his sisters who knew him as a boy. Grace has never seen him and thus will not know one way or the other.' She is clever, our Bess, I'll give her that," Cecily said.

"I wonder what made her change her mind," Grace said. "She was so adamant he was an imposter every time we talked."

Tom wiped his brow. The sun was hot and his worsted jacket was making him sweat uncomfortably. He took it off, loosed the ties of his shirt underneath and looked around for some shade. "There is more to this story, but if we may find a cooler spot, I would be grateful."

Cecily led the way to a pond with a bubbling spring. "Hellowe, or Heghelow in the old English, is from *belle eau* in French," Cecily explained as they removed their shoes and stockings, sat around the mossy edge of the lake and slipped their feet into its cool water. "It means beautiful water, and I suppose this was it." With its border of yellow-flag iris and loosestrife and the ash trees shading it, the small lake was indeed a lovely spot. "But I interrupted you, Tom. Pray tell us more."

"It seems Henry's spies uncovered a tale of a young boy from Tournai—in Hainault, part of the Burgundian territories—whose father was naught but a boatman on the river there. He was taken from his parents at a young age by the bishop of that city, and from there it seems he disappeared. He went by the name of Piers or Pierrequin Werbecque or perhaps Osbeck. Here in England he is being called Perkin Warbeck." Tom paused as the news was digested by his companions.

"I don't believe it," Cecily scoffed. "How could Aunt Margaret be duped like that? How could he have learned the graces of a prince by being a boatman's son? 'Tis preposterous!"

"Certes, he is not a boatman's son, Cis," Grace said softly. "Aunt Margaret told me of our brother being safely hid in the castle at Guisnes and now being found. John believed it, too. 'Tis why Henry tortured and killed him. We had it from Sir Edward Brampton, who had just returned from Calais and came to the abbey. When I was at Malines, our aunt was convinced 'twas Dickon—even though, 'tis true, she had not yet set eyes on him." She shook her head. "Nay, I fear Henry is grasping at straws."

During the ensuing pause, Tom put a blade of grass between his thumbs and blew a raucous note with it. A large frog hopped off a lily pad and into the water with a plop and, across the pond, a heron lifted effortlessly into the air.

Cecily frowned. "I cannot conceive why Henry would condone this visit by Grace. It would appear to be tempting fate."

"You are wrong!" Grace exclaimed, the light dawning. "I think this means Bess does believe this is Dickon, and Henry needs her on his side. Certes, he will expect me to report publicly that the man is an imposter. I may only be a bastard member of the family, but I am still a member of the family, and I will give Henry's disavowal of Richard credence, don't you see?"

Cecily let out a long breath of accord. "Aye, and Bess will believe *you*, Henry guesses. I think you have the measure of it, Grace."

Tom grinned and patted his wife's knee. "Not just a pretty face, are you, sweetheart?"

Cecily watched an iridescent dragonfly hover near her knee. "Then it seems to me you must prepare to return to our formidable aunt, my dear sister. Oh—and I forgot to tell you the rest of the letter, Tom. Bess wishes you to escort Grace, *naturellement*, as well as two or more armed guards from here for good measure. Henry is sending envoys to Maximilian, and you may take ship with them. I assume you will also want Edgar?"

Grace looked at Tom. He was plainly astonished by this new turn of events but did not say anything except, "When are we to leave?"

GRACE AND TOM were shocked when, during the voyage, they realized Henry had duped Bess by agreeing to send Grace to see this Perkin Warbeck. Tom had learned from one of the clerks traveling with the envoys that his master, William Warham, was coming to expose Perkin as a fraud in public at the court and shame Maximilian and Margaret into renouncing the man and giving him up to Henry.

"So much for the 'great love' Henry bears her," Grace scoffed when Tom relayed this piece of news at an inn in Sluis, the port closest to Bruges. She pondered the information as they readied for bed, and suddenly she let out a little cry. "I have it!" she said. "Henry is so certain that Warham's brilliant oration will convince everyone of Dickon's falsity that I will not dare to deny it." Tom gave a rueful sigh and took off his jacket; he had other, more lusty thoughts on his mind than unraveling King Henry's twisted one. But Grace rattled on. "I have heard Warham speak, and he is magnificent, in truth. Aye, Henry thinks I will be forced to return home and confirm the man is Perkin Warbeck and not Richard of York or be ridiculed. Ah, but he is a whey-faced vassal! And he is no match for me," she announced smugly.

They had taken lodgings separate from Henry's official party and were told they were welcome to travel with the envoys to Malines upon the morrow. When the innkeeper and his wife learned they were lodging the half sister to England's queen, and niece to their beloved duchess, they gave up their quarters to Grace and Tom with much bowing and awed glances.

Believing her puzzling done, Tom unlaced his wife's bodice and cupped his hands over her breasts, kissing the nape of her neck. She squirmed from his hold and swung round to face him. "I am in no mood for loving, Tom. Henry has put us in a difficult position." She frowned, still suspicious of Henry's motives. "I have in no way abandoned the possibility that my brother Dickon is alive and at Aunt Margaret's court. Until I am given proof that he is an imposter, he has my undying loyalty. A pox on Henry— he is just afraid."

But Tom ignored her rejection and bent to kiss her neck, lifting her chemise and sliding his hand between her thighs, making her forget Henry, Warham and even Dickon in his ardent pursuit of her undivided attention.

THE AUDIENCE CHAMBER at the ducal palace was crowded when the English embassy arrived two days later. Grace and Tom were eyed curiously by the bystanders nearest the door, where they chose to remain unheralded while William Warham and Edward Poynings approached the dais and gave their names to the chamberlain. Sixteen-year-old Philip, duke of Burgundy, sat ramrod straight in his high-backed throne under a purple and gold satin canopy, the double-headed eagle coat of arms on the wall behind his head. Grace was struck by his beauty—he had an oval face with dark eyes, a strong nose and a full mouth, all framed by fine golden hair falling to his shoulders, enhancing his fair complexion. Beside him sat his stepgrandmother Margaret in a deep blue belted gown, its fashionable square neck trimmed with pearls, and the kirtle underneath of pale blue silk.

A hush came over the court as the two Englishmen knelt before Philip, who had only recently been given the reins of government by his father and regent, Maximilian. Philip acknowledged the envoys with a nod and extended his hand for them to kiss. All was pleasant and courteous until Warham rose and was given leave to speak.

After the usual high-flown platitudes and greetings on behalf of Henry to the duke in passable French, Warham got to the meat of the matter. "It has come to our notice that you are harboring a man pretending to be the late Prince Richard, duke of York. He is, in truth, a commoner—*sordido genere*," he said, using Latin for emphasis. The painted hall reverberated with a gasp of astonishment, and all eyes turned to Margaret. Grace saw her aunt blanch, her eyes narrow and her hands grip the arms of her chair so tightly that her knuckles showed as white as the sleeves of her chemise. Afraid he might be silenced, Warham plunged on: "The real duke of York perished with his older brother at the hands of their uncle, the usurper Richard of Gloucester. Indeed it would have served King Richard no purpose to kill the older and let the younger live to challenge him—do you not agree, your grace? It is therefore impossible that this man, who we now know to be naught but a boatman's son from Tournai—" Another gasp went up and whisperings began, and Philip became noticeably agitated. He looked to his councilors, grouped to the side of the dais, but court etiquette forbade them from interfering with the message from a foreign herald.

But Philip had reckoned without Margaret, who got to her feet and, pointing an accusing finger at Warham, cried: "You may tell your master King Henry that when he can show us the bodies of my nephews we will consider his words. Tell him that!" And she sat down hard, her legs giving way. Philip's cheeks were tinged with pink and he was clearly at a loss, but his upbringing—which, ironically, had been carried out mostly by Margaret herself—would not allow him to stop the Englishman. He waved an elegant beringed hand Warham's way. Warham, well aware of the hostile vibrations in the room, bowed and countered Margaret's words by announcing, "My master, his grace King Henry of England, invites you to come and visit the chapel where they are buried." At which Margaret let out a barely suppressed guffaw.

"What lie is this?" Grace murmured, and Tom laid a hand on her arm to silence her.

Warham now delivered the most damning portion of his message, his voice less certain now: " 'Tis well known to the king's grace and all the people of England that Madame la Duchesse has regularly contrived to discover scoundrel nephews from among her brothers' children." He cited Lambert Simnel, posing as the earl of Warwick. "Certes, this Perkin Warbeck and the other are naught but boys fit for washing pots and"—he paused, eyeing a possible escape, before he gave Henry's final pronouncement—"the fruit of her own secret pregnancies."

Bedlam ensued as Margaret staggered to her feet and would have stumbled down the dais in her hurry to strike the unfortunate Warham had Philip not restrained her, while Edward Poynings propelled the stunned Warham through the jostling crowd, which hissed and spat at them but did not deter their departure. They passed close to Grace, who turned away, hoping they would not single her and Tom out, but Warham had his hands up to protect his face and Poynings's eyes were fixed squarely on the door.

"What insults!" Grace whispered. "How could Henry have ordered such insults to be cast at her in public? 'Tis monstrous!" She tried to see over the people in front of her to the dais, but once again she cursed her lack of inches. "Can you see her, Tom? Poor Aunt Margaret. Is she well?"

"Aye, her attendants are with her and Philip is conferring with his councilors. Let us go into the garden and wait while I leave word with her chamberlain that you are here." He gave her his arm and they withdrew from the hall, thinking on the extraordinary scene they had just witnessed.

. . .

MARGARET WAS ASTONISHED but delighted to receive her niece at her
court in Malines later that day. Seemingly undeterred by her earlier ordeal,
she greeted Grace with affection in her elegant solar, its wide casements
overlooking the peaceful gardens. After stooping to kiss Grace's cheek, she
turned to Tom and gave him an avising that made his hair stand on end.

"So this is your husband, Grace," she said finally. "He is about the same
height as your father, my dear." Observing the two of them standing side
by side, she gave a rueful sigh and remarked, "Such a waste of a tall man."
She turned and sank down gratefully into her favorite chair. Her legs hurt
her these days, if the truth be known, and her height caused her back to
ache from the moment she rose from her great tester bed to the time she
fell back into it after kneeling in prayer for an hour before she retired. And
to exacerbate the problem, the dramatic events in the great hall had given
her a pounding headache.

"Sit, sit!" she invited Grace, and she sent for refreshment and her headache powders in her accented but perfect French. "Tell me why you are
come at this diplomatically difficult time. Certes, it cannot be for the love
of your old aunt." She went off into a cackle of loud laughter that made her
chief attendant, Henriette, smile. But then she was all seriousness again.
"In truth, I have borne such an insult from Henry's ambassador that I
know not where to throw myself. I dare say Dr. Warham's words were
fed to him by that measle Henry, but he has caused an uproar among our
councilors." She chuckled. "In truth, I wanted to kill the prating pizzle."

Grace was shocked by Margaret's coarse language, but Tom hid a grin.
"We were there, Madame la Grande," Grace said. "We could not believe
what we were hearing, although, in truth, we knew a little of what Warham would say from a conversation Tom had with a clerk on the ship."

Margaret frowned. "If Henry thinks he will embarrass Philip into surrendering Richard, he is wrong. Philip is my grandson, and he will stand
by me, mark my words. Everyone here believes Richard is the duke of
York—and I do above all. He is my darling boy!"

Grace seized the opening. "That is why I am come, Aunt Margaret,"
Grace said, reaching down to scratch the ears of a wolfhound that had chosen to lay its huge head on her foot. "The king and—more important—the
queen want me to judge for myself if he be our brother or no. Is he here?"

Margaret contemplated the tips of her steepled fingers before lifting her eyes to Grace's face, observing the flush on the young woman's cheeks. I would not be surprised if she were with child, she thought. How she had longed for a child those years she was married to Charles. She had even thought she had carried her lover's child at one point, but she had long since decided that God saw fit to punish that adultery by making her barren. And then along came Jehan, her secret boy—her dearest boy. And through several twists of fate, and a little careful planning on her part, she was now able to love him publicly.

"When I knew the envoy was expected from England, I sent Richard to my dower property of Dendermonde for safety," she finally replied. "I do not trust Henry as far as I can see a flea on a dog's ear! I would not put it past him to kidnap Richard and smuggle him back to England. My kind Philip has given my nephew a bodyguard, with a knight of the Golden Fleece as their captain, so he should be in good hands. I will take you there myself in a few days, if you can wait." She yawned, and Grace saw she had lost several teeth.

"Forgive us, *madame*," Grace said. "We are tiring you. We can come back later." She rose, waking the dog on her toes, which scrambled to its feet and ambled over to lick Margaret's hand. Grace longed to inspect the beautiful gardens laid out so neatly below while the sun shone.

"Nay, I should like to take a walk with you," Margaret replied, feeding the dog a sweetmeat. "Certes, Samson would like a walk, too, wouldn't you boy?" She rose and Samson wagged his tail and barked with excitement. "Henriette, pray have someone fetch my hat and then accompany us outdoors—and don't tell my doctors. I should not walk when 'tis hot, they tell me, or I shall fall prey to the plague," she told Grace. "But as 'tis ill-advised to sleep during the day as well, I know not which regimen to follow." She chuckled. "Come, let us brave the heat. You have much to tell me about my family. Tom, you will allow me to steal Grace for an hour, will you not?" It was a rhetorical question and Tom could do no more than bow and kiss her hand before leaving them.

The roses were a riot of color and Grace ran from bush to bush to compare each different scent. "It is so beautiful here, aunt. Is it your favorite home?" Grace asked.

"One of my favorites," Margaret said, enjoying her niece's company and joie de vivre more than she could have imagined. "But I like Binche the best. It is far from the center of things in Hainault, and I can be myself there." She led the way through the beds of flowers, and gardeners took off their straw hats and bowed as they passed by. "But I wanted to talk to you privately for two reasons, my dear. The first—and I hope it is not too painful for you to relive—is to ask how Johnny died? We heard news of it, but much later, and with little detail."

Grace pricked her thumb on a thorn as the unexpected question momentarily jolted her, and she sucked on it to compose her thoughts. "I saw him the day before his execution, and he was sore afraid," she told Margaret softly. "Cecily and I gave him what comfort we could, but it broke my heart to leave him." She paused and bent down to pick a heartsease, the violet and pink petals shining in the sun. "Then I was foolish enough to go to Smithfield," she said with a catch in her throat. "I swooned when they put the noose about his neck, so Edgar carried me away."

Margaret gasped and turned to face Grace. "You thought you could watch him die? You brave child. You loved him, did you not?"

Grace nodded, tears not far away. "As much as one can love for the first time, in truth. But he loved me only as a sister," she said.

"Oftimes, 'tis a longer-lasting love, Grace, so treasure it," Margaret told her.

"I promised I would not desert him," Grace whispered, "and I tried, truly I did. He saw me—from up there on the scaffold—and then he saw his mother. Ah, 'twas pitiful, and when he cried out to her I fainted with the horror of it all. So I was not so brave after all." Grace finally let the tears fall, but they were for herself and her weakness rather than for John. She sniffed and wiped her nose on the soft linen sleeve of her chemise, having unlaced the tight long sleeves of her overdress and left them in the solar to be cooler outdoors. "I learned later—certes, from his mother herself—that he had died by the noose and not from the disemboweling. Dame Haute had paid the executioners to let John die quickly."

"You kept your promise to him," Margaret soothed. "And now it seems you are fortunate to have a good man who loves you, my dear." She took Grace's arm and stepped across the manicured grass to seek out her favorite seat under an arbor.

"But I did not keep my promise, your grace," Grace suddenly remembered, sitting down beside her aunt. "He gave me a letter that was destined for—"

"Lord Lovell?" Margaret finished. "Aye, never fear. Another with the correct intelligence went a more secret route and arrived safely."

Grace tensed. "You mean John carried false information? He died carrying false information?" Anger rose in her chest and constricted her last words. "He was tortured, you know."

Margaret sighed. "You have much to learn about the ways of politics, my child. John was insistent upon returning home; he chafed at being here, for all home meant danger. I thought the harmless letter might throw Henry off the track, and I told John to destroy it if he was captured. I am sorry if he did not do as he was instructed." She took Grace's anguished face between her long, slender fingers and looked her straight in the eye. "There was no need for John to be tortured—if he had given it up once he was caught and feigned surprise at its contents, he might have escaped Henry's wrath. But you must understand, Grace, Henry was delighted to have an excuse to rid himself of Richard's son—bastard or no. The lad was destined to die the day Henry killed Richard on Redemore Plain." She dropped her hands and clenched her teeth: "As I believe all sons of the house of York are destined to do—unless we can unseat Henry. Can you not see the truth of this?"

But Grace's thoughts were still with John and the callous way he had been sacrificed. She did not know whether she believed her aunt or not. Her thoughts ran rampant wondering what awful wiles women of noble blood would employ to achieve their goals. Elizabeth Woodville, Margaret of Anjou, Scraggy Maggie and now her Aunt Margaret did not seem above scheming without regard for human life or limb. I do not belong among such people, Grace thought miserably. How I wish I could go back to the convent! But in her heart of hearts she knew she was deceiving herself. I do belong here; I am one of the York family and proud of it. And, she told herself now, I know I belong to Tom. I would not change anything, in truth.

Margaret waited for her niece's anger to subside before saying: "And now for the second reason I wanted to talk to you." She glanced at her attendants, who were standing at a discreet distance, and lowered her voice. "They do not speak English, but I never know. I can never be alone at this court, God have mercy. I hope one day a future duchess will see to it that things change, but I am too old to try," she said, shrugging. "But now, I need to know how the wind blows in England for Richard, my nephew and *your* half brother."

Grace pulled herself together and brushed the last of her tears aside. "There is much unrest in England, so I understand. There have been several hangings connected with Dickon's name, and some of Henry's own household have left the country."

Margaret nodded, smiling. "Henry must not be able to sleep these days," she enthused. "Clifford is lately arrived at Dendermonde and is with Richard—Dickon, you call him. Tell me more."

"The queen would not have sent me if she was certain he is not Dickon. Cecily, who is my constant companion, believes he is, but certes, her husband is one of Henry's closest advisers—and his uncle—so we must be careful. Besides, all of my sisters fare well under the Tudor. To exclude the real Richard, he must reverse the act of legitimacy, and then his queen and all her sisters would be like me again—bastards! Poor Henry, he is caught over a barrel." She laughed grimly. "And my mentor, the queen dowager, was convinced Dickon had survived. There had been doctors' reports that Ned was diseased—the jawbone, I heard—and Elizabeth said she had dreamed he was dead and so believed it." She spread her hands. "But unless a tomb has been uncovered more recently than Tom's quitting Warwick, where Henry was in consultation with Warham about the mission, there is no truth to Warham's statement about finding the princes' corpses."

Margaret let out a harsh laugh. "Just as I thought."

Grace paused and then took courage. "I must ask you, *madame*—for my own peace of mind, as well as to report back to England—how well did you know Dickon before he and Edward disappeared? You returned to England only once since your marriage, and then only for a few months, when Dickon was a small boy. Is it possible you are mistaken?"

Margaret shook her head vehemently, and the few folds of skin beneath her chin wobbled in the way of older women. "As God is my witness, I swear I knew him when I saw him. He is my nephew," she insisted, as the church bells rang for None. "Come, 'tis time to bend our knee in prayer."

Satisfied Margaret was not lying, Grace could hardly wait to meet her long-lost brother.

• • •

GRACE AND TOM were given mounts for their daylong ride to Dendermonde in eastern Flanders, journeying back the way they had come from
Bruges. The countryside was flat and fertile and Grace was delighted to
recognize many of her favorite wildflowers along the way. Although the
dowager duchess had told her guests that they would travel with a mere
handful of servants, the cavalcade that set out that hazy morning from
Malines made Grace feel she was on a royal progress. Margaret's escort
was flashy in scarlet, yellow and black, and she was carried on a gilded litter pulled by two of the largest horses she had ever seen. "They are bred
right here in Flanders," Margaret said. One might think she has forgotten
she is English, Grace mused, hearing the pride in her aunt's voice. But
she knew better. The number of white roses woven among her signature
marguerites on the canopy and curtains of the litter proclaimed her a
daughter of York, and when Grace had admired an enameled white rose
that Margaret always wore, she had been told it was a gift from her brother
Edward and Elizabeth upon her departure from England in Sixty-eight.
"So I would never forget," she explained. "And I never have."

Ragged children ran alongside the litter when the group passed through
hamlets, calling Margaret's name, her charity legendary in the region. She
did not disappoint them and flung coins into their waiting hands, pity in
her eyes.

"Are you anxious about this meeting?" Tom asked as they were told by
Guillaume de la Baume, Margaret's brawny chevalier, that the spires in
front of them were of the palace and the village church. Tom sat his horse
as if he had been born to it, and Grace enjoyed riding pillion behind him,
even if it was hard to carry on a conversation. "I know you hardly slept a
wink."

"Did I keep you awake, my dear? Aye, I confess I am looking forward to
this with a mixture of excitement and fear," Grace answered.

"Fear? He cannot harm us, Grace. Why are you frightened?"

"That I shall make a mistake. I want to be sure this is my brother. Can
you not see? 'Tis a heavy responsibility, for it may have a wide-reaching
effect on all our futures." She felt him pat the hand that was grasping him
round the waist and she snuggled into his back, once again loving the
safe haven his presence gave her. Little by little during the journey from
Hellowe to Malines, Tom had come to the reluctant conclusion that this

young man who had reappeared as if from the grave was indeed Richard of York. Otherwise, why was Henry—and therefore his master and others of Henry's council—so afraid of him? No proof existed of the boys' deaths since their disappearance—no confessions, no secret orders and, above all, no bodies. King Richard must have sent them somewhere for safekeeping, he reasoned, or if the older one had died naturally, then the younger had been spirited away.

Chevalier de la Baume led Margaret up the steps of the palace and through the studded oak door into the great hall, and they were followed by Margaret's attendants and then Grace and Tom with her new maid, Enid. Standing by the fireplace at the far end of the hall, and the center of attention, was a young man with fair hair enjoying a joke with several companions, among whom Tom recognized Sir Robert Clifford.

The entrance of the dowager duchess brought the conversation to an abrupt halt, and all bowed over soft leather ankle boots, their sleeves trailing to the ground. Separating himself from the group, Richard came forward, happy to see his aunt. After executing another flourishing bow, his bright red hat showing off a rich brooch with a deep red ruby and three teardrop pearls, he went to kiss Margaret on both cheeks. Her affection for him was manifest in the way she stroked his cheek and played with his hair. He looked beyond her to where Grace and Tom now stood alone and moved confidently to greet the newcomers, still holding Margaret's hand. It seemed Margaret had not warned him whom she was bringing with her, as if she wanted to test him. His smile, therefore, was genuine, and his hand was extended in friendship as his associates moved closer to hear the introduction.

Grace found her knees wobbling and her heart racing, and she was not aware she was staring at him until he cocked his head and felt to see if his hat was on straight. Dear god, she thought as a memory stirred, can it be the man from that long-ago dream? She blushed and gave him a graceful curtsy. Tom bowed, his soft felt bonnet over his heart.

"God's greeting," Richard said in French, bowing only slightly, as befitted a duke of the royal blood. "Your grace, who are these charming visitors?"

"This, my dearest boy, is your half sister, the Lady Grace," Margaret told him gleefully. "And the handsome man at her side is her husband,

Master Tom Gower. I have that right?" she looked at Tom, who nodded. "It seems your father was busy the year you were born, Richard. You two are a brace of months apart in age, but you have never met because Grace was discovered only after your father died. She grew up among nuns until your aunt Elizabeth rescued her," she explained.

He was fully informed now, and the fine eyebrows shot up and a smile—it almost looked like relief, Grace thought—suffused his clean-shaven face. Indeed, so invisible was Richard's beard, Grace would have guessed he was younger than his twenty years. But it was his small stature, too, that made him seem so youthful, she decided. There was an odd cast to his left eye—Grace wondered if it was a trick of the light—and the brow was creased. Certes, she breathed with mounting excitement, like my father's.

"My sister? My half sister?" Richard cried enthusiastically, his gaze sweeping her from head to toe. "God's mercy, but I have a beauty for a sister," he said, making Grace blush again.

She smiled happily at him. "God's greeting to you, too, brother," she replied in less confident French. "If it will not offend you, may we speak English?"

She thought she detected a tiny pause before he answered with a mere whisper of an accent, "With all my heart, sister." Certes, he had an excuse, Grace told herself. He had been shut away in the castle of Guisnes for so many years, and perhaps he had had French guardians. He continued to smile, one corner of his mouth turning up more easily than the other. "I am delighted to see one of my own family. It has been so long, I know not if I would recognize them or they me." He turned to Tom and held out his hand. "God's greeting, Master Gower. And I must present my loyal friends: Anthony de la Forsa; Master Taylor and his son, John; and perhaps you know Sir Robert Clifford—lately come from England—and George Neville." The introductions were made and the men excused before Richard turned to Margaret. "Come, *madame*, let us go somewhere less public."

Grace felt giddy. He is my brother, she exulted; it must be why I feel thus, and he *was* the man in her dream, she was almost certain. She took Tom's arm, and he whispered: "Afraid now, Grace? You should see your face; 'tis as readable as a page of a book."

"Oh, pish!" came the response.

Richard led the way with Margaret to the palace's private apartments
and the small group was escorted by two of his new bodyguards in the
York colors of murrey and blue. Grace nudged Tom to take notice, but he
was busy admiring the vaulted ceilings and brilliantly painted columns
of the large rooms they passed through. Richard was almost half a head
shorter than his tall aunt, but as they conversed together, Grace could see
a similarity in their profiles. Elizabeth had told her Margaret resembled
her brother, Edward, more than she did her other brothers, but having
met only Uncle Richard, Grace could not know. It did seem to her that
they had an affection for each other that surely could only come from their
being kin. She gazed happily at Richard's back. After all this time and all
the rumors, conjectures and doubts, she was finally face to face with him.
That it was her half brother Richard, she had not a doubt. But she knew
she must tread carefully and search for further proof before Bess—and,
certes, Henry—would believe her. She hoped she would have enough time
to make that possible.

THEY DINED INFORMALLY in Margaret's solar well into the summer
night, the last rays of the sun disappearing just before nine o'clock. Two
musicians had played while they ate cold roast duck, rabbit pie, flampayns
and custards, washing it down with wine from Beaune, in the southern
part of the duchy. Comfits of dates and ginger in sugar and wafers were
brought in and were accompanied by the spicy hippocras that comprised
the voide. Once the platters and trenchers were removed and the musicians had withdrawn, Margaret had Richard sit on a footstool next to her
and invited Tom and Grace to use the large satin cushions on the floor.
Henriette and her husband, Guillaume, were their sole attendants that
night and sat conversing quietly in the window seat.

"I trust both of them with my life," Margaret told her young audience.
"And as neither has bothered to learn English since being in my service—
let me see—twenty or more years now, we may speak freely." She ruffled
Richard's curls as if he were a young boy, and Grace noticed that Richard
seemed not to notice. She could not imagine Tom allowing his mother,
let alone an aunt, caress his head thus. It puzzled her, but not for long, as
they talked for another hour about the English court and Richard's other
sisters. At one point early on Grace mentioned Elizabeth and, almost as

if he had needed the nudging, Richard's demeanor changed, as though he were mustering the courage to ask about his mother's recent death. "Aunt Margaret tells me you were one of only two attending my mother in her exile. In so much as I remember her, I thank you for your good service to her," he told Grace. "She was a dutiful mother to us all."

"What do you remember of her, Richard?" Grace asked, thinking his description of Elizabeth a trifle odd. "I confess most of what I know of you is from her, and she talked about your merry humor and how you loved to sing. Our sister, the queen, had a different story." She chuckled. "She said when you were in sanctuary, you were always underfoot."

Richard nodded. "Aye, certes, I must have been a handful. Perhaps I missed my brother. I still enjoy music, although I play the virginals now rather than sing." He did not pursue the subject but rose and went to the bowl of fruit and eyed the array of cherries, plums and oranges. Grace held her breath, then gulped when he selected an orange. Hadn't Elizabeth told her that was his favorite fruit? Aye, and that he liked the flavor of mint and hated the smell of cloves. She must be watchful while she was here.

"How were you taken from the Tower, my lord?" Tom asked suddenly, making everyone jump, as he had said very little.

"*Vir sapit qui pauca loquitur*," Richard remarked wryly. Tom looked to Grace for a translation, but it was Richard who helped him out, while expertly peeling the orange with his bone-handled knife. " 'Tis a wise man that speaks little."

Before he could answer Tom's question, however, Margaret preempted him. "He was drugged and does not remember, do you, Richard?" she said.

"Aye, aunt," he agreed. "When I awoke, I was on a ship. I was told I was being sent away to safety by 'friends.' As you may imagine, I was too young and afraid to object. I was moved from place to place, and then I was at Guisnes, where I was treated well but sworn to secrecy until the time came to tell my story. That is all there is to tell."

"And Edward," Grace said softly. "Where was Ned?"

"He was put to death," Richard said dully. "They said he had a wasting sickness and would not survive the journey." He sucked on an orange slice and began to pace about the room. "I never saw him again," he murmured, and Grace imagined she heard a catch in his throat.

"Enough for tonight, *mes enfants*," Margaret said, breaking the mood with forced cheerfulness. " 'Tis trying for Richard to talk about, and I for one need my bed." She turned to Henriette. "Show my niece and her husband to their quarters, *madame*," she instructed in French. "I think you will be comfortable in my granddaughter Margarethe's room, Grace. I hope you like pink?" She laughed, waiting until they had risen before kissing Grace warmly.

In their pink and gold chamber, Tom was grateful for a servant's help in untying his points and removing his padded gipon while Enid readied her mistress for bed. She was as round as Grace was tall, but she did not gossip, possibly because she was silent and did not make friends easily. Cecily had told her that the other servants were probably suspicious of her Welsh origins, but Grace found her respectful, and the woman went about her business deftly and without complaint. She was the perfect maid, Grace had told Cecily, after Matty had been dismissed when it was discovered she carried a child by one of Hellowe's grooms.

Snuggled in Tom's arms, Grace could hardly keep her eyes open. "Certes, I shall sleep well tonight. Is this not the most comfortable bed you have ever been in?" she asked sleepily. "I am so happy, I know not how to thank God for bringing me here, and for my brother's resurrection."

Tom was quiet. He was not passing judgment on Richard of York just yet, as, in Tom's opinion, the story of his escape needed further details. He was, however, impressed that Richard, who Henry claimed was a common boatman's son, spoke Latin.

GRACE AND MARGARET stood at the window overlooking the courtyard to watch the hunters mount their impatient horses for a morning in the woods and fields. Dogs yelped and bayed, straining at the ends of their handlers' leashes to be let free to seek the scent of some unsuspecting quarry. Richard was given a leg up by a groom, and Grace noted the easy way he wore his magnificent royal blue jacket trimmed in gold braid; only one of noble blood could carry off such finery and draw all eyes to him. She found Tom among the group, keeping his mount calm while searching the upper windows for a glimpse of her. She waved when he caught sight of her and blew him a kiss.

Margaret sighed. "I remember on a day like today when I went hunting with my stepdaughter, Mary. How she loved to ride, and how sad that it was what killed her in the end." Then she chuckled. "And I shall tell you a secret, Grace. The day I am remembering was one where I found myself alone with my heart's desire—my one true love—in the middle of the forest."

"Anthony Woodville, was it not, your grace?" Grace said softly. "The queen dowager told me," she said by way of explanation and hoped Margaret would not be angry.

Margaret's bony hand trembled on the window ledge, and a sadness suffused the duchess's face. She nodded. "Aye, 'twas he—my Lancelot." She fingered an ornament on her belt, a bronze marguerite that Grace had noticed before. "That day he wore a gift boldly on his cap that I had given him in secret, and I chided him for it." She shook her head. " 'Twas so many years ago now, and I have not thought of him for a long time. My mind has been full of Richard—my White Rose, I call him." She waved gaily to the man in question, who raised his hat and waved it back. A horn blew in the distance and, with shouts of anticipation and a clattering of hoofs, the party took off while Grace leaned out as far as she could to watch them go.

When the noise died away, Margaret asked, "How do you like your brother, Grace?"

Grace slapped at several flies that seemed to be targeting her face and pulled her head back in. "Certes, I like him very well indeed," she enthused. "He has a bearing that can only come from being a king's son, in truth. He is cultured and pleasant to talk to, and I cannot wait to tell Cecily and Bess all about him."

"And Henry. You must tell Henry, Grace. We must make him believe Richard is Edward's son," Margaret said.

Grace frowned. "Make him believe? I do not need to make him believe. He will see for himself ere long, if I understand correctly. You said last night Richard will one day return, when you have been able to give him the money and the men."

Margaret rubbed her eyes. There was something in the air at Dendermonde that made her eyes itch and water. "Mercy, child! You need not inform Henry of that. Let us see what Henry does when you give him the bad news." She stared at the mantel and gave an unpleasant chuckle.

Grace did not think Margaret would appreciate that she could not tell

Henry anything but what he wanted to hear, so she said: "Do you know him, aunt? He is a cold fish—although I do believe he loves Bess—and mean with his money. He penny-pinches while he governs and yet thinks nothing of gambling vast sums for his own personal amusement. He has hanged more than a dozen men for even talking about Dickon, so afraid he is that men might flock to a York standard again."

"You are very observant, niece. My compliments," Margaret said. "I met Henry of Richmond when I was a girl, but then he was sent away and I only knew his sour-faced mother."

They were ensconced in Margaret's private study—her sanctuary, where only Henriette was allowed to attend her. Seeing Grace peering at her collection of books under lock and key, Margaret handed her the key and told her to help herself. Grace chose a book of St. Brigid's visions, its vivid illuminations of the Nativity depicting a blond Virgin, as described by the saint.

"That was my mother's," Margaret observed. "I read it now, but when I was your age I read Master Chaucer's tales and the French romances. I think Proud Cis your grandmother, despaired of me." She chuckled.

Grace put the book down and sat on a cushion in front of Margaret. "Did you know William Caxton died last year?" she asked. "His apprentice Master de Worde is now the proprietor at the Sign of the Red Pale."

Margaret crossed herself. "He was a good friend," she said sadly. "But he will not be forgotten."

A knock on the door made her brighten. "Ah, it must be time for dinner. Come," she called. Henriette and a second lady spread a spotless white cloth on the table and placed the elegant saltcellar at the head before the many dishes were brought in. As Grace smelled the fish that sat upon one platter, its iridescent eye seeming to stare directly at her, her stomach heaved.

"Your pardon, aunt," she gasped and ran to the tiny garderobe behind the screen in the corner of the room, where she retched into a basin. What is wrong with me? she thought, remembering she had felt ill the morning before. She shivered. Perhaps she had caught the plague? Dear God, no, she prayed, feeling under her arms for any swelling. The sickness passed after a few minutes and she wiped her mouth on a drying cloth and reentered the room.

"I knew I was right," Margaret said, smiling at her. "How long has it been that you are with child, my dear?"

Grace blushed. "Certes, that is why I am ill!" she exclaimed, unconsciously putting a protective hand on her belly. "I have had no one to ask since I suspected. I feared 'twas the plague," she said, relieved. She sat down on the bench at the table, eyeing the food with trepidation. "I was certain before we left England, but I did not want to hope too much, and so I said nothing to anyone—not even Tom," she said shyly. "I had a *fausse couche* earlier this year, you see."

"I lost two babes like that, Grace, so I know the heartache," Margaret answered, patting her niece's hand. "Judging from the healthy glow of you at the moment, however, I am sure all will be well this time, and we shall pray to Saint Elizabeth together for your safe delivery. 'Tis certain you will deliver in winter—under the sign of the goat, which can mean a weakly child—so you must be healthy and strong for the babe to survive. Certes, I think you should go back to England as soon as you can. Too much travel may affect your humors and cannot be good for the child.

"Besides, the sooner you can report on Richard to the English court, the better," she finished, her own ambitions bubbling to the surface again.

Grace gave her a small smile but said nothing.

AND YET MARGARET was loath to let Grace go.

"If Richard were an imposter," Grace reasoned with Tom one wet morning in August, "Aunt Margaret would not risk us staying long enough to unmask him. You cannot deny it."

Tom agreed, although he was distracted. He chafed at lingering in Flanders. He missed his duties with the viscount and worried he would lose his rank if he stayed away much longer. He had pressed Grace to leave a fortnight before, but he had not yet uncovered the true measure of his wife's stubbornness. This time abroad was the longest stretch they had spent together, and he marveled at the change in Grace from their first meeting at Sheriff Hutton. He was at once proud of her spirit and afraid where it might lead. She had risked her life to help John, and it appeared she was in danger of repeating the situation with this so-called duke of York. One minute Tom believed in the man as truly as Grace did, yet in the next he was troubled by him. It was all too neat and tidy, his practical Yorkshire side told him. Aye, he was beautifully mannered, spoke Latin, French and English, sat a horse like a nobleman and was duly knowledgeable about his family and his life before the Tower. And Margaret had accepted him— as had the Irish nobles and the king of France before her. But it seemed to Tom that Richard was too much the perfect prince. It had occurred to Tom, but not to Grace, that they were never allowed to be alone with Richard. Richard's group of courtiers or Margaret was always there to prevent too private a conversation.

Late in their visit Margaret had invited members of several noble families to join them for an evening of feasting and dancing. Margaret hoped the event would send a far-reaching message that King Edward's bastard daughter Grace had accepted Richard as her own brother in front of dozens of influential people. When Margaret waved farewell to her niece one humid August day, she was already thinking about other and more important individuals she needed to win over to her White Rose cause.

Richard graciously bade farewell to the couple and kissed Grace warmly. "Until we meet again, sister," he murmured, "and if God is good, upon English soil."

"Aye, God willing," Grace replied.

"We are counting on you, Lady Grace," Margaret called as the little retinue turned its horses towards the gate.

Tom sighed inwardly. He knew he had the time on the journey home to persuade Grace to tell the king only what he wanted to hear. He did not know she had already made up her mind.

24

Malines

AUGUST 1493

*T*o her most noble catholic majesty Isabella, queen of Castile and Aragon, we *send you greetings from our northern city of Malines and pray God's grace is upon you and your family,"* Margaret dictated to her secretary in high-flown Latin phrases to win over the Spanish queen. Margaret enjoyed using her Latin and took pains with every word.

Richard sat close by her, his eyes fixed on a new painting the duchess had acquired by the Florentine master Botticelli. The Virgin was holding the plump Christ child on her lap and plucking a wheat stalk from the hand of an angel, who stood vigil over them. Did my mother ever look at me with the same glow of pride that Botticelli has so vividly painted into the Madonna's face? Richard wondered. The woman busily writing beside him was the only mother he remembered, and he loved her with all his heart and knew she loved him. It was why he sat here so miserably now, wondering what was to become of him. Could one love so blindly? Every day was exhausting as he acted out the charade in which Margaret had so carefully rehearsed him. After Grace had left—and, he admitted to himself, he had liked Grace greatly—he felt more at ease in his new role than he had thought possible. Was he beginning to believe he was indeed Richard, duke of York? Was there much difference between being the son of the duke of Clarence and Richard, the son of his Uncle Edward? He had never met either man, so what did it matter? He did believe he was Jehan or John, bastard son of Clarence and adopted son of Jehan Werbeque and Nicaise, sometimes called Katherine, de Faro, but it was quite another thing to convince people he was the rightful king of England. He shivered, and Margaret turned to him anxiously. "Are you feverish, dearest boy?" she asked and he shook his head. She smiled. "It must be twenty past the hour and simply an angel passing by," she said and continued with her letter.

"*Last year, the earls of Desmond and Kildare, the chief lords of Ireland, wrote to me that the second son of Edward, late King of England, my most beloved brother, by name Richard Plantagenet, duke of York, who everyone thought was dead, was still alive, and was with those earls in Ireland, safe and held in great honor. They affirmed this with letters reinforced with their seals and with a sacred oath. They prayed I might be willing to bring help and assistance to this same duke of York. These things seemed to me to be ravings and dreams.*" She smiled. "I like that line," she muttered, and Richard finally came out of his reverie and grunted diligently.

"*Afterward this duke of York was received by the King of France as the son of King Edward and as his cousin.*" That had not been part of her plan, but how she had thanked God and her special saint, Anthony of Padua, for the serendipitous happening. "*And I sent certain men there who would have recognized him as easily as his mother or his nurse, since from their first youth they had been in service and had intimate familiarity with King Edward and his children.*"

Aye, although she did not name them for Isabella, she had taken a chance on those men, for any one of them might have decided Richard was an imposter. "*These men, too, with a most sacred oath, affirmed that this man was the second son of King Edward.*" She paused again. And now the most important part, she thought, as she watched the secretary catch up to her last words.

"Let me see, how shall I phrase your finally coming out of France to my court?" Margaret asked, excitement in her voice as she drummed her long fingers on the table. "How does this sound? *Tandem ipse Dux Eborancensis ex*

Francia ad me venit," she translated, and Richard nodded eagerly. "Aye, Heer Braun, that is as good as any," she told the clerk.

"*I recognized him as easily as if I had last seen him yesterday or the day before,*" she continued, and then stopped. "I had better admit that the last time I saw you was when you were only a boy. I do not want anyone to call me a dissembler. Put brackets around this next phrase, *mein heer, 'for I had seen him once long ago in England . . . Then I recognized him by private conversations and acts between him and me in times past, which undoubtedly no other person would have been able to guess at.*'" She turned and winked at Richard, who gave her a small smile and crossed himself. He was certain the fires of Hell had been awaiting him for several years now—and what was one more lie? It was a comfort to know his aunt would be there, too!

After regaling Isabella with a few more convictions that this indeed was her long-lost nephew, Richard, Margaret chose to end the letter on a note that might appeal to Isabella's feminine side.

"*I, indeed, for my part, when I gazed on this only male remnant of our family— who had come through so many perils and misfortunes—was deeply moved, and out of this natural affection, into which both necessity and the rights of blood were drawing me, I embraced him as my only nephew and my only son.*" She lifted her shoulders and let out a deep sigh. When she turned to Richard again, she had tears running down her cheeks. He could do no more than reach out his arms to her and hold her close.

"Now, Richard," she whispered, " 'tis your turn to make her recognize you. I shall leave you to write your own letter."

25

England

1494

The scene outside Grace and Tom's chamber window was silent and white. Grace was lying-in and, although custom ordained the shuttering of casements to keep out the Devil, she could not bear the gloom and begged Tom to open one of the shutters so she could watch the snowflakes float effortlessly towards the ground, covering branches and bushes in soft, fluffy mantles of purity.

Alice Gower had insisted that Grace be rested before her ordeal, as Grace had come down with a fever and cold at Christmas and missed the festivities at Sheriff Hutton, where they had all been invited. "Tom, you are to be gentle with Grace for the next few weeks," she had advised her son one morning after shooing Grace away from the barn. There was frost on the roof of the byre and ice in the water trough, and Grace's hands were red from cold. Her head was pounding and her nose running, but she could not forsake the poor cows when the milkmaid had failed to appear that morning. Bundling her daughter-in-law up in her own woolen shawl,

Alice hurried her back to the warm kitchen in the manor house and told her sternly to stay where she was.

Grace thought back fondly to the scene as she lay snug in the bed Tom had fetched for them from Sheriff Hutton, a belated wedding gift from his uncle, Sir John. Tom had been almost as enthusiastic about taking her home to Yorkshire as he had been when she told him she was carrying their child. In fact, she remembered, he had been close to tears at the announcement. With time to daydream, she spent hours reliving the past—especially the past six months, when she had met her half brother in Flanders and, upon her arrival back in England, had been certain she was with child.

"What would you do if I said you were going to be a father, Tom?" she asked him coyly one night after he had made love to her at Pasmer's Place. She laughed out loud now when she remembered his reaction. He had immediately moved a foot away from her and gently pulled her chemise down to cover her nakedness. "F-f-father?" he whispered as he accomplished his task, his eyes glistening with unshed tears. "I am going to be a father? When, how . . . ?"

Grace giggled. "Foolish boy. You know very well how. But I do believe the babe will be born under the sign of the goat. A good omen for a farmer and his wife," she teased, knowing he thought of himself more as a knight than a farmer.

Tom counted on his fingers. "Five months from now," he said eagerly. Then his face paled. "But sweetheart, all those nights when we made love—and sometimes none too gently—why did you not tell me sooner? You could have harmed the child."

"Foolish boy," Grace said again. "Nature has a way of protecting the babe. And besides, 'tis good for the mother's humors to know her man still desires her," she said, purposefully running her finger down his chest to his belly and around his sensitive navel until she saw her goal achieved. She bent and kissed his prick and, whispering of his love, he rolled her on top of him and gently pushed up into her. "There, you see, 'tis as it always is," she said as she felt her own passion mount. "You want our child to know what love is, do you not? Then, dear husband, I pray do not delay any further," she muttered as a wave of pleasure made her gasp.

Grace smiled now, remembering and caressing her enormous belly.

Dear Saint Sibylline, at least this child will know both her parents, she thought. There had come a time when lovemaking had become too difficult, and the two of them had found other ways of pleasuring each other. She never got tired of feeling the baby kick, and right now she could feel a little hand or foot moving under her hand. She thought back to the first time the child had quickened and how thrilling the sensation had been. She frowned, but that day was also when she had had the terrifying audience with Henry and his mother. She did not want to think dark thoughts while she was so close to birthing, but the memory of those two faces glaring down at her from their higher position on the little dais was still so fresh, it burned on her mind and entered her nightmares.

She and Tom had returned to Hellowe after leaving Flanders and found only the two Welles daughters in residence. Jack and Cecily had joined the Lady Margaret at Collyweston to greet the King for his monthlong stay in Northampton. Tom had ridden immediately to join his master, leaving Grace happily tending her garden and playing with little Anne and Elizabeth. A fortnight later a messenger had arrived to instruct Grace to join Tom at Collyweston and report on her observations at the Malines court. Bess had arrived from Greenwich and was anxious to see Grace, Tom's letter explained. She rode pillion behind one of the escorts and enjoyed the shade of the woods until the road ran alongside fields, some freshly reaped and dotted with sheaves and stooks that allowed further ripening of the grain in the hot late August sun. They passed hedgerows of intertwined blackthorn, with its blue-bloomed sloe berries, and thorny brambles, which still flowered pink or showed its juicy fruit. And here and there carpets of red poppies reigned supreme in those yet unharvested fields of wheat and barley. The drone of bees, the cacophony of birdsong and the bleating of sheep were all sounds that accompanied them, and Grace knew that she was happiest in the countryside.

Once at Collyweston, Grace had passed a pleasant hour with the queen and Cecily and told them faithfully of her impressions of Richard. Bess, seated on a small dais in a gilded chair, had not said a word during her retelling, but Cecily had interrupted with a hundred questions and great excitement. When Grace came to the end, eyeing the queen with her characteristic cocked head, Bess finally spoke. "I am sorry that you should be so deceived by this foul dissembler, Grace. I had thought you a better judge of people than that."

Even Cecily's smile had faded as she'd watched her older sister's stern face. "Come now, Bess," she said, clearly irritated. "We both know Grace is not a dissembler. She has no reason to be." Grace threw her a grateful glance before giving Bess her full attention again.

"Henry has uncovered a diabolical deception, which you must have known about while you were with Aunt Margaret," Bess began. "This popinjay is naught but a boatman's son dressed in fine clothes playing a pernicious part in Margaret's mummery. To believe otherwise is to have treasonous thoughts," Bess told them coldly, though her voice trembled.

Grace flushed and plucked nervously at her gown, noticing a dark stain on the damask and pushing the offending fold between her knees. "Dear sister, would you have wanted me to lie to you? You asked for my impression, and I have told you. 'Tis only *my* impression—"

Cecily jumped to her feet, interrupting her. "Christ's nails, Bess," she swore, making Bess's eyes fly wide. "*You* asked Grace to go to Burgundy and report what she saw and heard. I see nothing treasonous in what she has said, and we know Grace does not lie. I have to confess that I am half convinced myself. Are you going to tell me that we are *both* traitors?"

Tears suddenly coursed down Bess's face, and Grace knew in an instant how compromised her sister must be. She got up and knelt by the queen's side, taking her hands and chafing them. "Do not weep, Bess. You have only done your duty by your husband, and Cis and I understand, don't we Cecily?" she turned and frowned a warning at the still-indignant Cecily. "You have been kind enough to caution me that, should the king question me, I must tell a different tale. True?"

Bess nodded vigorously and then managed a smile. "I do not know how you do it, Grace. You are always such a comfort." She pulled herself together and wiped her eyes on a lawn kerchief. "Believe what you will, my dear, but no one at court—except perhaps my other foolish sister—"

"Do you mean *me*, your grace?" Cecily cried. "Do you call *me* foolish?"

Bess ignored her outburst and continued as though there had been no interruption: "No one believes it, because it is not prudent to believe it."

"Believe what, my dear?" a voice from the doorway froze the three sisters in their positions, until all fell on their knees in front of the king.

"Forgive us for the intrusion, but your steward knocked and was not heard for the din in here. 'Twas as noisy as a morning at Billingsgate, was it not, Mother?"

Grace's heart sank into her knees as she saw Lady Margaret follow her son into the room. Cardinal Morton, as Henry's favorite adviser, was never far from the duo, and soon his portly form joined them in, it seemed to Grace, an unholy trinity. The little tableau was completed by Henry's pet, a white-whiskered monkey that capered beside him on a golden chain.

"Aye, fishwives is an apt comparison," Lady Margaret said with amusement. "Lady Welles, my brother has not revealed to me this side of you," she said to Cecily, who looked appropriately sheepish. "I believe I must have been fortunate not to have sisters."

"Believe what?" Henry repeated to his wife, almost running over his mother's words and raising Bess to her feet.

Bess blushed and hesitated. It was plain she was desperately forming a satisfactory answer. Grace's heart went out to her, and she stepped forward and curtsied to the king again, who had ushered his mother to the chair on the dais and was ministering to her.

"By your leave, your grace, may I speak?" Grace said, so softly that Henry asked her to repeat herself. "May I explain?" she asked. Henry nodded, puzzled.

"Her grace, Bess, the queen—my sister . . ." She paused. Oh, no, I am rambling again, she thought, and she prayed to the Virgin to guide her words. "Her grace was explaining why our brother, Richard of York, who is at the court at Malines, is not really our brother, but an imposter. I had just finished telling her of my visit to our Aunt Margaret—"

Henry's eyes narrowed and he jutted his head forward. "So, my lady, were you as convinced of his falsity as the rest of us? 'Twould be foolish if you were not, don't you think?"

Grace stared at him miserably. "I cannot lie to you or my sister, the queen, your grace. I was not . . . entirely . . . unconvinced," she whispered. "But my opinion is of such little value compared with your ambassadors'."

Cecily hurried forward and stood between her sisters. "Lady Grace is right, my liege. 'Tis her word against your own ambassadors'. Do not forget, poor Grace never set eyes on Richard before her visit. Therefore, her opinion can be of no value to anyone, and that is why the queen was advising her to forsake him and believe—as we all do—that this Perkin *est un poseur*," she ended in Henry's favorite French. She took her sisters' hands and gave them a meaningful squeeze.

"Is this true, madam?" Henry asked his wife.

"Aye, your grace," Bess replied, looking up at him and loosing Cecily's hand. She gave him one of her sweetest smiles and stepped up onto the dais to peck him on the cheek. "Do not chastise Grace, my dear husband. 'Twas I who sent her—and with your permission. She is young and has no influence with anyone at court. She was taken in by the man, like so many others who are less informed than you are."

Grace was aware that Lady Margaret was boring holes in her with her piercing dark eyes—black as a crow's feather when she was angered. She hoped the woman was only staring at the stain on her gown and could not see her trembling legs beneath.

Henry bent and whispered something to his mother, and she whispered back. He nodded and fixed his eyes on Grace. "It would please us if you would leave the court for a spell, Lady Grace." He watched impassively as all the color drained from Grace's cheeks. "I shall ask Lord John to excuse your husband his duties until this matter with Warbeck is resolved once and for all, which"—he smirked at Cardinal Morton—"when Philip of Burgundy feels the burden of the sanctions I shall place on trade with him, should happen in the very near future. I command you not to speak of your impressions to anyone outside this circle, do you understand?"

Now Grace's legs did give way, and she fell to her knees, trembling. "Do not punish my husband, your grace," she begged, her tears splashing onto the blue and red tiles. "He is not of the same mind as I. He should not be disgraced because of me."

Henry softened for a moment. "Come, child, 'tis not a weeping matter. Your husband will keep his place, but he must take responsibility for keeping you from court for a spell. No doubt he has family somewhere who will take you in."

Grace nodded miserably and, getting to her feet, she would have stumbled had Cecily not taken her arm and led her from the room as several pairs of eyes watched them go in silence.

And so Tom had finally taken his wife home to the wolds, where she was far removed from worldly events. When he saw how frightened she was, he had not chastised her but assured her that although she had not yet met her brother-in-law, Edmund, who now owned the Gower manor, he and his mother were eager to welcome her.

And so she did not hear how Richard went as Edward's son and prince of England to the Holy Roman Emperor Frederick's funeral in Vienna in November. Nor did she hear how he sat at the right hand of Maximilian, now emperor, who had finally accepted Margaret's nephew as duke of York and rightful king of England.

JUST AS TOM had predicted, his family welcomed Grace with open hearts. Alice Gower was the first to greet her, clucking around the diminutive Grace like a hen with her chick. "Well met, my dear, oh, well met!" she kept saying. First she kissed Grace on both cheeks and then decided to curtsy, unsure how to treat a lady of royal blood who was now a member of her own family.

Grace tried to be serious, but soon she was laughing and gladly taking the older woman's arm into the familiar hall. She looked around her in wonder; the pleasant room looked exactly as she remembered it. She never thought that day ten years ago after her mishap in the stream that she would ever return. Alice was chattering on as they climbed the staircase to a small chamber she had prepared for the young couple. She swore she had seen a bright new star that night after Grace and Cecily's unexpected visit and told Grace she was not surprised when Tom had taken her to wife.

" 'Twas a portent, Lady Grace, that told me we had not seen the last of you," she explained. "Now come into my solar and meet your sister Cat, who is visiting from York," she trilled, steering the weary Grace down a short passageway and into a sun-filled solar that looked over the southern fields of the Gower land.

Tom came bounding up the stairs two at a time and, overtaking his mother and Grace, called out for his sister. Throwing down her spindle, with which she was idly playing while waiting impatiently to meet Grace, Cat flung herself into her brother's arms. Her linen cap was knocked flying, revealing a thick braid of exactly the same colored hair as Tom's. Only when Tom put her down could Grace see that there the resemblance between the siblings ended. Where Tom was big-boned and handsome, with a strong jaw and wide shoulders, Cat was just like her name, lithe and graceful, with a sweet face and huge blue eyes. When Edmund followed Tom into the room, breathless from his run from the field where he was supervising the haying, Grace was astonished to see a medium-built, dark-haired man with a ruddy complexion whose features could only be described as regular. How did three such different children spring from the same parents, she wondered?

Tom grinned and drew Grace to him. "Cat, Edmund, may I present my wife, Lady Grace Plantagenet—or plain Dame Gower, if 'tis all the same to her. Is she not as fair as I told you?"

"Aye, that she is!" Edmund said, his voice a rich baritone with a slight Yorkshire burr. He smiled, and he was suddenly handsome, with Alice Gower's dimples making him look surprisingly boyish for his thirty years. "You have done well for yourself, my clay-brained, clodhopping brother. God's greeting to you, sister," he finished, taking Grace's hand and pressing it to his lips: "You are right welcome in our house."

Grace couldn't control a giggle at the description of Tom, and when Cat saw that Grace was not offended, she elbowed her brother out of the way, curtsied and then gave Grace a quick embrace, blushing as she did so. "I am glad to meet you, too, sister," she murmured and moved to her mother's side before Grace had a chance to react.

"What do you think of my family, Grace?" Tom asked, going to the two women and putting a protective arm around each.

"I like them very much, Tom," Grace replied, smiling happily at them all. "I like them very much indeed."

THE SUN WAS just sending out its first golden rays over the snowy fields when Grace, only half awake, heaved herself out of her warm bed and onto the jakes, thinking she had been relieving herself in her sleep. Then she knew her time had come.

"Tom, Tom!" she whispered into the room, bathed in a rosy glow, her breath visible in the cold air. " 'Tis time. The babe is coming." A movement from the pallet on the floor told her Tom had heard her and in a flash he was by her side, shivering despite his warm cloak.

"Sweet Christ, what should I do?" Tom cried, helping her up and back into bed. "Stay here and don't move," he ordered her, which made her smile. Where would she go? "I will fetch Mother and Enid." Gratefully, he ran from the room, his palms now sweating with anxiety and his stomach churning. Grace could hear him knocking on his mother's door but before Alice had time to answer Enid had bustled into the room carrying firewood to rekindle the embers in the hearth. Before he had died, Tom's father had spent a small fortune opening up the central chimney of the manor house so fireplaces could be installed in the upstairs chambers, and then Edmund had replaced all the old horn panes in the leaded windows with glass, which allowed the sunlight to brighten and warm the rooms, even on a winter's day.

Enid soon had the fire blazing, while Alice called out to Tom to send Edgar for the midwife from Westow. Then she came hurrying in, all smiles and clucking, plumping up the pillows and straightening the bed covers. "Enid, I pray you, open all the doors and windows a crack. I know 'tis cold, but we must let any evil spirits escape who may be hiding in the house. Nothing must harm this child." Grace knew Alice was remembering the loss of her first grandchild and its mother the year before, when Edmund had been widowed. She admired Alice's pragmatic perspective on life: *"The Lord giveth and the Lord taketh away. They are in Heaven now and free of all earthly toils,"* she had written to Tom.

"Have Jack bring water from the well to boil," Alice commanded. "I have prepared clean cloths—you will find them in a basket in my solar," she said, shooing Enid out of the room as Grace suddenly groaned with an unfamiliar pain. "Hurry, woman! There is no time to lose."

Enid did as she was told and was back in two shakes of a lamb's tail. Grace was dismayed by the intensity of her spasms, but at the moment they were irregular and short. She wanted Tom beside her, but Alice would not hear of it. " 'Tis not customary for a man to be anywhere near a birthing chamber, my dear," she tut-tutted. "He can wait downstairs, just as his father did. The midwife will be here anon, if the snow is not too deep."

Alice gave Grace sips of a potion made from myrtle, horehound and dried mare's blood that was thought to shorten the labor, but it was late in the winter afternoon before Grace was helped onto the birthing chair. She had lost all sense of time, her chemise was soaked through with sweat and her hair hung in a damp plait down her back. She leaned against the hard, sloping wooden chairback, her legs straddling the seat, and attempted to understand the commands of the midwife, a gnarled old woman with a broad Yorkshire brogue. With her purple nose, sporting a hideous wart from which sprouted several long hairs, and her wheezing cackle, which revealed only a single tooth in her gums, Grace thought she must be a dobby, the Yorkshire name for a goblin. As her pains came closer together and intensified, she became more terrified of the woman and screamed more from fear than pain. She became delirious, shrieking that this woman would steal her child and feed it to the wolves. Alice was concerned poor Goody Watling would leave in a huff, but the old wise woman only cackled again and told her, "Tak noa gawm, I tak nowt higg," which Alice translated to Grace as, "Pay no mind, I take no offense."

"Can she not speak English?" Grace muttered before she was overtaken by another contraction.

"Push, hinny, push! Aye, open thy lisk," she ordered, spreading Grace's legs wider. "Tha mun rive a mickle, but tha's nowt going to dee," the midwife assured her, feeling for the baby's head. "The barn is a-coming. Tha mun push agin." To help out, Alice reiterated, "Push once more on the next pain, child; the babe is almost here. See? Oh, so much black hair!"

Grace didn't think she wanted to look, but when she saw the crown and knew she would soon hold her child, she put her whole effort into expelling it and freeing herself from the agony of the past few hours. The tiny mite slithered into the waiting hands of the midwife, who declared with pride: "Tha hast a dowter, lady. A strang barn, by gum," and she turned the baby upside down and smacked breath into her. Furious at being so ill-treated after nine months in a cozy cocoon, the child wailed her displeasure, making all four women smile.

"Pray go and tell Tom he has a daughter, Mother Gower," Grace said wearily, watching as the baby's cord was cut and bracing herself for the rest of the after-birthing ritual.

But in no time at all Grace was back in her bed wearing a clean chemise, the child tucked into the crook of her arm. She watched in amazement as the tiny fingers flexed and unflexed and the rosebud mouth began to work in anticipation of her mother's breast. Had she and Tom really produced such a miracle of nature? she marveled. Every feature was perfect in her eyes, despite the flattened head and nose, and her only disappointment was that her child did not have Tom's flaxen hair.

There was a knock at the door, and Tom looked in. Grace had to chuckle. "Why husband, you look almost as untidy as I do," she declared, loving Tom's sheepish grin. "Has the wait been such an ordeal? Come and meet your daughter. Goody Watling says she's 'strang.' "

"Aye, strong. She told me on her way out," he said, tiptoeing to Grace's side with a grin he could not contain. He bent over and kissed her lovingly on the lips, not heeding the tiny blood vessels that had burst in labor peppering her face. She looked more beautiful than he had ever seen her, he assured her. "Oh, pish!" she retorted, making him laugh. Then he picked up the tiny bundle that wriggled in protest at being snatched from its mother's warm breast, but who calmed the moment Tom put her upon his broad chest and gently jigged her up and down.

"Thank you, Grace," he said, stroking the dark head snuggled under his chin and inhaling the new baby's scent. "You have made me the happiest man on earth."

PART FOUR

. . . *Among each degree and each estate*
To know a tapster from a lady, a lord from a lad.
Then shall truth and falsehood fall at debate,
And right shall judge and set aside flattery and guile
And falsehood for ever be put in exile.

—FROM *INSTRUCTIONS TO HIS SON*,
PETER IDLE, ESQUIRE OF KENT
AND FIFTEENTH-CENTURY POET

26

England

1 4 9 7

Tom came riding to the manor unannounced one late afternoon in July. Edgar saw him first from the stable, where he was polishing the reins of Edmund's horse. He jumped up from his perch on the water trough and, not heeding the trailing leather lead that he had managed to wrap around his leg, tried to run towards Tom. With a shout of annoyance and a few well chosen oaths, he ended up flat on his face among the chickens, which immediately scattered to safety with fearful squawking. On hearing his cries, Alice went to the front door and saw her younger son trot into the stableyard, his head thrown back in laughter.

"Tom! My dear boy," she cried and then called up to the second-story window. "Grace, 'tis Tom come home to us. Are the girls with you or Enid?"

Grace let out a whoop when she saw that it was indeed Tom dismounting on the wooden block that Edgar had placed for him. Tom slapped the groom on the shoulder and plucked a long dangling straw from his tunic, still laughing. "Such a simpkin, Edgar," he said jovially, and Edgar hung his head, feeling ashamed of himself. Then he took charge of the horse and led it to the trough to drink.

Like a rabbit from its hole, Grace bolted from the house and into Tom's arms. He whirled her round and round as if she were goosedown and planted kisses on her face until she begged him to set her down. "Where are my babes?" he asked, linking his arm in hers and going to greet his mother. "Where are Susannah and Bella?"

"They were asleep, but I doubt they are now, after this racket," Grace said, laughing and pulling him towards the house. "How good it is to see you, my dearest! How long can you stay this time?"

"Not long, Grace, but let me tell all when we are inside."

Alice had hurried inside the hall before them and was pouring some good Yorkshire ale into the horn cups when Tom and Grace pulled out a bench and sat at the long table. Edmund's new wife, Rowena, slipped into the room and stood passively by her mother-in-law, awaiting a task. Tom greeted her warmly, and the girl gave a small smile but said nothing. Alice sighed. Rowena was with child, but that was all that could be said for this namby-pamby young daughter of a distant cousin in Scarborough. Grace was kind to her, but Alice found that at her age her patience was beginning to wear thin, and she tended to snap at the child. But nothing pleased Alice more than a family gathering like this, and when Edmund came in from baling the hay, she would be in her element.

"Papa, papa!" a little girl's voice called from the top of the staircase, and Tom swept up the dark, curly-haired Susannah before she had reached the bottom. Her plump little arms clung to his neck and she snuggled into his broad chest, giggling.

"Just like his father with Cat," Alice whispered to Grace. "How George doted on his daughter." She sighed. George was dead these ten years and she still missed him. He had been well enough to give his beloved Cat away to her York merchant a few months before his death, and they were now keeping a fine house and raising a baby boy near the Layerthorpe Gate. "Ah, here is Enid with Bella," she said, nodding to the top of the stairs, her eyes lighting up. Grace knew Alice was partial to her third grandchild, and it was because Isabella's birth had not been as easy as Susannah's. Thanks to Goody Watling, warts and all, the child had survived. Grace had taken a fever and had not been able to suckle her baby. A wet nurse was found in the village, and Alice had insisted on paying for her out of what was left from her own meager family inheritance. "What do I need at this time in my life, Grace?" Alice had declared as she bathed her daughter-in-law's hot, dry skin with sweet rosemary water while Grace attempted to refuse the kindness. "Certes, if I cannot give to my own grandchild, who should I give to, pray tell? Now, not another word, child. The babe will be taken care of, and that is all there is to it! Praise be to God, both you and she are still alive."

Tom had insisted on a wet nurse for the first child, as befitted a noblewoman of Grace's rank, he had said, but when she conceived Isabella, Grace told him she hoped she could suckle the next and pass on the money saved to Edmund, who had been more than generous to take them in. She had been melancholy following Bella's birth and her illness, and so she did not refuse Alice's kind offer. Tom sent money every month, but Henry had not given Grace a penny when she left court. Instead, Cecily had pressed several rose nobles into her hand before the couple had ridden off quietly from Collyweston that early September day almost four years ago. Grace had been distraught at leaving Cecily, and the two women had clung together for several minutes, promising to pray daily for each other and write often. Anxious to remove Grace from danger and leave, Tom had cleared his throat to interrupt them.

"No one knows the true reason for your going, Grace," Cecily assured her. "Jack understands that your family tradition requires Gower children to be born at Westow, and as his family's lying-in house of Bonthorpe is sacrosanct, as I discovered to my utmost discomfort"—she grimaced—"he is at ease with letting Tom accompany you."

"Promise me one thing, Cis," Grace urged. "If you can only lie about your true belief in our brother, then do not speak of him at all. Certes, until he comes. I fear for your mortal soul."

Cecily had gripped Grace's arm and hissed: "I lie because I fear for my *life*, sister. You would do well to follow my lead. Henry isn't above hanging us both. And never, I repeat, *never* suggest to anyone that Dickon may invade—nay, not even to those you love. There are spies everywhere, Grace, so lace your lips together and trust no one. Underneath Henry's cool exterior is a frightened man, and fear makes a man dangerous, Grace.

Jack has told me tales—" She had broken off, certain her point had been made.

Cecily had been right. In the fall and winter of Ninety-four, several plots had been uncovered that smacked of Yorkist collusion, and on Valentine's Day of Ninety-five—a day usually kept for lovers—Lady Margaret's own brother-in-law, Sir William Stanley, had been executed as part of a conspiracy to place the so-called duke of York upon the throne. This was the same William Stanley who sat with his force watching which way the wind would blow at Bosworth Field and chose to come in on Henry's side when King Richard made his desperate bid to reach Henry and dispense with him personally. A grateful Tudor had made this turncoat a Knight of the Garter and Lord Chamberlain and as chamberlain had taken Grace to visit John in prison at Collyweston. But Sir William was heard to say that if he was certain the young man was indeed Edward's son, then he would not bear arms against him. Grace had been saddened to hear that the man who betrayed Stanley was one of the men she had met laughing with her brother at Dendermonde, Sir Robert Clifford. Cecily was right; there were spies everywhere—even among one's friends. Indeed, the air was rife with rumors of invasion, and Henry ferreted out many loyal Yorkists, who were condemned as spies and either tortured or executed in an attempt to stem the unrest.

Tom came home when his duties allowed and filled Grace in on all the court gossip; however, it was a letter from Cecily that brought the first real news: "*Our grandmother Cecily has passed away just three weeks after her eightieth birthday. The court is,* naturellement, *in deep mourning.*" Grace had not known the old duchess of York well at all, but nonetheless she said a prayer for the matriarch of the York family that day at her prie-dieu—the same one Elizabeth had used at Bermondsey.

Not long after Proud Cis's death, Tom told her that Henry had created his son Harry, duke of York, aiming to snub all those in Europe who were fêting the false duke of York. And Bess had given birth to another daughter, Mary, just months after one of the coldest winters anyone could remember.

Their little Isabella had been born in April 1495; then, in July, Tom reported that Richard, duke of York, had finally made his move. With soldiers, arms and supplies sent with him by Duchess Margaret and Maximilian, he had attempted to land at Deal in Kent. He had been assured that the Kentishmen would rise up with him, but those he had sent ashore were completely routed by Henry's men and most were put to death on the spot. Richard and the rest of his force fled with their small fleet to Ireland, but due to Henry's clever politics in that part of his kingdom, Richard now found himself unwanted there.

After failing to win the earls of Kildare and Desmond to his banner again, the young man was forced to take to the sea once more and find safe haven—this time in Scotland—with Burgundy's ally, James. And thus, yet another royal ruler welcomed this handsome young man to his court, with his beautiful manners, fine clothes and noble bearing, and accepting without doubt that he was the son of Edward of England come to life. James welcomed with enthusiasm any chance he had to worry Henry on his northern borders, and he promised Richard he would join him in invading England if it would feather his own nest.

James held welcome jousts in his honor when Richard came to him at the sandstone clifftop castle at Stirling in November 1495, and by January 1496 he had honored Richard by giving him a wife, Katherine Gordon, a daughter of the earl of Huntly, who was Scotland's most powerful lord after the king. Not eight months later they were blessed with a son, Henry's spies told him—it was said the young couple were so smitten with each other when they first met at Advent tide that they did not wait to tie the knot before finding a bed and conceiving a child. Now Henry had another prickle in his side that he could not leave to fester.

The young prince and his beautiful bride were given leave to take up residence in the royal hunting lodge at Falkland, which was secluded in a forest in the shadow of the two heather-covered mounds that comprised the Lomond Hills. So much in love had they become, according to the spies' reports, that Richard was reluctant to leave his idyllic situation to accomplish the very goal he had gone to Scotland to achieve: invade England and take back his crown. Unbeknownst to Richard during those months of his leisure away from court, James had, in fact, come to some sort of a reluctant truce with Henry, but that did not deter James from keeping his promise to his new friend. And thus, in a cold September rain in 1496, Richard finally rode into England with his proud satin banner of the White Rose hanging limp on its staff above him. James expected Englishmen to be there to rally to the cause, but no one ran to greet the young duke of York and his ragtag band of foreign mercenaries. So disgusted were the Scots by this wild goose chase that they chose to treat the invasion like any other border raid and began pillaging and killing innocent villagers where they could before making their way back across the River Tweed towards home.

When Grace heard of all these disasters, she wept for Richard. Tom comforted her, but he tactfully suggested that perhaps the English did not care to have a new king. Perhaps they were contented with Henry now, and certes, with the news of the way James and Richard's armies had attacked the people of Northumberland, the English were in no mind to accept a prince who treated his own subjects thus.

"But 'twas not his fault, Tom," an indignant Grace had said. " 'Twas that savage Scottish king's. We know they are all wild beasts north of the border. My poor brother must be at their mercy. I hope he can escape back to Aunt Margaret and try again."

Tom did not have the heart to tell her that her half brother was on a fool's errand. In the spring, Henry had faced a rebellion by fifteen thousand Cornishmen who resented the taxes levied on them to finance Henry's fight against their allies, the Scots. In June, the Cornish army had marched unchecked through the south of England to London, where they had challenged the city. Henry soon put them to rout at a battle on Blackheath, executed the leaders and demonstrated to the rest of the country how intolerant he was of dissension. He had also sent the fleet north to guard the Tweed so no more incursions would go undefended.

Aye, the king was concerned, Lord Welles had told his gentlemen of the chamber, but he was forewarned and forearmed. Whatever this Perkin Warbeck attacked England with, it would be no match for Henry's forces, Tom knew. Besides, Henry had a greater reason to want to be free of Perkin Warbeck and keep his kingdom stable: in October the year before, he had finally concluded the arrangements with Ferdinand and Isabella of Spain to betroth Arthur to the infanta Catherine, and nothing as paltry as a pretender should ruin this superb alliance.

As TOM AND Grace strolled along the path to the field where Edmund was supervising the hay baling, Tom decided she did not need to know everything just yet. Instead, he bent to pick Grace's favorite tricolored heartsease from a clump under the low stone wall that marked the northern boundary of the manor's lands and whistled to Freya, who had her nose in a rabbit hole. To the south and east, the Gower fields stretched down the hill to a brook and up the other side into stands of beech and oak trees. He and Edmund knew every inch of the property, and he was always moved by its beauty when he returned.

"I wanted to tell you some news privately, sweetheart," he said, offering her the flower and kissing her fingers as she took it from him. Grace slowed her step, a frown creasing her sun-stained brow. He was used to his nut-brown wife, as he teasingly called her, and although she might be disdained at court, he thought she looked natural and healthy, and he thanked God several times a day that she had given him two thriving daughters. He turned to look back along the path and grinned. Edgar had Susannah on his shoulders, and the little girl was squealing with delight when he alternately galloped and then slowed to a walk. It was plain the groom adored the child, and through Edgar's patience, Tom was pleased his daughters would grow up without the fear of horses that Grace had never lost.

"What news, husband?" Grace asked eagerly. " 'Tis good, I hope."

"I have good news and bad news; which shall go first?"

Grace made a face. "Tell me the good, so I may smile through the bad," she answered.

"It seems my lord Welles has rewarded me for my efforts at Blackheath. Even though I was only doing my knightly duty by defending our banner, I fought well enough to have been knighted. My lady, you are now staring at Sir Thomas Gower!" he cried, laughing at her gap-mouthed face. She gave a shriek and jumped into his arms, almost bowling him over and making Freya bark and race around them in excited circles.

"Tom, Tom, you should have written and told me. Oh, how proud I am of you, my dearest," she said, letting herself back down onto the ground. "Your mother will be delighted. Look at you, husband—you are as red as a robin's breast!" She took his hand and kissed his palm, flirting with him under her lashes. "I wonder if nights with knights are any different than with ordinary men?"

"Soft, Grace," Tom admonished her, chuckling. "Not in front of Susannah!"

"So, now you may tell me the bad news, for nothing will break my merry mood, I promise."

"I trust you will understand that 'twas not my decision, but the queen's," Tom began, taking her arm and continuing their pace. "You are called back to court, Grace, because the queen wants you to attend her in Lady Cecily's stead. One of the Welleses' daughters has been stricken with a malady the doctors are unable to recognize. The queen has sent the viscountess to Hellowe to be with her child for the summer. I am to escort you to London in a week's time."

"A week?" Grace said, her voice faltering. It had not occurred to her that she would return to life at court, as she thought Henry had made it clear she was no longer welcome there. She had grown to love Yorkshire and its blunt but good-hearted people, and she looked on Alice as her mother. Other than Enid, there were no nursemaids or attendants in charge of her children, which meant she was at liberty to watch them grow and change—take their first steps, say their first words and, aye, she could even take care of their dirty linens. And she had nothing to wear. Her court gowns must be old-fashioned now—they were none too fashionable when she was there, except for the beautiful brown silk gown that Elizabeth had afforded for the audience at Westminster with her cousin of Luxembourg all those years ago.

"God's bones, Tom!" she exclaimed, startling her husband with her vehemence and unusual oath. "Am I to be a servant for the rest of my life? Grace go here, Grace go there, Grace attend this one, Grace attend that one? I have my own family now, and I am still a king's daughter. Can I not live in peace here? Edmund is pleased with my help; the children are strong and love the farm life. The only part I hate is your long absences. Oh, Tom, how can I leave my two little ones? 'Twould break my heart."

"Come down from your high horse, sweetheart," Tom replied, stopping her and taking her hands. "Certes, you are invited to bring the girls with you. Your sister is most pleased to invite them, and calls them her dear nieces. 'Twill not be for very long, and as the viscount must be with the king and the king and queen will be at Shene throughout August, we shall see each other more often. 'Tis an honor to serve the queen, and you dare not refuse her grace's command, my love—you must see that."

Grace relaxed the stubborn line of her mouth into a reluctant smile.

Certes, she could not refuse, and she told him so. "But your mother will be desolate, in truth. She adores Susannah and Bella. She will soon have Edmund's child to love, I suppose." She sighed. "Let us go and tell Mother the news and promise Edmund we shall return in time to help with the harvest. It looks to be a fine one this year."

She stopped and waited for Edgar to catch up to them and then scooped up the bright-eyed Susannah and swung her into Tom's waiting arms.

THE SMALL PARTY left Westow on a day that showed off the Yorkshire landscape to perfection. When Grace looked back at Alice, Edmund and Rowena waving from the upper field in front of the stone manor house, she saw them framed by an azure sky above, a dark green forest to the east and green and gold fields in front of them. The corn was ripening nicely, and St. Swithun had been kind this year and had not sent the rain on his feast day. The grain would be plentiful and not plagued with mold from too much rain. Tears stung her eyes as she gave one final wave before the figures turned away and went back to their work on the farm.

Edgar had fashioned a special basket for Bella that held the baby safely in front of him on his large rouncy, and Enid was riding pillion so that she could monitor her charge's needs. But it seemed the gentle swaying of the basket kept the child sleeping for much of the day, meaning Grace and Enid had to minister to a wakeful bundle for their five nights upon the road. Their route took them through the center of England, and Grace was saddened by the names of places they passed by that were synonymous with battles fought in the struggle of Lancaster against York—Towton, Wakefield, Stoke, Northampton, St. Albans and Barnet—where many of her own family had lost their lives. She clutched Tom around the waist and shuddered, not wanting to imagine what it must have been like to see one's husband, sweetheart or brother march off to fight. Tom patted her hand. "Are you cold, hinny?" he asked as they left the village of Barnet behind on their last leg of the journey to London. She smiled, loving it when he used the northern endearment, which he tended to do after spending time at home.

"Nay, Tom. I was thinking about the terrible waste of life that battles cause. 'Twas at Barnet where the great earl of Warwick lost his life, was it not?"

"Aye, and his brother, John Neville," Tom said. "The two were laid out for all to see at Saint Paul's, my uncle told me. But better to die in battle than on the scaffold, in truth. Although, as befitted their noble rank, they would have been spared the usual traitor's death, unlike the leaders of the Cornishmen after the debacle at Blackheath." Grace shivered again. She thought of John for the first time in a long while and smelled again the sickly scent of burning flesh and hair. "And the foolish followers of the Warbeck fellow who were taken at Deal."

"Do not call him that, I beg of you, Tom. Not in front of me," Grace said. "Believe what you will, but until someone proves otherwise, I shall think of him always as my brother."

Tom sighed. He hoped he would not have to lecture her again about keeping silent on the subject when she was with the king and queen. While she remained at court, she would have to become accustomed to hearing the man referred to as Perkin Warbeck, or by Henry's favorite moniker: "the boy." There was even a rumor that Warbeck was the result of a liaison between Margaret and her confessor, Henri de Berghes, the bishop of Cambrai, although Tom had dismissed it as ridiculous. He squeezed Grace's hand again, and she did not reject him but laid her cheek on his long back, the kersey tunic soft against her skin.

And thus they rode into London, past the fields and gardens of the immense St. Bartholomew's Priory to where the Aldersgate gaped like a mouth in the twenty-foot-high city wall. The smell of the ditch before the wall made Susannah cry "Pooh!" and Bella held her little nose. The sentries came to attention upon seeing the queen's banner and cleared a path for the small meinie. Before them, carts drawn by oxen, piled high with tuns of wine or sacks of flour, lumbered through the hulking stone gate upon which was set the rotting haunch of a man whose body had been hacked into quarters and, together with his head, pilloried thus on each of London's gates. Grace averted her eyes and was glad when Tom pointed out St. Paul's spire to Susannah to divert her attention from the carcass.

To avoid the crowds in the center of the city, Tom chose to keep close to the inside of the wall around to the east and thus to the Tower. He had received word along the way that the court was still at the Tower following the Cornish rebellion scare, and Grace was not looking forward to going there. All she knew about it was that, despite being a royal palace, it was the place where Ned and Dickon had disappeared and still housed her unfortunate cousin, Ned of Warwick.

With its wide moat and low curtain wall, the Tower looked more like a fortress than a palace. They crossed one drawbridge to an island gate, called Lion Tower, and then over another bridge to the Middle Tower before reaching the gate in the high Byward Tower. Soon the children were stretching their legs on the manicured grass by the Garden Tower, which the royal lodgings abutted.

Tom led them to the entrance to the queen's apartments and they climbed the staircase to the second floor, where they found the suite of apartments to be richly decorated and with leaded windows that looked out onto the flower gardens below. The massive central White Tower was in front of them, where the king was staying this time, and Grace was glad Bess was not residing in the same building with him.

"Lady Grace Plantagenet, your grace," Bess's chamberlain barked as Tom escorted his wife into the queen's presence, two-year-old Bella in his arms and Grace holding Susannah's hand. She had taught Susannah how to curtsy during the last week at Westow, but the little girl was so overawed by the magnificence of the chamber and the beautiful woman seated before them that she stood rooted to the spot. Grace sank into an accustomed reverence, thinking her daughter had followed suit. She heard Bess's soft laughter and looked up anxiously.

"She reminds me of you the first time I saw you at court, dear Lady Grace," Bess said, waving her hand to indicate that Grace should rise. "You were just as overwhelmed. Come here, poppet," she beckoned to Susannah, who Grace realized was still on her feet gazing about her in wonder. "Come and tell me your name, and your brother's . . ."

Susannah needed no second bidding. Deciding she liked this goddess in her blue and black patterned silk gown with its shiny golden trim, and ignoring the bevy of attendants clucking their tongues around her, she skipped over and clambered up on Bess's lap before Grace could stop her. One of the ladies attempted to gently remove the child, who was now comfortably seated on the queen's knee.

"My name is Susannah," she said, eyeing the diamond and pearl pendant that swung temptingly from the front of Bess's velvet headdress.

Grace hurried forward, smiling an apology. "She tends to be too forward," she explained. "I beg your pardon, your grace. Susannah, get down and make your reverence—"

"My dear sister," Bess interrupted her, "I have four children of my own, as you know. Leave her be, I beg of you. Cannot an aunt make her niece's acquaintance? Sweet Jesu, but she is the image of you, Grace." She tickled Susannah's nose with her finger. "Aye, we are talking about you, little poppet. Now, you have not yet told me your brother's name."

Grace stepped back and let her child answer. "It's not a brother," Susannah scoffed, rolling her eyes to the ceiling painted with golden stars. "She's Bella, and she's a girl."

"Susannah!" Grace exclaimed sternly, plucking the girl from Bess's knee and setting her down. "You must show the queen of England respect. Now make your obeisance at once!"

Trembling, Susannah curtsied low, her eyes on the ground. Grace's heart melted. "Beg her grace's pardon, sweeting," she whispered in her ear. " 'Tis all you need to do."

Big brown eyes met Bess's dark blue ones, which had more than a merry twinkle in them, and Susannah lost her fear once more. "I am sorry, your grace," she said, addressing Bess as her mother had taught her. "I shan't do it again."

"You may call me Aunt Bess when we are alone, my dear, because I think you and I are going to be friends." Bess rose and, bending down, kissed Susannah on the top of her head and then opened her arms to Grace. "It has been too long, sister," she said after they embraced. "And I see marriage agrees with you. You look the picture of health and—if I may say—prettier than ever." She smiled past Grace at Tom, who was standing patiently with Bella. "Sir Thomas, my compliments. It seems you make my sister happy." She paused before adding, "and you make very pretty babes!"

Tom colored and, amused, Grace went to his side, stroking his cheek. "You should not flatter him so, your grace. 'Twill go to his head. But aye, we are very happy. I thank you for noticing."

When Tom eventually left them to seek out his own quarters and find his master, he breathed a sigh of relief. So far, so good, he thought. Now if only Grace can keep silent about Warbeck, we should have a pleasant few weeks.

. . .

THE CHILDREN WERE playing in the nursery, well attended by nursemaids, when Grace went to the inner ward for her afternoon walk in the
garden. Bess liked to nap at that time, and Grace could escape her duties,
tuck her overdress up into her belt and either pull a few weeds or deadhead
the roses when the weather permitted. This afternoon she chose to explore
her surroundings and wandered through the archway into Water Lane and
under the bridge room to the king's water gate, where there was the usual
hustle and bustle from the wharf as provisions were unloaded and trans-
ported into the inner ward. Scores of people populated the Tower, giving a
livelihood to bowyers, armorers, smiths, potters, cordwainers, carpenters
and coopers. Grace had forgotten how hectic life inside a castle could be
after her years at Gower House, and she looked about her with curiosity.
Hoping to get a view of the river over the curtain wall, Grace climbed the
steps by the round gate tower, but she was stopped by a guard who barred
her path with his halberd.

"Begging your pardon, mistress, but no one is permitted up here, on
account it be a prisoner I be guarding."

Grace made to turn back, but her curiosity got the better of her. "Who
is your prisoner, sir? Someone of importance?" she asked, noting that the
man's iron kettle helm was a size too large and almost covered his eyes.

"Lord Edward of Warwick, mistress. Bin 'ere now these dozen years,
poor sod." He made a circular motion with his finger to his temple. "Not
all there, he ain't. Only a boy when 'e come, 'e was. Feel sorry for 'im, I do.
Not that he's chained nor nothin', but I feel sorry for 'im."

Grace's heart was in her throat. Little Ned! His desperate cries for help
echoed in her mind as she recalled his wriggling body being carried off
by Sir Robert Willoughby at Grafton. What had he done wrong? Born to
the wrong father, she thought, shaking her head; he could still inherit the
throne, despite Uncle George's attainder. How cruel Henry is, she thought
angrily, descending the steps. Then she stopped and turned back to
the man.

"Is he allowed family visitors? Or food? Or a letter, perhaps?" she asked,
giving him her most angelic smile.

"Aye, 'is sister, Lady Margaret, visits 'im once in a blue moon, but that's
it. As for a letter, well, it couldn't 'urt, could it? Why, you want to write

one?" He chortled, eyeing her muddy old-fashioned gown and shoes. "Can you write, mistress?"

"Have a care, sirrah," Grace retorted. "I am the queen's sister and attendant, the Lady Grace."

The man stumbled back, clutching his throat as if struck. "Beg pardon, mistr— I mean me lady. I meant no 'arm. It's just that . . ." and he gave her old blue gown another quizzical look.

Grace smiled. "You were doing your duty, 'tis all. But I would dearly like to visit my cousin upon the morrow. I have not seen Ned since they took him away, and I would not want him to think we had forgotten him."

"I'll be 'ere this time tomorrow, me lady. You'll have to get permission from Sir Simon, you will. He'll let you see 'im for a few minutes, I dare say."

"Sir Simon Digby? Come now, as constable he is far too busy to take time with me," she said, giving him an innocent look. "Besides, I shall be there for only a few minutes, to cheer my cousin. Can this not be just between you and me?" And she reached into the little pouch at her waist. "I'll make it worth your while."

THE NEXT DAY, her new friend, who said his name was Harry Turner, turned the heavy iron key of the stout oak door to let her in. She pressed a coin into his hand and slipped past him into a large vaulted chamber whose once brightly painted plaster walls were now faded and chipped. A handsome tester bed and a long oak table, chair and matching footstool were the only furnishings, except for an exquisitely decorated prie-dieu, whose triptych panels were open, displaying the annunciation, nativity and crucifixion in brilliant hues. A large book of hours lay upon the attached stand below the paintings and two silver candleholders were skillfully mounted on either side. A window was open to the warm summer air and overlooked the river. Grace noticed, however, that iron bars reminded the occupant every minute of every day that he was a prisoner. All this Grace took in at a glance, as she was aware of the door being locked behind her, and then of a man silhouetted against the light of the window, so she could not see his face.

"Ned?" she said quietly. " 'Tis your long-lost cousin, Grace."

The man bowed quickly. "Nay, my lady," he replied in an accent that proclaimed him a Londoner. "I am Robert Cleymond, my lord of Warwick's—er—servant," he stumbled over the word and Grace assumed he should have said "keeper." "My master is taking the air on the turret, which he does every day at this time. He expects you, but he must have been distracted."

When Grace's eyes became accustomed to the light, she saw that the man had straggly gray hair and a long, lugubrious face. He would not be her choice to spend each and every day with in captivity, but by the time she left the room she thought he was not unkind to her cousin.

"It has been twelve years, Master Cleymond. I can wait a few more minutes, in truth," she said pleasantly. "How is his lordship?"

Cleymond bent over slightly when he spoke and rubbed his hands as though he were constantly washing them, making Grace uncomfortable. It was only a habit, she told herself, but it irked her. "He is well, my lady, and gives me no cause to worry. He suffers somewhat from the cold in the winter, 'tis all. We share the bed, but even so he shivers every night before he sleeps. I report once a week to Sir Simon and receive my instructions. I have served the earl faithfully these past years." More handwashing and unctuous grinning made Grace impatient.

"And his mind?" she insisted. "The guard indicated the earl was—"

Suddenly a door next to the bed opened and Edward, earl of Warwick, almost fell into the room from the narrow spiral staircase that led from the roof. He clucked his tongue and shook his dirty blond head as he hurried towards Grace. A guard followed him in, closed and locked the small door and then stood sentinel by it.

"Cleymond, why didn't you fetch me the moment my cousin arrived?" Ned complained, and Grace noticed he had picked up the London vernacular. He reached for her hand and cradled it. "Grace, my dear cousin, I wouldn't have recognized you. It has been ever so long."

What a handsome man, Grace thought, remembering the scrawny boy she had known. But then she had heard Uncle George had been handsome. She was expecting a skeleton who had been given only weevilly bread and ale all these years, but he was of medium build and his mien was not unhealthy. There were holes in his hose and his short gown was badly stained. How shameful that no one had thought to make him presentable for her—not even a clean shirt.

"We were but children at Sheriff Hutton, cousin," Grace said, taking his hand to her cheek. "Come, let us stand close to the window as we talk. I do so love to watch the boats."

"Aye, so do I!" he enthused. "So many of them. I sit for hours and wonder where they are all going and who is in them. 'Tis a game I play, isn't it, Cleymond?"

"Aye, my lord," Cleymond replied, smiling, but Grace heard the boredom in his voice as he muttered, "interminably."

"Then I shall play with you, Ned," Grace cried, leaning out as far as the bars would allow. "Who do you suppose that boat belongs to?" She pointed to a canopied barge below, drawing Ned closer so Cleymond might not listen.

"The man in the moon!" Ned cried. "I have seen him often. They say the moon is made of green cheese, but I do not believe them. The man would die just eating green cheese."

Grace's heart sank. Sweet Jesu, he is mad, she thought. And how could he not be, captive in one room all these years, with never a moment alone—not even at night. She was about to make a guess of her own, when she heard Ned whisper: "I am not as mad as they think me, Grace. It amuses me to make them believe so. I am so starved of any company that I must divert myself any way I can. Cleymond is my friend, I think, but let us not take a chance. I pray you, speak quickly, for we may not have long together. I know from Harry, my kindly guard, that Digby knows not of your visit as yet, but he will if Cleymond reports it. You take a chance, in truth, but as you are a woman, perhaps your visit will not be."

Grace felt her hackles rise in fear. Sir Simon Digby, the Tower constable, was fiercely loyal to Henry, she had learned from Bess. She groaned inwardly, and thought of Tom's admonishment to her only the day before, when the king and queen had celebrated Mass together and they had had a moment to talk. "Do nothing to incur the king's displeasure, Grace. Stay by the queen and be a good mother to the girls. With the news that Perkin has set sail from Scotland, his grace is as irritable as a horse with a burr under its saddle." Not knowing that Henry and James had made a truce, which had made Perkin's presence at the Scottish court awkward, she had been surprised by this information. She asked Tom if her brother was expected to invade from the sea and perhaps James by land from the

North. Tom had shaken his head. "James sent him away in a small ship with his wife and babe. 'Tis thought he will go to Ireland, although with Desmond and Kildare to heel, the man will not have friends there." Seeing her anxious expression, he put paid to any more questions. "Now soft, hinny, and get you back to the queen's side before someone overhears us." He took her hands and changed the subject. "I miss your sweet body next to me at night, my dearest, and if there were not so many to see us now, I would take you right here on the grass if I could." Grace had giggled, and he had bent and kissed her long and hard.

Now, Grace knew she must tell Ned as much as she could as they continued their game out of the window. She was shocked by how little he knew of the world outside his lonely tower room, although he was allowed to receive and send letters—provided they were first read by Digby. But it seemed none but his sister Margaret had kept up a correspondence with her sibling, and as she was now wife to Sir Reginald Pole and not often at court, she spoke mostly of her own family.

"You can hear the lions from here," Ned suddenly said, interrupting her story about Richard at Aunt Margaret's court. "Listen."

Grace frowned. "Have you heard anything I have told you, Ned?"

"The lions are roaring again, Cleymond. Can you go and stop them?" he cried, putting his hands to his ears. He clutched at Grace. "They frighten me, cousin. They are kept in the tower over there." He pointed upriver, to the Lion Tower by the drawbridge. "They are in cages, just like me."

"Now, now, my lord." Cleymond came forward and gently took his elbow, leading him to the bed. " 'Tis time for you to rest. Lady Grace can come again another day."

He pulled off Ned's soft round-toed shoes and lifted his legs onto the bed. Coming back to the nonplussed Grace, he murmured: "Best leave now. When the lions roar, he can hear nothing else," he said, using the same finger motion to his temple the guard had used the day before. He closed the window to shut off the sound from the menagerie. Then he knocked on the chamber door and asked the guard to unlock it. When he turned to usher Grace out and saw she was kneeling by the bed kissing Ned's hand, he clucked his tongue but dared not comment.

"I shall come again, I promise," Grace whispered.

Ned focused his pale blue eyes on her and smiled. "Aye, I know you will.

And bring your brother, Richard, with you," he murmured and closed his weary lids. "I should dearly love to see him again."

Grace's heart thumped. He had heard what she said, she thought, full of hope; at least he had grasped some of it. As she passed Cleymond, she said softly, "You seem a kind man, Master Cleymond. I regret I was unaware I should ask permission for this visit," she lied. "I pray you, let it go unreported. I meant no harm."

The man gave her an obsequious little bow.

"WE ARE TO leave for Shene finally," Bess told Grace when Grace reappeared from her adventure at the Byward Tower. "With Perkin languishing in Ireland, it cannot be long before Kildare or Desmond captures him, and thus Henry believes we are now safe to leave this castle. It cannot come too quickly for me," she confided. "Every time I walk past the Garden Tower, I think of our little brothers . . ." She stopped and shook her head sadly.

Grace held her tongue. She would have liked to remind Bess that perhaps one of those boys was "languishing in Ireland," but for once her mind was on another captive of the Tower.

"Have you seen Ned—our cousin Ned of Warwick?" Grace said suddenly, and Bess started.

Fingering a large gold cross set with smooth rubies, Bess shook her head. "Nay, I am ashamed to say. I had forgotten all about him since the Simnel affair," she admitted. Then her eyes widened and she stared at Grace. "Why? Have you?"

Grace bent and stroked the spaniel lying at her feet to avoid Bess's gaze. "I was just wondering, 'tis all," she said nonchalantly. "A guard mentioned he was still imprisoned here and that his mind wanders. When shall we leave for Shene?"

"On the morrow. Have you not noticed the activity in our lodgings? Or have you spent all afternoon deepening the color of your skin?" Bess teased. "In truth, de Puebla asked me if you were from his country the other day, as he had not seen you at court before. He was covered in confusion and actually blushed when I told him you were my half sister."

"Tomorrow," Grace repeated, trying to sound pleased. But she was upset she would have to break her promise to Ned. Perhaps she could send him a letter. Aye, that was what she would do. Harry the guard would deliver it; she was sure of it. She tickled the spaniel between the pads of its paws and smiled when she got the reaction she was expecting. The leg jerked twice in its slumber, but the dog did not wake. "Who is de Puebla?" she asked.

"He is the Spanish ambassador, who seems to live in Henry's pocket at the moment. They are hard at work making sure the treaty between us and Spain includes the betrothal of Arthur and Catherine." She lowered her voice. " 'Tis why it is imperative that this boy in Ireland is captured. Ferdinand and Isabella are stalling in case he does prove . . ." She paused, testing Grace. Bess had been assured by Cecily that Grace was no longer obsessed with the mystery, and yet Bess watched for any reaction. But Grace's expression remained impassive, and the queen breathed more easily.

Another attendant approached, making Bess clear her throat and tell Grace brightly: "De Puebla has such bad breath, in truth, perhaps because he enjoys eating uncooked onions." She wrinkled her nose and clucked her tongue and then changed the subject. "When we are at Shene, my dear Lady Grace, I must insist we fit you for a new gown or two; that one is shockingly outdated and, dare I say, shabby. Do you not agree?"

So, Grace thought, nodding absently, *Henry is afraid of losing his alliance with Spain because of Richard. No wonder he is concocting such an elaborate tale about him being a boatman's son.* Then she felt a chill run up her spine. *Dear God! He cannot let Richard live if he captures him, can he?*

Cousin Ned was forgotten in her anxiety to find Tom and ensure he shared her bed that night. Bess took pity on the couple and gave them her generous permission to take her chamber, as Henry had asked her to come to him. Everything was packed and ready to go, although the bed was a permanent fixture at the palace and the feather mattress would be washed and aired after the queen was gone. Bess had been strict about the sanitary conditions in her lodgings while she was at the Tower; London was always ripe for outbreaks of plague during the summer, and she would usually spend those months at Greenwich or Shene to be out of its deadly reach. But Henry had been concerned for his family during the Cornish rebellion in June and moved them all into his most impregnable fortress as the rebels had drawn ever closer to London.

After spending an hour with the children in the nursery, Grace walked through the pretty gardens with their meandering pathways, low brick walls and tiny bridges, to a building abutting the White Tower, where many of the squires and knights were housed. She knocked at the door and asked for Tom and was told he was attending Lord Welles in the king's council chamber.

"But he must come through that door to return to his lodging here, my lady," the helpful steward told her. "Perhaps you should wait in my office. Or I might give him a message."

She thanked him and said she would wait outside for a little while, and he disappeared inside. Several young men were loitering about in the sunshine, and she did not notice that she was an object of curiosity until a bold squire carrying a bow chose to accost her with a flourishing bow and a lascivious wink. "And who might you be, my pretty one?" he said, clearly liking what he saw and sidling closer. "I would dearly like to take you behind that tree and steal a kiss or two. Will you indulge me, sweetheart?" He ran his finger down her neck while his comrades whistled and egged him on.

Grace could not believe this was happening to her in broad daylight, and in full view of the queen's lodgings. She cursed her folly for refusing Enid's company. She felt acutely vulnerable for her lack of inches, but even though the man was a foot taller, she slapped his hand from her and tried to walk away. Too late she realized it was her drab gown, unaccompanied status and unladylike sunburned complexion that had allowed him to think her a commoner.

"Not so fast, little wanton," her seducer growled, and he pulled her to him. "I asked nicely, did I not? Surely you will not deny me one—" He got no further. Had he bothered to notice the silence that had fallen on the group behind him, he might have been warned that he was in trouble. A huge hand plucked him from the ground and flung him four feet into a flower bed. Before he could take in what had happened, the giant had grabbed his jacket and lifted him up to within inches of an angry unshaven face, complete with unclean teeth and foul breath.

"She be my mistress, your lordship," Edgar spat, making the young man blink away the spittle. "She ain't no wench. She be the queen's sister, the Lady Grace. If my mistress weren't 'ere, I'd hollow you out a new arsehole with your own pretty dagger. Do I make myself clear?"

Grace had collapsed in a heap on the grass and watched as the man nodded slowly, his spindly legs dangling like a dead chicken's high above the ground.

"Put him down, Edgar," she thought she ordered, but she was shocked by the squeak that actually left her mouth. She cleared her throat. "Put him down," she said more firmly this time.

Edgar shook his victim once more for good measure and dropped him like a stone. The man picked up his bow and ran through an archway towards the butts, checking over his shoulder to make sure Edgar was not following. Edgar shook his fist at him and then turned to confront the others, who had magically melted back into the house. He went to help Grace, but she was already on her feet, feeling foolish that she had not been able to avoid the scene. And I thought I was brave, she chided herself, shaking her head.

"Once again I have to thank you for saving me, Edgar," she said, smiling wanly. " 'Twas foolish of me to come alone, in truth, but 'tis only a stone's throw from the queen's apartment and 'tis the middle of the day. But no matter." She patted his hand. "Where did you come from, pray?"

Edgar grinned. "It be my duty to know where you be at all times, milady. I'd done finished me work in the stable, and I were biding the time with the cordwainer's daughter at her lodging yonder." He jerked his head in its direction. "I sees you leave the queen's place and go crossed the garden. As you say, mistress, it were foolish."

Tom appeared at that moment from the king's quarters. When he saw Grace his face broke into a smile, and he walked quickly towards her.

"Say not a word," Grace whispered to Edgar out of the corner of her mouth. "Swear you will not."

"I'll be mum, never fear, milady," he muttered back. "If the master knew, he'd 'ave the lad's guts for garters, and that's the truth." He touched his fingers to his temple, gave a little bow and ambled off back to the cordwainer's house.

Grace held out her hands to Tom and put the unpleasant encounter with the young squire behind her. "We leave on the morrow, my love. You have the queen's permission to do what you will with me tonight—and in her bed!" She tried to look demure from under her lashes. "I was ever so shocked by her suggestion. But I am commanded to do her bidding, and so I am her messenger."

Taking her outstretched hands, Tom threw back his head and laughed. Grace noticed he had not trimmed his beard straight under his chin. "Do not play Mistress Innocent with me," he said. Then, lowering his voice, he added: "My trollop of a wife."

Grace's eyes flew wide and she looked about them. "Tom! Have a care, someone might be—" But she did not finish, for he had picked her up and planted a kiss on her open mouth. Wrapping her arms about his neck, she nuzzled into his cheek, feeling the soft beard on her skin, which always aroused her. "Do not start what you cannot finish, husband. Your trollop of a wife would like nothing more than to be ravished right here and now in full view of the whole palace. I have such a hunger for you, Tom."

"And I you, sweetheart. But let us wait until I can pleasure you privily. I have much to do for the viscount this afternoon. We leave for Woodstock with the king in two days." He kissed her again and set her down. An amused whistle floated from a casement above them, but the head disappeared when they looked up.

Later that night, the knotted ropes of Bess's bed proved up to the task of supporting them in the most vigorous lovemaking they had yet enjoyed. Grace was surprised the guard was not called to investigate the noise she knew she was producing each time Tom discovered a different way to bring her to climax—sometimes by his mounting her, but more often the other way round. Grace found she liked being in control of her husband's hard, well-built body. She was tired of feeling small and feeble all day, as Bess towered over her or servants ran to take anything that seemed too heavy for her to carry. Bringing Tom to ecstasy from above him gave her a sense of power, and she learned to hold him at the peak of pleasure until *she* made the decision for him to release into her.

"I swear you have had lessons at one of those infamous Southwark stews," he moaned after surrendering completely to her newfound prowess. "You could not have spent every day for four years inside the abbey." And he moaned again, gripping her buttocks and driving deeper.

When she finally rolled off him, she giggled as she gently wiped his perspiring body with the covering sheet and snuggled into him. "Certes, I learned everything I know from the Bermondsey brotherhood," she whispered, biting his ear, and Tom made a sound of horrified surprise. "Did I tell you of Brother Damien and his special service to the prior?"

Tom propped himself up on one elbow and tweaked her nose. "Nay, and I do not want to hear it." He let out a feigned sigh of disappointment. "What happened to the young, naive Grace I met at Sheriff Hutton a dozen years ago?"

Grace yawned and turned over to sleep. "She discovered she was a trollop," she murmured. "But I do not think her husband cares."

"Wanton!" Tom cried, playfully slapping her buttocks. "And, by the Rood, you are right."

By the Rood, 'tis the second time I have been called wanton today, Grace thought drowsily, but said nothing. Safe in Tom's arms, the first time did not seem to matter anymore, although she acknowledged she had learned a valuable lesson.

THE NEXT DAY, after the furniture, carpets, tapestries, silver, chests of clothes and jewels were laden into shouts and barges, a fanfare of shawms announced to the Tower populace that the queen's household was ready to leave.

Tom left her side as soon as the cock crowed, promising to be on the wharf to kiss his daughters farewell. He lifted them into the barge and waited until Grace arrived with the queen before relinquishing his hold on them and saying good-bye to his wife.

Henry escorted his queen to the private Watergate with her attendants, who would make the first part of the journey by boat to Lambeth and thence by road to Shene along the south bank of the river. They kissed tenderly, Grace saw, after one of the only nights they had spent together since Grace had arrived. Baby Bella was sitting on her cushion, good as gold, but Susannah was already making friends with the master of the oarsmen, and Grace had to pull her back. She wanted nothing to attract Henry's attention to her. She had managed to be at the Tower for more than a fortnight without crossing paths with Henry once.

"The king goes to Woodstock to hunt for the rest of the summer," Bess said wistfully when she joined Grace on the barge, and she blew Henry a kiss. "He seems to love that place, although there is not enough room for both our households, and thus we cannot be together. But he promises me that my children will visit, and so I shall look forward to that."

Grace felt sorry for motherly Bess, whose three older children had already been set up in their own households—Arthur at Ludlow, Margaret and Harry at Eltham Palace. She knew she was lucky to have her own daughters in the same place with her, and Bess had spoiled them already in the short time they had been there. Bella and little Mary were almost the same age and toddled about together happily, until naughty Susannah would play havoc by tripping them up and making them cry. Grace stroked Bella's fair hair under its linen coif and the child raised her big blue eyes adoringly to her mother. As she did with Alice Gower, this child tugged at Grace's heart and she feared she favored her, but certes, Susannah did not lack for parental attention, for Tom worshipped his older daughter, perhaps because she was the spitting image of his wife.

Another fanfare sounded as the lines were untied from the dock and the oarsmen, in perfect unison, lowered their oars into the slots on the gunwale and the master began to beat out a rhythm. Cheers and shouts of farewell accompanied the vessel as it slowly pulled into the middle of the river. Grace glanced up at the circular Byward Tower and said a prayer for Ned. She had scribbled a note and, as she had predicted, the guard had been glad to take it when a groat had been pressed into his palm.

Her thoughts were interrupted by loud shouts from the shore. "God speed, good Queen Bess," the Londoners cried. "Farewell and God speed."

Grace put her hand into her sister's and whispered. "How they love you, Bess."

Bess turned her face to Grace, her eyes brimming. "Do you really think so, Grace? I confess, I do not know why."

"I do," Grace told her, smiling. Bess lived her chosen motto *humble and reverent*, and her subjects loved her for it. And 'tis just as well, she thought, for they will never love Henry.

27

Leprous Island

IRELAND, AUGUST 1497

Right noble lady, dowager duchess of Burgundy, princess of England and my dearest aunt, I greet you well from somewhere near Kinsale in Ireland.

I was invited here by Sir James Ormond and in good faith hoped for succor as well as a force to help me towards England. But God in His wisdom had other plans. Sir James was killed in an ambush before I landed, and the country is much in King Henry's power. You should know, also, that I am come with my beloved wife, Katherine, and our son, for whom we thank God each day. The people of Ireland suffer greatly from famine, and we have to pay the same for five ounces of wheat as a peck in happier times. We cannot tarry long.

Richard looked up at his wife, sitting on a crude stool and crooning a lullaby to their son, also named Richard. She caught his eye and smiled. Richard's heart leapt into his throat and his prick stirred, as it did every time he looked at her. What rapture they had enjoyed in the huge bed at Falkland! Night after night he had pleasured her until both had lain back exhausted and had to be shaken awake by the servants in the mornings. He smiled back at her, but then looked away and frowned, nibbling at his quill.

He could not tell Aunt Margaret that he had lain awake all night in the lice-ridden pallet and thought of escaping to Spain. The support he had been led to believe he could muster in Ireland was not here—unless one counted the few score wild Irishmen who had followed him to the tiny island—and James of Scotland had forsaken him, he knew that now. He dared not return to Burgundy and incur his aunt's wrath—nay, more important, her disappointment. And so what was he supposed to do? The charming Spanish ambassador at the Scottish court had made it sound as though he would be welcomed by their Spanish majesties, Ferdinand and Isabella. They would send ships to fetch him. Perhaps he could launch an invasion from Spain, Ayala had suggested. *Perhaps I could just disappear,* Richard had immediately thought. *Dear Saint Patrick—perhaps the Irish saint could intercede for him—show me the way. I am so close to England here; I know I should fulfill my duty to my aunt and my friends Maximilian and Philip and launch my feeble army in the ships I have here. But what awaits me there now?* The men of Northumberland were loath to greet me, let alone join me, last year. A shiver went through him. That had been the closest he had ever come to battle, and the idea of it chilled him to his soul. *And if the men of the north had no use for him, then why should the Cornishmen be any different? Certes, I am on a fool's errand, I feel it in my bones. I am a simple seaman,* one voice insisted. *I am naught but Piers Werbecque, son of a boatman. What do I know of fighting, or of leading men into battle or, God help me, of being a king? Ah, wounds of Christ, who am I, and what am I doing?*

Then he looked again at Katherine and his son, and his sense of honor returned. He sat up and held his head high as his other voice told him that he was indeed an English prince, albeit not the one he was pretending to be. *She believes I am Richard, duke of York, and took me to husband as such,* he mused. *She trusts me to protect her and the boy. Besides, why should I not be king? I would be kinder to my subjects than Henry,* he thought. *And she expects to be queen of England, in truth.* He imagined them both in robes of state and with crowns upon their heads, and he knew they would look the part. *How can I deny her all of that by running* away? He shook off his lethargy. Nay, I shall take ship for Cornwall and see what fate has in store, he decided, dipping his pen in the ink and continuing his letter.

Take heart, dear aunt, for with my brave Irishmen ready to fight with me, I shall set sail when the wind is fair and make for England. King Henry should look to his crown. And now I must see to the victualing of the fleet.

He chuckled as he wrote the last word; two small fishing boats and a Breton pinnace were all he had at his disposal.

When next I write, I shall report of my triumph upon English soil, I have not a doubt. All duty and honor are yours, madam.

Richard, your White Rose

28

Shene and London

AUTUMN 1497

The many-towered palace of Shene seemed to shimmer in the hazy afternoon sun, and Grace knew it for her favorite of the royal residences. Inside, the rooms were gaily painted with bright reds and blues and dotted with thousands of flowers. Other rooms were warmly paneled with the popular linen-fold carving in the ancient English oak. Most of the royal apartments gave a view of the river flowing gently past reeded banks in which lived watervoles and otters, moorhens, coots and herons. The snowy white egrets stalked along the opposite bank, which was now covered in bright purple loosestrife. Life itself might pass the inhabitants by, Grace thought as she watched her girls collect daisies with Enid.

So intent was she on making a daisy chain, Grace did not notice a boat with the king's colors floating from upstream until it had almost reached the dock. She jumped up and called to Enid to watch the girls, holding out the half-made chain to Susannah. "I must go back inside and let the queen know that a messenger has arrived," she told the little girl, who shrugged and wandered off in search of more daisies.

Grace ran along the passageway to Bess's apartments and, barely waiting to knock, she slipped in and curtsied low. Bess was choosing a thread from among her embroidery silks and talking to Anne and Catherine, her two younger sisters now both wives of earls, who had rejoined the household recently.

"Henry has sent a messenger, your grace. Perhaps 'tis news of the children coming."

Bess set down her needlework and wiped beads of perspiration off her upper lip. Despite the river breezes, it was a very warm September day, and when the messenger was ushered into the queen's presence, dark patches were visible under his arms.

"Your highness, I bring a message from his grace, the king," he began on bended knee. The other attendants went about their business, playing music, plying their needles or reading, thinking, too, that it was news of the children.

"It seems the man called Perkin has invaded England," he began unsteadily, and at once everyone in the room froze midtask. Bess put her hand to her mouth, and Grace sat down with a thump on a stool. "I shall endeavor to recount all that was told to me, your grace, and beg your indulgence if, in my haste, I forget a detail."

Bess nodded, her face the color of her snow-white plastron. "Go on, sir," she murmured. Anne fanned the queen with her kerchief, but Bess waved her away impatiently. "Go on," she said again.

And so for half an hour, the messenger told the assembled ladies how Perkin Warbeck, decked out in cloth-of-gold, had landed with four ships at St. Michael's Mount in Cornwall and how the "rebellious Cornishmen deserted their tin mines and flocked to his standard." He left his wife and baby son on the Mount, it was thought, and, after landing at St. Ives, made his way to Bodmin, where King Henry had ordered the sheriff to stop them. "By then, 'tis said, the invader had eight thousand men marching with him," the messenger announced ominously.

"Eight thousand?" Bess exclaimed as a collective gasp went up. "Who would follow this imposter thus?"

"Those who believe he is Richard, duke of York," Grace said quietly from her perch next to her. "Those who think he should be king of England."

Bess looked at her sharply, wondering if there was more to her statement than fact. But Grace met her gaze, and as her expression did not change, Bess turned back to the man. "I pray you, sir, tell us this rascally fellow fell before the king's forces."

The man looked down at his feet and played with the feather in his bonnet, which he clutched in front of his potbelly. "Nay, your grace," he muttered. "The sheriff's men fled and Perkin entered Bodmin with trumpets and cheering. There he was proclaimed king—King Richard the Fourth, second son of Edward, late king . . ." He trailed off when he saw the queen's angry face and cringed, anticipating her reaction.

"You are lying!" Bess cried, pointing her finger at him, tears springing to her eyes. "How dare you tell me such lies? And if you are, I shall have you put on the rack." She stood up and the man was dismayed to see that she was half a head taller than he. He stepped back, aghast; he had heard the queen was a gentle, pious lady who never raised her voice. She was not quiet now, God help him. He tried again, stammering so badly that Grace felt sorry for him and stood between him and Bess.

"Soft, your grace," she counseled in a low voice. "The man is only doing what he was told. Why would he lie to you? 'Tis not in his interest. I pray you, give him a chance to explain. 'Tis clear as a summer's rain that Henry is still alive and well, or he would have told you that first. Do be reasonable and sit down." She coaxed her sister into the chair. "Let him tell his story."

Bess nodded. "You have done it again, haven't you?" she said, a small smile flitting across her face. When Grace inclined her head, puzzled, Bess whispered, "Sit down, dear diplomat, and let us listen." And she waved the man on.

"Perkin crossed the Tamar at Launceston unopposed and, as he continued across the boggy, craggy wilderness that was Dartmoor, he gathered men to him. Again, those sent against him—by the sheriff of Devon this time—were afraid to fight. And those under the banner of the White Rose came to the walls of Exeter and camped overnight, preparing to besiege the city. After several days, the rebel army's inexperienced leader did attempt to enter the city—using battering rams, fire and rocks against a sky-high wall—but his force failed in its first attempt. The next day, 'tis said,

Richard's men broke through the east gate and overran the high street before the defenders pushed them back. The last news we had was that Perkin's now diminished army was on the move to Taunton—in Somerset."

"Where was the king's grace?" Bess demanded. "Where *is* the king's grace, sir?"

The man finally grinned. "He musters his forces from all points of the kingdom, your grace. I left him at Woodstock, confident he did not have to do anything but warn Perkin that he was ready to march southwest and deal with him. One army was already dogging the man. As far as I know King Henry is still there—being that I left two days ago. My liege the king tells you to be of good cheer and that all will be righted by the end of the week. There is no danger to you or your children from the feigned lad, he told me to say." It was not his place to tell her that Henry had in fact ordered Simon Digby to fetch gunners and other troops to defend the Tower as a precaution. For now, she need only know the fellow was kept at bay in the West Country and that the king was safe.

"In other cheerful news," he continued, " 'tis thought that James of Scotland was supposed to worry us on the northern border at the same time that Perkin arrived in Cornwall, but he came in August—too early—and, hearing nothing, went away again. Now he has entered into negotiations with Henry. Certes, this Perkin has no friends left."

"Except for those eight thousand who stood with him at Exeter," Bess reminded him.

"Nay, fewer than that, your highness. Perkin lost nigh on five hundred, and daily they leave him to return to their homes."

"Good news, indeed, sir. You have done well," Bess said, dismissing the man.

Grace was pleased to hear the gentler tone in her sister's voice, although her head was reeling so wildly with this information, she wondered that she noticed it. Richard had come! He had got as far as Taunton, and Henry had not stopped him. Was it possible he could reach London, and that he might take back his crown? The notion was at once exhilarating and frightening.

"RIGHT WELL BELOVED *sister, I greet you with great sadness from Pasmer's Place,*" Cecily wrote to Bess, who was reading aloud to Grace in the sun-filled solar.

"*Two days ago, my sweet Anne was taken from us and is now with God and his an-gels.*" Bess's eyes filled with tears, as she remembered the death of her own child a few years before. Grace held her hand and urged her to continue. "*It pains me to suffer this loss alone, for my noble husband is still with the king at Taunton and was unable to join me in the vigil over our daughter's poor wracked body. Despite journeying to London to consult with the king's physicians as recommended by Lady Margaret, God keep her, we were unable to discover a cure for her ailment, nor indeed name the terrible sickness that kept her in bed for the past two months. We know not if it will be passed on to Elizabeth, but, God be praised, she is healthy and strong as I write. Anne will be buried at the St. Augustine church on the morrow.*

"*Dear Bess, I will wait to know when I should join you. My days hold no joy for me and are spent grieving and helping Elizabeth understand her sister's death.*" Bess paused and looked up at her newest acquisition from Brussels, a floor-to-ceiling tapestry of a noblewoman surrounded by her children in a flower garden. "Cecily never paid her girls much attention, in truth. One day I asked her if she was glad to be a mother, and she merely shrugged, saying it was a woman's lot to bear children. Certes, she feels differently now, poor Cis." She sighed and lowered her eyes to the letter once more.

"*Until then, I send my respects to you and my dear Grace, whom I miss greatly. Say a prayer for me, and ask our Holy Mother to intercede for Anne's soul before God. Your devoted Cecily.*"

Grace crossed herself, a tear dropping onto her new emerald gown. She would pray for Anne, but before that she prayed that she would never know the loss of a child.

Harry and Margaret were immediately sent for from Eltham. Bess was so distressed by Cecily's news that she needed to embrace her own children as soon as possible. In the meantime, Grace brought Susannah and Bella into the queen's presence more often, as Bess's melancholy lifted every time she saw the little girls. Susannah had no more qualms about climbing onto Bess's lap, and her chatter kept Bess smiling for many an hour over the next week. Grace was relieved when the two royal children and their retinues arrived one drizzly afternoon. Arthur, however, had earlier joined his father at Woodstock for the hunting and was now with him at Taunton.

"Arthur is so grown up, Grace, you will see. A good-looking boy with his red-gold hair, but not so handsome as Harry. However, I think England is fortunate that thoughtful Arthur and not intemperate Harry will be king," she confided later that day, after a special banquet was held in the prince and princess's honor and the household had enjoyed roasted kid, porpoise and a swan that had arrived complete with its snowy-white feathers. The tables were cleared and the floor swept of rushes and debris from the feast to make room for dancing. Harry and Margaret were showing off a new dance they had learned together, and thoroughly enjoying the attention.

"He is vain for an eight-year-old," Bess continued, "and already knows he is a prince among boys. Margaret is a plain Jane, in truth, but the two of them are so gifted in music and dance, and they love attention." She smiled indulgently. "And both are always asking for new and finer clothes. Henry does not seem to be able to refuse them—for all he is usually a little close with his purse strings."

A little, Grace thought scornfully, remembering the shabbiness of the apartment at Bermondsey and Elizabeth's worn-out gowns. She watched as the two children, clothed in silk and satin as luxurious as any of their royal mother or aunts would wear, tripped lightly along the great hall's floor to the music of viols, recorders and rebecs, which set feet tapping and heads nodding. Her position as Bess's chief companion and half sister was not disputed by the other ladies, and thus no one thought she was breaking with etiquette when she invited Susannah up to join in the dance. The courtiers were amused by the picture of the earnest Susannah—an exact miniature of her mother—painstakingly learning the steps to the country dance, and they clapped along in time to encourage the little girl. Grace did not notice that Harry and Margaret had stopped dancing. The prince stood with arms akimbo, a sullen frown on his face as he watched them, while Margaret stalked off to her mother with her nose in the air.

Bess sighed. "They are much indulged at Eltham, it would seem. They need their father's presence more." And, not for the first time, she added, "I wish we had more news from him."

A FEW DAYS later Henry obliged her with word that Perkin had fled the field at Taunton in the middle of the night, *"where he abandoned his army in all cowardice, like the baseborn varlet he is,"* Henry wrote. *"In two days he found sanctuary at Beaulieu Abbey, after trying to take ship in Southampton and finding all ways to the coast barred by my quick action. There he languishes, it is said, dressed as a monk, while five hundred of my men surround the place."*

"But certes, Henry cannot violate sanctuary!" Grace exclaimed. "So Richard is safe."

Bess said nothing. She knew her husband had frequently violated the safe haven that religious sanctuary was supposed to provide a person in terror of his life. Nay, Perkin was not safe, she knew.

"We are to go on a pilgrimage to Walsingham," Bess said, reading the rest of the letter to herself. "Henry thinks a progress—to include Lady Margaret and Harry—will prove to the populace that England is once again safe from invasion, now that Perkin is cornered. And in truth, I think he wants me far away from London."

Grace's heart sank at the mention of Margaret Beaufort. Travel with Scraggy Maggie was the last thing she wanted to do, but as Cecily's stand-in, she knew she had no choice. She still remembered the thin, stern face with its gold-rimmed spectacles glowering at her over Henry's shoulder on the day she was sent from court; she was certain the woman disliked her. Her mind began to contemplate what arrangements she needed to make for Susannah and Bella, when Bess's voice interrupted her thoughts.

"Where are you, sister?" she said, touching Grace's hand and making her jump. "Come out of the woods, I beg of you. Ah, that's better. I was saying that I would not require you to come on this progress for two reasons. I am more than well attended, and I know you would have to send Bella and Susannah somewhere, which might prove tiresome. But more than that, I believe it would be prudent to keep my mother-in-law out of your way until the Perkin affair is thoroughly resolved."

Grace grinned. "You mean keep me out of *her* way, my considerate sister," she teased. "In truth, I must confess I am much relieved on all counts. Where shall I attend you upon your return?"

Bess pondered the question for a moment and then replied: "You may as well stay here, for I shall ask Henry if we can celebrate Christmas at Shene. 'Tis so well suited for the festivities, and this year I shall do my best, for Henry's sake, to put this difficult year behind us."

GRACE STOOD ON the riverbank with Susannah and Bella by her side and waved farewell to the royal party as the barge was rowed away from the jetty and into the downstream current. Behind it a flotilla followed, laden with enough chests of clothes, jewelry and silver to serve the party on the short progress. September was drawing to an end and, to help lessen her daughters' sadness at being left behind, Grace had promised to take them to the Michaelmas Fair to celebrate the end of the harvest.

The sun was still low on the horizon when the last of the boats rounded the bend and disappeared from view. As she walked back to the palace, leaving the girls in Enid's capable hands, she thought about her final conversation with Bess the night before.

She had found herself alone with her sister for a few minutes in the queen's chamber. Bess was anxious, anticipating the monthlong progress, and paced up and down in front of the enormous canopied bed she shared with Grace. "I am certain Henry is doing the right thing by sending me away from London, but I wish we had more news from Taunton," she said. "I knew I could count on him to bring this to a bloodless end." Bloodless but for the five hundred lost at Exeter, Grace thought, but said nothing. "What a relief it must be to have the man in his sights—albeit in sanctuary. Praise be to God. He cannot remain there, 'tis certain, and then perhaps we shall have the truth. Indulge me, Grace," she said, suddenly stopping in front of her sister. "Once and for all, admit this Perkin cannot be our brother. No royal prince would walk—nay, run—away from his army in the middle of the night. 'Tis truly the mark of a coward and a common man. If he wanted to prove he was king to Englishmen, he would have behaved like one." It was her turn to cock her head quizzically.

"Believe what you will, Bess," Grace answered her, so low Bess could hardly hear her. "But I cannot lie to you, until we have a confession from him, I must remain true to the brother I met in Malines. If you can persuade me with proof otherwise, certes, I will admit I was wrong."

"Ah, Grace, you foolish girl." Bess sighed, taking Grace's hand. "Must I send you away again so you cannot cause more concern for Tom? Already I am protecting you from a possible false step with Lady Margaret. I love you dearly and cannot bear to part with you now that Cis is gone. Anne and Catherine are good girls, but they talk of naught but their clothes and their husbands. In truth, keeping my sisters close fills the void in my heart left by my children and by Henry's long absences, but 'tis not the same," she said wistfully, and Grace again marveled how Bess was still so enamored of her cold husband. "You may remain here with the steward and some of the household, but you must promise me not to cross the king, should he come when I am gone. If you cannot, then I must send you back to Westow now."

Grace saw genuine affection in her sister's eyes, and she raised Bess's hand to her cheek and gave her a grateful smile. "Fear not, Bess. I promise to be good, and Henry will have no cause to doubt me. Let us say no more about it, for it seems Richard's cause is lost and he will be sent away, will he not?"

Humoring Grace's naive grasp of the situation, Bess nodded. "Aye, I suppose he will."

Grace sighed now, her heart heavy as she made her way back to the empty apartment. The rooms and corridors were quiet except for a few servants who were sweeping the floors and airing out the palace. The brooms had stirred up the dust, and she grimaced with annoyance as a flea, disdaining the fur on the hem of her gown, found her ankle instead and took a bite. She stopped and scratched her leg, wondering if she should dare to write to Aunt Margaret and apprise her of the events of the past few weeks. But what if the letter fell into the wrong hands? Nay, the duchess must have her spies, she decided; she does not need me. She had promised Bess she would stay out of trouble, and she would keep her promise until . . . until when? she wondered. Until her conscience caused her to break it, she supposed.

ENID CAME RUNNING into the solar, breathless, her cap askew.

"It must be important, Enid," Grace said, her raised eyebrow showing her disapproval of Enid's behavior.

Enid curtsied, her matronly bosom heaving. "Beggin' pardon, my lady," she demurred but then hurried on. "Aye, there's important it is!" she said, her Welsh way with words becoming more exaggerated because she was excited. "Downstairs is a man with news from the West, look you. Thought you might want to hear it from him, as he did stop for refreshment and to rest his horse."

"Send him to me in the hall, Enid," Grace said, rising from the table where she was writing to Alice. "And fetch the steward to meet us there."

The messenger was unshaven and dusty when he was ushered into

Grace's presence. The young man gawped at his surroundings and kept bowing every few steps as he made his way to where Grace, the steward and the chaplain stood near the massive fireplace. He first addressed the steward, believing him to be the person of importance there, but Sir Hugh set him right.

"You are in the presence of the queen's sister, Lady Grace Plantagenet, lad. 'Tis she whom you must address."

Grace almost laughed at the surprise the man was unable to disguise as he eyed her up and down. "My lady," he said, bowing twice again and touching his forelock.

"Come, sir, I do not wish to keep you from your mission. What news do you have from the king?" Grace said, and she saw the messenger's face soften when he heard her friendly tone.

"I am come from the earl of Devon, my lady," he said. "The man who calls himself duke of York has been taken by the king at Beaulieu," he began.

"Taken? But he was in sanctuary. Was he taken by force? How did the king fetch the duke out?" Grace could not stop herself from asking the questions, although she heard the quick intake of breath from Sir Hugh next to her. "I meant to say Perkin Warbeck," she added hurriedly. Woe betide if her slip was passed on to the king.

"With cleverness, it seems," the messenger answered her. "He promised Perkin a pardon, so the man and his councilors agreed to put themselves in the king's hands." He lifted his shoulders and turned his palms up. "I ask you, what else could he do? When they came out of the abbey this Perkin was royally dressed in cloth-of-gold, like he was a king. 'Tis said many people who came to see him shouted insults and hissed at him."

Grace trembled for her brother. "Where is he now?" she whispered.

"He was taken by Richmond Herald back to Taunton, where the king awaited. God be praised, 'tis said he confessed that he was not who he claimed to be."

Grace gasped and would have fallen had not the chaplain, who had heard her confession several times in the past month, steadied her and murmured: "Do not lose faith, my lady."

Grace regained her composure then, thanked the messenger and commanded that he be fed and a fresh horse be given him. Then she left the steward in charge and, smiling her thanks to the priest, walked slowly out of the hall. Once out of sight, she raced up the stairs and along the passage to the solar, where she bolted the door behind her and fell to her knees, weeping.

He had confessed. The words ran round and round in her head as she conjured up the scene in Taunton. He was tortured, she suddenly realized. Certes, he must have been tortured!

BESS'S HOMECOMING TO Shene was a joyful one, despite the dank October day that caused the smoke from the bonfires to linger like ghostly fingers among the gnarled apple trees, now plucked bare of their rosy fruit. The pilgrim's prayers said at the shrine in Walsingham had been answered, a happy Bess told Grace when she greeted her sister with a hug. England was safe again, and Henry would be back in London soon, he had promised her.

"Grace!" a familiar voice called to her from the second vehicle. "Come, give me your greeting, too." A smile curved Grace's lips as she recognized Cecily's lovely face peering from behind the carriage curtain. She ran to greet her sister.

"Is the king's mother come with you?" Grace whispered as she kissed Cecily's cheek, and when she was told no, she breathed a sigh of relief.

"But she will be here for Yuletide, little one, so gird your loins," Cecily teased. "Sweet Jesu, but 'tis good to see you again. I can see you have been outside overly much of late—you are no longer resembling a Spaniard; in truth, you could pass for a Moor."

"Pish!" Grace responded, laughing. "I did help with the apple-picking, although I gathered those fallen. I did not climb the ladders, you will be glad to know. Oh, Cis," she said, quickly changing her tone, "how sorry I am for the loss of little Anne. I pray you found comfort at Walsingham."

Cecily's face fell and she squeezed Grace's hand as they processed behind the queen into the palace. "I was grateful for your prayers and your letter, Grace. I was happy I was able to join Bess on the pilgrimage and, aye, I derived some comfort from it."

"Did you walk the last mile barefoot from the Slipper Chapel? 'Tis then one pays the greatest penance, I have heard, and receives the greatest blessing. I wish with all my heart I could make the pilgrimage. Did you see the Virgin's milk?"

"Tell no one, Grace, but I believe 'twas naught but chalk and water. It did not look like milk from any woman's breast I know, in truth."

"Cecily!" Grace was aghast and crossed herself. "Have a care. Someone may take you for a Lollard. You well know the Virgin Mary gave the Widow Faverches the drops after she told the woman how to build the shrine. Certes, thousands have made the pilgrimage, and many have been cured or given comfort. How can you doubt the faith of so many?"

"Because I am becoming a snappish old woman," Cecily retorted, chuckling. "Pay me no mind, Grace. I hope you have had the kitchen ready a feast for us; I am ravenous."

Before the queen and her chattering attendants reached their respective quarters, Cecily was able to murmur: "You have heard the news about Richard, I suppose? Although I now do not believe he is Richard, and"—she gripped Grace's arm to stop her interrupting—"you *must* stop believing, too. We shall soon hear the truth from Henry, and we must bow to his wisdom and judgment, no matter how hard we may not wish to. Promise me you will, Grace."

Not another promise, Grace thought grimly. Although she felt like screaming, she found herself smiling sweetly instead. "As you wish, Cis," she replied, dutifully enough, but then added: "As soon as I hear the truth for myself."

THREE DAYS LATER, with Harry and Margaret again in attendance, Bess held a banquet celebrating their safe arrival home and for the deliverance from the threat of the pretender. Cecily helped Grace dress in the new fashion for the first time that night. Bess had been true to her word, and had paid for Grace to have two new gowns made. Grace had been overcome by the queen's generosity, especially as Bess often mended her own gowns and had no qualms about wearing them over and over again.

"Enough, I beg of you," Grace exclaimed as Cecily pulled hard on the laces of the boned bodice that seemed to compress her every rib and force her breasts upward to form soft mounds just visible above the edge. The kirtle was of stiff green and gold diamond-patterned satin and tied around her waist, from where it flared to the floor in a wide circle.

Grace looked at herself in the long silver mirror and made a face. "This fashion is for taller women," she complained. "It makes me look as if I have no legs."

"Patience, little sister," Cecily said, picking up the gown made of yards of silky black velvet trimmed in gold buckram that she put on Grace like a coat. The wide, open sleeves almost overpowered her, and Grace was critical when she stepped back to be admired. " 'Tis too much stuff, in truth, and so heavy." But as she twirled in a slow circle and caught a glimpse of herself in the mirror again, she smiled. "What do you think, Cis?"

"You are beautiful, Grace," Cecily said truthfully. " 'Tis unfortunate, though, that fashion dictates you cover up those magnificent locks. But cover them you must. I shall send Enid to you to plait it, although how she manages, I cannot imagine."

Bess was delighted with her half sister's new gown when her score of attendants were gathered around the door to the great hall. " 'Tis as well you are already wed, Grace, for I swear you will have every man here lusting for you this night," she said as she waited on the threshold to make her entrance.

The banquet lasted for two hours and, as was the queen's custom, was eaten in silence but for the lilting sounds of lutes, mandolins and gemshorns. As chief attendant, Cecily sat to Bess's left, but young Harry had the place of honor on his mother's right hand. Princess Margaret sat next to him, and Grace next to Cecily.

When the ewerers had offered the handbasins for the final finger-washing and the voide was being served, Bess allowed conversation to begin and the tables to be cleared for dancing.

Once again Prince Harry was the first on the dance floor and once again he partnered his sister, while the rest of the household watched and openly admired the pair, passing remarks to one another on Harry's fine leg or Margaret's perfectly demure countenance.

A flurry of activity at the far end of the hall caught Bess's attention and caused the music to peter out. The dancers stopped.

"What is it, Lady Anne?" the queen called to her sister, who was conversing with Lady Fitzwalter at the bottom of the dais steps. "Can you see?"

Grace had just returned from the garderobe and so stood quietly near the door, observing a small cloaked stranger flanked by two yeomen in the king's livery waiting in the shadow of the doorway. She recognized the man in front of the newcomer as Windsor Herald from the sunburst-out-of-clouds badge he wore, and she knew at once this party must be from the king.

The queen's chamberlain hurried forward upon hearing Bess's question. Bowing low, he told her: " 'Tis a retinue from Exeter, your grace. It appears the king has sent the pretender's wife to you, so the herald tells me. She requests an audience."

"Does she have a name?" Bess asked, taken aback, and the chamberlain turned and beckoned to the herald. As he moved forward, the stranger took two steps into the room and her hood fell back to reveal a young woman of about Grace's age with porcelain skin, large gray eyes and fair, almost woolly hair visible under her black velvet bonnet. She unhooked her mantle and immediately a young page stepped forward to take it from her. Her black satin gown, decorated with ribbons and accented in an amber fabric, was obviously new—a gift from the king, Grace later discovered.

Keeping her eyes respectfully on the floor, the young woman advanced towards the dais, the two guards flanking her, and sank into a deep reverence, remaining humbly on her knees.

"Lady Katherine Gordon, daughter of the earl of Huntly and kinswoman of James, king of Scotland, your grace," Windsor Herald intoned. "She was lately called wife of the pretender, Perkin Warbeck. I am commanded to bring her here by our merciful sovereign King Henry and place her in your protection."

Grace had slipped back into her seat, not wanting to miss a moment of this fascinating scene. Cecily glanced over at her and raised her eyebrows, her mouth open in surprise. A buzz began among the courtiers, who had closed ranks behind Katherine and were all trying to get a look at an intimate of the pretender.

"I am his lawful wife still, herald," Katherine Gordon said in her strong Scottish burr and, daring to look up at Bess, added, "if it please, your grace."

Bess avised the young woman for at least a minute as the court stood silently waiting. And then, to Grace's immense awe, the queen left her throne, glided down the steps of the dais and held out her hand to raise Katherine herself. Kissing the queen's fingers first and her tears flowing, the lovely Scottish noblewoman slowly got to her feet, using the proffered hand to guide her.

"You must be travel weary, Lady Katherine." Bess turned and looked straight at Grace. "My sister will be glad to relinquish her seat to you, will you not, Lady Grace?"

Grace could not stop her blush. She knew that Bess was trying to send her a message that spoke of her compassion for Grace's mistaken belief in Perkin but that also said, I am the queen and I accept this woman because she is a noblewoman and has been unjustly wedded to a deceiver. Grace left her seat, fully aware the whole room was watching her and, descending the steps, curtsied to Bess and stood aside. Katherine looked at her curiously and nodded her thanks.

But before Bess allowed Katherine to sit, she first presented Cecily, then Margaret and, finally, in a voice that could be heard throughout the hall, said, "And this is my second son, Prince Henry, the duke of York."

Cecily told Grace later that Katherine had gone white, well understanding the queen's implication. There is only one rightful duke of York in this land, she was saying, and he sits before you, my lady.

THE SOUND OF muffled sobs came to Grace as she passed the queen's wardrobe one dreary afternoon soon after Lady Katherine's arrival. Thinking it was one of the servants who ought not be in the storage room at that hour, she went in. In the jumble of chests, gowns, cloaks, curtains and other bric-a-brac and with only a tiny window to illuminate the space, it took her a few seconds to distinguish the figure slumped on top of a folded arras on the floor.

"Do you have permission to be in here, mistress?" Grace asked, not unkindly, thinking she was speaking to a maid. She was taken aback when Katherine Gordon's blotched face appeared. She sniffed loudly. Grace was surprised, the young woman was supposed to be supervised at all times, Bess had instructed. "We do not want her running off to bring us more trouble," the queen had told them. "She has powerful friends in Scotland, remember."

Grace knelt down beside Katherine, taking the women's frail body in her arms and rocking her like a baby. "There, there. Weeping has never harmed anyone, and 'tis time you had a good cry," she said as Katherine buried her head on Grace's shoulder and let her tears fall.

Gradually the sobs gave way to sniffles, and finally Grace felt the young woman pull away, searching for her kerchief in her voluminous sleeve. She was still wearing the same black and brown dress she had arrived in, but it was now rumpled and tear-stained. When she recognized Grace, she stiffened, fear in her eyes. "I pray you, Lady Grace, do not tell the queen I was here."

Grace had no intention of tattling on Katherine. She was much too curious to hear from Richard's wife how Henry had treated her—and her husband—when they had been captured. She patted Katherine's knee and put her finger to her lips. Before closing the door she peered up and down the passage to make sure no one else was wandering in that area of the palace. She pulled up an old footstool and told Katherine that she alone in the queen's train believed Richard to be the duke of York. Katherine was too distraught to be wary, and relief spread over her face.

Breathing a little more easily, Katherine told of her capture at St. Buryan's priory, where she had moved to with her son from the Mount not long after Richard left. "I thought 'twould be safer there, and the wee island is nay braw enough for a bairn of Dickon's age. Poor wee mite was crabbity all the time." Grace had a little trouble understanding Katherine's heavy brogue, but she listened intently.

"But there was a more important reason for my leaving Saint Michael's," Katherine confided, her chin trembling. "I was carrying our second child, but the uncomfortable sea voyages and all the distress of what would become of us made me ill. I lost the child at Saint Buryan's—a little girl, it was."

Grace's eyes filled with tears as she pictured the anguish this poor woman had suffered. Certes, no wonder she was all in black. "God rest her soul," she whispered, crossing herself. "I am heartily sorry for you, Lady Katherine."

Katherine smiled and continued with her tale. She said she had been taken from sanctuary by three important men sent by the king, one of whom was master of the household, and Grace grimaced upon hearing that once again Henry had violated sanctuary laws. "When they knew I was in mourning for the bairn, they allowed me to stay cloistered in a house nearby for a respectful few days before they took me to the king."

"Did you see your husband then?" Grace whispered. "Did Henry at least allow you to see him?"

Katherine hung her head, nodding. She could not look at Grace. "I am ashamed, my lady. I was so relieved to see Richard alive that I fell to my knees weeping and blessed the king for his mercy. He told me my husband had deceived me, and that he was naught but a lying scoundrel. I was shocked to hear this from the king's own mouth, even though it had been whispered in Scotland. But my kinsman James, and all my noble family believed Richard was the duke of York. Why should I not have? In all our time together, he treated me with all honor and love, and I cannot believe he is not a prince." She broke down again, and Grace waited patiently. She could imagine Henry standing, watching like a bird of prey, his cold face smug and his bony hands rubbing together in satisfaction. "Then the king raised me in all gentleness and made me face Richard—who had said nothing all this time," Katherine continued in a monotone. "We were alone with the king, and I wanted him with all my heart to deny the king's charge and to say that he *was* the duke of York, younger son of Edward, but he did not."

She turned away and stared at the wall. "Dear God, instead he told me he was not who he had said he was, and that others had led him to believe he was the duke when he knew he was not. And he then begged my for-giveness and asked the king to return me to my family. He did not want me to stay." She plucked at her gown, as if working up the courage to admit something terrible. Then she blurted out, "I called him accursed, wicked and a seducer. And I told him I loathed him. It was the last thing I said to him before they took him away. But I don't loathe him—I love him. Ah, by the sweet Virgin, I love him truly." She flung herself back down on the rolled-up arras, crying to her own St. Catherine that she wished she were dead.

"My dear Lady Katherine, certes you loathed him in that moment, and you had every right to tell him so," Grace reasoned, patting Katherine's heaving shoulders gently. Grace did not know how she could console Kath-erine until she understood what was in her own heart. Could it be that he has deceived me, too? she wondered miserably. If he had denied he was Richard to the person he loved most in all the world, then surely it must be true. Ever eager to solve a problem, she quickly came to a solution. "Have you not considered that perhaps he confessed to being a pretender in order to protect you and your son? Aye, Richard saw the way of things, once his military cause was lost and Henry had cornered him, and his only thoughts were of you and his son. If he persisted saying he was the duke of York, he would only make Henry angrier and more vengeful. Nay, 'tis clear as spring water Henry threatened that harm would come to you and the boy if Richard did not make the confession the king wanted to hear," she finished triumphantly, hoping to stay Katherine's noisy weeping. " 'Tis simple when you think about it," she reiterated. But she was missing something—something important. What was it? Then it dawned on her. "Your son? Where *is* your son?"

Katherine's muffled voice came from the folds of the tapestry. "They took him from me at Saint Buryan's. I have not seen him since." She sat up slowly, a glint of anger in her eyes. "The king promised the child would be sent to me here anon. I hope he keeps his promises."

Grace looked away, not wanting her doubt to add to the mother's distress. "You may be sure he is well cared for," she reassured her. "Now, wash your face and straighten your headdress. Your absence will have been noted by now. You can say you were lost in the labyrinth of corridors. Certes, I still do not know my way around them. But, I beg of you, do not tell anyone of our talk—I have brought enough trouble on myself and my family already."

She helped Katherine to her feet and propelled her to the door. "Go now, quickly, but know that you have a friend at court."

THE KING'S CAVALCADE rode slowly across the drawbridge, under the portcullis and gate behind and into the main courtyard late in the day on the eighteenth day of November—a day marked by heavy downpours that turned the road to the palace into a quagmire. They had been expecting Henry for two days, and Bess waited in her long audience chamber for her husband, her attendants fussing with her train and the blue velvet veil hanging down her back from her jeweled gabled headband. But Henry kept his wife waiting for another hour while he changed out of his wet traveling clothes and warmed his feet in front of the fire in his own chamber.

Grace was determined that no sign of any friendship with Katherine would be visible to the court, but while Henry took his time escorting his prisoner to London, she managed to reassure Katherine a few times that she had meant what she said. Now she had placed herself on the other side of Bess from where Katherine stood and was half hidden by the taller Anne and Cecily in the hope she would not be noticed. Why she needed to worry, she could not say, because she was sure the king would have eyes only for his wife.

She was mistaken, however, for when Henry was announced and stalked in on his long, strong legs—which Grace had once acknowledged to Cecily were his only good feature—his eyes scanned the group of ladies and briefly rested on Katherine Gordon's face before he focused his full attention on Bess. Grace was no judge, she admitted to herself, but was there a hint of lust in Henry's lashless eyes when he saw the Scottish woman? Nay, I must have been mistaken, she thought, watching him kiss each of Bess's hands, and then her lips, with ardor.

"Where is Perkin Warbeck, my lord?" Bess asked, smiling. "Is he locked up safely somewhere?"

"Nay, your grace. It pleases me to treat him as I would any guest who has had the friendship of kings and an emperor," Henry said, amused that his nonchalance was catching his wife and the assembled company off guard.

Bess was nonplussed and her smile faded. "But is he not an enemy? A traitor?"

"Certes, he is an invader whom we have vanquished, but as a foreigner he cannot be a traitor, can he? I have not decided what we shall do with him, but I shall, never fear. At this moment, however, he is travel weary—as am I, my dear. We shall rest and meet at supper, if that pleases you?" He lifted her hand to his lips again and waited for her response. He knew what it would be; his accommodating wife had never gainsaid him yet in their marriage, and he doubted she would begin now.

"Whatever pleases you pleases me, my lord," she said, smiling again. " 'Til supper, then."

Henry bowed, turned on his heel and hurried away before any other awkward questions about his odd treatment of the pretender could be raised.

"Extraordinary," Cecily murmured to Grace while they were still in their curtsy.

"Nay, 'tis not," Grace replied, a little glimmer of hope in her heart. "It means he is still not convinced one way or the other."

. . .

GRACE AND TOM strolled arm in arm around the queen's audience chamber, talking and admiring the view of the river from the long windows.
Others also took the opportunity to stretch their legs in the long hall, its
walls boasting murals of long-ago legends, as the rain continued outside.
Her sisters Anne and Catherine along with their husbands led the way,
and behind Grace and Tom several attendants, including Lady Katherine
Gordon, lollygagged in their wake.

Without warning the king appeared on the threshold and waited for
the courtiers to move aside and provide passage to the low dais at the far
end of the room. Following behind him, clothed in his own princely finery
and walking freely, was Perkin Warbeck. A gasp of surprise echoed around
the room when the man's identity was whispered. Grace caught sight of
Katherine Gordon's stricken face in the group opposite her as Perkin's eyes
scanned the many courtiers, searching for her. A look of relief came over
his handsome features when he found her, and he quickly turned his gaze
back to the king in front of him, Henry's pet monkey scampering along
on his golden chain beside him. The implication was not lost on the court,
whose eyes were now glued to Henry's other pet—the pretender. After the
initial murmuring, the room went quiet.

Grace saw Thomas of Dorset frown when he observed the man from
only a few feet away, and Grace could not decide if he was recognizing him
or not. The two were half brothers, albeit twenty-two years apart, and
Dorset had not often been in the little prince's presence during Edward's
reign. Would he recognize the boy of ten in a man now twenty-four? Would
she have picked Ned of Warwick out in a crowd from the nine-year-old boy
at Sheriff Hutton? She thought not.

Henry called for a stool for Perkin and allowed him to sit a few steps
down from the throne. "Lady Katherine, I pray you, approach us and greet
your husband," Henry said, his sallow face animated for once, his bony
fingers fondling the white-faced monkey. "And let us have music. 'Tis far
too sober in here."

Henry's cheerfulness astonished the court, and Grace wished Cecily
were present to discuss it. She frowned. Where was the queen? She assumed Cecily was in attendance, and later when she helped ready Bess for
bed, she found out.

"Henry thought it prudent for Bess to stay away from *le garçon*," Cecily said, emphasizing Henry's favorite French moniker for Perkin. "He said 'twas insulting to the queen to have to endure the company of a man who played the part of her beloved departed brother," Cecily whispered as they set out Bess's finest chemise. Another attendant was warming the mattress with hot stones, and sweet herbs were sprinkled on the soft white bed linen. The king would attend the queen tonight, they had been told, and Bess must be at her most alluring.

Grace nodded, but she was certain Henry was afraid that Bess might recognize Richard as her brother, and she knew Henry could not take that chance. But there were many others who could have told the king the truth, she thought. Many of King Edward's councilors were still at court—like Cardinal John Morton, and Prince Richard's attorney, Andrew Dymock, who was now Henry's solicitor. Certes, Richard's cousin and contemporary the earl of Arundel would have played with the prince in those far-off days. It seemed all had accepted the confession as the truth, and none was about to gainsay the king.

And ever since her clandestine conversation with Katherine, a niggling doubt that Richard was her half brother had crept like a worm into Grace's heart. She tried to squash it, prayed to St. Thomas to ease it, but it wriggled and squirmed its way into her waking thoughts, making her snappish even with Tom.

"My courses are due, 'tis all," she told him when he expressed concern. "It will pass."

Before Henry left Shene for Westminster after three days' rest, he called the queen's household together and, with Perkin standing between his two guardians high in the musicians' gallery, commanded Cardinal Morton, archbishop of Canterbury, to read the confession made at Taunton. The old man stepped forward and read it as he would a lesson from the Bible:

"First it is to be known that I was born in the town of Tournai in Flanders, and my father's name is John Osbeck: which said John Osbeck was controller of the town of Tournai. And my mother's name is Katherine de Faro." People frowned at the unfamiliar Osbeck name, but Grace remembered Tom saying Henry's spies had interchanged the name with Werbecque in their reports. Perhaps this was a sign that Henry had indeed tortured the unfortunate man into repeating only what he was told to say, she thought.

Morton droned on with a detailed list of Perkin's relatives and their rank, none of whom gave Grace a sense of where Perkin's advanced education could have been achieved, but her ears pricked up when Morton read: "*. . . afterward I was led by my mother to Antwerp to learn Flemish in a house of a cousin of mine . . . with whom I was the space of half a year.*" Then he fell sick for five months while with a merchant named Berlo in a house nearby the English merchants. "*After this the said Berlo set me with a merchant in Middelburg to service, with whom I dwelled from Christmas unto Easter; and then I went into Portugal in the company of Sir Edward Brampton's wife in a ship which was called the Queen's ship. And when I was come thither, I was put in service to a knight that dwelled in Lisbon which was called Pero Vaz da Cuhna, with whom I dwelled an whole year, which said knight had but one eye; and then because I desired to see other countries, I took license of him. And then I put myself in service with a Breton called Pregent Meno, the which brought me with him into Ireland. And when we were there arrived in the town of Cork, they of the town, because I was arrayed with some clothes of silk came until me and threped upon that I should be the duke of Clarence's son . . .*"

Grace glanced up at Perkin, but he stared straight ahead at the royal arms carved in the plaster high above the king's head. "*And for as much as I denied it, there was brought until me the Holy Evangelist and the Cross by the Mayor of the town; and there in the presence of him and others I took my oath as truth was that I was not the aforesaid duke's son, nor other of his blood.*"

The confession stated that Perkin was then urged to pretend he was King Richard's bastard, John, which he denied. Grace blanched at this and then felt Tom's hand lightly squeeze her shoulder in sympathy from behind her. She put up her hand and touched his gratefully.

Morton took a sip of wine and savored the absolute silence in the room. "*And then they advised me not to be afraid but that I should take it upon me boldly, and if I would so do they would aid and assist me with all their power against the king of England.*"

A gasp went up at this treasonous statement, and, as one, the heads swiveled from looking at Morton to Perkin. Still he remained motionless. The confession now implicated the earls of Desmond and Kildare in the plot, "*so that they might be revenged upon the king of England; and so against my will made me to learn English, and taught me what I should do and say.*" Is that true? Grace wondered. She was so confused, she began to question her sanity. She remembered him at Dendermonde describing his flight from the

Tower, the death of his brother, his kindly treatment at Guisnes. It had all seemed so genuine, and Aunt Margaret believed it, too. She brought her focus back to the archbishop, who was coming to the end.

". . . *and thence I went into France, and from thence into Flanders and from Flanders into Ireland. And from Ireland into Scotland and so into England.*" Morton looked over the top of his spectacles at the expectant courtiers and held up the document for all to see. "It is signed by the man up there—Piers Osbeck or Pierrequin Werbecque or whatever other name he falsely uses. The so-called duke of York," he cried scornfully, pointing at Perkin, who was now flushed pink.

A commotion in the group opposite spoiled Morton's dramatic moment, and Tom whispered, " 'Tis Perkin's wife. She has swooned."

"You ARE TO accompany Lady Katherine in the king's train tomorrow," Bess told Grace that night at the prie-dieu, where Bess had invited her to pray. "She is well enough now, but I sent her to bed early. Henry wants the couple to be seen in public."

Grace knew her sister well enough to recognize that Bess was nonplussed by this turn of events, but she merely nodded and waited. Why me? she wanted to ask. Does Henry suspect me still? I have given him no reason, she thought, unless someone saw me speaking to Katherine those few times and reported it. But she had been very careful.

"Henry asked me which of my ladies I could spare who would be kind to Lady Katherine, and I told him you were the only one I could trust." Bess half turned to make sure they were not overheard. "I also thought 'twas a chance for you to make amends with Henry, Grace. He knows you are the only one of my sisters who is unconvinced of Perkin's guilt. Perhaps you can be her confidante and—"

"And spy on her!" Grace hissed angrily. "How could you, Bess?"

"Be silent, sister," Bess warned, and for the first time Grace felt the power of the queen and was cowed. "If you do not do as I ask, I will send you from here in disgrace. And there will be no returning this time. Do I make myself clear?"

"Aye, your grace." Grace's voice was barely audible, and tears stung her eyes. "I will gladly accompany Lady Katherine."

" 'Tis well said," Bess answered. "All I ask is that you stay close while

Henry takes her with Perkin to Westminster. Your children will be safe with us here. You will all return for Christmas in a month's time, and I shall pray daily that by then you, too, dear Grace, will believe the man is not our brother."

"Aye, Bess," Grace assented again. Then, taking her courage in her hands, she begged a favor. " 'Tis my understanding—or perhaps 'tis naught but gossip—that Lady Katherine's child was removed from her custody before she was at Exeter. If Lady Katherine should mention this to me"—Grace held her thumb between her first two fingers to protect her lie—"what may I tell her? I know that as a mother, you—and I—would be bereft if the same were to happen to us."

Bess turned her head and stared at Grace. "A child, you say? 'Tis the first I have heard of it." She turned back to gaze on the vibrant portrait of her own St. Elizabeth, mother of John the Baptist and patron saint of all expectant mothers. Dear God, what has Henry done now?

"Aye. Katherine and Perkin"—Grace used the name to appease Bess—"have a son—Richard," she said. "He was with them when they landed in Cornwall." She dared not say more or Bess would guess she had had intimate conversation with Katherine. "I thought everyone knew," she said innocently.

"I will find out what I can, Grace, but I cannot promise anything. Henry is secretive and touchy about *le garçon*, as you know. I shall not see him privately before he leaves on the morrow, and at Christmas"—Bess drew a breath—"his mother will be with him."

Grace heard the resignation in the final statement and nodded. "I understand."

"Give Lady Katherine my assurance that the child is well cared for. 'Tis all I can do." And with that, Bess crossed herself and rose, signaling the end of the private conversation.

"God bless you, good Queen Elizabeth," Grace murmured, and she saw Bess smile.

29

London

WINTER 1497

Riding for all he was a free man and showing he was as at home in the saddle as any of the nobles who rode in Henry's train, Perkin seemed not to have a care in the world. Some way behind him, Grace rode pillion on her cousin Richard de la Pole's palfrey, with Katherine on her own horse alongside. The retinue was strung out for half a mile along the road to Lambeth, and for once the weather was kind. A milky sun penetrated the ever-present clouds, but the fields were boggy and the trees dripped moisture down unsuspecting necks as the riders brushed past the bare branches. It was cold enough for the horses' breath to plume from their nostrils, and Grace's feet on the pillion-saddle support were already numb. She hated November: the last of the leaves had fallen; mists and fogs rolled in; the dark, cold mornings often meant breaking ice in the wash basin; and the sun rarely shone. Even the birds were not singing, except for the unattractive cawing of jackdaws and crows, foraging what they could find in the fallow fields. The parting from Susannah and Bella had been hard for Grace, but with other children now to play with, they hardly knew she had left them.

The royal barge at Lambeth dock was waiting, and so was a small but vocal crowd, who jeered and booed Perkin as he dismounted and was helped into the vessel. How cruel Henry is, Grace thought angrily, although she had to confess that Perkin did not appear unduly discouraged. Katherine, on the other hand, could not stop the tears from coming, and as Grace maneuvered herself close to the young woman in preparation for embarking on the second barge, she whispered: "Courage, Lady Katherine. Take a leaf from your husband's book."

The mockery was worse on the Westminster side of the river, and Perkin suffered the ignominy of spittle and an egg. Henry pretended not to notice as he strode up the path to the king's gate and on into the palace. Grace was glad the citizenry did not know Katherine Gordon was in the king's train, but she was beginning to understand Henry's motive for including the pretender's wife. Certes, he wants her to see that England has forsaken Perkin, she concluded, and that his cause is lost. He is as wily as a fox, she decided, but she was still puzzled as to why he had not simply imprisoned or executed the man. Henry had not quibbled earlier that month when he chose to hang all the Flemings who had been captured at Deal during the first disastrous invasion attempt. In truth, his clemency gave her hope that perhaps deep down he could not bring himself to end the life of someone who might be King Edward's son. God's wounds, she thought scornfully, I hope he stews in his own juice.

More outings in London followed the arrival of the king at Westminster, and each time Perkin either rode amiably with whomever was alongside, or he rode in dignified silence, enduring the stares and ridicule of Londoners lining the streets or hanging from second-story windows. By then he was known by one name only—Perkin—in the manner of a lowly servant, and the name was cursed on every corner, at every market cross and in every tavern. The worst ride yet came on November twenty-eighth, Grace wrote to Cecily, when Perkin was *"forced to lead one of his followers—who had once been Henry's farrier—lashed to a horse all the way to the Tower. 'Twas said the man expected to be imprisoned or, worse, executed, but it pleased Henry to command Perkin to lead the farrier all the way back again to Westminster. For what purpose,*

Cis, I cannot tell except that more curses were heaped upon both men. Through all of it, Perkin was brave and dignified, so Tom tells me."

Two days earlier Henry decided to show off his captive to the various ambassadors who served their European masters at Westminster. This was nothing new, Tom told Grace when they had a chance to talk that morning after Mass. "The viscount says the Spanish ambassador—you know de Puebla, I think—is increasingly concerned with the king's indecision with regard to Perkin. He says de Puebla told my lord that Ferdinand and Isabella want no trace of doubt as to Arthur's claim to the throne. The alliance is in abeyance because of Perkin."

"A pox on Henry's alliance," Grace muttered. "Whether he be Richard or no, the unfortunate man has no right to be treated thus. So he is to be paraded again tonight?"

"Aye. But this time, Katherine is to be by his side," Tom said, looking at the subject of their discussion walking to the lodgings accompanied by two servants.

"She will be ecstatic," Grace exclaimed. "Although the black dress is decidedly travel-stained, we shall endeavor to have her looking her best for her husband tonight."

"Lady Katherine does not need ribbons and satins to be the most beautiful woman in the room," Tom mused, and was not prepared for the kick to his shins he received for his thoughtless remark. "You did not let me finish my sentence," he complained, grinning sheepishly. "I was going to say 'except for my wife, dearest Grace,' truly I was." And, taking off at a run, he avoided another playful blow.

As KATHERINE'S COMPANION, Grace stood by the young couple in a corner of the king's smaller audience chamber. Katherine looked paler tonight in her black dress, Grace thought, although it lent her an ethereal beauty. Perkin was arrayed in his cloth-of-gold suit, complete with a spice-studded orange pomander hanging from a ribbon around his neck. It was the first time Grace had been close enough to speak to him since their meeting in Dendermonde, but she dared not say anything to him, as all eyes were upon the little group.

Henry had entertained his guests at a feast earlier with fire-eaters, tumblers, jugglers, a bearded woman and a giantess from Flanders. Then he invited a privileged few into this room, where Diego, Henry's Spanish fool, poked fun at de Puebla in his native tongue, making the ambassador throw back his hairy head and roar with laughter. As a juggler tossed balls in the air, distracting the guests, no one was aware for a few moments that Perkin, his two escorts and Katherine, accompanied by two attendants, had been let into the room. Suddenly the Milanese Raimondo Soncino spotted them and, nudging Ambassador Trevisano, his friend from Venice, jerked his head in the couple's direction.

Katherine was trembling—Grace did not know if from touching her beloved husband again or from fright—and Perkin took her hand possessively. The admiration in the Italians' faces told Grace they found the couple beautiful to behold.

"I give you Lady Katherine Gordon of Huntley and her husband, Perkin," Henry announced, as if toasting them. "They are free to converse with you."

Grace took a step back and stood alongside the second attendant, with Perkin's men on her other side. Robert Jones was sewer of the chamber, and William Smyth was one of Henry's ushers of the chamber, and, as close associates of the king, they were commanded to be with Perkin everywhere. They did not look unkind, Grace thought, and William did not seem particularly alert. 'Twas odd that Henry had not chosen armed guards. Grace looked down at her feet, her square-toed shoes peeking out from under her green gown, and wished the sordid and humiliating scene would come to an end.

It eventually did, but not before Perkin whispered of his love to his wife by hiding behind the pomander that he pretended to sniff, and fondled her neck, stealing one desperate kiss. "How long must we live like this?" Katherine whispered. "And do you have news of our son?"

"What can you mean, my love?" came his puzzled reply. Then Perkin turned angry eyes towards the dais. "I thought he was with you all this time," he muttered through clenched teeth. "Christ's nails, where is he?" He looked at Grace, who had come between them and Smyth and Jones to keep the conversation private. "Do you know, Grace?"

Grace shook her head. "I am trying to discover his whereabouts." She saw Henry's eyes on them. "Have a care, the king is watching. I can do no more."

After making their reverences to the king, Katherine and Perkin bowed to the other spectators—that is how Grace described them later to Tom— and made their exits, in different directions. "They may stand close in public," Soncino whispered to Trevisano as Grace moved past them, "but they can never bed again. Too dangerous. *Molto pericoloso.*"

"Lady Grace, pray approach the throne." The king's command took Grace off-guard, as she was about to follow Katherine from the room. Her knees wobbled as she walked back to Henry and sank to her knees in a curtsy. Henry pointed to the golden chair next to him, where Bess would have sat had she been present. "Tell me, how does my lady of Huntly? She appears tired, but otherwise healthy. Am I correct?"

Grace smoothed her skirts and then clasped her hands in her lap. She was aware of many pairs of eyes on her, and she felt the blush start up from the edge of her square-necked bodice, Elizabeth's amber brooch pinned at its center. What could Henry want from her? She took a deep breath and then looked at the king, who was watching her with amusement. She opened her mouth, but nothing came out.

"Why are you so afraid of me, my lady?" he said quietly. "My wife always speaks so affectionately of you to me. Certes, you cannot doubt that I respect her opinion, and therefore I must look upon you as a dear sister, too. Aye, you were deluded all those years ago, but Bess tells me you are reformed—thanks to the guidance of your husband, *sans dout*. You should know my uncle thinks highly of Sir Thomas Gower and trusts him in all things. He has the opportunity to rise at court, if he—and you—play your cards right." He gave her a friendly smile. "I believe we can now trust you, can we not? Come, answer me, Grace, or has the cat run away with your tongue?"

Grace closed her mouth, astonished by his benevolence. "My duty is to you, your grace, and my sister," she said, a little hesitantly. Where was this leading? she wondered. "And I honor my husband with all my heart."

"And with your body, I trust," Henry said, leaning to her and winking. "You make a handsome couple, in truth. Your husband is a fortunate man."

Now Grace was completely perplexed. Was the king flirting with her? If he was, she was disgusted. Thank Heaven Tom has already left, she thought. "Th-thank you, your grace," was all she could think to say. She noticed that his velvet bonnet was making his forehead sweat in the heat of so many candles, and then she noticed his smile had faded and his myopic blue eyes glittered. Her stomach lurched.

"I would know what *le garçon* and his peahen were talking of earlier, Grace. I pray you, do not dissemble. I cannot expect you to swear on your little daughters' souls, but I do expect you to honor me with the truth."

Sweet Mary, he *is* threatening me, Grace realized, thunderstruck. I am his mouse: first the playing, then the pounce. She gripped her hands and felt Tom's ring digging into her finger. It gave her courage. "I will tell you readily, your grace," she said, leveling her gaze at him and taking Henry aback. "They spoke of their love, which seems to be considerable. And then they spoke of their son—the one who was taken from Lady Katherine at Saint Buryan's. Perkin was unaware—and dismayed—that the child was no longer in her care. Both expressed a desire to know if he is well." She forced a dazzling smile. "And as a father yourself, your grace, I cannot think you will blame them for that."

Now it was Henry's turn to open and shut his mouth, as Grace continued to smile. "You observed Lady Katherine's heavy eyes, your grace?" she said. "As her companion, I can tell you 'tis from overmuch weeping for her babe. I would dearly love to comfort her with word of his well-being and safety." Her heart was thumping so loudly at this outrageous speech that she was sure it was drowning out the lutes in one corner and the conversation around the rest of the room. Surely Henry could hear it?

Henry avised her for a full minute before his features softened a trifle. "I can see you know not how to lie, Lady Grace, and therefore I must thank you for your honesty. As a reward, and to comfort the noble gentlewoman in your care, I will tell you that the child has been sent into Wales to be cared for by trusted servants of mine. Unfortunately, Lady Katherine must understand that, for my subjects' protection, she will never see the boy again." He ignored her look of horror and continued. "I trust you can break the news to her gently. In truth, you are ridding me of an unpleasant duty, Grace, for it would have fallen to me—or the queen—to deliver the bad tidings." He rose, making Grace jump instantly to her feet, while the company stopped talking and waited expectantly. "My lords," he called, then turned to Grace and inclined his head, "and my lady, I bid you all a good night."

Before Grace could curtsy again, he strolled down the steps of the dais and disappeared among his councilors, leaving her—the only woman in the room—on her own. She fled down the back of the dais and out of the small door through which she had entered.

She had gone but a few dozen steps when a hand reached out from a doorway to pull her through it and into a small chamber, where a candle guttered as it lit a truckle bed covered with a worn counterpane. She had no time to scream before her mouth was stopped with Tom's kiss. He kicked the door shut behind her and held her so tightly she thought she would crack.

"What happened to you, sweetheart?" he whispered when he finally let her go. She was so relieved to see him and feel his strength that she started to cry. "What is it, hinny? Tell me."

He led her to the bed and gently sat her down upon it, cradling her against him. He could feel her trembling, and his mind ran rampant. Had someone insulted her? Had she been attacked in the corridor outside the king's audience chamber? Nay, he had been waiting all that time—and he had seen Lady Katherine and another attendant hurry by to their quarters. Certes, they would have all been surprised by an intruder, not only Grace. "What is it?" he coaxed.

Grace wiped her eyes and recounted the scene with Henry word for word. Tom drew in his breath. "He is still suspicious of you, in truth. But, my love, you answered him truthfully and, therefore, he cannot mistrust you. By the same token, you did not betray Katherine, either, for your honesty obtained the information she so craved." He patted her hand, and then he chuckled. "It appears to me, my beauty, that the king finds you desirable. I cannot help but be flattered."

"Tom!" Grace cried, and then lowered her voice. "How could you laugh? I did not know what to do . . . say." She paused. "But then I knew what he was doing. He was playing with me, and I took the bait. And now I must deliver the dire tidings to Katherine. I pray she has the courage to accept it—unless . . ." and her mind began to race, as it always did when an idea was forming.

"Unless?" Tom frowned. "There seems to be no way out of this, Grace."

"Unless we leave court and try to find the boy," Grace enthused, her tears forgotten. "We could use Enid to navigate around the Welsh hills. I must help Perkin, for he may be my brother. Certes, you must know who took—"

"No!" Tom said suddenly, a hint of anger in his frustrated exclamation. "No, Grace. There will be no more harebrained schemes, I pray you. You are not alone now. You have a duty to two children, who deserve to live in comfort and safety. I will not permit you to help this"—he wanted to say imposter, but he did not need to hurt Grace further—"this man or his wife, no matter how deserving. In fact, I forbid it."

Memories of their disagreements over John flooded Grace's mind, and Tom felt her stiffen beside him. He tried turning her head to kiss her, but she refused to move it, and he could see the stubborn set of her jaw and tears ready to spill. He sighed. "Please, sweetheart, let us kiss and use this time to discover each other again. 'Tis Advent and a time of chastity, I know, but it has been too long. I do not doubt that God will forgive us." He stroked her back, tugging at her laces. Even in times of tension between them, his desire for her never lessened.

"Nay, Tom. I cannot lie with you when I know that poor man cannot lie with his Katherine," Grace explained. "I am sorry. But their loss will be like a shadow between us."

Tom dropped his hand. "Ah, Grace. Once again I must share you with another man," he said bitterly. "The precious moments I had planned for us here are gone, I believe. I could force you, as is my right, but I made a vow to myself when we were wed that I would never exercise that right. And so I will leave you," he said, standing up and reaching for his doublet. At the door he turned and, for the first time since she had known him, she saw tears in his eyes. "Can you never put our love above all else? Must you always shelter weak creatures and put yourself at risk? It seems you are as elusive to me as the crown is for Perkin."

"Oh, Tom," Grace cried, running to him. "Do not leave me, I beg of you. I do not mean to hurt you, husband, truly I do not." It was her turn to stroke him, while he stood solid as the door at his back. "Your words have reached out and touched my foolish heart. Until this moment, I did not know how truly I love you. The scene in the audience chamber unnerved me, 'tis all, and living beside Lady Katherine these weeks has saddened me beyond belief." She reached up and took his face in her hands, feeling the soft beard between her fingers. "You do not know how many times a day I thank God for the love we have and are able to show each other." She went back to the bed and pulled off her stiff headdress and the cap underneath. Keeping his gaze, she unwound the glossy plait and allowed the freed curls to fall to her waist. "Stay a while, my dearest love, and you shall have my full attention, I swear."

A single tear escaped from Tom's eye before he groaned, "Ah, my sweet Grace," and went into her embrace.

Although Grace gave in readily to Tom's passion, she could not erase the memory of the two beautiful objects of Henry's disdain touching each other so tenderly and in such desperation earlier. How could she not offer them her friendship and comfort?

NO ONE REFUSED a royal invitation for Christmas at Shene. It was unthinkable, especially this Christmas, when Perkin would be a focal point. Once Mass was celebrated, the king, wearing his ceremonial crown according to the custom of centuries, had laid hands on several afflicted subjects, who were expected to heal from the blessing. Only then could the festivities of the twelve days begin.

Lying next to Cecily after another evening of entertainment by mummers, poets, musicians and the court jesters, Grace dreamed she was back at Bermondsey. She floated through the winter garden, heard a pig shriek in agony near the cowshed as it was sacrificed for the winter provisioning and saw a monk coming towards her, his face hidden in his cowl. As she reached out to throw back his hood, flames started licking at his habit and the sickly smell of burning flesh assailed her nostrils. Then, out of nowhere, crowds jeered and taunted the man, but he did not seem to notice them or the fire. "Water! Fetch water!" Grace screamed at the mob, and then she saw the man's face. It was John, and he was smiling at her, his face bathed in an eerie light. It was not fireglow she saw, but an unearthly, iridescent light. "Dearest John," she cried, "you have returned." He shook his head, and she thought he had never looked so happy. Shimmering as if in a mirage, a second figure appeared beside him, and Grace recognized his mother, Katherine Haute, who took his hand and gently pulled him away. "Look after yourself, Grace," John said, his habit on fire and yet the flames not consuming him. Then she realized the burning smell of flesh was her own and felt a searing pain in her leg. As the cacophony of voices deafened her, she thrashed at her fiery gown, trying to extinguish it.

"God's bones, Grace!" Cecily cursed sleepily. "Stop kicking me, I beg of you."

Grace's eyes flew open and she realized with relief that she had been dreaming. She crossed herself and then frowned, wrinkling her nose. " 'Tis no dream!" she exclaimed, sitting up and sniffing the air. "I smell smoke. Wake up, Cis!" An orange glow was reflected in the windowpanes from the king's apartments, and she could hear distant shouts. "I'm not dreaming, there *is* a fire!" she screamed. She jumped out of bed and fumbled in the dark for her cloak.

Cecily came awake instantly. "Where?" she cried, flinging off the bed-covers.

Grace flung open the casement, and then the shouts could be plainly heard. Although the walls were stone, the interior of the old palace was constructed mostly of wood. Indeed, Henry had remarked just that night, as the Yule log sent out a shower of sparks that set the floor rushes aflame in the great hall, that with its vulnerable hammer-beam roof Shene was a disaster waiting to happen. It would seem, Grace thought grimly as she lit a taper, that his prediction was correct.

The women ran from room to room, waking the queen's household, and Cecily and Grace helped Bess into an overdress and cloak to join them in her waiting chamber for news. Grace ran to the nursery to make sure Susannah and Isabella were safe and unafraid. The room was at the back of the palace, and when she entered all were undisturbed, as the noise and smoke had not penetrated those corridors. She held her candle aloft and for the hundredth time gazed in wonder at her sleeping children, curled up together in their tiny bed.

"There is a fire in the king's apartments, Margery," she whispered to the nursemaid. " 'Tis a long way off and under control, I feel certain. But perhaps we should take the children outside to safety."

Waking the older children and wrapping them in blankets, then each carrying the littlest, the two women made their way down the two flights of stairs to the door into the knot garden. Bella began crying at being so rudely awakened, which set off her cousin Mary, their wails adding to the chaos the little group found outside as dozens of servants and grooms ran back and forth with buckets of water from the river to douse the flames or damp down the adjoining buildings. The chapel wing was blazing, which included the wardrobe where Perkin slept with his guards, Grace realized. *Dear God, I pray he was not so foolish as to have set it. Why, he might have killed the king!* She dared not contemplate such folly.

An hour later, when the fire had been isolated to one part of the palace, the queen's household returned to their chambers and Grace let Bella and Susannah share her bed for what was left of the night, although few were able to sleep. As the day was dawning, Henry went to tell the queen that the fire had been contained but the wing was all but destroyed.

"It began in the wardrobe," Henry said, his arm about Bess. "A candle, *certainement*. Praise God no one was hurt."

"But that is where . . ." Bess paused, raising an eyebrow.

"Where *le garçon* sleeps? Aye, you have the measure of it, my dear. The two yeomen Kebyll and Sherwyn—his night guardians—slept beside him as always but swore they had snuffed their tapers," he said. "They were fortunate to get out alive. Very fortunate," he repeated grimly. His eyes scanned the room and found Lady Katherine, who looked quickly away. Grace felt the hairs on the back of her neck rise. *Had Katherine helped him? Nay, she has not been out of anyone's sight. Truly it must all be a cruel coincidence,* she decided. *Besides, it would have been certain suicide if indeed Perkin had set it.*

It was a mystery, the courtiers whispered, why Henry has not simply accused the man of attempting to kill the king and could thus have rid himself of this tiresome Perkin prickle. Once again, Henry hesitated.

Within days Henry had ordered that the palace be completely rebuilt. He said Shene belonged to a bygone era and that in looking forward to a new century, Richmond Palace would rise from the ruins in its stead.

30

Malines

JANUARY 1498

*H*enri de Berghes, bishop of Cambrai, waited for the dowager duchess to speak. He had been summoned to her private solar for her usual weekly confession and was surprised to find her waiting for him in her high-backed chair and not upon her knees at the prie-dieu. The exquisite triptych, commissioned from Hans Memling by Margaret, had not even been opened, nor were the two candles lit that illuminated the prayer book. The bishop's handsome features remained impassive as he contemplated his steepled fingers and allowed Margaret to gather her thoughts. They were alone, as was customary for a supplicant and her confessor, but on more than one occasion the dowager had used the time to confide other than her venial sins to him. About the same age, they shared a strong bond of piety and mutual respect that had allowed confidences to flow freely between them over the past ten years.

"My lord bishop, I have troubling news from England," Margaret began, her eyes sad. "It appears King Henry, not satisfied with capturing

Richard and torturing a confession from him, is subjecting him to the most degrading public derision while pretending to treat him as a guest at court."

"Aye, *madame*, I had heard such a rumor." Cambrai nodded. " 'Twould seem the king is afraid to imprison one who may be royal and yet he is afraid to be seen as weak by not confining him. The young duke of York is in grave danger, I fear." Margaret's mouth turned down and Cambrai was afraid she was about to cry. He had had no experience of dealing with a woman's tears—and especially not one this powerful—until the news had come of Richard's capture and confession. Then she had been inconsolable for many minutes during that particular meeting, and he had been relieved when anger overcame her tears and she cursed Henry, astounding Cambrai with her vitriol. Now he sent up a prayer to his favorite St. Peter to stem the flood that threatened to engulf her again. "How can I help you, *madame*?" he offered.

Margaret composed herself and gave him a wan smile. "I want you to go to the English court and make sure my darling nephew knows I still support him. I fear Maximilian and Philip are losing interest in his cause because of the despicable trading restraints Henry has imposed on Burgundy. I am certain that your erudition and spotless reputation will give Henry no reason to refuse you a private audience with Richard. Any letters I write will never reach him, and"—she drew a deep breath, her tears close now—"I want him to know that he still means everything in the world to me, but that without Maximilian and Philip's support, I cannot send an army to rescue him." She fingered the white rose brooch she always wore, and Cambrai knew this trinket was a constant reminder of her York family roots, from which she took her strength even after thirty years in her adopted land. "Will you go, my lord?" she cajoled. "For me?"

Cambrai thought quickly. A brilliant man from a fine family who had served both Duke Charles and Maximilian well, he was acutely aware that Richard, duke of York's future was not bright. And if the truth be told, he had never believed Margaret that this young man was the son of Edward of England. He could not believe he was a boatman's son, either, and it had irked him that although Margaret trusted him in all other matters temporal and spiritual, she would not reveal to him the man's true identity. If he went to the court as her emissary, he felt certain Henry would refuse to see him; if he went secretly, he might succeed, but at what cost once Henry's spies discovered the ruse? He would put his rather special life in danger, he suspected, and Cambrai had no intention of jeopardizing the power and luxury he had built up for himself. And yet how could he refuse the woman who had helped him get there?

"May I think on your request, *madame?*" He put a tiny emphasis on the word *request*, reminding her that he was not hers to command. "A visit to the English court must be carefully planned if it is to be successful, do you not agree? We must be better informed of the climate there before we endanger your nephew by putting our foot wrong."

To his immense relief, Margaret sighed, got to her feet and stretched out her hand in agreement. "Aye, my lord, we shall think on it and not do anything rash. Henry of England may not know what to do with Richard, but let us be sure we do."

31

London

SUMMER 1498

And still Henry could not make up his mind how to deal with the peacock called Perkin. He took his captive down to Kent with him during the month of April. After celebrating Easter at Canterbury, Henry subjected Perkin to the humiliation of witnessing the king receive the captured standard from the failed Deal landing in a ceremony that included a singing of the *Te Deum*. There seemed no end to Henry's debasing of his so-called guest.

When the court removed to the Tower in the middle of May, Katherine received a gift from the king that surprised even Cecily. A tawny gown over a black worsted kirtle, ribbons for her girdle and some white gauze to tuck around her neck were ordered for her, and for the first time since she was taken to Henry's presence in Exeter, Katherine did not wear black.

"Do you suppose his grace is softening towards us, Grace?" Katherine asked one morning after Mass as they were walking in the tidy knot garden in the inner ward of the Tower. The king was lodged in the Lanthorn

Tower this time and out of sight of the queen's apartments, which embold-ened Katherine to ask the question. "My husband has shown he plots no more and is contented to be a guest at court. 'Tis said his aunt in Flanders has abandoned him . . ."

"Nay!" Grace exclaimed. "Do not say so. He—you—are not forgotten, trust me. There can be no communication at present, 'tis all. The Holy Roman Emperor still works to have Perkin returned to Burgundy, so Tom tells me." True, the attempts at a diplomatic solution had lessened on the part of Maximilian since November, when trade sanctions had hit the Bur-gundian merchants hard, but Grace was convinced Margaret would never abandon her White Rose and believed what she was saying to Katherine. She changed the subject. "I can imagine your husband's face when he sees you in your new gown, Lady Katherine. In truth, you will turn the head of every man at court. You are truly beautiful."

Katherine dimpled. "The king is most kind. I cannot believe I warrant an expense such as this," she said, holding up one sumptuously decorated sleeve and fingering the braid and ribbons.

Grace merely smiled. Katherine was an innocent, she had decided. Had she not noticed the queen's worn-out clothes and wondered why the king did not allow his wife more of an allowance? Grace knew that Elizabeth's shoes were of the cheapest leather because she spent much of her income on her own sisters' upkeep and dowries. And the amounts she gave to help the poor and infirm often left her in debt. Then she had to beg Henry for a loan, which Grace told Cecily was degrading.

Grace looked at the radiant Katherine, who was admiring her new gar-ment, and prayed the young woman could avoid hearing the common gos-sip about the king's generosity. Even Viscount Welles had told Tom of his disapproval of his nephew's recent crass remarks about the Lady Katherine to his privy council at Westminster. "He would have her to mistress, if he could," Tom told Grace. " 'Tis only the Scottish treaty and the need to see the betrothal between James and little Margaret come to pass that keeps the king's hands off the woman." And Grace had noted it was the first time Tom had been openly critical of his sovereign.

"Such a champion of young and fragile ladies you are, Sir Thomas," she'd teased him. He had scratched his rumpled head of hair and given her his endearing sheepish grin, which made her stand on tiptoe to pull his face to hers to kiss. "I beg of you, husband, look to your own lady and not at others. Am I not enough of a handful? Not to mention Susannah and Bella."

Grace smiled as she thought of how he had picked her up by her waist then, and she'd wrapped her legs around him as they exchanged a kiss that might have led to further exploration but for their location in front of a window to one of the palace offices, where a balding accountant had tapped loudly on the window and embarrassed them.

Katherine's voice interrupted her thoughts and, as she turned to apologize, she saw Robert Cleymond stomping across the courtyard. Begging Katherine's pardon, she darted down the pathway to speak to him.

"My cousin of Warwick?" she murmured when he recognized her and bowed. "Is he well?"

Cleymond nodded, his smile guarded. "As well as can be expected under the circumstances. I am on my way to give my weekly report to Sir Simon, if you will excuse me, my lady." And he bowed again and would have passed on but Grace stayed him with a raised hand.

"Tell my cousin that I have kept my promise," she bade him. "I have prayed daily for his release, but I do not seem to have enough influence with the saints to matter. If my duties to the queen allow, I will try to visit him before we leave again, Master Cleymond." She inclined her head. "I am sorry to have kept you."

She thought she saw him smirk, but as he was an insignificant little man, she ignored it and returned to Katherine.

"Did you know my cousin, Edward of Warwick, languishes in the Byward Tower for crimes he never committed?" she asked by way of explanation for her absence. " 'Twas his manservant I spoke to. Sweet Jesu, Ned was only nine years old when he was imprisoned after Bosworth. I still remember his screams as he was taken away from all of us." She watched Katherine's eyes grow as big as bucklers. "But Henry has always been afraid of him—just as he is afraid of Perkin. Aye, Katherine, that is the other side of King Henry you do not see. 'Tis the side I hope you—or Perkin—never sees."

Katherine shivered. "Let us go inside, Grace. For all it is May, I am suddenly chilled."

· · ·

THE BARGES SWUNG sideways to the ebbing tide and the oarsmen brought them into shore with ease. Once safely tied, the queen and all her company processed into Westminster Palace to rejoin the king's court once more. Since the Tower, Henry had progressed to Woodstock and Hertford, and Bess had begged to be excused. In March she had lost a child she had carried for only a few months and it had weakened her constitution. And she still grieved.

As they wound their way up the spiral stone staircase to the queen's wing of the rambling palace, they could hear music floating up from the great hall. It sounded as though someone was playing the round organ and singing, but whether the voice was male or female, Grace could not decide, but was less than tuneful. Later, when Henry joined the queen in her small audience chamber for supper, Dick the Fool came tumbling into the room and then began to sing in a high falsetto, preening and posing before the king and queen.

"He mimics *le garçon*, my dear," Henry explained, grinning, and Grace winced at the demeaning moniker. He swiveled around to find Katherine in the group of ladies and called her forward. She sank to her knees in front of him, and his hand trembled as he put it out for her to kiss. "Your husband chose to give us a recital today, my dear Lady Katherine. He thinks because he was trained in a humble choir in Tournai that he can sing. Such arrogance. Would you believe he has even offered the wife of one of my ushers music lessons? 'Tis amusing, *n'est ce pas*? I have tasked Skelton to write a poem in praise of him. You shall be the first to hear it."

Katherine's eyes were now bright with tears, and she flinched.

"Your grace," Bess chided him gently. "Is this necessary?"

Henry's smile faded and he turned away, catching Grace's eye so unexpectedly she was unable to hide the anger in it. "I see I am unwelcome here tonight. I do not seem to please you, madam," he said to Bess, "or you, Lady Gordon," he said to Katherine, still on her knees, "nor indeed any of your ladies," he said straight to Grace. "I believe I shall retire, and so wish you all *bonne nuit*." He strode from the room, leaving Bess full of remorse in his wake.

GRACE'S ANGER MOUNTED further when John Skelton, poet laureate, entertained the court the next night with his verses that he titled *Against a Comely Groom*.

Katherine was told to stand with Perkin, facing the royal dais in the middle of the great hall upon the wide staircase leading back into the palace. Bess sat motionless on her throne, her eyes never wavering from the white hart badge of King Richard the Second engraved over the huge oak door at the other end of the hall. In anticipation of the poem, Henry's mood was merry, and he told some of his courtiers to be prepared to wager well later that night. "I am in the mood for a game of chance, sirs. Make ready the tables," he said, rubbing his hands and clinking his money pouch. "Now, Master Poet Laureate, pray entertain us. *Nom de Dieu*, I pay you well enough to scribble your lines," he cried. "Let us hear the droppings from that witty tongue of yours."

The hall was silent as a tall stick of a man came forward dressed in a flowing green and white robe that might have been fashionable in the Rome of Cicero and Virgil, and upon the breast of which was embroidered the word *Calliope*, his muse. A laurel wreath rested on top of his wispy white hair and his gleaming sharp, birdlike eyes roamed the room until they settled on the young couple standing alone upon the black and white marble flagstones. His pink cheeks flushed red and a slow smile spread from ear to ear, revealing several bright yellow teeth and an overactive tongue that darted in and out of his mouth like a reptile's. "He is relishing this," Cecily whispered to Grace. "He thinks no one should teach music but him. He thinks he is the sole recipient of the Muse's gifts, and he thinks Perkin has tried to usurp his position. God help our poor imposter."

"A sweet sugar loaf and sour bran bun
Be somewhat inform and shape alike,
The one for a duke, the other for dung,
A bit for a horse thereon to bite.
The groom's heart is too high to have any chance,
Except in his scale to snatch what he can;
Lo, Jack would be a gentleman!"

A guffaw from Henry accompanied the line about "his scale," and Perkin cast his eyes down to his feet, his toes nervously poking at the rushes. Grace's heart went out to him, but there was nothing she could do but listen to the rest of the scathing diatribe that had the court in stitches.

"He cannot find it in sharps and flats
Though he sings the notes from 'doh' to 'ti.'
He brags of his birth that was born full base
His music lacks measure, too sharp is his 'mi'
He trims his tenor o'er his deficiency."

There was even a line that referenced Katherine, who blushed from her bodice to her brow: *"Lord, how this Perkin is proud of his peahen."* Skelton pronounced the initial p's with a popping emphasis, gloating over his own prose.

When Skelton took his bow, Henry roared and encouraged the court to applaud with hands and feet thumping tables and the floor. Then he threw a rose noble to Skelton, who was ready and caught it deftly, bowing his thanks to his sovereign.

"I would see Perkin and his peahen dance," Henry cried, waving at the musicians to begin. "Something sprightly, I pray you."

Cecily drew in a sharp breath. " 'Tis beyond belief," she murmured to Grace.

"And look at his mother, beaming beside him," Grace answered.

Cecily was silent; her friendship with Margaret Beaufort had deepened during the years Grace had spent in Westow, but she could not blame Grace for her unkind comments. The woman had treated Elizabeth with disrespect and encouraged Henry to send Grace from court.

Grace could see that Perkin and Katherine used the time on the dance floor to their advantage, caressing each other's hands and brushing much too close during the crosses of the dance. They had been joined by others now, and so a few murmured remarks between the couple were not noticed, except by Grace—and possibly by Henry.

Later, as Grace and Katherine walked side by side up the staircase back to their quarters, Katherine whispered: "Richard can bear it no longer. He means to run away."

Grace stopped in her tracks. "He cannot! 'Tis too dangerous. Henry will surely kill him."

Katherine's chin trembled. "He says 'twould be preferable to dying of shame each day as he is doing. I tried to talk him out of it, but he is stubborn. It seems the locks on the door to the wardrobe room are being changed. His servants told him this today. He wonders if you would help us?" They were hidden in the doorway of a dark corridor, a flambeau lighting their way farther down the passageway. Grace nervously fingered her brooch—the gift from Elizabeth that always gave her courage. She thought quickly, which, Tom would have reminded her, often led to rash action on her part. But Tom was not there, and this man who had been, in name if not in person, so much a part of her life for the past twelve years needed her help. She could not refuse.

"Does he yet have a plan?" she asked Katherine, who shook her head.

How convenient that the locks would be changed, she thought. It would take the locksmith a day at least. Perkin was right to use the information to his advantage. If he could get past the two yeomen servants and whatever other guard might be outside the door, he could use the river to make his escape.

"I want to go with him," Katherine interrupted Grace's planning. "We shall go into Wales and find our son, and then we will flee to Europe."

"You plotted all this during the dance this evening?"

"Nay," Katherine admitted. "I have spoken with him a few times from the window in the wardrobe room at night when you—and his guards—are asleep. There is a ladder in the room, for fetching down items from high shelves, and Richard climbs it to reach the window. It is not far to the ground outside, but too far for him to jump, in truth. We can hear each other even though we whisper."

Grace raised an eyebrow. "Certes, Katherine, and I thought you would not say boo to a goose. I am awed by your daring."

Now Katherine drew herself up and leveled her gaze at Grace in the gloom. "I am Katherine Gordon, daughter of the earl of Huntly, and I grew up by the highlands of Scotland," she declared, her brogue thickening with every word. "I have climbed hills higher than you boast of in England, hunted in dense forests and sailed in a miserable boat to Ireland for weeks while close to my birthing time. I have more courage than anyone at this lily-livered court, in truth."

Grace let out a soft whistle—an unladylike sound learned at Westow to call off the sheepdogs—that made Katherine smile. "Then I fear I shall not be able to stop you from carrying out this audacious plan," she said, "because you will be a hindrance to Richard's escape, you see. A young man is more able to travel unnoticed and more quickly alone."

Katherine's eyes blazed. "I will go with my husband. I belong by his side, and I will die by his side if 'tis necessary. Would you not follow your love if you could?"

John's distraught face at the Newgate prison floated before Grace's eyes, and she remembered thinking she could save him. But in the end, she mused with shame, she didn't even try. She stared at the grim line of Katherine's mouth and the fire of resolve in her eyes and knew the Scotswoman was made of sterner stuff than she.

She leaned back against the door and thought for a moment, and Katherine checked the corridor again, but all was quiet. "I shall have Enid fetch me something from the apothecary to help me sleep," Grace whispered, gripping Katherine's arm. "My groom will engage the two Johns"—Grace's code name for Richard's guardians—"while we are at our supper and slip the powders in their ale. On the morrow, you will show me the window of the wardrobe and the lay of the land around it. Edgar shall be in attendance. Have you seen my groom? He is a giant. Perhaps Richard can climb down onto his shoulders?"

Katherine nodded, her eyes shining with excitement now. "Aye, 'tis possible. But why not go through the door when the old locks are removed?"

"How can we know how long it will take? As well, there would be too many opportunities for others to see him," Grace answered. "Other guards to steal past. Nay, 'tis simpler my way."

"Then we must get far away from Westminster as quickly as we can," Katherine told her. "They will look for us at ports and on ships for Flanders. But we shall be running in the opposite direction—towards Wales and our son."

Grace was again impressed with Katherine's pluck and quick intelligence. "You will need a boat—can Richard row?" Seeing Katherine nod eagerly, Grace went on: "Edgar shall make sure there is one tied up where it cannot be seen."

Voices nearby stopped them planning further, so Grace took Katherine's arm and walked confidently along the corridor to their apartments before they could be discovered. "If you talk to Richard tonight, you must advise him of our plan. All will be in place upon the first night the old locks are removed—whether they are replaced or no."

Katherine agreed, and Grace put her finger to her lips as they reached the door to the queen's bedchamber.

"Come!" Bess called. "Ah, there you are Grace. I was wondering what had kept you. You asked to comb my hair tonight, and I had to fight the other ladies off to keep my word." She looked from one woman to the other, but, seeing nothing suspicious, smiled and held out her ivory comb.

"Hounds!" Grace cried, waking from a heavy slumber and seeing the first light of dawn slanting through the shutters. Cecily sat up beside her, and they listened to the mournful sound of the baying dogs in the distance.

Controlling her excitement, Grace allowed Cecily and their two maids to run to the window and throw wide the casement. He must have escaped, she exulted. Sweet Mother of God, their plan must have worked. More shouting from the palace grounds accompanied the dogs' barking, and a guard below their window shouted to another: "Go to the abbey, Rob. Could be he took sanctuary."

"Addlepated ass," Rob retorted. "The abbey were the first place the king looked!"

In the next room, where Katherine slept with Bess's other two sisters—Catherine and Anne, there were voices and questions about the noise from below. Grace slipped on her soft slippers and threw a bed robe over her chemise and ran to see if Katherine was missing. She stopped still on the threshold when she saw her friend sitting up on her truckle bed and rubbing her eyes, eyes that were red from crying. Luckily, Anne and Catherine were leaning far out of their window while their maids hovered behind them trying to see. Grace ran to Richard's wife and knelt down beside her.

"What happened? Why are you still here?" she whispered.

Katherine glanced at the others and back at the door before answering: "He forbade me to go with him. Oh, Grace, I have never seen him so angry. He said our son would have a chance if I stayed, making it look as though he had escaped by himself. He said Henry would be kind to me. I begged him—I implored him, and I even tried to get into the boat, but to no avail." The tears began to flow, and Grace shook her.

"Soft, Katherine. You must go to the garderobe, take the washbasin and stay there until we are with the queen. I will make your excuses—'tis your time of the month or the like. But if they see you have cried already, they will know you were a part of the escape."

Katherine nodded and wiped her eyes on her linen chemise. Without another word, she followed Grace's advice, and no one saw her slip into the niche in the wall to use the privy. Then Grace joined her sisters at the window.

"What has happened to cause such a racket?" she asked, her eyes wide. "I will go and see to Bess. Maybe she knows." And she hurried out of the room and joined Cecily, also on her way to Bess's chamber.

They found the queen sitting rigid in her chair, staring at the window, which had been opened onto the Thames, letting the cool morning breeze into the large painted bedchamber. Her glorious fair hair was loose about her shoulders, which told her attendants that Henry had visited her that night. She turned her pale face and anxious eyes to her siblings as they ran in.

"Henry has just left," she said dully. "It seems the boy escaped last night. Perkin has run away."

Catherine, Anne and now their aunt Elizabeth of Suffolk all crowded into the room and heard the pronouncement. Escaped! they all mouthed at each other.

"How?" demanded Cecily. "Was he not locked in the king's wardrobe with the two guards?"

Bess nodded. "And with new locks on the door," she said, looking from one expectant face to the next. "Henry believes one of the two men must have passed Perkin a key—or failed to lock the door properly. The men were dead to the world when Will Smyth went to dress Perkin for the hunt today. Still in their cups from the night before, presumably." The women clucked their tongues and whispered questions among themselves.

Seeing her sister shivering, Grace placed a shawl about her shoulders. "If he left by the door, are there not guards outside to pass as well? Someone must have bribed them," she commented. Her heart was in her throat; her plan must have worked.

When Katherine Gordon entered the room, Grace gave her an approving glance and a subtle nod. She had tidied herself up, and the dark circles under her eyes could have been due to her courses. The attendants had forgotten about her, but now they silently glided out of the way, leaving a passage to Bess.

The queen held out her hand. "Come here, Lady Katherine," she said kindly. When Katherine knelt before her, Bess told her of Perkin's flight, and Grace was astonished to see Katherine blanch and sway, as if in shock. The woman has unlimited talents, she thought with grim amusement.

"G-gone, your grace?" Katherine whispered. "How c-can he be g-gone?"

Noises floated up to the group from the wharf below, and Grace went to the window and reported that large numbers of men were taking to boats and fanning out in both directions.

"The king is mounting a full-scale search," Bess told them, rising and seeing for herself. "He has sent horsemen as far as Poole and Lyme in the west, King's Lynn and Yarmouth in the east, and the channel ports shall all be alerted from Dover to Southampton. He cannot escape."

"But did he not confess he was a mariner? All he needs to do is change his clothes, dirty his face, use his other languages and climb aboard a merchant ship bound for Flanders," Grace remarked in what she hoped was a neutral tone. "Certes, he would try to return to his homeland, do you not think, your grace?"

Bess turned back from watching the flurry of activity below her and nodded. "My lord's thoughts exactly."

"How many hours do they believe he has been gone?" Cecily asked, and Bess shrugged. Cecily went to Katherine, who was now standing near the fireplace, and put her arm about her. "This must be a shock to you, Lady Katherine. But it proves your husband has no thought but of himself. Did he not think that he would be abandoning you—and that the king might be inclined to punish you just for being his wife? He is not worthy of you, my dear."

"Quite right, sister." Henry's voice startled the ladies, who all sank into curtsies. "*Le garçon* is not worthy to kiss Lady Katherine's feet, and I shall tell him so personally when I capture him—yet again. Rise, my lady," he said, putting his hand under Katherine's elbow and helping her up. He smiled into her eyes. "We cannot have this noble and gentle woman so insulted by one of such low birth, can we?"

Grace held her breath. Now that she knew Katherine Gordon better, she would not be surprised if she spat in Henry's face. But Katherine was less impetuous than Grace, and she cast her eyes down demurely and thanked the king for his kind attention. Grace heard her Aunt Elizabeth harrumph quietly behind her. The mother of John de la Pole, earl of Lincoln, once heir to the house of York and the fallen leader at Stoke, had no time for Henry Tudor, but with a second son who was rumored to be fomenting rebellion against the king, she dared not cross the man now. Grace breathed a sigh of relief; it appeared Katherine was not suspected in her husband's escape and that Henry had no intention of treating her any less kindly.

"The bells will ring for Mass shortly, ladies," Henry said pleasantly. "If you have not forgotten, 'tis the celebration of the Holy Trinity today. By the end of the day, I have no doubt we shall be thanking God the Father, God the Son and God the Holy Ghost for delivering us the foolish fugitive. Madam." He bowed to Bess, smiled benignly on the rest of the women and stalked from the room.

He is altogether too complacent, Grace thought suddenly. He has lost his caged bird, his personal popinjay and the safeguard against his overthrow, and yet he smiles and goes about his business as if he'd merely mislaid a coin of little value. She was puzzled; it made no sense. And then cold fingers reached around her heart. God help you, Perkin, if he catches you, she concluded: the escape is the excuse Henry needed to know what next to do with you. You were the king's guest, and you have scorned his hospitality. Now the hand gripped her heart in an icy vise, and she knew with certainty that Perkin's days in the sun were gone. She prayed to St. Peter, the fisherman, that Henry's far-reaching net would have a hole in it large enough for a minnow to swim through. And she prayed devoutly to the Holy Trinity that the tragic young man who tried to be king would know peace again aboard a ship bound for the ends of the earth.

But Grace's prayers were not heard. Four days later, although no one in the queen's wing knew it, Henry received a visit from Ralph Tracy, prior of the Carthusian charterhouse that was situated adjacent to Shene Palace, a mere twelve miles away.

Grace was in the wardrobe, searching for a gown that was sorely in need of a new hem that Bess had asked her to fetch. She was surprised to see Piers Courteys, the keeper of the king's wardrobe, seated on an old footstool and chewing the end of a quill, a piece of parchment lying across his knees. She ascertained he was taking inventory so she merely offered a "Good day to you, Master Courteys," and would have left him to his work, but he had stayed her.

" 'Tis Lady Grace, is it not?" he said pleasantly. "I have seen you in the company of Lady Katherine Gordon, have I not?" Grace nodded and Courteys lowered his voice and said, "Perhaps you would like to tell her that they have found her husband."

Grace gasped and went back to close the door to make sure no one would enter without notice. "Go on, sir," she begged him.

He let the scroll roll up and took the pair of spectacles off his nose. "Prior Tracy of Shene is now closeted with the king. 'Tis said he came to plead for the pretender's life."

"Shene?" Grace murmured. He only got as far as Shene, she thought, dismayed. "Is he still there?"

The man shrugged. "I have heard the prior interceded prettily, and his grace agreed to spare Perkin's life if he came out of sanctuary."

"Aye, but this time, certes, he will not be so merciful," Grace reflected gloomily. "He must surely imprison this man who so threatens—" She stopped herself and looked anxiously at the wardrobe master. "I speak too boldly, sir; forgive me. The appearance at court of one who claimed to be my half brother has been a test of my—nay, all of our resolves." She hoped the statement sounded noncommittal. She did not want the man tattling to Henry or any of Henry's entourage.

Courteys glanced over his shoulder. "I am discreet, my lady, and was ever loyal to your father, God rest his soul. I cannot say for certain that this man is indeed Prince Richard, whom I helped clothe on more than one occasion, but I do say that he reminds one of the young King Edward—but for his size, certes. Aye, the York family resemblance is there."

Grace's eyes widened. "Are you saying . . . ?"

"I shall not say anything more, my lady. 'Tis not prudent to make comparisons these days, if you value your life. All of us who served the little prince know it makes no sense to give our opinion on the matter." He tapped the side of his nose. "I will say that seeing young Gloucester—King Richard—all those years as I did, it was never my belief he had it in him to murder his brother's children." He leaned forward. "Prince Richard could have survived, is all."

"And thus, Perkin may indeed be who he said he was?"

Again he shrugged. "I could not say, my lady. He did not know me or his servant, Rodon, nor even his own brother, Thomas of Dorset, when they brought him before the king after his capture. Strange indeed." He busied himself with the inkpot in his writing kit, and Grace saw he did not want to communicate further; he had said enough.

"I thank you for the news, Master Courteys. You may count on my discretion, and I shall tell Lady Katherine in my own way." As she hurried back with the queen's dress, a sudden thought stopped her in her tracks. He had been tortured when he confessed, Master Courteys, she wanted to go back and tell him. Certes, he would have been too frightened to know anyone.

KATHERINE STOOD LIKE a statue next to Grace and Cecily on the top of the steps of Westminster Hall and stared down at the pathetic figure locked in chains and the stocks atop a scaffold made of empty wine barrels— Henry called it Perkin's empty throne—erected in the center of the room. On most days the hall was a concourse for merchants and others meeting to discuss business, but today, the Friday of Corpus Christi, courtiers and commoners flocked into the areas known as "Heaven" and "Hell" and left "Purgatory" to Perkin. They mocked him on all sides, calling him "king of an empty throne." Grace felt a tear roll down her cheek, but she dared not wipe it away, aware that Henry and his mother were somewhere, watching them watching.

"I cannot bear it," Katherine murmured, feeling for Grace's hand in the folds of Grace's gray dress. "He has been ill-treated, I can see. There is blood on his shirt, and his lip is misshapen."

"You must bear it, for his sake," Grace whispered back. "See how quietly he bears it. Like a prince, in truth." She felt Katherine's body straighten and saw how Perkin never took his eyes from his wife's face. "You are his strength at this moment, Katherine. Do not fail him."

Henry ordered Perkin to be led away after only two hours, and Grace breathed a sigh of relief. Perhaps the worst is over, she thought, and he will just be put in prison somewhere where he need not face the insults.

She was wrong. On Monday Perkin was taken into the city of London and pilloried at the Standard, a gigantic post upon which the citizens would tack random notices, bulletins and ballads. It stood by the conduit in front of one of the most famous taverns of the Chepe, The King's Head. That day the Standard's pinned-up papers told snippets of Perkin's life for those who could read. For those who could not, the town crier read aloud parts of the confession as Perkin stood helplessly above the crowd on the empty barrels from ten until three and endured derision from a multitude of curious and angry citizens.

This time, Henry allowed the women of the court to remain at Westminster, and when Katherine heard how her love had collapsed from standing in the hot sun for five hours, she, too, fainted. Even Bess was overcome with sympathy for the man and his gentle wife, and she commanded that Katherine be taken to her own chamber and placed in her bed. When Katherine awoke, Grace told her that Perkin was to be locked up for his lifetime in the Tower of London.

"I WANT TO leave court," Grace told Tom that night, when they met in the little garden beside St. Margaret's chapel. "I have never liked Henry, 'tis true, but now I hate him. I want to go far from here with our children and not allow them to witness such cruelty. Is it possible, Tom?" She snuggled into the crook of his arm as they sat on the grassy excedra and breathed in the scent of roses and lilies around them. "I miss Yorkshire; I miss your mother; and I long for that simpler life."

The heat of the day had dissipated only somewhat in the shadows of night, and Grace had worn her light worsted dress and left her long sleeves in her chamber. Tom could feel her skin beneath the fine lawn of her chemise as he turned her to him. "Then perhaps I should get you with child, sweetheart, so we shall have an excuse to return to your 'lying-in' manor at Westow," he teased. He kissed her tenderly. "Tell me you love me, Grace," he whispered. "I fear love has disappeared from this court, and I have a need to hear its name spoken tonight."

Grace hitched up her cumbersome skirts and straddled his lap. Looking straight into his eyes, midnight blue in the light of the moon, she told him she loved him with all her heart and mind and soul. Then she kissed him, gentling open his mouth with her lips and tongue and tasting the sweet hippocras they had shared earlier. With deft fingers she untied the bow of his codpiece and gently took him in her hand. With their passion mounting in the kiss, she guided him into her, slowly rising and falling in the rhythm of love.

· · ·

By the time the court reached Hedingham Castle on its way to Bury St. Edmunds, it was late July and Grace knew she was expecting a child. Although she had shared the good news with Bess, who whispered that she, too, was with child again, she wished Cecily had not gone to Hellowe with her husband and daughter to escape the worst of the heat, as she would have dearly loved to share the news with her favorite sister. Then again, she remembered, it might remind Cecily of her loss. It seemed the Welleses were in no hurry to try for an heir, Grace had mused on more than one occasion, and when she had brought up the subject one evening with Cecily as they listened to ten-year-old Elizabeth play her recorder, Cecily had raised a cynical eyebrow.

"My dear Grace, my husband is nearing fifty, and I fear his seed pod has all but dried up," she murmured. " 'Tis either that or I no longer have the desired effect upon him."

"Pish! Thomas Kyme cannot tear his eyes from you."

"Soft, Grace," Cecily chastised her, glancing about, but she dimpled all the same. "Do you think others notice?"

Grace shook her head and changed the subject. "Lilleth plays well. Has the dispensation for her betrothal to young Tom Stanley arrived from Rome?"

"Aye, but Jack will not act on it until Anne's mourning year is past."

Now, inside the Norman keep of Hedingham Castle, the earl of Oxford entertained the king lavishly. The de Veres had built and owned the castle since the Conqueror's time, and the aging earl—commander of Henry's van at Bosworth—was determined to leave an indelible impression upon the king's guest, Henri de Berghes, bishop of Cambrai. Having dined earlier in the queen's apartments in a separate building, the ladies were now present in the great hall for the entertainment—which included a dancing bear—and Grace could study the duchess's confessor, a rather aloof but handsome nobleman in his late forties. Oxford was regaling him and the king with yet another version of how he'd single-handedly killed John Howard, duke of Norfolk, in the battle when the steward came forward and announced the arrival of a visitor.

Ambassador de Puebla, who was conversing cozily with Katherine, sucked in a deep breath. *He is always fascinated by Katherine Gordon,* Grace had mentioned to Tom. Tom had explained that every tidbit the diplomat gleaned from those intimate moments with the lady was relayed to their royal majesties in Spain, who were waiting to see what Henry would do with Perkin before allowing their precious daughter to go to England and be married.

"It must be Digby," de Puebla murmured.

Now it was Grace's turn to draw a quick breath and, moving out of Katherine's earshot, she asked guilelessly: "Sir Simon Digby, constable of the Tower, *señor*?"

"He brings the pretender to show to Cambrai," he said behind his hand. "The bishop visits on behalf of the *duquesa diabólico*—how Henry calls Margaret," he said, chuckling. "The duchess and her stepson, Maximilian, hope to persuade Henry to release *el niño*. I am to be witness myself." He frowned. "But you do not need to know this, my lady—*y muy importante*, Lady Gordon needs not to know."

Henry's advisers were in a knot about him and, after kissing Bess's hand and waving the musicians to play on, he nodded to Cambrai and de Puebla before he marched from the room.

The next day word was whispered of a night of intense questioning. When Grace saw de Puebla hurrying towards the stables, she ran after him, catching him as he waited for his groom to bring his horse to the mounting block. He stared down at Grace in surprise, and she saw at once that he had not slept well.

"Señor Ambassador," she begged him, "is Perkin . . . is he . . . how is he?"

De Puebla shook his head gloomily, a drip from his nose threatening to fall on her. "Ah, my lady, I fear you would not recognize him today." He grimaced as Grace paled. "*Si*, and he once so handsome." He drew his sleeve across his face and sniffed. "I cannot tell you all—the meeting was secret, you know," he told her sternly, "but I understand you care about Lady Gordon and you would only console her, *no*?"

Grace nodded vigorously. "Aye," she agreed and waited.

The ambassador stepped down from the block and paced a few steps out of earshot of the groom. Grace hurried after him. "Digby brought him in. He had *pedenae*—you know, foots chains—and more around here"—he used his fingers to encircle his neck. "But his body . . . his face . . ." He shook his head again, tut-tutting. "He was *desfigurado*. I did not recognize him. His grace has make his face so no one say *el niño* looks like King Edward again. All broken," he explained, making a circular motion over his face. "His hands, his fingers . . . also broken."

Grace was horrified by the description, but she was on a mission and plunged ahead. De Puebla had probably divulged too much already, but she plucked up her courage and gave him her most beseeching look. "I am grateful to you, Doctor de Puebla. But just one more thing, I beg of you. Did Perkin change his confession?"

"*Sagrario!*" he exclaimed. "You are gone too far, Lady Grace." But when he saw her eyes well up and her mouth droop, he softened. "He say only that Duchess Margaret knew, like him, that"—he stopped and pondered on the actual phrase—"*si.*" He nodded, slowly repeating Perkin's words, " 'I am not the son of who I said I was.' Is all, milady, and I go now." He bowed perfunctorily and returned to the mounting block.

Grace was left standing stock-still, her head and shoulders drooping as low as her spirits. Surely in this interrogation, with Aunt Margaret's envoy as witness, he had a chance to deny his previous confession—tell Cambrai it had been made under torture—but he hadn't. Sweet Jesu, he hadn't!

She wanted to run, feel the wind in her face and the grass beneath her feet and find a place far from anyone where she could vent her anger and sorrow. Instead, she turned back to the imposing square keep and took deliberate steps to regain her composure. She had to think of Katherine now. Lovely Katherine, who had stayed true in her heart to the man she loved. Perhaps she already knew he was not who he said he was and did not care. Perhaps all she wanted was to lie with him and become as one with him again. To feel his body next to hers, see the love in his eyes, hear the passion in his voice and hold her cherished face in his hands once more. Grace gasped, picturing it. Dear God, what should she tell Katherine? That her beautiful husband's face was battered beyond recognition, and those hands that had caressed her were crippled? Her thoughts returned to the young couple dancing for Henry and how Perkin had defied the king by talking to Katherine behind his pomander, whispering words of love as he inhaled the spicy scent of cloves . . .

"Cloves!" Grace suddenly cried out to a crow cawing overhead. Sweet Jesu, why did I not remember then? Elizabeth told me her son Richard loathed the smell of cloves.

She felt the blood drain from her face as the sad realization sank in. She had recently suspected Perkin was not her brother, but she had always hoped that he was. And now she felt betrayed not only by him but by Aunt Margaret as well. She lifted her eyes to Heaven and whispered: "How foolish I have been all this time!"

IT WAS AS well that Grace was not at court when a letter of apology to Henry arrived from Duchess Margaret at the end of September. It seemed she had either abandoned her White Rose or—as de Puebla wrote to his sovereigns—she hoped to buy his life with her admission of collusion.

For Perkin, his fate appeared to be to lie in a small, locked room—not completely devoid of furnishings—with one small barred window high up in the wall of the Byward Tower, directly beneath, he would learn later, Edward, earl of Warwick.

32

England

1499

*C*ecily was glad of Grace's company that Yuletide at Hellowe, as the viscount had decided to stay in London at Pasmer's Place and be available to Henry during the ongoing negotiations between England and Spain. Due to Grace's delicate condition and to ease her burden on the long journey into Lincolnshire, Bess had insisted that Susannah and Bella remain at Greenwich in the royal nursery to keep young Harry and two-year-old Mary company. Susannah had not complained, especially as her cousins Harry and Margaret would be joining them from Eltham for the festivities. But Bella clung to her mother, her big blue eyes pleading to be taken.

"Please can I go, Mother?" she lisped, her corn-colored hair curling around her chubby face under her blue linen cap. It was all Grace could do not to pick her up and cover her cheeks with kisses. Enid attempted to distract the girl with a rag doll, but she flung it across the room and burst into tears. "I want to go with you! I want to go with you!" she cried, clinging to Grace's skirts.

"Let her go with you, Grace." Tom's cheerful voice from the doorway caused Susannah, impervious to her sister's screams, to drop the wooden blocks she was stacking and rush headlong towards him. He reached down and swung her high into the air, leaving her breathless. Then he smacked a kiss on her laughing mouth and put her down again. He walked to Grace's side, put his arm around her thick waist and pecked her on the cheek. "Enid is going with you anyway, so why not take the child? Susannah will not mind, will you sweeting?"

"Certes, *no*," Susannah answered, rolling her eyes. "She is such a baby."

She sounded so like her mother, Tom could not help laughing. "I can come and see her from Sithes Lane from time to time," he assured Grace. "Perhaps it would be good for the two to learn to be apart. It will come soon enough. Susannah is of an age when we should send her to another house, even if you disapprove, my love. We have only to find someone willing to take on such an imp," he teased his daughter.

"I am not an imp," she answered, throwing her arms around him and giggling.

Grace glanced down at Bella, whose tear-stained face brightened as she sensed her mother yielding. "Ah, well, I suppose it would not inconvenience Cecily to have another small mouth to feed," she said, enjoying the look of pure delight on Bella's cherubic face. "You would not mind, Enid?" she asked her servant. "But you must promise to be good, Bella, or I shall send you back here in disgrace."

"I promise, I promise!" Bella shrieked, jumping about. "Thank you, Papa."

Tom picked up both girls and balanced them on his arms. "Give your father a kiss farewell, my poppets. I have already stayed away too long from Lord Welles." The girls gave him loud, wet kisses and squirmed to get down. Then he took Grace by the waist, caressing her belly and grinning. "How now, my pillicock! Do I get a kiss?"

"Tom!" Grace pretended to be shocked. "Do not encourage the children to learn such words too soon." She lifted her face to his and they shared a tender, if not passionate, kiss. "Write to me whenever you come and see Susannah, and keep yourself safe—and out of trouble, my love."

"And you, Grace. God go with you. Look after your mother, Bella. I am counting on you," he said, wagging his finger at his youngest.

"I will, Father," Bella answered earnestly. "Cross my heart and hope to die."

They all laughed, and Grace sent her husband a loving look that could last him a month.

Ensconced in Cecily's warm solar, painted window coverings shutting out the cold rain, the two sisters watched as Elizabeth Welles painstakingly taught Bella her first few notes on the recorder. The journey had been uneventful, thanks to the viscount's generous loan of a carriage and two armed escorts. A few vagabonds had accosted them out of Monkswood near Huntingdon, but as soon as the soldiers' swords had been raised and Edgar's pikestaff had knocked one of the thieves to his knees, they took off with their tails between their legs. Bella's eyes had been as big as saucers as she peered around the carriage curtain from her warm spot under the furs next to her mother.

"Edgar hit the man," she declared gleefully. "He fell over."

Enid pulled her back inside the carriage without more ado. "There's naughty you are," she admonished her. "Alarming your mother, look you."

Other than a dreary half day spent digging the carriage out of the mud near Stamford, Grace's journey ended uneventfully six days later.

The Yule log had been brought in and holly and ivy decorated the great hall in readiness for the first night of Christmas. Grace was well rested after sleeping for twelve hours, and when she rose to greet Cecily and the household, she was ready to join in the festivities.

"Lilleth, take Bella to the hall for the lighting of the Yule log. Aunt Grace and I shall be down anon," Cecily told her daughter, who obeyed without a word. "She's a good girl, but so sad, Grace. She misses her sister greatly—I am happy you decided to bring Bella." She sighed. "Losing a child is a dreadful thing."

"Dear Cis, I cannot imagine your sorrow. But Lilleth will grow to be a healthy woman and give you many grandchildren, I don't doubt."

Cecily grimaced. "God's bones, Grace, do not age me too quickly! I have no wish to have grandchildren until I am ancient." They both laughed gratefully.

Now that they were alone, Grace broached the subject of Perkin.

"I confess I was wrong all this time, Cis," she began, causing Cecily to chuckle. "Why the laughter, pray? Ah, certes, because I am always so stubborn. Aye, perhaps I am, but now let me admit my folly, and promise you won't mock me for it."

"I promise," Cecily murmured. " 'Tis about Tom, I suppose."

"Then you suppose wrong, sister," Grace retorted. " 'Tis about Perkin."

"You mean our brother Richard?"

"Nay, I mean Perkin. I know now he is not our brother, much to my sorrow. Oh, I wanted him so much to be, but he is not. Let me tell you why."

When she had finished, Cecily took her in her arms and consoled her. "Let us hope this foolish business is over and we can all get on with our lives," she said. "It has consumed us—and divided us—for too long."

Grace lifted her head. "But does it not make you wonder who he really is, Cis?" she said eagerly. "He cannot be a boatman's son. So who is he?"

"Certes, Grace, I could give a tinker's arse. And, if you take my advice, neither should you. Now let us go and join the girls."

"FEEL HER BROW, Grace," Cecily said with a worried frown. " 'Tis like a fire in there."

Grace rested the back of her hand on Lilleth's forehead and shook her head. "Aye, 'tis hotter than I have known with my little ones. Sweetheart, how long have you had this fever?" she asked the girl, whose face was the color of the covering sheet.

"Since before supper," Lilleth whispered. "It hurts here, Mother," she said, putting her hand to her neck. " 'Tis hard to swallow."

Inflammation of the throat, thought Grace, who had suffered through a few in her childhood at the convent. She went to Bella's side of the bed and felt her daughter's forehead. "She's cool," she told Cecily. "But perhaps I should take her to our bed tonight?"

"Aye, and I shall stay with Lilleth." Cecily nodded. "Open your mouth, sweeting. Aye, 'tis swollen back there, and red," she told Grace, holding the candle high and peering down her daughter's throat. "I shall send for some milk, poppet. It will soothe you."

Lilleth was shivering. " 'Tis cold, Mother. Please give me another coverlet."

Cecily hurried Grace into their chamber to fetch a fur blanket and

Grace gently tucked Bella into bed. " 'Tis best you stay here in your condition and get some sleep, Grace. I shall send for the physician in Lincoln. See if he can balance Lilleth's humors. It must be the yellow bile that causes the fever. She needs bleeding." Fear had crept into her voice now. "You are better at potions than I; what would you give her?"

"Brother Benedictus at the abbey believed in the benefits of yarrow and elder to break the fever, and root of goldenseal for a swollen throat," Grace told her.

When Cecily left the room, Grace went down on her knees. *"Ave Maria, gratia plena,"* she began, murmuring the rote prayers that comforted her in telling the rosary. As she repeated the prayers over and over, she was able to think on another plane, selfishly begging the Virgin to spare her own child in case Lilleth's illness was catching. The two children had shared a bed since she and Bella had reached Hellowe, and played closely together. Lilleth was a sturdy girl, but Bella was thin and tiny, like Grace. Grace could not count how many parents she knew who had lost a child. She accepted that it was God's will for the young and the feeble to be called to Him so often. Hale one day; dead the next. But not *her* child, she prayed. She reached the *pater noster* bead and whispered the words out loud in case God could hear her better. Then she ended with: "Do not let Lilleth die, dear Lord. Cecily has suffered the loss of one child already. Certes, you cannot need the sister so soon."

Yawning, she climbed into bed and snuggled Bella to her. As she drifted off into slumber, she felt her baby kick with heartwarming strength inside her, and it gave her hope.

Her sleep was disturbed by Bella's restless movements and shallow breaths, and she came awake with a start, fear crawling in her heart. Dawn was creeping over the frosty meadows, turning the landscape into a sparkling wonderland, but Grace had no time for its beauty. Her child was ailing, she knew it. Softly climbing out of bed so as not to waken Bella, she took a piss in the jakes and then pulled on her bed robe and slippers. She waddled down the corridor to the nursery, her hand cradling her aching back. Enid and one of Cecily's attendants were ministering to Lilleth, but Cecily was slumped asleep in a chair by the window.

"How does she?" Grace whispered to Enid, who was applying a cool cloth to Lilleth's forehead.

"Bad she is, my lady, and too hot," Enid replied sadly. "Had a fit in the middle of the night, look you. Aye, was a bad one."

"A fit? You mean a spasm? Has the physician been sent for?" Enid nodded. "Good," Grace said, looking down at Lilleth, whose eyes were staring dully at her. "Sweet child, does your throat still pain you?" The girl nodded. She was having trouble breathing, and as she moved her head from side to side, the morning light revealed rosy marks on her neck and throat. Without warning she sat up and, before Enid was ready with the basin, Lilleth vomited onto the floor, moaning in pain as she did so. The noise awoke Cecily, who jumped up guiltily and ran to her daughter's side. Seeing Grace, she chastised her sister for coming back into the room. "Get you gone, Grace, you foolish woman. See to your child and protect your baby," she commanded. "Doctor Rollins will be here anon. A groom rode through the night for him."

Grace embraced her sister and reluctantly obeyed. Cecily clung to her for a moment and whispered: "Pray for her, my dearest."

The doctor arrived by midmorning and, using his fleems, bled poor Lilleth but could not give Cecily good news. After examining the thick dark blood in the bowl and peering down the girl's throat, he grimaced and stepped back to tell the viscountess that he believed her daughter was suffering from the rosy fever or, as he intoned gravely, "what they call the scarlet fever."

No sooner had he uttered the words that brought dread to all present than Lilleth began to convulse again, gasping for breath, her limbs writhing like so many serpents under the covers and her head thrashing from side to side. Once calmed, she seemed to fall into a stupor, her eyes half open and her pupils dilated.

Grace stayed all day in her chamber watching over Bella, who was beginning to develop the same high fever. How she wished Tom was there, and how she wished practical Alice Gower were there to support her. She could hear the comings and goings from the room along the corridor and at one point during the day Cecily came to see her. Her face was drawn and her eyes haggard. " 'Tis the scarlet fever, I think, Grace, and Lilleth will most surely die," she said, breaking down and crying for the first time. "I cannot bear this. How cruel is this God of ours? And how I despise him," she seethed between sobs, sinking into a chair. Grace flinched at the sacrilege but could understand Cecily's anger. "Jack will blame me." When she saw Grace's puzzled frown, she blurted out: "I am certain he thinks I have made a cuckold of him with Thomas. I swear upon all that is holy, we have not had carnal knowledge of each other. We have only kissed and spoken of our love. He has not confronted me, but I am certain Jack believes we are guilty. And now he will think God is punishing me for my sin, and he will blame me for Lilleth's death." More tears poured down her face and onto her apron.

Grace was not used to seeing stoic Cecily cry, and she was deeply moved. She ran to kneel beside her, gathering her sister into her arms. "Soft, dearest Cis, you are imagining things. Lord Welles was all kindness when he saw me off in his carriage, and he sent his dearest love to you. I warrant you have dreamed this up because you do feel guilty about your affection for Thomas. But feeling and acting are two different things. You are not the first to love another man, Cis, and God knows it," she insisted, taking her sister's face between her hands and looking into her tearful blue eyes.

Cecily let her sobs subside and used her linen apron to wipe her nose. "You do not think he hates me, Grace? I could not bear him to hate me. He is a good man, in truth, but I do not love him." Her chin trembled again. "I love Thomas," she wailed and buried her head in her hands.

"I know, I know." Grace's calm voice was soothing. "But Thomas is not the concern here, Cecily. You must hold up and go back to your daughter's side. I wish I could be with you, but I fear Bella is on the verge of the same fever, and I am needed here."

Cecily sniffed and pulled herself together. "Are you certain, Grace?" she asked, going to the sleeping Bella and laying her hand on the child's forehead. "She is hot, there is no denying it. I will send in Doctor Rollins."

The hours dragged by, and before the bell rang for Compline, Grace heard the agonized cry of a woman who has surely lost her child. She picked up her skirts, ran to the nursery and flung open the door. Taking in the scene, she gently pulled the distraught Cecily off Lilleth's body, now lying peaceful and cool beneath the soiled covers. The priest had been sent for at supper, and he had given the comatose child her last rites. Now he carefully covered the lifeless face with the sheet and led those present in prayer. On their knees, Grace felt Cecily's body leaning against her and prayed that her sister would do the same for her when the time came—as it surely must.

Whether Doctor Rollins's bleeding came early enough for Bella, or whether Bella did not contract so virulent a form of the disease, the sisters did not know, but Grace's pleas to God for mercy were heard and the little girl pulled through. Her body was covered with a rosy rash after the second day of fever, and she had bouts of nausea and flux, but she had no spasms and by the third day her fever lessened and her breathing improved.

Once Bella was out of danger, Grace stood with Cecily on the steps of the rambling manor house as the steward and some of the male retainers accompanied Elizabeth Welles's small coffin to the village church for burial. Grace's unborn child moved in her womb, and she was reminded again that the circle of life was forever turning.

CECILY'S DUTY WAS to mourn with her husband, so she shared the journey to London with Grace, who was to resume her position in Bess's train at Greenwich until her own lying-in. Leaving Pasmer's Place after resting for one night, Grace and Bella were accompanied to Greenwich by Tom in a hired boat.

"I am glad to leave the house, in truth," Tom told Grace as she enjoyed his protective arm and the fur-lined cloak around her. "Lord John was not himself these past two days. He was ill-tempered and complained of aching muscles and a headache. He took the death of his daughter hard, and you should know 'tis not only ladies who cry, Grace. The viscount's red eyes gave away his grief, and I suspect his humors became unbalanced. Too much of the black bile causing melancholy, I suspect."

Grace listened idly, gazing at the faraway tower of Bermondsey Abbey to the south and remembering her hour with John on the riverbank after Stoke. She thought she recognized the spot and sighed.

"Was that little sigh for his lordship, Grace?" Tom teased her. "Daydreaming again?"

Grace started. 'Twas what John had said to her the first time they talked alone, on the ramparts of Sheriff Hutton. The day came rushing back with all its youthful fantasies, but with it came the memory of John calling: "Tom! Tom Gower. I pray you go with me," and of her taking note of Tom for the first time. A soft smile curved her mouth. "I was thinking how much I love being with you, Tom Gower," she replied, and although it was not exactly what she had been thinking, the sentiment was true.

To the left of them, the Tower rose white against the bright blue winter sky, and Grace shivered. She could see the window of her cousin of Warwick's room in the Byward Tower and wondered where Perkin was imprisoned. Somewhere less comfortable than Ned's apartment, where he would be forgotten, she guessed. She asked Tom if anything more had been heard of Perkin since his appearance before the bishop of Cambrai six months earlier, and Tom shrugged. "Not a peep," he said, "and I pray you are not—"

"Nay," she interrupted, taking a deep breath. "You need have no more worry on that score, husband." And, snuggling closer to him, she repeated what she had told Cecily.

"Praise be to God," Tom muttered. "I am sorry for you, Grace. You had your heart set on finding your brother, but 'tis a relief to know we may put this behind us now." He kissed the top of her bowed head and knew a peace he had not dreamed of during these years of turmoil when John and Perkin had intruded on their lives.

THEY HAD NOT been more than half a day at Greenwich when Tom recognized the viscount's lawyer, John Cutler, hurrying towards the palace from the wharf. He frowned as he watched from one of the smaller antechambers in the king's lodgings and made his way closer to the audience chamber. Thus he was able to hear as the man breathlessly told the king that his well-beloved stepuncle, John, Viscount Welles, was dead. All the color drained from Tom's face. How could his master have met his Maker so quickly? He remembered the testiness, the complaints about aching back and legs and the persistent dry cough. Surely 'twas not enough to kill a man of the viscount's strength?

But it was, and when Cecily heard the news, she went into shock. She took to her bed, and Grace watched over her for days. Bess was already lying-in, and she demanded a report on her sister every hour from her prone position on the curtained bed in her shuttered room. The royal physicians and astrologers looked grave, hoping these were not bad omens for the baby Bess was about to deliver. " 'Tis not an auspicious beginning to a royal life," Henry's astrologer, William Parron, told him. "If Lady Welles herself should die, then it would be an especially ill-fated time for the queen to give birth."

Henry had finally lost his temper with his soothsayer. "What is the queen supposed to do, you addlepate, unconceive the child?"

All honor had been accorded John, Viscount Welles, and no expense spared to convey him in a long procession to his last resting place in Westminster Abbey, where his body lay in state while monks and abbots said Masses for his soul for a night and a day. Grace could not help but compare all this pomp and ceremony to the paltry arrangements Henry had made for his mother-in-law, who had once worn the crown of England.

THE FIRST PERSON to greet Grace upon her return to court was Katherine Gordon. She was watching from her perch in the window seat of the long hall and pounced on her friend as soon as Grace entered. Grace bit her tongue; she did not know when or if she would ever tell Katherine of her change of heart, although during the journey back from Hellowe, Cecily had come to the same conclusion as Grace: Katherine knew her husband was not Richard. Grace noted that Katherine had filled out and lost the haunted look in her eyes and was cheered.

"I have had a letter from Richard," Katherine whispered, taking Grace's arm and leading her away from the others. With Bess confined to her chamber, her attendants were somewhat aimless between shifts of sitting with the queen, and were playing music, cards or fox and geese, and some of the younger ones were flirting outrageously with blushing squires and pages. Where is Lady Margaret? Grace wondered, looking about her. Ah, there she was, conversing with Grace's half sister Catherine Courtenay, countess of Devon. It was one of those times when she was thankful for her lack of inches, so she could hide herself behind the wide sleeves of other attendants.

"How wonderful for you, Katherine," Grace enthused. "Are his spirits good, despite his circumstance?"

"He says that I may visit him due to his good behavior." Katherine's eyes shone, and Grace was struck once again by the Scotswoman's extraordinary beauty. "Certes, I have to be attended when I am in the room with him, and no doubt there will be guards outside, but I can see him! The king is allowing it; he is so kind. Oh, Grace, please will you go with me?"

Grace's face fell. "I cannot leave court again so soon, Katherine. And

I shall be lying-in within a few weeks. Maybe my sister Catherine can accompany you."

Katherine made a face. "The countess does not care for me, I can tell. I shall wait until you are ready." She gave a wry grin. "In truth, Richard is not going anywhere, is he?"

SURROUNDED BY TWO dozen people, including the king and his mother, attendants, physicians and midwives, Queen Elizabeth gave birth to a son at the gray dawn on the twenty-first day of February. It had not been an easy birth, and the physicians had shaken their heads at the sanguine temperament of the baby after such long labor distress, while the astrologers had consulted the stars and their charts and muttered predictions for the child born under the sign of the fishes. The royal couple named the baby Edmund, and although Henry meant to honor his father, the queen and her sisters knew it was to honor their Uncle Edmund who had been cruelly killed at Wakefield the same day as their grandfather, Richard, duke of York.

Not three weeks later, in a smaller chamber not far from Bess's, Grace went into labor. Enid hardly had time to hurry Susannah and Bella back to the nursery and fetch the midwife before the Gowers' third daughter slipped easily into practiced hands and cried lustily to be wrapped and held in her mother's arms. Tom was delighted with the child, and even more pleased when Grace told him she would like to call her Alice, after his mother. Watching his daughter trying to squirm free of her swaddling bands, he chuckled. "She is as busy as my mother, in truth." He bent and kissed his wife tenderly, taking her hand and holding it to his cheek. "I am so proud to be your husband, Grace. God and his saints smiled on me when you were sent to Sheriff Hutton."

Grace nodded and smiled but said nothing. Her tired body needed rest, and she closed her eyes. As she did whenever Sheriff Hutton was mentioned, she thought of John. But now she thought of the injustice of his death and how he, like Perkin, had been manipulated by the woman both looked upon as their aunt. How odd, she mused, that all three of us have been used by powerful women, but none so dreadfully as poor Perkin. She drifted off into sleep and dreamed of Perkin climbing a ladder, his face pale with fear and the sound of men jeering all around him.

. . .

THE TWO WET nurses chattered away as their charges nuzzled at the full breasts offered them, and Bess and Grace could not help but entwine hands as they watched their new offspring share a feeding moment.

"Your Alice is beautiful," Bess said, admiring the fine dark hair and chubby cheeks. "She is as strong as an ox. See how she kicks as she suckles. She will be a handful, Grace."

Grace chuckled. Alice was indeed giving the wet nurse's stomach a drubbing, but the young woman did not seem to mind and grinned up at the queen. She looked at baby Edmund, whose placid stare at nothing in particular accompanied a lackluster attempt at sucking, and Bess clucked her concern.

"Eat well, sweeting," she murmured, bending down and allowing the child to wrap his hand around her little finger. It seemed to give him confidence, and he smacked down on his wet nurse's tit and gave an impression of concentration. Grace and Bess both laughed.

"Bess, I have a favor to ask," Grace said when they moved away and allowed the surrogate mothers to do their job.

"Another?" Bess teased, smiling mischievously. "What is it now, sister?"

"Katherine Gordon has been given leave to visit her husband and has asked that I accompany her," she began and paused, waiting for an immediate refusal. When it did not come, she persevered, although she saw Bess's face flush pink. "I did not think I wanted to go, but I can now. Certes, I would not do this without your permission, Bess." She was not ready to admit to the queen—and thus Henry—that she had been wrong all these years. Henry did not deserve it.

Bess walked to the door and Grace's heart sank. She should never have approached the queen before she was fully recovered and churched.

"May I trust you, Grace?" Bess asked softly without turning back. "May I trust that you will not attempt to help the man escape?"

Grace gripped the sides of her gown, sweat breaking out on her upper lip. Did Henry know she had helped at Westminster? Had Perkin confessed after being tortured so horribly?

"H-help him escape?" Grace stammered, hoping she sounded shocked. "How could I do that, your grace? He is locked in the Tower of London, the strongest fortress in all of England."

Bess looked back over her shoulder at Grace's cocked head and guileless brown eyes. "Aye, Grace, you may go," she said simply. "I will always be in your debt for the service you gave my mother." Without another word, she left the room.

IN MID-MAY, AFTER Grace's churching, she and Katherine left Greenwich one morning in a small barge with Edgar and Bess's earnest young secretary, Geoffrey, and an escort of three of the queen's yeomen. Both women were quiet during the hour-long journey on a mounting tide, contemplating the impending visit. Grace was remembering Tom's admonition to her upon hearing of the plan: "Do not do or say anything foolish. The king will be watching you." They had been strolling up the hill behind the palace to the ivy-covered castle tower, built earlier in the century by Duke Humphrey of Gloucester. They could look up the river to the spires of London from the top of it, and it was one of Grace's favorite places to visit when the weather was fine, as it was that day, when flocks of twittering birds flew overhead and the grassy hillside was filled with the snowy blossoms of hawthorn and the brilliant yellow of broom. She smiled to herself now, when she recalled how she'd answered Tom. She had caught him unawares and tripped up his lanky six-foot frame, which sent him rolling several feet down the hill. Then she pounced on him and tickled his chest mercilessly with her chin, making him writhe and laugh at the same time. She had discovered this vulnerability early in their lovemaking, and she adored the way he could not control his laughter when she attacked him.

"Stop! I beg of you, stop!" he cried between breaths, and catching her wrists in his big hands, he flipped her over onto her back as if he were playing with a puppy. "Ah, now I have you, wench!" he cried, and proceeded to cover her face and neck with kisses.

It was her turn to laugh and tell him to stop, and soon articles of clothing were strewn about them and with Grace in nothing but her petticoat and Tom in his shirt and hose, they came together for the first time since Grace went to Hellowe for Christmas. She could feel a hard clump of earth digging into her back, which caused her to arch up, unwittingly bringing herself even more pleasure. A speckled songthrush repeated its musical warble on a hawthorn bough as if inspired by the sensuous sounds from below. Then they had lain on their backs, delighting in the warmth of the sun on their bare torsos.

Katherine's soft accented voice broke into Grace's reverie of that idyllic afternoon. "There is the Tower," she murmured, moving instinctively closer to Grace. " 'Tis a beautiful yet fearsome place. I pray poor Richard has a wee window at least."

A man named Thomas Astwood met them at the bottom of the Byward Tower, and Grace was somehow cheered to know Perkin was close by Ned. Showing the ladies a good deal of deference, Thomas informed them before he led them up the staircase of the riverside twinned gate tower that he had the honor of being Perkin's servant. Katherine pleaded with the young secretary to wait below with Edgar, taking his hand and pressing it between her own. He melted in her expressive eyes, and once again Grace admired the steely resolve of the young Scotswoman.

They passed a guardroom, where the open door revealed the apparatus for raising and lowering the portcullis, and went up a few more steps to an iron-studded oak door. The guard outside sprang to his feet, fumbled for the right key on his ring then inserted it in the keyhole. The door complained on its rusty hinges and the noise alerted the prisoner, who had shackles around his ankles and a chain around his neck and was seated on the crude wooden chair.

"Visitors, Perkin!" the guard barked. "Get up—they be ladies." He grinned and Grace turned her face away from his blackened teeth and the open sore on one of his cheeks.

Katherine gave a little cry of anguish when she saw Perkin attempting to stand while hampered by the heavy chains, and she ran to help him up. Grace stepped quietly into the vaulted chamber, followed by Astwood, who scurried to fetch the stool from the corner and place it for her. She glanced around the room. It was clean enough, despite a thin film of slime descending from the small barred window, open to all weathers. At least Perkin had a proper bed with a straw mattress and a blanket, Grace thought, relieved; she had expected him to be sleeping on a pile of straw on the floor. Astwood's pallet was stored beneath the bed. There was a table on which were the remains of some bread and cheese, and a chipped pottery cup. Astwood hurriedly pushed the tin jakes under the bed and out of sight.

Clanking, and hampered by the painful constraints, Perkin shuffled towards Grace and bowed as gracefully as though he were back at Henry's court. Once the light fell on him, she was horrified by his appearance; he was gaunt, had aged, and his nose was so crushed, she would not have recognized him. The dull eye was more marked, and one of his front teeth was broken off at an angle, marring his once brilliant smile. He had not bathed for months, she ascertained from the layer of grime on the exposed parts of him and from his greasy, matted hair. It was all she could do not to turn away to hide her pity.

"Lady Grace, I am grateful to you for bringing my wife here," he said, his voice husky with unchecked emotion. "I am certain 'tis you we have to thank for this unexpected visit."

Grace shook her head. "Nay, sir. 'Tis her grace the queen whom you should thank, not I," was all she could murmur, so shocked was she by the change in him. Katherine stroked his matted hair as though she did not notice. "Grace is too modest, my dearest. She always is. She is called 'Grace the gracious' by the other attendants. Aye, you did not know that, did you, dear Grace?" she said, her happy smile brightening the room. "Come, my love, let us sit and talk," she cajoled.

They sat down on the bed, never taking their eyes off each other. Katherine lovingly traced what remained of his once elegant fingers, and Grace felt tears pricking her eyes. Were they tears of sadness for herself or joy for them? They seemed happy at this moment, she thought. She found herself looking at him differently. Certes, he does not resemble the man I met in Burgundy, but even with his injuries, she now saw him through more critical eyes.

"*Je vous remerci aussi*"—Perkin reverted to French so Astwood would not understand—"for helping me flee last summer. If I ever get out of here, I will reward your groom—Edgar, I think is his name? He has courage—as do you, Grace."

Grace smiled her thanks, but before she could answer a voice from above their heads startled the women, and they both looked up to find the source. Perkin and Astwood grinned conspiratorially.

" 'Tis Edward of Warwick," Perkin said. "He bored a hole in the floor of his room when he was told I was below. We have been talking each day about this and about that, and"—he winked at his servant—"it gives me great comfort, does it not, Thomas?"

Astwood winked back at him. "Aye, sir."

Grace saw the wink and was puzzled. "About what?"

Astwood put his finger to his lips and glanced back at the locked door. "We cannot say, my lady. But before long, you will know, I don't doubt."

"Richard! Who is there with you?" Ned's voice was now recognizable to Grace, and she forgot the men's cryptic remarks.

" 'Tis I, Grace, cousin Ned," Grace cried, going over to where she could now see the hole in the vaulting. "How glad I am to hear your voice."

"Was Cleymond not clever to devise this way of talking to Perkin?" Ned enthused. "We have been planning such a scheme, you would not believe."

Grace frowned. "What scheme, cousin?" she called in as loud a whisper as she dared.

"Aye, Richard, what scheme?" Katherine asked her husband, concern in her face. He shook his head and would not say.

Astwood hurried to the corner and, cupping his hand spoke as though talking to a child: "Remember, my lord, no one—not even your cousin here—must know. 'Tis our secret." He turned to Grace and wound his finger against his temple: "Poor man, he knows not a goose from a capon."

"What do you say, Thomas?" Ned said. "I did not hear the last part."

"Nothing, my lord. I was addressing the Lady Grace." Thomas all but pushed Grace away from her spot under the hole, telling Ned: "You must move the chest back now, my lord, or someone will hear us." The occupants of the lower room kept silent as they heard the sound of furniture moving above them, and then all was quiet again.

Astonished by this turn of events, Grace wandered back to her stool and sat down hard upon it. It seemed to her the two servants were encouraging the prisoners to communicate, and she had the distinct impression they were not merely comforting each other. But then again, maybe she was wrong; she was always too ready to unravel a mystery, she knew, and perhaps she was reading more into this little scene than there was.

"Have I disappointed you, Grace?" Perkin's unexpected question roused her from her reflections.

She stared at him for a moment before answering, knowing full well his meaning. " 'Tis not for me to judge you, Perkin. Only the king and God may do that," she countered. It was a lame answer to a most forthright question, she knew, but how could she tell this broken man that aye, she was disappointed in him, and that she had been deceived like everyone else. "You would disappoint me only if you have not been true to yourself, to Katherine and"—she hesitated to add—"to your son."

"Ah, Grace, I wish it were as simple as that." Perkin sighed. "You want me to tell you that I am your half brother Richard, do you not? But I am naught but a poor boy from Tournai who is not who he pretended to be. 'Tis the truth, sad to say."

Grace looked from him to Katherine, expecting her to register horror at this admission, but she merely continued to stroke his hair, and then Grace knew for certain Katherine was fully aware she was not the wife of Richard, duke of York, but she loved her husband anyway. At least she would not have to pretend with Katherine any longer.

"Sad? You should be angry," Grace cried, standing up. "You have been cruelly treated by everyone, and now your life is in the king's hands." She saw the fear in Katherine's face and calmed down. "And you used me," she said sadly. "I truly believed you were my brother."

Perkin shrugged and then winced as the chain caught on a scab on his neck and it began to bleed. "I regret I duped you, Grace, and I truly wish I were your brother. But I will tell you the worst crime I have committed in all this was betraying Aunt Margaret's trust in me," he said sadly. "I did not mean to tell the king that she knew I was from Tournai." He leaned forward, an urgency in his voice. "If you ever see her, Grace, pray tell her I am sorry for that."

"Aye, if I ever see her again," Grace replied, but she chose not to add, *although she does not deserve your loyalty,* in my opinion.

Perkin, giving her a grateful smile, turned his attention once more to Katherine, whispering in her ear and making her smile. Grace watched them for a moment, wondering why it was she and not Perkin who was so angry. *Aye, I have put myself—and Edgar—in danger for him,* but she was free and Perkin was not. *She had Tom, the children and a life to look forward to; all Perkin has are these few precious moments with the woman he loves,* she realized sadly. She wished she could leave them alone, but it was expressly forbidden, and so as best she could, she turned and faced the other way.

It was while they waited for the signal that the visit was at an end that she vowed Henry would never know from her that he had been right about Perkin all along.

EVEN WITH PERKIN safely behind bars and seemingly resigned to his fate as a perpetual prisoner, Henry took no chances. That summer, he rounded up two of those who he knew had formed the core of the conspiracy to place Perkin on the throne. Accused of receiving damning letters from the pretender and hiding them from the king, Irishman John Atwater and his son, Philip, who had first acclaimed Perkin as duke of York, were taken from Cork and sent to London. John Taylor would soon follow, after extradition from France.

Henry left London on a progress to the Isle of Wight in late July, leaving Bess and her household at Greenwich. Bess and Grace watched their new babies closely through the dangerous summer months together, when plague and the new sweating sickness often took away precious children as their first victims. Tom was now attached to Cecily's household, and he was in the train that wended its way first to Collyweston and then to Hellowe so Cecily could oversee the management of the estates in Lincolnshire.

"You are kind to Tom," Grace told her sister as they walked together to the Welleses's barge, the blue bucket and golden chain banner fluttering above it. "I hope you will find employment for him, as I will be loath to leave you."

"I have it in mind to put him in charge of the manor at Theydon Bois in Essex, Grace. 'Tis one of my dower properties, and I have neglected it of late. We shall have to go there next spring, where I have no doubt you will put your husbandry skills to work," she said, chuckling. "You have lost your ugly brown color, praise God, and look like a lady again."

"Pish!" Grace retorted. " 'Tis hard for me to believe a pale face is the sign of a lady. 'Tis how one comports oneself, your mother always told me."

"Ah, yes, Mother," Cecily mused. "I never wished to be like her, but I wish now I had her ability to produce so many children."

"Pish," Grace repeated more gently. "You still have many child-bearing years ahead. Henry will find you another husband anon, and there will be other babes, never fear," she said as she watched Cecily being helped into the carriage. "Farewell and God speed."

Tom settled Cecily in the barge when he took Grace once more in his arms and kissed her. "Write to me of the children. Know that I will miss you all, but we shall be back before you know it. Three months at the most, my love."

33

London

AUTUMN 1499

Tom was right, but the world turned upside down for Henry in those three months. Grace told her husband of the messenger who had ridden to Greenwich from Winchester with the news that Henry had returned to the ancient capital unexpectedly from his progress in the Isle of Wight. He remained there for three weeks and it was only now, in October, that the queen was told the reason why.

"It seems a plot was uncovered at the Tower in early August," Grace explained as soon as Tom had seen Cecily safely to her lodgings. Grace was unable to sit still as she talked. "Some men—I know not who, although they mentioned Thomas Astwood—had been meeting together since early summer to persuade Perkin and Warwick to overthrow Sir Simon and take the Tower for themselves."

Tom could not forbear to smile. " 'Take the Tower,' Grace?" he queried. "How? How could two prisoners—one who was chained—take the strongest fortress in England? You are not making sense, my dear. And who is Thomas Astwood, pray?"

Grace took a deep breath. "I will try to tell you, if you would not keep interrupting me and asking questions," she complained. "Thomas Astwood is Perkin's servant. I told you about him. But there were others who came to visit Perkin—a priest among them who may have come from Duchess Margaret, they say—and someone smuggled in a file and then a false shackle, so Perkin could free himself of his chains. There was even talk of a code book," Grace whispered behind her hand.

It was all Tom could do not to laugh out loud at his wife's obvious delight in these intrigues. Instead he told her, "I can see you learned well at Elizabeth Woodville's school of scheming," and instantly regretted it.

Grace flounced across the room and stood with her back to him, her arms crossed in defiance. "I shall tell you nothing more, husband, if you will not take me seriously," she protested. "And to think I had arranged for us to spend the night together."

Tom was on his feet in a second and cradled her against him. "How I love you when you pout, my dearest," he whispered, and was cheered when she sagged against him and covered his hands with hers. "Certes, I want to hear every detail of this plot. 'Twould seem that someone betrayed the prisoners, am I right?"

Grace nodded and allowed him to lead her back to the settle. "It seems there were those about London who believed they could free Perkin and Warwick and, by securing the Tower, could put Perkin on the throne."

"I can see how Perkin would agree to escaping, but Warwick? Where does he fit in? He must not even know Perkin. Why would he agree to put his life in danger for a stranger?"

"If Perkin is not Richard, then Warwick is next in line to the Yorkist throne, remember?" Grace said. "Besides, Ned *does* know Perkin."

Tom watched Grace's face redden, and sighed. "You did not tell me everything about that meeting at the Tower, did you, Grace?"

"I did not think it was important," Grace blustered. She played with her rosary beads for a moment and then described the means of communication between the two captives. "Their servants knew about it, and 'tis clear to me that Ned's servant preyed on his poor master's innocent mind in the matter. Perhaps he tempted Ned with the crown? Perkin's servant, Astwood, seemed to genuinely care for his master, but Robert Cleymond made me uncomfortable. I think he was spying for Sir Simon and betrayed Perkin and Warwick."

"You have a wild imagination, my girl," Tom told her sternly.

Grace was indignant. "Certes, I do not," she retorted. "Then tell me why this Cleymond measle has disappeared, while the rest have been detained, if he is not guilty."

Tom frowned. "When did he disappear? Perhaps he sought sanctuary."

"I know not," Grace said. There was a pause while they puzzled on the facts. "Does it not appear strange to you, Tom, that if Sir Simon knew of the plot in the first days of August, that Henry allowed the conspirators to continue with their actions for so long? It seems they recruited more and more people to help—both inside and outside the Tower—and the constable looked the other way. And Henry stayed for three weeks in Winchester—seemingly ignorant of the affair, for he did nothing. Nothing."

Tom gave a long, low whistle. "By all that is holy," he said slowly. "It would seem the king may have given Perkin and Warwick enough rope to hang themselves."

Grace frowned. "Rope to hang themselves? Don't speak in riddles, Tom," she said, and then the light dawned. "You mean . . . Sweet Jesu, he now has a reason to destroy them—permanently!"

Tom nodded. "The viscount told all of us who served him many times over that nothing would stop Henry's ambition to join England with Spain through this marriage between Catherine and Arthur." He paused, taking Grace's hands before letting the ax fall. "I regret to say this, but I believe your cousin and Perkin must now be condemned." Grace let a cry of anguish escape before she buried her head in Tom's chest. "I hope I am wrong, sweetheart," he said, "but it looks plain as a pikestaff to me."

THE COURT WAS at Westminster at Martinmas, the final feast of the winter provisioning, when Grace saw Henry for the first time since he had left for his progress in late July. "He has aged twenty years," she whispered to Cecily, as she took a share of roast pheasant from their mess to her trencher. " 'Tis good to know he suffers, too."

Henry was in good spirits after a banquet that included several different fish dishes, pies of larks, plovers and thrushes, roasted peacocks, haunches of beef, venison and the traditional meat of Martinmas: mutton. Then came flampayns, custards and finally a frumenty. After the usual entertainment of performers and freaks, he called forth William Parron to read from the book he had commissioned the astrologer to write, *The Fateful Meaning of the Stars*. Parron bowed solemnly to the king and then the company and chose to read a passage that left no one in doubt as to the subject. He spoke of the fate of *"those who are unlucky under the stars, the law and causation and justice say they must be beheaded or hanged, or others burned or drowned . . ."* He looked out at the silent courtiers who were heeding every word, and when he went on to mention a man *"not of base birth"* whose stars were so ill-crossed he should expect nothing but imprisonment, death and the destruction of his property, they understood he was speaking of Edward of Warwick. Some years before, the soothsayer had told of awesome omens that had appeared at the time of Richard, duke of York's birth, and now he confirmed for all to hear that those omens had predicted the unlucky prince would never reach manhood. His implication was loud and clear: Perkin could therefore not be that same prince, and thus deserved whatever fate the king chose for him for his pretense.

But Warwick was a different matter; he was as royal as Henry himself and had a better claim to the throne, and history was watching what Henry would decide to do with him.

"A prince may imprison another prince or lord because he fears he will cause insurrection, or that insurrection will come through him, and that is without sin," Parron intoned, stroking his long white beard. Now a rustling could be heard around the hall as neighbor nudged neighbor and those in attendance gave one another knowing looks. Henry sat impassively through all this, as though Parron's words left him no other choice but to follow the stars.

As superstitious as any God-fearing person, Grace did not doubt these predictions were real, but she scorned Henry's cowardice. Lily-livered craven, she thought, and felt her heart constrict. Poor cousin Ned, who had never harmed a fly and had spent the best part of his life in captivity, was to lose his life, as Tom had predicted. And Perkin, whom Grace guessed had never wished to be set upon this path to becoming a king, would follow suit. 'Tis truly a tragedy, Grace wanted to cry out; let them both live— they are naught but mawmets and have never wished anyone harm. Then she remembered Katherine. Sweet Jesu, she must be overcome with worry, she thought. I must find and console her.

Happily, she saw that Katherine had found Tom, and Grace made her way over to them. The strain on Katherine's face spoke volumes, and Tom gave his wife a quick nod of understanding. "Come, Katherine," Grace told the trembling woman, "before the king notices we are gone, let us find somewhere more private and talk about what all this means."

It MEANT THAT the very next day, Chief Justice Fineux informed the king and his councilors that Warwick, Perkin and others had conspired to commit treasonous acts against the king's grace. Perkin, John and Philip Atwater of Cork and John Taylor—who had come to the Castelo de São Jorge in Lisbon ten years before to begin the priming of a pretender—were arraigned on Saturday the sixteenth at the White Hall at Westminster.

Bess commanded that all her attendants be present in her waiting chamber that day, and then drew Grace aside. The queen had lost weight, her hair was graying quickly, her once beautiful skin had lost its creaminess and deep lines had appeared in her face. Dear God, she does not look healthy, Grace thought anxiously, although Bess's blue eyes were still clear and honest, and her wan smile did not lack genuine warmth.

"You must watch over Lady Gordon particularly today, Grace. She may likely swoon, or perhaps have a fit of apoplexy," Bess murmured. "Henry has warned me the outcome of the trial is already assured."

Grace widened her eyes. "Already assured? Is Perkin not to have a jury? Perhaps they will not find him guilty. After all, how can he be called 'traitor' when Henry has proven he is foreign-born?"

Bess gave an impatient sigh. "Ah, Grace, I had hoped you would be reasonable about this," she chided her. "You have shown me loyalty and given me snippets about Katherine here and there. 'Twas all I asked of you, and you complied. Do not fight me—or Henry—on this, I beg of you," she urged. "The sordid affair is over. You do understand that there can be only one ending, don't you?"

Bess was right; there was only one way to freedom for the broken man who had called himself a prince: by leaving this world and entering the next. Grace hung her head. "Aye, your grace," she acquiesced bitterly. " 'Tis a tragic one nonetheless, you must agree." Plucking up her courage, she said, "In truth, I have kept my promise to you, sister, but now, I beg of you, keep your promise to me. What news is there of Katherine and Perkin's son?"

Bess was taken aback, and for a second Grace thought she would be dismissed again—sent from court for insulting the queen—but then the gentle woman's face softened, and she nodded. "I did promise you, didn't I? Tell Katherine her little boy is well and is loved by a modest Welsh couple in the Gower region. They have several other children, so Richard does not lack for company," she said. "Are you satisfied now, my small but persistent sister?"

Grace gave her a sheepish smile, reached up and kissed her on the cheek. "Thank you, your grace. As loving a mother as you are, I knew you could not forbear to comfort another."

Bess had been witness to Katherine Gordon's spirit, as had Grace, and she was not surprised when Katherine remained calm when the courtier sent from Henry informed the queen's court of the verdict on Perkin and his comrades. "Guilty, all of them," he said with glee. "My lord of Oxford presided and Perkin's two judges read the charge of treason. 'Tis said Perkin pleaded guilty."

Katherine let out a groan. "Ah, foolish boy," she murmured as Grace looked at her anxiously.

"He will be hanged, drawn and quartered at Tyburn, as will Taylor and the other two," the man continued cheerfully. "They took him straightway back to the Tower."

Katherine swayed for a moment but then stiffened her back on the window seat where she sat with Grace and crossed herself, as did Grace. "God have mercy on him," she whispered. "Certes, the king has none."

The king was not merciful on Warwick, either. Brought before his peers in the Great Hall of Westminster three days after Perkin's trial, he was supposed to be examined, but he did not even receive that courtesy.

" 'Twas rumored the poor man merely repeated the charges of treason that were put to him and just put his faith in the king," Tom told Grace a few days later, when they were finally able to share a bed again. The court had been so filled with peers from all corners of the realm who were commanded to be at Warwick's trial that people were often three to a bed in the palace. But Cecily, unable to bear listening to the accounts of the mockery that was her cousin Ned's trial, had begged leave of Bess and gone to Pasmer's Place.

"There are those who believe his mind is that of a child and that he could not have conspired the way it has been suggested. They say he stood like a prince when they sentenced him to the same fate as Perkin and said, 'I have faith in God and in the king's mercy,' " Tom murmured, winding one of Grace's curls around his finger.

Grace felt the tears at the sides of her eyes run down her cheeks and wet the pillow. "I do not believe Henry even knows the word. But they should not give Ned a commoner's execution, should they?" She sniffed, moving closer into Tom's protective hold. They lay thus for a few minutes, both silent in their thoughts, Grace's full of sorrow and Tom's full of desire after a long dry spell. He stroked her back but when he attempted to lift her chemise, she forestalled him. "Please, Tom, just hold me tonight," she begged him, taking his wandering hand and clasping it firmly around her waist. "Make the nightmares go away. I cannot even imagine how those men are holding on to their sanity. How I wish I could see both of them before they die and offer them what comfort I can. They have had little in this life, in truth."

Tom groaned inwardly. Why must she always play the angel of mercy? he thought. But then, he chided himself, is not her kindness one of the reasons you adore her? He felt sleep coming on but before closing his eyes he whispered in her ear the words she wanted to hear: "Perhaps Lady Margaret would intercede for you with the king, Grace. She has come to like me, I believe. I will ask her for you on the morrow." He yawned. "But now, try to sleep, my love."

From Tom's rhythmic breathing Grace knew after only a few minutes that he was asleep, and once again marveled at it. She lay awake for an hour or two, reliving scenes from her unexpected life at court: the summer at Sheriff Hutton and her stirrings of love for John; her time with Elizabeth at Bermondsey; her unexpected marriage to Tom; her adventure in disguise to Malines, and the second one to meet her so-called half brother; John's capture and their last moments in the Newgate. Then the scene at Smithfield came back to haunt her, the shadow of the scaffold with its gibbet looming over the crowd. Dear God, now two others who had been part of her new life were to meet similar fates. She remembered again the boy Ned struggling in Robert Willoughby's grasp at Ormond's Inn that day he was taken from the family, and his sister Margaret's fear that she would never see him again. Then she thought of her visit with him at the Tower. He was cheerful enough, considering his years of captivity, and she remembered thinking he might not be as daft as people said. But he did not know the ways of the world, Grace admitted. How could he, only watching it float past his window on the river? Nay, he could not have planned such a complicated conspiracy to set himself and Perkin free. She imagined him at his trial, tall and handsome, looking at all the nobles and bishops around him and not recognizing a soul. How demeaning for one of his lineage, and how terrifying! He probably did not know what he was saying when he did not deny his guilt. Her heart ached for him, as it did for Perkin.

Ah, Perkin! Or was he Perkin? Her desperate need to fit in with her family, and her obsession with her half brother, had sometimes led her to act rashly, she knew now, but she had been so convinced Richard was alive when Sir Edward Brampton came to Bermondsey. She could remember Elizabeth's joy at the news and her own excitement when she finally met Richard at Dendermonde. She had been certain then that he was indeed Richard. But had wishes and feelings colored her judgment? She tried to piece the puzzle together, remembering the instances when she had been swayed one way or the other: from the man's noble demeanor, his likeness to her family and his acceptance by so many in positions of power to his public confession and private denial to her; from his lack of knowing Dorset and other court familiars of the young Dickon to the pomander of Dickon's hated cloves and his dreadful singing voice. But something did not add up to his being a boatman's son, either. So who was he? And why was she the only person who wanted to know?

Sweet St. Sibylline, but she was simply too tired to unravel the threads tonight. She heard the watch cry one of the clock, and her eyes finally closed. Turning onto her other side, she felt Tom stir in his sleep, missing her. And then she slept.

Perkin's status as condemned man meant Grace was allowed only half an hour with him in a damp, filthy cell belowground. In the ambient glow of a guttering rushlight the guard had left in a niche near the door, she could not see what she was standing on, but it felt slimy and the stench was almost unbearable. Thank Heaven Katherine had not come with her, she thought; she was right to demur.

The king had reluctantly allowed the visit, thanks to Lady Margaret's cajoling. Tom had appealed to the love she had for Viscount Welles and the good service he had given Lady Margaret's half brother. He had thought it prudent to ask on behalf of Lady Gordon as well as for Grace, knowing from Grace that Henry had a soft spot for Katherine and might grant the Tower visit more readily.

Henry had virtually spat at Tom. "Aye, let them see the false prince one more time. Perhaps when Lady Gordon sees how low he has sunk— even lower than whence he came—she will know him for who he really is: Piers Werbecque, a poor boatman's son from Tournai. Pah!" He waved Tom away. "Half an hour, no more!" he cried.

But when the small boat docked at the Tower wharf from Westminster and Katherine looked up at the towering stone walls, she balked. "I cannot go, Grace," she whispered. "I shall not bring him the comfort he needs today, for I know I shall only weep at the sight of him."

And looking at the pathetic figure on the soggy straw, chained to the wall, the hackles almost too heavy for his emaciated arms and legs, it was all Grace, too, could do not to weep. She saw the disappointment on his grimy face when she and not Katherine was let into the cell. She was aware of movement to the left of her and realized Perkin was not alone. She held the light above her head and whispered her name. "I hope I do not disturb you, sir," she said, not recognizing the man shivering in the other corner.

" 'Tis John Atwater, Grace. He who would have made me king in Ireland," Perkin told her, his voice a monotone although his teeth were chattering. "He was my friend—until this. We die together on the morrow."

Grace choked on her response, but went closer to him so they could converse quietly. She wished she had brought more than a few groats with her, so she could pay the jailer to give him a clean shirt in which to meet his Maker. "God have mercy on you, Perkin. I will pray daily for you," was all she could say, pulling her shawl about her in the chilling damp and putting the light in its sconce.

"In truth, I shall be happier where I am going than stuck in this filthy hole," Perkin said, laughing harshly. "Last night I was bitten twice by a rat,

God damn it to Hell." Grace picked up her skirts and shrank against the
wall. "Fear not, Grace, they come only at night—although how they know
the difference down here, I know not." He changed the subject, desperation in his voice as he knew they had so little time. "Where is Katherine?"
he asked. "I have so much I want to tell her. They said she would come."

Thank you sweet Sibylline for the dark, Grace thought, feeling herself
color as she was about to tell a lie. She held her thumbs between her fingers
and prayed for forgiveness. " 'Tis the woman's curse that has kept her from
you. The queen is strict about the customary seclusion."

Perkin nodded, crying to the heavens: "My ill luck continues, I fear.
God, why do you hate me so?" He softened. "Then you will have to relay
my words to her, if you will be so kind."

Grace's eyes were becoming used to the darkness, and she saw that a
small amount of light was coming through a grating from the room on
the ground floor above them. She reached out and stroked his cold cheek
and his shivering stopped. He merely gazed at her with his odd eyes, and
a memory of a long-ago dream stirred. She could feel the foul water ooz-
ing from the muddy floor and seeping into her thin leather shoes, and she
wished she had worn her pattens.

"When did you know I was not Richard?" he whispered out of
nowhere.

Grace withdrew her hand quickly. " 'Twas not one thing, exactly. I was
forced to believe your confession—it was so detailed—although I defended
you with Tom and my sisters, because I was certain 'twas not gained without pressure." She saw him nod absently. "But there was one tiny mistake
you made—a tiny fact about you that I was privy to through those years
serving Queen Elizabeth—that convinced me."

Perkin harrumphed. "I made many mistakes. The first was being born
at the wrong time and in the wrong place. Nay, being born at all!" He gave
a short bark of laughter, as if enjoying a joke. " 'Twas not so hard to pierce
my disguise in my mind, but once on the path 'twas hard to go back. So
what was it? I am curious."

"Prince Richard hated the smell of cloves, so the queen told me. The
night you were with Katherine and whispering to her while holding the
orange pomander to your nose—"

Perkin burst out laughing—a painful, unpleasant sound. "Do you hear,

John? I was undone by a few cloves and an orange." Then he let out an agonized cry. "Sweet Virgin, Mother of God, what have I done to deserve this?" He beckoned her closer. "Ah, Grace, if you knew how the demons do torment me in the dark!" he muttered, not wanting Atwater to hear. "I fear the scaffold with every fiber of my being. To have the hood blind me, feel the noose about my neck, hear the creak of the trap beneath my feet and know it will soon fall open—"

"Soft, Perkin," Grace interrupted him, sitting on her haunches and taking his face between her hands. "Think only of the blessed release from all this. You deserve to fly to Heaven and take your place with those who know earthly pain no more." She could feel his tears on her fingers but she kept her hands on his cheeks until he calmed. "Our time is short. Is there aught more I can do for you? May I carry a message with me? A token for Katherine?"

"You will convey my duty and love to my wife," Perkin said solemnly. "Tell her the happiest times of my life, and what sustains me in this hour of my death, are those halcyon days at the lodge at Falkland, riding with her in the forest, reading with her by firelight, watching the birds circling above us as we sat upon the hill looking across the Forth all the way to Arthur's seat." He let the tears flow, not heeding that it might be unmanly, and poured his heart out. "But most of all, I treasure lying with her and conceiving our son together. 'Twas Heaven on earth, tell her, and when I stand on the scaffold tomorrow, I shall imagine I am standing in the heather of East Lomond, smelling the scent of wild bluebells and hearing the larks singing high and curlews crying again. She will be with me forever then." He was sobbing now, making the jailer take notice outside, stick his nose through the grille on the door and growl, "Time be nearly up, my lady."

Ignoring the guard, Grace tore off a piece of her petticoat and, using Perkin's tears to moisten it, cleansed his face a little. "I will tell her all that you said, my dear 'brother,' " she said, her tears coming now. "I wish you were my brother, in truth, for I could have none better. Is there aught more I can do for you?"

"Dear Grace," Perkin murmured, catching her hand awkwardly with his manacled one and carrying it to his lips. "Why do you do this for me? Now you know I am not your brother, why do you care?"

Grace stood then. "I do it for Katherine—her love is true—and I do it for you, because like me, your life has been forced upon you, and we have been made to become what we are not. I must go where I am told because of who I am, when all I crave is a life of quiet on a farm."

"And I would have spent mine on the deck of a ship charting unknown lands," he whispered back. Suddenly, a scene among roses flashed before Grace's eyes, and she saw again Aunt Margaret's secret smile as she read from a letter to Grace and John. Aunt Margaret knew Perkin long before he fled from France to her court, she realized with a jolt. "Aunt Margaret must—," she spoke out loud.

Perkin grasped her skirt. "Aye, I beg of you, Grace, Aunt Margaret must be told that I never forgot my pledge to her all those years ago. Tell her that. She will know what I mean."

Grace nodded, although puzzled. "Aunt Margaret? Besides giving you shelter after France and helping you with men and ships upon your first attempt at an invasion, had she helped you before? Certes, she has abandoned you to your fate now."

"Never say so, Grace!" Perkin hissed so vehemently she took a step back. "She sent me messages during those months in the Tower through a priest who was in her service. She did not abandon me. She loves me. But she has no power to free me. Now, if you care at all, I beg of you, carry my message to her."

"Aye," Grace whispered. "I promise." Then she took a deep breath as she heard the guard's key in the lock. "Who are you in truth?" she said.

"Ask Aunt Margaret, for I cannot tell you," Perkin muttered. "Now, go!"

Grace bent down swiftly and kissed him on the forehead, flinching at the vile odor of him. "God grant you his mercy," she told him, deciding not to add, *and give you a swift end*. Then, giving Atwater a quick blessing, she hurried from the room without a backwards look.

"God bless you, Grace Plantagenet," Perkin called after her. "And *adieu*."

The guard leered at Grace as he led her back out into the fresh air, where Edgar and Katherine were anxiously awaiting her. Her fur hem was coated with the cell slime and her feet were wet through. She reached into the small pouch at her waist and gave the guard two groats. "If 'tis possible, sirrah, can you see to it that he is clean for his ordeal tomorrow. After all," she said, eyeing him, "we do not know for certain he is not the duke of York."

The guard was pleased to get the money and laughed. "We have orders to clean both prisoners, my lady. Sir Simon's orders included fresh shirts and hose. What a waste!" He guffawed and disappeared back into the blackness of the dungeon.

Edgar walked a step behind her, ready to support his mistress, whom he had once before seen deathly white. He would be there to catch her ere she fell this time, too, he thought. Grace walked in a daze along Water Lane to the Byward Tower gate and, as she passed behind the portcullis room, she saw Margaret, Countess of Salisbury, coming towards her carrying a basket and a book.

"Good day to you, Lady Grace," Margaret said, surprised. "Are you here to see my brother, too? I have brought him food and a prayer book." There was a catch in her throat, and Grace could see she had been crying.

Grace was glad Margaret had come in time to see Ned. Margaret lived most of the year on her husband's estates, but must have heard of her brother's trial and come quickly.

"I had hoped to see him—I was not certain anyone else would come, but now that you are here, certes, he will be happier to see you," Grace said. "Pray tell him he is in my prayers, and that I do not doubt Henry will pardon him. 'Tis the talk at court," she lied, and was glad to see hope in the woman's eyes. "No doubt we shall see you at court until—"

"No doubt," the other woman finished with a small smile of understanding. "I shall look forward to praying with you, dear Grace," she said. "My brother needs our prayers."

Grace chose not to add, *As does Perkin.* She merely nodded, bowed and walked on.

TOM MET THEM on the Westminster wharf when the boat returned from the Tower and walked both women back into the palace. Grace turned to thank Edgar for his escort and, in an unusual gesture, he grasped her hand and kissed it.

"How now, Edgar, what ails you?" Grace said kindly, although she wanted nothing more than a moment with Tom to tell him of her ordeal at the Tower.

"You be the best mistress in London," the big man answered. "Nay, the best in all England. To go alone into such a place as that"—he jerked his thumb back towards the Tower—"to comfort that Perkin fellow. My lady here told me of it, mistress, and when you'd come out, we could smell the dungeon from a mile away. It must've been something awful down there, but you didn't care. That Perkin be a lucky man."

"Aye, so he is, Edgar," Katherine answered before the stunned Grace could say anything. "My husband never had a truer friend—and neither have I." She gave Edgar one of her sweetest smiles and Edgar almost toppled into the Thames with embarrassment.

Tom chuckled, reaching to grip the man's hand. "And we are fortunate to have such a loyal servant, Edgar. I thank you for the compliment, on behalf of my speechless wife." All Grace could do was smile her thanks and take Tom's proffered arm.

Watching Katherine disappear up the spiral staircase to the royal apartments, Grace related the events of the morning as quickly as she could. She was still upset, so Tom took her in his arms. "Certes, you do smell foul, my love, but I am so proud of you, I know not how to express it. 'Tis evident to me that you will want to extend your kindness to this man tomorrow, and I cannot deny you. In fact, I will escort you myself—for I know if I did not, you would not hesitate to disguise yourself with the apprentices, it being Saint Clement's Day. What say you, O best mistress in England? Shall we go together?"

"Oh, Tom, I did not dare to dream you would agree to it," Grace said, burying her face in his blue wool doublet and inhaling his familiar, comforting scent. "I think I can bear it, if you are there." She lifted her head. "And then let us take the children home to Westow for Christmas. Bess will let me go—sadly, there will be no need to watch Katherine after tomorrow."

"I AM TO stay away," Katherine sobbed later that evening, after she and Grace had been dismissed from the queen's chamber. Grace thought it wise to tell Bess that she and Tom would go to Tyburn, and Bess had shrugged. She was not feeling well, and her head ached. "Go with my blessing, Grace," she said, her voice listless. "Sir Giles Daubeney has invited Henry to hunt nearby his lodge, Hampton Court, and I expect Arthur, Harry and Margaret to visit me—if my head heals."

Grace broached the subject of Katherine, and Bess frowned. "She should not witness the execution. Henry has expressly forbidden it; he believes it is for her own good. He has her well-being in mind, and I commend him for it."

Grace said nothing. She saw the resignation in Bess's eyes, and her heart went out to her gentle, temperate sister. She knows, Grace thought; she knows about Henry's penchant for Katherine. Grace's hatred for Henry grew even more. She was convinced that Henry did not have Lady Gordon's well-being in mind this time; he was afraid that the beautiful, tormented wife of the condemned man would curry pity with the crowd and make him look malevolent.

"My dear Katherine, 'twould serve your husband nothing for you to be there," Grace said now. "Supposing he sees you? It will make his ordeal even worse knowing you are watching." Grace did not entirely believe what she was saying, but she had to give Katherine just cause for obeying Henry. "If he should . . . if he resists . . . should he not behave in a dignified way," she tried to find the right words, "and you were there, it would mortify him. Do you see?"

Katherine nodded and leaned her head on Grace's shoulder. "You must promise to tell me all," she murmured, and Grace patted her hand. "Certes, I shall," she replied. "And, thank God—and the people of London—for changing the king's mind about the manner of his death. A simple hanging is more merciful, I promise you."

Grace and Tom set off on horseback from the Westminster stableyard as soon as they had broken their fast—Tom in a servant's livery and Grace in a gown Edgar had borrowed from a laundress.

With the groom on a sturdy rouncy behind them, Tom urged his horse into a canter along the muddy paths between the fields that stretched from the palace up to the village of Tyburn, so called for the meeting of two small streams that converged there and flowed the short way into the Thames. A roaring noise began to get their attention from the east as they neared the hamlet, and soon they recognized the sound of hundreds of voices upon the road out of London.

At the back of the village, Tom spotted a gnarled old apple tree out of sight of the nearest dwelling and quickly dismounted with Grace. Leaving Edgar to wait with the animals, he and Grace finished the journey on foot.

Rounding the tiny church, they were confronted by an already sizeable throng crowding the notorious hanging tree in the middle of the road that led to the north.

"How close do you want to be, sweetheart?" Tom asked, putting his arm around Grace protectively and wishing he had his shortsword with him. "Closer? Then hold on tight."

People glanced indifferently at the couple as they fought their way to within spitting distance of the gallows, as the noise grew louder, and the spectators already there began to feel the pressure of more bodies angling for a view.

"There must be more than five hundred souls," Grace whispered. "Although I cannot see much from down here," she complained.

" 'Ere, mistress, you can have this pail if you likes," a man near them said. He had just been to the well, but he cheerfully tipped the contents onto the already muddy ground and turned it upside down for Grace to stand on.

"Thank you, sir," Tom said, helping Grace up. She turned and gave him a brilliant smile and was amused to see the rough old farmer blush.

" 'Tis not often I see eye to eye with my husband," Grace told him, and then felt ashamed for jesting on such a day. The man guffawed and dug his neighbor in the ribs.

Straining her eyes over as many heads as she could, Grace could see several men on horseback at the head of the procession. Then she heard the people around her cheering: "Here he comes, the pretender prince. Perkin, Perkin, Perkin . . ." They chanted in unison, now all standing on tiptoe or jumping up and down to see the captives.

The armed escorts rode their mounts slowly around the base of the scaffold, pushing back the crowds so there would be room for the hanging party. "Move back, move back!" the riders shouted, and a scream of pain went up from a woman whose foot was trodden on by one of the horses.

Tom held tight to Grace, and his height and her bucket anchor caused people to move around them instead of pushing them aside. Then Grace saw the two horses pulling the hurdles, and she put one hand to her mouth to stifle a cry and pointed with the other. "There he is," she whispered. "Dear God, look at him."

Spread-eagled upon the wooden hurdle, Perkin had been dragged by a horse through the muck-filled streets of London from the Tower to Tyburn. The journey had taken two hours and he had endured poking, spitting, rotten vegetables, an occasional stone and, worst of all, the heckling, taunts and derision of a city angry at this mawmet who had disturbed their peace and insulted their king. "Perkin, Perkin, Perkin . . . Hang him, hang him, hang him," they cried, enjoying the little chant they had invented.

A hush came over the throng as the second horse arrived and both prisoners were untied and tipped off the hurdles into the mud, clothed only in shirts and hose. Elderly John Atwater could barely stand and needed support, but Perkin got up from the dirt and stood tall, facing his mockers. He looked at the leering men and women eager for the day's entertainment and swallowed. He asked for water but was refused. A priest mumbled prayers in his ear and then called them out to him as he was pushed, his hands still tied, up the steps to the stage. He was calm, Grace noticed, and she could see that his shirt had been clean before the hurdling. He gazed out at the sea of upturned faces and began to speak. At first no one heard him, but as the shouting abated they listened.

" 'Tis his confession," Grace murmured to Tom. "Dear God, he is repeating his confession."

"I am a stranger born, from Tournai in Picardy . . . and I was never that person I said I was—the second son of King Edward, nor"—his voice and his head dropped so only a few heard—"none of his blood." Then he jerked up his head and told the spectators that he never wished to be named the prince but that "John Atwater here present and others were to blame."

A gasp of disgust rose from those in the front who had heard. "He blames the poor bastard who follows—" one man began, but he was cut off by Atwater himself.

"What he says is true," Atwater cried as loudly as his weakness allowed. "He did not wish it."

Perkin looked down gratefully on the Irishman, and when he raised his eyes again, by a miracle he found Grace's small, sweet face, wet with tears and radiating pity, gazing back at him. It gave him courage and the strength to cry out: "I beg God and the king and all others whom I have offended to forgive me." His eyes begged for her forgiveness, and Grace nodded her acceptance.

The spectators' raucous jeering had subsided during the confession, and now Perkin's final apology seemed to have garnered their grudging sympathy, for they stood quietly watching him. He nodded to the hangman, who secured the noose that hung from the crossbar around Perkin's neck and turned him to the ladder. With his hands tied behind him, it was no easy task to mount each rung, but with the hangman's help he reached the top.

"*In manus tuas, Domine, commendo spiritum meum,*" he cried to the heavens as a crow cawed on the topmost point of the gibbet.

Before Grace could close her eyes the ladder was kicked away, and the young man who might have been a king swung free, his legs dancing as the noose constricted his airway and he fought valiantly for breath. Grace stumbled off the bucket and buried herself in Tom's embrace, weeping uncontrollably. "Is he dead?" she asked after the cheering began again for Atwater's turn.

Tom could not tell her that it would take Perkin at least an hour to die up there; prison had so emaciated the young man's body, there was not enough weight to have broken his neck.

"Aye, sweetheart, he is gone. He died with dignity and patience," he told her and, thanking the man for his bucket, led the trembling Grace away before the traitor Atwater met his more grisly end.

The final indignity imposed on the pretender by Henry, which may have been lost on Perkin, was that he died the common criminal's death. His head was cut off, speared on a pole and displayed upon London Bridge for the carrion to feast upon and as a warning to other would-be traitors. Even then, there were Londoners who stared up at the blackened head, its blond hair lifting with the breeze, and wondered if he had really been Richard, duke of York.

FIVE DAYS LATER upon Tower Green Henry rid himself of yet another York prince. Edward of Warwick, too, had the original traitor's death sentence of hanging, drawing and quartering commuted and, in deference to his rank, was sentenced to be beheaded instead. What was so surprising was that there was no public shaming of his body, which was conveyed with all respect to Bisham Abbey in Berkshire, where the young man was laid to rest in the family vault. And even more surprising, Grace told Tom, was that Henry paid the bill.

Others in the conspiracy were executed, imprisoned or, surprisingly, pardoned.

Robert Cleymond was never found.

A LIGHT SNOW was falling when the Gower family left the inn at York on the last few miles of their journey to Westow, and when the road branched off a little north of the city, Grace called out to Susannah, who was riding in her favorite place in front of Tom, almost hidden in the folds of his fur-lined cloak.

"You see that other road, sweeting? 'Tis the road to Sheriff Hutton, where there is a big castle. 'Tis where I met your father for the first time."

"How old were you, Mother?" Susannah asked, swiveling round as best she could.

"I was only twelve. Your father was tall and skinny and interested only in hunting, fishing and archery," Grace told her, squeezing Tom's waist in fun. "He had a big dog called Jason then. It was sad when Jason died, but he was old for a dog, and one day he did not wake."

"Doggie," Bella said suddenly from her perch in front of Edgar, who had Enid riding pillion on his big rouncy. Enid and Grace took turns holding baby Alice, who found the gentle rocking of the horse's gait soporific and slept a good deal of the day. "I want a doggie."

"Then you shall have one," Tom exclaimed. "We shall go to Sheriff Hutton and see what the kennels hold. 'Tis a perfect gift for the new year," he said over his shoulder to Grace. "What say you, sweetheart? When we take up residence at Cecily's manor in Essex, the girls will have a new playmate, and Freya will be left in peace."

"I'd rather have a lamb," Grace teased him. "Oh, Tom, I am so looking forward to being at Westow again." She laughed at the girls, who were sticking out their tongues and catching the crystal snowflakes as they floated down more heavily now. "I hope we get there before there are drifts."

"Only a league more, my love. I hope Mother has mulled wine for us; we shall be in need of it after this."

No one at the manor heard the hooves in the falling snow until a dairymaid saw the group riding up the hill past the copse towards the stables. She picked up her skirts and ran full tilt to the kitchen door, shrieking at the top of her voice. "Mistress Gower, Mistress Gower, they are come!"

The double oak doors into the hall were thrown open and Alice, Edmund and his wife and their child stood grouped on the steps down to the courtyard, calling out their welcomes.

Grace's heart lifted. Her journey from deep sorrow after the deaths of both Perkin and Ned to the happy anticipation of reaching Westow had taken several days to achieve on the road north. Tom had shouldered the lion's share of the children's well-being and allowed her to be melancholy, and soon the joy of being close to Tom's family again overcame her sadness and she began to look forward instead of back.

"Oh, Tom," she whispered as he lifted her off the uncomfortable pillion seat for the final time and carried her like a bride over the threshold and into the warm hall. " 'Tis so good to be home."

"Mother, take care of Grace, I beg of you," he said after he had embraced his doting parent. "I must fetch Susannah."

Alice took Grace in her arms, tears in her eyes. "It has been so long, hinny," she said, and Grace noticed that her hair was now completely white. "We have missed you all."

Enid was next to dismount, and Edgar took the precious bundle from her and carried the baby to Grace's waiting arms.

"Thank you, Edgar," she said, smiling at him. "You are the best servant in the world."

Edgar grinned from ear to ear and bowed his way from the door. Slipping on the icy steps and with arms flailing, he tottered backwards into the snow.

Susannah and Bella stood on the steps and giggled. "Thilly Edgar," Bella said, but without a moment's hesitation the two girls held hands, skipped down the steps and tried to help him up, leaving the grown-ups laughing.

Alice bustled them all into the hall, pulling off Grace's wet cloak and clucking in her usual fashion about dry clothes and hot baths. Baby Alice was beginning to squirm, and Grace knew loud screams of hunger would soon follow, so she nudged her mother-in-law towards the inviting fire.

"Tarry a moment, Mother," Grace said, laughing. "I want you to meet your namesake." She eased the damp coverlet from around the baby's wriggling body, still tightly wrapped in swaddling bands. "But be warned, she is as busy as you are," she said and held her out to the older woman. Alice

Gower, meet Alice Gower," she murmured softly as Tom came to her side and put his arm around her.

Baby Alice chose that moment to let forth a torrent of frustrated babbling, and the older Alice began to laugh, taking the squirming child into her strong arms.

"Aye, Alice meet Alice," Tom repeated, grinning. "Did I not say she is just like you?"

EPILOGUE

Many a man thinks he is seeing something,
And it is completely different from what it seems to be.
Whoever misapprehends, misjudges.

—GEOFFREY CHAUCER,
THE MERCHANT'S TALE

Essex and Burgundy

1 5 0 0

*E*arly in the year following Perkin's death, Cecily moved from Hellowe to her dower property near Theydon in Essex, and she found room for Grace, Tom and their children at the rambling Park Hall, putting Tom in charge of the estates. Grace was not surprised when Thomas Kyme rode back into Cecily's life that spring. The betrothal was a merry affair, and it was not long afterwards that Cecily kept her word to Grace.

"I have not forgotten my promise," Cecily said as they strolled arm in arm through the woods at the back of the house. They inhaled the heady scent of bluebells, which were blooming so profusely after a wet April the two women had trouble not trampling on the plants. Grace bent to pick one and presented it to Cecily. Grace knew exactly what promise her sister was alluding to and her heart leapt, though she waited for the confirmation. "When the sheep-shearing is done, I can let Tom take you to see Aunt Margaret. Is that soon enough? You have been very patient, in truth," Cecily said, accepting the bluebell and waving it front of her nose. "Heavenly," she exclaimed. "There is nowhere else on earth so beautiful as England in May, don't you think?"

"Nowhere," Grace agreed, beaming. "I hoped you had not forgotten, Cis. 'Tis true, my guilt was growing, although it is not a journey I look forward to making. Certes, Aunt Margaret will have had her own reports of Perkin's death, but the last thing he begged me to do was tell her that he had died bravely and, other than his one slip of the tongue, that her name had never passed his lips."

" 'Tis still a mystery to me why he did not denounce her in his public confession. Certes, an idiot could deduce it was she who must have pushed him to pose as Dickon. Then, when she apologized to Henry for deceiving him, why did Perkin not cry foul?" Cecily shook her head and then abruptly stopped, pointing silently at a fallow deer grazing on a patch of grass, its dappled brown coat well camouflaged against the undergrowth. Too late, the animal heard the approaching women and lifted its head for a second's perusal of danger before leaping away through the brush.

"Beautiful," Grace murmured in awe, and then answered her sister's question with a nonchalant: "I know not." Had Margaret elicited an oath from him? Had he known more than he admitted? These were questions she had pondered all these months, and she wondered if she had the courage to ask her aunt. Now, it seemed, she would get the chance. She felt a shiver of anticipation and drew her short mantle closer around her shoulders. Perhaps the real story of Margaret's White Rose would finally be revealed.

"Sweet Jesu on His cross! That old crone of a soothsayer in Winchester spoke the truth. Remember what she foretold?" Cecily said, stopping abruptly and gripping Grace's arm, her eyes wide with excitement. "She said you would be bound up with two young men, both of whom would be executed. Certes, 'twas John and Perkin. We talked about her when John was caught, but have you thought of the prophecy since?"

Grace's hand covered her mouth. "Nay," she whispered in to it. "What can it mean?"

Seeing her sister's fear, Cecily joked: "It means the old woman earned her groat that day, 'tis all. If it did not haunt you, then 'tis best forgotten." She grunted. " 'Tis as well Henry did not hear of it or he would be employing her at the palace, replacing Will Parron." She continued walking, taking Grace's arm firmly and changing the subject. "What would you say if I told you I am with child?"

MEMORIES OF HER first visit to Burgundy surged through Grace's head as the small merchant ship was pulled close to the wharf at Bruges by the men on shore, who wrapped the huge bow and stern lines around the sturdy wooden piles and hauled in the vessel while chanting rhythmically. She wondered what had become of the Gerards family, and then she remembered her companion, Judith, Master Caxton's kin. She had heard the printer's business was thriving even after his death, and this news would be sure to please Aunt Margaret.

She watched the great crane that was the city's pride and joy lower its hook into the hold of the ship at the next wharf and emerge toting a netful of barrels, which were swung over the side and lowered carefully to the waiting dockhands. Tom had been gone for an hour, hiring horses for the journey, and Edgar waited for him by Grace's small traveling chest near the gangplank. One of Cecily's tiring women, who had been sent along so Enid could stay behind with the children, stood a few yards away from Grace. The poor young woman, who had never been more than a few miles from Theydon Bois, was still gray from the sea voyage and clutching in fear the small purse that was attached to her belt.

Grace was so engrossed in the wharfside activity next door, she did not see Tom sprint up the gangway until he put his arm around her and made her jump. "A penny for your thoughts, sweetheart," he said, chuckling. "Are you practicing your speech for the duchess? Come, 'tis time to go ashore. We have many miles to travel before we see her, in truth, so you will have ample opportunity to practice."

Soon the small English party was trotting through the Burg, where the city hall abutted the Church of the Holy Blood, then along a canal towards the Ghentpoort, the southern gate of the city. It would take them three days to reach Binche, one of Margaret's dower towns in Hainault, where the duchess would be awaiting them. It was drizzling, and Grace pulled up the hood of her cloak and leaned into Tom's back upon the sturdy palfrey he had chosen for them. With little Edith riding pillion, Edgar was astride a strong rouncy, leading a packhorse laden with the traveling gear. The loud Belfort bells rang a carillon as they crossed the last canal bridge and passed under the twin-towered gate, and the women stopped their ears with their fingers against the din.

The congestion eased once they turned onto the road south, and Tom led them on a route suggested by the duchess in her letter of invitation to Grace. After two nights upon the road, they approached the small city of Binche from Mons to its west, so called for the hill that rose high above the flat landscape, upon which sat a church and an impregnable castle. Tom rose up in his stirrups and pointed enthusiastically towards the walled city in the far distance, also on a hill. Even higher than the ten-foot-thick wall at the southern end of the city rose the turrets of a gleaming white palace and the spire of the Abbaye de Bonne Esperance. All around the walls were gently rolling fields dotted with cows, and a small river bordered one side. It seemed a peaceful place, and Grace could understand why her aunt would spend most of her days here now. They entered under the Mons road gateway and joined farmers and other travelers wending their way to the marketplace in front of the town hall. Tom was pointed to a lane that led to the palace gate, close to St. Ursmer's church.

Tom escorted Grace to the staircase outside the small but attractive palace, leaving Edgar to tend to the horses. The black and white tiled floor of the entry hall was spread with sweet-smelling rushes and two guards stood to attention, their halberds polished and their livery immaculate. Margaret's new chamberlain, with thick gray hair and a brush of a mustache, came hurrying forward to greet the visitors. When he learned their names he bowed solemnly to Grace and then snapped his fingers at a page and instructed him to show Edgar and Edith the way to Lady Grace's lodgings with the baggage. With a ducklike gait on his short, stubby legs, the steward led the way through several rooms painted in varying patterns of green, gold and scarlet, each with long windows showing off the rose garden below. Grace noticed how often the marguerite and white rose were repeated in the patterns and smiled. There was no doubt who lived here, she thought. A new detached building bordered one side of the garden, and it appeared the chamberlain was leading them to it.

"Her grace is expecting you, *madame*," he said in French. "She has been unwell of late, so she is often lying in her chamber. *Monsieur* may wait in the library."

Grace had a hard time imagining her aunt anything but stately, hale and lavishly dressed, so she was shocked upon entering Margaret's solar to see her reclined upon a settle next to the window, still in her chemise and satin chamber robe. Her gray hair was no longer shaved high on her forehead but had started to sprout back, giving her the appearance of an unkempt wolfhound. The rest of it was braided under a winged cap, in the Dutch fashion. Certes, Grace realized, sinking into a deep reverence, it has been almost ten years since I saw her last and she must be . . . Grace frowned, trying to remember.

"Fifty-six, niece," Margaret said in English, startling Grace into lifting her head before being given permission. "I am fifty-six, but I swear I feel ninety-five most days. Come, give your old aunt a kiss." Blushing for being second-guessed, Grace rose, amusing Margaret even more. "I do not claim to have the gift of sight, but I know shocked surprise when I see it." She laughed. "I swear, raising my grandchildren—and now Maximilian has me caring for his grandchildren when there is no one else—has put these lines on my face and these gray hairs on my head. All those years when I was governing Burgundy in Charles's absence, the headaches we had seem so much simpler when compared to raising children at my advanced age." She patted the settle and shifted her legs off the cushions and onto the floor.

Grace first kissed her aunt's hand and then her cheek before sitting down gingerly at the other end of the bench. She had not said a word so far, her feelings for the duchess still conflicted. "Aye, I can understand, your grace," she finally said. "I now have three little girls and they have given me one or two gray hairs, in truth."

"Three daughters?" Margaret sighed. "How fortunate you are." She turned to look over her shoulder. "Henriette," she addressed her lady in waiting in French, "you remember my niece, Lady Grace? Aye, I see that you do. Will you please pour wine for us?"

Without a word, Henriette de la Baume abandoned her needlework and went to the table to comply. She, too, had aged, Grace saw, but she was still a beautiful woman. The two murmured a greeting as Grace reached for a cup.

"Let us drink to the new century, and you can tell me news of my family in England," the duchess said. "I would rather not talk about the reason for your visit today, Grace. Instead, if you can wait until this infernal rain stops, I would dearly love to show you my garden. There is a spot where I am happiest and can hear the worst of news. I am expecting you to stay for a few days at least, so we have all the time in the world." She sounded calm, but her jaw was clenched and her fingers played nervously with her ever-present belt ornament, causing Grace to wonder if it was also worn in bed. Grace knew the older woman was putting off hearing about the untimely demise of her dearest White Rose, and she understood the reluctance—even though, by the end, Grace had placed the blame for Perkin's tragic life and death squarely on these bony old shoulders.

"As you wish, aunt," came her dutiful reply. "I do not wish to burden you."

Margaret waved her hand dismissively. "You do not burden me, my dear. I shall enjoy your company—and that of your husband. Now tell me about my nieces—I heard Cecily lost her husband and, more important, her daughters. How sad."

"Not so sad, Aunt Margaret," Grace replied, unbending a little, and proceeded to update the duchess on the happy developments in Essex.

UPON THE AFTERNOON of the next day, the sun reappeared and sparkled on the raindrops still clinging to the myriad roses that filled the garden. "I am first and foremost an Englishwoman," Margaret declared, steadying herself on Grace's arm. "There are roses in all my gardens."

Grace was glad when they reached the duchess's favorite seat, as Margaret's height made it awkward for Grace to be a support.

"You must be the smallest member of my family," Margaret had remarked as they began down the path. "Are you sure you are Edward's child? Nay, do not answer such an impertinent question. I am showing exceedingly bad manners, but you are so charming and easy to be with that I feel I have known you for a long time and can talk frankly with you."

Grace noted that Henriette and the other two attendants who had accompanied them into the garden were walking together in the opposite direction, knowing their mistress needed to speak to Grace privately. Tom had been happy to accompany the falconer and another huntsman who were hawking for hares and small game that day. There was nothing to disturb aunt and niece that afternoon, except the incessant cawing of two very noisy crows.

"Flap off!" Margaret cried at them, launching a pebble in their general direction. "Foolish, I know, but I hate those birds. I think they bring bad luck."

"Nay, 'tis magpies that bring bad luck, Aunt Margaret—one at least," Grace answered, smoothing her brown and yellow kirtle over her knees. "But there was a crow at Tyburn the day that Perkin died," she whispered. "Do you want to hear of it now, aunt?"

Margaret nodded sadly. "Tell me everything. Leave nothing out, my child. I must pay penance for helping him to his ghastly death; the details will provide me with the pain I need to feel to purge my guilty soul."

And so Grace recounted the final scene in Perkin's filthy prison, including the all-important message that made Margaret cry out in anguish. Grace hurried on to describe his journey from the Tower to Tyburn and his last confession from the scaffold.

"And he never mentioned my name?" Margaret whispered, holding her breath. "Not even once? Not even when he might have cursed me from the scaffold?"

Grace shook her head. "Only once—under torture—and he was consumed by guilt." She wanted to ask what the message meant but knew she had no right to intrude.

"Did all believe he was a boy from Tournai and not Richard, duke of York? Did he tell you who he really was?" Margaret reached out and grasped Grace's hand, and Grace was surprised by the strength in it.

"In the end I, too, knew he was Perkin Warbeck, aunt, even though I wanted with all my heart for him to be my half brother. But it seemed there were too many clues that he was not." She felt Margaret loose her wrist. "On the scaffold his final words were 'I am heartily sorry for the deception. I am not who I said I was.' He was so calm, so dignified, that the crowd stopped jeering, and I saw more than one woman weep for him."

A tear rolled down the old woman's face. "Ah, my little Jehan," she murmured, "so, you kept your promise." Grace leaned forward, her ears alert.

"Jehan? Who is Jehan? I thought he was Perkin—Pierrequin," Grace said, more forcefully than she had intended. "Was he not Perkin Warbeck?" Her hands were clammy and her heart was pounding. She knew there was yet more to this mystery, she thought triumphantly.

Margaret leaned her back against the tree behind her and closed her eyes. "He did not tell you? Not even when you went to see him and all was lost?" Grace shook her head. "He was braver than I thought—and more loyal, God rest his soul."

Grace waited less patiently than was her wont, until eventually the duchess spoke again. "A long time ago, I brought a little boy from Tournai to live with me here in Binche. I was unable to bear children, and this child, Jehan, meant everything to me. But he was not just any little boy from Tournai," she said, opening her eyes and looking straight at Grace. "And if you swear by all that is holy never to tell a soul, I will reveal his true identity to you."

"Cer-certes, I swear," Grace whispered, crossing herself and holding her hand over her heart. Margaret's eyes went to the hand and flinched. Jehan had done exactly that when she had exhorted a promise from him fifteen years ago. How she wished she could take it back! She would have her dearest boy with her now.

"You and I are the only two people who will know this, Grace, now that Jehan and my brother Edward are dead."

Edward? My father? What does my father have to do with Perkin Warbeck, if indeed he was not Richard? Grace wondered.

"It seems my other brother, George, spent an illicit night with a young woman once. The result was my Jehan. Poor George, his guilt must have been great, because when he knew he was to die, he begged Edward to continue payments to the boy's mother, as he, George, had done since the baby's birth five years before. Edward, himself full of remorse for putting his own brother to death, came up with the idea of easing his conscience by asking George's favorite—and childless—sister to take the boy in and care for him: me. He knew I would not be able to resist nor deny the offer."

Grace did a little calculation and realized this birth must have occurred close to her own. And thus the boy was of a similar age to Prince Richard, as Perkin had claimed all along. As Grace absorbed the gist of the story, the pieces began to fall into place. She gripped the edge of the bench and whispered: "If Pierrequin was Uncle George's bastard, then he was my cousin. Oh, Sweet Jesu, and poor Ned's half brother." Then her eyes widened and she gasped. "Dear God, Ned died plotting to put his own bastard brother on the throne!" She felt dizzy with the horrible irony of it all. She got to her feet and walked a few paces away. Suddenly she turned: "Did

Pierrequin know who he really was, Aunt Margaret?" she asked bitterly. "Was he tortured and hanged while he was already weighted down with his secret?"

Margaret put her head in her hands and began to cry softly. Grace had to creep closer to hear her when she began to speak. "Aye, God help me," she said between her fingers. "I told him in Ninety-four when he fled France to my court. I told him a few steps from where you are standing," she said, lifting her head and waving one hand in the direction of the wall embrasure. "He knew." She did not tell Grace how, over many days and through many tears, she had coaxed and cajoled her White Rose to do her bidding and pretend he was the duke of York. How she'd reminded him of his promise of all those years before, or how she'd dangled the throne of England like a carrot under his nose. It all made sense at the time, she told herself; it was the opportunity to wreak revenge on the hated Henry Tudor and restore the throne to York. But in the end, it was all for naught, and her beloved boy was gone. She let her tears fall; she felt old and worn out.

Grace was pacing again, her anger growing, but she held it in check because she had more questions to ask. "But if he was Clarence's child, born in England, wherefore was he also a boy from Tournai?"

Margaret wiped her eyes with her long silk sleeve and pulled herself together. "It seems the girl's parents were respectable Flemish weavers in London. To avoid scandal, they sent their daughter with the baby to be married to a boatman in Tournai. One Jehan Werbecque. We paid the woman handsomely for me to take her son one day when the stepfather was not home. They had too many mouths to feed, and the woman was sickly. I do believe she was ignorant of the identity of her lover that drunken night at the tavern; she knew only that money came from a rich man somewhere. As far as she knew, I was sent from the bishop to put the child in the choir school. She did not know my name." She paused, biting her bottom lip. "I was glad to take little Jehan away. His mother was not kindly, and the man beat him, so the boy told me."

Grace let out a whistle—an ill-bred sound that made Margaret frown. "And so, much of Henry's confession that he made Pierrequin—Jehan—sign was true?" she asked. Margaret nodded, and Grace gasped. "What about Sir Edward Brampton, and the admiral in Portugal?"

"All true. I had to send Jehan from me after Bosworth. I was afraid someone would find out I had another York son in my house and the boy would be in danger. Certes, Henry of Richmond could never sleep soundly while York heirs were still running around. Jehan thought he was a simple lad from Tournai at that point and accepted the plan I had made. Sir Edward and his wife thought Jehan was a charity case and were pleased to be in my debt." A sneer curved her cracked lips. "It must have been Brampton who gave away Jehan's name to Henry. I cannot think how else Henry's spies knew to search in Tournai. But I have no proof." She sighed. "Poor Jehan. All he really wanted to do in life was be a mariner. Ah, the letters he wrote to me about the voyages he took, the dreams of sailing with someone like Cristoforo Columbo or da Gama—'twas when he was happiest." Grace nodded, remembering Perkin's sad admission.

The bell for Compline rang from St. Ursmer's church tower and Margaret crossed herself. "*Ave Maria*, pray for me a sinner," she muttered, slumping in her seat.

Grace swung around, her anger showing now. "Aye, aunt," Grace agreed. "You should seek Our Lady's forgiveness. You have destroyed lives with your desire to avenge our family." Margaret flinched at Grace's harsh tone, but she let her continue. "Not only John and Perkin but Perkin's wife and their little son." She paused and tried to calm herself. "But your secret is safe with me, although I would like to know what has stopped Jehan's mother from giving away his true lineage? From all I have heard, Katherine de Faro is not to be trifled with, and she and the boatman were very sure Jehan was their missing son, or so Henry told all of England."

"Not Nicaise Farou, Grace—Nicaise was her *petit nom*. She was Jehan's stepmother. Frieda died soon after I took Jehan, and Nicaise became Madame Werbecque. So you see, with Edward, George and Jehan also dead, you and I are the only ones to know whose son he is!"

Grace nodded disconsolately. She wished she didn't know. If she had known sooner, she would have made sure Perkin had escaped from Westminster more successfully than he had. It was only because she came to realize he was not Richard, duke of York, and she felt sorry for him and Katherine, that she agreed to help him as far as she could without risking her own and Tom's future. If he could have reached the coast, he could have taken a ship back to Portugal. He could be riding high upon a mast and sighting new lands over distant horizons. Poor Perkin. After all he suffered, he went to his grave knowing he was naught but a bastard son of an attainted father. A bastard, just like me, she grimaced. No wonder I cared so much; no wonder I felt such kinship. How proud she had always been of her York lineage, but now she was repelled by its ambition, and its members were naught but lechers and liars, it seemed.

She made up her mind on the spot. "Tom and I will leave you on the morrow, madam," she pronounced, a hint of bitterness in her tone. "I miss my children, and knowing what I now know makes me all the more determined to take them away from court and let them live long and happy, where men—or women"—she paused, sending an accusing look Margaret's way—"cannot play fox and geese with their lives. I have done my duty by my cousin, and I pray he rests in peace now."

Margaret lifted her head and, with a hint of a smile, remarked, "Your father would have been proud of you, Grace. You have more wisdom than any of us. May God go with you on your journey home." She drew herself up to her full height and put out her hand proudly, and the chastened aunt was once again Margaret of England, dowager duchess of Burgundy. "I pray you, find Chevalier de la Baume and send him to me. I shall need him to return to the palace." Grace curtsied and kissed Margaret's ringless fingers lightly. "And so I bid you farewell, my child. May God bless you."

"*Adieu*, your grace," Grace responded with a finality that told Margaret her niece would not return to Burgundy.

STARING BACK AT the walled city receding in the morning light, Grace went over the extraordinary story she had been told the day before. She could never tell Tom; she would keep her promise to the duchess, although she did not know what purpose the secret served now.

How could a mother give up her child for money? she wondered, returning to the part of the boy's early tale that saddened her the most. The thought of handing Susannah to a stranger and taking a few coins in return made her stomach heave. She must have been so desperate, she thought, this Frieda. A memory stirred . . .

"Frieda!" she suddenly cried.

Tom jumped. "Did you say something, sweetheart?"

"Nay, nay," she answered hurriedly, her mind reeling from the revelation.

Sweet Jesu and St. Sibylline! she mouthed. Perkin was unknowingly who he said he was. He was indeed a king's son! He was *Edward's* bastard, not George's. Certes, it happened that night in London when Edward and Will Hastings played a trick on the intoxicated George and came back boasting of it to Elizabeth. Edward had sired the bastard on Frieda, as Katherine Hastings had surmised upon hearing Will conspiring to pay the girl off on Edward's behalf.

If it weren't so tragic, she might have laughed. Your secret is safe with me, Father, she thought ruefully, casting her eyes heavenward. Even Aunt Margaret will never know the truth. Ha! And she doesn't deserve to, Grace decided; she will have to wait until Judgment Day.

With a satisfied smile, she snuggled up against Tom.

"Let us hurry home, Tom," she said. "I have never had such a hunger to hold my children."

Author's Note

*I*f the Perkin Warbeck story had been invented by a novelist, scornful readers might have left the book on the shelf or consigned it to the wastepaper basket as preposterous and implausible. As a novelist, I am in awe of and humbled by the facts and am now a believer in the old adage "truth is stranger than fiction."

And the truth of the matter is that, until we can produce the body of young Richard, duke of York, we shall never know if Perkin was the prince or a pretender. *The King's Grace* is my interpretation of the facts and my best guess—and as the mystery of the princes in the Tower is still unsolved, a guess that is as good as any. I would urge anyone still intrigued to study the sources for themselves. I guarantee you will come up with yet another take on this fascinating tale. My job was to read as much as I could about the events and people involved and faithfully follow them and my instincts.

For the facts: Perkin Warbeck was first noticed in history in 1491, when Irish Yorkist supporters in Cork claimed to recognize a young seaman, dressed in silks, as the son of Edward IV. Soon King Charles of France, Maximilian of Austria, Philip of Burgundy and James of Scotland all recognized his lineage, giving Henry VII of England a nasty scare. His greatest mentor, though, was Margaret of York, dowager duchess of Burgundy, who would have been his aunt—if he was Prince Richard. It is thought by historians that these royal heads of Europe had political motives behind recognizing the young man, and indeed he was a thorn in Henry's side for eight years until the king captured and hanged him.

Perkin did end up at the court of James of Scotland, who was so convinced of the man's authenticity that he gave Perkin his own kinswoman, Katherine Gordon, as a bride. I visited Scotland for the first time in 2007 and walked the Lomond Hills while staying in the charming village of Falkland, where the old palace/hunting lodge still stands. "Richard" and his Katherine spent more than a year there—an idyllic place for an extended honeymoon.

After attempting to invade England from the north with James and failing to rouse any support, Perkin was forced to leave Scotland once Henry and James signed a truce in 1497. James could not be seen supporting an enemy of his new ally, so Perkin and Katherine set sail with their little son, landed in Ireland to recruit more troops and eventually sailed for Cornwall. I walked along the wall at Exeter in Devon, where Perkin had his momentary military success before being cornered by Henry's far superior forces near Taunton. There was something about Perkin's midnight flit across the countryside to Beaulieu Abbey in the New Forest, abandoning his followers and his wife and son, that made me believe this young man had no real desire for kingship. He sounded like a frightened boy fulfilling other people's ambitions, and so for me he became a tragic figure, doomed from the moment Henry's lieutenants took him back to Taunton for questioning. Much has been written about his confession there—some of the original* I have used in the book—and of Henry's spies tracing Perkin's story back to Tournai and the boatman on the Scheldt. But despite the details in the confession, there were many who still questioned why such a puppet was able to affect the trappings of nobility and pass for royal. Being versed in English, French and Latin was not conducive to being a boatman's son, nor were his noble bearing, ease of conversation with royalty or abilities on horseback and with a sword. These were inher-

---

*Historians are unsure of the reason for the discrepancies in the names of Perkin's family name of "Osbeck" instead of "Werbeque" and "Kateryn de Faro" instead of "Nicaise Farou." I have attempted to explain it away in my narrative, as it is still confusing scholars.

ently noble traits—not to be picked up in a few months with the help of a tutor.

Perkin did become a "guest" at Henry's court for all those months, and Henry indeed paraded him through London and put him and Katherine on display during court festivities as though they were a freak show. And yet he was fed and clothed and considered "free" to ride and walk where he wanted—albeit with a constant escort. I could not resist using some of the poem about Perkin by Henry's poet laureate John Skelton, although, with the help of my friend Catherine Thibedeau, the language is updated a little. Perhaps the verses were the final insult that led him to escape from Westminster. He did escape from Westminster and manage to get to Shene—but whether he had help from Katherine (and Grace) we do not know! The fire that burned some of Shene—and convinced Henry to rebuild and rename the palace Richmond—did begin in the king's wardrobe, where it was thought Perkin had slept with his guards.

From all the accounts of the story that I read, I got the distinct impression that Perkin and Warwick died so Henry could satisfy Ferdinand and Isabella of Spain that it was safe to send their daughter to England to marry his heir. Sir Simon Digby was alerted to the plot to take over the Tower on August 3 and informed Henry, who was on his progress to the Isle of Wight, but who did not bother to return to the mainland until August 24. Then nothing was done until the end of October, by which time Henry was being pressured by Spain to make a decision on the Perkin problem, and Henry had John Taylor in his custody as well as Atwater, father and son. Someone betrayed the plotters—and there were more plotters than I have mentioned in the book—and, to me, Robert Cleymond looked like the culprit. He disappeared and was never charged.

As far as I could, I have placed the major characters in the right places at the right times. Oddly enough, very little information remains about Elizabeth of York's movements, nor of her character during her all-too-short life as queen of England. After losing Edmund in 1500, she rejoiced finally in the marriage between Catherine of Aragon and Arthur, Prince of Wales, in November 1501. But more tragedy struck this much beloved queen when Arthur inexplicably died six months later. She became pregnant again in the summer of 1502 and gave birth to another daughter on February 2, 1503, who died that same day. Nine days later, on her thirty-eighth birthday, Elizabeth died and was buried in the new chapel built by Henry in Westminster Abbey. Henry joined her six years later. (As a sweet footnote, the queen of hearts on our playing cards today is, as John predicts, a representation of Elizabeth of York.)

Her sister Cecily, who was reputed to have been even more beautiful than Elizabeth suffered the three losses I write about in the book. We are not sure exactly when her daughters died, but according to Welles family expert Nita Knapp, Elizabeth (Lilleth) was still alive in 1498, as the papal dispensation for her marriage to Thomas Stanley was given then. However, at the time of Viscount Welles's death in February 1499, no mention was made in his will of his daughters, and so it is presumed neither was living. In her many years of researching this family, Nita discovered that Anne was buried in London but as Elizabeth was not and there is no record of death or burial, I chose to have Elizabeth die in Lincolnshire, separate from Anne. On a happier note, Cecily did marry her Thomas Kyme, a gentleman of Lincolnshire closely associated with the Welles family. She had two children with him. As her marriage was to a commoner, Henry stripped Cecily of much of her Welles inheritance, and it was this fact and the fact that the marriage was described by seventeenth-century historian Thomas Fuller as *"rather for comfort than credit"* that made me take the dramatic liberty of suggesting Cecily and Thomas were in love rather more sooner than after John Welles's death. Cecily died in 1507.

As for Grace, we know only one fact about her existence, and it is from the Arundel collection of manuscripts at the British Library (Arundel MS 26 folio 29v), where it was written: *"Maistres Grace, a bastard dowghter of Kyng Edwarde, and among an other gentilwoman"* were the only mourners upon the funeral barge of Elizabeth Woodville in June 1492, along with Elizabeth's chaplain and her cousin, Edward Haute.* I was intrigued as to why the dowager queen would have sanctioned Grace as a mourner—a signal honor—when the girl was a bastard of King Edward's. I decided Elizabeth must have taken to the young woman, and so I chose Grace to be our eyes and ears at court during the Perkin Warbeck mystery. No one has been able to trace Grace's story, which gave me license to imagine one. The Gower family was prolific in that area of Yorkshire around Sheriff Hutton,

---

* I have used Elizabeth's will as she wrote it on April 10, 1492.

and when I was researching there we stayed at a delightful inn in Westow. Finding a branch of the family had lived at Westow in the fifteenth century, I was determined to make it Tom's home, although the only name I ran across in my research of the period was a George Gower of Westow, and thus Alice, Edmund, Cat and Tom are also figments of my imagination.

Central to the Perkin Warbeck story was Margaret of York, and it was Ann Wroe's research into the Burgundian archives that brought to light the existence of Margaret's "secret boy." He was under her wing at her palace at Binche from 1478 to 1485, when he and his tutor-chaplain disappeared from her accounts. Ann's conjecture that he may have been a bastard child of Edward or George of Clarence became the basis for my Perkin, although, I repeat, this is purely conjecture. Curiously, when Margaret remodeled Binche in the late 1490s, one of the rooms was named in the plans as "Richard's Room." The letters between nephew and aunt are invented—it was a way to depict Perkin's life before he and Grace crossed paths in England so that he was not a stranger to the reader. However, the letter to Isabella from Margaret is reproduced from the original Latin, thanks to Ann Wroe's generous permission. The one Perkin wrote, and that I allude to, at about the same time is also extant. Henry did nickname Margaret "the diabolical duchess," due to her lifelong ambition to overthrow him and put the York family back on the throne. It is thought that her letter of apology to him in September 1499 was a desperate attempt to spare her White Rose's life—to no avail. Margaret died in 1503 aged fifty-seven.

Katherine Gordon remained at the English court and married twice more during Henry VIII's reign, but her son by Perkin Warbeck was never restored to her. There is a family named Perkins near Swansea in South Wales who claim to be descended from a Richard Perkins, son of Perkin Warbeck.

It is thought that Henry and Elizabeth were tolerably happy together, despite Margaret Beaufort's iron influence on her son, and indeed when Arthur died the husband and wife were said to have comforted each other greatly in their loss, and when his wife died, Henry spared no expense on a lavish funeral and tomb for her in Westminster Abbey. He did not remarry, although he kept Katherine Gordon close, and he is said to have aged twenty years during the Perkin Warbeck dilemma. Even though he helped negotiate the papal dispensation for it, Henry did not live to see his son, Henry, marry Catherine of Aragon. He died on April 22, 1509, and Catherine and Henry VIII were married on June 11. The rest, as they say, is history.

Newburyport, Massachusetts

Glossary

all-night—a snack before bedtime served to the king by one of his lords

argent—heraldic term for silver

arras—tapestry or wall hanging

attaint—imputation of dishonor or treason; estates of attainted lords were often forfeited to the crown

avise—to look closely, study a person

bailey—outer wall of a castle

barbe or *wimple*—widow's headdress, resembling a nun's wimple

basse danza—slow, stately dance

bill-man—soldier with long bladed weapon

blackjack—a large jug usually made of leather and coated with tar

buckler—small round shield

burthen—refrain or chorus of a song

butt—barrel for wine

butts—archery targets

caravel—medieval sailing ship

catafalque—funeral chariot

caul—mesh hair covering, often jeweled or decorated, often encasing braids wound on either side of the head

certes—for sure; of course

chausses—leggings

churching—first communion given to a woman following the period of seclusion after giving birth

coif—scarf tied around the head

Compline law—no talking after this final service of the day

conduit—drinking fountain in a town or city with piped-in water

coney—rabbit or rabbit fur

cote or *cotehardie*—long gown worn by men and women

crackows—fashionable long-pointed shoes, said to have originated in Krakow, Poland

crenellation—indentation at top of battlement wall

cutpurse—thief or mugger

donzel—knight in training; young squire

ewerer—water-pourer and holder of handwashing bowls at table

excedra—low, grass-covered wall that could be used as a seat in a garden

flampayn—an egg pie with meat, like a quiche

fleem—thin knife for bloodletting

fox and geese—medieval board game

frumenty—dish made with hulled wheat and boiled in milk, like creamed wheat

galingale—aromatic root of the ginger family

garderobe—inside privy where clothes were often stored

gemshorn—musical instrument of polished, hollowed goat's horn

gipon—close-fitting padded tunic

gittern—plucked, gut-stringed instrument similar to a guitar

gong farmer—man who removes waste from privies and carts it outside city

groat—silver coin worth about fourpence

halberd—a long weapon, often carried by guards

hennin—tall conical headdress from which hangs a veil; steepled hennins were as much as two feet high, while butterfly hennins sat on the head like wings with the veil draped over a wire frame

herber—a flower or herb garden

hippocras—sweet, spicy wine

houppelande—full-length or knee-length tunic or gown with full sleeves and train *jennet*—saddle horse, often used by women

jerkin—jacket

jupon—see *gipon*

kersey—coarse woollen cloth

kirtle—woman's gown or outer petticoat

leman—lover, sweetheart and often mistress

Lollard—religious reformer, follower of John Wyclif, who was considered a heretic

lurcher—large hunting dog

malmsey—kind of wine

mammet or *mawmet*—puppet or dressed-up figure who is a tool of another

meinie—group of attendants on a lord

mess—platter of food shared by a group of people

mural tower—tall tower in the curtain wall, ideal in defense of castle

murrey—heraldic term for purple-red (plum)

obit—memorial service for the dead

osier—willow shoot used for baskets

palfrey—small saddle horse

pantler—household officer in charge of the pantry

patten—wooden platform strapped to the sole of a shoe

pavane—a slow, stately dance

pennon—triangular flags attached to a lance or staff; often rallying points during battle

pibcorn—hornpipe

pillicock—slang term for a wanton

pillion—a pad placed at the back of a saddle for a second rider

pipkin—earthenware or metal pot

plastron—gauzy material tucked for modesty into the bodice of a gown

points—lacing with silver tips used to attach hose to undershirt or gipon

portcullis—heavy, grilled gate able to be raised or lowered from the gatehouse

puling—whining; crying in a high, weak voice

rebec—a three-stringed instrument played with a bow

rouncy—a packhorse used by travelers or men-at-arms

sackbut—early form of trombone

salet—light, round helmet

sanctuary—place of protection for fugitives; haven (perhaps in an abbey), usually for noblewomen and their children, who pay to stay

sarcenet—a fine, soft silk fabric

scarlet—a high-quality broadcloth, usually dyed red with expensive kermes, an insect

scrip—a leather or hemp satchel carried by shepherds

seneschal—steward of a large household

sennight—a week (seven nights)

settle—high-backed sofa

shawm—wind instrument making a loud, penetrating sound often used on castle battlements

shout—a sailing barge carrying grain, building stone and timbers, common on the Thames

skep—beehive made of straw or wicker

solar—living room often doubling as a bedroom

squint—small window in a wall between a room and a chapel; often women would participate in a service through it

staple town—center of trade in a specified commodity (e.g., Calais for wool)

stewpond—private pond stocked with fish for household use

stews—brothel district

stomacher—stiff bodice

subtlety—dessert made of hard, spun colored sugar formed into objects or scenes

surcote—loose outer garment of rich material, often worn over armor

suzerain—feudal overlord

symphonie—hurdy-gurdy, played by turning a handle producing a drone

tabard—short tunic bearing the coat of arms of a knight worn over chain mail

tabbied—moiré effect on grosgrain taffeta

tabor—small drum

threped—Scottish for "insisted upon"

timbre—medieval percussion instrument, forerunner of tambourine

trencher—stale bread used as a plate

tric-trac—form of backgammon

tun—barrel

tussie-mussie—aromatic pomander

vair—a composite of white ermine and gray squirrel; a fur prized by the nobility

verjuice—sour fruit juice used for cooking and medicines

viol or vielle—a stringed instrument, the ancestor of the viola da gamba

voide—the final course of a feast, usually hippocras wine and wafers or comfits

worsted—spun from long fleece, a smooth, lightweight wool for summer

Bibliography

Arthurson, Ian. *The Perkin Warbeck Conspiracy.* Stroud, Gloucestershire, UK: Sutton Publishing, 1994.

Baldwin, David. *Elizabeth Woodville, Mother of the Princes in the Tower.* Stroud, Gloucestershire, UK: Sutton Publishing, 2002.

Bennett, Michael. *Lambert Simnel and the Battle of Stoke.* New York: St. Martin's Press, 1987.

Calmette, Joseph. *The Golden Age of Burgundy.* Trans. Doreen Weightman. London: Phoenix Press, 2001.

Chrimes, S. B. *Henry VII.* Berkeley and Los Angeles: University of California Press, 1972.

Cosman, Madeleine Pelner. *Medieval Wordbook.* New York: Checkmark Books, 1996.

Gairdner, James. *Henry the Seventh.* London: MacMillan and Co., 1920.

Gairdner, James, ed. *Letters and Papers Illustrative of the Reigns of Richard III and Henry VII.* London: Her Majesty's Stationery Office, 1863; Kraus Reprint Ltd., 1965.

———. *The Paston Letters.* Stroud, Gloucestershire, UK: Sutton Publishing, 1986.

Hammond, P. W. *Food and Feast in Medieval England.* Stroud, Gloucestershire, UK: Sutton Publishing, 1993.

Hartley, Dorothy. *Lost Country Life*. London: Macdonald & Janes Publishers, 1979.

Kleyn, Diana. *Richard of England*. Oxford: Kensal Press, 1990.

Leyser, Henrietta. *Medieval Women: A Social History of Women in England 1450–1500*. London: Weidenfeld & Nicolson, 1989.

Newman, Paul B. *Daily Life in the Middle Ages*. Jefferson, N.C.: McFarland & Company, 2001.

Norris, Herbert. *Medieval Costume and Fashion*. London: J. M. Dent & Sons, 1927.

Reeves, Compton. *Pleasures and Pastimes in Medieval England*. Oxford: Oxford University Press, 1998.

Scofield, Cora L. *The Life and Reign of Edward IV* (2 vols.). London: Frank Cass & Co., 1967.

Speed, J. *The Counties of Britain: A Tudor Atlas* (pub. 1611). London: Pavilion Books, 1995.

Thomas, A. H., and I. D. Thornley, eds. *Great Chronicle of London*. London: G. W. Jones, 1938.

Uden, Grant. *A Dictionary of Chivalry*. Ipswich, Suffolk: W. S. Cowell, 1968.

Warkworth, John. *The Chronicles of the White Rose of York*. J. A. Giles, ed. London: James Bohn, 1843.

Weightman, Christine. *Margaret of York*. Stroud, Gloucestershire, UK: Sutton Publishing, 1989.

Williamson, Audrey. *The Mystery of the Princes*. Stroud, Gloucestershire, UK: Sutton Publishing, 1981.

Wroe, Ann. *The Perfect Prince*. New York: Random House, 2003.

Also, for information on Sir Edward Brampton:

The Jewish Historical Society of England Journal, *Transactions*, Sessions 1945–1951, vol. XVI.

Roth, Cecil. *Sir Edward Brampton, Governor of Guernsey and the Mystery of Richard, Duke of York*, a talk given to the Fellowship of the White Boar at Claxton Hall on February 11, 1959.

The King's Grace

For Discussion

1. Review the quote from Aesop's fable about the wolf in sheep's clothing at the Prologue of this story. What connections can you make between this and *The King's Grace*? Which characters are deceptive? Which characters are deceived? Can deception ever yield positive results?

2. Margaret of York's "secret boy" is given several names throughout this story—Jehan, Pierrequin, Perkin Warbeck, Richard of York (Dickon). Who is he? Which identity do you think he would choose for himself if it were up to him?

3. The mystery of the princes in the Tower has yet to be solved. What do *you* think happened to Ned and Dickon? Did they waste away in captivity, or did they perish at the hands of Richard III? Or Henry VII? Or the Duke of Buckingham? Who are the other likely suspects?

4. Choose one adjective you think best sums up the character of Grace Plantagenet and share it with the group. Were you surprised by how others in your group perceived Grace? Is she a likable or sympathetic heroine? Were there any points in the story when you wished that you could intervene to prevent Grace from making a mistake?

5. *The King's Grace* is full of examples of political ambition, scheming, betrayal, and accusations of treason. Are these things endemic to a monarchy of days gone by, or do you see these in contemporary democracies or other governments as well?

6. Why did Elizabeth Woodville (Dame Grey) agree to a marriage between Bess and Henry VII if she was such a loyal Yorkist? What do you make of Bess's change of heart and alliances toward Henry?

7. How do you view the other arranged marriages in this novel? Are they fair? Purposeful? Fulfilling? Based on your reading of this novel,

what do you make of attitudes about marriage during this time? What about attitudes regarding fidelity, sex, or love?

8. Elizabeth Woodville advises Cecily on page 74, ". . . unlike those who do not have our privilege, we are not born to do as we please. There is a price to pay for our nobility." What is that price? Is it worth paying? Is there any freedom in being born of royal blood?

9. Who has the most power in this story? Are there different kinds of power? How is gender related to power in the novel?

10. What value does a piece of historical fiction such as *The King's Grace* hold for you? How might your understanding of this time period and these characters be different if you had read a nonfiction account of this story? What does fiction provide that nonfiction cannot? Where might fiction fall short?

11. Grace has several vivid dreams throughout this story. Discuss the images and messages in these dreams. Are they ominous? Do they give Grace reliable impressions or interpretations of her world?

12. Why do you think Perkin Warbeck never reveals his true identity to Henry VII or others at court?

A Conversation with Anne Easter Smith

Grace Plantagenet loves to solve a mystery and put together the pieces in the puzzle of her family history. You seem to enjoy doing the same through your extensive research. Do you feel a kind of kinship to Grace in this regard?
Oh, yes! Just keeping track of all the real characters and making sure I have them in the right place at the right time is a challenge. Thanks to my trusty wall chart, I can keep some sort of order to my research, but it is time-consuming. And always one piece of information leads to another and another, and soon hours have gone by while I fit facts together.

This is your third novel about the house of York. Did you know when you wrote your first novel, *A Rose for the Crown*, that this family would inspire you to write multiple books about them? How many more do you intend to write?

I had no intention of writing another book after *A Rose for the Crown*, to be honest! But in order to have that published, I was unable to turn down an offer that included a second. By the time *Margaret (Daughter of York)* was finished, I felt as though I was on a roll, and so my agent and I proposed two more books to round out the York family story. The fourth book is being researched and will be about the matriarch of the house of York in the fifteenth century, Duchess Cecily.

You write in the author's note that Grace comes from a mere mention in the historical manuscripts. How difficult was it to imagine the life a central character we know so little about and to connect her to characters whose lives are more richly documented?

You must write a backstory for a character like that, and in some ways it gives me freedom to create who I want from it. I found Grace's historical anonymity a wonderful way to tell the story of the better known royals.

When filling in the gaps that historical evidence cannot provide, how do you make the determination whether or not an imagined event, dialogue, or action is authentic or possible? What questions do you ask yourself? Do you consult others for verification?

Ah, this is a dilemma for the novelist. I can only speak for myself and say that I try to be true to my characters from impressions I get from the facts I have gleaned from biographers, historians, and the contemporary accounts (those are the "others" you refer to). As long as my characters stay true to themselves, imagined events and dialogue should feel plausible.

Did you come across any stumbling blocks in trying to piece together this story?

Oh, dear, many! Perkin's is an exceptionally complex tale with no resolution as of today, and I had several "plot blocks" along the way. There was the day I called my editor, Trish, begging for help as I lay in a fetal position on the floor with four different versions of his story around me! In the end, I went with my gut feeling that this young man must not have been a mere boatman's son but nobly born and hidden. Historian Ann Wroe's discovery of Margaret of Burgundy's "secret boy" in the Burgundian archives of her household accounts convinced me that there was more than a charitable connection between them.

What responsibilities do you, as a writer of historical fiction, feel toward your audience? Do you think those responsibilities would be different if you were a nonfiction writer?

I love this question, because I believe strongly that the role of a good historical novelist is to pique a reader's interest in the material enough so that he or she rushes off to the library and does more research on the subject. I look at myself as a conduit to greater knowledge of the period. I also feel responsible for the accuracy of the facts as we know them. We can take dramatic license with those we don't know—within reason, of course—under the banner of fiction. If I were writing nonfiction, however, I would feel a great responsibility not to make conjectures—I try to avoid those kinds of writers in my research!

All three of your novels feature a female protagonist. Do you find it easier to write from a women's perspective, or do you choose these women because their stories might not necessarily be told otherwise?

Both. To be honest, I have reached my advanced age—which shall be unspecified—and I still have a hard time knowing how men think, so I have thought it best to stick with something I know. They say write what you know, so that's what I did. Besides, I think medieval women were fabulous and many forgotten, so why not tell their stories and the history they lived through their eyes?

Describe your process. Do you gather all the research and map out your story before you begin, or do you make discoveries as you write?

Now you will reveal me as being undisciplined, because I make but a rough outline! I had no experience in book writing before I launched into *A Rose for the Crown* and did not know about plot outlines, chapter lengths, and such. Of course, I am lucky enough to have history as my skeleton time line, but how I put the flesh on the bones is often up to my characters, who have minds of their own—I kid you not! Grace was quite stubborn at very awkward times, and I had to ask Tom to chivvy her out of trouble quite often. What a sweetheart he was! As for the research—it happens every single day I am writing. I think I have everything I need, but then halfway through a paragraph, I find I need to know a silly little thing like how to color lips in the middle of winter when the usual berry stain isn't available. That took me an hour, and when I had no luck, I left it out! (I have since found out that beets were used—but were they available in England in the fifteenth century? You see what I mean?)

What are you working on next?
As I mentioned, my fourth book is about Cecily of York, also known as the Rose of Raby and Proud Cis. She and Richard, duke of York, were betrothed at a very young age and by all accounts had a strong, happy marriage with thirteen children, two of whom became king and another the wealthiest duchess in Europe. I have visited Rouen, where they lived during the end of the Hundred Years War when Richard was governor of Normandy, and then Dublin, where Richard was also sent as governor by Henry VI and where Cecily had George of Clarence. Before Henry married Margaret of Anjou, Cecily was the first lady of England.

Enhance Your Book Club

1. Play a round of Balderdash featuring the words in the glossary. Have members in the group write false definitions for words like *catafalque, excedra, houppelande,* and *sackbut,* including the correct definition. Members vote on the definition they think is correct. Get one point if you are able to identify the correct definition and one point for every vote your false definition gets.
2. Provide a bowl of Richard of York's favorite fruit—oranges—and scent your home with cloves!
3. Research the characters of historical basis in the novel: Richard III, Henry VII, Edward IV, and Margaret of York. Where and how are these characters portrayed in other works?